LAURA INGALLS WILDER

Laura Ingalls Wilder and Almanzo J. Wilder, in the winter of 1885
COURTESY THE LAURA INGALLS WILDER HOME ASSOCIATION, MANSFIELD, MISSOURI

LAURA INGALLS WILDER

THE LITTLE HOUSE BOOKS

Volume Two

By the Shores of Silver Lake
The Long Winter
Little Town on the Prairie
These Happy Golden Years
The First Four Years

Caroline Fraser, *editor*

THE LIBRARY OF AMERICA

The paper used in this publication meets the
minimum requirements of the American National Standard for
Information Sciences—Permanence of Paper for Printed
Library Materials, ANSI Z39.48—1984.

Distributed to the trade in the United States
by Penguin Group (USA) Inc.
and in Canada by Penguin Books Canada Ltd.

Library of Congress Control Number: 2012904472
ISBN: 978-1-59853-161-9

The Library of America—230

Manufactured in the United States of America

Contents

BY THE SHORES OF SILVER LAKE

CONTENTS

CHAPTER I

Unexpected Visitor

LAURA was washing the dishes one morning when old Jack, lying in the sunshine on the doorstep, growled to tell her that someone was coming. She looked out, and saw a buggy crossing the gravelly ford of Plum Creek.

"Ma," she said, "it's a strange woman coming."

Ma sighed. She was ashamed of the untidy house, and so was Laura. But Ma was too weak and Laura was too tired and they were too sad to care very much.

Mary and Carrie and baby Grace and Ma had all had scarlet fever. The Nelsons across the creek had had it too, so there had been no one to help Pa and Laura. The doctor had come every day; Pa did not know how he could pay the bill. Far worst of all, the fever had settled in Mary's eyes, and Mary was blind.

She was able to sit up now, wrapped in quilts in Ma's old hickory rocking chair. All that long time, week after week, when she could still see a little, but less every day, she had never cried. Now she could not see even the brightest light any more. She was still patient and brave.

Her beautiful golden hair was gone. Pa had shaved it close because of the fever, and her poor shorn head looked like a boy's. Her blue eyes were still beautiful, but they did not know what was before them, and Mary herself could never look through them again to tell Laura what she was thinking without saying a word.

"Who can it be at this hour in the morning?" Mary wondered, turning her ear toward the sound of the buggy.

"It's a strange woman alone in a buggy. She's wearing a brown sunbonnet and driving a bay horse," Laura answered. Pa had said that she must be eyes for Mary.

"Can you think of anything for dinner?" Ma asked. She meant for a company dinner, if the woman stayed till dinnertime.

There was bread and molasses, and potatoes. That was all. This was springtime, too early for garden vegetables; the cow was dry and the hens had not yet begun to lay their summer's eggs. Only a few small fish were left in Plum Creek. Even the little cottontail rabbits had been hunted until they were scarce.

Pa did not like a country so old and worn out that the hunting was poor. He wanted to go west. For two years he had wanted to go west and take a homestead, but Ma did not want to leave the settled country. And there was no money. Pa had made only two poor wheat crops since the grasshoppers came; he had barely been able to keep out of debt, and now there was the doctor's bill.

Laura answered Ma stoutly, "What's good enough for us is good enough for anybody!"

The buggy stopped and the strange woman sat in it, looking at Laura and Ma in the doorway. She was a pretty woman, in her neat brown print dress and sunbonnet. Laura felt ashamed of her own bare feet and limp dress and uncombed braids. Then Ma said slowly, "Why, Docia!"

"I wondered if you'd know me," the woman said. "A good deal of water's gone under the bridge since you folks left Wisconsin."

She was the pretty Aunt Docia who had worn the dress with buttons that looked like blackberries, long ago at the sugaring-off dance at Grandpa's house in the Big Woods of Wisconsin.

She was married now. She had married a widower with two children. Her husband was a contractor, working on the new railroad in the west. Aunt Docia was driving alone in the buggy, all the way from Wisconsin to the railroad camps in Dakota Territory.

She had come by to see if Pa would go with her. Her husband, Uncle Hi, wanted a good man to be storekeeper, bookkeeper and timekeeper, and Pa could have the job.

"It pays fifty dollars a month, Charles," she said.

A kind of tightness smoothed out of Pa's thin cheeks and his blue eyes lighted up. He said slowly, "Seems like I can draw good pay while I'm looking for that homestead, Caroline."

Ma still did not want to go west. She looked around the kitchen, at Carrie and at Laura standing there with Grace in her arms.

"Charles, I don't know," she said. "It does seem providential, fifty dollars a month. But we're settled here. We've got the farm."

"Listen to reason, Caroline," Pa pleaded. "We can get a hundred and sixty acres out west, just by living on it, and the land's as good as this is, or better. If Uncle Sam's willing to give us a farm in place of the one he drove us off of, in Indian Territory, I say let's take it. The hunting's good in the west, a man can get all the meat he wants."

Laura wanted so much to go that she could hardly keep from speaking.

"How could we go now?" Ma asked. "With Mary not strong enough to travel."

"That's so," said Pa. "That's a fact." Then he asked Aunt Docia, "The job wouldn't wait?"

"No," Aunt Docia said. "No, Charles. Hi is in need of a man, right now. You have to take it or leave it."

"It's fifty dollars a month, Caroline," said Pa. "And a homestead."

It seemed a long time before Ma said gently, "Well, Charles, you must do as you think best."

"I'll take it, Docia!" Pa got up and clapped on his hat. "Where there's a will, there's a way. I'll go see Nelson."

Laura was so excited that she could hardly do the housework properly. Aunt Docia helped, and while they worked she told the news from Wisconsin.

Her sister, Aunt Ruby, was married and had two boys and a beautiful little baby girl named Dolly Varden. Uncle George was a lumberjack, logging on the Mississippi. Uncle Henry's folks were all well, and Charley was turning out better than had been expected, considering how Uncle Henry had spared the rod and spoiled that child. Grandpa and Grandma were still living in the old place, their big log house. They could afford a frame house now, but Grandpa declared that good sound oak logs made better walls than thin sawed boards.

Even Black Susan, the cat that Laura and Mary had left behind when they rode away from their little log house in the woods, was still living there. The little log house had changed hands several times, and now it was a corncrib, but nothing would persuade that cat to live anywhere else. She went right on living in the corncrib, sleek and plump from rats she caught, and there was hardly a family in all that country that didn't have one of her kittens. They were all good mousers, big-eared and long-tailed like Black Susan.

Dinner was ready in the swept, neat house when Pa came back. He had sold the farm. Nelson was paying two hundred dollars cash for it, and Pa was jubilant. "That'll square up all we owe, and leave a little something over," he said. "How's that, Caroline!"

"I hope it's for the best, Charles," Ma replied. "But how——"

"Wait till I tell you! I've got it all figured out," Pa told her. "I'll go on with Docia tomorrow morning. You and the girls stay here till Mary gets well and strong, say a couple of months. Nelson's agreed to haul our stuff to the depot, and you'll all come out on the train."

Laura stared at him. So did Carrie and Ma. Mary said, "On the train?"

They had never thought of traveling on the train. Laura knew, of course, that people did travel on trains. The trains were often wrecked and the people killed. She was not exactly afraid, but she was excited. Carrie's eyes were big and scared in her peaked little face.

They had seen the train rushing across the prairie, with long, rolling puffs of black smoke streaming back from the engine. They heard its roar and its wild, clear whistle. Horses ran away, if their driver could not hold them when they saw a train coming.

Ma said in her quiet way, "I am sure we will manage nicely with Laura and Carrie to help me."

CHAPTER 2

Grown Up

THERE was a great deal of work to be done, for Pa must leave early next morning. He set the old wagon bows on the wagon and pulled the canvas cover over them; it was almost worn out but it would do for the short trip. Aunt Docia and Carrie helped him pack the wagon, while Laura washed and ironed, and baked hardtack for the journey.

In the midst of it all, Jack stood looking on. Everyone was too busy to notice the old bulldog, till suddenly Laura saw him standing between the house and the wagon. He did not frisk about, cocking his head and laughing, as he used to do. He stood braced on his stiff legs because he was troubled with rheumatism now. His forehead was wrinkled sadly and his stub-tail was limp.

"Good old Jack," Laura told him, but he did not wag. He looked at her sorrowfully.

"Look, Pa. Look at Jack," Laura said. She bent and stroked his smooth head. The fine hairs were gray now. First his nose had been gray and then his jaws, and now even his ears were no longer brown. He leaned his head against her and sighed.

All in one instant, she knew that the old dog was too tired to walk all the way to Dakota Territory under the wagon. He was troubled because he saw the wagon ready to go traveling again, and he was so old and tired.

"Pa!" she cried out. "Jack can't walk so far! Oh, Pa, we can't leave Jack!"

"He wouldn't hold out to walk it for a fact," Pa said. "I'd forgot. I'll move the feedsack and make a place for him to ride here in the wagon. How'll you like to go riding in the wagon, huh, old fellow?"

Jack wagged one polite wag and turned his head aside. He did not want to go, even in the wagon.

Laura knelt down and hugged him as she used to do when she was a little girl. "Jack! Jack! We're going west! Don't you want to go west again, Jack?"

Always before he had been eager and joyful when he saw Pa putting the cover on the wagon. He had taken his place under it when they started, and all the long way from Wisconsin to Indian Territory, and back again to Minnesota, he had trotted there in the wagon shade, behind the horses' feet. He had waded through creeks and swum rivers, and every night while Laura slept in the wagon he had guarded it. Every morning, even when his feet were sore from walking, he had been glad with her to see the sun rise and the horses hitched up; he had always been ready for the new day of traveling.

Now he only leaned against Laura and nudged his nose under her hand to ask her to pet him gently. She stroked his gray head and smoothed his ears, and she could feel how very tired he was.

Ever since Mary and Carrie, and then Ma, had been sick with scarlet fever, Laura had been neglecting Jack. He had always helped her in every trouble before, but he could not help when there was sickness in the house. Perhaps all that time he had been feeling lonely and forgotten.

"I didn't mean it, Jack," Laura told him. He understood; they had always understood each other. He had taken care of her when she was little, and he had helped her take care of Carrie when Carrie was the baby. Whenever Pa had gone away, Jack had always stayed with Laura to take care of her and the family. He was especially Laura's own dog.

She did not know how to explain to him that he must go now with Pa in the wagon and leave her behind. Perhaps he would not understand that she was coming later on the train.

She could not stay with him long now because there was so much work to be done. But all that afternoon she said to him, "Good dog, Jack," whenever she could. She gave him a good supper, and after the dishes were washed and the table set for an early breakfast, she made his bed.

His bed was an old horse blanket, in a corner of the lean-to at the back door. He had slept there ever since they moved into this house, where Laura slept in the attic and he could not climb the attic ladder. For five years he had slept there, and Laura had kept his bed aired and clean and comfortable. But lately she had forgotten it. He had tried to scratch it up and arrange it himself, but the blanket was packed down in hard ridges.

He watched her while she shook it out and made it comfortable. He smiled and wagged, pleased that she was making his bed for him. She made a round nest in it and patted it to show him that it was ready.

He stepped in and turned himself around once. He stopped to rest his stiff legs and slowly turned again. Jack always turned around three times before he lay down to sleep at night. He had done it when he was a young dog in the Big Woods, and he had done it in the grass under the wagon every night. It is a proper thing for dogs to do.

So wearily he turned himself around the third time and curled down with a bump and a sigh. But he held his head up to look at Laura.

She stroked his head where the fine gray hairs were, and she thought of how good he had always been. She had always been safe from wolves or Indians because Jack was there. And how many times he had helped her bring in the cows at night. How happy they had been playing along Plum Creek and in the pool where the fierce old crab had lived, and when she had to go to school he had always been waiting at the ford for her when she came home.

"Good Jack, good dog," she told him. He turned his head to touch her hand with the tip of his tongue. Then he let his nose sink onto his paws and he sighed and closed his eyes. He wanted to sleep now.

In the morning when Laura came down the ladder into the lamplight, Pa was going out to do the chores. He spoke to Jack, but Jack did not stir.

Only Jack's body, stiff and cold, lay curled there on the blanket.

They buried it on the low slope above the wheat field, by the path he used to run down so gaily when he was going with Laura to bring in the cows. Pa spaded the earth over the box and made the mound smooth. Grass would grow there after they had all gone away to the west. Jack would never again sniff the morning air and go springing over the short grass with his ears up and his mouth laughing. He would never nudge his nose under Laura's hand again to say he wanted her to pet him. There had been so many times that she might have petted him without being asked, and hadn't.

"Don't cry, Laura," Pa said. "He has gone to the Happy Hunting Grounds."

"Truly, Pa?" Laura managed to ask.

"Good dogs have their reward, Laura," Pa told her.

Perhaps, in the Happy Hunting Grounds, Jack was running gaily in the wind over some high prairie, as he used to run on the beautiful wild prairies of Indian Territory. Perhaps at last he was catching a jack rabbit. He had tried so often to catch one of those long-eared, long-legged rabbits and never could.

That morning Pa drove away in the rattling old wagon behind Aunt Docia's buggy. Jack was not standing beside Laura to watch Pa go. There was only emptiness to turn to instead of Jack's eyes looking up to say that he was there to take care of her.

Laura knew then that she was not a little girl any more. Now she was alone; she must take care of herself. When you must do that, then you do it and you are grown up. Laura was not very big, but she was almost thirteen years old, and no one was there to depend on. Pa and Jack had gone, and Ma needed help to take care of Mary and the little girls, and somehow to get them all safely to the west on a train.

CHAPTER 3

Riding in the Cars

WHEN the time came, Laura could hardly believe it was real. The weeks and months had been endless, and now suddenly they were gone. Plum Creek, and the house, and all the slopes and fields she knew so well, were gone; she would never see them again. The last crowded days of packing, cleaning, scrubbing, washing and ironing, and the last minute flurry of bathing and dressing were over. Clean and starched and dressed-up, in the morning of a weekday, they sat in a row on the bench in the waiting room while Ma bought the tickets.

In an hour they would be riding on the railroad cars.

The two satchels stood on the sunny platform outside the waiting-room door. Laura kept an eye on them, and on Grace, as Ma had told her to. Grace sat still in her little starched white lawn dress and bonnet, her feet in small new shoes sticking straight out. At the ticket window, Ma carefully counted money out of her pocketbook.

Traveling on the train cost money. They had not paid anything to travel in the wagon, and this was a beautiful morning to be riding in the wagon along new roads. It was a September day and small clouds were hurrying in the sky. All the girls were in school now; they would see the train go roaring by and know that Laura was riding in it. Trains went faster than horses can run. They went so terribly fast that often they were wrecked. You never knew what might happen to you on a train.

Ma put the tickets inside her mother-of-pearl pocketbook and carefully snapped shut its little steel clasps. She looked so nice in her dark delaine dress with white lace collar and cuffs. Her hat was black straw with a narrow turned-up brim and a white spray of lilies-of-the-valley standing up at one side of the crown. She sat down and took Grace on her lap.

Now there was nothing to do but wait. They had come an hour early to be sure not to miss the train.

Laura smoothed her dress. It was brown calico sprinkled with small red flowers. Her hair hung down her back in long, brown braids, and a red ribbon bow tied their ends together. There was a red ribbon around the crown of her hat too.

Mary's dress was gray calico with sprays of blue flowers. Her wide-brimmed straw hat had a blue ribbon on it. And under the hat, her poor short hair was held back from her face by a blue ribbon tied around her head. Her lovely blue eyes did not see anything. But she said, "Don't fidget, Carrie, you'll muss your dress."

Laura craned to look at Carrie, sitting beyond Mary. Carrie was small and thin in pink calico, with pink ribbons on her brown braids and her hat. She flushed miserably because Mary found fault with her, and Laura was going to say, "You come over by me, Carrie, and fidget all you want to!"

Just then Mary's face lighted up with joy and she said, "Ma, Laura's fidgeting, too! I can tell she is, without seeing!"

"So she is, Mary," Ma said, and Mary smiled in satisfaction.

Laura was ashamed that in her thoughts she had been cross with Mary. She did not say anything. She got up and she was passing in front of Ma without saying a word. Ma had to remind her, "Say 'Excuse me,' Laura."

"Excuse me, Ma. Excuse me, Mary," Laura said politely, and she sat down beside Carrie. Carrie felt safer when she was between Laura and Mary. Carrie was really afraid of going on a train. Of course she would never say that she was frightened, but Laura knew.

"Ma," Carrie asked timidly, "Pa will surely meet us, won't he?"

"He is coming to meet us," Ma said. "He has to drive in from the camp, and it will take him all day. We are going to wait for him in Tracy."

"Will he—will he get there before night, Ma?" Carrie asked.

Ma said she hoped so.

You can not tell what may happen when you go traveling on a train. It is not like starting out all together in a wagon. So Laura said bravely, "Maybe Pa's got our homestead picked out, already. You guess what it's like, Carrie, and then I'll guess."

They could not talk very well, because all the time they were waiting, and listening for the train. At long, long last, Mary said she thought she heard it. Then Laura heard a faint, faraway hum. Her heart beat so fast that she could hardly listen to Ma.

Ma lifted Grace on her arm, and with her other hand she took tight hold of Carrie's. She said, "Laura, you come behind me with Mary. Be careful, now!"

The train was coming, louder. They stood by the satchels on the platform and saw it coming. Laura did not know how they could get the satchels on the train. Ma's hands were full, and Laura had to hold onto Mary. The engine's round front window glared in the sunshine like a huge eye. The smokestack flared upward to a wide top, and black smoke rolled up from it. A sudden streak of white shot up through the smoke, then the whistle screamed a long wild scream. The roaring thing came rushing straight at them all, swelling bigger and bigger, enormous, shaking everything with noise.

Then the worst was over. It had not hit them; it was roaring by them on thick big wheels. Bumps and crashes ran along the freight cars and flat cars and they stopped moving. The train was there, and they had to get into it.

"Laura!" Ma said sharply. "You and Mary be careful!"

"Yes, Ma, we are," said Laura. She guided Mary anxiously, one step at a time, across the boards of the platform, behind Ma's skirt. When the skirt stopped, Laura stopped Mary.

They had come to the last car at the end of the train. Steps went up into it, and a strange man in a dark suit and a cap helped Ma climb up them with Grace in her arms. "Oopsy-daisy!" he said, swinging Carrie up beside Ma. Then he said, "Them your satchels, ma'am?"

"Yes, please," Ma said. "Come, Laura and Mary."

"Who is he, Ma?" Carrie asked, while Laura helped Mary up the steps. They were crowded in a small place. The man came pushing cheerfully past them, with the satchels, and shouldered open the door of the car.

They followed him between two rows of red velvet seats full of people. The sides of the car were almost solidly made of windows; the car was almost as light as outdoors, and chunks of sunshine slanted across the people and the red velvet.

Ma sat down on one velvet seat and plumped Grace on her lap. She told Carrie to sit beside her. She said, "Laura, you and Mary sit in this seat ahead of me."

Laura guided Mary in, and they sat down. The velvet seat

was springy. Laura wanted to bounce on it, but she must behave properly. She whispered, "Mary, the seats are red velvet!"

"I see," Mary said, stroking the seat with her fingertips. "What's that in front of us?"

"It's the high back of the seat in front, and it's red velvet too," Laura told her.

The engine whistled, and they both jumped. The train was getting ready to go. Laura knelt up in the seat to see Ma. Ma looked calm and so pretty in her dark dress with its white lace collar and the sweet tiny white flowers on her hat.

"What is it, Laura?" Ma asked.

Laura asked, "Who was that man?"

"The brakeman," Ma said. "Now sit down and——"

The train jerked, jolting her backward. Laura's chin bumped hard on the seat back, and her hat slid on her head. Again the train jerked, not so badly this time, and then it began to shiver and the depot moved.

"It's going!" Carrie cried out.

The shivering grew faster and louder, the depot slid backward, and under the car the wheels began to beat time. A rub-a-dubdub, a rub-a-dubdub, the wheels went, faster and faster. The lumberyard and the back of the church and the front of the schoolhouse went by, and that was the last of that town.

The whole car swayed now, in time to the clackety-clacking underneath it, and the black smoke blew by in melting rolls. A telegraph wire swooped up and down beyond the window. It did not really swoop, but it seemed to swoop because it sagged between the poles. It was fastened to green glass knobs that glittered in the sunshine and went dark when the smoke rolled above them. Beyond the wire, grasslands and fields and scattered farmhouses and barns went by.

They went so fast that Laura could not really look at them before they were gone. In one hour that train would go twenty miles—as far as the horses traveled in a whole day.

The door opened, and a tall man came in. He wore a blue coat with brass buttons, and a cap, with

CONDUCTOR

in letters across its front. At every seat he stopped and took tickets. He punched round holes in the tickets with a small machine in his hand. Ma gave him three tickets. Carrie and Grace were so little that they could ride on the train without paying.

The Conductor went on, and Laura said low, "Oh, Mary! so many shining brass buttons on his coat, and it says CONDUCTOR right across the front of his cap!"

"And he is tall," Mary said. "His voice is high up."

Laura tried to tell her how fast the telegraph poles were going by. She said, "The wire sags down between them and swoops up again," and she counted them. "One—oop! two—oop! three! That's how fast they're going."

"I can tell it's fast, I can feel it," Mary said happily.

On that dreadful morning when Mary could not see even sunshine full in her eyes, Pa had said that Laura must see for her. He had said, "Your two eyes are quick enough, and your tongue, if you will use them for Mary." And Laura had promised. So she tried to be eyes for Mary, and it was seldom that Mary need ask her, "See out loud for me, Laura, please."

"Both sides of the car are windows, close together," Laura said now. "Every window is one big sheet of glass, and even the strips of wood between the windows shine like glass, they are so polished."

"Yes, I see," and Mary felt over the glass and touched the shining wood with her fingertips.

"The sunshine comes slanting in the south windows, in wide stripes over the red velvet seats and the people. Corners of sunshine fall on the floor, and keep reaching out and going back. Up above the windows the shiny wood curves in from the walls on both sides, and all along the middle of the ceiling there's a higher place. It has little walls of tiny, long, low windows, and you can see blue sky outside them. But outside the big windows, on both sides, the country is going by. The stubble fields are yellow, and haystacks are by the barns, and little trees are yellow and red in clumps around the houses.

"Now I will see the people," Laura went on murmuring. "In front of us is a head with a bald spot on top and side whiskers. He is reading a newspaper. He doesn't look out of the windows at all. Farther ahead are two young men with their hats on.

They are holding a big white map and looking at it and talking about it. I guess they're going to look for a homestead too. Their hands are rough and calloused so they're good workers. And farther ahead there's a woman with bright yellow hair and, oh, Mary! the brightest red velvet hat with pink roses——"

Just then someone went by, and Laura looked up. She went on, "A thin man with bristly eyebrows and long mustaches and an Adam's apple just went by. He can't walk straight, the train's going so fast. I wonder what— Oh, Mary! He's turning a little handle on the wall at the end of the car, and water's coming out!

"The water's pouring right into a tin cup. Now he's drinking it. His Adam's apple bobs. He's filling the cup again. He just turns the handle, and the water comes right out. How do you suppose it— Mary! He's set that cup on a little shelf. Now he's coming back."

After the man had gone by, Laura made up her mind. She asked Ma if she could get a drink of water, and Ma said she might. So she started out.

She could not walk straight. The lurching car made her sway and grab at the seat backs all the way. But she got to the end of the car and looked at the shining handle and spout, and the little shelf under them that held the bright tin cup. She turned the handle just a little, and water came out of the spout. She turned the handle back, and the water stopped. Under the cup there was a little hole, put there to carry away any water that spilled. Laura had never seen anything so fascinating. It was all so neat, and so marvelous, that she wanted to fill the cup again and again. But that would waste the water. So after she drank, she only filled the cup part way, in order not to spill it, and she carried it very carefully to Ma.

Carrie drank, and Grace. They did not want any more, and Ma and Mary were not thirsty. So Laura carried the cup back to its place. All the time the train was rushing on and the country rushing back, and the car swaying, but this time Laura did not touch one seat that she passed. She could walk almost as well as the Conductor. Surely nobody suspected that she had never been on a train before.

Then a boy came walking along the aisle, with a basket on his arm. He stopped and showed it to everyone, and some people took things out of it and gave him money. When he reached Laura, she saw that the basket was full of boxes of candy and of long sticks of white chewing gum. The boy showed them to Ma and said, "Nice fresh candy, ma'am? Chewing gum?"

Ma shook her head, but the boy opened a box and showed the colored candy. Carrie's breath made an eager sound before she knew it.

The boy shook the box a little, not quite spilling the candy out. It was beautiful Christmas candy, red pieces and yellow pieces and some striped red-and-white. The boy said, "Only ten cents, ma'am, one dime."

Laura, and Carrie too, knew they could not have that candy. They were only looking at it. Suddenly Ma opened her purse and counted out a nickel and five pennies into the boy's hand. She took the box and gave it to Carrie.

When the boy had gone on, Ma said, excusing herself for spending so much, "After all, we must celebrate our first train ride."

Grace was asleep, and Ma said that babies should not eat candy. Ma took only a small piece. Then Carrie came into the seat with Laura and Mary and divided the rest. Each had two pieces. They meant to eat one and save the other for next day, but some time after the first pieces were gone, Laura decided to taste her second one. Then Carrie tasted hers, and finally Mary gave in. They licked those pieces all away, little by little.

They were still licking their fingers when the engine whistled long and loud. Then the car went more slowly, and slowly the backs of shanties went backward outside it. All the people began to gather their things together and put on their hats, and then there was an awful jolting crash, and the train stopped. It was noon, and they had reached Tracy.

"I hope you girls haven't spoiled your dinners with that candy," Ma said.

"We didn't bring any dinner, Ma," Carrie reminded her.

Absently Ma replied, "We're going to eat dinner in the hotel. Come, Laura. You and Mary be careful."

CHAPTER 4

End of the Rails

PA WAS not there at that strange depot. The brakeman set down the satchels on the platform and said, "If you'll wait a minute, ma'am, I'll take you to the hotel. I'm going there myself."

"Thank you," Ma said gratefully.

The brakeman helped unfasten the engine from the train. The fireman, all red and smeared with soot, leaned out of the engine to watch. Then he yanked a bell rope. The engine went on by itself, puffing and chuffing under the bell's clanging. It went only a little way, then it stopped, and Laura could not believe what she saw. The steel rails under the engine, and the wooden ties between them, turned right around. They turned around in a circle there on the ground till the ends of the rails fitted together again, and the engine was facing backwards.

Laura was so amazed that she could not tell Mary what was happening. The engine went clanging and puffing on another track beside the train. It passed the train and went a little way beyond. The bell clanged, men shouted and made motions with their arms, and the engine came backing, bump! into the rear end of the train. All the cars slam-banged against each other. And there stood the train and the engine, facing back toward the east.

Carrie's mouth was open in amazement. The brakeman laughed at her in a friendly way. "That's the turntable," he told her. "This is the end of the rails, and we have to turn the engine around so it can take the train back down the line."

Of course, they would have to do that, but Laura had never thought of it before. She knew now what Pa meant when he spoke of the wonderful times they were living in. There had never been such wonders in the whole history of the world, Pa said. Now, in one morning, they had actually traveled a whole week's journey, and Laura had seen the Iron Horse turn around, to go back the whole way in one afternoon.

For just one little minute she almost wished that Pa was a

railroad man. There was nothing so wonderful as railroads, and railroad men were great men, able to drive the big iron engines and the fast, dangerous trains. But of course not even railroad men were bigger or better than Pa, and she did not really want him to be anything but what he was.

There was a long line of freight cars on another track beyond the depot. Men were unloading the cars into wagons. But they all stopped suddenly and jumped down from the wagons. Some of them yelled, and one big young man began to sing Ma's favorite hymn. Only he did not sing its words. He sang:

"There is a boarding house
Not far away
Where they have fried ham and eggs
Three times a day.

"Wow! How the boarders yell
When they hear that dinner bell!
Whoop! How those eggs do smell!
Three times——"

He was singing out these shocking words, and some other men were too, when they saw Ma and stopped. Ma walked on quietly, carrying Grace and holding Carrie's hand. The brakeman was embarrassed. He said quickly, "We better hurry, ma'am, that's the dinner bell."

The hotel was down a short street beyond a few stores and vacant lots. A sign over the sidewalk said, "Hotel," and under it a man stood swinging a hand bell. It kept on clanging, and all the men's boots made a beating sound on the dusty street and the board sidewalk.

"Oh, Laura, does it look like it sounds?" Mary asked trembling.

"No," Laura said. "It looks all right. It's just a town, and they're just men."

"It sounds so rough," Mary said.

"This is the hotel door now," Laura told her.

The brakeman led the way in, and set down the satchels. The floor needed sweeping. There was brown paper on the walls, and a calendar with a big shiny picture of a pretty girl in a bright yellow wheat field. All the men went hustling through an open door into a big room beyond, where a long table was covered with a white cloth and set for dinner.

The man who had rung the bell told Ma, "Yes, ma'am! We've got room for you." He put the satchels behind the desk and said, "Maybe you'd like to wash up, ma'am, before you eat?"

In a little room there was a washstand. A large china pitcher stood in a big china bowl, and a roller towel hung on the wall. Ma wet a clean handkerchief and washed Grace's face and hands and her own. Then she emptied the bowl into a pail beside the washstand and filled the bowl with fresh water for Mary and again for Laura. The cold water felt good on their dusty, sooty faces, and in the bowl it turned quite black. There was only a little water for each; then the pitcher was empty. Ma set it neatly in the bowl again when Laura was through. They all wiped on the roller towel. A roller towel was very convenient because its ends were sewed together and it ran around on its roller so that everyone could find a dry place.

Now the time had come to go into the dining room. Laura dreaded that, and she knew that Ma did, too. It was hard to face so many strangers.

"You all look clean and nice," Ma said. "Now remember your manners." Ma went first, carrying Grace. Carrie followed her, then Laura went, leading Mary. The noisy clatter of eating became hushed when they went into the dining room, but hardly any of the men looked up. Somehow Ma found empty chairs; then they were all sitting in a row at the long table.

All over the table, thick on the white cloth, stood screens shaped like beehives. Under every screen was a platter of meat or a dish of vegetables. There were plates of bread and of butter, dishes of pickles, pitchers of syrup, and cream pitchers and bowls of sugar. At each place was a large piece of pie on a small plate. The flies crawled and buzzed over the wire screens, but they could not get at the food inside.

Every one was very kind and passed the food. All the dishes kept coming from hand to hand up and down the table to Ma. Nobody talked except to mutter, "You're welcome, ma'am," when Ma said, "Thank you." A girl brought her a cup of coffee.

Laura cut Mary's meat into small pieces for her and buttered her bread. Mary's sensitive fingers managed her knife and fork perfectly, and did not spill anything.

It was a pity that the excitement took away their appetites. The dinner cost twenty-five cents, and they could eat all they wanted to eat; there was plenty of food. But they ate only a little. In a few minutes all the men finished their pie and left, and the girl who had brought the coffee began to stack up the plates and carry them into the kitchen. She was a big, good-natured girl with a broad face and yellow hair.

"I guess you folks are going out to homestead?" she asked Ma.

"Yes," Ma said.

"Your man working on the railroad?"

"Yes," Ma said. "He's coming here to meet us this afternoon."

"I thought that's the way it was," the girl said. "It's funny your coming out here this time of year, most folks come in the spring. Your big girl's blind, ain't she? That's too bad. Well, the parlor's on the other side of the office; you folks can set in there if you want to, till your man comes."

The parlor had a carpet on the floor and flowered paper on the walls. The chairs were cushioned in dark red plush. Ma sank into the rocking chair with a sigh of relief. "Grace does get heavy. Sit down, girls, and be quiet."

Carrie climbed into a big chair near Ma, and Mary and Laura sat on the sofa. They were all quiet, so that Grace would go to sleep for her afternoon nap.

The center table had a brass-bottomed lamp on it. Its curved legs ended in glass balls on the carpet. Lace curtains were looped back from the window, and between them Laura could see the prairie, and a road going away across it. Perhaps that was the road that Pa would come on. If it was, they would all go away on that road, and somewhere, far beyond the end of it that Laura could see, some day they would all be living on the new homestead.

Laura would rather not stop anywhere. She would rather go on and on, to the very end of the road, wherever it was.

All that long afternoon they sat quiet in that parlor while Grace slept, and Carrie slept a little, and even Ma dozed. The sun was almost setting when a tiny team and wagon came into sight on the road. It slowly grew larger. Grace was awake now, and they all watched from the window. The wagon grew life-size, and it was Pa's wagon, and Pa was in it.

Because they were in a hotel, they could not run out to meet him. But in a moment he came in saying, "Hullo! Here's my girls!"

CHAPTER 5

Railroad Camp

EARLY next morning they were all in the wagon going west. Grace sat between Ma and Pa on the spring seat, and Carrie and Laura sat with Mary between them on a board laid across the wagon box.

Traveling on the cars was rich and swift but Laura preferred the wagon. For this one day's trip, Pa had not put on the cover. The whole sky was overhead and the prairie stretched away on all sides with farms scattered over it. The wagon went slowly, so there was time to see everything. And they could all talk comfortably together.

The only noise was the horses' feet clop-clopping and the little creaking sounds of the wagon.

Pa said that Uncle Hi had finished his first contract and was moving to a new camp farther west. He said, "The men have cleared out already. There's only a couple of teamsters left beside Docia's folks. They'll have the last of the shanties down and be hauling off the lumber in a couple of days."

"Are we moving on then, too?" Ma asked.

"In a couple of days, yes," Pa answered. He had not looked for a homestead yet. He would get one farther west.

Laura did not find much to see out loud for Mary. The horses followed the road that went straight across the prairie. Always beside it was the railroad grade of raw earth. To the north the fields and houses were the same as at home, except that they were newer and smaller.

The freshness of the morning wore off. All the time little jolts and jiggles came up from the wagon through the hard board that they were sitting on. It seemed that the sun had never climbed so slowly. Carrie sighed. Her peaked little face was pale. But Laura could do nothing for her. Laura and Carrie must sit on the ends of the board where the jiggling was hardest because Mary must be in the middle.

At last the sun was overhead, and Pa stopped the horses by a little creek. It was good to feel still. The little creek talked to itself, the horses munched their oats in the feed-box at the back of the wagon, and on the warm grass Ma spread a cloth and opened the lunch box. There was bread and butter and good hardboiled eggs, with pepper and salt in a paper, to dip the bitten eggs into.

Noon ended too soon. Pa led the horses to drink from the creek, while Ma and Laura picked up the eggshells and bits of paper, to leave the place tidy. Pa hitched the horses to the wagon again and sang out, "All aboard!"

Laura and Carrie wished they could walk for a while. But they did not say so. They knew that Mary could not keep up with the wagon, and they could not let her sit in it alone and blind. They helped her climb up, and sat down beside her on the board.

The afternoon was longer than the morning. Once Laura said, "I thought we were going west."

"We are going west, Laura," Pa said, surprised.

"I thought it would be different," Laura explained.

"Just you wait till we get out beyond settled country!" said Pa.

Once Carrie sighed, "I'm tired." But she straightened up quickly and said, "Not so very tired." Carrie did not mean to complain.

One little jolt is nothing at all. They had hardly noticed two miles and a half of little jolts when they rode to town from Plum Creek. But all the little jolts from sunrise to noon, and then all the little jolts from noon to sunset, are tiring.

Dark came, and still the horses plodded on, and the wheels kept turning and the hard board went on jarring. Stars were overhead. The wind was chilly. They would all have been asleep if the jolting board had let them sleep. For a long time nobody said anything. Then Pa said, "There's the light of the shanty."

Far ahead there was a little twinkle on the dark land. The stars were larger but their light was cold. The tiny twinkle was warm.

"It's a little yellow spark, Mary," Laura said. "It's shining from far away in the dark to tell us to keep on coming, there's a house there, and folks."

"And supper," said Mary. "Aunt Docia's keeping supper hot for us."

Very slowly the light twinkled larger. It began to shine steady and round. After a long time it was square cornered.

"You can see it's a window now," Laura told Mary. "It's in a long, low house. There are two other long, low dark houses in the dark. That's all I can see."

"That's all of the camp," Pa said. He told the horses, "Whoa."

The horses stopped right then, without another step. The jiggling and jolting stopped. Everything stopped; there was only the still, cold dark. Then lamplight flared out of a doorway and Aunt Docia was saying, "Come right in, Caroline and girls! Hurry and put up your team, Charles; supper's waiting!"

The chilly dark had settled in Laura's bones. Mary and Carrie moved stiffly too, and they stumbled, yawning. In the long room, the lamp shone on a long table and benches and rough board walls. It was warm there and smelled of supper on the stove. Aunt Docia said, "Well, Lena and Jean, aren't you going to say anything to your cousins?"

"How do you do?" Lena said. Laura and Mary and Carrie all said, "How do you do?"

Jean was only a little boy, eleven years old. But Lena was a year older than Laura. Her eyes were black and snappy, her hair was black as black can be, and it curled naturally. The short wisps curled around her forehead, the top of her head was wavy, and the ends of her braids were round curls. Laura liked her.

"Do you like to ride horseback?" she asked Laura. "We've got two black ponies. We ride them, and I can drive them too. Jean can't because he's too little. Pa won't let him take the buggy. But I can, and tomorrow I'm going for the washing and you can come if you want to, do you?"

"Yes!" Laura said. "If Ma'll let me." She was too sleepy to ask how they could go in a buggy for the washing. She was so sleepy that she could hardly stay awake to eat supper.

Uncle Hi was fat and good-natured and easygoing. Aunt Docia talked very fast. Uncle Hi tried to calm her down, but every time he tried, Aunt Docia only talked faster. She was angry because Uncle Hi had worked hard all summer and had nothing to show for it.

"He's worked like a nailer all summer!" she said. "He's even worked his own teams on the grade, and both of us saving and scrimping and pinching till the job was finished, and now it's finished and the company says we owe them money! They say we're in debt to them for our summer's hard work! And on top of that they want us to take another contract, and Hi takes it! That's what he does! He takes it!"

Uncle Hi tried to calm her down again, and Laura tried to stay awake. All the faces wavered and the voice raveled out thin; then her neck jerked her head up. When supper was over, she staggered up to help do the dishes, but Aunt Docia told her and Lena to run along to bed.

There was no room in Aunt Docia's beds for Laura and Lena, nor for Jean. He was going to stay in the bunkhouse with the men, and Lena said, "Come along, Laura! We're going to sleep in the office tent!"

Outdoors was very large and dim and chilly. The bunkhouse lay low and dark under the big sky, and the little office tent was ghostly in the starlight. It seemed far away from the lamplit shanty.

The tent was empty. There was only grass underfoot and canvas walls sloping up to a peak overhead. Laura felt lost and lonesome. She would not have minded sleeping in the wagon, but she did not like to sleep on the ground in a strange place, and she wished that Pa and Ma were there.

Lena thought it was great fun to sleep in the tent. She flopped down right away, on a blanket spread on the ground. Laura mumbled sleepily, "Don't we undress?"

"What for?" Lena said. "You only have to put on your clothes again in the morning. Besides, there aren't any covers."

So Laura lay down on the blanket and was sound asleep. Suddenly she jerked awake with a frightful start. From the huge blackness of the night came again a wild, shrill howl.

It was not an Indian. It was not a wolf. Laura did not know what it was. Her heart stopped beating.

"Aw, you can't scare us!" Lena called out. She said to Laura, "It's Jean, trying to scare us."

Jean yelled again, but Lena shouted, "Run away, little boy! I wasn't brought up in the woods to be scared by an owl!"

"Yah!" Jean called back. Laura began to unstiffen and fell asleep.

CHAPTER 6

The Black Ponies

SUNSHINE, coming through the canvas onto Laura's face, woke her. She opened her eyes just as Lena opened hers, and looking at each other they laughed.

"Hurry up! We're going for the washing!" Lena sang out, jumping up.

They hadn't undressed, so they did not need to dress. They folded the blanket and their bedroom work was done. They went skipping out into the large, breezy morning.

The shanties were small under the sunny sky. East and west ran the railroad grade and the road; northward the grasses were tossing tawny seed plumes. Men were tearing down one of the shanties with a pleasant racket of clattering boards. On picket lines in the blowing grasses, the two black ponies, with blowing black manes and tails, were grazing.

"We've got to eat breakfast first," Lena said. "Come on, Laura! Hurry!"

Everyone except Aunt Docia was already at the table. Aunt Docia was frying pancakes.

"Get yourselves washed and combed, you lie-abeds! Breakfast's on the table and no thanks to you, lazy miss!" Aunt Docia, laughing, gave Lena a spank as Lena went by. This morning she was as good-natured as Uncle Hi.

Breakfast was jolly. Pa's great laugh rang out like bells. But afterward what stacks of dishes there were to wash!

Lena said the dishes were nothing to what she had been doing; dishes three times a day for forty-six men, and between times the cooking. She and Aunt Docia had been on their feet from before sunrise till late at night, and still they couldn't keep up with all the work. That's why Aunt Docia had hired the washing out. This was the first time that Laura had ever heard of hiring out the washing. A homesteader's wife did Aunt Docia's washing; she lived three miles away, so they'd have a six-mile drive.

Laura helped Lena carry the harness to the buggy, and lead

the willing ponies from their picket lines. She helped put the harness on them, the bits into their mouths, the hames on the collars clasping their warm black necks, and the tailpieces under their tails. Then Lena and Laura backed the ponies in beside the buggy pole, and fastened the stiff leather traces to the whiffletrees. They climbed into the buggy and Lena took the lines.

Pa had never let Laura drive his horses. He said she was not strong enough to hold them if they ran away.

As soon as Lena had the lines, the black ponies started gaily trotting. The buggy wheels turned swiftly, the fresh wind blew. Birds fluttered and sang and flew dipping over the tops of the blowing grasses. Faster and faster went the ponies, faster went the wheels. Laura and Lena laughed with joy.

The trotting ponies touched noses, gave a little squeal and ran.

Up sailed the buggy, almost jerking the seat from under Laura. Her bonnet flapped behind her tugging at its strings around her throat. She clutched onto the seat's edge. The ponies were stretched out low, running with all their might.

"They're running away!" Laura cried out.

"Let 'em run!" Lena shouted, slapping them with the lines. "They can't run against anything but grass! Hi! Yi! Yi, yi, yee-ee!" she yelled at the ponies.

Their long black manes and tails streamed on the wind, their feet pounded, the buggy sailed. Everything went rushing by too fast to be seen. Lena began to sing:

> "I know a young man fair to see,
> Take care! Oh, take care!
> And he can very obliging be.
> Beware! Oh, beware!"

Laura had not heard the song before, but she was soon singing the refrain with all her voice.

> "Take care, dear girl, he's a-fooling you!
> Take care! Oh, take care!
> Trust him not for he won't prove true,
> Beware! Oh, beware!"

"Hi, yi, yi, yi yipee-ee!" they yelled. But the ponies couldn't go faster, they were going as fast as they could.

"I wouldn't marry a farmer (Lena sang)
He's always in the dirt,
I'd rather marry a railroad man
Who wears a striped shirt!

"Oh, a railroad man, a railroad man,
A railroad man for me!
I'm going to marry a railroad man,
A railroader's bride I'll be!"

"I guess I better breathe them," she said. She pulled at the lines till she made the ponies trot, and then they slowed to a walk. Everything seemed quiet and slow.

"I wish I could drive," Laura said. "I always wanted to, but Pa won't let me."

"You can drive aways," Lena offered generously.

Just then the ponies touched noses again, squealed and ran.

"You can drive on the way home!" Lena promised. Singing and whooping, they went racing on across the prairie. Every time Lena slowed the ponies to get their breath, they got it and ran again. In no time at all, they reached the homesteader's claim shanty.

It was a tiny room, boarded up-and-down, and its roof sloped all one way, so that it looked like half of a little house. It was not as big as the wheat stacks beyond it, where men were threshing wheat with a noisy, chaff-puffing machine. The homesteader's wife came out to the buggy, lugging the basket of washing. Her face and arms and her bare feet were as brown as leather from the sun. Her hair straggled uncombed and her limp dress was faded and not clean.

"You must excuse the way I look," she said. "My girl was married yesterday, and here come the threshers this morning, and this wash to do. I been hustling since before sun-up, and here the day's work hardly started and my girl not here any more to help me."

"Do you mean Lizzie got married?" Lena asked.

"Yes, Lizzie got married yesterday," Lizzie's mother said

proudly. "Her Pa says thirteen's pretty young, but she's got her a good man and I say it's better to settle down young. I was married young myself."

Laura looked at Lena, and Lena looked at her. On the way back to camp they did not say anything for some time. Then both spoke at once.

"She was only a little older than I am," said Laura, and Lena said, "I'm a year older than she was."

They looked at each other again, an almost scared look. Then Lena tossed her curly black head. "She's a silly! Now she can't ever have any more good times."

Laura said soberly, "No, she can't play any more now."

Even the ponies trotted gravely. After a while Lena said she supposed that Lizzie did not have to work any harder than before. "Anyway, now she's doing her own work in her own house, and she'll have babies."

"Well," Laura said, "I'd like my own house and I like babies, and I wouldn't mind the work, but I don't want to be so responsible. I'd rather let Ma be responsible for a long time yet."

"And besides, I don't want to settle down," Lena said. "I'm not ever going to get married, or if I do, I'm going to marry a railroader and keep on moving west as long as I live."

"May I drive now?" Laura asked. She wanted to forget about growing up.

Lena gave her the lines. "All you have to do is hold the lines," Lena said. "The ponies know the way back." At that instant, the ponies touched noses and squealed.

"Hold onto them, Laura! Hold onto them!" Lena screeched.

Laura braced her feet and hung onto the lines with all her might. She could feel that the ponies didn't mean any harm. They were running because they wanted to run in the windy weather; they were going to do what they wanted to do. Laura hung onto them and yelled, "Yi, yi, yi, yip-ee!"

She had forgotten the basket of clothes, and so had Lena. All the way back to camp across the prairie they went whooping and singing, the ponies went running, trotting, and running again. When they stopped by the shanties to unhitch and picket the ponies, they found all the top layers of the clean washing on the buggy floor under the seats.

Guiltily they piled and smoothed them and lugged the heavy

basket into the shanty where Aunt Docia and Ma were dishing up the dinner.

"You girls look as if butter wouldn't melt in your mouths," said Aunt Docia. "What have you been up to?"

"Why, we just drove out and brought back the washing," said Lena.

That afternoon was even more exciting than the morning. As soon as the dishes were washed, Lena and Laura ran out again to the ponies. Jean had gone on one of them. He was riding away at a run across the prairie.

"No fair!" Lena yelled. The other pony was galloping in a circle, held by its picket rope. Lena grabbed its mane, unsnapped the rope, and sailed right up from the ground onto the back of the running pony.

Laura stood watching Lena and Jean race in circles, yelling like Indians. They rode crouching, their hair streaming back, their hands clutched in the flying black manes and their brown legs clasping the ponies' sides. The ponies curved and swerved, chasing each other on the prairie like birds in the sky. Laura would never have tired of watching them.

The ponies came galloping and stopped near her, and Lena and Jean slid off.

"Come on, Laura," Lena said generously. "You can ride Jean's pony."

"Who says she can?" Jean demanded. "You let her ride your own pony."

"You better behave or I'll tell how you tried to scare us last night," said Lena.

Laura took hold of the pony's mane. But the pony was much larger than she was, its back was high, and the pony was strong. Laura said, "I don't know if I can. I never did ride horseback."

"I'll put you on," said Lena. She held her pony by the forelock with one hand, and bending down she held her other hand for Laura to step onto.

Jean's pony seemed larger every minute. It was big and strong enough to kill Laura if it wanted to, and so high that to fall off it would break her bones. She was so scared to ride it that she had to try.

She stepped onto Lena's hand, she scrambled up the warm, slippery, moving mass of pony, while Lena boosted. Then she got one leg over the pony's back and everything began moving rapidly. Dimly she heard Lena saying, "Hang onto his mane."

She was holding onto the pony's mane. She was hanging onto deep handfuls of it with all her might, and her elbows and her knees were holding onto the pony, but she was jolting so that she couldn't think. The ground was so far beneath that she didn't dare look. Every instant she was falling, but before she really fell she was falling the other way, and the jolting rattled her teeth. Far off she heard Lena yell, "Hang on, Laura!"

Then everything smoothed into the smoothest rippling motion. This motion went through the pony and through Laura and kept them sailing over waves in rushing air. Laura's screwed-up eyes opened, and below her she saw the grasses flowing back. She saw the pony's black mane blowing, and her hands clenched tight in it. She and the pony were going too fast but they were going like music and nothing could happen to her until the music stopped.

Lena's pony came pounding along beside her. Laura wanted to ask how to stop safely but she could not speak. She saw the shanties far ahead, and knew that somehow the ponies had turned back toward the camp. Then the jolting began again. Then it stopped, and there she sat on the pony's back.

"Didn't I tell you it's fun?" Lena asked.

"What makes it jolt so?" Laura asked.

"That's trotting. You don't want to trot, you want to make your pony gallop. Just yell at it, like I did. Come on, let's go a long ways this time, you want to?"

"Yes," said Laura.

"All right, hang on. Now, yell!"

That was a wonderful afternoon. Twice Laura fell off; once the pony's head hit her nose and made it bleed, but she never let go of the mane. Her hair came unbraided and her throat grew hoarse from laughing and screeching, and her legs were scratched from running through the sharp grass and trying to leap onto her pony while it was running. She almost could, but not quite, and this made the pony mad. Lena and Jean always started the ponies to running and then swung up. They raced each other from the ground, trying which could sooner mount and reach a certain mark.

They did not hear Aunt Docia calling them to supper. Pa

came out and shouted, "Supper!" When they went in, Ma looked at Laura in shocked amazement and said mildly, "Really, Docia, I don't know when Laura's looked so like a wild Indian."

"She and Lena are a pair," said Aunt Docia. "Well, Lena hasn't had an afternoon to do as she liked since we came out here, and she won't have another till the summer's over."

CHAPTER 7

The West Begins

EARLY next morning they were all in the wagon again. It had not been unloaded so everything was ready to go.

Nothing was left of the camp but Aunt Docia's shanty. Over the worn-out grass and the dead spots where shanties had been, surveyors were measuring and driving stakes for a new town that would be built.

"We'll be along as soon as Hi gets his business settled," Aunt Docia said.

"I'll see you at Silver Lake!" Lena called to Laura, while Pa chirruped to the horses and the wheels began to turn.

The sun shone brightly on the uncovered wagon, but the wind was cool and riding was pleasant. Here and there, men were working in their fields, and now and then a team and wagon passed.

Soon the road curved downward through rolling land and Pa said, "The Big Sioux River's ahead."

Laura began to see out loud for Mary. "The road's going down a low bank to the river, but there aren't any trees. There's just the big sky and grassy land, and the little, low creek. It's a big river sometimes, but now it's dried up till it's no bigger than Plum Creek. It trickles along from pool to pool, by dry gravel stretches and cracked dry mud flats. Now the horses are stopping to drink."

"Drink hearty," Pa said to the horses. "There's no more water for thirty miles."

Beyond the low river the grassy land was low curve behind curve and the road looked like a short hook.

"The road pushes against the grassy land and breaks off short. And that's the end of it," said Laura.

"It can't be," Mary objected. "The road goes all the way to Silver Lake."

"I know it does," Laura answered.

"Well, then I don't think you ought to say things like that,"

Mary told her gently. "We should always be careful to say exactly what we mean."

"I was saying what I meant," Laura protested. But she could not explain. There were so many ways of seeing things and so many ways of saying them.

Beyond the Big Sioux there were no more fields, no houses, no people in sight. There really was no road, only a dim wagon trail, and no railroad grade. Here and there Laura glimpsed a little wooden stake, almost hidden in the grasses. Pa said they were surveyors' stakes for the railroad grade that was not started yet.

Laura said to Mary, "This prairie is like an enormous meadow, stretching far away in every direction, to the very edge of the world."

The endless waves of flowery grasses under the cloudless sky gave her a queer feeling. She could not say how she felt. All of them in the wagon, and the wagon and team, and even Pa, seemed small.

All morning Pa drove steadily along the dim wagon track, and nothing changed. The farther they went into the west, the smaller they seemed, and the less they seemed to be going anywhere. The wind blew the grass always with the same endless rippling, the horses' feet and the wheels going over the grass made always the same sound. The jiggling of the board seat was always the same jiggling. Laura thought they might go on forever, yet always be in this same changeless place, that would not even know they were there.

Only the sun moved. Without ever seeming to, the sun moved steadily upward in the sky. When it was overhead, they stopped to feed the horses and to eat a picnic lunch on the clean grass.

It was good to rest on the ground after riding all the morning. Laura thought of the many times they had eaten under the sky, while they were traveling all the way from Wisconsin to Indian Territory and back again to Minnesota. Now they were in Dakota Territory going farther west. But this was different from all the other times, not only because there was no cover on the wagon and no beds in it, but some other reason. Laura couldn't say how, but this prairie was different.

"Pa," she asked, "when you find the homestead, will it be like the one we had in Indian Territory?"

Pa thought before he answered. "No," he said finally. "This is different country. I can't tell you how, exactly, but this prairie is different. It feels different."

"That's likely enough," Ma said sensibly. "We're west of Minnesota, and north of Indian Territory, so naturally the flowers and grasses are not the same."

But that was not what Pa and Laura meant. There was really almost no difference in the flowers and grasses. But there was something else here that was not anywhere else. It was an enormous stillness that made you feel still. And when you were still, you could feel great stillness coming closer.

All the little sounds of the blowing grasses and of the horses munching and whooshing in their feedbox at the back of the wagon, and even the sounds of eating and talking could not touch the enormous silence of this prairie.

Pa talked about his new job. He would be the company storekeeper, and the timekeeper at Silver Lake camp. He would run the store and he would keep straight in his books the charge account of every man on the job, and know exactly how much money was due each man for his work, after his board bill and his account at the store had been subtracted. And when the paymaster brought the money each payday, Pa would pay every man. That was all he had to do, and for that he would be paid fifty dollars every month.

"And best of all, Caroline, we're among the very first out here!" said Pa. "We've got the pick of the land for our homestead. By George, our luck's turned at last! First chance at new land, and fifty dollars a month for a whole summer to boot!"

"It is wonderful, Charles," said Ma.

But all their talking did not mean anything to the enormous silence of that prairie.

All that afternoon they went on, mile after mile, never seeing a house or any sign of people, never seeing anything but grass and sky. The trail they followed was marked only by bent and broken grasses.

Laura saw old Indian trails and buffalo paths worn deep in the ground and now grassed over. She saw strange large depressions, straight-sided and flat-bottomed, that had been buffalo wallows, where now the grass was growing. Laura had never seen a buffalo, and Pa said it was not likely that she would ever see one. Only a little while before the vast herds of thousands of buffaloes had grazed over this country. They had been the Indians' cattle, and white men had slaughtered them all.

On every side now the prairie stretched away empty to far, clear skyline. The wind never stopped blowing, waving the tall prairie grasses that had turned brown in the sun. And all the afternoon, while Pa kept driving onward, he was merrily whistling or singing. The song he sang oftenest was:

"Oh, come to this country,
And don't you feel alarm,
For Uncle Sam is rich enough
To give us all a farm!"

Even baby Grace joined in the chorus, though she did not bother to follow the tune.

"Oh, come away! Come away!
Come away, I say!
Oh, come away! Come away!
Come right away!
Oh, come to this country
And have no fear of harm
Our Uncle Sam is rich enough
To give us all a farm!"

The sun was lowering in the west when a rider appeared on the prairie behind the wagon. He came following behind not very fast, but coming a little nearer mile after mile while the sun was slowly sinking.

"How much farther is it to Silver Lake, Charles?" Ma asked.

"About ten miles," said Pa.

"There isn't anybody living nearer, is there?"

"No," said Pa.

Ma did not say anything more. Neither did anyone else. They kept glancing back at that rider behind them, and each time they looked, he was a little nearer. He was surely following them and not meaning to overtake them until the sun sank. The sun was so low that every hollow between the low prairie swells was filled with shadow.

Each time that Pa glanced back, his hand made a little motion, slapping the horses with the lines to hurry them. But no team could pull a loaded wagon as fast as a man could ride.

The man was so near now that Laura could see two pistols in leather holsters on his hips. His hat was pulled low over his eyes, and a red bandana was tied loosely around his neck.

Pa had brought his gun west, but it was not in the wagon now. Laura wondered where it was, but she did not ask Pa.

She looked back again and saw another rider coming on a white horse. He wore a red shirt. He and the white horse were far behind and small, but they came fast, galloping. They overtook the first rider, and the two came on together.

Ma said in a low voice, "There's two of them now, Charles."

Mary asked frightened, "What is it? Laura, what's the matter?"

Pa looked back quickly, and then he was comfortable. "Everything's all right now," he said. "That's Big Jerry."

"Who's Big Jerry?" Ma asked.

"He's a half-breed, French and Indian," Pa answered carelessly. "A gambler, and some say a horse thief, but a darned good fellow. Big Jerry won't let anybody waylay us."

Ma looked at him astonished. Her mouth opened and then it shut; she did not say anything.

The riders came up beside the wagon. Pa lifted his hand and said, "Hullo, Jerry!"

"Hullo, Ingalls!" Big Jerry answered. The other man gave them all a snarling look and went galloping on ahead, but Big Jerry rode along by the wagon.

He looked like an Indian. He was tall and big but not one bit fat, and his thin face was brown. His shirt was flaming red. His straight black hair swung against his flat, high-boned cheek as he rode, for he wore no hat. And his snow-white horse wore no saddle nor bridle. The horse was free, he could go where he wanted to go, and he wanted to go with Big Jerry wherever Big Jerry wanted to ride. The horse and the man moved together as if they were one animal.

They were beside the wagon only a moment. Then away

they went in the smoothest, prettiest run, down into a little hollow and up and away, straight into the blazing round sun on the far edge of the west. The flaming red shirt and the white horse vanished in the blazing golden light.

Laura let out her breath. "Oh, Mary! The snow-white horse and the tall, brown man, with such a black head and a bright red shirt! The brown prairie all around—and they rode right into the sun as it was going down. They'll go on in the sun around the world."

Mary thought a moment. Then she said, "Laura, you know he couldn't ride into the sun. He's just riding along on the ground like anybody."

But Laura did not feel that she had told a lie. What she had said was true too. Somehow that moment when the beautiful, free pony and the wild man rode into the sun would last forever.

Ma still feared that the other man might be lying in wait to rob them, but Pa told her, "Don't worry! Big Jerry's gone ahead to find him and stay with him till we get into camp. Jerry'll see that nobody molests us."

Ma looked back to see that her girls were all right, and she held Grace snugly on her lap. She did not say anything because nothing she could say would make any difference. But Laura knew that Ma had never wanted to leave Plum Creek and did not like to be here now; she did not like traveling in that lonely country with night coming on and such men riding the prairie.

The wild calls of birds came down from the fading sky. More and more dark lines streaked the pale-blue air overhead—straight lines of wild ducks, and long flying wedges of wild geese. The leaders called to their flocks behind them, and each bird answered in turn. The whole sky twanged, "Honk? Honk! Honk! Quanck? Quanck. Quanck."

"They're flying low," said Pa. "Settling down for the night on the lakes."

There were lakes ahead. A thin silvery line at the very edge of the sky was Silver Lake, and little glimmers south of it were the Twin Lakes, Henry and Thompson. A wee dark blob between them was the Lone Tree. Pa said it was a big cottonwood, the only tree to be seen between the Big Sioux River and the Jim; it grew on a little rise of ground no wider than a road, between the Twin Lakes, and it grew big because its roots could reach water.

"We'll get some seeds from it to plant on our homestead," Pa said. "You can't see Spirit Lake from here, it's nine miles northwest of Silver Lake. You see, Caroline, what fine hunting country this is. Plenty of water and good feeding ground for wild fowl."

"Yes, Charles, I see," said Ma.

The sun sank. A ball of pulsing, liquid light, it sank in clouds of crimson and silver. Cold purple shadows rose in the east, crept slowly across the prairie, then rose in heights on heights of darkness from which the stars swung low and bright.

The wind, which all day long had blown strongly, dropped low with the sun and went whispering among the tall grasses. The earth seemed to lie breathing softly under the summer night.

Pa drove on and on beneath the low stars. The horses' feet went softly thump-thumping on the grassy ground. Far, far ahead a few tiny lights pricked through the dark. They were the lights of Silver Lake camp.

"Don't need to see the trail for these next eight miles," Pa told Ma. "All a man's got to do is keep driving toward the lights. There's nothing between us and camp but smooth prairie and air."

Laura was tired and chilly. The lights were far away. They might be stars after all. The whole night was a glittering of stars. Close overhead and down on all sides great stars glittered in patterns on the dark. The tall grass rustled against the turning wagon wheels; it kept on rustling, rustling against the wheels that kept on turning.

Suddenly Laura's eyes jerked open. There was an open doorway and light streaming out. And in the dazzle of lamplight Uncle Henry was coming, laughing. So this must be Uncle Henry's house in the Big Woods when Laura was little, for that was where Uncle Henry was.

"Henry!" Ma exclaimed.

"It's a surprise, Caroline!" Pa sang out. "I thought I wouldn't tell you Henry's out here."

"I declare, it takes my breath, I am so surprised," said Ma.

And then a big man was laughing up at them, and he was

Cousin Charley. He was the big boy who had bothered Uncle Henry and Pa in the oat field, and been stung by thousands of yellow jackets. "Hello, Half-pint! Hello, Mary! And here's baby Carrie, a big girl now. Not the baby any longer, uh?" Cousin Charley helped them down from the wagon, while Uncle Henry took Grace and Pa helped Ma over the wheel, and here came Cousin Louisa, bustling and talking and herding them all into the shanty.

Cousin Louisa and Charley were both grown up now. They were keeping the boarding shanty, cooking for the men who were working on the grade. But the men had eaten supper long ago, and now they were all sleeping in the bunkhouses. Cousin Louisa talked about all this, while she dished up the supper she had been keeping hot on the stove.

After supper Uncle Henry lighted a lantern and led the way to a shanty that the men had built for Pa.

"It's all new lumber, Caroline, fresh and clean as a whistle," Uncle Henry said, holding up the lantern so they could see the new board walls and the bunks built up against them. There was a bunk on one side for Ma and Pa, and on the other side two narrow bunks, one above the other, for Mary and Laura and Carrie and Grace. The beds were already spread in the bunks; Cousin Louisa had seen to that.

In no time at all, Laura and Mary were cuddled on the rustling fresh hay-mattress with the sheet and quilts drawn up to their noses, and Pa blew out the lantern.

CHAPTER 8

Silver Lake

THE sun had not yet risen next morning when Laura let down the pail into the shallow well by Silver Lake. Beyond the lake's eastern shore the pale sky was bordered with bands of crimson and gold. Their brightness stretched around the south shore and shone on the high bank that stood up from the water in the east and the north.

Night was still shadowy in the northwest, but Silver Lake lay like a sheet of silver in its setting of tall wild grasses.

Ducks quacked among the thick grasses to the south-west, where the Big Slough began. Screaming gulls flew over the lake, beating against the dawn wind. A wild goose rose from the water with a ringing call, and one after another the birds of his flock answered him as they rose and followed. The great triangle of wild geese flew with a beating of strong wings into the glory of the sunrise.

Shafts of golden light shot higher and higher in the eastern sky, until their brightness touched the water and was reflected there.

Then the sun, a golden ball, rolled over the eastern edge of the world.

Laura breathed a long breath. Then hurriedly she pulled up the pail of water, and carrying it she hurried back toward the shanty. The new shanty stood alone by the lake shore, south of the cluster of shanties that was the graders' camp. It shone yellow in the sunshine; a little house almost lost in the grasses, and its little roof sloped all one way, as if it were only half a roof.

"We have been waiting for the water, Laura," Ma said, when Laura went in.

"Oh, but Ma! the sunrise! You should have seen the sunrise!" Laura exclaimed. "I just had to watch it."

She began quickly to help Ma get breakfast, and while she hurried she told how the sun came up beyond Silver Lake, flooding the sky with wonderful colors while the flocks of wild geese flew dark against them, how thousands of wild ducks almost covered the water, and gulls flew screaming against the wind above it.

"I heard them," Mary said. "Such a clamoring of wild birds, it was like bedlam. And now I see it all. You make pictures when you talk, Laura."

Ma smiled at Laura too, but she only said, "Well, girls, we have a busy day before us," and she laid out their work.

Everything must be unpacked and the shanty made tidy before noon. Cousin Louisa's beds must be aired and returned, and Ma's ticking mattresses stuffed with fresh clean hay. Meanwhile, from the company store Ma brought yards of bright-figured calico for curtains. She made a curtain and they hung it across the shanty, shutting the bunks in behind it. Then she made another curtain and hung it between the bunks; so there were two bedrooms, one for her and Pa, the other for the girls. The shanty was so small that the curtains touched the bunks, but when the bunks were made up with Ma's mattresses and featherbeds and patchwork quilts, it all looked fresh and bright and snug.

Then in front of the curtain was the room to live in. It was very small, with the cookstove at the end by the door. Ma and Laura placed the drop-leaf table against the side wall, before the open front door. Mary's rocking chair and Ma's they put on the other side of the room. The floor was bare ground, with humps of obstinate grass roots in it, but they swept it clean. The wind blew softly in from the open doorway, and the railroad shanty was very pleasant and homelike.

"This is another kind of little house with only half a roof and no window," said Ma. "But it's a tight roof, and we don't need a window, so much air and light come through the doorway."

When Pa came to dinner, he was pleased to see everything so nicely settled and arranged. He tweaked Carrie's ear and swung Grace up in his hands; he could not toss her, under that low roof.

"But where's the china shepherdess, Caroline?" he asked.

"I haven't unpacked the shepherdess, Charles," said Ma. "We aren't living here, we're only staying till you get our homestead."

Pa laughed. "I've got plenty of time to pick the right one too! Look at all this great prairie with nobody on it but the railroad graders and they'll go away before winter comes. We can just about take our pick of the land."

"After dinner," Laura said, "Mary and I are going to take a walk and look at the camp and the lake and everything." She took the water pail and ran out bareheaded to get fresh water from the well for dinner.

The wind was blowing steady and strong. Not a cloud was in the huge sky, and far and wide on the immense land there was nothing but shimmering light passing over the grasses. And down wind came the sound of many men's voices, singing.

The teams were coming into camp. In a long, dark, snake-like line as they came over the prairie, horses plodding side by side in their harness, and men marching, bareheaded and bare-armed, brown-skinned in their striped blue-and-white shirts and gray shirts and plain blue shirts, and all of them were singing the same song.

They were like a little army coming across the vast land under the enormous empty sky, and the song was their banner.

Laura stood in the strong wind, looking and listening, till the last of the column came into the crowd that gathered and spread around the camp's low shanties, and the song blurred into the sound of all their hearty voices. Then she remembered the water pail in her hand. She filled it from the well as quickly as she could, and ran back, slopping water on her bare legs in her hurry.

"I just had—to watch the—teams coming into camp," she panted. "So many of them, Pa! And all the men were singing!"

"Now, Flutterbudget, catch your breath!" Pa laughed at her. "Fifty teams and seventy-five or eighty men are only a small camp. You ought to see Stebbins' camp west of here; two hundred men and teams according."

"Charles," Ma said.

Usually everyone knew what Ma meant when she said in her gentle way, "Charles." But this time Laura and Carrie and Pa all looked at her wondering. Ma shook her head just the least bit at Pa.

Then Pa looked straight at Laura and said, "You girls keep away from the camp. When you go walking, don't go near where the men are working, and you be sure you're back here before they come in for the night. There's all kinds of rough men working on the grade and using rough language, and the less you see and hear of them the better. Now remember, Laura. And you too, Carrie." Pa's face was very serious.

"Yes, Pa," Laura promised, and Carrie almost whispered, "Yes, Pa." Carrie's eyes were large and frightened. She did not want to hear rough language, whatever rough language might be. Laura would have liked to hear some, just once, but of course she must obey Pa.

So that afternoon when they set out for their walk they went away from the shanties. They set out along the lake shore toward the Big Slough.

The lake lay at their left shimmering in the sunshine. Little silvery waves rose and fell and lapped upon the shore as the wind ruffled the blue water. The shore was low, but firm and dry, with little grasses growing to the water's edge. Across the glittering lake, Laura could see the east bank and the south bank, rising up as tall as she was. A little slough came into the lake from the northeast, and Big Slough went on toward the southwest in a long curve of tall wild grasses.

Laura and Mary and Carrie walked slowly along on the green shore by the rippling silver-blue water, toward the wild Big Slough. The grasses were warm and soft to their feet. The wind blew their flapping skirts tight against their bare legs and ruffled Laura's hair. Mary's sunbonnet and Carrie's were tied firmly under their chins, but Laura swung hers by its strings. Millions of rustling grass-blades made one murmuring sound, and thousands of wild ducks and geese and herons and cranes and pelicans were talking sharply and brassily in the wind.

All those birds were feeding among the grasses of the sloughs. They rose on flapping wings and settled again, crying news to each other and talking among themselves among the grasses, and eating busily of grass roots and tender water plants and little fishes.

The lake shore went lower and lower toward Big Slough, until really there was no shore. The lake melted into the slough, making small ponds surrounded by the harsh, rank slough grass that stood five and six feet tall. Little ponds glimmered between the grasses and on the water the wild birds were thick.

As Laura and Carrie pushed into the slough grasses, suddenly harsh wings ripped upward and round eyes glittered; the whole air exploded in a noise of squawking, quacking, quonking. Flattening their webbed feet under their tails, ducks and geese sped over the grass-tops and curved down to the next pond.

Laura and Carrie stood still. The coarse-stemmed slough grass rose above their heads and made a rough sound in the wind. Their bare feet sank slowly into ooze.

"Oo, the ground is all soft," Mary said, turning back quickly. She did not like mud on her feet.

"Go back, Carrie!" Laura cried. "You'll mire down! The lake is in here among the grasses!"

The soft, cool mud sucked around her ankles as she stood, and before her the little ponds glimmered among the tall grasses. She wanted to go on and on, into the slough among the wild birds, but she could not leave Mary and Carrie. So she turned back with them to the hard, higher prairie where waist-high grasses were nodding and bending in the wind, and the short, curly buffalo grass grew in patches.

Along the edge of the slough they picked flaming red tiger lilies, and on higher ground they gathered long branching stems of purple buffalo bean pods. Grasshoppers flew up like spray before their feet in the grasses. All kinds of little birds fluttered and flew and twittered balancing in the wind on the tall, bending grass stems, and prairie hens scuttled everywhere.

"Oh, what a wild, beautiful prairie!" Mary sighed with happiness. "Laura, have you got your sunbonnet on?"

Guiltily Laura pulled up her sunbonnet from where it hung by its strings down her neck. "Yes, Mary," she said.

Mary laughed. "You just now put it on. I heard you!"

It was late afternoon when they turned back. The little shanty, with its roof slanting all one way, stood all by itself and small at the edge of Silver Lake. Tiny in the doorway, Ma shaded her eyes with her hand to look for them, and they waved to her.

They could see the whole camp, scattered along the lake shore north of the shanty. First was the store where Pa was working with the big feed store behind it. Then the stable for the work teams. The stable was built into a swell of the prairie, and its roof was thatched with slough grass. Beyond it was the long, low bunkhouse where the men slept, and still farther away was Cousin Louisa's long boardinghouse shanty, with supper smoke already rising from its stovepipe.

Then for the first time Laura saw a house, a real house, standing all by itself on the lake's northern shore.

"I wonder what that house can be and who lives there," she said. "It isn't a homestead because there's no stable and no land plowed."

She had told Mary all that she saw, and Mary said, "What a pretty place it is with the clean, new shanties and the grass and the water. There's no use wondering about that house; we can ask Pa about it. Here comes another flock of wild ducks."

Flock after flock of ducks and long lines of wild geese were coming down from the sky and settling to stay all night on the lake. And the men were making a racket of voices as they came from their work. In the shanty's doorway again, Ma waited till they reached her, wind-blown and full of the fresh air and sunshine, bringing her their armfuls of tiger lilies and purple bean pods.

Then Carrie put the big bouquet in a pitcher of water while Laura set the table for supper. Mary sat in her rocking chair with Grace in her lap and told her about the ducks quacking in the Big Slough and the great flocks of wild geese going to sleep on the lake.

CHAPTER 9

Horse Thieves

ONE night at supper Pa spoke hardly at all. He only answered questions. At last Ma asked, "Aren't you feeling well, Charles?"

"I'm all right, Caroline," Pa answered.

"Then what is the matter?" Ma demanded.

"Nothing," Pa said. "Nothing to worry you about. Well, the fact is, the boys have got word to look out for horse thieves tonight."

"That's Hi's affair," Ma said. "I hope you'll let him tend to it."

"Don't worry, Caroline," Pa said.

Laura and Carrie looked at each other and then at Ma. After a moment Ma said gently, "I wish you'd out with it, Charles."

"Big Jerry's been in camp," Pa said. "He's been here a week, and now he's gone. The boys say he's in with the gang of horse thieves. They say every time Big Jerry visits a camp the best horses are stolen after he leaves. They think he stays just long enough to pick out the best teams and find out what stalls they're in, and then he comes back with his gang in the night and gets away with them in the dark."

"I always heard you can't trust a half-breed," Ma said. Ma did not like Indians; she did not like even half-Indians.

"We'd all have been scalped down on the Verdigris River, if it hadn't been for a full-blood," said Pa.

"We wouldn't have been in any danger of scalping if it hadn't been for those howling savages," said Ma, "with fresh skunk skins around their middles." And she made a sound that came from remembering how those skunk skins smelled.

"I don't think Jerry steals horses," Pa said. But Laura thought he said it as if he hoped that saying it would make it so. "The real trouble is, he comes to camp after payday and wins all the boys' money playing poker. That's why some of them would be glad to shoot him."

"I wonder Hi allows it," said Ma. "If there's anything as bad as drink, it's gambling."

"They don't have to gamble if they don't want to, Caroline," Pa said. "If Jerry wins their money, it's their own fault. There never was a kinder-hearted man than Big Jerry. He'd give the shirt off his back. Look how he takes care of Old Johnny."

"That's so," Ma admitted. Old Johnny was the water boss. He was a little, wizened, bent-backed old Irishman. He had worked on railroads all his life, and now he was too old to work. So the company had given him the job of carrying water to the men.

Every morning and again after dinner, little old Johnny came to the well to fill his two large, wooden water pails. When they were full he set his wooden yoke across his shoulders and stooping, he hooked into the pails the two hooks that hung from short chains at each end of the yoke. Then with a grunt and groan, he straightened up. The chains lifted the heavy pails from the ground and Johnny steadied them with his hands while he bore their weight on his shoulders. He trotted under the weight with short, stiff steps.

There was a tin dipper in each water pail. When he got to the men working on the grade, Johnny would trot along the line of work, so that any thirsty man could help himself to a drink of water without stopping work.

Johnny was so old that he was little, stooped and shrunken. His face was a mass of wrinkles, but his blue eyes twinkled cheerily and he always trotted as quickly as he could so that no thirsty man need wait for a drink.

One morning before breakfast, Big Jerry had come to the door and told Ma that Old Johnny had been sick all night.

"He's so little and old, ma'am," Big Jerry said. "The meals at the boarding shanty don't agree with him. Would you give him a cup of hot tea and a bit of breakfast?"

Ma put several of her hot, light biscuits on a plate and beside them she put a fried mashed-potato cake and a slice of crisply fried salt pork. Then she filled a little tin pail with hot tea and gave it all to Big Jerry.

After breakfast Pa went to the bunkhouse to see Old Johnny, and later he told Ma that Jerry had taken care of the poor old man all night. Johnny said that Jerry had even spread his own blanket over him to keep him warm and gone without any covering himself in the cold.

"He couldn't take better care of his own father than he did of Old Johnny," Pa said. "For that matter, Caroline, I don't know but what we're beholden to him ourselves."

They all remembered how Big Jerry had come out of the prairie on his white horse when the strange man was following them and the sun was setting.

"Well," Pa said, getting up slowly, "I've got to go sell the boys the ammunition for their guns. I hope Jerry don't come back to camp tonight. If he just rode up to see how Old Johnny is, rode up to the stable to put his horse in, they'd shoot him."

"Oh, no, Charles! Surely they wouldn't do that!" Ma exclaimed.

Pa pulled on his hat. "The one that's doing most of the talking's already killed one man," he said. "He got off easy on a plea of self-defense, but he's served a term in State's prison. And Big Jerry cleaned him out, last payday. He hasn't got the nerve to face Big Jerry, but he'll bushwhack him if he gets the chance."

Pa went to the store, and Ma soberly began to clear the table. While Laura washed the dishes, she thought of Big Jerry and his white horse. She had seen them many times, galloping over the brown prairie. Big Jerry always wore a bright red shirt, he was always bareheaded, and his white horse never wore a strap.

The night was dark when Pa came from the store. He said that half a dozen men with loaded guns were lying in wait around the stable.

It was bedtime. There was not a light in the camp. The dark shanties, low against the land, could hardly be seen; only if you knew where to look, you could see them darker in the dark. There was a little starshine on Silver Lake, and all around it stretched the black prairie, flat under the velvet-dark sky sparkling with stars. The wind whispered cold in the dark, and the grass rustled as if it were afraid. Laura looked and listened, and hurried shivering into the shanty again.

Behind the curtain Grace was sleeping and Ma was helping Mary and Carrie to bed. Pa had hung up his hat and sat down on the bench, but he was not taking off his boots. He looked up when Laura came in, and then he got up and put on his coat. He buttoned it all the way up and turned up its collar so that his gray shirt did not show. Laura did not say a word. Pa put on his hat.

"Don't sit up for me, Caroline," he said cheerfully.

Ma came from behind the curtain, but Pa was gone. She went to the doorway and looked out. Pa had disappeared in the darkness. After a minute Ma turned around and said, "Bedtime, Laura."

"Please, Ma, let me stay up too," Laura begged.

"I believe I won't go to bed," said Ma. "Not for a while, anyway. I'm not sleepy. It's no use to go to bed when you're not sleepy."

"I'm not sleepy, Ma," Laura said.

Ma turned down the lamp and blew it out. She sat down in the hickory rocker that Pa had made for her in Indian territory. Laura went softly on her bare feet across the ground and sat close beside Ma.

They sat in the dark, listening. Laura could hear a thin, faint humming in her ears; it seemed to be the sound of her listening. She could hear Ma's breathing and the slow breathing of Grace, asleep, and the faster breathing of Mary and Carrie lying awake behind the curtain. The curtain made a faint sound, moving a little in the air from the open doorway. Outside the doorway there was an oblong of sky and stars above the faraway edge of dark land.

Out there the wind sighed, the grass rustled, and there was the tiny, ceaseless sound of little waves lapping on the lake shore.

A sharp cry in the dark jerked all through Laura; she almost screamed. It was only the call of a wild goose, lost from its flock. Wild geese answered it from the slough, and a quacking of sleepy ducks rose.

"Ma, let me go out and find Pa," Laura whispered.

"Be quiet," Ma answered. "You couldn't find Pa. And he doesn't want you to. Be quiet and let Pa take care of himself."

"I want to do something. I'd rather do something," Laura said.

"So would I," said Ma. In the dark her hand began softly to stroke Laura's head. "The sun and the wind are drying your hair, Laura," Ma said. "You must brush it more. You must brush your hair a hundred strokes every night before you go to bed."

"Yes, Ma," Laura whispered.

"I had lovely long hair when your Pa and I were married," Ma said. "I could sit on the braids."

She did not say any more. She went on stroking Laura's rough hair while they listened for the sound of shooting.

There was one shining large star by the black edge of the doorway. As time went on, it moved. Slowly, it moved from east to west, and more slowly still the smaller stars wheeled about it.

Suddenly Laura and Ma heard footsteps, and in an instant the stars were blotted out. Pa was in the doorway. Laura jumped up, but Ma only went limp in the chair.

"Sitting up, Caroline?" Pa said. "Pshaw, you didn't need to do that. Everything's all right."

"How do you know that, Pa?" Laura asked. "How do you know Big Jerry——"

"Never mind, Flutterbudget!" Pa stopped her cheerfully. "Big Jerry's all right. He won't be coming into camp tonight. I wouldn't be surprised though, if he rode in this morning on his white horse. Now go to bed. Let's get what sleep we can before sunrise." Then Pa's great laugh rang out like bells. "There'll be a sleepy bunch of men working on the grade today!"

While Laura was undressing behind the curtain and Pa was taking off his boots on the other side of it, she heard him say in a low voice to Ma, "The best of it is, Caroline, there'll never be a horse stolen from Silver Lake camp."

Sure enough, early that morning Laura saw Big Jerry riding by the shanty on his white horse. He hailed Pa at the store and Pa waved to him; then Big Jerry and the white horse galloped on and away toward where the men were working.

There never was a horse stolen from Silver Lake camp.

CHAPTER 10

The Wonderful Afternoon

EARLY every morning while Laura washed the breakfast dishes, she could look through the open door and see the men leaving the boarding shanty and going to the thatched stable for their horses. Then there was a rattling of harness and a confusion of talking and shouts, and the men and teams went out to the job leaving quietness behind them.

All the days went by, one like another. On Mondays Laura helped Ma do the washing and bring in the clean-scented clothes that dried quickly in the wind and sunshine. On Tuesdays she sprinkled them and helped Ma iron them. On Wednesdays she did her task of mending and sewing though she did not like to. Mary was learning to sew without seeing; her sensitive fingers could hem nicely, and she could sew quilt-patches if the colors were matched for her.

At noon the camp was noisy again with all the teams and the men coming in to dinner. Then Pa came from the store, and they all ate in the little shanty with the wind blowing against it and the wide prairie outside the door. Softly colored in all shades from dark brown to russet and tan, the prairie rolled in gentle swells to the far edge of the sky. The winds were blowing colder at night, more and more wild birds were flying southward, and Pa said that winter would not be long in coming. But Laura did not think about winter.

She wanted to know where the men were working and how they made a railroad grade. Every morning they went out, and at noon and at night they came back, but all that she saw of working was a smudge of dust that came up from the tawny prairie in the west. She wanted to see the men building the railroad.

Aunt Docia moved into the camp one day, and she brought two cows. She said, "I brought our milk on the hoof, Charles. It's the only way to get any, out here where there aren't any farmers."

One of the cows was for Pa. She was a pretty, bright-red cow named Ellen. Pa untied her from the back of Aunt Docia's wagon, and handed the halter rope to Laura. "Here, Laura," he said. "You're old enough to take care of her. Take her out where the grass is good, and be sure to drive down the picket pin good and firm."

Laura and Lena picketed the cows not far apart in good grass. Every morning and every evening they met to take care of the cows. They led them to drink from the lake, and moved the picket pins to fresh grass, and then they did the milking, and while they milked they sang.

Lena knew many new songs and Laura learned them quickly. Together, while the milk streamed into the bright tin pails, they sang:

"A life on the ocean wave,
A home on the rolling deep,
The pollywogs wag their tails
And the tears roll down their cheeks."

Sometimes Lena sang softly, and so did Laura.

"Oh, I wouldn't marry a farmer,
He's always in the dirt,
I'd rather marry a railroad man
Who wears a striped shirt."

But Laura liked the waltz songs best. She loved the Broom song, though they had to sing "broom" so many times to make the tune swing.

"Buy a broo-oom, buy a broom, broom!
Buy a broom, broom, buy a broom, broom!
Will you buy of this wandering Bavarian a broom?
To brush off the insects
That come to annoy you,
You'll find it quite useful
By night and by day."

The cows stood quiet, chewing their cuds, as though they were listening to the singing until the milking was done.

Then with the pails of warm, sweet-smelling milk, Laura and Lena walked back toward the shanties. In the mornings the men were coming out of the bunkhouse, washing in the basins on the bench by the door and combing their hair. And the sun was rising over Silver Lake.

In the evenings the sky flamed with red and purple and gold, the sun had set, and the teams and men were coming in, dark along the dusty road they had worn on the prairie, and singing. Then quickly Lena hurried to Aunt Docia's shanty, and Laura to Ma's, because they must strain the milk before the cream began to rise, and help get supper.

Lena had so much work to do, helping Aunt Docia and Cousin Louisa, that she had no time to play. And Laura, though she did not work so hard, was busy enough. So they hardly ever met except at milking time.

"If Pa hadn't put our black ponies to work on the grade," Lena said one evening, "you know what I'd do?"

"No, what?" Laura asked.

"Well, if I could get away, and if we had the ponies to ride, we'd go see the men working," said Lena. "Don't you want to?"

"Yes, I want to," Laura said. She did not have to decide whether or not she would disobey Pa, because they couldn't do it anyway.

Suddenly one day at dinner Pa set down his teacup, wiped his mustache, and said, "You ask too many questions, Flutter-budget. Put on your bonnet and come up to the store along about two o'clock. I'll take you out and let you see for yourself."

"Oh, Pa!" Laura cried out.

"There, Laura, don't get so excited," Ma said quietly.

Laura knew she should not shout. She kept her voice low. "Pa, can Lena go too?"

"We will decide about that later," said Ma.

After Pa had gone back to the store, Ma talked seriously to Laura. She said that she wanted her girls to know how to behave, to speak nicely in low voices and have gentle manners and always be ladies. They had always lived in wild, rough places, except for a little while on Plum Creek, and now they were in a rough railroad camp, and it would be some time before this country was civilized. Until then, Ma thought it best that they keep themselves to themselves. She wanted Laura to stay away from the camp, and not get acquainted with any of the rough men there. It would be all right for her to go quietly with Pa to see the work this once, but she must be well-behaved and ladylike, and remember that a lady never did anything that could attract attention.

"Yes, Ma," Laura said.

"And Laura, I do not want you to take Lena," said Ma. "Lena is a good, capable girl, but she is boisterous, and Docia has not curbed her as much as she might. If you must go where those rough men are working in the dirt, then go quietly with your Pa and come back quietly, and say no more about it."

"Yes, Ma," Laura said. "But——"

"But what, Laura?" Ma asked.

"Nothing," said Laura.

"I don't know why you want to go anyway," Mary wondered. "It's much nicer here in the shanty, or taking a little walk by the lake."

"I just want to. I want to see them building a railroad," Laura said.

She tied on her sunbonnet when she set out and resolved to keep it tied on. Pa was alone in the store. He put on his broad-brimmed hat and padlocked the door, and they went out on the prairie together. At that time of day when there were no shadows the prairie looked level, but it was not. In a few minutes its swells hid the shanties, and on the grassy land there was nothing to be seen but the dusty track of the road and the railroad grade beside it. Against the sky ahead rose up the smudge of dust, blowing away on the wind.

Pa held onto his hat and Laura bent her head in the flapping sunbonnet, and they trudged along together for some time. Then Pa stopped and said, "There you are, Half-pint."

They were standing on a little rise of the land. Before them the railroad grade ended bluntly. In front of it, men with teams and plows were plowing onward toward the west, breaking a wide strip of the prairie sod.

"Do they do it with plows?" Laura said. It seemed strange to her to think that men with plows went ahead into this country that had never been plowed to build a railroad.

"And scrapers," said Pa. "Now watch, Laura."

Between the plowing and the blunt end of the grade, teams and men were going slowly around in a circle, over the end of the grade and back to cross the plowed strip. The teams were pulling wide, deep shovels. These were the scrapers.

Instead of one long shovel handle, each scraper had two short handles. And a strong half-hoop of steel curved from one side of the scraper to the other side. The team was hitched to this curve of steel.

When a man and his team came to the plowed land, another man took hold of the scraper handles and held them just high enough to thrust the round shovel point into the loose earth of the plowed ground while the team went on and earth filled the scraper. Then he let go of the handles, the full scraper sat level on the ground, and the horses pulled it on around the circle, up the side of the grade.

On the grade's blunt end the men who drove the team caught hold of the scraper's handles and tipped the whole scraper over in a somersault inside the curving steel that the horses were hitched to. All the dirt was left right there, while the team drew the empty scraper down the grade and on around the circle to the plowed land again.

There the other man caught hold of the handles and held them just high enough to thrust the round shovel point into the loose earth until the scraper was filled again. And on around the circle it came sliding behind the team, up the steep slope of the grade, and somersaulting over again.

Team after team came around the circle, scraper after scraper tipped over. The teams never stopped coming, the scrapers never stopped filling and tipping.

As the loose soil was scraped from the plowed land, the curve widened out so that the scrapers passed over freshly plowed ground ahead, while the plow teams came back and plowed again the ground that had been scraped.

"It all goes like clockwork," said Pa. "See, no one stands still, no one hurries.

"When one scraper is filled another is on the spot to take its place, and the scraper holder is there to grab the handles and fill it. The scrapers never have to wait for the plows, and the plows go just so far ahead before they come back to plow again the ground that has been scraped. They are doing great work. Fred is a good boss."

Fred stood on the dump watching the teams and scrapers circling, and the plows coming around inside the circle and moving out ahead of it again. He watched the dumping of the scrapers and the dirt rolling down, and with a nod or a word he told each driver when to dump his scraper, so that the grade would be even, and straight, and level.

For every six teams, one man did nothing but stand and watch. If a team slowed, he spoke to the driver and he drove faster. If a team went too fast, he spoke to that driver and that driver held his horses back. The teams must be spaced evenly, while they kept on going steadily around the circle, over the plowed land and to the grade and over it and back to the plowed land again.

Thirty teams and thirty scrapers, and all the four-horse teams and the plows, and all the drivers and the scraper holders, all were going round and round, all in their places and all moving in time, there on the open prairie, just like the works of a clock as Pa had said, and on the prow of the new railroad grade in the dust, Fred, the boss, kept it all going.

Laura would never have tired of watching that. But farther west there was more to see. Pa said, "Come along, Half-pint, and see how they make a cut and a fill."

Laura walked with Pa along the wagon track, where the crushed dead grasses were like broken hay in the dust where wagon wheels had passed. Farther to the west, beyond a little rise of the prairie, more men were building another piece of the railroad grade.

In the little dip beyond the rise they were making a fill, and farther on they were making a cut through higher ground.

"You see, Laura," Pa said, "where the ground is low, they make the grade higher, and where the ground is high they cut through it to make the grade level. A railroad roadbed has to be as level as it can be for the trains to run on."

"Why, Pa?" Laura asked. "Why can't the trains just run over the prairie swells?" There were no real hills, and it seemed a waste of hard work to cut through all the little rises and fill in all the little hollows, just to make the roadbed level.

"No, it saves work, later on," Pa said. "You ought to be able to see that, Laura, without being told."

Laura could see that a level road would save work for horses, but a locomotive was an iron horse that never got tired.

"Yes, but it burns coal," said Pa. "Coal has to be mined, and that's work. An engine burns less coal running on a level than it does going up and down grades. So you see it takes more work and costs more money now to make a level grade, but later on there'll be a saving in work and money, so they'll be used for building something else."

"What, Pa? What else?" Laura asked.

"More railroads," said Pa. "I wouldn't wonder if you'll live to see a time, Laura, when pretty nearly everybody'll ride on railroads and there'll hardly be a covered wagon left."

Laura could not imagine a country with so many railroads, nor one so rich that nearly everybody could ride on trains, but she did not really try to imagine it because now they had come to high ground where they could see the men working at the cut and the fill.

Right across the prairie swell where the trains would run, the teams with plows and the teams with scrapers were cutting a wide ditch. Back and forth went the big teams pulling the plows, and round and round went the teams hauling the scrapers, all steadily moving in time with each other.

But here the scrapers did not go in a circle; they went in a long, narrow loop, into the cut and out again at one end, and at the other end they went over the dump.

The dump was a deep ditch at the end of the cut, and crossways to it. Heavy timbers shored up the sides of this ditch and made a flat platform over the top of it. There was a hole in the middle of this platform, and earth had been graded high on each side of the ditch, to make a road level with the platform.

Out of the cut came the teams steadily walking one behind another pulling the loaded scrapers. They went up the grade to the top of the dump and they went across the platform. They passed over the hole, one horse walking on each side of it, while into the hole the driver dumped the scraper-load of dirt. Going steadily on, down the steep grade and around, they went back into the cut to fill the scrapers again.

All the time, a circle of wagons was moving through the dump, under the hole in the platform. Every time a scraper dumped its load, a wagon was under the hole to catch the dirt. Each wagon waited till five scraper-loads had poured down into it, then it moved on and the wagon behind it moved under the hole and waited.

The circle of wagons came out of the dump and curved back to climb up over the end of the high railroad grade that was coming toward the cut. Every wagon, as it passed over the grade, dumped its dirt and made the grade that much longer. The wagons had no wagon-boxes; they were only platforms of heavy planks. To dump the dirt the teamster turned those planks over, one at a time. Then he drove onward, down over the end to the fill and back in the endless circle, through the dump to be loaded again.

Dust blew from the plows and the scrapers, and from the dump and the end of the hill. A great cloud of dust rose all the time, up over the sweating men and the sweating horses. The men's faces and arms were black with sunburn and dust, their blue and gray shirts were streaked with sweat and dust, and the horses' manes and tails and hair were full of dust and their flanks were caked with muddy sweat.

They all went on, steadily and evenly, circling into the cut and out while the plows went back and forth, and circling under the dump and back over the end to the fill and under the dump again. The cut grew deeper and the fill grew longer while the men and teams kept on weaving their circles together, never stopping.

"They never miss once," Laura marveled. "Every time a scraper dumps, there's a wagon underneath to catch the dirt."

"That's the boss's job," Pa said. "He makes them keep time just like they were playing a tune. Watch the boss, and you'll see how it's done. It's pretty work."

On the rise above the cut and on the end of the fill and along the circles, the bosses stood. They watched the men and the teams and kept them moving in time. Here they slowed one team a little, there they hurried another. No one stopped and waited. No one was late at his place.

Laura heard the boss call out from the top of the cut. "Boys! Move along a little faster!"

"You see," Pa said, "it's nearing quitting time, and they'd all slowed down a little. They can't put that over on a good boss."

The whole afternoon had gone while Pa and Laura watched those circles moving, making the railroad grade. It was time to go back to the store and the shanty. Laura took one last, long look, and then she had to go.

On the way, Pa showed her the figures painted on the little grade-stakes that were driven into the ground in a straight line where the railroad grade would be. The surveyors had driven those stakes. The figures told the graders how high to build the grade on low ground, and how deep to make the cuts on high ground. The surveyors had measured it all and figured the grade exactly, before anyone else had come there.

First, someone had thought of a railroad. Then the surveyors had come out to that empty country, and they had marked and measured a railroad that was not there at all; it was only a railroad that someone had thought of. Then the plowmen came to tear up the prairie grass, and the scraper-men to dig up the dirt, and the teamsters with their wagons to haul it. And all of them said they were working on the railroad, but still the railroad wasn't there. Nothing was there yet but cuts through the prairie swells, pieces of the railroad grade that were really only narrow, short ridges of earth, all pointing westward across the enormous grassy land.

"When the grade's finished," Pa said, "the shovel-men will come along with hand shovels, and they'll smooth the sides of the grade by hand, and level it on top."

"And then they'll lay the rails," Laura said.

"Don't jump ahead so fast, Flutterbudget." Pa laughed at her. "The railroad ties have got to be shipped out here and laid before it's time for the rails. Rome wasn't built in a day, and neither's a railroad, nor anything else worth having."

The sun was so low now that each prairie swell began to have its shadow lying eastward, and out of the large, pale sky the flocks of ducks and the long wedges of geese were sliding down to Silver Lake to rest for the night. The clean wind was blowing now with no dust in it, and Laura let her sunbonnet slip down her back so that she could feel the wind on her face and see the whole great prairie.

There was no railroad there now, but someday the long steel tracks would lie level on the fills and through the cuts, and trains would come roaring, steaming and smoking with speed.

The tracks and the trains were not there now, but Laura could see them almost as if they were there.

Suddenly she asked, "Pa, was that what made the very first railroad?"

"What are you talking about?" Pa asked.

"Are there railroads because people think of them first when they aren't there?"

Pa thought a minute. "That's right," he said. "Yes, that's what makes things happen, people think of them first. If enough people think of a thing and work hard enough at it, I guess it's pretty nearly bound to happen, wind and weather permitting."

"What's that house, Pa?" Laura asked.

"What house?" Pa asked.

"That house, that real house." Laura pointed. All this time she had been meaning to ask Pa about that house standing by itself on the North shore of the Lake, and she had always forgotten.

"That's the surveyors' house," Pa said.

"Are they there now?" Laura asked.

"They come and go," said Pa. They had almost reached the store, and he went on. "Run on along home now, Flutterbudget. I've got work to do on the books. Now you know how a railroad grade's made, be sure to tell Mary all about it."

"Oh, I will, Pa!" Laura promised. "I'll see it out loud for her, every bit."

She did her best, but Mary only said, "I really don't know, Laura, why you'd rather watch those rough men working in the dirt than stay here in the nice clean shanty. I've finished another quilt patch while you've been idling."

But Laura was still seeing the movement of men and horses in such perfect time that she could almost sing the tune to which they moved.

CHAPTER II

Payday

TWO weeks had gone by and now Pa worked every evening after supper in his little office at the back of the store. He was making out the time-checks.

From the time-book he counted up the days each man had worked, and figured how much he had earned. Then Pa figured up how much the man owed the store; to that he added the man's board-bill at the cook-shanty. He subtracted that amount from the man's wages, and made out his time-check.

On payday Pa would give each man his time-check and the money due him.

Always before, Laura had helped Pa with his work. When she was very little, in the Big Woods, she had helped him make the bullets for his gun; in Indian Territory she had helped finish the house, and on Plum Creek she had helped with the chores and the haying. But she could not help him now, for Pa said that the railroad company would not want anyone but him to work in the office.

Still she always knew what he was doing, for the store was in plain sight from the shanty's doorway and she saw everyone who came and went.

One morning she saw a fast team come dashing up to the store's door, and a man in fine clothes got quickly out of the buggy and hurried into the store. Two more men waited in the buggy, watching the door and looking around them on every side as if they were afraid.

In a little while the first man came out and got into the buggy. After another look all around, they drove away quickly.

Laura ran out of the shanty toward the store. She was sure that something had happened there. Her heart was beating wildly, and it gave a great flop when she saw Pa, safe and sound, come out of the store.

"Where are you going, Laura?" Ma had called after her, and now Laura answered, "Nowhere, Ma."

Pa came into the shanty and swung the door shut behind him. He took a heavy canvas bag out of his pocket.

"I want you to take care of this, Caroline," he said. "It's the men's pay. Anybody that tried to steal it would come to the office."

"I'll take care of it, Charles," Ma said. She wrapped the bag in a clean cloth and worked it deep into her open sack of flour. "Nobody'll ever think of looking there for it."

"Did that man bring it, Pa?" Laura asked.

"Yes. That was the paymaster," said Pa.

"Those men with him were afraid," Laura said.

"Oh, I wouldn't say that. They were only guarding the paymaster to keep him from being robbed," Pa said. "He's carrying a good many thousand dollars in cash to pay all the men in the camps, and somebody might try to get it. But those men had guns enough on them and in the buggy. They had no need to be afraid."

As Pa went back to the store, Laura saw the handle of his revolver showing from his hip pocket. She knew he was not afraid, and she looked at his rifle over the door and his shotgun standing in the corner. Ma could use those guns. There was no fear that robbers could get that money.

That night Laura woke up often, and often she heard Pa stirring too, in the bunk on the other side of the curtain. The night seemed darker and full of strange sounds, because that money was in the flour-sack. But no one would think of looking for it there, and no one did.

Early in the morning, Pa took it to the store. This was payday. After breakfast all the men gathered around the store, and one by one they went inside. One by one they came out again, and stood in little groups, talking. They would not work that day; it was payday.

At supper Pa said he must go back to the office again. "Some of the men don't seem to understand why they got only two weeks' pay," he said.

"Why don't they get paid for the whole month?" Laura asked him.

"Well, you see, Laura, it takes time to make out all those time-checks and send them in, and then the paymaster has to bring out the money. I'm paying the men their wages now up to the fifteenth, and in another two weeks I'll pay them up to now. Some of them can't get it through their thick heads that they've got to wait two weeks for their pay. They want to be paid right up to yesterday."

"Don't fret about it, Charles," said Ma. "You can't expect them to understand how business is handled."

"And they don't blame you, do they, Pa?" said Mary.

"That's the worst of it, Mary. I don't know," Pa answered. "Anyway I've got some bookwork to do at the office."

The supper dishes were soon washed, and Ma sat rocking Grace to sleep, with Carrie snuggled beside her. Laura sat beside Mary in the doorway, watching the light fade from the waters of the lake. She was seeing it out loud for Mary.

"The last light is shining pale in the middle of the smooth lake. All around it the water is dusky, where the ducks sleep, and the land is black beyond. The stars are beginning to twinkle in the gray sky. Pa has lighted his lamp. It shines out yellow from the back of the black store. Ma!" she cried out. "There's a big crowd of men—look."

The men were crowding around the store. They did not say anything, and there was not even any sound of their feet on the grass. Only the dark mass of men was growing larger very fast.

Ma rose quickly and laid Grace on the bed. Then she came and looked out over Laura's head and Mary's. She spoke softly. "Come inside, girls."

When they obeyed her she shut the door, all but a crack. She stood looking out through the crack.

Mary sat in the chair with Carrie, but Laura peeped under Ma's arm. The crowd was close around the store. Two men went up the step and pounded on the door.

The crowd was quiet. The whole dusky twilight was quiet for a moment.

Then the men pounded again on the door and one called, "Open the door, Ingalls!"

The door opened, and there in the lamplight stood Pa. He shut the door behind him, and the two men who had knocked stepped backward into the crowd. Pa stood on the step with his hands in his pockets.

"Well, boys, what is it?" he asked quietly.

A voice came from the crowd. "We want our pay."

Other voices shouted. "Our full pay!" "Come across with that two weeks' pay you kept back!" "We're going to get our pay!"

"You'll have it two weeks from now, just as soon as I can get your time-checks made out," said Pa.

The voices shouted again. "We want it now!" "Quit stalling!" "We're going to have it now!"

"I can't pay you now, boys," Pa said, "I won't have the money to pay you till the paymaster comes again."

"Open up the store!" somebody answered. Then the whole crowd yelled. "That's it! That's good enough— Open the store! Open up that store!"

"No, boys. I won't do that," Pa said coolly. "Come in tomorrow morning, and I'll let each man have all the goods he wants, on his account."

"Open up that store or we'll open it for you!" came a shout. A growl rumbled from the crowd. The whole mass of men moved in toward Pa as if that growl moved them.

Laura ducked under Ma's arm, but Ma's hand clenched on her shoulder and pulled her back.

"Oh, let me go! They'll hurt Pa! Let me go, they'll hurt Pa!" Laura screamed in a whisper.

"Be still!" Ma told her in a voice Laura had never heard before.

"Stand back, boys. Don't crowd too close," said Pa. Laura heard his cold voice and stood trembling.

Then she heard another voice behind the crowd. It was deep and strong, not loud, but plainly heard. "What's up, boys?"

In the dark Laura could not see the red shirt, but only Big Jerry was so tall. He stood head and shoulders above the shadowy figures of the crowd. Beyond them in the dusk was a pale blur that would be the white horse. A confusion of voices answered Big Jerry, then he laughed. His laugh was big and booming.

"You fools!" Big Jerry laughed. "What's the fuss about? You want the goods out of the store? Well, tomorrow we'll take what we want of them. They'll still be here. Nobody'll stop us when we get started."

Laura was hearing rough language. Big Jerry was using it. What he said was all mixed with swear words and with other words she had never heard. She hardly heard them now, because she felt all broken up; she felt as if everything was smashed like a dropped plate when Big Jerry took sides against Pa.

The crowd was all around Big Jerry now. He was calling some of the men by their names and talking to them about drinking and playing cards. Some of the crowd went with him toward the bunkhouse, then the rest of it broke into smaller pieces and scattered away in the dark.

Ma shut the door. "Bedtime, girls," she said.

Laura went trembling to bed as Ma told her to do. Pa did not come. Now and then she heard an outbreak of loud, rough voices from the camp, and sometimes singing. She knew she would not sleep till Pa came.

Then her eyes opened suddenly. It was morning.

Beyond Silver Lake the sky was burning gold and one line of red cloud lay across it; the lake was rosy, and wild birds flew up clamoring. The camp was noisy too. All around the boarding shanty the men were gathered in a milling crowd, talking excitedly.

Ma and Laura stood outdoors at the corner of the shanty watching. They heard a shout and saw Big Jerry jump onto his white horse.

"Come on, boys!" he shouted. "All aboard for the fun!"

The white horse reared and whirled and reared again. Big Jerry gave a wild whoop, the white horse broke into a run, and away they went over the prairie toward the west. All the men rushed to the stable and in a minute man after man was on his horse and following Big Jerry. The whole crowd went streaming away on the horses and was gone.

A great, cool quietness came over the camp and over Laura and Ma. "Well!" Ma said.

They saw Pa walking from the store toward the boarding shanty. Fred, the foreman, came out of it and met him. They talked a minute. Then Fred went to the stable, got on his horse, and galloped away to the west.

Pa was chuckling. Ma said she did not know what there was to laugh about.

"That Big Jerry!" Pa's laugh rang out. "By gum, if he didn't lead 'em all away to do their devilment somewhere else!"

"Where?" Ma asked sharply.

Pa was sober then. "There's a riot at Stebbins' camp. Everybody's flocking there from all the camps. You're right, Caroline, it's no laughing matter."

All day the camp was quiet. Laura and Mary did not go for their walk. There was no telling what might be happening at Stebbins' camp, nor when that dangerous crowd would come back. Ma's eyes were anxious all day, her lips were tight, and now and then she sighed without knowing it.

After dark the men came. But they rode into camp more quietly than they had left it. They ate supper in the boarding shanty and then they went to bed in the bunkhouse.

Laura and Mary were still awake when Pa came late from the store. They lay quiet in their bunk and heard Pa and Ma talking beyond the lamplit curtain.

"Nothing to worry about now, Caroline," Pa said. "They're tired out and everything's quiet." He yawned, and sat down to take off his boots.

"What did they do, Charles? Was anybody hurt?" Ma asked.

"They strung up the paymaster," said Pa. "And one man was hurt bad. They put him in a lumber wagon and started back east with him to find a doctor. Don't get so upset, Caroline. We better thank our stars we got off so easy. It's all over."

"I don't get upset till it is over," Ma said. Her voice was shaking.

"Come here," said Pa. Laura knew that now Ma was sitting on Pa's knee. "There, I know you don't," he said to her. "Never mind, Caroline. The grading's pretty near done, these camps'll be closing down and gone before long, and next summer we'll be settled on the homestead."

"When are you going to pick it out?" said Ma.

"Quick as the camps close. I don't have a minute away from the store till then," said Pa. "You know that."

"Yes, I know, Charles. What did they do about the men that —killed the paymaster?"

"They didn't kill him," Pa said. "It was this way. You see, it's the same at Stebbins' camp as here; the office is a lean-to at the back of the store. It has one door into the store and that's all. The paymaster stayed in the office with the money and kept the door locked. He paid the men through a little opening beside the door.

"Stebbins has got over three hundred and fifty men drawing pay there, and they wanted their pay up to now, like the men here wanted it. When they got paid only to the fifteenth, they acted ugly. Most of them wear guns, and they were in the store, threatening to shoot up the place unless they got their full pay.

"In the melee, a couple of men got to quarreling and one of them hit the other over the head with the weight from the scales. He dropped like a struck ox, and when they dragged him out into the air they couldn't bring him back to his senses.

"So the crowd started out with a rope, after the man that hit him. They trailed him easy enough into the slough, and then they couldn't find him in the high grass. They threshed around looking for him through that slough grass taller than their heads, till I guess they'd ruined any trail he'd left.

"They kept on hunting him till past noon, and lucky for him they didn't find him. When they got back to the store, the door was locked. They couldn't get in. Somebody had loaded the hurt man into a wagon and headed back east to look for a doctor.

"By this time men were piling into the place from all the other camps. They ate everything they could get hold of in the boarding shanty and most of them were drinking. They kept pounding on the store door and yelling to the paymaster to open up and pay them, but nobody answered.

"A crowd of near a thousand drunken men is an ugly thing to deal with. Somebody caught sight of that rope and shouted, 'Hang the paymaster!' The whole crowd took it up and kept on yelling, 'Hang him! Hang him!'

"A couple of men got on top of the lean-to roof and tore a hole in the shingles. They left the end of the rope dangling over the edge of the roof and the crowd grabbed hold of it. The two fellows dropped down onto the paymaster and got the noose around his neck."

"Stop, Charles. The girls are awake," said Ma.

"Pshaw, that's all there is to it," Pa said. "They hauled him up once or twice, is all. He gave in."

"They didn't hang him?"

"Not enough to hurt much. Some of the crowd was breaking down the store door with neck-yokes, and the storekeeper opened it. One of the fellows in the office cut the rope and let the paymaster down, and opened up the pay-window and the paymaster paid every man what he claimed was due him. A good many men from the other camps crowded in and drew pay, too. There wasn't any bothering with time-checks."

"Shame on him!" Laura cried out. Pa drew back the curtain. "What did he do it for? I wouldn't! I wouldn't!" she went on, before Pa or Ma could say a word. There she was, sitting up on her knees in bed, her fists clenched.

"You wouldn't what?" said Pa.

"Pay them! They couldn't make me! They didn't make you!"

"That mob was bigger than ours. And the paymaster didn't have Big Jerry to help him," said Pa.

"But you wouldn't have, Pa," Laura said.

"Sh!" Ma hushed them. "You'll wake Grace. I'm thankful the paymaster was sensible. Better a live dog than a dead lion."

"Oh, no, Ma! You don't mean that!" Laura whispered.

"Anyway, discretion is the better part of valor. You girls go to sleep," Ma murmured.

"Please, Ma," Mary whispered. "How could he pay them? Where did he get the money, when he'd already paid out what he had?"

"That's so, where did he?" Ma asked.

"From the store. It's a big store and it had already taken in most of what the men had been paid; they spend as fast as they get," said Pa. "Now mind your Ma, girls, and go to sleep." He let the curtain fall.

Very softly under the quilt Mary and Laura talked until Ma blew out the lamp. Mary said she wanted to go back to Plum Creek. Laura did not answer that. She liked to feel the great wild prairie all around the little shanty. Her heart beat strong and fast; she could hear in her mind again the savage fierce sound of that crowd's growl and Pa's cold voice saying, "Don't crowd too close." And she remembered the sweating men and sweating horses moving strongly through clouds of dust, building the railroad in a kind of song. She did not want ever to go back to Plum Creek.

CHAPTER 12

Wings Over Silver Lake

THE weather grew colder and the sky was full of wings and great birds flying. From East to West, from North to South, and as far up into the blue sky as eyes could see, were birds and birds and birds sailing on beating wings.

At evening down they came endlessly from the sky, sliding down long slopes of air to rest on the water of Silver Lake.

There were great, gray geese. There were smaller, snow-white brant that looked like snow at the water's edge. There were ducks of many kinds; the large mallards with a shimmering of purple and green on their wings, the redheads, the bluebills, the canvasbacks, and teals and many others whose names Pa did not know. There were herons, and pelicans, and cranes. There were little mud-hens, and the small hell-divers that peppered the water thickly with their little black bodies. When a shot cracked, hell-divers up-ended and vanished quicker than winking. They went far down in the water and stayed there a long time.

At sunset the whole large lake was covered with birds of all kinds speaking in every kind of bird's voice to each other before they went to sleep for a night of rest on their long journey from north to south. The winter was driving them; the winter was coming behind them from the north. They knew it and started early so that they could rest on the way. All night they rested, comfortable on the water that held them so softly, and when dawn came, up they rose again to swim onward in the high air with their rested, strong wings.

One day Pa came from hunting, bringing a great, snow-white bird.

"I'm sorry, Caroline," he said soberly. "I would not have done it if I'd known. I've shot a swan. It was too beautiful to kill. But I had no idea it was a swan. I never saw one flying before."

"It can't be helped now, Charles," Ma told him. They all stood looking sorrowfully at the beautiful, snowy bird that would never fly again. "Come," said Ma. "I'll pluck its feathers and you skin it. We'll cure the skin with the swan's-down on."

"It's bigger than I am," Carrie said. The swan was so large that Pa measured it. Its feathery white wings measured eight feet from tip to tip.

Another day Pa brought a pelican to the shanty to show Ma what it was like. He opened the long bill and dead fish fell out of the pouch of skin underneath it. Ma snatched up her apron and pressed it to her face, and Carrie and Grace held their noses.

"Take it away, Charles, quick!" said Ma through the apron. Some of those fish were fresh, and some were fish that had been dead a long, long time. Pelicans were not fit to eat. Even their feathers smelled so strongly of rotten fish that Ma could not save them for pillows.

Pa shot all the ducks and geese that they could eat, but he shot nothing else except hawks. Sometimes he shot a hawk because hawks kill other birds. Every day Laura and Ma plucked feathers from the scalded skins of the ducks and geese that Pa shot for dinner.

"We'll soon have enough for another feather bed," said Ma. "Then you and Mary can sleep in feathers this winter."

All those golden autumn days the sky was full of wings. Wings beating low over the blue water of Silver Lake, wings beating high in the blue air far above it. Wings of geese, of brant, of ducks and pelicans and cranes and heron and swans and gulls, bearing them all away to green fields in the South.

The wings and the golden weather and the tang of frost in the mornings made Laura want to go somewhere. She did not know where. She wanted only to go.

"Let's go West," she said one night after supper. "Pa, can't we go West when Uncle Henry does?"

Uncle Henry and Louisa and Charley had earned money enough to go West. They were going back to the Big Woods to sell their farm, and in the spring, with Aunt Polly, they were all driving West to Montana.

"Why can't we?" Laura said. "There's all the money you've earned, Pa; three hundred dollars. And we've got the team and wagon. Oh, Pa, let's go on West!"

"Mercy, Laura!" Ma said. "Whatever—" She could not go on.

"I know, little Half-pint," said Pa, and his voice was very

kind. "You and I want to fly like the birds. But long ago I promised your Ma that you girls should go to school. You can't go to school and go West. When this town is built there'll be a school here. I'm going to get a homestead, Laura, and you girls are going to school."

Laura looked at Ma, and then again at Pa, and she saw that it must happen; Pa would stay on a homestead, and she would go to school.

"You'll thank me some day, Laura. And you too, Charles," Ma said gently.

"Just so you're content, Caroline, I'm satisfied," said Pa. That was true, but he did want to go West. Laura turned back to the dishpan and went on washing the supper dishes.

"Another thing, Laura," said Pa. "You know Ma was a teacher, and her mother before her. Ma's heart is set on one of you girls teaching school, and I guess it will have to be you. So you see you must have your schooling."

Laura's heart jerked, and then she seemed to feel it falling, far, far down. She did not say anything. She knew that Pa and Ma, and Mary too, had thought that Mary would be a teacher. Now Mary couldn't teach, and— "Oh, I won't! I won't!" Laura thought. "I don't want to! I can't." Then she said to herself, "You must."

She could not disappoint Ma. She must do as Pa said. So she had to be a school teacher when she grew up. Besides, there was nothing else she could do to earn money.

CHAPTER 13

Breaking Camp

Now all the vast, low earth rippled softly in gentle colors under a faded sky. Grasses were golden-stemmed, and over the prairie they spread a coverlet of buff and tan and brown and warm brownish gray; only the sloughs were darker with green. The birds were fewer, and hurrying. Often at sunset a long flock talked anxiously, high above Silver Lake, and instead of sinking to eat and rest on the water that must have tempted them so much, the tired leader fell back, another took his place, and they went on flying southward. Winter's cold was not far behind them and they could not pause to rest.

In the frosty mornings and the chilly evenings when they went to milk the cows, Laura and Lena wore shawls snug over their heads and pinned under their chins. Their bare legs were cold and the wind nipped their noses, but when they squatted down to milk the warm cows, the shawls covered them cosily and their feet warmed under them. And they sang while they milked.

"Where are you going, my pretty maid?
I'm going a-milking, sir, she said.
May I go with you, my pretty maid?
Oh, yes, if you please, kind sir, she said.

"What is your fortune, my pretty maid?
My face is my fortune, sir, she said.
Then I can't marry you, my pretty maid.
Nobody asked you, sir, she said."

"Well, I guess we won't be seeing each other again for a long time," Lena said one evening. The grading job at Silver Lake was nearly finished. Next morning early, Lena and Jean and Aunt Docia were leaving. They were going away before sun-up because they were getting away with three big wagon-loads of goods from the company's stores. They would not tell anybody where they were going, for fear the company would catch them.

"I wish we'd had time to ride the black ponies again," Laura said.

"Gosh!" Lena spoke that wicked word boldly, "I'm glad this summer's over! I hate houses." She swung the milk pail and chanted. "No more cooking, no more dishes, no more washing, no more scrubbing! Whoop-ee!" Then she said, "Well, good-by. I guess you're going to stay right here as long as you live."

"I guess so," Laura said miserably. She was sure that Lena was going out West. Maybe even to Oregon. "Well, good-by."

Next morning Laura milked the lone cow by her lonely self. Aunt Docia had driven away with a load of oats from the feed room. Lena had driven a wagonload of goods from the store, and Jean still another big load of scrapers and plows. Uncle Hi would follow them as soon as he settled with the company.

"I guess Hi's debt is big enough this time with all those goods charged to him," Pa said.

"Shouldn't you have stopped it, Charles?" Ma worried.

"It's not my look-out," said Pa. "My orders were to let the contractor take anything he wanted, and charge it to him. Oh, come, Caroline! It wasn't stealing. Hi hasn't got away with any more than's due him for his work here and at the camp on the Sioux. The company cheated him there, and he's got even here. That's all there is to it."

"Well," Ma sighed, "I'll be glad when these camps are gone and we're settled again."

Every day the camp was noisy with men drawing their last pay and leaving. Wagon after wagon went away to the east. Every night the camp was emptier. One day Uncle Henry, Louisa and Charley started the long drive back to Wisconsin, to sell the farm. The boarding shanty and the bunkhouse were deserted, the store was empty, and Pa was only waiting till the company man came to check his bookkeeping.

"We'll have to go East somewhere to spend the winter," he said to Ma. "This shanty's too thin for zero weather, even if the company'd let us stay in it, and even if we had any coal."

"Oh, Charles," Ma said, "you haven't even found the homestead yet, and if we have to spend the money you've earned, just living till spring——"

"I know. But what can we do?" said Pa. "I can find the homestead all right before we leave, and file on it next spring. Maybe next summer I can get a job to live on and pay for the lumber to build us a shanty. I could make a sod shanty, but even so it will take all we've got to live till spring, with the prices of supplies out here, and coal. No, we'd better go East for the winter."

It was so hard to get ahead. Laura tried to cheer up, but she couldn't. She did not want to go back East again. She hated to leave Silver Lake to go East. They had got as far as Silver Lake and she wanted to hang on there, not to be pushed back. But if they must be, they must; next spring they could start again. It would do no good to complain.

"Don't you feel well, Laura?" Ma asked her.

"Oh, yes, Ma!" she answered. But she felt so heavy and dark that trying to be cheerful only made her more miserable.

The company man had come to check Pa's bookkeeping, and the last wagons from the West were going by. Even the lake was almost empty of birds and the sky was bare, except for one hurrying streak of flyers. Ma and Laura mended the wagon-cover and baked bread for the long drive.

That evening Pa came whistling from the store, and blew into the shanty like a breeze.

"How'd you like to stay here all winter, Caroline?" he sang out, "in the surveyors' house!"

"Oh, Pa! Can we?" Laura cried.

"You bet we can!" said Pa. "If your Ma wants to. It's a good, sound, weather-tight house, Caroline. The head surveyor was at the store just now, and he says they thought they had to stay and they laid in coal and provisions enough to last them through, but if I'll take charge and be responsible for the company tools till spring, they'll go out for the winter. The company man's agreed.

"There's flour and beans and salt meat and potatoes, and even some canned stuff, he told me. And coal. We can have the whole of it for nothing, just for staying out here this winter. We can use the stable for the cow and team. I told him I'd let him know early tomorrow morning. What do you say, Caroline?"

They all looked at Ma and waited. Laura could hardly keep still in her excitement. To stay at Silver Lake! Not to have to go back East, after all! Ma was disappointed; she had been wanting to go back to settled country. But she said, "It does seem Providential, Charles. There's coal, you say?"

"I wouldn't think of staying without it," said Pa. "But the coal's there."

"Well, supper's on the table," said Ma. "Wash up and eat before it gets cold. It does look like a good chance, Charles."

At supper they talked of nothing else. It would be pleasant to live in a snug house; the shanty was cold with wind blowing through its cracks, though the door was shut and a fire was in the stove.

"Don't it make you feel rich—" Laura began.

"Doesn't," said Ma.

"Doesn't it make you feel rich, Ma, just to think of the whole winter's provisions laid in, already?" said Laura.

"Not a penny going out till spring," said Pa.

"Yes, Laura, it does," Ma smiled. "You're right, Charles, of course; we must stay."

"Well, I don't know, Caroline," Pa said. "In some ways maybe we'd better not. So far as I know, we won't have a neighbor nearer than Brookings. That's sixty miles. If anything happened——"

A knock at the door startled them all. In answer to Pa's "Come in!" a big man opened the door. He was bundled in thick coats and a muffler. His short beard was black, his cheeks were red, and his eyes were as black as the eyes of the little papoose in Indian territory whom Laura had never forgotten.

"Hullo, Boast!" Pa said. "Come up to the fire; it's chilly to-night. This is my wife and girls. Mr. Boast has filed on a home-stead out here, and he's been working on the grade."

Ma gave Mr. Boast a chair by the fire and he held his hands out to the warmth. One hand was bandaged. "Did you hurt your hand?" Ma asked kindly.

"Only a sprain," said Mr. Boast, "but the heat feels good on it." Turning to Pa he went on, "I'm needing some help, Ingalls. You remember my team that I sold Pete? He paid me part down and said he'd pay the rest next payday. But he's kept putting it off, and now I'm darned if he hasn't skipped out with the team. I'd go after him and take them, but his son's with him and they'd put up a fight. I don't want trouble with two toughs at once, and me with a lame hand."

"There's enough of us around yet to tend to it," said Pa.

"I don't mean that," said Mr. Boast, "I don't want any trouble."

"Then just where do I come in?" Pa asked.

"I was thinking. There's no law out here, no way to collect a debt, no officers, not even a county. But maybe Pete don't know that."

"Oho!" said Pa. "You want me to make out some papers to serve on him?"

"I've got a man that'll act as sheriff and serve them," Mr. Boast said. His eyes twinkled as much as Pa's, but the twinkles were not alike. Mr. Boast's eyes twinkled small and black, Pa's twinkled wide and blue.

Pa laughed out loud and slapped his knee. "What a joke! Lucky I've got some legal cap left. I'll make out your papers, Boast! Go get your sheriff!"

Mr. Boast hurried away while Ma and Laura hastily cleared the table. Pa squared up to it and wrote on a large sheet of paper, red-lined down the sides.

"There!" he said finally, "that looks important. And finished just in time."

Mr. Boast was knocking at the door. Another man was with him, wrapped in a big overcoat, a cap pulled low over his eyes and a muffler wrapped around his neck and across his mouth.

"Here you are, Sheriff!" Pa said to him. "Serve this writ of attachment and bring back the team or the money, dead or alive, with costs of this suit at law!" Their laughter seemed to shake the shanty.

Pa looked at the cap and muffler that hid the man's face. "Lucky for you it's a cold night, Sheriff!" he said.

When the two men shut the door behind them, and Pa stopped laughing, he said to Ma, "That was the head surveyor, or I'll eat my hat!" He slapped his thigh and roared again.

In the night Mr. Boast's voice and Pa's woke Laura. At the door Mr. Boast was saying, "I saw your light and stopped by to tell you it worked. Pete was so scared he'd have turned over the money and the team both. That crook's got reason to be scared of the law. Here are the costs, Ingalls. The surveyor wouldn't take any; he said the fun of it more than paid him."

"You keep his share," said Pa. "I'll take mine. The dignity of this court must be upheld!"

When Mr. Boast laughed, Laura and Mary and Carrie and Ma all burst out laughing. They couldn't help it. Pa's laugh was like great bells ringing; it made you feel warm and happy. But Mr. Boast's laugh made everybody laugh.

"Hush, you'll wake Grace," Ma said.

"What's the joke?" Carrie asked. She had been asleep and had only heard Mr. Boast laugh.

"What are you laughing at?" Mary asked her.

"Mr. Boast's laugh tickles," Carrie said.

In the morning Mr. Boast came to breakfast. The camp was gone and there was nowhere else to eat. The surveyors started East that morning in their buggy, and the last teamster passed. Mr. Boast was the last man to go; he had had to wait until his hand was better so that he could drive his team. His hand was worse that morning because it had been chilled in the night, but he started east anyway. He was going to Iowa to be married.

"If you folks are going to stay here all winter, I don't know but I'll bring Ellie back and stay too," he said, "if we can make it before winter sets in."

"Be glad to have you, Boast," said Pa. Ma said, "We would, indeed."

Then they watched Mr. Boast's wagon going, and heard its rattling die away on the wagon track to the East.

The whole prairie was empty now and not even one flock of birds was in the cold sky.

As soon as Mr. Boast's wagon was out of sight, Pa brought his team and wagon to the door.

"Come, Caroline!" he called. "Nobody's left in camp but us, and this is moving day!"

CHAPTER 14

The Surveyors' House

THERE was no need to pack anything, for the surveyors' house stood on the North shore of the lake not half a mile from the shanty. Laura could hardly wait to see it. When she had helped to put everything neatly into the wagon, and Mary and Carrie and Ma and Grace were in it, Laura said to Pa, "Please, can't I run ahead?"

" 'May,' Laura," Ma said. "Really, Charles, don't you think——"

"Nothing can hurt her," Pa said. "We'll have her in sight all the way. Follow the lake shore, Flutterbudget, and don't worry, Caroline; we'll be there in two shakes of a lamb's tail."

So Laura ran ahead. Straight against the steady wind she ran. Her shawl flapped in the wind behind her and the cold of the wind poured through her. She felt her blood thin and chill in the wind, and then she felt it warm and pulsing strong, and her breath throbbed hard in her chest.

She passed the spoiled spots where the camp had been. The earth was hard under her pounding feet, and rough with dead grass. No one else was anywhere near. Everybody had gone now. The prairie, the whole vast prairie, and the great sky and the wind were clear and free.

Even the wagon was left behind now. But it was coming. Laura looked back, and Pa waved to her. When she stopped running she could hear the sound of the wind in the grasses and the lippety-lapping of the lake water. She hoppity-skipped on the short dry grass along the shore. She could shout if she wanted to. No one else was there. She shouted, "It's ours! All ours!"

The shout seemed loud in her throat, but in the air it was thin. The wind took it away perhaps. Or the stillness of the empty land and sky would not be disturbed.

The surveyors' boots had worn a path through the grasses. It was smooth and soft to Laura's feet. She bent her shawled head to the wind and padded along the path, hurrying. It would be fun to see the surveyors' house all by herself.

It stood up in front of her suddenly. It was a big house, a real house with two stories, and glass windows. Its up-and-down boards were weathering from yellow to gray, and every crack was battened, as Pa had said. The door had a china knob. It opened into the lean-to over the back door.

Laura opened the door and peeped in. Then she pushed the door back, along the curved mark it had worn in the board floor, and she went in. This house had board floors; not as comfortable to bare feet as the earth floor of the shanty, but not so much work to keep clean.

The largeness of the empty house seemed to wait and listen. It seemed to know that Laura was there, but it had not made up its mind about her. It would wait and see. Against its walls the wind made a lonely sound, but that was outside the house. She tiptoed across the lean-to and opened a door on its farther side.

Laura looked at the large front room. Its board walls were still yellow inside, and sunshine from its west window slanted yellow on the floor. A cool light came in from the window to the east beside the front door. The surveyors had left their stove! It was a larger stove than the one that Ma had brought from Plum Creek; it had six lids on top and two oven doors, and it stood all set up with its stovepipe in place.

Spaced on the wall beyond it were three doors. All of them were shut.

Laura tiptoed across the wide floor, and softly opened one door. There was a small room, with a bedstead in it. This room had a window, too.

Softly Laura opened the middle door. She was surprised. Steeply up in front of her went a stair, just the width of the door. She looked up, and saw the underside of a slanting roof high overhead. She went up a few steps, and a big attic opened out on both sides of the stairs. It was twice as big as the large room downstairs. A window in each gable end lighted the whole empty place under the roof.

That made three rooms already, and still there was another door. Laura thought that there must have been a great many surveyors to need so much space. This would be by far the largest house she had ever lived in.

She opened the third door. A squeal of excitement came out of her mouth and startled the listening house. There before her eyes was a little store. All up the walls of that small room were shelves, and on the shelves were dishes, and pans and pots, and boxes, and cans. All around under the shelves stood barrels and boxes.

The first barrel was nearly full of flour. The second held corn meal. The third had a tight lid, and it was full of pieces of fat, white pork held down in brown brine. Laura had never seen so much salt pork at one time. There was a wooden box full of square soda crackers, and a box full of big slabs of salted fish. There was a large box of dried apples, and two sacks full of potatoes, and another big sack nearly full of beans.

The wagon was at the door. Laura ran out, shouting, "Oh, Ma, come quick and see! There's so many things— And a big attic, Mary! And a stove, and crackers, soda crackers!"

Ma looked at everything and she was pleased. "It's very nice, I'm sure," she said. "And so clean. We can get settled here in a jiffy. Bring me the broom, Carrie."

Pa didn't even have to set up a stove. He put Ma's stove in the lean-to outside the back door, where the coal was. For a minute they all admired the great heap of coal. Then while Pa built a fire they arranged the table and chairs in the large front room. Ma set Mary's rocking chair by the open oven door. Already that good stove was giving off heat, and in the warm corner Mary sat holding Grace and amusing her, to keep her out of the way while Ma and Laura and Carrie were busy.

Ma made the big bed on the bedstead in the bedroom. She hung her clothes and Pa's on nails in the wall there, and covered them neatly with a sheet. Upstairs in the large, low attic Laura and Carrie made two neat beds on the bedsteads there, one for Carrie and the other for Laura and Mary. Then they carried their clothes and their boxes upstairs; they hung the clothes on the gable wall by one window, and under it they set their boxes.

Everything was neat now, so they went downstairs to help Ma get supper. Pa came in bringing a large, shallow packing box.

"What's that for, Charles?" Ma asked, and Pa said, "This is Grace's trundle bed!"

"It's the only thing we needed!" Ma exclaimed.

"The sides are high enough to hold her covers tucked in," said Pa.

"And low enough to go under our bed in the daytime, like any trundle bed," said Ma.

Laura and Carrie made up a little bed for Grace in the packing box, and slid it under the big bed, and pulled it out again for the night. The moving-in was done.

Supper was a feast. The surveyors' pretty dishes made the table gay. Little sour cucumber pickles, from a jar the surveyors had left, made the warmed-over roast duck and fried potatoes taste different. And after they were eaten, Ma stepped into the pantry and brought out— "Guess what?" she said.

She set before each of them a little dish of canned peaches, and two soda crackers! "We'll have a treat," she said, "to celebrate living in a house again."

It was fine to be eating in such a large place, with a board floor, and the glass windows glittering black against the night outside. Slowly, slowly they ate the smooth, cool peaches and the sweet golden juice, and carefully licked their spoons.

Then the dishes were quickly cleared away and washed in the handy pantry. The table's leaves were dropped, the red-and-white checked cloth spread, and the bright-shining lamp set on its center. Ma settled with Grace in the rocking chair, and Pa said, "This makes a fellow feel like music. Bring me the fiddle box, Laura!"

He tightened and tuned the strings and rosined the bow. Winter evenings were coming again when Pa played the fiddle. He looked around contentedly at them all and at the good walls that would keep them comfortable.

"I must manage something for curtains," Ma said.

Pa paused with the bow poised above the fiddle. "Don't you realize, Caroline, that our nearest neighbor to the east is sixty miles away and our nearest west is forty miles? When winter shuts down, they might as well be farther off. We've got the world to ourselves! I saw only one flock of wild geese today, flying high and fast. They weren't stopping at any lakes; not they! They were hurrying South. Looked to me like the last flock of the season. So even the geese have left us."

His fiddle bow touched the strings and he began to play. Softly Laura began to sing:

> "One night when the winds blew bitter,
> Blew bitter across the wild moor,
> Young Mary she came with her child,
> Wandering home to her own father's door,
> Crying, Father, O pray let me in!
> Take pity on me I implore
> Or the child in my arms will die
> From the winds that blow across the wild moor.
> But her father was deaf to her cries
> Not a voice nor a sound reached the door
> But the watch dogs did howl
> And the village bells tolled
> And the winds blew across the——"

Pa stopped. "That song doesn't fit!" he exclaimed. "What was I thinking of! Now here's something worth singing."

Merrily the fiddle sang and Pa sang with it. Laura and Mary and Carrie sang too, with all their might.

> "I've traveled about a bit in my time
> And of troubles I've seen a few
> But found it better in every clime
> To paddle my own canoe.
>
> "My wants are few. I care not at all
> If my debts are paid when due.
> I drive away strife in the ocean of life
> While I paddle my own canoe.
>
> "Then love your neighbor as yourself
> As the world you go traveling through
> And never sit down with a tear or a frown
> But paddle your own canoe!"

"That's what we'll be doing this winter," said Pa. "And we've done it a good many times before. Haven't we, Caroline?"

"Yes, Charles," Ma agreed. "And we haven't always been so comfortable and so well provided for."

"Everything snug as bugs in a rug," said Pa, tuning the fiddle. "I piled bags of oats across one end of the stable to make a small place for the cow and the team. They'll have all they can eat, too, and they'll be warm and cosy. Yes, we've got everything to be thankful for."

Then he played the fiddle again. He played on and on, jigs and reels and hornpipes and marches. Ma laid Grace in her little trundle bed and shut the door. Then she sat idly rocking, listening to the music. Ma and Mary and Laura and Carrie listened until they were full, full of music. No one spoke of bedtime, because this was their first evening in the new house, all by themselves on the prairie.

At last Pa laid the fiddle and the bow in the fiddle box. As he shut down the lid, a long, mournful, lonely howl came from the night outside the window. Very near, it was.

Laura sprang to her feet. Ma rushed to comfort Grace's screaming in the bedroom. Carrie sat frozen white, with big, round eyes.

"It's—it's only a wolf, Carrie," Laura said.

"There, there!" said Pa. "A fellow'd think you'd never heard a wolf before. Yes, Caroline, the stable door is well fastened."

CHAPTER 15

The Last Man Out

NEXT morning the sun shone but the wind was colder and there was a feeling of storm in the air. Pa had come from doing the chores and was warming his hands by the stove, while Ma and Laura put breakfast on the table, when they heard a wagon rattling.

It stopped by the front door. The driver shouted and Pa went out to him. Through the window Laura saw them talking in the cold wind.

In a moment Pa came back and hurriedly put on his overcoat and his mittens while he said, "We've got a neighbor I didn't know about last night. An old man, sick and all alone. I'm going out there now, I'll tell you all about it when I get back."

He drove away with the stranger and it was some time before he came walking home.

"Brrrr! It's getting colder," he said, dropping his coat and mittens on a chair and bending over the stove to warm himself before he unwound his muffler. "Well, it's a good job done.

"That teamster's the last one out. He came all the way from the Jim River and didn't find a soul. Everyone along the line is going. Last night, when dark caught him, he saw a light about two miles North of the grade and drove to it on the chance of finding a place to stay all night.

"Well, Caroline, he found a claim shanty and an old man all by himself. His name is Woodworth. He has consumption, and came out here to take the prairie-climate cure. He's been living on his claim all summer and was going to stay all winter.

"Well, he's so feeble, the teamster tried to get him to go out. Told him it's his last chance, but Woodworth wouldn't go. So when the teamster saw our smoke this morning, he stopped to see if he couldn't get somebody to help him persuade the old man.

"Caroline, he was skin and bones. But bound and determined to stick to the prairie cure. Said it was the one cure the doctors recommended as pretty near a sure-fire thing."

"Folks come from all over the world to take it," said Ma.

"Yes, I know, Caroline. It's true enough, I guess, these prairies are about the only thing that cures consumption. But if you'd seen him, Caroline. No, he wasn't in any shape to stay alone in a claim shanty, fifteen miles from a neighbor. The place for him is with his own folks.

"Anyhow, the teamster and I packed him up and loaded him and his things into the wagon. Lifted him in, as easy as if he was Carrie, here. In the end he was glad to be going. He'll be a sight more comfortable with his folks in the East."

"He'll nearly freeze to death, riding in a wagon this cold day," Ma said, putting more coal on the fire.

"He's dressed warmly, wearing a good overcoat. We wrapped him in blankets besides and heated a bag of oats for his feet. He'll make it all right. That teamster is one fine fellow."

Thinking of that old man going out with the last teamster, Laura really knew how deserted the country was. It would take them two long days to get to the Big Sioux River. All the way between the Big Sioux and the Jim, there was nobody at all except them, there in the surveyors' house.

"Pa, did you see wolf tracks this morning?" Laura asked.

"Yes, plenty of them, all around the stable," said Pa. "Big tracks too. Must be buffalo wolves. But they couldn't get in. All the birds have gone South, and the antelope were scared away by the men working on the grade, so the wolves will have to move on too. They won't stay where they can't kill anything to eat."

After breakfast he went to the stable, and as soon as the housework was done Laura put on her shawl and went too. She wanted to see the wolf tracks.

She had never seen such huge ones, and deep. Those wolves must be very big and heavy. "Buffalo wolves are the largest wolves on the prairie and very fierce," Pa told her. "I'd hate to meet one without a gun."

He was looking the stable over carefully, to see that every board was nailed fast. He drove in more nails, to make the walls solid, and he put an extra bolt on the door. "If one gets broken, the other might hold," he said.

Snow began to fall while Laura handed him nails and he hammered them in. The wind blew strong and keen, but it was a straight wind, not a blizzard wind. Still it was so cold that they could not talk.

At supper in the warm house Pa said, "I don't believe the winters are going to be so bad out here. Seems like the blizzards sort of draw down through western Minnesota. We are farther west out here, and they say that three degrees west is as good as one degree south."

After supper they all gathered in the warmth of the stove. Ma rocked Grace slowly to and fro, and Laura brought Pa the fiddle box. Now the happy winter evenings were begun.

"Hail Columbia, happy land! (Pa sang with the fiddle)
Hail, ye heroes, Heaven born band!
Firm, united let us be,
Rallying 'round our liberty,
As a band of brothers joined
Peace and safety we shall find."

He looked at Mary sitting quietly with beautiful empty eyes and folded hands in her rocking chair by the oven. "What shall I play for you, Mary?"

"I would like to hear 'Highland Mary,' Pa."

Softly Pa played a verse. "Now, Mary! Help sing!" he said, and they sang together.

"How sweetly bloomed the gay, green birk,
How rich the hawthorn's blossom,
As underneath their fragrant shade
I clasped her to my bosom.

"The golden hours on angel wings
Flew o'er me and my dearie
For dear to me as light and life
Was my sweet Highland Mary!"

"It's sweet," Mary said when the last note died away.

"It's sweet but it's sad," said Laura. "I like 'Coming Through the Rye.' "

"I'll play it," Pa said, "but I won't sing it alone. It isn't fair for me to do all the entertaining."

So gaily all together they sang the lively song. And Laura got up and pretended to be wading across a creek, holding her skirts above her ankles and laughing back over her shoulder, singing:

"Ilka lassie has her laddie,
Nane, they say, ha'e I,
Yet all the lads they smile at me
When coming through the Rye!"

Then Pa's fiddle twinkled short, gay little notes, and he sang:

"I'm Captain Jinks of the Horse Marines!
I feed my horse on corn and beans,
And I often go beyond my means
To court the girls all in their teens,
For I'm Captain Jinks of the Horse Marines,
I'm Captain in the Army!"

Pa nodded at Laura, and she went on singing with the fiddle:

"I am Mrs. Jinks of Madison Square,
I wear fine clothes and I curl my hair,
The Captain went on a regular tear
And they kicked him out of the Army!"

"Laura!" Ma said. "Charles, do you think that is a nice song for a girl to sing?"

"She sang it well," said Pa. "Now, Carrie, you must do your share. Get out here with Laura and see what you can do."

He showed them how to hold hands and step to the tune of a polka. Then he played it and they danced while he sang:

"First! the heel and then the toe,
That's the way the steps do go,
First the heel and then the toe,
That's the way the steps do go,
First-the-heel-and-then-the-toe——"

Faster and faster he played, and faster they danced, with higher and higher steps, back and forth and whirling back again till they were breathless and hot with dancing and laughing.

"Now then," said Pa, "try a bit of a waltz," and the music flowed smoothly in gliding long waves. "Just float on the music," Pa sang to them softly. "Just float on the music, glide smoothly and turn."

Laura and Carrie waltzed across the room and back, and around and around the room, while Grace sat up in Ma's lap and watched them with round eyes and Mary listened quietly to the music and the dancing feet.

"That's fine, girls," said Pa. "We must have more of it this winter. You're growing up now and you must know how to dance. You're going to be fine dancers, both of you."

"Oh, Pa, you aren't stopping!" Laura cried.

"It's long past bedtime," said Pa. "And there'll be plenty more long, cosy evenings before spring."

Bitter cold came down the stairway when Laura opened the door. She hurried up the steps, carrying the lighted lantern, and behind her Mary and Carrie hurried. There was a little warmth around the stovepipe that came up from the room below, and close to it they undressed and with shivering fingers pulled their nightgowns over their underflannels. Chattering, they crawled into their cold beds and Laura blew out the lantern.

In the dark she and Mary cuddled together, and slowly the blankets lost their chill. All around the house the black cold of the night was as high as the sky and as wide as the world, and there was nothing in it but the lonely wind.

"Mary," Laura whispered. "I guess the wolves have gone. I didn't hear them howl, did you?"

"I hope they have," Mary answered drowsily.

CHAPTER 16

Winter Days

THE weather grew colder. Silver Lake was frozen. Snow fell, but always the wind blew the ice clean, drifting the snow into the tall grass of the sloughs and driving it into waves on the low shores.

On the whole white prairie nothing moved but blowing snow, and the only sound in the vast silence was the sound of the wind.

In the snug house Laura and Carrie helped Ma with the housework, and Grace played, running about the big room with toddling short steps. Whenever she was tired of play she climbed into Mary's lap, for that was the warmest place and Mary would always tell her a story. Listening to stories, Grace would fall asleep. Then Ma laid her in her trundle bed by the stove, and they all settled down for a cosy afternoon of knitting and sewing and crocheting.

Pa did the chores and walked the trap line he had set along the edge of Big Slough. In the lean-to he skinned foxes and coyotes and muskrats, and stretched the furs on boards to dry.

The prairie was so desolate and the wind so cold that Mary did not go out at all. She loved to sit sewing in the pleasant, warm house, taking tiny, even stitches with the needle that Laura threaded for her.

At twilight Mary did not put away her sewing. She told Laura, "I can sew when you can't see to, because I see with my fingers."

"You sew more beautifully than I can, anytime," Laura told her. "You always could."

Even Laura liked the cosy afternoons of rocking and stitching and talking a little, though she never would truly enjoy sewing as Mary did. Often she was restless in the house. Then she would walk from window to window, looking into a whirl of snowflakes and listening to the wind, till Ma said gently, "I declare I don't know what gets into you, Laura."

When the sun shone, no matter how cold it was, Laura must

go out. When Ma would let them go, she and Carrie, well wrapped up in coats and hoods, with shoes and mittens and mufflers on, went sliding on Silver Lake. Holding hands, they ran a little way and then slid on the dark, smooth ice. First on one foot, then on the other, with little runs between slides, they went back and forth, breathless and warm and laughing.

Those were glorious days when they were out in the glitter of the sharp cold. Then it was good to come into the warm, close house, and good to eat supper, and through the evening of music and singing and dancing, Laura was the merriest of all.

One stormy day Pa brought a wide, square board in by the stove, and with his pencil he marked it off in small squares inside a plain border.

"Whatever are you making, Pa?" Laura asked, and he answered, "Wait and see."

He heated the tip of the poker red-hot in the stove, and carefully he burned black every alternate little square.

"Curiosity killed a cat, Pa," Laura said.

"You look pretty healthy," said Pa. Tantalizing, he sat there whittling until he had made twenty-four small squares of wood. Half of them he laid on the hot stove, turning them until they were burned black all over.

Then he ranged all these pieces in the squares on the board, and set the board on his knees.

"Now, Laura!" he said.

"Now what?" said Laura.

"These are checkers, and this is a checker board. Pull up your chair, and I'll show you how to play checkers."

She learned so well that before that storm ended she had beaten Pa in one game. But after that, they did not play so immoderately. Ma did not care to play, nor Carrie, so after one game Pa always put the board away.

"Checkers is a selfish game," he said, "for only two can play it. Bring me the fiddle, Flutterbudget."

CHAPTER 17

Wolves on Silver Lake

THERE came a night when moonlight shone silver clear. The earth was endless white and the wind was still.

Beyond every window the white world stretched far away in frosty glitter, and the sky was a curve of light. Laura could not settle down to anything. She didn't want to play games. She hardly heard even the music of Pa's fiddle. She did not want to dance, but she felt that she must move swiftly. She must be going somewhere.

Suddenly she exclaimed, "Carrie! Let's go slide on the ice!"

"In the night, Laura?" Ma was astonished.

"It's light outdoors," Laura replied. "Almost as light as day."

"It will be all right, Caroline," Pa said. "There's nothing to hurt them, if they don't stay too long and freeze."

So Ma told them, "You may go for a quick run. Don't stay until you get too cold."

Laura and Carrie hurried into their coats and hoods and mittens. Their shoes were new and the soles thick. Ma had knit their stockings of woolen yarn, and their red flannel underclothes came down over their knees and buttoned in a snug band around each stocking. Their flannel petticoats were thick and warm, and their dresses and their coats were wool, and so were their hoods and mufflers.

Out of the warm house they burst into the breath-taking air that tingled with cold. They ran a race on the snowy path down the low hill to the stables. Then they followed the path that the horses and the cow had made when Pa led them through the snow to water at the hole he had cut in the lake ice.

"We mustn't go near the water hole," Laura said, and she led Carrie along the lake shore until they were well away from it. Then they stopped and looked at the night.

It was so beautiful that they hardly breathed. The great round moon hung in the sky and its radiance poured over a silvery world. Far, far away in every direction stretched motionless flatness, softly shining as if it were made of soft light.

In the midst lay the dark, smooth lake, and a glittering moonpath stretched across it. Tall grass stood up in black lines from the snow drifted in the sloughs.

The stable lay low and dark near the shore, and on the low hill stood the dark, small, surveyors' house, with the yellow light in the window twinkling from its darkness.

"How still it is," Carrie whispered. "Listen how still it is."

Laura's heart swelled. She felt herself a part of the wide land, of the far deep sky and the brilliant moonlight. She wanted to fly. But Carrie was little and almost afraid, so she took hold of Carrie's hand and said, "Let's slide. Come on, run!"

With hands clasped, they ran a little way. Then with right foot first they slid on the smooth ice much farther than they had run.

"On the moonpath, Carrie! Let's follow the moonpath," Laura cried.

And so they ran and slid, and ran and slid again, on the glittering moonpath into the light from the silver moon. Farther and farther from shore they went, straight toward the high bank on the other side.

They swooped and almost seemed to fly. If Carrie lost her balance, Laura held her up. If Laura was unsteady, Carrie's hand steadied her.

Close to the farther shore, almost in the shadow of the high bank, they stopped. Something made Laura look up to the top of the bank.

And there, dark against the moonlight, stood a great wolf!

He was looking toward her. The wind stirred his fur and the moonlight seemed to run in and out of it.

"Let's go back," Laura said quickly, as she turned, taking Carrie with her. "I can go faster than you."

She ran and slid and ran again as fast as she could, but Carrie kept up.

"I saw it too," Carrie panted. "Was it a wolf?"

"Don't talk!" Laura answered. "Hurry!"

Laura could hear their feet running and sliding on the ice. She listened for a sound behind them, but there was none. Then they ran and slid without a word until they came to the path by the water hole. As they ran up the path, Laura looked back but she could see nothing on the lake nor on the bank beyond.

Laura and Carrie didn't stop running. They ran up the hill to the house, opened the back door and ran into the lean-to. They ran across that, burst through the door into the front room and slammed it shut behind them. Then leaned against it, panting.

Pa sprang to his feet. "What is it?" he asked. "What has frightened you?"

"Was it a wolf, Laura?" Carrie gasped.

"It was a wolf, Pa," Laura gulped, catching her breath. "A great, big wolf! And I was afraid Carrie couldn't run fast enough but she did."

"I should say she did!" Pa exclaimed. "Where is this wolf?"

"I don't know. It is gone," Laura told him.

Ma helped them take off their wraps. "Sit down and rest! You are all out of breath," she said.

"Where was the wolf?" Pa wanted to know.

"Up on the bank," Carrie said, and Laura added, "The high bank across the lake."

"Did you girls go clear there?" Pa asked in surprise. "And ran all the way back after you saw him! I had no idea you would go so far. It is a good half-mile."

"We followed the moonpath," Laura told him. Pa looked at her strangely. "You would!" he said. "I thought those wolves had gone. It was careless of me. I'll hunt them tomorrow."

Mary sat still, but her face was white. "Oh, girls," she almost whispered. "Suppose he had caught you!"

Then they all sat silent while Laura and Carrie rested.

Laura was glad to be safe in the warm room with the desolate prairie shut out. If anything had happened to Carrie, it would have been her fault for taking her so far across the lake.

But nothing had happened. She could almost see again the great wolf with the wind ruffling the moonlight on his fur.

"Pa!" she said in a low voice.

"Yes, Laura?" Pa answered.

"I hope you don't find the wolf, Pa," Laura said.

"Why ever not?" Ma wondered.

"Because he didn't chase us," Laura told her.

"He didn't chase us, Pa, and he could have caught us."

A long, wild, wolf howl rose and faded away on the stillness.

Another answered it. Then silence again.

Laura's heart seemed to turn over with a sickening flop and she found herself on her feet. She was glad of Ma's steadying hand on her arm.

"Poor girl! You are nervous as a witch and no wonder," Ma said softly.

Ma took a hot flatiron from the back of the stove, wrapped it tightly in a cloth and gave it to Carrie.

"It is bedtime," she said. "Here is the hot iron for your feet."

"And here is yours, Laura," as she wrapped another. "Be sure you put it in the middle of the bed so Mary's feet can reach it too."

As Laura shut the stair door behind them, Pa was talking earnestly to Ma. But Laura could not hear what he said for the ringing in her ears.

CHAPTER 18

Pa Finds the Homestead

AFTER breakfast next morning Pa took his gun and set out. All that morning Laura was listening for a shot and not wanting to hear it. All morning she remembered the great wolf sitting quiet in the moonlight that shimmered through his thick fur.

Pa was late for dinner. It was long past noon when he stamped the snow from his feet in the lean-to. He came in and put his gun on the wall, and hung his cap and coat on their nail. His mittens he hung, by their thumbs, to dry on the line behind the stove. Then he washed his face and hands in the tin basin on the bench, and before the small glass that hung above it he combed his hair and his beard.

"Sorry I kept dinner waiting, Caroline," he said. "I was gone longer than I thought. Went farther than I intended."

"It doesn't matter, Charles; I've kept dinner warm," Ma replied. "Come to the table, girls! Don't keep Pa waiting."

"How far did you go, Pa?" Mary asked.

"Better than ten miles, all told," said Pa. "Those wolf tracks led me a chase."

"Did you get the wolf, Pa?" Carrie wanted to know. Laura did not say anything.

Pa smiled at Carrie and said, "Now, now, don't ask questions. I'll tell you all about it. I went across the lake, followed the marks you girls made last night. And what do you suppose I found in that high bank where you saw the wolf?"

"You found the wolf," Carrie said confidently. Laura still said nothing. Her food was choking her; she could hardly swallow the smallest mouthful.

"I found the wolves' *den*," said Pa. "And the biggest wolves' tracks I ever saw. Girls, there were two big buffalo wolves at that den last night."

Mary and Carrie gasped. Ma said, "Charles!"

"It's too late to be scared now," Pa told them. "But that's

what you girls did. You went right up to the wolves' den and there were the wolves.

"Their tracks were fresh, and all the signs show plain as day what they were doing. It's an old den, and from their size they're no young wolves. I'd say they'd been living there for some years. But they haven't been living there this winter.

"They came down from the northwest sometime yesterday evening and went pretty straight to that den. They stayed around it, in and out of it, maybe till this morning. I followed their tracks from there, down along Big Slough and out on the prairie, southwest.

"From the time they left the old den, those wolves never stopped. They trotted along, side by side, as if they had started on a long journey and knew where they were going. I followed them far enough to be sure that I couldn't get a shot at them. They've left for good."

Laura took a deep breath as though she had forgotten to breathe till now. Pa looked at her. "You are glad they got away, Laura?" he asked.

"Yes, Pa, I am," Laura answered. "They didn't chase us."

"No, Laura, they didn't chase you. And for the life of me, I can't figure out why they didn't."

"And what were they doing at that old den?" Ma wondered.

"They were just looking at it," said Pa. "My belief is they came back to visit the old place where they lived before the graders came in and the antelope left. Maybe they used to live here before the hunters killed the last buffalo. Buffalo wolves were all over this country once, but there's not many left now, even around here. The railroads and settlements kept driving them farther west. One thing's certain if I know anything about wild animal tracks; those two wolves came straight from the west and went straight back west, and all they did here was to stop one night at the old den. And I wouldn't wonder if they're pretty nearly the last buffalo wolves that'll ever be seen in this part of the country."

"Oh, Pa, the poor wolves," Laura mourned.

"Mercy on us," Ma said briskly. "There's enough to be sorry for, without being sorry for the feelings of wild beasts! Be thankful the brutes didn't do any worse than scare you girls last night."

"That isn't all, Caroline!" Pa announced. "I've got some news. I've found our homestead."

"Oh, where, Pa! What's it like? How far is it?" Mary and Laura and Carrie asked, excited. Ma said, "That's good, Charles."

Pa pushed back his plate, drank his tea, wiped his mustache, and said, "It is just right in every way. It lies south of where the lake joins Big Slough, and the slough curves around to the west of it. There's a rise in the prairie to the south of the slough, that will make a nice place to build. A little hill just west of it crowds the slough back on that side. On the quarter section there's upland hay and plow land lying to the south; and good grazing on all of it, everything a farmer could ask for. And it's near the townsite, so the girls can go to school."

"I'm glad, Charles," said Ma.

"It's a funny thing," Pa said. "Here I've been looking around this country for months and never finding a quarter section that just exactly suited me. And that one was lying there all the time. Likely enough I wouldn't have come across it at all, if this wolf chase hadn't taken me across the lake and down along the slough on that side."

"I wish you had filed on it last fall," Ma worried.

"Nobody'll be in here this winter," Pa said confidently. "I'll get out to Brookings and file on that claim next spring before anybody else is looking for a homestead."

CHAPTER 19

Christmas Eve

IT HAD snowed all day and soft, large flakes were still falling. The winds were quiet so that the snow lay deep on the ground, and Pa took the shovel with him when he went to do the evening chores.

"Well, it's a white Christmas," he said.

"Yes, and we're all here and all well, so it's a merry one," said Ma.

The surveyors' house was full of secrets. Mary had knitted new, warm socks for Pa's Christmas present. Laura had made him a necktie from a piece of silk she found in Ma's scrap bag. Together in the attic, she and Carrie had made an apron for Ma from one of the calico curtains that had hung in the shanty. In the scrap bag they found a piece of fine, white muslin; Laura had cut a small square from it, and secretly Mary had hemmed the square with her fine stitches and made a handkerchief for Ma. They put it in the apron pocket. Then they had wrapped the apron in tissue paper and hidden it under the quilt blocks in Mary's box.

There had been a blanket, striped across the ends in red and green. The blanket was worn out, but the striped end was good, and from it Ma had cut bed shoes for Mary. Laura had made one, and Carrie the other, seaming and turning and finishing them neatly with cords and tassels of yarn. The shoes were hidden carefully in Ma's bedroom so that Mary would not find them.

Laura and Mary had wanted to make mittens for Carrie, but they had not enough yarn. There was a little white yarn, and a little red, and a little blue, but not enough of any color to make mittens.

"I know!" Mary said. "We'll make the hands white, and the wrists in red and blue strips!" Every morning while Carrie was making her bed in the attic, Laura and Mary had knitted as fast as they could; when they heard her coming down stairs, they hid the mittens in Mary's knitting basket. The mittens were there now, finished.

Grace's Christmas present was to be the most beautiful of all. They had all worked at it together in the warm room, for Grace was so little that she didn't notice.

Ma had taken the swan's skin from its careful wrappings, and cut from it a little hood. The skin was so delicate that Ma trusted no one else to handle that; she sewed every stitch of the hood herself. But she let Laura and Carrie piece out the lining, of scraps of blue silk from the scrap bag. After Ma sewed the swan's-down hood to the lining, it would not tear.

Then Ma looked again in the scrap bag, and chose a large piece of soft blue woolen cloth, that had once been her best winter dress. Out of it she cut a little coat. Laura and Carrie sewed the seams and pressed them; Mary put the tiny stitches in the hem at the bottom. Then on the coat Ma sewed a collar of the soft swan's-down, and put narrow swan's-down cuffs on the sleeves.

The blue coat trimmed with the white swan's-down, and the delicate swan's-down hood with its lining as blue as Grace's eyes, were beautiful.

"It's like making doll's clothes," Laura said.

"Grace will be lovelier than any doll," Mary declared.

"Oh, let's put them on her now!" Carrie cried, dancing in her eagerness.

But Ma had said the coat and the hood must be laid away until Christmas, and they were. They were waiting now for tomorrow morning to come.

Pa had gone hunting. He said he intended to have the biggest jack rabbit in the territory for the Christmas dinner. And he had. At least, he had brought home the very biggest rabbit they had ever seen. Skinned and cleaned and frozen stiff, it waited now in the lean-to to be roasted tomorrow.

Pa came in from the stable, stamping the snow from his feet. He broke the ice from his mustache and spread his hands in the warmth above the stove.

"Whew!" he said. "This is a humdinger of a cold spell for the night before Christmas. It's too cold for Santa Claus to be out," and his eyes twinkled at Carrie.

"We don't need Santa Claus! We've all been—" Carrie began, then she clapped her hand over her mouth and looked quickly to see if Laura and Mary had noticed how nearly she had told secrets.

Pa turned around to warm his back in the heat from the oven, and he looked happily at them all.

"We're all snug under cover anyway," he said. "Ellen and Sam and David are warm and comfortable too, and I gave them an extra feed for Christmas Eve. Yes, it's a pretty good Christmas, isn't it, Caroline?"

"Yes, Charles, it is," said Ma. She set the bowl of hot corn meal mush on the table, and poured out the milk. "Come now, and eat. A hot supper will warm you quicker than anything else, Charles."

At supper they talked about other Christmases. They had had so many Christmases together, and here they were again, all together and warm and fed and happy. Upstairs in Laura's box there was still Charlotte, the rag doll from her Christmas stocking in the Big Woods. The tin cups and the pennies from Christmas in Indian Territory were gone now, but Laura and Mary remembered Mr. Edwards who had walked forty miles to Independence and back, to bring those presents from Santa Claus. They never had heard of Mr. Edwards since he started alone down the Verdigris River, and they wondered what had become of him.

"Wherever he is, let's hope he's as lucky as we are," said Pa. Wherever he was, they were remembering him and wishing him happiness.

"And you're here, Pa," Laura said. "You're not lost in a blizzard." For a moment they all looked silently at Pa, thinking of that dreadful Christmas when he almost had not come home and they feared he never would.

Tears came into Ma's eyes. She tried to hide them, but she had to brush them away with her hand. They all pretended not to notice. "It's just thankfulness, Charles," Ma said, blowing her nose.

Then Pa burst out laughing. "That was the joke on me!" he said. "Starving to death for three days and nights, and eating the oyster crackers and the Christmas candy, and all the time I was under the bank of our own creek, not a hundred yards from the house!"

"I think the best Christmas was the time there was the Sunday-school Christmas Tree," said Mary. "You're too little to remember, Carrie, but Oh! how wonderful that was!"

"It wasn't really as good as this one," Laura said. "Because now Carrie is old enough to remember, and now we have Grace." There was Carrie—the wolf didn't hurt her. And there on Ma's lap sat the littlest sister Grace, with her hair the color of sunshine and eyes as blue as violets.

"Yes, this is best after all," Mary decided. "And maybe next year there'll be a Sunday school here."

The mush was gone. Pa scraped the last drop of milk from his bowl and drank his tea. "Well," he said, "we can't have a tree, for there isn't so much as a bush on Silver Lake. We wouldn't want one anyway, just for ourselves. But we can have a little Sunday-school celebration of our own, Mary."

He went to get his fiddle box, and while Ma and Laura washed the bowls and the pot and set them away, he tuned the fiddle and rosined the bow.

Frost was thick on the windowpanes and frost furred the cracks around the door. Thickly against the clear upper edges of the windowpanes the snowflakes fluttered. But lamplight was bright on the red-and-white tablecloth, and the fire glowed behind the open drafts of the stove.

"We can't sing so soon after eating," said Pa. "So I'll just limber up the fiddle."

Merrily he played, "Away Down the River on the O-hi-o!" And, "Why Chime the Bells So Merrily." And,

"Jingle bells, jingle bells,
Jingle all the way!
Oh, what fun it is to ride,
In a one-hoss open sleigh!"

Then he stopped and smiled at them all. "Are you ready to sing now?"

The voice of the fiddle changed; it was going to sing a hymn. Pa played a few notes. Then they all sang:

"Yes, a brighter morn is breaking,
Better days are coming on.
All the world will be awaking

In a new and golden dawn.
And many nations shall come and say,
Come, let us go up to the mountain of the Lord!
And He will teach us, will teach us of His ways,
And we will walk in His paths."

The fiddle's voice wandered away, Pa seemed to be playing his thoughts to himself. But a melody grew out of them and throbbed softly until they all joined in and sang:

"The sun may warm the grass to life,
The dew the drooping flower;
And eyes grow bright and watch the light
Of autumn's opening hour;
But words that breathe of tenderness
And smiles we know are true
Are warmer than the summertime
And brighter than the dew.

"It is not much the world can give
With all its subtle art;
And gold and gems are not the things
To satisfy the heart;
But Oh, if those who cluster round
The altar and the hearth,
Have gentle words and loving smiles,
How beautiful the earth!"

Through the music, Mary cried out, "What's that?"

"What, Mary?" Pa asked.

"I thought I heard— Listen!" Mary said.

They listened. The lamp made a tiny purring sound, and the coals softly settled a little in the stove. Past the little space above the white frost on the windows, falling snowflakes twinkled in the lamplight shining through the glass.

"What did you think you heard, Mary?" Pa asked.

"It sounded like— There it is again!"

This time they all heard a shout. Out in the night, in the storm, a man shouted. And shouted again, quite near the house.

Ma started up. "Charles! Who on earth?"

CHAPTER 20

The Night Before Christmas

PA LAID the fiddle in its box, and opened the front door quickly. Snow and cold swirled in, and again a husky shout. "Hullo-o-o, Ingalls!"

"It's Boast!" Pa cried. "Come in! Come in!" He snatched his coat and cap, jerked them on and went out into the cold.

"He must be nearly frozen!" Ma exclaimed, and she hurried to put more coal on the fire. From outside came voices and Mr. Boast's laugh.

Then the door opened and Pa called, "Here's Mrs. Boast, Caroline. We're going to put up the horses."

Mrs. Boast was a great bundle of coats and blankets. Ma hurried to help her take off layer after layer of wrappings. "Come to the stove! You must be nearly frozen."

"Oh, no," a pleasant voice answered. "The horse was warm to sit on and Robert wrapped me so tightly in all these blankets, the cold couldn't reach me. He even led the horse so my hands would be under cover."

"This veil is frozen just the same," said Ma, unwinding yards of frosted woolen veil from Mrs. Boast's head. Mrs. Boast's face appeared, framed in a fur-edged hood. Mrs. Boast did not look much older than Mary. Her hair was soft brown, and her long-lashed eyes were blue.

"Did you come all this way on horseback, Mrs. Boast?" Ma asked her.

"Oh, no. Only about two miles. We were coming in a bobsled, but we got stuck in the snow in a slough. The team and the sled fell down through the snow," she said. "Robert got the team out but we had to leave the sled."

"I know," said Ma. "The snow drifts over the top of the tall slough grass, and you can't tell where the slough is. But the grass underneath won't hold up any weight." She helped Mrs. Boast out of her coat.

"Take my chair, Mrs. Boast. It's in the warmest place," Mary urged her. But Mrs. Boast said she would sit beside Mary.

Pa and Mr. Boast came into the lean-to with a great stamping of snow from their feet. Mr. Boast laughed, and in the house everyone laughed, even Ma.

"I don't know why," Laura said to Mrs. Boast. "We don't even know what the joke is, but when Mr. Boast laughs——"

Mrs. Boast was laughing too. "It's contagious," she said. Laura looked at her blue, laughing eyes and thought that Christmas would be jolly.

Ma was stirring up biscuit. "How do you do, Mr. Boast," she said. "You and Mrs. Boast must be starved. Supper will be ready in a jiffy."

Laura put slices of salt pork in the frying pan to parboil, and Ma set the biscuits in the oven. Then Ma drained the pork, dipped the slices in flour and set them to fry, while Laura peeled and sliced potatoes.

"I'll raw-fry them," Ma said to her low, in the pantry, "and make milk gravy and a fresh pot of tea. We can make out well enough for food, but what will we do about the presents?"

Laura had not thought of that. They had no presents for Mr. and Mrs. Boast. Ma whisked out of the pantry to fry the potatoes and make the gravy, and Laura set the table.

"I don't know when I've enjoyed a meal more," said Mrs. Boast, when they had eaten.

"We didn't look for you until spring," said Pa. "Winter is a bad time to make such a drive."

"We found that out," Mr. Boast answered. "But I tell you, Ingalls, the whole country is moving West in the spring. All Iowa is coming, and we knew we must be ahead of the rush or some claim jumper would be on our homestead. So we came, weather or no weather. You should have filed on a homestead last fall. You'll have to rush it in the spring, or you'll find no land left."

Pa and Ma looked soberly at each other. They were thinking of the homestead that Pa had found. But Ma only said, "It's getting late, and Mrs. Boast must be tired."

"I am tired," Mrs. Boast said. "It was a hard drive, and then to leave the sled and come on horseback through the snowstorm. We were so glad to see your light. And when we came nearer, we heard you singing. You don't know how good it sounded."

"You take Mrs. Boast in with you, Caroline, and Boast and I will bunk down here by the fire," Pa said. "We'll have one more song, then all you girls skedaddle."

He raised the fiddle again from its nest in the box and tried it to see that it was in tune. "What'll it be, Boast?"

" 'Merry Christmas Everywhere,' " said Mr. Boast. His tenor voice joined Pa's bass. Mrs. Boast's soft alto and Laura's soprano and Mary's followed, then Ma's contralto. Carrie's little treble piped up happily.

"Merry, Merry Christmas everywhere!
Cheerily it ringeth through the air;
Christmas bells, Christmas trees,
Christmas odors on the breeze.

"Why should we so joyfully
Sing with grateful mirth?
See the Sun of Righteousness
Beams upon the earth!

"Light for weary wanderers,
Comfort for the oppressed;
He will guide his trusting ones,
Into perfect rest."

"Good night! Good night!" they all said. Ma came upstairs to get Carrie's bedding for Pa and Mr. Boast. "Their blankets are sopping wet," she said. "You three girls can share one bed for one night."

"Ma! What about the presents?" Laura whispered.

"Never mind, I'll manage somehow," Ma whispered back. "Now go to sleep, girls," she said aloud. "Good night, sleep tight!"

Downstairs Mrs. Boast was softly singing to herself, "Light for weary wanderers . . ."

CHAPTER 21

Merry Christmas

When Laura heard the door shut as Pa and Mr. Boast went out to do the morning chores, she dressed chattering in the cold and hurried downstairs to help Ma get breakfast.

But Mrs. Boast was helping Ma. The room was warm from the glowing stove. Mush was frying on the long griddle. The teakettle was boiling and the table was set.

"Merry Christmas!" Ma and Mrs. Boast said together.

"Merry Christmas," Laura answered but she was staring at the table. At each place, the plate was turned bottom-up over the knife and fork, as usual. But on the plates' bottoms were packages, small packages and larger packages, some wrapped in colored tissue paper and others in plain wrapping paper tied with colored string.

"You see, Laura, we didn't hang up stockings last night," said Ma, "so we will take our presents off the table at breakfast."

Laura went back upstairs, and told Mary and Carrie about the Christmas breakfast table. "Ma knew where we hid all the presents but hers," she said. "They are all on the table."

"But we can't have presents!" Mary wailed horrified. "There isn't anything for Mr. and Mrs. Boast!"

"Ma will fix it," Laura answered. "She told me so last night."

"How can she?" Mary asked. "We didn't know they were coming! There isn't anything we could give them."

"Ma can fix anything," said Laura. She took Ma's present from Mary's box and held it behind her when they all went downstairs together. Carrie stood between her and Ma while quickly Laura put the package on Ma's plate. There was a little package on Mrs. Boast's plate, and another on Mr. Boast's.

"Oh, I can't wait!" Carrie whispered, squeezing her thin hands together. Her peaked face was white and her eyes were big and shining.

"Yes, you can. We've got to," said Laura. It was easier for Grace, who was so little that she did not notice the Christmas table. But even Grace was so excited that Mary could hardly button her up.

"Mewy Cwismas! Mewy Cwismas!" Grace shouted, wriggling, and when she was free she ran about, shouting, until Ma told her gently that children must be seen and not heard.

"Come here, Grace, and you can see out," said Carrie. She had blown and wiped a clear space in the frost on the window-pane, and there they stayed, taking turns at looking out, till at last Carrie said, "Here they come!"

After a loud stamping-off of snow in the lean-to, Pa and Mr. Boast came in.

"Merry Christmas! Merry Christmas!" they all cried.

Grace ran behind Ma and clung to her skirts, peeping around them at the strange man. Pa picked her up and tossed her, just as he used to toss Laura when Laura was little. And Grace screamed with laughter just as Laura used to. Laura had to remember hard that she was a big girl now or she would have laughed out loud too. They were all so happy in the warmth full of good smells of cooking, and with company there for Christmas in the snug house. The light from the frost-furred windows was silvery, and just as they all sat down to that exciting Christmas table, the eastern window turned golden; outdoors the stillness of the whole vast snowy prairie was full of sunshine.

"You first, Mrs. Boast," said Ma, for Mrs. Boast was company. So Mrs. Boast opened her package. In it was a lawn handkerchief edged with narrow crocheted lace. Laura recognized it; it was Ma's best Sunday handkerchief. Mrs. Boast was delighted, and so surprised that there was a gift for her.

So was Mr. Boast. His present was wristlets, knitted in stripes of red and gray. They fitted him perfectly. They were the wristlets that Ma had knitted for Pa. But she could knit some more for Pa, and the company must have Christmas presents.

Pa said his new socks were exactly what he needed; the cold from the snow had been going right through his boots. And he admired the necktie that Laura had made. "I'll put this on, right after breakfast!" he said. "By George, now I'll be all dressed up for Christmas!"

Everyone exclaimed when Ma unwrapped her pretty apron.

She put it on at once, and stood up for them all to see. She looked at the hem, and smiled at Carrie. "You hem very nicely, Carrie," she said, then she smiled at Laura, "And Laura's gathers are even, and well sewed. It is a nice apron."

"There's more, Ma!" Carrie cried out. "Look in the pocket!"

Ma took out the handkerchief. She was so surprised. And to think that the very morning she gave away her Sunday best handkerchief, she was given another one; it was as if this had been planned, though none of them had planned it. But of course this could not be said in Mrs. Boast's hearing. Ma only looked at the handkerchief's tiny hem and said, "Such a pretty handkerchief too! Thank you, Mary."

Then everyone admired Mary's bed shoes, and how they had been made of the ends of a worn-out blanket. Mrs. Boast said she was going to make some for herself, as soon as any of her blankets wore out.

Carrie put on her mittens and softly clapped her hands. "My Fourth of July mittens! Oh, see my Fourth of July mittens!" she said.

Then Laura opened her package. And in it was an apron, made of the same calico as Ma's! It was smaller than Ma's apron, and had two pockets. A narrow ruffle was all around it. Ma had cut it out of the other curtain, Carrie had sewed the seams, Mary had hemmed the ruffle. All that time, Ma hadn't known and Laura hadn't known that each was making an apron for the other from those old curtains, and Mary and Carrie had been almost bursting with the two secrets.

"Oh, thank you! Thank you all!" Laura said, smoothing down the pretty white calico with the little red flowers scattered over it. "Such tiny stitches in the ruffle, Mary! I do thank you."

Then came the best part of all. Everyone watched while Ma put the little blue coat on Grace and smoothed the swan's-down collar. She put the lovely white swan's-down hood over Grace's golden hair. A bit of the blue silk lining showed around Grace's face and matched her shining eyes. She touched the fluffy soft swan's-down on her wrists, and waved her hands and laughed.

She was so beautiful and so happy, blue and white and gold and alive and laughing, that they could not look at her long enough. But Ma did not want to spoil her with too much attention. So, too soon, she quieted Grace and laid away the coat and hood in the bedroom.

There was still another package beside Laura's plate, and she saw that Mary and Carrie and Grace each had one like it. All at once, they unwrapped them, and each found a little pink cheesecloth bag full of candy.

"Christmas candy!" Carrie cried and "Christmas candy!" Laura and Mary said at the same time.

"However did Christmas candy get here?" Mary asked.

"Why, didn't Santa Claus get here on Christmas Eve?" said Pa. So, almost all at once, they said, "Oh, Mr. Boast! Thank you! Thank you, Mr. and Mrs. Boast!"

Then Laura gathered up all the paper wrappings, and she helped Ma set on the table the big platter of golden, fried mush, a plate of hot biscuits, a dish of fried potatoes, a bowl of codfish gravy and a glass dish full of dried-apple sauce.

"I'm sorry we have no butter," said Ma. "Our cow gives so little milk that we can't make butter any more."

But the codfish gravy was good on the mush and the potatoes, and nothing could taste better than hot biscuits and applesauce. Such a breakfast as that, like Christmas, came only once a year. And there was still the Christmas dinner to come, on that same day.

After breakfast, Pa and Mr. Boast went with the team to get Mr. Boast's bobsled. They took shovels to dig the snow away so that the horses could pull it out of the slough.

Then Mary took Grace on her lap in the rocking chair, and while Carrie made the beds and swept, Ma and Laura and Mrs. Boast put on their aprons, rolled up their sleeves, and washed the dishes and got dinner.

Mrs. Boast was great fun. She was interested in everything, and eager to learn how Ma managed so well.

"When you haven't milk enough to have sour milk, however do you make such delicious biscuits, Laura?" she asked.

"Why, you just use sour dough," Laura said.

Mrs. Boast had never made sour-dough biscuits! It was fun to show her. Laura measured out the cups of sour dough, put in the soda and salt and flour, and rolled out the biscuits on the board.

"But how do you make the sour dough?" Mrs. Boast asked.

"You start it," said Ma, "by putting some flour and warm water in a jar and letting it stand till it sours."

"Then when you use it, always leave a little," said Laura. "And put in the scraps of biscuit dough, like this, and more warm water," Laura put in the warm water "and cover it," she put the clean cloth and the plate on the jar, "and just set it in a warm place," she set it in its place on the shelf by the stove. "And it's always ready to use, whenever you want it."

"I never tasted better biscuits," said Mrs. Boast.

With such good company, the morning seemed to go in a minute. Dinner was almost ready when Pa and Mr. Boast came back with the bobsled. The enormous jack rabbit was browning in the oven. Potatoes were boiling, and the coffee pot bubbled on the back of the stove. The house was full of the good smells of roasting meat, hot breads, and coffee. Pa sniffed when he came in.

"Don't worry, Charles," said Ma. "You smell coffee, but the kettle is boiling to make your tea."

"Good! Tea is a man's drink in cold weather," Pa told her.

Laura spread the clean white tablecloth, and in the center of the table she set the glass sugar bowl, the glass pitcher full of cream, and the glass spoonholder full of silver spoons all standing on their handles. Around the table Carrie laid the knives and forks, and filled the water glasses, while Laura set all the plates in a pile at Pa's place. Then at each place, all around the table, she cheerfully put a glass sauce dish holding half a canned peach in golden syrup. The table was beautiful.

Pa and Mr. Boast had washed and combed their hair. Ma put the last empty pot and pan in the pantry, and helped Laura and Mrs. Boast whisk the last full dish to the table. Quickly she and Laura took off their work aprons and tied on their Christmas aprons.

"Come!" said Ma. "Dinner is ready."

"Come, Boast!" said Pa. "Sit up and eat hearty! There's plenty more down cellar in a teacup!"

Before Pa, on the big platter, lay the huge roasted rabbit with piles of bread-and-onion stuffing steaming around it. From a dish on one side stood up a mound of mashed potatoes, and on the other side stood a bowl of rich, brown gravy.

There were plates of hot Johnny cake and of small hot biscuits. There was a dish of cucumber pickles.

Ma poured the strong brown coffee and the fragrant tea, while Pa heaped each plate with roast rabbit, stuffing, and potatoes and gravy.

"This is the first time we ever had jack rabbit for Christmas dinner," Pa said. "The other time we lived where jack rabbits grow, they were too common, we had them every day. For Christmas we had wild turkey."

"Yes, Charles, and that was the most we did have," said Ma. "There was no surveyors' pantry to get pickles and peaches out of, in Indian Territory."

"Seems to me this is the best rabbit I ever tasted," said Mr. Boast. "The gravy is extra good too."

"Hunger is the best sauce," Ma replied modestly. But Mrs. Boast said, "I know why the rabbit's so good. Mrs. Ingalls lays thin slices of salt pork over it when she roasts it."

"Why, yes, I do," Ma agreed. "I think it does improve the flavor."

They all took big second helpings. Then Pa and Mr. Boast took big third helpings, and Mary and Laura and Carrie did not refuse, but Ma took only a bit of stuffing and Mrs. Boast just one more biscuit. "I declare, I'm so full I can't eat another mouthful," she said.

When Pa took up the fork from the platter again, Ma warned him. "Save some room, Charles, you and Mr. Boast."

"You don't mean there's more to come?" said Pa.

Then Ma stepped into the pantry and brought out the dried-apple pie.

"Pie!" said Pa, and, "Apple pie!" said Mr. Boast. "Jumping Jehoshaphat, I wish I'd known this was coming!"

Slowly they each ate a piece of that apple pie, and Pa and Mr. Boast divided the one piece left over.

"I never hope to eat a better Christmas dinner," said Mr. Boast, with a deep sigh of fullness.

"Well," Pa said. "It's the first Christmas dinner anybody ever ate in this part of the country. I'm glad it was a good one. In time to come, no doubt a good many folks will celebrate Christmas around here, and I expect they'll have fancier fixings in some ways, but I don't know how they can have more solid comfort than we've got, for a fact."

After a while he and Mr. Boast got up reluctantly, and Ma began to clear the table. "I'll do the dishes," she said to Laura. "You run help Mrs. Boast get settled."

So Laura and Mrs. Boast put on their coats and hoods, mufflers and mittens, and went out into the glittering, biting cold. Laughing, they plowed and plunged through snow, to the tiny house nearby that had been the surveyors' office. At its door Pa and Mr. Boast unloaded the bobsled.

The little house had no floor, and it was so small that the double bedstead just fitted across one end. In the corner by the door Pa and Mrs. Boast set up the stove. Laura helped Mrs. Boast carry the feather bed and quilts and make the bed. Then they set the table against the window opposite the stove, and pushed two chairs under it. Mrs. Boast's trunk squeezed between the table and the bed and made another seat. A shelf above the stove and a box beside it held the dishes, and just room enough was left for the door to open against the table.

"There!" Pa said, when all was done. "Now you folks are settled, come on over. Not even the four of us can get in here, but there's plenty of room at the other house, so that's headquarters. How about a game of checkers, Boast?"

"You go along," Mrs. Boast told them. "Laura and I will come in a minute."

When they were gone, Mrs. Boast took a full paper bag from under the dishes. "It's for a surprise," she told Laura. "Popcorn! Rob doesn't know I brought it."

They smuggled the bag into the house and hid it in the pantry, whispering to tell Ma what it was. And later, when Pa and Mr. Boast were absorbed in checkers, quietly they heated fat in the iron kettle and poured in a handful of the shelled popcorn. At the first crackle, Pa looked around quickly.

"Popcorn!" he exclaimed. "I haven't tasted popcorn since—if I'd known you'd brought popcorn, Boast, I'd have routed it out before now."

"I didn't bring popcorn," said Mr. Boast. Then he cried out, "Nell, you rascal!"

"You two go on with your game!" Mrs. Boast told him, laughing at him with her blue eyes. "You're much too busy to notice us."

"Yes, Charles," said Ma. "Don't let us disturb your checkers."

"I've got you beat anyway, Boast," said Pa.

"Not yet you haven't," Mr. Boast contradicted.

Ma dipped the snowy kernels from the kettle into a milkpan, and Laura carefully salted them. They popped another kettleful, and the pan would hold no more. Then Mary and Laura and Carrie had a plateful of the crispy crackly melting-soft corn, and Pa and Ma and Mr. and Mrs. Boast sat around the pan, eating and talking and laughing, till chore-time and suppertime and the time when Pa would play the fiddle.

"Every Christmas is better than the Christmas before," Laura thought. "I guess it must be because I'm growing up."

CHAPTER 22

Happy Winter Days

THE Christmasy feeling lasted day after day. Every morning Mrs. Boast did her breakfast work quickly and came to spend her time with "the other girls," as she said. She was always merry and full of fun and always so pretty, with her soft dark hair and laughing blue eyes and the bright color in her cheeks.

That first week the sun shone brightly, there was no wind, and in six days the snow was all gone. The prairie showed bare and brown, and the air seemed warm as milk. Mrs. Boast had cooked the New Year's dinner.

"You can all crowd into my little place for once," she said.

She let Laura help her move things. They put the table on the bed and opened the door wide against the wall. Then they set the table in the exact middle of the house. One corner of it almost touched the stove, and the other end was almost against the bed. But there was room for them all to come in, single file, and sit around it. Mrs. Boast sat by the stove and served the food from its hot top.

First, there was oyster soup. In all her life Laura had never tasted anything so good as that savory, fragrant, sea-tasting hot milk, with golden dots of melted cream and black specks of pepper on its top, and the little dark canned oysters at its bottom. She sipped slowly, slowly from her spoon, to keep that taste going over her tongue as long as she could.

And with this soup, there were little round oyster crackers. The little oyster crackers were like doll-crackers, and they tasted better because they were so light and small.

When the last drop of soup was gone, and the last crackers divided and crunched, there were hot biscuits with honey, and dried-raspberry sauce. And then a big dishpan full of tender salty popcorn, that had been keeping hot on the back of the stove.

That was the New Year's dinner. It was light but filling. There was something fashionable about it because it was so odd and new, so different, and so daintily served on Mrs. Boast's pretty dishes and brand-new tablecloth.

Afterward they sat talking in the little house, with the soft air coming in and beyond the open door, the brown prairie stretching far away and the soft blue sky curving down to meet it.

"I've never tasted finer honey, Mrs. Boast," said Pa. "I'm glad you brought it out from Iowa."

"The oysters too," said Ma. "I don't know when I've had such a treat as this dinner."

"It's a good beginning for 1880," Pa declared. "The seventies haven't been so bad, but it looks like the eighties'll be better. If this is a sample of a Dakota winter, we're all lucky we came West."

"This is certainly a fine country," Mr. Boast agreed. "I'm glad I've got my claim filed on a hundred and sixty acres of it, and I wish you had, Ingalls."

"I'll have it before I'm a week older," said Pa. "I've been waiting for the land office to open at Brookings, to save me more than a week's travel to Yankton and back. They said the Brookings office would open the first of the year, and by Jove, with weather like this I'm starting tomorrow! If Caroline says so."

"I do, Charles," Ma said quietly. Her eyes, her whole face, were shining with gladness because now, so soon, Pa would surely have their homestead.

"That settles it," said Pa. "Not that I figure there's any danger of being too late, but it might as well be done and over with."

"The sooner the better, Ingalls," Mr. Boast said. "I tell you, you've got no notion what the rush is going to be this spring."

"Well, nobody'll be there quicker than I'll be," Pa answered. "Starting before sun-up, I ought to show up at the land office bright and early day after tomorrow morning. So if you folks want to send any letters back to Iowa, get 'em fixed up and I'll take 'em along and mail them in Brookings."

That ended New Year's dinner. Mrs. Boast and Ma were writing letters that afternoon, and Ma packed a lunch for Pa to take with him. But at nightfall a wind full of snow was blowing and frost began to creep up the windowpanes again.

"This is no kind of weather to go anywhere," Pa said. "Don't worry about the homestead, Caroline. I'll get it."

"Yes, Charles, I know you will," Ma replied.

In the stormy weather Pa tended his trap lines and stretched skins to dry. Mr. Boast hauled brushwood from Lake Henry and chopped it up to burn, for he had no coal. And every day Mrs. Boast came.

Often when the sun was shining, she and Laura and Carrie, well wrapped-up, played in the deep snow together. They wrestled and ran and threw snowballs, and one day they made a snowman. And hand in hand in the sharp, bright cold the three of them ran and slid on the ice of Silver Lake. Laura had never laughed so much.

Late one afternoon, when they had been sliding and were coming home warm and breathless, Mrs. Boast said, "Laura, come over to my house a minute."

Laura went with her and Mrs. Boast showed her a tall stack of newspapers. She had brought all those New York Ledgers from Iowa.

"Take as many as you can carry," she said. "When you get them read, bring them back and get some more."

Laura ran all the way home with an armful of papers. She burst into the house and dropped them in Mary's lap.

"See, Mary! See what I've brought!" she cried. "Stories! They're all stories!"

"Oh, hurry up and get the supper work done so we can read," Mary said eagerly. But Ma said, "Never mind the work, Laura! Read us a story!"

So while Ma and Carrie got supper, Laura began to read to them all a wonderful story, about dwarfs and caves where robbers lived and a beautiful lady who was lost in the caves. At the most exciting part she came suddenly to the words, "To be continued." And there was not another word of that story.

"Oh, dear me, we never will know what became of that lady," Mary lamented. "Laura, why do you suppose they print only part of a story?"

"Why do they, Ma?" Laura asked.

"They don't," said Ma. "Look at the next paper."

Laura looked, at the next and the next and next. "Oh, here it is!" she cried. "And more—and more— It goes right on down through the pile. It's all here, Mary! Here it says, 'The End.' "

"It's a continued story," said Ma. Laura and Mary had never before heard of a continued story, but Ma had.

"Well," Mary said contentedly. "Now we can save the next part for tomorrow. Every day we can read one part, and that will make the stories last longer."

"That's my wise girls," said Ma. So Laura did not say that she would rather read as fast as she could. She laid the papers carefully away. Every day she read one more part of the story, and then they wondered until next day what would happen next to the beautiful lady.

On stormy days, Mrs. Boast brought her sewing or knitting, and those were cosy days of reading and talking. One day Mrs. Boast told them about whatnots. She said that everyone in Iowa was making whatnots, and she would show them how.

So she told Pa how to make the shelves, three-cornered, to fit in a corner. He made five shelves of graduated sizes, the largest at the bottom and the smallest at the top, all fastened solidly with narrow strips of board between them. When he had finished, the whatnot fitted snugly into a corner of the room and stood firmly on three legs. Its top shelf was as high as Ma could easily reach.

Then Mrs. Boast cut a curtain of pasteboard to hang from the edge of each shelf. She scalloped the bottom of the pasteboard, a large scallop in the middle and a smaller scallop at each side. The pieces of pasteboard and the scallops were graduated like the shelves, from large at the bottom to small at the top.

Next Mrs. Boast showed them how to cut and fold small squares of heavy wrapping paper. They folded each square cornerwise and then across, and pressed it smooth. When dozens of the squares were folded, Mrs. Boast showed Laura how to sew them in rows on the pasteboard, close together, with points down. Each row overlapped the row below it, and each point must lie between two points of the row below it, and the rows must follow the scallops' curves.

While they worked in the snug, cosy house, they told stories and sang and talked. Ma and Mrs. Boast talked mostly about the homesteads. Mrs. Boast had seeds enough for two gardens; she said she would divide with Ma, so Ma need not worry about seeds. When the town was built, there might be seeds in town to sell, but again there might not. So Mrs. Boast had brought plenty from the gardens of her friends in Iowa.

"I'll be thankful when we're settled," Ma said. "This is the last move we're going to make. Mr. Ingalls agreed to that before we left Minnesota. My girls are going to have schooling and lead a civilized life."

Laura did not know whether or not she wanted to be settled down. When she had schooling, she would have to teach school, and she would rather think of something else. She would rather sing than think at all. She could hum very softly without interrupting the talk, and then often Ma and Mrs. Boast and Mary and Carrie would sing with her. Mrs. Boast had taught them two new songs. Laura liked "The Gypsy's Warning."

"Do not trust him, gentle lady,
Though his voice be low and sweet,
Heed not him who kneels before you,
Gently pleading at your feet,
Now thy life is in the morning,
Cloud not this, thy happy lot,
Listen to the gypsy's warning,
Gentle lady, heed him not."

The other new song was, "When I Was One and Twenty, Nell, and You Were Seventeen." It was Mr. Boast's favorite song. He had been twenty-one when he met Mrs. Boast, and she had been seventeen. Her name was really Ella, but Mr. Boast called her Nell.

At last the five pasteboard pieces were neatly covered with rows above rows of the little paper points, and no stitches showed except along the top of the top row. Then Mrs. Boast sewed a wide strip of the brown paper above these stitches and folded it over to hide them.

Finally, they tacked each pasteboard curtain to its shelf. The stiff scallops, covered with the stiff little paper points, hung down stiffly. Then Pa carefully painted the whole whatnot, and all the little paper points, a rich, dark brown. When the paint dried, they set the whatnot in the corner behind Mary's chair.

"So that's a whatnot," Pa said.

"Yes," said Ma. "Isn't it pretty?"

"It's a neat job," said Pa.

"Mrs. Boast says they're all the rage in Iowa," she told him.

"Well, she ought to know," Pa agreed. "And there's nothing in Iowa too good for you, Caroline."

But the best time of all was after supper. Every evening Pa played the fiddle, and now Mr. Boast's and Mrs. Boast's beautiful voices rounded out the singing. Gaily Pa played and sang:

"When I was young and single,
I could make the money jingle
And the world went well with me then, O then!
The world went well with me then.

"I married me a wife, O then! O then!
I married me a wife, O then!
I married me a wife, she was the joy of my life,
And the world went well with me then!"

The song went on to say that she was not such a good wife after all, so Pa never sang the rest of it. His eyes twinkled at Ma while the music laughed and whirled and then he would sing:

"She can make a cherry pie,
Billy boy! Billy boy!
She can make a cherry pie,
Charming Billy.
She can make a cherry pie
With a twinkle in her eye
But she's a young thing
And cannot leave her mother."

The music would go rollicking while only Pa and Mr. Boast sang:

"I bet my money on the bob-tailed mare
And you bet yours on the gray!"

Even in songs Ma did not approve of gambling, but her toe could not stop tapping while Pa played such tunes.

Then every evening they all sang one round. Mr. Boast's tenor would begin, "Three blind mice," and go on while Mrs. Boast's alto began, "Three blind mice," then as she went on Pa's bass would join in, "Three blind mice," and then Laura's soprano, and Ma's contralto, and Mary and Carrie. When Mr. Boast reached the end of the song he began it again without stopping, and they all followed, each behind the other, going round and round with words and music.

"Three blind mice! Three blind mice!
They all ran after the farmer's wife
She cut off their tails with the carving knife,
Did you ever hear such a tale in your life
Of three blind mice?"

They kept on singing until someone laughed and then the song ended ragged and breathless and laughing. And Pa would play some of the old songs, "to go to sleep on," he said.

"Nellie was a lady, last night she died,
Oh, toll the bell for lovely Nell,
My old—Vir-gin-ia bride."

And,

"Oh, do you remember sweet Alice, Ben Bolt?
Sweet Alice with eyes so brown,
Who wept with delight when you gave her a smile,
And trembled with fear at your frown?"

And,

"Oft in the stilly night,
Ere slumber's chain has bound me,
Sweet memory brings the light
Of other days around me."

Laura had never been so happy, and for some reason she was happiest of all when they were singing,

"Ye banks and braes of Bonny Doon,
How can ye bloom sae fresh and fair?
How can ye chaunt, ye little birds,
And I sae weary, full of care?"

CHAPTER 23

On the Pilgrim Way

ONE Sunday evening Pa's fiddle was singing a Sunday tune and they were all singing heartily with it,

"When cheerful we meet in our pleasant home
And the song of joy is swelling,
Do we pause to think of the tears that flow
In sorrow's lonely dwelling?
Let us lend a hand——"

The fiddle stopped suddenly. Outdoors a strong voice was singing:

"—to those who are faint and weary,
Let us lend a hand to those on the pilgrim way."

The fiddle squawked in amazement as Pa dropped it on the table and hurried to the door. The cold burst in and the door slammed behind him. Outside it there was an outburst of voices; then the door flung open and two snowy men stumbled in while Pa said behind them, "I'll see to putting up your team, be with you right away."

One of the men was tall and thin. Between his cap and muffler Laura saw blue, kind eyes. Before she knew what she was doing she heard herself screaming, "Reverend Alden! Reverend Alden!"

"Not Brother Alden!" Ma exclaimed. "Why, Brother Alden!"

He had taken off his cap and now they could all see his pleasant eyes and his dark brown hair.

"We are pleased to see you, Brother Alden," Ma said. "Come to the fire. This is a surprise!"

"You are no more surprised than I am, Sister Ingalls," said the Reverend Alden. "I left you folks settled on Plum Creek. I had no idea you were 'way out West. And here are my little country girls grown into women!"

Laura could not say a word. Her throat was choked with the joy of seeing Reverend Alden again. But Mary said politely,

"We are glad to see you again, sir." Mary's face was shining with gladness; only her sightless eyes were blank. They startled Reverend Alden. He looked quickly at Ma, and then at Mary again.

"Mr. and Mrs. Boast, our neighbors, Reverend Alden," said Ma.

Reverend Alden said, "You were all doing some fine singing when we drove up," and Mr. Boast said, "You did some fine singing yourself, sir."

"Oh, I wasn't the one who joined in," said Reverend Alden. "That was Scotty, here. I was too cold, but his red hair keeps him warm. Reverend Stuart, these are old, good friends of mine, and their friends, so we are all friends together."

Reverend Stuart was so young that he was not much more than a big boy. His hair was flaming red, his face was red with cold, and his eyes were a sparkling cold gray.

"Set the table, Laura," Ma said quietly, tying on her apron. Mrs. Boast put on an apron too, and they were all busy, poking up the fire, setting the kettle to boil for tea, making biscuits, frying potatoes, while Mr. Boast talked to the visitors who stood in the way, thawing themselves by the stove. Pa came from the stable with two more men, who owned the team. They were homesteaders, going out to settle on the Jim River.

Laura heard Reverend Alden say, "We two are just passengers. We hear there's a settlement on the Jim, a town named Huron. The Home Missionary Society sent us out to look over the ground and make ready to start a church there."

"I guess there's a townsite marked out on the railroad grade," said Pa. "But I never heard of any building there, except a saloon."

"All the more reason we should get a church started," Reverend Alden answered cheerfully.

After the travelers had eaten supper, he came to the door of the pantry where Ma and Laura were washing the dishes. He thanked Ma for the good supper and then he said, "I am sorry indeed, Sister Ingalls, to see the affliction that has come to Mary."

"Yes, Brother Alden," Ma answered sadly. "Sometimes it is hard to be resigned to God's will. We all had scarlet fever in our place on Plum Creek, and for a while it was hard to get along. But I'm thankful that all the children were spared to us.

Mary is a great comfort to me, Brother Alden. She has never once repined."

"Mary is a rare soul, and a lesson to all of us," said Reverend Alden. "We must remember that whom the Lord loveth, He chasteneth, and a brave spirit will turn all our afflictions to good. I don't know whether you and Brother Ingalls know that there are colleges for the blind. There is one in Iowa."

Ma took tight hold of the edge of the dishpan. Her face startled Laura. Her gentle voice sounded choked and hungry. She asked, "How much does it cost?"

"I don't know, Sister Ingalls," Reverend Alden answered. "I will make inquiries for you if you like."

Ma swallowed and went on washing dishes. She said, "We can't afford it. But perhaps, later—if it doesn't cost too much, we might somehow manage, sometime. I always wanted Mary to have an education."

Laura's heart beat hard and thick. She could feel its beating in her throat, and wild thoughts fluttered so fast in her mind that she did not know what any of them were.

"We must trust in the Lord to do all things for our best good," said Reverend Alden. "Shall we have a short prayer meeting, all of us together, when you've finished the dishes?"

"Yes, Brother Alden, I should like that," said Ma. "I am sure we all would."

When the dishes were done and their hands washed, Ma and Laura took off their aprons and smoothed their hair. Reverend Alden and Mary were talking together earnestly while Mrs. Boast held Grace, and Mr. Boast and the two homesteaders were talking to Reverend Stuart and Pa about the wheat and oats he intended to raise as soon as he could get his sod broken. When Ma came in, Reverend Alden stood up and said they would all have the refreshment of prayer together before saying good night.

They all knelt down by their chairs, and Reverend Alden asked God, Who knew their hearts and their secret thoughts, to look down on them there, and to forgive their sins and help them to do right. A quietness was in the room while he spoke. Laura felt as if she were hot, dry, dusty grass parching in a drought, and the quietness was a cool and gentle rain falling on her. It truly was a refreshment. Everything was simple now that she felt so cool and strong, and she would be glad to work hard and go without anything she wanted herself, so that Mary could go to college.

Then Mr. and Mrs. Boast thanked Brother Alden and went home, and Laura and Carrie brought Carrie's bed downstairs. Ma made it down on the floor by the stove.

"We've only the one bed," Ma apologized, "and I'm afraid there are not covers enough for it."

"Don't worry, Sister Ingalls," said Reverend Alden. "We'll use our overcoats."

"We'll be very comfortable, I'm sure," said Reverend Stuart. "And glad we are to have found you folks here. We thought we had to go all the way to Huron, until we saw your light and heard you singing."

Upstairs, Laura helped Carrie unbutton in the dark. She tucked the hot flatiron close against Mary's feet in the bed. As they all snuggled tight together to get warm under the icy-cold covers, they heard Pa and the travelers still talking and laughing around the fire.

"Laura," Mary whispered, "Reverend Alden told me there are colleges for blind people."

"What, for blind people?" Carrie whispered.

"Colleges," whispered Laura, "where they get college educations."

"How can they?" Carrie asked. "I thought you had to read, to study."

"I don't know," Mary said. "Anyway, I couldn't go. It must cost something. I don't suppose there's any chance I could."

"Ma knows," Laura whispered. "Reverend Alden told her too. Maybe you can, Mary. I do hope you can." She took a deep breath and promised, "I will study hard, so I can teach school and help."

In the morning the travelers' voices and a clatter of dishes woke her and she sprang out of bed to dress and hurry downstairs to help Ma.

Outdoors was crisp and cold. Sunshine gilded the frosty windows, and in the house everyone was hearty and cheerful. How the travelers did enjoy that breakfast! They praised everything they ate. The biscuits were light and flaky, the fried potatoes were brown and finely hashed, the slices of fat pork were thin and crisp, and the gravy was smooth and brown and creamy. There was hot brown-sugar syrup, and plenty of fragrant steaming tea.

"This meat is delicious," Reverend Stuart said. "I know it is just fat salt pork, but I never tasted any like it. Would you tell me how you cook it, Sister Ingalls?"

Ma was surprised, and Reverend Alden explained, "Scotty's going to stay out here in this missionary field. I've only come out to get him started. He'll be baching and doing his own cooking."

"Do you know how to cook, Brother Stuart?" Ma asked, and he said he expected to learn by experience. He had brought supplies; beans, flour, salt, tea, and salt pork.

"The meat is easy," said Ma. "Cut the slices thin, and set them to parboil in cold water. When the water boils, pour it off. Then roll the slices in flour and fry them brown. When they are crisp, take them out onto a platter, and pour some of the fat off. Save it to use for butter. Then brown some flour in the fat left in the frying pan, pour in some milk, and keep stirring it as it boils until the gravy is just right."

"Would you mind writing it down?" said Reverend Stuart. "How much flour, and how much milk?"

"Goodness!" said Ma. "I never measure, but I guess I can make a stab at it." She got a sheet of paper and her little pearl-handled pen and the ink bottle, and wrote down her receipts for fried salt pork and gravy, and for sour-dough biscuits and bean soup and baked beans, while Laura cleared the table quickly and Carrie ran to ask Mr. and Mrs. Boast to come over for a preaching service.

It seemed odd to have church on Monday morning, but the travelers were starting on the last stage of their journey to Huron, and no one wanted to lose this opportunity to hear a sermon.

Pa played the fiddle, and they all sang a hymn. Reverend Stuart, with Ma's receipts in his pocket, made a short prayer for guidance in all their worthy endeavors. Then Reverend Alden preached the sermon. After that, Pa's fiddle gaily and sweetly played and they all sang:

"There is a happy land, far, far away,
Where saints in glory stand, bright, bright as day,
Oh, to hear the angels sing glory to the Lord, our
King . . ."

When the team and wagon were ready to start, Reverend Alden said, "You have had the first church service in this new town. In the spring I will be back to organize a church." And he said to Mary and Laura and Carrie, "We will have a Sunday school too! You can all help with a Christmas Tree next Christmas."

He climbed into the wagon and went away, leaving them with that to think about and look forward to. Wrapped in shawls and coats and mufflers, they stood watching the wagon going westward on the untouched snow and leaving the marks of its wheels behind it. The cold sun shone brightly and the white world glittered millions of tiny, sharp points of light.

"Well," Mrs. Boast said through a fold of shawl drawn across her mouth, "it's nice to have had the first church service here."

"What is the name of the town that's going to be here?" Carrie asked.

"It doesn't have a name yet, does it, Pa?" said Laura.

"Yes," Pa answered. "It's De Smet. It's named for a French priest who came pioneering out here in the early days."

They went into the warm house. "That poor boy'll ruin his health, most likely," said Ma. "Baching all by himself and trying to live on his own cooking." She meant Reverend Stuart.

"He's Scotch," said Pa, as if that meant that he would be all right.

"What did I tell you, Ingalls, about the spring rush?" said Mr. Boast. "Two homesteaders in here already, and March hardly begun."

"That struck me too," said Pa. "I'm making tracks for Brookings tomorrow morning, rain or shine."

CHAPTER 24

The Spring Rush

"NO MUSIC tonight," Pa said that evening at the supper table. "Early to bed and early to rise, and day after tomorrow our claim's filed on the homestead."

"I'll be glad, Charles," said Ma. After all the bustle of last night and this morning, the house was quiet and composed again. The supper work was done, Grace slept in the trundle bed, and Ma was packing the lunch that Pa would eat on the way to Brookings.

"Listen," Mary said. "I hear somebody talking."

Laura pressed her face to a windowpane and shut out the lamplight with her hands. Against the snow she saw a dark team and a wagon full of men. One of them shouted again, then another jumped to the ground. Pa went to meet him and they stood talking. Then Pa came in and shut the door behind him.

"There's five of them, Caroline," he said. "Strangers, on their way to Huron."

"There isn't room for them here," said Ma.

"Caroline, we've got to put them up for the night. There isn't any other place they can stay or get a bite to eat. Their team is tired out and they're greenhorns. If they try to get to Huron tonight, they'll lose themselves on the prairie and maybe freeze to death."

Ma sighed. "Well, you know best, Charles."

So Ma cooked supper for the five strange men. They filled the place with their loud boots and loud voices, and their bedding piled in heaps, ready to make their beds on the floor by the stove. Even before the supper dishes were finished, Ma took her hands from the dishwater and said quietly, "It's bedtime, girls."

It was not bedtime, but they knew that she meant they were not allowed to stay downstairs among those strange men. Carrie followed Mary through the stair door, but Ma held Laura back to slip into her hand a strong sliver of wood. "Push this into the slot above the latch," Ma said. "Push it in well and leave it there. Then no one can lift the latch and open the door. I want the door to be locked. Don't come down till I call you tomorrow morning."

In the morning, Laura and Mary and Carrie lay in bed after the sun was up. Downstairs they heard the strangers talking, and breakfast dishes clattering.

"Ma said not to come till she called us," Laura insisted.

"I wish they'd go away," said Carrie. "I don't like strangers."

"I don't either, and neither does Ma," Laura said. "It takes them a long time to get started, because they're greenhorns."

At last they were gone, and at dinner Pa said he would go to Brookings tomorrow. "No use starting unless I start early," he said. "It's a long day's trip, and there's no sense in starting after sun-up and having to camp out overnight in this cold."

That night more strangers came. The next night there were more. Ma said, "Mercy on us, aren't we to have one night in peace by ourselves?"

"I can't help it, Caroline," said Pa. "We can't refuse folks shelter, when there's nowhere else they can stay."

"We can charge them for it, Charles," Ma said firmly. Pa did not like to charge folks for shelter and a meal, but he knew that Ma was right. So he charged twenty-five cents a meal, and twenty-five cents for shelter overnight, for man or horse.

There was no more singing, no more comfortable suppers or cosy evenings. Every day more strangers crowded around the supper table and every night as soon as all the dishes were washed, Laura and Mary and Carrie had to go up to the attic and fasten the door behind them.

The strangers came from Iowa, from Ohio, from Illinois and Michigan, from Wisconsin and Minnesota and even from faraway New York and Vermont. They were going to Huron or to Fort Pierre or even farther West, looking for homesteads.

One morning Laura sat up in bed, listening. "Where's Pa, I wonder?" she said. "I don't hear Pa's voice. That's Mr. Boast talking."

"Maybe he's gone to get the homestead," Mary guessed.

When at last the loaded wagons went away to the West and Ma called the girls downstairs, she said that Pa had started before sun-up. "He didn't want to go and leave us in this rush," she said, "but he had to. Someone else will get the homestead if he doesn't hurry. We had no idea that people would rush in here like this, and March hardly begun."

This was the first week in March. The door was open, and the air felt like spring.

"When March comes in like a lamb, it goes out like a lion," said Ma. "Come, girls, there's work to be done. Let's get this house in order before more travelers come."

"I wish nobody'd come till Pa gets back," Laura said while she and Carrie washed the stacks of dishes.

"Maybe nobody will," Carrie hoped.

"Mr. Boast is going to look after things while your Pa's gone," Ma said. "He asked Mr. and Mrs. Boast to stay here. They'll sleep in the bedroom, and Grace and I'll go upstairs with you girls."

Mrs. Boast came to help. That day they cleaned the whole house and moved the beds. They were all very tired, when in the last of the sunset they saw a wagon coming from the East. There were five men in it.

Mr. Boast helped them put their horses in the stable. Mrs. Boast helped Ma cook their suppers. They had not finished eating, when another wagon brought four men. Laura cleared the table, washed the dishes, and helped put supper on the table for them. While they were eating, a third wagon brought six men.

Mary had gone upstairs to be away from the crowd. Carrie sang Grace to sleep in the bedroom with the door shut. Laura cleared the table again and washed the dishes again.

"This is the worst yet," Ma said to Mrs. Boast when they met in the pantry. "There isn't room for fifteen on the floor, we'll have to put some beds in the lean-to. And they'll have to use their robes and blankets and coats for bedding."

"Rob will tend to it, I'll speak to him," said Mrs. Boast. "Mercy me, that's not another wagon?"

Laura had to wash the dishes again and reset the table again. The house was so full of strange men, strange eyes and strange voices and bulky coats and muddy boots, that she could hardly get through the crowd.

At last they were all fed, and for the last time the last dish was washed. Ma with Grace in her arms followed Laura and Carrie to the stairs, and carefully fastened the door behind them. Mary was sleeping in bed, and Laura could not keep her eyes open while she undressed. But as soon as she lay down, she was awakened by the noise downstairs.

There was loud talking and walking. Ma sat up to listen. The downstairs bedroom was still, so Mr. Boast must think that the noise was all right. Ma lay down again. The noise grew louder. Sometimes it almost stopped, then suddenly it burst out. A crash shook the house, and Laura sat straight up, crying out, "Ma! What's that?"

Ma's voice was so low that it seemed louder than all the shouting downstairs. "Be quiet, Laura," she said. "Lie down."

Laura thought she could not sleep. She was so tired that the noise tormented her. But another crash woke her out of a sound sleep. Ma said, "It's all right, Laura. Mr. Boast is there." Laura slept again.

In the morning Ma gently shook her awake, and whispered, "Come Laura, it's time to get breakfast. Let the others sleep."

They went downstairs together. Mr. Boast had taken up the beds. Tousled, sleepy and red-eyed, the men were getting into their boots and coats. Ma and Mrs. Boast hurried breakfast. The table was small, there were not dishes enough, so that Laura set the table and washed the dishes three times.

At last the men were gone, and Ma called Mary, while she and Mrs. Boast cooked more breakfast and Laura washed dishes and set the table once more.

"My, such a night!" Mrs. Boast exclaimed.

"What was the matter?" Mary wondered.

"I think they were drunk," Ma said, tight-lipped.

"I should say they were!" Mr. Boast told her. "They brought bottles and a jug of whisky. I thought once I would have to interfere, but what could I do against a crowd of fifteen drunks? I decided to let them fight it out, unless they set the house afire."

"I'm thankful they didn't," said Ma.

That day a young man drove up to the house with a load of lumber. He had hauled the boards from Brookins, to build a store on the townsite. Pleasantly he urged Ma to board him while he was building, and Ma could not refuse because there was no other place where he could eat.

Next came a man and his son from Sioux Falls. They had

brought lumber to build a grocery store. They begged Ma to board them, and after she had agreed she said to Laura, "Might as well be hung for a sheep as a lamb."

"If Ingalls doesn't hurry back, we'll have a town here before he comes," said Mr. Boast.

"I only hope he's not too late to file on the homestead," Ma replied anxiously.

CHAPTER 25

Pa's Bet

THAT day did not seem real. Laura's eyelids felt sandy and she yawned all the time, yet she did not feel sleepy. At noon young Mr. Hinz and the two Mr. Harthorns came to dinner. In the afternoon their hammers could be heard pounding on the framework of the new buildings. It seemed a long time since Pa had gone.

He did not come that night. All the next day he did not come. That night he did not come. And now Laura was sure that he was having a hard time to get the homestead. Perhaps he might not get it. If he did not get it, perhaps they would go west to Oregon.

Ma would not let any more strangers sleep in the house. Only Mr. Hinz and the two Harthorns bunked down on the floor by the stove. The weather was not so cold that men would freeze, sleeping in their wagons. Ma charged twenty-five cents just for supper, and far into the night she and Mrs. Boast cooked and Laura washed dishes. So many men came to eat that she did not try to count them.

Late in the afternoon of the fourth day Pa came home. He waved as he drove by to put the tired team in the stable, and he walked smiling into the house. "Well, Caroline! Girls!" he said. "We've got the claim."

"You got it!" Ma exclaimed joyfully.

"I went after it, didn't I?" Pa laughed. "Brrr! It's chilly, riding. Let me get to the stove and warm myself."

Ma shook down the fire and set the kettle boiling for tea. "Did you have any trouble, Charles?" she asked.

"You wouldn't believe it," said Pa. "I never saw such a jam. It looks like the whole country's trying to file on land. I got to Brookings all right the first night, and next morning when I showed up at the Land Office I couldn't get anywheres near the door. Every man had to stand in line and wait his turn. So many were ahead of me that my turn didn't come that day."

"You didn't stand there all day, Pa?" Laura cried.

"Yep, Flutterbudget. All day."

"Without anything to eat? Oh, no, Pa!" said Carrie.

"Pshaw, that didn't worry me. What worried me was the crowds. I kept thinking maybe somebody ahead of me is getting my quarter section. Caroline, you never saw such crowds. But my worry then wasn't a patch to what came later."

"What, Pa?" Laura asked.

"Let a fellow get his breath, Flutterbudget! Well, when the Land Office closed I went along in the jam to get supper at the hotel, and I heard a couple of men talking. One had filed on a claim near Huron. The other said De Smet was going to be a better town than Huron, and then he mentioned the very piece I picked out last winter. He told the numbers. He was going to file on it first thing next morning. He said it was the only piece left vacant anywhere near this townsite. So he was going to have it, though he'd never seen it.

"Well, that was enough for me. I had to beat him to that claim. At first I thought I'd be up bright and early next morning, and then I figured I wouldn't take any chances. So as soon as I got some supper, I made tracks for the Land Office."

"I thought it was closed," said Carrie.

"It was. I settled right down on the doorstep to spend the night."

"Surely you didn't need to do that, Charles?" said Ma, handing him a cup of tea.

"Need to do that?" Pa repeated. "I wasn't the only man who had that idea, not by a blamed sight. Lucky I got there first. Must have been forty men waiting there all night, and right next to me were those two fellows that I'd heard talking."

He blew on the tea to cool it, and Laura said, "But they didn't know you wanted that piece, did they?"

"They didn't know me from Adam," said Pa, drinking the tea, "till a fellow came along and sang out, 'Hello, Ingalls! So you weathered the winter on Silver Lake. Settling down at De Smet, uh?' "

"Oh, Pa!" Mary wailed.

"Yes, the fat was in the fire then," said Pa. "I knew I wouldn't have a chance if I budged from that door. So I didn't. By sun-up the crowd was doubled, and a couple of hundred men must have been pushing and shoving against me before the Land Office opened. There wasn't any standing in line that day, I tell you! It was each fellow for himself and devil take the hindmost.

"Well, girls, finally the door opened. How about some more tea, Caroline?"

"Oh, Pa, go *on!*" Laura cried. "Please."

"Just as it opened," said Pa, "the Huron man crowded me back. 'Get in! I'll hold him!' he said to the other fellow. It meant a fight, and while I fought him, the other'd get my homestead. Right then, quick as a wink, somebody landed like a ton of brick on the Huron man. 'Go in, Ingalls!' he yelled. 'I'll fix 'im! Yow-ee-ee!' "

Pa's long, catamount screech curled against the walls, and Ma gasped, "Mercy! Charles!"

"And you'll never guess who it was," said Pa.

"Mr. Edwards!" Laura shouted.

Pa was astounded. "How did you guess it, Laura?"

"He yelled like that in Indian Territory. He's a wildcat from Tennessee," Laura remembered. "Oh, Pa, where is he? Did you bring him?"

"I couldn't get him to come home with me," said Pa. "I tried every persuasion I could think of, but he's filed on a claim south of here and must stay with it to keep off claim jumpers. He told me to remember him to you, Caroline, and to Mary and Laura. I'd never have got the claim if it hadn't been for him. Golly, that was a fight he started!"

"Was he hurt?" Mary asked anxiously.

"Not a scratch. He just started that fight. He got out of it as quick as I ducked inside and started filing my claim. But it was some time before the crowd quieted down. They ——"

"All's well that ends well, Charles," Ma interrupted.

"I guess so, Caroline," Pa said. "Yes, I guess that's right. Well, girls, I've bet Uncle Sam fourteen dollars against a hundred and sixty acres of land, that we can make out to live on the claim for five years. Going to help me win the bet?"

"Oh, yes, Pa!" Carrie said eagerly, and Mary said, "Yes, Pa!" gladly, and Laura promised soberly, "Yes, Pa."

"I don't like to think of it as gambling," Ma said in her gentle way.

"Everything's more or less a gamble, Caroline," said Pa. "Nothing is certain but death and taxes."

CHAPTER 26

The Building Boom

THERE was no time for a good, long talk with Pa. Already the sunshine from the western window slanted far across the floor, and Ma said, "We must be getting supper. The men will be here soon."

"What men?" Pa asked.

"Oh, wait, Ma, please, I want to show him," Laura begged. "It's a surprise, Pa!" She hurried into the pantry, and from the almost empty sack of beans where it was hidden, she pulled out the little sack full of money. "Look, Pa, look!"

Pa felt the little sack in amazement. He looked at their faces, all shining with smiles. "Caroline! What have you girls been up to?"

"Look inside, Pa!" Laura cried. She could not wait while he untied the little sack. "Fifteen dollars and twenty-five cents!"

"I'll be jiggered!" Pa said.

Then while Laura and Ma started to get supper, they told him all that had happened while he was away. Before they had finished talking, another wagon pulled up at the door. There were seven strangers at supper that night; another dollar and seventy-five cents. And now that Pa was at home, the strangers could sleep on the floor around the stove. Laura did not care how many dishes she washed, nor how sleepy and tired she was. Pa and Ma were getting rich, and she was helping.

In the morning she was surprised. There was hardly time to talk; so many men were there for breakfast, she could hardly wash the dishes fast enough, and when at last she could empty the dishpan and hang it up there was hardly time to sweep and scrub the muddy floor before she must begin peeling potatoes for dinner. She had only a glimpse of the sunny, cold, blue-and-white-and-brown March day outdoors, while she emptied the dishpan. And she saw Pa driving a load of lumber toward the townsite.

"What on earth is Pa doing?" she asked Ma.

"He's putting up a building on the townsite," said Ma.

"Who for?" Laura asked, beginning to sweep. Her fingers were shrunken in ridges, from being so long in the dishwater.

" 'For whom', Laura," Ma corrected her. "For himself," and she tugged through the doorway an armful of bedding that she was taking outdoors to air.

"I thought we were going to move to the claim," Laura said when Ma came in.

"We have six months before we must build on the homestead," said Ma. "Lots in town are going so fast your Pa thinks he can make money by building on one. He's using the lumber from the railroad shanties and putting up a store building to sell."

"Oh, Ma, isn't it wonderful, all the money we're making!" Laura said, sweeping vigorously while Ma gathered another armful of bedding.

"Draw the broom, Laura; don't flip it, that raises the dust," said Ma. "Yes, but we mustn't count chickens before they're hatched."

That week the house filled with steady boarders, men who were building houses on the townsite or on their homestead claims. From dawn until far into the night, Ma and Laura hardly had time to catch their breaths. All day long there was a racket of wagons passing. Teamsters were hauling lumber from Brookings as fast as they could, and yellow skeletons of buildings rose every day. Already you could see Main Street growing up from the muddy ground along the railroad grade.

Every night beds covered the floor of the big room and the lean-to. Pa slept on the floor with the boarders so that Mary and Laura and Carrie could move into the bedroom with Ma and Grace, and more boarders' beds covered the whole floor of the attic.

The supplies were all gone, and now Ma had to buy flour and salt and beans and meat and corn meal, so she did not make so much money. Supplies cost three and four times as much as they cost in Minnesota, she said, because the railroad and the teamsters charged so much for the hauling. The roads were so muddy that the teamsters could not haul large loads. Anyway, she made a few cents' profit on every meal, and any little bit they could earn was better than nothing.

Laura did wish she could get time to see the building that Pa was putting up. She wished she could talk to him about the building, but he ate with the boarders and hurried away with them. There was no time for talking now.

Suddenly, there on the brown prairie where nothing had been before, was the town. In two weeks, all along Main Street the unpainted new buildings pushed up their thin false fronts, two stories high and square on top. Behind the false fronts the buildings squatted under their partly shingled, sloping roofs. Strangers were already living there; smoke blew gray from the stovepipes, and glass windows glinted in the sunshine.

One day Laura heard a man say, through the clattering at the dinner table, that he was putting up a hotel. He had got in the night before with a load of lumber hauled from Brookings. His wife was coming out on the next load. "We'll be doing business within a week," he said.

"Glad to hear it, sir," Pa said. "What this town needs is a hotel. You'll be doing a land-office business, as quick as you can get started."

As suddenly as the hurry had begun, it ended. One evening Pa and Ma and Laura and Mary and Carrie and Grace sat down to supper. No one else was there. Around them was their own house again; no one else was in it. A beautiful quiet was there, peaceful and cool, like the silence when a blizzard stops, or the restfulness of rain after a long fever of drought.

"I declare! I didn't know I was so tired," Ma sighed peacefully.

"I'm glad you and the girls are through working for strangers," said Pa.

They did not talk much. It was so pleasant to eat supper again alone.

"Laura and I counted up," said Ma. "We made over forty dollars."

"Forty-two dollars and fifty cents," said Laura.

"We'll put it aside and hang onto it if we can," said Pa. If they could save it, Laura thought, it would be that much toward sending Mary to college.

"I expect the surveyors to show up any day now," Pa went on. "Better be ready to move so I can turn over this house to them. We can live in town till I can sell the building."

"Very well, Charles. We'll wash the bedding tomorrow and start getting ready to pack," said Ma.

Next day Laura helped to wash all the quilts and blankets. She was glad to lug the loaded basket out to the clothesline in the sweet, chilly March weather. Teamsters' wagons were slowly pulling along the muddy road toward the west. Only an edging of ice remained around the shores of Silver Lake and among the dead slough grass. The lake water was blue as the sky, and far away in the shimmering sky an arrow of tiny black dots came up from the south. Faintly from far away came the wild, lonely sound of the wild geese calling.

Pa came hurrying to the house. "First spring flock of geese's in sight!" he said. "How about roast goose for dinner?" He hurried away with his gun.

"Mm, it will be good," Mary said. "Roast goose with sage stuffing! Won't you like that, Laura!"

"No, and you know I don't," Laura answered. "You know I don't like sage. We'll have onion in the stuffing."

"But I don't like onion!" Mary said crossly. "I want sage!"

Laura sat back on her heels where she was scrubbing the floor. "I don't care if you do. We won't have it! I guess I can have what I want sometimes!"

"Why, girls!" Ma said astonished. "Are you quarreling?"

"I want sage!" Mary insisted.

"And I want onion!" Laura cried.

"Girls, girls," Ma said in distress. "I can't think what's got into you. And I never heard of anything so silly! You both know we have no sage, nor onion either."

The door opened, and Pa came in. Soberly he put his gun in its place.

"Not a goose within gunshot," he said. "The whole flock rose when it came to Silver Lake and kept on going north. They must have seen the new buildings and heard the noise. Looks like hunting's going to be slim around here from now on."

CHAPTER 27

Living in Town

ALL around the unfinished, little town the endless prairie lay greening in the sunshine for new grass was starting everywhere. Silver Lake was blue, and the large white clouds in the sky were mirrored in the clear water.

Slowly Laura and Carrie walked on either side of Mary toward the town. Behind them came the loaded wagon, Pa and Ma and Grace riding in it, and the cow Ellen tied behind. They were all moving to Pa's building in town.

The surveyors had come back. Mr. and Mrs. Boast were gone to their claim. There was nowhere to live except in Pa's unfinished building, and in all the hustle, bustle and busyness of the town there was no one that Laura knew. She did not feel all alone and happy on the prairie now; she felt lonely and scared. The town's being there made the difference.

Men were busily working on the new buildings all up and down Main Street. Shavings and sawdust and ends of boards were scattered on the muddy and trampled young grass in the street, and wheels had cut deep ruts through it. Through the frames of buildings that did not have the siding on yet, and down alleys between the buildings, and beyond both ends of the street, the clean, green prairie rippled far away and quiet under the clear sky, but the town was troubled and noisy with rasping saws and pounding hammers and the thud of boxes and sharp crash of boards unloaded from wagons, and men loudly talking.

Timidly Laura and Carrie waited to let Pa's wagon come up, and they led Mary along beside it until they came to the corner where Pa's building was.

The tall false fronts loomed up, cutting off half the sky. Pa's building had a front door, with a glass window at each side. The door opened into one long room. Far at its other end was a back door, and near it a side window. The floor was wide boards, and the walls were boards with daylight coming through the cracks and knotholes. That was all.

"This place isn't very warm nor tight, Caroline," Pa said. "I haven't had time to put on the siding nor to ceil the inside, and there's no cornice under the eaves to cover that big crack. But we'll be warm enough, now that spring has come, and I'll soon get the building finished."

"You must build a stair, so we can get into the loft," said Ma. "Now I shall just stretch a curtain across to make two rooms so we will have a place to sleep until you can put up a partition. Warm as this weather is, we don't need siding and ceiling."

Pa put Ellen and the horses in a small stable at the back of the lot. Then he set up the stove and stretched a rope for Ma's curtain. Ma hung sheets on it while Laura helped Pa set up the bedstead. Then Carrie helped her make the beds while Mary amused Grace and Ma got supper.

The lamplight shone on the white curtain while they ate, but the end of the long room was shadowy and the chilly air coming through all the cracks made the lamp flicker and the curtain move. There was too much empty space in that building but all the time Laura felt that strangers were close outside it. Lamplight shone out of strangers' windows, footsteps passed with a lantern, and voices were talking though she could not hear the words. Even when the night was still, she felt crowded by so many other people so near. She lay in bed with Mary in the dark and airy room, and stared at the vague white curtain and listened to the stillness and felt trapped in town.

Sometime in the night she dreamed of wolves' howling, but she was in bed and the howling was only the wind. She was cold. She was too cold to wake up. The covers seemed very thin. She snuggled closer to Mary and burrowed her cold head under the thin covers. In her sleep she was tight and shivering, till finally she grew cosily warm. The next she knew, she heard Pa singing.

> "Oh, I am as happy as a big sunflower
> That nods and bends in the breezes!
> And my heart is as light as the wind that blows
> The leaves from off the treeses!"

Laura opened one eye and peeked from under the covers. Snow fell softly onto her face, a great lot of snow.

"Ow!" she said.

"Lie still, Laura!" said Pa. "All you girls lie still. I'll shovel you out in a minute. Soon as I get this fire started and the snow off Ma."

Laura heard the stove lids clatter. She heard the scratch of a match and the crackle of burning kindling. She did not stir. The covers were heavy over her and she was warm as toast.

Soon Pa came behind the curtain. "There's a good foot of snow on these beds!" he exclaimed. "But I'll have it off in three jerks of a lamb's tail. Lie still now, girls!"

Laura and Mary lay perfectly still while Pa shoveled the snow off their covers, and the cold came through them. They lay shivering and watching while with his shovel he took the snow off Carrie and Grace. Then he went to the stable to shovel out Ellen and the horses.

"Get up, girls!" Ma called. "Bring your clothes and dress by the fire."

Laura jumped out of the warm bed and grabbed her clothes from the chair where she had laid them the night before. She shook the snow off them and ran barefoot over snow scattered on the cold floor, to the stove beyond the curtain. As she ran she said, "Wait, Mary. I'll come back in a minute and shake the snow off your clothes."

She shook out her petticoats and her dress so quickly that the snow had no time to melt on them. Quickly she shook her stockings and emptied the snow from her shoes, and put them on. She hurried so fast that when she was dressed she was quite warm. Then she shook the snow from Mary's clothes and helped her quickly to the warmth that the oven gave out.

Carrie came running with little squeals and jumps. "Oo, the snow burns my feet!" she said, laughing though her teeth chattered from cold. It was so exciting to wake up in a snowdrift that she wouldn't wait in bed until Laura could shake her clothes. Laura helped button her up, then they put on their coats, and with the stove shovel and the broom they scooped and swept back the snow into piles in the far corners of the long room.

Snow lay in piles and drifts all along the street. Every lumber pile was a mountain of snow, and from the drifts the bare timbers of unfinished buildings stuck up thin and yellow. The sun was up, and all the slopes of snow were rosy and all the hollows blue. Through every crack the air came in as cold as ice.

Ma warmed her shawl by the fire, wrapped it snugly around Grace, and brought her to Mary, in the rocking chair pulled close to the oven. The hot stove made the air fairly warm all around it. Ma set the table almost against the stove, and breakfast was ready when Pa came back.

"This building's a pretty good sieve!" Pa said. "Snow blew through every crack and in under the eaves. That was a genuine blizzard while it lasted."

"To think we went all winter without a blizzard, and now we get one in April," Ma marveled.

"Lucky it struck in the night when folks were under cover," said Pa. "If it had hit in the daytime, somebody would have been lost and frozen sure. Nobody looks for a blizzard at this time of year."

"Well, the cold can't last long," Ma encouraged herself. " 'April showers bring May flowers.' What will an April blizzard bring?"

"For one thing, a partition," said Pa. "I'll have a partition up to keep in the heat around this stove before I'm a day older."

And he did. All day by the stove he sawed and hammered. Laura and Carrie helped hold the boards, and in Mary's lap Grace played with the shavings. The new partition made a little room, with the stove and the table and the beds in it, and its window looking out at all the green prairie covered with snow.

Then Pa brought in more snowy lumber and he began ceiling the walls. "I'll stop some of the cracks anyway," he said.

All over the town there was sawing and hammering inside the other buildings. Ma said, "I'm sorry for Mrs. Beardsley, keeping a hotel while it's being built over her head."

"That's what it takes to build up a country," said Pa. "Building over your head and under your feet, but building. We'd never get anything fixed to suit us if we waited for things to suit us before we started."

In a few days the snow was gone and spring came back again. The wind from the prairie brought a smell of damp ground and young grass, the sun rose earlier every day, and faintly all day the blue sky clanged with the wild birds' calls. High in the sky Laura could see them flying, flock after flock dark and small in the shimmering air.

They did not gather thickly any more on Silver Lake. Only a few very tired flocks settled late after sunset in the sloughs and rose to the sky again before the sun rose. Wild birds did not like the town full of people, and neither did Laura.

She thought, "I would rather be out on the prairie with the grass and the birds and Pa's fiddle. Yes, even with wolves! I would rather be anywhere than in this muddy, cluttered, noisy town, crowded by strange people." And she said, "Pa, when are we going to move to the homestead?"

"Soon as I sell this building," said Pa.

More and more wagons came in every day. Teams and wagons pulled along the muddy street, past the windows. All day there was the noise of hammers and of boots and voices. The shovel gangs were leveling the railroad grade, the teamsters were unloading ties and steel rails. In the evenings they were loudly drinking in the saloons.

Carrie liked the town. She wanted to go out into it and see everything, and for hours she stood looking out of the windows. Sometimes Ma let her cross the street to visit two little girls who lived there, but oftener the little girls came to see her, for Ma did not like to let Carrie out of her sight.

"I declare, Laura, you are so restless you give me the fidgets," Ma said one day. "You are going to teach school, so why not begin now? Don't you think it would be nice if you taught Carrie and Louizy and Annie every day? It would keep Carrie at home and be good for you all."

Laura did not think it would be nice. She did not want to do it at all. But she said obediently, "Yes, Ma."

She thought she might as well try. So next morning when Louizy and Annie came to play with Carrie, Laura told them that they would have a school. She seated them all in a row and set them a lesson to study in Ma's old primer.

"You study that for fifteen minutes," she told them, "and then I will hear you recite."

They looked at her with wide eyes, but they did not say anything. They put their heads together and studied, while Laura sat in front of them. There never was such a long fifteen minutes. At last Laura heard their spelling lesson, and then she set them a lesson in arithmetic. Whenever they fidgeted she told them they must sit still, and she made them raise their hands for permission to speak.

"You all did very nicely, I'm sure," Ma smiled in approval, when at last it was time to get dinner. "You may come every morning, and Laura will teach you. Tell your mother I shall step across the street this afternoon and tell her about our little school."

"Yes, ma'am," Louizy and Annie answered weakly. "Good-by, ma'am."

"With diligence and perseverance, Laura, I think you will be a very good teacher," Ma praised Laura, and Laura answered, "Thank you, Ma." She thought, "I've got to be a teacher, so I might as well try hard to be a good one."

Every morning little brown-haired Annie and red-headed Louizy came more reluctantly; every day it was harder to teach them. They fidgeted so that Laura despaired of ever making them sit still, and she could not make them study. One day they did not come.

"Perhaps they are too young to appreciate schooling, but I wonder at their mother," said Ma.

"Don't be discouraged, Laura," Mary said. "Anyway, you have taught the first school in De Smet."

"I'm not discouraged," Laura said cheerfully. She was so glad to be free from teaching that she began to sing while she swept the floor.

From the window Carrie cried out. "Look, Laura! Something's happening! Maybe that's why they don't come."

In front of the hotel a crowd was gathering. More and more men came from all directions, and the sound of their voices was loud and excited. Laura remembered the payday crowd that had threatened Pa. In a minute she saw Pa breaking through the crowd and coming home.

He came in looking sober. "What do you say to moving out to the claim right away, Caroline?" he asked.

"Today?" Ma asked.

"Day after tomorrow," said Pa. "It will take me that long to put up a claim shanty."

"Sit down, Charles, and tell me what is wrong," Ma said quietly.

Pa sat down. "There's been a murder."

Ma's eyes opened wide and she caught her breath. She said, "Here?"

"South of town." Pa got up. "A claim jumper killed Hunter. He used to work on the grade. He drove out yesterday to his homestead, he and his father. When they drove up to his claim shanty, a man opened the door and looked out at them. Hunter asked him what he was doing there, and he shot Hunter dead. He tried to shoot the old man, but he whipped up the team and got away. Neither one of them had a gun. The old man got to Mitchell and brought officers out this morning, and they arrested the fellow. Arrested him!" Pa said furiously. "Hanging's too good for him. If we'd only known in time!"

"Charles," Ma said.

"Well," said Pa, "I think we'd better get onto our claim before somebody jumps it."

"So do I," Ma agreed. "We will move as soon as you can put up any kind of shelter."

"Fix me up a snack to eat, and I'll start now," said Pa. "I'll go get a load of lumber and a man to help and put up the shanty this afternoon. We'll move tomorrow."

CHAPTER 28

Moving Day

"WAKE up, sleepyhead!" Laura sang out, and with both hands she rolled Carrie back and forth under the quilts. "It's moving day! Get up quick, we're moving to the homestead!"

Quickly they all ate breakfast, wasting no time in talk, and quickly Laura washed the dishes and Carrie dried them, while Ma packed the last box and Pa hitched up the team. This was the gladdest moving day that Laura had known. Ma and Mary were glad because this was the end of traveling; they were going to settle on the homestead and never move again. Carrie was glad because she was eager to see the homestead, Laura was glad because they were leaving town, Pa was glad because he always liked moving, and Grace sang and shouted in gladness because all the others were glad.

As fast as the dishes were wiped, Ma packed them in the tub so they would ride safely. Pa loaded the trunk, the packed boxes and the tub of dishes into the wagon. Then Ma helped him take down the stovepipe, and they put it and the stove into the wagon box. He laid the table and the chairs on top of all, and then he looked at the load and tugged his beard.

"I'll have to make two trips so we can all ride," he said. "Get the rest of the stuff ready and I'll be back."

"But you can't unload the stove by yourself," Ma objected.

"I'll manage," said Pa. "What goes up must come down, and I'll rig up some skids; there's lumber out there."

He climbed into the wagon and drove away. Then Ma and Laura rolled the bedding into tight rolls. They took down Ma's big bedstead and the two smaller new bedsteads that Pa had bought in town, and they packed the lamps carefully in a box, right side up so that they would not spill the kerosene. They stuffed the lamp chimneys with paper and wrapped them in towels and packed them beside the lamps. Everything was ready and waiting before Pa came back.

He put the bedstead and the boxes in the wagon, and laid the rolls of bedding on them. Then Laura handed him the fiddle box and he tucked it carefully among the quilts. On top of all he laid the whatnot, on its back so that it could not be scratched. Then he brought Ellen and tied her behind the wagon.

"Now, Caroline, up you go!" He handed Ma over the wagon wheel to the spring seat. "Catch!" and he tossed Grace into Ma's lap. "Now, Mary," he said gently, and he helped her to the board laid close behind the seat, while Laura and Carrie clambered to their places beside her.

"Now then," said Pa, "we will soon be home."

"For pity's sake, Laura, put on your sunbonnet!" Ma exclaimed. "This spring wind will ruin your complexion." And she pulled Grace's little bonnet farther forward to protect her fair, soft skin. Mary's face was far back in her bonnet, and so was Ma's, of course.

Slowly Laura pulled up her own bonnet by its strings, from where it hung down her back, and as its slatted sides came past her cheeks they shut out the town. From the tunnel of the bonnet she saw only the green prairie and blue sky.

She kept on looking at them, while she held onto the back of the spring seat and joggled to the wagon's jolting over the wind-dried ruts of mud. While she was looking, suddenly into the sunny green and blue came two brown horses with flowing black manes and tails, trotting side by side in harness. Their brown flanks and shoulders gleamed in the sunshine, their slender legs stepped daintily, their necks were arched and their ears pricked up, and they tossed their heads proudly as they went by.

"Oh, what beautiful horses!" Laura cried. "Look, Pa! Look!" She turned her head to watch them as long as she could. They drew a light wagon. A young man stood up in the wagon, driving, and a taller man stood behind him with a hand on his shoulder. In a moment the backs of the men and the wagon loomed up so that Laura could no longer see the horses.

Pa had turned around in the seat to watch them too. "Those are the Wilder boys," he said. "Almanzo's driving, and that's his brother Royal with him. They've taken up claims North of town, and they've got the finest horses in this whole country. By George, you seldom see a team like that."

With all her heart Laura wished for such horses. She supposed she never could have them.

Pa was driving South now, across the green prairie and down a gentle slope toward Big Slough. The ranker, coarse grass of the slough filled its straggling hollow, and up from a water pool flapped a heron with dangling long legs.

"How much do they cost, Pa?" Laura asked.

"What, Flutterbudget?" said Pa.

"Horses like those."

"A matched team like that? Not a penny under two hundred and fifty dollars, maybe three hundred," said Pa. "Why?"

"Nothing. I was just wondering," Laura replied. Three hundred dollars was so much money that she could hardly imagine it. Only rich people could pay such a sum for horses. Laura thought that if ever she were rich, what she would have would be two sleek brown horses with black manes and tails. She let her bonnet fly back in the wind and thought of riding behind such fast horses.

Far to the West and South, Big Slough widened and spread. On the other side of the wagon it ran narrow and marshy to the narrow tip of Silver Lake. Quickly Pa drove across the narrow part and up to the higher ground beyond.

"There it is!" he said. The little claim shanty stood bright in its newness in the sunlight. It looked like a yellow toy on the great rolling prairie covered with rippling young grass.

Ma laughed at it when Pa helped her from the wagon. "It looks like half of a woodshed that has been split in two."

"You are wrong, Caroline," Pa told her. "It is a little house only half built, and that half unfinished. We'll finish it now, and build the other half soon."

The little house and its half a slanting roof were built of rough boards with cracks between. There were no windows and no door for the doorway, but there was a floor. And a trap door in the floor opened into a cellar.

"I couldn't do more than dig the cellar and put up rough walls yesterday," said Pa. "But now we're here! Nobody can jump our claim. And I'll soon fix things up for you, Caroline."

"I'm glad to be home, Charles," said Ma.

Before sunset they were all settled in the funny little house. The stove was up, the beds were made, the curtain was hung to make two tiny rooms of the one small room. Supper was cooked and eaten, the dishes washed, and darkness was falling softly on the prairie. No one wanted the lamp lighted, the spring night was so beautiful.

Ma sat gently rocking by the doorless doorway, holding Grace in her lap and Carrie close beside her. Mary and Laura sat together on the threshold. Pa sat just outside the doorway, in a chair on the grass. They did not talk. They sat looking, while stars came out one by one and frogs were croaking in the Big Slough.

A little wind was whispering. The darkness was velvety soft and quiet and safe. All over the huge sky the stars were twinkling merrily.

Then Pa said softly, "I feel like music, Laura."

Laura brought the fiddle box from its safe place under Ma's bed. Pa took the fiddle from its nest and tuned it lovingly. Then they sang to the night and the stars:

"Oh, drive dull care away,
For weeping is but sorrow.
If things are wrong today,
There's another day tomorrow.

"So drive dull care away
And do the best you can.
Put your shoulder to the wheel
Is the motto for every man."

"I am going to put up the little shepherdess just as soon as the roof is finished over our heads," said Ma.

Pa's fiddle answered her with little notes running like water in the sunshine and widening into a pool. The moon was rising. The creamy light crept up the sky and the stars melted in it. Cool and silvery, the moonlight lay over the wide, dark land, and softly Pa sang with the fiddle:

"When the stars are brightly beaming
And the sighing winds are still,
When the twilight shadows hover o'er the lea,
There's a tiny candle gleaming
From the cottage 'neath the hill
And I know that little beacon shines for me."

CHAPTER 29

The Shanty on the Claim

"THE first thing to do is to dig a well," said Pa next morning. He shouldered his spade and shovel and went whistling toward the slough while Laura cleared the breakfast table and Ma rolled up her sleeves.

"Now, girls," she said cheerfully, "all together with a will, and we'll soon have things to rights."

But even Ma was puzzled that morning. The little claim shanty was as full as it would hold. Everything must be carefully fitted into the space. Laura and Carrie and Ma lifted and tugged the furniture this way and that, and stood and thought, and tried again. Mary's rocking chair and the table were still outdoors when Pa came back.

"Well, Caroline, your well's all dug!" he sang out. "Six feet deep, and good, cold water in quicksand. Now I'll hammer together a cover for it, so Grace can't fall in, and that'll be done." He looked at the disorder and pushed back his hat to scratch his head. "Can't you get it all in?"

"Yes, Charles," said Ma. "Where there's a will, there's a way."

It was Laura who thought how to fit in the beds. The trouble was that they now had three bedsteads. When they stood side by side, there was not room for Mary's rocking chair. Laura thought of setting the little bedsteads together, tight in the corner, and putting the foot of the big bedstead against them, with its headboard against the other wall.

"Then we'll hang a curtain around our beds," she said to Ma, "and another curtain across beside yours, and that leaves room for the rocking chair against your curtain."

"That's my smart girl!" said Ma.

Against the foot of Laura's and Mary's bed, the table fitted under the window that Pa was sawing in that wall. Ma's rocking chair went in beside the table, and the whatnot fitted in that corner, behind the door. In the fourth corner stood the stove, with the dish cupboard made of a packing box behind it, and the trunk fitted between the stove and Mary's rocking chair.

"There!" said Ma. "And the boxes will go under the beds. It couldn't be better!"

At dinner Pa said, "Before night I'll finish this half of a house." And he did. He put in a window beside the stove, to the south. He hung in the doorway a door bought from the lumberyard in town. Then all over the outside of the shanty he put black tar paper, fastening it down with lath.

Laura helped him unroll the wide, black, tarry-smelling paper down over the slanting roof and the walls of fresh, clean, pine-scented boards, and she helped him cut it and she held it down in the wind while he nailed on the lath. Tar-paper was not pretty, but it stopped all the cracks and kept out the wind.

"Well, there's one good day's work done," Pa said when they sat down to supper.

"Yes," said Ma. "And tomorrow we'll finish unpacking and be finally settled. I must do a baking too. It's a blessing to have yeast once more. I feel as though I never want to see another sour-dough biscuit."

"Your light bread is good and so are your sour-dough biscuits," Pa told her. "But we won't have either if I don't rustle something to bake them with. Tomorrow I'll haul a load of wood from Lake Henry."

"May I go with you, Pa?" Laura asked.

"Me, too?" Carrie begged.

"No, girls," said Pa. "I'll be gone quite a while and Ma will need you."

"I wanted to see trees," Carrie explained.

"I don't blame her," said Ma. "I would like to see some trees again myself. They would rest my eyes from all this prairie with not a tree. Not even a bush to be seen in any direction."

"This country's going to be covered with trees," Pa said. "Don't forget that Uncle Sam's tending to that. There's a tree claim on every section, and settlers have got to plant ten acres of trees on every tree claim. In four or five years you'll see trees every way you look."

"I'll be looking in all directions at once then," Ma smiled. "There's nothing more restful than shady groves in the summertime, and they'll break the wind too."

"Well, I don't know," said Pa. "Trees spread, and you know what it was like back in the Big Woods of Wisconsin, grubbing out stumps and breaking our backs on the sprouting hoe to keep a little land clear for crops. It's restful to have clear prairie land like this, if you're going to farm. But Uncle Sam don't seem to look at it that way, so don't worry, Caroline; you're going to see plenty of trees all over this country. Likely they'll stop the wind and change the climate, too, just as you say."

They were all too tired for music that night. Soon after supper they were all asleep, and bright and early next morning Pa drove away toward Lake Henry.

The whole world was gay in the early sunshine when Laura led Ellen to drink at the well. All over the prairie the little white blossoms of wild onion were dancing in the wind. Down the slope of the little hill below the shanty, patches of wild crocus spread yellow and blue in the young grass, and everywhere the sheep-sorrel uncurled its little pink-lavender flowers above sleek clover-shaped leaves. Laura bent down to pick them as she walked, and slowly nibbled the delightfully fresh, sour little stems and petals.

From the grassy swell where she picketed Ellen she could see the town beyond to the north. Big Slough curved between and spread wide southwest, covering acres upon acres with its rough high grass. All the rest of the whole enormous prairie was a green carpet flowered with spring blossoms.

Big girl as she was, Laura spread her arms wide to the wind and ran against it. She flung herself on the flowery grass and rolled like a colt. She lay in the soft, sweet grasses and looked at the great blueness above her and the high, pearly clouds sailing in it. She was so happy that tears came into her eyes.

Suddenly she thought, "Have I got a grass stain on my dress?" She stood up and anxiously looked, and there was a green stain on the calico. Soberly she knew that she should be helping Ma, and she hurried to the little dark tar-paper shanty.

"It's tiger-striped," she said to Ma.

"What is, Laura?" Ma asked, looking up startled. She was putting her books on the bottom shelves of the whatnot.

"This shanty," said Laura. "Striped with yellow lath on the tar paper."

"Tigers are yellow with black stripes," Mary objected.

"You girls unpack your boxes now," said Ma. "We'll arrange all our pretty things on these upper shelves."

On the shelf above the books there was room for Mary's and Laura's and Carrie's little glass boxes. Each box had frosted flowers on its side and colored flowers on the lid. The three made that shelf all bright and gay.

Ma stood the clock on the fourth shelf. Its brown wooden case spread up in a carved lacy pattern from its round glass face, and behind glass painted with gilt flowers its brass pendulum wagged to and fro, tick-tock, tick-tock.

On the smallest, very top shelf above the clock, Laura set her white china jewel box with the tiny gold cup and saucer on its top, and Carrie put beside it her brown-and-white china dog.

"It's very pretty, I'm sure," Ma approved. "When the door is shut, the whatnot quite dresses up the room. Now for the china shepherdess." Then she looked around quickly and exclaimed, "Mercy! Is my bread-sponge risen already?"

The bread-sponge was lifting the lid of the pan. Ma hurriedly floured the breadboard, and kneaded the dough. Then she got dinner. She was putting the pan of light biscuits in the oven when Pa came driving the wagon up the hill. Behind him the wagon box was piled high with willow brush that he had brought for summer fuel, for there were no real trees at Lake Henry.

"Hello, Flutterbudget! Let dinner wait, Caroline!" he called. "I've got something to show you as soon as I picket the team."

Quickly he slipped the harness off the horses and dumped it across the wagon tongue. He hurried the horses away to their picket ropes, and came hurrying back. Then he lifted a horse blanket from the front of the wagon box.

"There you are, Caroline!" he beamed. "I covered them so they wouldn't dry out in the wind."

"What, Charles?" Ma and Laura craned to see into the wagon box, and Carrie climbed up the wheel. "Trees!" Ma exclaimed.

"Little trees!" Laura shouted. "Mary! Pa's brought little trees!"

"They're cottonwoods," Pa said. "They all grew from seeds of the Lone Tree that we saw across the prairie when we were coming out from Brookings. It's a giant of a tree when you get close to it. It's seeded all along the edge of Lake Henry. I dug enough of these seedlings to make a windbreak clear around the shanty. You're going to have your trees growing, Caroline, quick as I can get them set in the ground."

He took his spade out of the wagon and said, "The first one's your tree, Caroline. Pick it out and tell me where you want it."

"Just a minute," Ma answered. She hurried to the stove and shut its draft and set back the pot of potatoes. Then she picked out her tree. "I want it right here by the door," she said.

With his spade, Pa cut a square in the sod and lifted the grass. He dug a hole and loosened the soft soil until it was fine and crumbly. Then carefully he lifted the little tree and carried it without shaking the earth from its roots.

"Hold the top straight, Caroline," he said. Ma held the small tree straight by its top, while with his spade Pa sifted earth over its roots until the hole was filled. Then he stamped the earth down firmly, and stood back. "Now you can look at a tree, Caroline. Your own tree. We'll give each one of 'em a pailful of water after dinner. But first we'll get their roots in the ground. Come, Mary, it's your turn next."

Pa dug another hole in a straight line with the first. He brought another tree from the wagon, and Mary carefully held it upright while Pa planted it. That was Mary's tree.

"Yours is next, Laura," said Pa. "We'll make a square windbreak, all around the house. Ma's tree and mine by the door, and a tree for each of you girls on each side of ours."

Laura held her tree while Pa planted it. Then Carrie held hers. The four little trees stood up straight from the patches of dark earth in the grass.

"Now Grace must have hers," said Pa. "Where's Grace?" He called to Ma, "Caroline, bring Grace out here to plant her tree!"

Ma looked out of the shanty. "She's out there with you, Charles," she said.

"I guess she's behind the house, I'll get her," Carrie said, and she ran, calling, "Grace!" In a minute she came from behind the shanty, her eyes large and scared and the freckles standing out from her pale face. "Pa, I can't find her!"

"She must be close by," said Ma, and she called, "Grace! Grace!" Pa shouted too, "Grace!"

"Don't stand there! Go look for her, Carrie! Laura, go!" Ma said. She exclaimed, "The well!" and ran down the path.

The cover was on the well, so Grace had not fallen into it.

"She can't be lost," Pa said.

"I left her outdoors. I thought she was with you," said Ma.

"She can't be lost," Pa insisted. "She wasn't out of my sight a minute." He shouted, "Grace! Grace!"

Laura ran panting up the hill. She could not see Grace anywhere. Along the edge of the Big Slough toward Silver Lake she looked, and over the flowery prairie. Quickly, quickly she looked, again and again, seeing nothing but wild flowers and grasses. "Grace! Grace!" she screamed. "Grace!"

Pa met her on the slope as she ran down and Ma came up gasping for breath. "She must be in sight, Laura," Pa said. "You must have missed seeing her. She can't be—" Terribly he exclaimed, "The Big Slough!" He turned and ran.

Ma ran after him, calling back, "Carrie, you stay with Mary! Laura, look for her, go look!"

Mary stood in the doorway of the shanty calling, "Grace! Grace!" More faintly from Big Slough came Pa's shouts and Ma's, "Grace! Where are you? Grace!"

If Grace was lost in the Big Slough, how could anyone find her? The old, dead grass stood higher than Laura's head, over acres and acres, for miles and miles. The deep mud sucked at bare feet, and there were water holes. Laura could hear, where she stood, the sound of the coarse slough grass in the wind, a muffling sound that almost smothered even Ma's shrill call, "Grace!"

Laura felt cold and sick.

"Why don't you look for her?" Carrie cried. "Don't stand there! Do something! I'm going myself!"

"Ma told you to stay with Mary," said Laura. "So you'd better stay."

"She told you to look!" Carrie screamed. "Go look! Go look! Grace! Grace!"

"Shut up! Let me think!" Laura screeched, and she started running across the sunny prairie.

CHAPTER 30

Where Violets Grow

LAURA was running straight toward the south. Grass whipped soft against her bare feet. Butterflies fluttered over the flowers. There wasn't a bush nor a weed that Grace could be hidden behind. There was nothing, nothing but grass and flowers swaying in the sunshine.

If she were little and playing all by herself, Laura thought, she wouldn't go into the dark Big Slough, she wouldn't go into the mud and the tall grass. Oh, Grace, why didn't I watch you? she thought. Sweet pretty little helpless sister—"Grace! Grace!" she screamed. Her breath caught and hurt in her side.

She ran on and on. Grace must have gone this way. Maybe she chased a butterfly. She didn't go into Big Slough! She didn't climb the hill, she wasn't there. Oh, baby sister, I couldn't see you anywhere east or south on this hateful prairie. "Grace!"

The horrible, sunny prairie was so large. No lost baby could ever be found on it. Ma's calling and Pa's shouts came from Big Slough. They were thin cries, lost in wind, lost on the enormous bigness of the prairie.

Laura's breathing hurt her sides under the ribs. Her chest was smothering and her eyes were dizzy. She ran up a low slope. Nothing, nothing, not a spot of shadow was anywhere on the level prairie all around her. She ran on, and suddenly the ground dropped before her. She almost fell down a steep bank.

There was Grace. There, in a great pool of blue, sat Grace. The sun shone on her golden hair blowing in the wind. She looked up at Laura with big eyes as blue as violets. Her hands were full of violets. She held them up to Laura and said, "Sweet! Sweet!"

Laura sank down and took Grace in her arms. She held Grace carefully and panted for breath. Grace leaned over her arm to reach more violets. They were surrounded by masses of violets blossoming above low-spreading leaves. Violets covered the flat bottom of a large, round hollow. All around this lake of violets, grassy banks rose almost straight up to the prairie-level. There in the round, low place the wind hardly disturbed the fragrance of the violets. The sun was warm there, the sky was overhead, the green walls of grass curved all around, and butterflies fluttered over the crowding violet-faces.

Laura stood up and lifted Grace to her feet. She took the violets that Grace gave her, and clasped her hand. "Come, Grace," she said. "We must go home."

She gave one look around the little hollow while she helped Grace climb the bank.

Grace walked so slowly that for a little while Laura carried her. Then she let her walk, for Grace was nearly three years old, and heavy. Then she lifted her again. So, carrying Grace and helping her walk, Laura brought her to the shanty and gave her to Mary.

Then she ran toward the Big Slough, calling as she ran. "Pa! Ma! She's here!" She kept on calling until Pa heard her and shouted to Ma, far in the tall grass. Slowly, together, they fought their way out of Big Slough and slowly came up to the shanty, draggled and muddy and very tired and thankful.

"Where did you find her, Laura?" Ma asked, taking Grace in her arms and sinking into her chair.

"In a—" Laura hesitated, and said, "Pa, could it really be a fairy ring? It is perfectly round. The bottom is perfectly flat. The bank around it is the same height all the way. You can't see a sign of that place till you stand on the bank. It is very large, and the whole bottom of it is covered solidly thick with violets. A place like that couldn't just happen, Pa. Something made it."

"You are too old to be believing in fairies, Laura," Ma said gently. "Charles, you must not encourage such fancies."

"But it isn't—it isn't like a real place, truly," Laura protested. "And smell how sweet the violets are. They aren't like ordinary violets."

"They do make the whole house sweet," Ma admitted. "But they are real violets, and there are no fairies."

"You are right, Laura; human hands didn't make that place," Pa said. "But your fairies were big, ugly brutes, with horns on their heads and humps on their backs. That place is an old buffalo wallow. You know buffaloes are wild cattle. They paw up the ground and wallow in the dust, just as cattle do.

"For ages the buffalo herds had these wallowing places. They pawed up the ground and the wind blew the dust away. Then another herd came along and pawed up more dust in the same place. They went always to the same places, and——"

"Why did they, Pa?" Laura asked.

"I don't know," Pa said. "Maybe because the ground was mellowed there. Now the buffalo are gone, and grass grows over their wallows. Grass and violets."

"Well," Ma said. "All's well that ends well, and here it is long past dinnertime. I hope you and Carrie didn't let the biscuits burn, Mary."

"No, Ma," Mary said, and Carrie showed her the biscuits wrapped in a clean cloth to keep warm, and the potatoes drained and meally-dry in their pot. And Laura said, "Sit still, Ma, and rest. I'll fry the salt pork and make the gravy."

No one but Grace was hungry. They ate slowly, and then Pa finished planting the windbreak. Ma helped Grace hold her own little tree while Pa set it firmly. When all the trees were planted, Carrie and Laura gave them each a full pail of water from the well. Before they finished, it was time to help get supper.

"Well," Pa said at the table. "We're settled at last on our homestead claim."

"Yes," said Ma. "All but one thing. Mercy, what a day this has been. I didn't get time to drive the nail for the bracket."

"I'll tend to it, Caroline, as soon as I drink my tea," Pa said.

He took the hammer from his toolbox under the bed, and drove a nail into the wall between the table and the whatnot. "Now bring on your bracket and the china shepherdess!" he said.

Ma brought them to him. He hung the bracket on the nail and stood the china shepherdess on its shelf. Her little china shoes, her tight china bodice and her golden hair were as bright as they had been so long ago in the Big Woods. Her china skirts were as wide and white; her cheeks as pink and her blue eyes as sweet as ever. And the bracket that Pa had carved for Ma's Christmas present so long ago was still without a scratch, and even more glossily polished than when it was new.

Over the door Pa hung his rifle and his shotgun, and then he hung on a nail above them a bright, new horseshoe.

"Well," he said, looking around at the snugly crowded shanty. "A short horse is soon curried. This is our tightest squeeze yet, Caroline, but it's only a beginning." Ma's eyes smiled into his eyes, and he said to Laura, "I could sing you a song about that horseshoe."

She brought him the fiddle box, and he sat down in the doorway and tuned the fiddle. Ma settled in her chair to rock Grace to sleep. Softly Laura washed the dishes and Carrie wiped them while Pa played the fiddle and sang.

"We journey along quite contented in life
And try to live peaceful with all.
We keep ourselves free from all trouble and strife
And we're glad when our friends on us call.
Our home it is happy and cheerful and bright,
We're content and we ask nothing more.
And the reason we prosper, I'll tell to you now,
There's a horseshoe hung over the door.

"Keep the horseshoe hung over the door!
It will bring you good luck evermore.
If you would be happy and free from all care,
Keep the horseshoe hung over the door!"

"It sounds rather heathenish to me, Charles," Ma said.

"Well, anyway," Pa replied, "I wouldn't wonder if we do pretty well here, Caroline. In time we'll build more rooms on this house, and maybe have a driving team and buggy. I'm not going to plow up much grass. We'll have a garden and a little field, but mostly raise hay and cattle. Where so many buffalo ranged, must be a good country for cattle."

The dishes were done. Laura carried the dishpan some distance from the back door and flung the water far over the grass where tomorrow's sun would dry it. The first stars were pricking through the pale sky. A few lights twinkled yellow in the little town, but the whole great plain of the earth was shadowy. There was hardly a wind, but the air moved and whispered to itself in the grasses. Laura almost knew what it said. Lonely and wild and eternal were land and water and sky and the air blowing.

"The buffalo are gone," Laura thought. "And now we're homesteaders."

CHAPTER 31

Mosquitoes

"WE MUST build a stable for the horses," Pa said. "It won't always be warm enough for them to stay outdoors and a bad storm might come even in summer. They must have shelter."

"Ellen too, Pa?" Laura asked.

"Cattle are better off outdoors in the summer," Pa told her. "But I like to have horses in a stable at night."

Laura held boards for Pa. She handed him tools and brought nails while he built the stable, at the west of the house against the little hill. It would be sheltered there on the west and the north, when the cold winter winds were blowing.

The days were warm. Mosquitoes came out of the Big Slough at sundown and sang their high, keen song all night as they swarmed around Ellen, biting her and sucking the blood until she ran around and around on her picket rope. They went into the stable and bit the horses until they pulled at their halters and stamped. They came into the claim shanty and bit everyone there until great blotches raised on faces and hands.

Their singing and the sting of their bites made night a torment.

"This will never do," Pa said. "We must have mosquito bar on the windows and door."

"It's the Big Slough," Ma complained. "The mosquitoes come from there. I wish we were farther away from it."

But Pa liked the Big Slough. "There are acres and acres of hay there, that anyone can have for the cutting," he told Ma. "No one will ever take up homesteads in the Big Slough. There is only upland hay on our place, but with the Big Slough so near, we can always cut hay there and have all we need.

"Besides, all the prairie grass is full of mosquitoes too. I'll go to town today and get some mosquito bar."

Pa brought yards of pink mosquito bar from town and strips of lumber to make a frame for a screen door.

While he made the door, Ma tacked mosquito bar over the

windows. Then she tacked it to the door frame and Pa hung the screen door.

That night he built a smudge of old, damp grass, so the smoke would drift before the stable door. Mosquitoes would not go through the smoke.

Pa made another smudge so Ellen could stand in its smoke and she went at once and stayed there.

Pa made sure there was no dry grass near the smudges and built them up so they would last all night.

"There!" he said, "I guess that fixes the mosquitoes."

CHAPTER 32

Evening Shadows Fall

SAM and David stood quietly, resting in the stable, with the smoke screen before the door.

Ellen, on her picket rope, lay comfortably in the smoke from the smudge. No mosquitoes could get at them.

There was not one of the singing pests inside the claim shanty. They could not come through the mosquito bar over the door and windows.

"Now we are all snug," Pa said, "settled at last on our homestead. Bring me the fiddle, Laura, and we'll have a little music!"

Grace was safely in her bed with Carrie beside her.

Ma and Mary sat rocking gently in the shadows. But moonlight shone through the southern window and touched Pa's face and hands and the fiddle as the bow moved smoothly over the strings.

Laura sat near Mary and watched it as she thought how the moonlight would be shining in the fairy ring where the violets grew. It was just the night for fairies to be dancing there.

Pa was singing with the fiddle:

"In Scarlet town where I was born,
There was a fair maid dwellin';
And every youth cried 'Well-a-wa.'
Her name was Barbary Allen.

"All in the merry month of May,
When green buds they were swellin'
Young Johnnie Grove on his death bed lay
For love of Barbary Allen."

Laura drew the curtain as she and Mary joined Carrie and Grace in their tiny bedroom.

And, as she fell asleep still thinking of violets and fairy rings and moonlight over the wide, wide land, where their very own homestead lay, Pa and the fiddle were softly singing:

"Home! Home! Sweet, sweet home,
Be it ever so humble
There is no place like home."

THE LONG WINTER

CONTENTS

CHAPTER I

Make Hay While the Sun Shines

THE mowing machine's whirring sounded cheerfully from the old buffalo wallow south of the claim shanty, where bluestem grass stood thick and tall and Pa was cutting it for hay.

The sky was high and quivering with heat over the shimmering prairie. Half-way down to sunset, the sun blazed as hotly as at noon. The wind was scorching hot. But Pa had hours of mowing yet to do before he could stop for the night.

Laura drew up a pailful of water from the well at the edge of the Big Slough. She rinsed the brown jug till it was cool to her hand. Then she filled it with the fresh, cool water, corked it tightly, and started with it to the hayfield.

Swarms of little white butterflies hovered over the path. A dragon-fly with gauzy wings swiftly chased a gnat. On the stubble of cut grass the striped gophers were scampering. All at once they ran for their lives and dived into their holes. Then Laura saw a swift shadow and looked up at the eyes and the claws of a hawk overhead. But all the little gophers were safe in their holes.

Pa was glad to see Laura with the water jug. He got down from the mowing machine and drank a mouthful. "Ah! that hits the spot!" he said, and tipped up the jug again. Then he corked it, and setting it on the ground he covered it with cut grass.

"This sun almost makes a fellow want a bunch of sprouts to make a shade," he joked. He was really glad there were no trees; he had grubbed so many sprouts from his clearing in the Big Woods, every summer. Here on the Dakota prairies there was not a single tree, not one sprout, not a bit of shade anywhere.

"A man works better when he's warmed up, anyway!" Pa said cheerfully, and chirruped to the horses. Sam and David plodded on, drawing the machine. The long, steel-toothed blade went steadily whirring against the tall grass and laid it down flat. Pa rode high on the open iron seat, watching it lie down, his hand on the lever.

Laura sat in the grass to watch him go once around. The

heat there smelled as good as an oven when bread is baking. The little brown-and-yellow-striped gophers were hurrying again, all about her. Tiny birds fluttered and flew to cling to bending grass-stems, balancing lightly. A striped garter snake came flowing and curving through the forest of grass. Sitting hunched with her chin on her knees, Laura felt suddenly as big as a mountain when the snake curved up its head and stared at the high wall of her calico skirt.

Its round eyes were shining like beads, and its tongue was flickering so fast that it looked like a tiny jet of steam. The whole bright-striped snake had a gentle look. Laura knew that garter snakes will not harm anyone, and they are good to have on a farm because they eat the insects that spoil crops.

It stretched its neck low again and, making a perfectly square turn in itself because it could not climb over Laura, it went flowing around her and away in the grass.

Then the mowing machine whirred louder and the horses came nodding their heads slowly in time with their feet. David jumped when Laura spoke almost under his nose.

"Whoa!" Pa said, startled. "Laura! I thought you'd gone. Why are you hiding in the grass like a prairie chicken?"

"Pa," Laura said, "why can't *I* help you make hay? Please let me, Pa. Please."

Pa lifted his hat and ran his fingers through his sweat-damp hair, standing it all on end and letting the wind blow through it. "You're not very big nor strong, little Half-Pint."

"I'm going on fourteen," Laura said. "I can help, Pa. I know I can."

The mowing machine had cost so much that Pa had no money left to pay for help. He could not trade work, because there were only a few homesteaders in this new country and they were busy on their own claims. But he needed help to stack the hay.

"Well," Pa said, "maybe you can. We'll try it. If you can, by George! we'll get this haying done all by ourselves!"

Laura could see that the thought was a load off Pa's mind and she hurried to the shanty to tell Ma.

"Why, I guess you can," Ma said doubtfully. She did not like to see women working in the fields. Only foreigners did that. Ma and her girls were Americans, above doing men's work.

But Laura's helping with the hay would solve the problem. She decided, "Yes, Laura, you may."

Carrie eagerly offered to help. "I'll carry the drinking water out to you. I'm big enough to carry the jug!" Carrie was almost ten, but small for her age.

"And I'll do your share of the housework, besides mine," Mary offered happily. She was proud that she could wash dishes and make beds as well as Laura, though she was blind.

The sun and hot wind cured the cut grass so quickly that Pa raked it up next day. He raked it into long windrows, then he raked the windrows into big haycocks. And early the next morning, while the dawn was still cool and meadow-larks were singing, Laura rode to the field with Pa in the hayrack.

There Pa walked beside the wagon and drove the horses between the rows of haycocks. At every haycock he stopped the horses and pitched the hay up into the hayrack. It came tumbling loosely over the high edge and Laura trampled it down. Up and down and back and forth she trampled the loose hay with all the might of her legs, while the forkfuls kept coming over and falling, and she went on trampling while the wagon jolted on to the next haycock. Then Pa pitched more hay in from the other side.

Under her feet the hay climbed higher, trampled down as solid as hay can be. Up and down, fast and hard, her legs kept going, the length of the hayrack and back, and across the middle. The sunshine was hotter and the smell of the hay rose up sweet and strong. Under her feet it bounced and over the edges of the hayrack it kept coming.

All the time she was rising higher on the trampled-down hay. Her head rose above the edges of the rack and she could have looked at the prairie, if she could have stopped trampling. Then the rack was full of hay and still more came flying up from Pa's pitchfork.

Laura was very high up now and the slippery hay was sloping downward around her. She went on trampling carefully. Her face and her neck were wet with sweat and sweat trickled down her back. Her sunbonnet hung by its strings and her braids had come undone. Her long brown hair blew loose in the wind.

Then Pa stepped up on the whiffletrees. He rested one foot on David's broad hip and clambered up onto the load of hay.

"You've done a good job, Laura," he said. "You tramped the hay down so well that we've got a big load on the wagon."

Laura rested in the prickly warm hay while Pa drove near to the stable. Then she slid down and sat in the shade of the wagon. Pa pitched down some hay, then climbed down and spread it evenly to make the big, round bottom of a stack. He climbed onto the load and pitched more hay, then climbed down and leveled it on the stack and trampled it down.

"I could spread it, Pa," Laura said, "so you wouldn't have to keep climbing up and down."

Pa pushed back his hat and leaned for a minute on the pitchfork. "Stacking's a job for two, that's a fact," he said. "This way takes too much time. Being willing helps a lot, but you're not very big, little Half-Pint." She could only get him to say, "Well, we'll see." But when they came back with the next load he gave her a pitchfork and let her try. The long fork was taller than she was and she did not know how to use it, so she handled it clumsily. But while Pa tossed the hay from the wagon she spread it as well as she could, walking around and around on the stack to pack it tightly. In spite of the best she could do, Pa had to level the stack for the next load.

Now the sun and the wind were hotter and Laura's legs quivered while she made them trample the hay. She was glad to rest for the little times between the field and the stack. She was thirsty, then she was thirstier, and then she was so thirsty that she could think of nothing else. It seemed forever till ten o'clock when Carrie came lugging the jug half-full.

Pa told Laura to drink first but not too much. Nothing was ever so good as that cool wetness going down her throat. At the taste of it she stopped in surprise and Carrie clapped her hands and cried out, laughing, "Don't tell, Laura, don't tell till Pa tastes it!"

Ma had sent them ginger-water. She had sweetened the cool well-water with sugar, flavored it with vinegar, and put in plenty of ginger to warm their stomachs so they could drink till they were not thirsty. Ginger-water would not make them sick, as plain cold water would when they were so hot. Such a treat made that ordinary day into a special day, the first day that Laura helped in the haying.

By noon, they had hauled all the hay and finished the stack. Pa topped it himself. It takes great skill to round the top of a haystack so that it will shed rain.

Dinner was ready when they went to the shanty. Ma looked sharply at Laura and asked, "Is the work too hard for her, Charles?"

"Oh, no! She's as stout as a little French horse. She's been a great help," said Pa. "It would have taken me all day to stack that hay alone, and now I have the whole afternoon for mowing."

Laura was proud. Her arms ached and her back ached and her legs ached, and that night in bed she ached all over so badly that tears swelled out of her eyes, but she did not tell anyone.

As soon as Pa had cut and raked enough hay for another stack, he and Laura made it. Laura's arms and legs got used to the work and did not ache so badly. She liked to see the stacks that she helped to make. She helped Pa make a stack on each side of the stable door and a long stack over the whole top of the dugout stable. Besides these, they made three more big stacks.

"Now all our upland hay is cut, I want to put up a lot of slough hay," Pa said. "It doesn't cost anything and maybe there'll be some sale for it when new settlers come in next spring."

So Pa mowed the coarse, tall grass in Big Slough and Laura helped him stack that. It was so much heavier than the bluestem grass that she could not handle it with the pitchfork, but she could trample it down.

One day when Pa came clambering up to the top of the load, she told him, "You've left a haycock, Pa."

"I have!" said Pa, surprised. "Where?"

"Over there, in the tall grass."

Pa looked where she pointed. Then he said, "That isn't a haycock, Half-Pint; that's a muskrat house." He looked at it a moment longer. "I'm going to have a closer look at that," he said. "Want to come along? The horses'll stand."

He pushed a way through the harsh, tall grass and Laura followed close behind him. The ground underfoot was soft and marshy and water lay in pools among the grass roots.

Laura could see only Pa's back and the grasses all around her, taller than she was. She stepped carefully for the ground was growing wetter. Suddenly water spread out before her in a shimmering pool.

At the edge of the pool stood the muskrats' house. It was taller than Laura, and far larger than her arms could reach around. Its rounded sides and top were rough, hard gray. The muskrats had gnawed dry grass to bits and mixed the bits well with mud to make a good plaster for their house, and they had built it up solidly and smoothly and rounded the top carefully to shed rain.

The house had no door. No path led to it anywhere. In the grass-stubble around it and along the muddy rim of the pool, there was not one paw-print. There was nothing to tell how the muskrats went in and out of their house.

Inside those thick, still walls, Pa said, the muskrats were sleeping now, each family curled in its own little room lined softly with grass. Each room had a small round doorway that opened onto a sloping hall. The hallway curved down through the house from top to bottom and ended in dark water. That was the muskrats' front door.

After the sun had gone, the muskrats woke and went pattering down the smooth mud-floor of their hallway. They plunged into the black water and came up through the pool to the wide, wild night under the sky. All night long, in the starlight or moonlight, they swam and played along the edges of the water, feeding on roots and stems and leaves of the water-plants and grasses. When dawn was coming ghostly gray, they swam home. They dived and came up through their water-door. Dripping, they went up the slope of their hallway, each to his own grass-lined room. There they curled comfortably to sleep.

Laura put her hand on the wall of their house. The coarse plaster was hot in the hot wind and sunshine, but inside the thick mud walls, in the dark, the air must be cool. She liked to think of the muskrats sleeping there.

Pa was shaking his head. "We're going to have a hard winter," he said, not liking the prospect.

"Why, how do you know?" Laura asked in surprise.

"The colder the winter will be, the thicker the muskrats build the walls of their houses," Pa told her. "I never saw a heavier-built muskrats' house than that one."

Laura looked at it again. It was very solid and big. But the sun was blazing, burning on her shoulders through the faded, thin calico and the hot wind was blowing, and stronger than the damp-mud smell of the slough was the ripening smell of grasses parching in the heat. Laura could hardly think of ice and snow and cruel cold.

"Pa, how can the muskrats know?" she asked.

"I don't know how they know," Pa said. "But they do. God tells them, somehow, I suppose."

"Then why doesn't God tell us?" Laura wanted to know.

"Because," said Pa, "we're not animals. We're humans, and, like it says in the Declaration of Independence, God created us free. That means we got to take care of ourselves."

Laura said faintly, "I thought God takes care of us."

"He does," Pa said, "so far as we do what's right. And He gives us a conscience and brains to know what's right. But He leaves it to us to do as we please. That's the difference between us and everything else in creation."

"Can't muskrats do what they please?" Laura asked, amazed.

"No," said Pa. "I don't know why they can't but you can see they can't. Look at that muskrat house. Muskrats have to build that kind of house. They always have and they always will. It's plain they can't build any other kind. But folks build all kinds of houses. A man can build any kind of house he can think of. So if his house don't keep out the weather, that's *his* look-out; he's free and independent."

Pa stood thinking for a minute, then he jerked his head. "Come along, little Half-Pint. We better make hay while the sun shines."

His eyes twinkled and Laura laughed, because the sun was shining with all its might. But all the rest of that afternoon they were rather sober.

The muskrats had a warm, thick-walled house to keep out cold and snow, but the claim shanty was built of thin boards that had shrunk in the summer heat till the narrow battens hardly covered the wide cracks in the walls. Boards and tar-paper were not very snug shelter against a hard winter.

CHAPTER 2

An Errand to Town

ONE morning in September the grass was white with frost. It was only a light frost that melted as soon as sunshine touched it. It was gone when Laura looked out at the bright morning. But at breakfast Pa said that such an early frost was surprising.

"Will it hurt the hay?" Laura asked him, and he said, "Oh, no. Such a light frost will only make it dry faster when it's cut. But I'd better get a hustle on, for it won't be long now till it's too late to make hay."

He was hustling so fast that afternoon that he hardly stopped to drink when Laura brought him the water-jug. He was mowing in Big Slough.

"You cover it up, Half-Pint," he said, handing back the jug. "I'm bound and determined to get this patch mowed before sundown." He chirruped to Sam and David and they started again, drawing the whirring machine. Then suddenly the machine gave a clattering kind of yelp and Pa said, "Whoa!"

Laura hurried to see what had happened. Pa was looking at the cutter-bar. There was a gap in the row of bright steel points. The cutter-bar had lost one of its teeth. Pa picked up the pieces, but they could not be mended.

"There's no help for it," Pa said. "It means buying another section."

There was nothing to say to that. Pa thought a minute and said, "Laura, I wish you'd go to town and get it. I don't want to lose the time. I can keep on mowing, after a fashion, while you're gone. Be as quick as you can. Ma will give you the five cents to pay for it. Buy it at Fuller's Hardware."

"Yes, Pa," Laura said. She dreaded going to town because so many people were there. She was not exactly afraid, but strange eyes looking at her made her uncomfortable.

She had a clean calico dress to wear and she had shoes. While she hurried to the house, she thought that Ma might let her wear her Sunday hair-ribbon and perhaps Mary's freshly ironed sunbonnet.

"I have to go to town, Ma," she said, rushing in breathless.

Carrie and Mary listened while she explained and even Grace looked up at her with big, sober blue eyes.

"I will go with you to keep you company," Carrie volunteered.

"Oh, can she, Ma?" Laura asked.

"If she can be ready as soon as you are," Ma gave permission.

Quickly they changed to fresh dresses and put on their stockings and shoes. But Ma saw no reason for hair-ribbons on a week day and she said Laura must wear her own sunbonnet.

"It would be fresher," Ma said, "if you took care to keep it so." Laura's bonnet was limp from hanging down her back and the strings were limp too. But that was Laura's own fault.

Ma gave her five cents from Pa's pocketbook and with Carrie she hurried away toward town.

They followed the road made by Pa's wagon-wheels, past the well, down the dry, grassy slope into Big Slough, and on between the tall slough-grasses to the slope up on the other side. The whole shimmering prairie seemed strange then. Even the wind blowing the grasses had a wilder sound. Laura liked that and she wished they did not have to go into town where the false fronts of the buildings stood up square-topped to pretend that the stores behind them were bigger than they were.

Neither Laura nor Carrie said a word after they came to Main Street. Some men were on the store porches and two teams with wagons were tied to the hitching posts. Lonely, on the other side of Main Street, stood Pa's store building. It was rented and two men sat inside it talking.

Laura and Carrie went into the hardware store. Two men were sitting on nail kegs and one on a plow. They stopped talking and looked at Laura and Carrie. The wall behind the counter glittered with tin pans and pails and lamps.

Laura said, "Pa wants a mowing-machine section, please."

The man on the plow said, "He's broke one, has he?" and Laura said, "Yes, sir."

She watched him wrap in paper the sharp and shining three-cornered tooth. He must be Mr. Fuller. She gave him the five cents and, taking the package in her hand, she said, "Thank you," and walked out with Carrie.

That was over. But they did not speak until they had walked out of town. Then Carrie said, "You did that beautifully, Laura."

"Oh, it was just buying something," Laura replied.

"I know, but I feel funny when people look at me. I feel . . . not scared, exactly . . ." Carrie said.

"There's nothing to be scared of," Laura said. "We mustn't ever be scared." Suddenly she told Carrie, "I feel the same way."

"Do you, really? I didn't know that. You don't act like it. I always feel so safe when you're there," Carrie said.

"You are safe when I'm there," Laura answered. "I'd take care of you. Anyway, I'd try my best."

"I know you would," Carrie said.

It was nice, walking together. To take care of their shoes, they did not walk in the dusty wheel-tracks. They walked on the harder strip in the middle where only horses' hoofs had discouraged the grass. They were not walking hand in hand, but they felt as if they were.

Ever since Laura could remember, Carrie had been her little sister. First she had been a tiny baby, then she had been Baby Carrie, then she had been a clutcher and tagger, always asking "Why?" Now she was ten years old, old enough to be really a sister. And they were out together, away from even Pa and Ma. Their errand was done and off their minds, and the sun was shining, the wind was blowing, the prairie spread far all around them. They felt free and independent and comfortable together.

"It's a long way around to where Pa is," Carrie said. "Why don't we go this way?" and she pointed toward the part of the slough where they could see Pa and the horses.

Laura answered, "That way's through the slough."

"It isn't wet now, is it?" Carrie asked.

"All right, let's," Laura answered. "Pa didn't say to go by the road, and he did say to hurry."

So they did not follow the road that turned to cross the slough. They went straight on into the tall slough grass.

At first it was fun. It was rather like going into the jungle-picture in Pa's big green book. Laura pushed ahead between the thick clumps of grass-stems that gave way rustling and closed again behind Carrie. The millions of coarse grass-stems and their slender long leaves were greeny-gold and golden-green in their own shade. The earth was crackled with dryness underfoot, but a faint smell of damp lay under the hot smell of the grass. Just above Laura's head the grass-tops swished in the wind, but down at their roots was a stillness, broken only where Laura and Carrie went wading through it.

"Where's Pa?" Carrie asked suddenly.

Laura looked around at her. Carrie's peaked little face was pale in the shade of the grass. Her eyes were almost frightened.

"Well, we can't see him from here," Laura said. They could see only the leaves of the thick grass waving, and the hot sky overhead. "He's right ahead of us. We'll come to him in a minute."

She said it confidently but how could she know where Pa was? She could not even be sure where she was going, where she was taking Carrie. The smothering heat made sweat trickle down her throat and her backbone, but she felt cold inside. She remembered the children near Brookings, lost in the prairie grass. The slough was worse than the prairie. Ma had always been afraid that Grace would be lost in this slough.

She listened for the whirr of the mowing machine, but the sound of the grasses filled her ears. There was nothing in the flickering shadows of their thin leaves blowing and tossing higher than her eyes, to tell her where the sun was. The grasses' bending and swaying did not even tell the direction of the wind. Those clumps of grass would hold up no weight at all. There was nothing, nothing anywhere that she could climb to look out above them, to see beyond them and know where she was.

"Come along, Carrie," she said cheerfully. She must not frighten Carrie.

Carrie followed trustfully but Laura did not know where she was going. She could not even be sure that she was walking straight. Always a clump of grass was in her way; she must go to right or left. Even if she went to the right of one clump of grass and to the left of the next clump, that did not mean that she was not going in a circle. Lost people go in circles and many of them never find their way home.

The slough went on for a mile or more of bending, swaying

grasses, too tall to see beyond, too yielding to climb. It was wide. Unless Laura walked straight ahead they might never get out of it.

"We've gone so far, Laura," Carrie panted. "Why don't we come to Pa?"

"He ought to be right around here somewhere," Laura answered. She could not follow their own trail back to the safe road. Their shoes left almost no tracks on the heat-baked mud, and the grasses, the endless swaying grasses with their low leaves hanging dried and broken, were all alike.

Carrie's mouth opened a little. Her big eyes looked up at Laura and they said, "I know. We're lost." Her mouth shut without a word. If they were lost, they were lost. There was nothing to say about it.

"We'd better go on," Laura said.

"I guess so. As long as we can," Carrie agreed.

They went on. They must surely have passed the place where Pa was mowing. But Laura could not be sure of anything. Perhaps if they thought they turned back, they would really be going farther away. They could only go on. Now and then they stopped and wiped their sweating faces. They were terribly thirsty but there was no water. They were very tired from pushing through the grasses. Not one single push seemed hard, but going on was harder than trampling hay. Carrie's thin little face was gray-white, she was so tired.

Then Laura thought that the grasses ahead were thinner. The shade seemed lighter there and the tops of the grasses against the sky seemed fewer. And suddenly she saw sunshine, yellow beyond the dark grass stems. Perhaps there was a pond there. Oh! perhaps, perhaps there was Pa's stubble field and the mowing machine and Pa.

She saw the hay stubble in the sunshine, and she saw haycocks dotting it. But she heard a strange voice.

It was a man's voice, loud and hearty. It said, "Get a move on, Manzo. Let's get this load in. It's coming night after awhile."

Another voice drawled lazily, "Aw-aw, Roy!"

Close together, Laura and Carrie looked out from the edge of the standing grass. The hayfield was not Pa's hayfield. A strange wagon stood there and on its rack was an enormous load of hay. On the high top of that load, up against the blinding sky, a boy was lying. He lay on his stomach, his chin on his hands and his feet in the air.

The strange man lifted up a huge forkful of hay and pitched it onto the boy. It buried him and he scrambled up out of it, laughing and shaking hay off his head and his shoulders. He had black hair and blue eyes and his face and his arms were sunburned brown.

He stood up on the high load of hay against the sky and saw Laura. He said, "Hello there!" They both stood watching Laura and Carrie come out of the tall standing grass—like rabbits, Laura thought. She wanted to turn and run back into hiding.

"I thought Pa was here," she said, while Carrie stood small and still behind her.

The man said, "We haven't seen anybody around here. Who is your Pa?" The boy told him, "Mr. Ingalls. Isn't he?" he asked Laura. He was still looking at her.

"Yes," she said, and she looked at the horses hitched to the wagon. She had seen those beautiful brown horses before, their haunches gleaming in the sun and the black manes glossy on their glossy necks. They were the Wilder boys' horses. The man and the boy must be the Wilder brothers.

"I can see him from here. He's just over there," the boy said. Laura looked up and saw him pointing. His blue eyes twinkled down at her as if he had known her a long time.

"Thank you," Laura said primly and she and Carrie walked away, along the road that the Morgan team and the wagon had broken through the slough grass.

"Whoa!" Pa said when he saw them. "Whew!" he said, taking off his hat and wiping the sweat from his forehead.

Laura gave him the mowing-machine section, and she and Carrie watched while he opened the tool-box, took the cutter-bar from the machine, and knocked out the broken section. He set the new one in its place and hammered down the rivets to hold it. "There!" he said. "Tell your Ma I'll be late for supper. I'm going to finish cutting this piece."

The mowing machine was humming steadily when Laura and Carrie went on toward the shanty.

"Were you much scared, Laura?" Carrie asked.

"Well, some, but all's well that ends well," Laura said.

"It was my fault. I wanted to go that way," said Carrie.

"It was my fault because I'm older," Laura said. "But we've learned a lesson. I guess we'll stay on the road after this."

"Are you going to tell Ma and Pa?" Carrie timidly asked.

"We have to if they ask us," said Laura.

CHAPTER 3

Fall of the Year

PA AND Laura stacked the last load of slough hay on a hot September afternoon. Pa intended to mow another patch next day, but in the morning rain was falling.

For three days and nights the rain fell steadily, slow, weepy rain, running down the windowpanes and pattering on the roof.

"Well, we must expect it," Ma said. "It's the equinoctial storm."

"Yes," Pa agreed, but uneasily. "There's a weather change, all right. A fellow can feel it in his bones."

Next morning the shanty was cold, the windowpanes were almost covered with frost, and all outdoors was white.

"My goodness," Ma said shivering, while she laid kindling in the stove. "And this is only the first day of October."

Laura put on her shoes and a shawl when she went to the well for water.

The air bit her cheeks and scorched the inside of her nose with cold. The sky was coldly blue and the whole world was white. Every blade of grass was furry with frost, the path was frosted, the boards of the well were streaked with thick frost, and frost had crept up the walls of the shanty, along the narrow battens that held the black tar-paper on.

Then the sun peeped over the edge of the prairie and the whole world glittered. Every tiniest thing glittered rosy toward the sun and pale blue toward the sky, and all along every blade of grass ran rainbow sparkles.

Laura loved the beautiful world. She knew that the bitter frost had killed the hay and the garden. The tangled tomato vines with their red and green tomatoes, and the pumpkin vines holding their broad leaves over the green young pumpkins, were all glittering bright in frost over the broken, frosty sod. The sod corn's stalks and long leaves were white. The frost had killed them. It would leave every living green thing dead. But the frost was beautiful.

At breakfast Pa said, "There'll be no more haying, so we'll

get in our harvest. We can't get much from a first year on sod-ground, but the sods will rot this winter. We'll do better next year."

The plowed ground was tumbled slabs of earth still held together by the grass-roots. From underneath these sods, Pa dug small potatoes and Laura and Carrie put them into tin pails. Laura hated the dry, dusty feeling of earth on her fingers. It sent shivers up her backbone but that couldn't be helped. Someone must pick up the potatoes.

She and Carrie trudged back and forth with their pails, till they had filled five sacks full of potatoes. That was all the potatoes there were.

"A lot of digging for a few potatoes," said Pa. "But five bushels are better than none, and we can piece out with the beans."

He pulled the dead bean-vines and stacked them to dry. The sun was high now, all the frost was gone, and the wind was blowing cool over the brownish and purple and fawn-colored prairie.

Ma and Laura picked the tomatoes. The vines were wilted down, soft and blackening, so they picked even the smallest green tomatoes. There were enough ripe tomatoes to make almost a gallon of preserves.

"What are you going to do with the green ones?" Laura asked, and Ma answered, "Wait and see."

She washed them carefully without peeling them. She sliced them and cooked them with salt, pepper, vinegar, and spices.

"That's almost two quarts of green tomato pickle. Even if it's only our first garden on the sod and nothing could grow well, these pickles will be a treat with baked beans this winter," Ma gloated.

"And almost a gallon of sweet preserves!" Mary added.

"Five bushels of potatoes," said Laura, rubbing her hands on her apron because they remembered the horrid dusty feeling.

"And turnips, lots of turnips!" Carrie cried. Carrie loved to eat a raw turnip.

Pa laughed. "When I get those beans threshed and winnowed and sacked there'll be pretty near a bushel of beans. When I get those few hills of corn cut, husked, and stored down cellar in a teacup, we'll have quite a harvest."

Laura knew that it was a very small harvest. But the hay and corn would winter the horses and the cow through till spring, and with five bushels of potatoes and nearly a bushel of beans and Pa's hunting they could all live.

"I must cut that corn tomorrow," Pa said.

"I see no special rush, Charles," Ma remarked. "The rain is over and I never saw nicer fall weather."

"Well, that's so," Pa admitted. The nights were cool now and the early mornings were crisp, but the days were sunny-warm.

"We could do with some fresh meat for a change," Ma suggested.

"Soon as I get the corn in I'll go hunting," said Pa.

Next day he cut and shocked the sod corn. The ten shocks stood like a row of little Indian tepees by the haystacks. When he had finished them, Pa brought six yellow-gold pumpkins from the field.

"The vines couldn't do much on tough sod," he made excuse, "and the frost caught the green ones, but we'll get a lot of seed out of these for next year."

"Why such a hurry to get the pumpkins in?" Ma asked.

"I feel in a hurry. As if there was need to hurry," Pa tried to explain.

"You need a good night's sleep," said Ma.

A misty-fine rain was falling next morning. After Pa had done the chores and eaten breakfast, he put on his coat and the wide-brimmed hat that sheltered the back of his neck.

"I'll get us a brace of geese," he said. "I heard them flying over in the night. There'll be some in the slough."

He took down his shotgun and sheltering it under his coat he went out into the weather.

After he had gone Ma said, "Girls, I've thought of a surprise for Pa."

Laura and Carrie turned round from the dishpan and Mary straightened up from the bed she was making. "What?" they all asked her.

"Hurry and get the work done," said Ma. "And then, Laura, you go to the corn-patch and bring me a green pumpkin. I'm going to make a pie!"

"A pie! But how . . ." Mary said, and Laura said, "A *green* pumpkin pie? I never heard of such a thing, Ma."

"Neither did I," said Ma. "But we wouldn't do much if we didn't do things that nobody ever heard of before."

Laura and Carrie did the dishes properly but in a hurry. Then Laura ran through the cool, misty rain to the corn-patch and lugged back the biggest green pumpkin.

"Stand by the oven door and dry yourself," said Ma. "You're not very big, Laura, but you're old enough to put on a shawl without being told."

"I went so fast I dodged between the raindrops," Laura said. "I'm not much wet, Ma, honestly. Now what do I do?"

"You may cut the pumpkin in slices and peel them while I make the piecrust," said Ma. "Then we'll see what we'll see."

Ma put the crust in the pie pan and covered the bottom with brown sugar and spices. Then she filled the crust with thin slices of the green pumpkin. She poured half a cup of vinegar over them, put a small piece of butter on top, and laid the top crust over all.

"There," she said, when she had finished crimping the edges.

"I didn't know you could," Carrie breathed, looking wide-eyed at the pie.

"Well, *I* don't know yet," said Ma. She slipped the pie into the oven and shut the door on it. "But the only way to find out is to try. By dinnertime we'll know."

They all sat waiting in the tidy shanty. Mary was busily knitting to finish warm stockings for Carrie before cold weather. Laura was sewing two long breadths of muslin together to make a sheet. She pinned the edges together carefully and fastened them with a pin to her dress at the knee. Carefully holding the edges even, she whipped them together with even, tiny stitches.

The stitches must be close and small and firm and they must be deep enough but not too deep, for the sheet must lie smooth, with not the tiniest ridge down its middle. And all the stitches must be so exactly alike that you could not tell them apart, because that was the way to sew.

Mary had liked such work, but now she was blind and could not do it. Sewing made Laura feel like flying to pieces. She wanted to scream. The back of her neck ached and the thread twisted and knotted. She had to pick out almost as many stitches as she put in.

"Blankets are wide enough to cover a bed," she said fretfully. "Why can't sheets be made wide enough?"

"Because sheets are muslin," said Mary. "And muslin isn't wide enough for a sheet."

The eye of Laura's needle slipped through a tiny hole in her thimble and ran into her finger. She shut her mouth hard and did not say a word.

But the pie was baking beautifully. When Ma laid down the shirt that she was making for Pa and opened the oven, the rich smell of baking pie came out. Carrie and Grace stopped to look in while Ma turned the pie so that it would brown evenly.

"It's doing nicely," Ma said.

"Oh, won't Pa be surprised!" Carrie cried.

Just before dinnertime Ma took the pie from the oven. It was a beautiful pie.

They kept dinner waiting until almost one o'clock, but Pa did not come. When he was hunting, he paid no attention to mealtimes. So at last they ate dinner. The pie must wait till suppertime when Pa would come with fat geese to roast for tomorrow.

All afternoon the slow rain fell steadily. When Laura went to the well for water, the sky was low and gray. Far over the prairie the brown grasses were sodden with rain and the tall slough grass stood dripping, bent a little under the steady pressure of the falling rain.

Laura hurried back from the well. She did not like to look at the outdoors when all the grass was weeping.

Pa did not come home until suppertime. He came empty-handed except for his gun. He did not speak or smile and his eyes were wide-open and still.

"What is wrong, Charles?" Ma asked quickly.

He took off his wet coat and his dripping hat and hung them up before he answered. "That is what I'd like to know. Something's queer. Not a goose nor a duck on the lake. None in the slough. Not one in sight. They are flying high above the clouds, flying fast. I could hear them calling. Caroline, every kind of bird is going south as fast and as high as it can fly. All of them, going south. And no other kind of game is out. Every living thing that runs or swims is hidden away somewhere. I never saw country so empty and still."

"Never mind," Ma said cheerfully. "Supper's ready. You sit close by the fire, Charles, and dry yourself. I'll move the table up. Seems to me it's growing chilly."

It was growing chilly. The cold crept under the table, crawling up from Laura's bare feet to her bare knees under her skirts. But supper was warm and good and in the lamplight all the faces were shining with the secret of the surprise for Pa.

Pa did not notice them. He ate hungrily but he did not notice what he ate. He said again, "It's queer, not a duck nor a goose coming down to rest."

"Likely the poor things want to get to sunshine," Ma said. "I'm glad we're snug, out of the rain, under this good roof."

Pa pushed back his empty plate and Ma gave Laura a look that said, "Now!" Smiles spread over all their faces but Pa's. Carrie wriggled in her chair and Grace bounced on Ma's lap, while Laura set down the pie.

For an instant Pa did not see it. Then he said, "Pie!"

His surprise was even greater than they had expected. Grace and Carrie and even Laura laughed out loud.

"Caroline, however did you manage to make a pie?" Pa exclaimed. "What kind of pie is it?"

"Taste it and see!" said Ma. She cut a piece and put it on his plate.

Pa cut off the point with his fork and put it in his mouth. "Apple pie! Where in the world did you get apples?"

Carrie could keep still no longer. She almost shouted, "It's pumpkin! Ma made it of green pumpkin!"

Pa took another small bite and tasted it carefully. "I'd never have guessed it," he said. "Ma always could beat the nation cooking."

Ma said nothing, but a little flush came up in her cheeks and her eyes kept on smiling while they all ate that delicious pie. They ate slowly, taking small bites of the sweet spiciness to make it last as long as they could.

That was such a happy supper that Laura wanted it never to end. When she was in bed with Mary and Carrie, she stayed awake to keep on being happy. She was so sleepily comfortable and cosy. The rain on the roof was a pleasant sound.

A splash of water on her face dimly surprised her. She was sure it could not be rain, for the roof was overhead. She snuggled closer to Mary and everything slid away into dark, warm sleep.

CHAPTER 4

October Blizzard

LAURA woke up suddenly. She heard singing and a queer slapping sound.

"Oh, I am as happy as a big sunflower (Slap! Slap!)
That nods and bends in the breezes, Oh! (Slap! Slap!)
And my heart (Slap!) is as light (Slap!) as the wind that blows (Slap! Slap!)
The leaves from off the treeses, Oh! (Slap! SLAP!)"

Pa was singing his trouble song and slapping his arms on his chest.

Laura's nose was cold. Only her nose was outside the quilts that she was huddled under. She put out her whole head and then she knew why Pa was slapping himself. He was trying to warm his hands.

He had kindled the fire. It was roaring in the stove, but the air was freezing cold. Ice crackled on the quilt where leaking rain had fallen. Winds howled around the shanty and from the roof and all the walls came a sound of scouring.

Carrie sleepily asked, "What is it?"

"It's a blizzard," Laura told her. "You and Mary stay under the covers."

Careful not to let the cold get under the quilts, she crawled out of the warm bed. Her teeth chattered while she pulled on her clothes. Ma was dressing, too, beyond the curtain, but they were both too cold to say anything.

They met at the stove where the fire was blazing furiously without warming the air at all. The window was a white blur of madly swirling snow. Snow had blown under the door and across the floor and every nail in the walls was white with frost.

Pa had gone to the stable. Laura was glad that they had so many haystacks in a row between the stable and the shanty. Going from haystack to haystack, Pa would not get lost.

"A b-b-b-b-blizzard!" Ma chattered. "In Oc-October I n-n-never heard of . . ."

She put more wood in the stove and broke the ice in the water pail to fill the teakettle.

The water pail was less than half-full. They must be sparing of water for nobody could get to the well in that storm. But the snow on the floor was clean. Laura scooped it into the washbasin and set it on the stove to melt, for washing in.

The air by the stove was not so cold now, so she rolled Grace in quilts and brought her to the stove to dress her. Mary and Carrie shiveringly dressed themselves, close to the open oven. They all put on their stockings and shoes.

Breakfast was waiting when Pa came back. He blew in with a howl of wind and swirling snow.

"Well, those muskrats knew what was coming, didn't they, Laura?" he said as soon as he was warm enough to speak. "And the geese too."

"No wonder they wouldn't stop at the lake," said Ma.

"The lake's frozen by now," Pa said. "Temperature's down near zero and going lower."

He glanced at the wood box as he spoke. Laura had filled it last night, but already the wood was low. So as soon as he had eaten breakfast, Pa wrapped himself well and brought big armfuls from the woodpile.

The shanty was growing colder. The stove could not warm the air inside the thin walls. There was nothing to do but sit huddled in coats and shawls, close to the stove.

"I'm glad I put beans to soak last night," said Ma. She lifted the lid of the bubbling kettle and quickly popped in a spoonful of soda. The boiling beans roared, foaming up, but did not quite run over.

"There's a little bit of salt pork to put in them too," Ma said.

Now and then she spooned up a few beans and blew on them. When their skins split and curled, she drained the soda-water from the kettle and filled it again with hot water. She put in the bit of fat pork.

"There's nothing like good hot bean soup on a cold day," said Pa. He looked down at Grace, pulling at his hand. "Well, Blue-Eyes, what do you want?"

"A tory," Grace said.

"Tell us the one about Grandpa and the pig on the sled," Carrie begged. So, taking Grace and Carrie on his knees, Pa began again the stories that he used to tell Mary and Laura in the Big Woods when they were little girls. Ma and Mary knitted busily, in quilt-covered rockers drawn close to the oven, and Laura stood wrapped in her shawl, between the stove and the wall.

The cold crept in from the corners of the shanty, closer and closer to the stove. Icy-cold breezes sucked and fluttered the curtains around the beds. The little shanty quivered in the storm. But the steamy smell of boiling beans was good and it seemed to make the air warmer.

At noon Ma sliced bread and filled bowls with the hot bean broth and they all ate where they were, close to the stove. They all drank cups of strong, hot tea. Ma even gave Grace a cup of cambric tea. Cambric tea was hot water and milk, with only a taste of tea in it, but little girls felt grown-up when their mothers let them drink cambric tea.

The hot soup and hot tea warmed them all. They ate the broth from the beans. Then Ma emptied the beans into a milk-pan, set the bit of fat pork in the middle, and laced the top with dribbles of molasses. She set the pan in the oven and shut the oven door. They would have baked beans for supper.

Then Pa had to bring in more wood. They were thankful that the woodpile was close to the back door. Pa staggered in breathless with the first armful. When he could speak he said, "This wind takes your breath away. If I'd thought of such a storm as this, I'd have filled this shanty with wood yesterday. Now I'm bringing in as much snow as wood."

That was almost true. Every time Laura opened the door for him, snow swirled in. Snow fell off him and the wood was covered with snow. It was snow as hard as ice and as fine as sand, and opening the door made the shanty so cold that the snow did not melt.

"That's enough for now," Pa said. If he let in any more cold, the wood he brought would not make enough heat to drive the cold out.

"When you get that snow swept up, Laura, bring me the fiddle," he said. "Soon as I can thaw out my fingers, we'll have a tune to drown the yowl of that wind."

In a little while he was able to tune the strings and rosin the bow. Then he set the fiddle to his shoulder and sang with it.

"Oh, If I were young again,
I'd lead a different life,
Lay up some money and buy some land
And take Dinah for my wife.
But now I'm getting old and gray
I cannot work any more.
Oh carry me back
Oh, carry me back
To the old Virginia shore.
So carry me 'long and carry me 'long
And carry me till I die . . ."

"For pity's sakes!" Ma broke in. "I'd as soon listen to the wind." She was trying to keep Grace warm and Grace was struggling and whimpering. Ma set her down. "There, run if you're bound to! You'll be glad enough to come back to the stove."

"I'll tell you what!" Pa exclaimed. "Laura and Carrie, you get out there with Grace and let's see you quick-step march! It'll warm up your blood."

It was hard to leave the shelter of their huddled shawls, but they did as Pa said. Then his strong voice rang out with the singing fiddle:

"March! March! Ettrick and Teviotdale!
Why, my lads, dinna ye march forward in order?
March! March! Eskdale and Liddesdale!
All the blue bonnets are over the border!
Many a banner spread flutters above your head,
Many a crest that is famous in story."

Round and round they marched, Laura and Carrie and Grace, singing with all their might, thumping loud thumps of their shoes on the floor.

"Mount, and make ready, then,
Sons of the mountain glen,
Fight! for your homes and the old Scottish glory!"

They felt that banners were blowing above them and that they were marching to victory. They did not even hear the storm. They were warm to the tips of their toes.

Then the music ended and Pa laid the fiddle in its box. "Well, girls, it's up to me to march out against this storm and make the stock comfortable for the night. Blamed if that old tune don't give me the spunk to like fighting even a blizzard!"

Ma warmed his coat and muffler by the oven while he put away the fiddle-box. They all heard the wind howling furiously.

"We'll have hot baked beans and hot tea waiting when you get back, Charles," Ma promised him. "And then we'll all go to bed and keep warm, and likely the storm'll be over by morning."

But in the morning Pa sang again his sunflower song. The window was the same white blur, the winds still drove the scouring snow against the shivering little shanty.

The blizzard lasted two more long days and two more nights.

CHAPTER 5

After the Storm

ON THE fourth morning, there was a queer feeling in Laura's ears. She peeped from the quilts and saw snow drifted over the bed. She heard the little crash of the stove lid and then the first crackling of the fire. Then she knew why her ears felt empty. The noise of the blizzard had stopped!

"Wake up, Mary!" she sang out, poking Mary with her elbow. "The blizzard's over!"

She jumped out of the warm bed, into air colder than ice. The hot stove seemed to give out no heat at all. The pail of snow-water was almost solidly frozen. But the frosted windows were glowing with sunshine.

"It's as cold as ever outside," Pa said when he came in. He bent over the stove to thaw the icicles from his mustache. They sizzled on the stove-top and went up in steam.

Pa wiped his mustaches and went on. "The winds tore a big piece of tar-paper off the roof, tight as it was nailed on. No wonder the roof leaked rain and snow."

"Anyway, it's over," Laura said. It was pleasant to be eating breakfast and to see the yellow-glowing windowpanes.

"We'll have Indian summer yet," Ma was sure. "This storm was so early, it can't be the beginning of winter."

"I never knew a winter to set in so early," Pa admitted. "But I don't like the feel of things."

"What things, Charles?" Ma wanted to know.

Pa couldn't say exactly. He said, "There's some stray cattle by the haystacks."

"Are they tearing down the hay?" Ma asked quickly.

"No," said Pa.

"Then what of it, if they aren't doing any harm?" Ma said.

"I guess they're tired out by the storm," said Pa. "They took shelter there by the haystacks. I thought I'd let them rest and eat a little before I drove them off. I can't afford to let them tear down the stacks, but they could eat a little without doing any harm. But they aren't eating."

"What's wrong then?" Ma asked.

"Nothing," Pa said. "They're just standing there."

"That's nothing to upset a body," said Ma.

"No," Pa said. He drank his tea. "Well, I might as well go drive them off."

He put on his coat and cap and mittens again and went out.

After a moment Ma said, "You might as well go with him, Laura. He may need some help to drive them away from the hay."

Quickly Laura put Ma's big shawl over her head and pinned it snugly under her chin with the shawl-pin. The woolen folds covered her from head to foot. Even her hands were under the shawl. Only her face was out.

Outdoors the sun-glitter hurt her eyes. She breathed a deep breath of the tingling cold and squinted her eyes to look around her. The sky was hugely blue and all the land was blowing white. The straight, strong wind did not lift the snow, but drove it scudding across the prairie.

The cold stung Laura's cheeks. It burned in her nose and tingled in her chest and came out in steam on the air. She held a fold of the shawl across her mouth and her breath made frost on it.

When she passed the corner of the stable, she saw Pa going ahead of her and she saw the cattle. She stood and stared.

The cattle were standing in sunshine and shadow by the haystacks—red and brown and spotted cattle and one thin black one. They stood perfectly still, every head bowed down to the ground. The hairy red necks and brown necks all stretched down from bony-gaunt shoulders to monstrous, swollen white heads.

"Pa!" Laura screamed. Pa motioned to her to stay where she was. He went on trudging, through the low-flying snow, toward those creatures.

They did not seem like real cattle. They stood so terribly still. In the whole herd there was not the least movement. Only their breathing sucked their hairy sides in between the rib bones and pushed them out again. Their hip bones and their shoulder bones stood up sharply. Their legs were braced out, stiff and still. And where their heads should be, swollen white lumps seemed fast to the ground under the blowing snow.

On Laura's head the hair prickled up and a horror went down her backbone. Tears from the sun and the wind swelled out her staring eyes and ran cold on her cheeks. Pa went on slowly against the wind. He walked up to the herd. Not one of the cattle moved.

For a moment Pa stood looking. Then he stooped and quickly did something. Laura heard a bellow and a red steer's back humped and jumped. The red steer ran staggering and bawling. It had an ordinary head with eyes and nose and open mouth bawling out steam on the wind.

Another one bellowed and ran a short, staggering run. Then another. Pa was doing the same thing to them all, one by one. Their bawling rose up to the cold sky.

At last they all drifted away together. They went silently now in the knee-deep spray of blowing snow.

Pa waved to Laura to go back to the shanty, while he inspected the haystacks.

"Whatever kept you so long, Laura?" Ma asked. "Did the cattle get into the haystacks?"

"No, Ma," she answered. "Their heads were . . . I guess their heads were frozen to the ground."

"That can't be!" Ma exclaimed.

"It must be one of Laura's queer notions," Mary said, busily knitting in her chair by the stove. "How could cattle's heads freeze to the ground, Laura? It's really worrying, the way you talk sometimes."

"Well, ask Pa then!" Laura said shortly. She was not able to tell Ma and Mary what she felt. She felt that somehow, in the wild night and storm, the stillness that was underneath all sounds on the prairie had seized the cattle.

When Pa came in Ma asked him, "What was wrong with the cattle, Charles?"

"Their heads were frozen over with ice and snow," Pa said. "Their breath froze over their eyes and their noses till they couldn't see nor breathe.

Laura stopped sweeping. "Pa! Their own breath! Smothering them," she said in horror.

Pa understood how she felt. He said, "They're all right now, Laura. I broke the ice off their heads. They're breathing now and I guess they'll make it to shelter somewhere."

Carrie and Mary were wide-eyed and even Ma looked horrified. She said briskly, "Get your sweeping done, Laura. And Charles, for pity's sake, why don't you take off your wraps and warm yourself?"

"I got something to show you," Pa said. He took his hand carefully out of his pocket. "Look here, girls, look at what I found hidden in a haystack."

Slowly he opened his hand. In the hollow of his mitten sat a little bird. He put it gently in Mary's hands.

"Why, it's standing straight up!" Mary exclaimed, touching it lightly with her finger-tips.

They had never seen a bird like it. It was small, but it looked exactly like the picture of the great auk in Pa's big green book, *The Wonders of The Animal World.*

It had the same white breast and black back and wings, the same short legs placed far back, and the same large, webbed feet. It stood straight up on its short legs, like a tiny man with black coat and trousers and white shirt front, and its little black wings were like arms.

"What is it, Pa? Oh, what is it?" Carrie cried in delight and she held Grace's eager hands. "Mustn't touch, Grace."

"I never saw anything like it," said Pa. "It must have tired out in the storm winds and dropped down and struck against the haystack. It had crawled into the hay for shelter."

"It's a great auk," Laura declared. "Only it's a little one."

"It's full-grown, it isn't a nestling," said Ma. "Look at its feathers."

"Yes, it's full-grown, whatever it is," Pa agreed.

The little bird stood up straight on Mary's soft palm and looked at them all with its bright black eyes.

"It's never seen humans before," said Pa.

"How do you know, Pa?" Mary asked.

"Because it isn't afraid of us," Pa said.

"Oh, can we keep it, Pa? Can't we, Ma?" Carrie begged.

"Well, that depends," Pa said.

Mary's finger-tips touched the little bird all over, while Laura told her how white its smooth breast was and how very black its back and tail and little wings. Then they let Grace carefully touch it. The little auk sat still and looked at them.

They set it on the floor and it walked a little way. Then it pushed its webbed feet tiptoe against the boards and flapped its little wings.

"It can't get going," said Pa. "It's a water-bird. It must start from the water where it can use those webbed feet to get up speed."

Finally they put it in a box in the corner. It stood there looking up at them, with its round, bright black eyes and they wondered what it ate.

"That was a queer storm all around," said Pa. "I don't like it."

"Why, Charles, it was only a blizzard," Ma said. "We'll likely have nice warm weather now. It's beginning to warm up a little already."

Mary took up her knitting again and Laura went on sweeping. Pa stood by the window and after awhile Carrie led Grace away from the little auk and they looked out too.

"Oh, look! Jackrabbits!" Carrie exclaimed. All around the stable, dozens of jackrabbits were hopping.

"The rascals have been living on our hay, all through the storm," Pa said. "I ought to take my gun and get us a rabbit stew."

But he had been standing at the window looking at them without making a move toward his gun.

"Please let them go, Pa, this one time," Laura pleaded. "When they came because they had to, they had to find shelter."

Pa looked at Ma, and Ma smiled. "We aren't hungry, Charles, and I'm thankful we all got through that storm."

"Well, I guess I can spare the jackrabbits a little hay!" said Pa. He took the water pail and went to the well.

The air that came in when he opened the door was very cold, but the sun was already beginning to melt the snow on the south side of the shanty.

CHAPTER 6

Indian Summer

THERE were only slivers of ice on the water pail next morning and the day was sunny and warm. Pa took his traps to set them for muskrats in Big Slough, and Carrie and Grace played outdoors.

The little auk would not eat. It did not utter a sound, but Carrie and Laura thought that it looked up at them desperately. It would die without food, but it did not seem to know how to eat anything that they offered it.

At dinnertime Pa said that the ice was melting on Silver Lake; he thought that the strange little bird could take care of itself on the open water. So after dinner Laura and Mary put on their coats and hoods and they went with Pa to set the little auk free.

Silver Lake was ruffling pale blue and silver under the warm, pale sky. Ice was around its edges and flat gray cakes of ice floated on the ripples. Pa took the little auk from his pocket. In its smooth black coat and neat white shirt-front of tiny feathers, it stood up on his palm. It saw the land and the sky and the water, and eagerly it rose up on its toes and stretched out its little wings.

But it could not go, it could not fly. Its wings were too small to lift it.

"It does not belong on land," said Pa. "It's a water-bird."

He squatted down by the thin white ice at the lake's edge and reaching far out he tipped the little bird from his hand into the blue water. For the briefest instant, there it was, and then it wasn't there. Out among the ice cakes it went streaking, a black speck.

"It gets up speed, with those webbed feet," said Pa, "to lift it from the . . . There it goes!"

Laura barely had time to see it, rising tiny in the great blue-sparkling sky. Then, in all that glittering of sunlight, it was gone. Her eyes were too dazzled to see it any more. But Pa stood looking, still seeing it going toward the South.

They never knew what became of that strange little bird that came in the dark with the storm from the far North and went southward in the sunshine. They never saw nor heard of another bird like it. They never found out what kind of bird it was.

Pa still stood looking far away across the land. All the prairie curves were softly colored, pale browns and tan and fawn-gray and very faint greens and purples, and far away they were gray-blue. The sunshine was warm and the air hazy. Only a little cold was around Laura's feet, near the thin, dry ice at the lake's edge.

Everything was still. No wind stirred the gray-bleached grass and no birds were on the water or in the sky. The lake faintly lapped at the rim of that stillness.

Laura looked at Pa and she knew he was listening too. The silence was as terrible as cold is. It was stronger than any sound. It could stop the water's lapping and the thin, faint ringing in Laura's ears. The silence was no sound, no movement, no thing; that was its terror. Laura's heart jumped and jumped, trying to get away from it.

"I don't like it," Pa said, slowly shaking his head. "I don't like the feel of the weather. There's something . . ." He could not say what he meant and he said again, "I don't like it. I don't like it at all."

Nobody could say, exactly, that anything was wrong with that weather. It was beautiful Indian summer. Frosts came every night and sometimes a light freeze, but all the days were sunny. Every afternoon Laura and Mary took long walks in the warm sunshine, while Carrie played with Grace near the house.

"Get yourselves full of sunshine while you can," Ma said. "It will soon be winter and you'll have to stay indoors."

Out in the bright soft weather they were storing up sunshine and fresh air, in themselves, for the winter when they could not have any.

But often, while they were walking, Laura quickly looked at the north. She did not know why. Nothing was there. Sometimes in the warm sunshine she stood still and listened and she was uneasy. There was no reason why.

"It's going to be a hard winter," Pa said. "The hardest we ever saw."

"Why, Charles," Ma protested. "We're having fine weather

now. That one early storm is no reason why the whole winter will be bad."

"I've trapped muskrats a good many years," said Pa, "and I never saw them build their walls so thick."

"Muskrats!" said Ma.

"The wild things know, somehow," Pa said. "Every wild creature's got ready for a hard winter."

"Maybe they just made ready for that bad storm," Ma suggested.

But Pa was not persuaded. "I don't like the feel of things, myself," he said. "This weather seems to be holding back something that it might let loose any minute. If I were a wild animal, I'd hunt my hole and dig it plenty deep. If I were a wild goose, I'd spread my wings and get out of here."

Ma laughed at him. "You *are* a goose, Charles! I don't know when I've seen a more beautiful Indian summer."

CHAPTER 7

Indian Warning

ONE afternoon a little crowd of men gathered in Harthorn's store in town. The trains, which had been stopped by the blizzard, were running again, and men had come in to town from their claims to buy some groceries and hear the news.

Royal and Almanzo Wilder had come from their homesteads, Almanzo driving his own fine team of matched Morgans, the best team in all that country. Mr. Boast was there, standing in the middle of the little crowd and setting it laughing when he laughed. Pa had walked in with his gun on his arm, but he had not seen so much as a jackrabbit, and now he was waiting while Mr. Harthorn weighed the piece of salt pork that he had had to buy instead.

No one heard a footstep, but Pa felt that someone was behind him and he turned to see who it was. Then suddenly Mr. Boast stopped talking. All the others looked to see what Mr. Boast saw, and they stood up quickly from the cracker boxes and the plow. Almanzo slid down from the counter. Nobody said anything.

It was only an Indian, but somehow the sight of him kept them all quiet. He stood there and looked at them, at Pa, at Mr. Boast, at Royal Wilder and each of the other men, and finally at Almanzo.

He was a very old Indian. His brown face was carved in deep wrinkles and shriveled on the bones, but he stood tall and straight. His arms were folded under a gray blanket, holding it wrapped around him. His head was shaved to a scalp-lock and an eagle's feather stood up from it. His eyes were bright and sharp. Behind him the sun was shining on the dusty street and an Indian pony stood there waiting.

"Heap big snow come," this Indian said.

The blanket slid on his shoulder and one naked brown arm came out. It moved in a wide sweep, to north, to west, to east, and gathered them all together and swirled.

"Heap big snow, big wind," he said.

"How long?" Pa asked him.

"Many moons," the Indian said. He held up four fingers, then three fingers. Seven fingers, seven months; blizzards for seven months.

They all looked at him and did not say anything.

"You white men," he said. "I tell-um you."

He showed seven fingers again. "Big snow." Again, seven fingers. "Big snow." Again seven fingers. "*Heap* big snow, many moons."

Then he tapped his breast with his forefinger. "Old! Old! I have seen!" he said proudly.

He walked out of the store to his waiting pony and rode away toward the west.

"Well, I'll be jiggered," Mr. Boast said.

"What was that about seven big snows?" Almanzo asked. Pa told him. The Indian meant that every seventh winter was a hard winter and that at the end of three times seven years came the hardest winter of all. He had come to tell the white men that this coming winter was a twenty-first winter, that there would be seven months of blizzards.

"You suppose the old geezer knows what he's talking about?" Royal wanted to know. No one could answer that.

"Just on the chance," Royal said, "I say we move in to town for the winter. My feed store beats a claim shanty all hollow for wintering in. We can stay back there till spring. How'd it suit you, Manzo?"

"Suits me," said Almanzo.

"How do you feel about moving in to town, Boast?" Pa asked.

Mr. Boast slowly shook his head. "Don't see how we could. We've got too much stock, cattle and horses, and chickens. There's no place in town to keep them even if I could afford to pay rent. We're fixed pretty well for the winter on the claim. I guess Ellie and I better stay with it."

Everyone was sober. Pa paid for his groceries and set out, walking quickly toward home. Now and then he looked back at the northwest sky. It was clear and the sun was shining.

Ma was taking bread from the oven when Pa came in. Carrie

and Grace had run to meet him; then came in with him. Mary went on quietly sewing but Laura jumped up.

"Is anything wrong, Charles?" Ma asked, tipping the good-smelling loaves from the pan onto a clean white cloth. "You're home early."

"Nothing's wrong," Pa answered. "Here are your sugar and tea and a bit of salt pork. I didn't get a rabbit. Not a thing's wrong," he repeated, "but we're moving to town as quick as we can. I've got to haul in hay, first, for the stock. I can haul one load before dark if I hustle."

"Goodness, Charles!" Ma gasped, but Pa was on his way to the stable. Carrie and little Grace stared at Ma and at Laura and at Ma again. Laura looked at Ma and Ma looked helplessly at her.

"Your Pa never did such a thing before," Ma said.

"Nothing's wrong, Ma. Pa said so," Laura answered. "I must run help him with the hay."

Ma came out to the stable, too, and Pa talked to her while he slapped the harness on the horses.

"It's going to be a hard winter," Pa said. "If you must have the truth, I'm afraid of it. This house is nothing but a claim shanty. It doesn't keep out the cold, and look what happened to the tar-paper in the first blizzard. Our store building in town is boarded and papered, sided on the outside and ceiled on the inside. It's good and tight and warm, and the stable there is built warm too."

"But what's the need to hurry so?" Ma asked.

"I feel like hurrying," Pa said. "I'm like the muskrat, something tells me to get you and the girls inside thick walls. I've been feeling this way for some time, and now that Indian . . ."

He stopped.

"What Indian?" Ma asked him. She looked as if she were smelling the smell of an Indian whenever she said the word. Ma despised Indians. She was afraid of them, too.

"There's some good Indians," Pa always insisted. Now he added, "And they know some things that we don't. I'll tell you all about it at supper, Caroline."

They could not talk while Pa pitched hay from the stack and Laura trampled it down in the rack. The hay rose higher under her fast-moving legs until the load was tall above the horses' backs.

"I'll handle it by myself in town," Pa said. "Town's no place for a girl to be doing a boy's work."

So Laura slid down from the high top of the load into what was left of the haystack, and Pa drove away. The Indian summer afternoon was warm and sweet-smelling and still. The low ripples of softly-colored land stretched far away and the sky was gentle over them. But under the softness and gentleness there was something waiting. Laura knew what Pa meant.

"'Oh, that I had the wings of a bird!'" Laura thought of those words in the Bible. If she had had the wings of a bird, she, too, would have spread them and flown, fast, fast, and far away.

She went soberly to the house to help Ma. None of them had wings; they were only moving to town for the winter. Ma and Mary did not mind, but Laura knew she would not like to live among so many people.

CHAPTER 8

Settled in Town

PA'S store building was one of the best in town. It stood by itself on the east side of Main Street. Its false front was tall and square-cornered, with one upstairs window in it. Downstairs there were two windows with the front door between them.

Pa did not stop the loaded wagon there. He turned the corner to Second Street, that was only a road, and drove in behind the store to its lean-to door. There was a good wooden stable with one haystack already beside it, and beyond them, on Second Street, Laura saw a house newly built of fresh boards. Pa's stable and store building had already weathered gray, like the other stores on Main Street.

"Well, here we are!" said Pa. "It won't take us long to get settled in."

He untied Ellen, the cow, and her big calf from behind the wagon, and Laura led them to their stalls in the stable, while Pa unloaded the wagon. Then he drove it on to the stable and began to unhitch the horses.

The lean-to's inside door opened under the stairs that went up from the back room. The narrow, back room would be the kitchen, of course, and it had a window, in its other end, looking out across the road that was Second Street and on across vacant lots to the side of a little vacant store. Farther over the prairie to the northeast, Laura could see the two-story depot.

Ma stood in the bare front room, looking at it and thinking where to put all their things.

In the big, empty room stood a coal heater and a shiny boughten desk and boughten chair.

"Why, where did that desk and chair come from?" Laura exclaimed.

"They're Pa's," said Ma. "Judge Carroll's new partner has a desk so Judge Carroll let Pa have his old desk and chair and the coal heater for part of the rent."

The desk had drawers and a top with pigeonholes under a

marvelous flexible cover made of narrow slats of wood that could be pulled, curving down, or pushed up again. When it was pushed up it disappeared.

"We'll put the rocking chairs by the other window," Ma went on. "Then Mary'll have the sunshine all afternoon and I can see to read to us until sundown. We'll do that first thing, Mary, so you can settle down and keep Grace out of our way."

Ma and Laura set the rocking chairs by the window. Then they edged the table through the doorways and put it between the coal heater and the door to the kitchen. "That will be the warm place to eat," said Ma.

"Can we put up the curtains now?" Laura asked. The two windows were like strange eyes looking in. Strangers went by in the street, and across the street stood the staring store buildings. Fuller's Hardware was there, with the drugstore beside it, and Power's Tailor Shop, and Loftus' Groceries, Dry Goods and General Merchandise.

"Yes, the sooner the better," said Ma. She unpacked the muslin curtains and she and Laura put them up. A wagon went by while they did it and suddenly five or six boys came down Second Street and after a moment as many girls.

"School's out for the day," said Ma. "You and Carrie'll be going to school tomorrow." Her voice was glad.

Laura did not say anything. No one knew how she dreaded meeting strangers. No one knew of the fluttering in her breast and the gone feeling in her stomach when she had to meet them. She didn't like town; she didn't want to go to school.

It was so unfair that *she* had to go! Mary wanted to be a schoolteacher, but she couldn't be because she was blind. Laura didn't want to teach, but she must do it to please Ma. Probably all her life she must go among strange people and teach strange children; she would always be scared and she must never show it.

No! Pa had said she must never be afraid and she would not be. She would be brave if it killed her. But even if she could get over being afraid, she could not like strange people. She knew how animals would act, she understood what animals thought, but you could never be sure about people.

Anyway, the curtains at the windows kept strangers from looking in. Carrie had set the plain chairs around the table.

The floor was bright, clean pine boards, and the large room looked very pleasant when Laura and Ma had laid a braided-rag rug before each door.

Pa was setting up the cookstove in the kitchen. When he had put the stovepipe together, straight and solid, he brought in the dry-goods-box cupboard and set it against the wall on the other side of the doorway.

"There!" he said. "The stove and the cupboard'll both be handy to the table in the other room."

"Yes, Charles, that's well thought out," Ma praised him. "Now, when we get the beds upstairs, we'll soon be through."

Pa handed up the pieces of the bedsteads while Ma and Laura drew them through the trap-door at the top of the stairs. He crowded the fat featherbeds through, and the blankets, quilts, and pillows, and then he and Carrie went to fill the strawticks from the haystack. They must fill the strawticks with hay, because there was no straw in this new country where no grain had yet been raised.

Under the attic roof, a building-paper partition made two rooms. One had a window to the west and one to the east. From the eastern window at the top of the stairs, Ma and Laura could see the far sky line and the prairie, the new house and the stable, and Pa and Carrie busily stuffing hay into the strawticks.

"Pa and I will have this room at the head of the stairs," Ma decided. "You girls can have the front one."

They set up the bedsteads and laid in the slats. Then Pa pushed the fat, crackling strawticks up to them and Laura and Carrie made the beds while Ma went down to get supper.

The sunset was shining on the western window and flooding the whole room with golden light while they leveled the sweet-smelling, crackling hay in the strawticks and laid the featherbeds on top and stroked them softly smooth. Then, one on each side of a bed, they spread the sheets and the blankets and quilts, drawing them even and folding and tucking them in square at the corners. Then each plumped up a pillow and set it in place and the bed was made.

When the three beds were done, there was nothing more to do.

Laura and Carrie stood in the warm-colored, chilly sunset

light, looking out of the window. Pa and Ma were talking in the kitchen downstairs and two strange men were talking in the street. Farther away, but not very far, someone was whistling a tune and there were many little sounds besides that, all together, made the sound of a town.

Smoke was coming up from behind the store fronts. Past Fuller's Hardware, Second Street went west on the prairie to a lonely building standing in the dead grasses. It had four windows and the sunset was shining through them, so there must be even more windows on the other side. It had a boarded-in entry, like a nose, in its front-gable end and a stovepipe that was not smoking. Laura said, "I guess that's the schoolhouse."

"I wish we didn't have to go," Carrie almost whispered.

"Well, we do have to," said Laura.

Carrie looked at her wonderingly. "Aren't you . . . scared?"

"There's nothing to be *scared* of!" Laura answered boldly. "And if there was, we wouldn't be scared."

Downstairs was warm from the fire in the cookstove, and Ma was saying that this place was so well-built that it took hardly any fire to heat it. She was getting supper, and Mary was setting the table.

"I don't need any help," Mary said happily. "The cupboard is in a different place, but Ma put all the dishes in the same places in the cupboard, so I find them just as easily as ever."

The front room was spacious in the lamplight when Ma set the lamp on the supper-table. The creamy curtains, the varnished yellow desk and chair, the cushions in the rocking chairs, the rag rugs and the red tablecloth, and the pine color of the floor and walls and ceiling were gay. The floor and the walls were so solid that not the smallest cold draft came in.

"I wish we had a place like this out on the claim," Laura said.

"I'm glad we have it in town where you girls can go to school this winter," said Ma. "You couldn't walk in from the claim every day, if the weather was bad."

"It's a satisfaction to me to be where we're sure of getting coal and supplies," Pa declared. "Coal beats brushwood all hollow for giving steady heat. We'll keep enough coal in the lean-to to outlast any blizzard, and I can always get more from the lumberyard. Living in town, we're in no danger of running short of any kind of supplies."

"How many people are there in town now?" Ma asked him.

Pa counted up. "Fourteen business buildings and the depot; and then Sherwood's and Garland's and Owen's houses—that's eighteen families, not counting three or four shacks on the back streets. Then the Wilder boys are baching in the feed store, and there's a man named Foster moved in with his ox team and staying at Sherwood's. Count them all, there must be as many as seventy-five or eighty people living here in town."

"And to think there wasn't a soul here this time last fall," said Ma. Then she smiled at Pa. "I'm glad you see some good at last, Charles, in staying in a settled place."

Pa had to admit that he did. But he said, "On the other hand, all this costs money and that's scarcer than hen's teeth. The railroad's the only place a man can get a dollar for a day's work and it's not hiring anybody. And the only hunting left around here is jackrabbits. Oregon's the place to be nowadays. The country out there'll be settled up, too, pretty soon."

"Yes, but now is the time for the girls to be getting some schooling," Ma said firmly.

CHAPTER 9

Cap Garland

LAURA did not sleep very well. All night, it seemed, she knew that the town was close around her and that she must go to school in the morning. She was heavy with dread when she woke and heard steps going by in the street below and strange men speaking. The town was waking up too; the storekeepers were opening their stores.

The walls of the house kept strangers outside. But Laura and Carrie were heavyhearted because they must go out of the house and meet strangers. And Mary was sad because she could not go to school.

"Now Laura and Carrie, there's no cause to worry," Ma said. "I'm sure you can keep up with your classes."

They looked at Ma in surprise. She had taught them so well at home that they knew they could keep up with their classes. They were not worried about that. But they only said, "Yes, Ma."

They hurried to wash the dishes and make their bed and hurriedly Laura swept their bedroom floor. Then they dressed carefully in their woolen winter dresses and nervously combed their hair and braided it. They tied on their Sunday hair-ribbons. With the steel buttonhook they buttoned their shoes.

"Hurry up, girls!" Ma called. "It's past eight o'clock."

At that moment, Carrie nervously jerked one of her shoe-buttons off. It fell and rolled and vanished down a crack of the floor.

"Oh, it's gone!" Carrie gasped. She was desperate. She could not go where strangers would see that gap in the row of black buttons that buttoned up her shoe.

"We must take a button off one of Mary's shoes," Laura said.

But Ma had heard the button fall, downstairs. She found it and sewed it on again, and buttoned the shoe for Carrie.

At last they were ready. "You look very nice," Ma said, smiling. They put on their coats and hoods and took their schoolbooks. They said good-by to Ma and Mary and they went out into Main Street.

The stores were all open. Mr. Fuller and Mr. Bradley had finished sweeping out; they stood holding their brooms and looking at the morning. Carrie took hold of Laura's hand. It helped Laura, to know that Carrie was even more scared than she was.

Bravely they crossed wide Main Street and walked steadily on along Second Street. The sun was shining brightly. A tangle of dead weeds and grasses made shadows beside the wheel-tracks. Their own long shadows went before them, over many footprints in the paths. It seemed a long, long way to the schoolhouse that stood on the open prairie with no other buildings near.

In front of the schoolhouse strange boys were playing ball, and two strange girls stood on the platform before the entry door.

Laura and Carrie came nearer and nearer. Laura's throat was so choked that she could hardly breathe. One of the strange girls was tall and dark. Her smooth, black hair was twisted into a heavy knot at the back of her head. Her dress of indigo blue woolen was longer than Laura's brown one.

Then suddenly Laura saw one of the boys spring into the air and catch the ball. He was tall and quick and he moved as beautifully as a cat. His yellow hair was sun-bleached almost white and his eyes were blue. They saw Laura and opened wide. Then a flashing grin lighted up his whole face and he threw the ball to her.

She saw the ball curving down through the air, coming swiftly. Before she could think, she had made a running leap and caught it.

A great shout went up from the other boys. "Hey, Cap!" they shouted. "Girls don't play ball!"

"I didn't think she'd catch it," Cap answered.

"I don't want to play," Laura said. She threw back the ball.

"She's as good as any of us!" Cap shouted. "Come on and play," he said to Laura, and then to the other girls, "Come on, Mary Power and Minnie! You play with us, too!"

But Laura picked up the books she had dropped and took

Carrie's hand again. They went on to the other girls at the schoolhouse door. Those girls would not play with boys, of course. She did not know why she had done such a thing and she was ashamed, fearful of what these girls must be thinking of her.

"I'm Mary Power," the dark girl said, "and this is Minnie Johnson." Minnie Johnson was thin and fair and pale, with freckles.

"I'm Laura Ingalls," Laura said, "and this is my little sister, Carrie."

Mary Power's eyes smiled. They were dark blue eyes, fringed with long, black lashes. Laura smiled back and she made up her mind that she would twist up her own hair tomorrow and ask Ma to make her next dress as long as Mary's.

"That was Cap Garland that threw you the ball," Mary Power said.

There was no time to say anything more, for the teacher came to the door with the hand-bell, and they all went in to school.

They hung their coats and hoods on a row of nails in the entry, where the broom stood in a corner by the water-pail on its bench. Then they went into the schoolroom.

It was so new and shining that Laura felt timid again, and Carrie stood close to her. All the desks were patent desks, made of wood varnished as smooth as glass. They had black iron feet and the seats were curved a little, with curving backs that were part of the desks behind them. The desk-tops had grooves to hold pencils and shelves underneath them for slates and books.

There were twelve of these desks in a row up each side of the big room. A large heating stove stood in the middle of the room, with four more desks in front of it and four more behind it. Almost all those seats were empty. On the girls' side of the room, Mary Power and Minnie Johnson sat together in one of the back seats. Cap Garland and three other big boys sat in back seats on the boys' side—a few little boys and girls sat in front seats. They had all been coming to school, for a week now, and knew where to sit, but Laura and Carrie did not.

The teacher said to them, "You're new, aren't you?" She was a smiling young lady, with curled bangs. The bodice of her black dress was buttoned down the front with twinkling jet buttons. Laura told her their names and she said, "And I'm Florence Garland. We live back of your father's place, on the next street."

So Cap Garland was Teacher's brother and they lived in the new house out on the prairie beyond the stable.

"Do you know the Fourth Reader?" Teacher asked.

"Oh, yes, ma'am!" Laura said. She did indeed know every word of it.

"Then I think we'll see what you can do with the Fifth," Teacher decided. And she told Laura to take the back seat in the middle row, across the aisle from Mary Power. Carrie she put in front, near the little girls, and then she went up to her desk and rapped on it with her ruler.

"The school will come to attention," she said. She opened her Bible. "This morning I will read the twenty-third Psalm."

Laura knew the Psalms by heart, of course, but she loved to hear again every word of the twenty-third, from " 'The Lord is my shepherd: I shall not want,' " to, " 'Surely goodness and mercy shall follow me all the days of my life: and I will dwell in the house of the Lord forever.' "

Then Teacher closed the Bible and on all the desks the pupils opened their textbooks. School work had begun.

Every day Laura liked the school more. She had no seatmate, but at recess and noontimes she was with Mary Power and Minnie Johnson. After school they walked to Main Street together, and by the end of that week they were meeting in the mornings and walking together to school. Twice Cap Garland urged them to play ball with the boys at recess, but they stayed inside the schoolhouse and watched the game through the window.

The brown-eyed, dark-haired boy was Ben Woodworth who lived at the depot. His father was the sick man that Pa had sent out with the last teamster the year before. The "prairie cure" had truly almost cured his consumption of the lungs and he had come West again for more for it. He was the depot agent now.

The other boy was Arthur Johnson. He was thin and fair like his sister Minnie. Cap Garland was strongest and quickest. Inside the window, Laura and Mary and Minnie all watched him throwing the ball and leaping to catch it. He was not as handsome as black-haired Ben, but there was something about him. He was always good-natured and his grin was like a flash of light. It was like the sun coming up at dawn; it changed everything.

Mary Power and Minnie had gone to schools in the East, but Laura found it easy to keep up with them in their lessons. Cap Garland was from the East, too, but even in arithmetic he could not beat Laura.

Every night after supper she put her books and her slate on the red-checkered tablecloth in the lamplight, and she studied next day's lessons with Mary. She read the arithmetic problems aloud, and Mary did them in her head while she worked them on the slate. She read the history lesson and the geography to Mary until both of them could answer every question. If ever Pa could get money enough to send Mary to the college for the blind, Mary must be ready to go.

"And even if I never can go to college," Mary said, "I am learning as much as I can."

Mary and Laura and Carrie were all enjoying school so much that they were sorry when Saturday and Sunday interrupted it. They looked forward to Monday. But when Monday came Laura was cross because her red flannel underwear was so hot and scratchy.

It made her back itch, and her neck, and her wrists, and where it was folded around her ankles, under her stockings and shoetops, that red flannel almost drove her crazy.

At noon she begged Ma to let her change to cooler underthings. "It's too hot for my red flannels, Ma!" she protested.

"I know the weather's turned warm," Ma answered gently. "But this is the time of year to wear flannels, and you would catch cold if you took them off."

Laura went crossly back to school and sat squirming because she must not scratch. She held the flat geography open before her, but she wasn't studying. She was trying to bear the itching flannels and wanting to get home where she could scratch. The sunshine from the western windows had never crawled so slowly.

Suddenly there was no sunshine. It went out, as if someone had blown out the sun like a lamp. The outdoors was gray, the windowpanes were gray, and at the same moment a wind crashed against the schoolhouse, rattling windows and doors and shaking the walls.

Miss Garland started up from her chair. One of the little Beardsley girls screamed and Carrie turned white.

Laura thought, "It happened this way on Plum Creek, the Christmas when Pa was lost." Her whole heart hoped and prayed that Pa was safe at home now.

Teacher and all the others were staring at the windows, where nothing but grayness could be seen. They all looked frightened. Then Miss Garland said, "It is only a storm, children. Go on with your lessons."

The blizzard was scouring against the walls, and the winds squealed and moaned in the stovepipe.

All the heads bent over the books as Teacher had told them to do. But Laura was trying to think how to get home. The schoolhouse was a long way from Main Street, and there was nothing to guide them.

All the others had come from the East that summer. They had never seen a prairie blizzard. But Laura and Carrie knew what it was. Carrie's head was bowed limply above her book, and the back of it, with the white parting between the braids of fine, soft hair, looked small and helpless and frightened.

There was only a little fuel at the schoolhouse. The school board was buying coal, but only one load had been delivered. Laura thought they might outlive the storm in the schoolhouse, but they could not do it without burning all the costly patent desks.

Without lifting her head Laura looked up at Teacher. Miss Garland was thinking and biting her lip. She could not decide to dismiss school because of a storm, but this storm frightened her.

"I ought to tell her what to do," Laura thought. But she could not think what to do. It was not safe to leave the schoolhouse and it was not safe to stay there. Even the twelve patent desks might not last long enough to keep them warm until the blizzard ended. She thought of her wraps and Carrie's, in the entry. Whatever happened she must somehow keep Carrie warm. Already the cold was coming in.

There was a loud thumping in the entry. Every pupil started and looked at the door.

It opened and a man stumbled in. He was bundled in overcoat, cap, and muffler, all solid white with snow driven into the woolen cloth. They could not see who he was until he pulled down the stiffened muffler.

"I came out to get you," he told Teacher.

He was Mr. Foster, the man who owned the ox team and had come in from his claim to stay in town for the winter at Sherwood's, across the street from Teacher's house.

Miss Garland thanked him. She rapped her ruler on the desk and said, "Attention! School is dismissed. You may bring your wraps from the entry and put them on by the stove."

Laura said to Carrie, "You stay here. I'll bring your wraps."

The entry was freezing cold; snow was blowing in between the rough boards of the walls. Laura was chilled before she could snatch her coat and hood from their nail. She found Carrie's and carried the armful into the schoolhouse.

Crowded around the stove, they all put on their wraps and fastened them snugly. Cap Garland did not smile. His blue eyes narrowed and his mouth set straight while Mr. Foster talked.

Laura wrapped the muffler snugly over Carrie's white face and took firm hold of her mittened hand. She told Carrie, "Don't worry, we'll be all right."

"Now, just follow me," said Mr. Foster, taking Teacher's arm. "And keep close together."

He opened the door, led the way with Miss Garland. Mary Power and Minnie each took one of the little Beardsley girls. Ben and Arthur followed them closely, then Laura went out with Carrie into blinding snow. Cap shut the door behind them.

They could hardly walk in the beating, whirling wind. The schoolhouse had disappeared. They could see nothing but swirling whiteness and snow and then a glimpse of each other, disappearing like shadows.

Laura felt that she was smothering. The icy particles of snow whirled scratching into her eyes and smothered her breathing. Her skirts whipped around her, now wrapped so tightly that she could not step, then whirled and lifted to her knees. Suddenly tightening, they made her stumble. She held tightly to Carrie, and Carrie, struggling and staggering, was pulled away by the wind and then flung back against her.

"We can't go on this way," Laura thought. But they had to.

She was alone in the confusion of whirling winds and snow except for Carrie's hand that she must never let go. The winds struck her this way and that. She could not see nor breathe, she stumbled and was falling, then suddenly she seemed to be lifted and Carrie bumped against her. She tried to think. The others must be somewhere ahead. She must walk faster and keep up with them or she and Carrie would be lost. If they were lost on the prairie they would freeze to death.

But perhaps they were all lost. Main Street was only two blocks long. If they were going only a little way to north or south they would miss the block of stores and beyond was empty prairie for miles.

Laura thought they must have gone far enough to reach Main Street, but she could see nothing.

The storm thinned a little. She saw shadowy figures ahead. They were darker gray in the whirling gray-whiteness. She went on as fast as she could, with Carrie, until she touched Miss Garland's coat.

They had all stopped. Huddled in their wraps, they stood like bundles close together in the swirling mist. Teacher and Mr. Foster were trying to talk, but the winds confused their shouts so that no one could hear what they said. Then Laura began to know how cold she was.

Her mittened hand was so numb that it hardly felt Carrie's hand. She was shaking all over and deep inside her there was a shaking that she could not stop. Only in her very middle there was a solid knot that ached, and her shaking pulled this knot tighter so that the ache grew worse.

She was frightened about Carrie. The cold hurt too much, Carrie could not stand it. Carrie was so little and thin, she had always been delicate, she could not stand such cold much longer. They must reach shelter soon.

Mr. Foster and Teacher were moving again, going a little to the left. All the others stirred and hurried to follow them. Laura took hold of Carrie with her other hand, that had been in her coat pocket and was not quite so numb, and then suddenly she saw a shadow go by them. She knew it was Cap Garland.

He was not following the others to the left. With hands in

his pockets and head bent, he went trudging straight ahead into the storm. A fury of winds thickened the air with snow and he vanished.

Laura did not dare follow him. She must take care of Carrie and Teacher had told them to follow her. She was sure that Cap was going toward Main Street, but perhaps she was mistaken and she could not take Carrie away from the others.

She kept tight hold of Carrie and hurried to follow Mr. Foster and Teacher as fast as she could. Her chest sobbed for air and her eyes strained open in the icy snow-particles that hurt them like sand. Carrie struggled bravely, stumbling and flopping, doing her best to stay on her feet and keep on going. Only for instants when the snow-whirl was thinner could they glimpse the shadows moving ahead of them.

Laura felt that they were going in the wrong direction. She did not know why she felt so. No one could see anything. There was nothing to go by—no sun, no sky, no direction in the winds blowing fiercely from all directions. There was nothing but the dizzy whirling and the cold.

It seemed that the cold and the winds, the noise of the winds and the blinding, smothering, scratching snow, and the effort and the aching, were forever. Pa had lived through three days of a blizzard under the bank of Plum Creek. But there were no creek banks here. Here there was nothing but bare prairie. Pa had told about sheep caught in a blizzard, huddled together under the snow. Some of them had lived. Perhaps people could do that, too. Carrie was too tired to go much farther, but she was too heavy for Laura to carry. They must go on as long as they could, and then . . .

Then, out of the whirling whiteness, something hit her. The hard blow crashed against her shoulder and all through her. She rocked on her feet and stumbled against something solid. It was high, it was hard, it was the corner of two walls. Her hands felt it, her eyes saw it. She had walked against some building.

With all her might she yelled, "Here! Come here! Here's a house!"

All around the house the winds were howling so that at first no one heard her. She pulled the icy stiff muffler from her mouth and screamed into the blinding storm. At last she saw a shadow in it, two tall shadows thinner than the shadowy wall she clung to—Mr. Foster and Teacher. Then other shadows pressed close around her.

No one tried to say anything. They crowded together and they were all there—Mary Power and Minnie, each with a little Beardsley girl, and Arthur Johnson and Ben Woodworth with the small Wilmarth boys. Only Cap Garland was missing.

They followed along the side of that building till they came to the front of it, and it was Mead's Hotel, at the very north end of Main Street.

Beyond it was nothing but the railroad track covered with snow, the lonely depot and the wide, open prairie. If Laura had been only a few steps nearer the others, they would all have been lost on the endless prairie north of town.

For a moment they stood by the hotel's lamplit windows. Warmth and rest were inside the hotel, but the blizzard was growing worse and they must all reach home.

Main Street would guide all of them except Ben Woodworth. No other buildings stood between the hotel and the depot where he lived. So Ben went into the hotel to stay till the blizzard was over. He could afford to do that because his father had a regular job.

Minnie and Arthur Johnson, taking the little Wilmarth boys, had only to cross Main Street to Wilmarth's grocery store and their home was beside it. The others went on down Main Street, keeping close to the buildings. They passed the saloon, they passed Royal Wilder's feed store, and then they passed Barker's grocery. The Beardsley Hotel was next and there the little Beardsley girls went in.

The journey was almost ended now. They passed Couse's Hardware store and they crossed Second Street to Fuller's Hardware. Mary Power had only to pass the drugstore now. Her father's tailor shop stood next to it.

Laura and Carrie and Teacher and Mr. Foster had to cross Main Street now. It was a wide street. But if they missed Pa's house, the haystacks and the stable were still between them and the open prairie.

They did not miss the house. One of its lighted windows made a glow that Mr. Foster saw before he ran into it. He went on around the house corner with Teacher to go by the clothesline, the haystacks, and the stable to the Garland house.

Laura and Carrie were safe at their own front door. Laura's hands fumbled at the doorknob, too stiff to turn it. Pa opened the door and helped them in.

He was wearing overcoat and cap and muffler. He had set down the lighted lantern and dropped a coil of rope. "I was just starting out after you," he said.

In the still house Laura and Carrie stood taking deep breaths. It was so quiet there where the winds did not push and pull at them. They were still blinded, but the whirling icy snow had stopped hurting their eyes.

Laura felt Ma's hands breaking away the icy muffler, and she said, "Is Carrie all right?"

"Yes, Carrie's all right," said Pa.

Ma took off Laura's hood and unbuttoned her coat and helped her pull out of its sleeves. "These wraps are driven full of ice," Ma said. They crackled when she shook them and little drifts of whiteness sifted to the floor.

"Well," Ma said, " 'All's well that ends well.' You're not frost-bitten. You can go to the fire and get warm."

Laura could hardly move but she stooped and with her fingers dug out the caked snow that the wind had driven in between her woolen stockings and the tops of her shoes. Then she staggered toward the stove.

"Take my place," Mary said, getting up from her rocking chair. "It's the warmest."

Laura sat stiffly down. She felt numb and stupid. She rubbed her eyes and saw a pink smear on her hand. Her eyelids were bleeding where the snow had scratched them. The sides of the coal heater glowed red-hot and she could feel the heat on her skin, but she was cold inside. The heat from the fire couldn't reach that cold.

Pa sat close to the stove holding Carrie on his knee. He had taken off her shoes to make sure that her feet were not frozen and he held her wrapped in a shawl. The shawl shivered with Carrie's shivering. "I can't get warm, Pa," she said.

"You girls are chilled through. I'll have you a hot drink in a minute," said Ma, hurrying into the kitchen.

She brought them each a steaming cup of ginger tea.

"My, that smells good!" said Mary and Grace leaned on Laura's knee looking longingly at the cup till Laura gave her a sip and

Pa said, "I don't know why there's not enough of that to go around."

"Maybe there is," said Ma, going into the kitchen again.

It was so wonderful to be there, safe at home, sheltered from the winds and the cold. Laura thought that this must be a little bit like Heaven, where the weary are at rest. She could not imagine that Heaven was better than being where she was, slowly growing warm and comfortable, sipping the hot, sweet, ginger tea, seeing Ma, and Grace, and Pa and Carrie, and Mary all enjoying their own cups of it and hearing the storm that could not touch them here.

"I'm glad you didn't have to come for us, Pa," Laura said drowsily. "I was hoping you were safe."

"So was I," Carrie told Pa, snuggling against him. "I remembered that Christmas, on Plum Creek, when you didn't get home."

"I did, too," Pa said grimly. "When Cap Garland came into Fuller's and said you were all heading out to the open prairie, you can bet I made tracks for a rope and lantern."

"I'm glad we got in all right," Laura woke up to say.

"Yes, we'd have had a posse out looking for you, though we'd have been hunting for a needle in a haystack," said Pa.

"Best forget about it," said Ma.

"Well, he did the best he could," Pa went on. "Cap Garland's a smart boy."

"And now, Laura and Carrie, you're going to bed and get some rest," said Ma. "A good long sleep is what you need."

CHAPTER 10

Three Days' Blizzard

WHEN Laura's eyes opened in the morning she saw that every clinched nail in the roof overhead was furry-white with frost. Thick frost covered every windowpane to its very top. The daylight was still and dim inside the stout walls that kept out the howling blizzard.

Carrie was awake too. She peeked anxiously at Laura from under the quilts on the bed by the stovepipe where she and Grace slept. She blew out a breath to see how cold it was. Even close to the stovepipe her breath froze white in the air. But that house was so well-built that not one bit of snow had been driven through the walls or the roof.

Laura was stiff and sore and so was Carrie. But morning had come and they must get up. Sliding out of bed into the cold that took her breath away, Laura snatched up her dress and shoes and hurried to the top of the stairs. "Ma, can we dress down there?" she called, thankful for the warm, long red flannels under her flannel nightgown.

"Yes, Pa's at the stable," Ma answered.

The cookstove was warming the kitchen and the lamplight made it seem even warmer. Laura put on her petticoats and dress and shoes. Then she brought down her sisters' clothes and warmed them and carried Grace downstairs wrapped in quilts. They were all dressed and washed when Pa came in with the milk half frozen in the pail.

After he had got his breath and melted the frost and snow from his mustaches, he said, "Well, the hard winter's begun."

"Why, Charles," Ma said. "It isn't like you to worry about winter weather."

"I'm not worrying," Pa replied. "But it's going to be a hard winter."

"Well, if it is," said Ma, "here we are in town where we can get what we need from the stores even in a storm."

There would be no more school till the blizzard was over. So, after the housework was done, Laura and Carrie and Mary studied their lessons and then settled down to sew while Ma read to them.

Once she looked up and listened and said, "It sounds like a regular three days' blizzard."

"Then there won't be any more school this week," said Laura. She wondered what Mary and Minnie were doing. The front room was so warm that the frost on the windows had melted a little and turned to ice. When she breathed on it to clear a peephole she could see against the glass the blank white swirling snow. She could not even see Fuller's Hardware store, across the street, where Pa had gone to sit by the stove and talk with the other men.

Up the street, past Couse's Hardware store and the Beardsley Hotel and Barker's grocery, Royal Wilder's feed store was dark and cold. No one would come to buy feed in that storm, so Royal did not keep up the fire in the heater. But the back room, where he and Almanzo were baching, was warm and cosy and Almanzo was frying pancakes.

Royal had to agree that not even Mother could beat Almanzo at making pancakes. Back in York state when they were boys and later on Father's big farm in Minnesota they had never thought of cooking; that was woman's work. But since they had come West to take up homestead claims they had to cook or starve; and Almanzo had to do the cooking because he was handy at almost anything and also because he was younger than Royal who still thought that he was the boss.

When he came West, Almanzo was nineteen years old. But that was a secret because he had taken a homestead claim, and according to law a man must be twenty-one years old to do that. Almanzo did not consider that he was breaking the law and he knew he was not cheating the government. Still, anyone who knew that he was nineteen years old could take his claim away from him.

Almanzo looked at it this way: the Government wanted this land settled; Uncle Sam would give a farm to any man who had the nerve and muscle to come out here and break the sod and stick to the job till it was done. But the politicians far away in Washington could not know the settlers so they must make rules to regulate them and one rule was that a homesteader must be twenty-one years old.

None of the rules worked as they were intended to. Almanzo knew that men were making good wages by filing claims that fitted all the legal rules and then handing over the land to the rich men who paid their wages. Everywhere, men were stealing the land and doing it according to all the rules. But of all the homestead laws Almanzo thought that the most foolish was the law about a settler's age.

Anybody knew that no two men were alike. You could measure cloth with a yardstick, or distance by miles, but you could not lump men together and measure them by any rule. Brains and character did not depend on anything but the man himself. Some men did not have the sense at sixty that some had at sixteen. And Almanzo considered that he was as good, any day, as any man twenty-one years old.

Almanzo's father thought so too. A man had the right to keep his sons at work for him until they were twenty-one years old. But Almanzo's father had put his boys to work early and trained them well. Almanzo had learned to save money before he was ten and he had been doing a man's work on the farm since he was nine. When he was seventeen, his father had judged that he was a man and had given him his own free time. Almanzo had worked for fifty cents a day and saved money to buy seed and tools. He had raised wheat on shares in western Minnesota and made a good crop.

He considered that he was as good a settler as the government could want and that his age had nothing to do with it. So he had said to the land agent, "You can put me down as twenty-one," and the agent had winked at him and done it. Almanzo had his own homestead claim now and the seed wheat for next year that he had brought from Minnesota, and if he could stick it out on these prairies and raise crops for four years more he would have his own farm.

He was making pancakes, not because Royal could boss him any more but because Royal could not make good pancakes and Almanzo loved light, fluffy, buckwheat pancakes with plenty of molasses.

"Whew! listen to that!" Royal said. They had never heard anything like that blizzard.

"That old Indian knew what he was talking about," said Almanzo. "If we're in for seven months of this . . ." The three pancakes on the griddle were holding their bubbles in tiny holes near their crisping edges. He flipped them over neatly and watched their brown-patterned sides rise in the middle.

The good smell of them mixed with the good smells of fried salt pork and boiling coffee. The room was warm and the lamp with its tin reflector, hung on a nail, lighted it strongly. Saddles and bits of harness hung on the rough board walls. The bed was in one corner, and the table was drawn up to the stove hearth so that Almanzo could put the pancakes on the white ironstone plates without moving one step.

"This can't last seven months. That's ridiculous," said Royal. "We're bound to have some spells of good weather."

Almanzo replied airily, "Anything can happen and most usually does." He slid his knife under the edges of the pancakes. They were done and he flipped them onto Royal's plate and greased the griddle again with the pork rind.

Royal poured molasses over the cakes. "One thing can't happen," he said. "We can't stick it out here till spring unless they keep the trains running."

Almanzo poured three more rounds of batter from the batter pitcher onto the sizzling griddle. He lounged against the warm partition, by the stovepipe, waiting for the cakes to rise.

"We figured on hauling in more hay," he said. "We've got plenty of dry feed for the team."

"Oh, they'll get the trains through," Royal said, eating. "But if they didn't we'd be up against it. How about coal and kerosene and flour and sugar? For that matter, how long would my stock of feed last, if the whole town came piling in here to buy it?"

Almanzo straightened up. "Say!" he exclaimed. "Nobody's going to get my seed wheat! No matter what happens."

"Nothing's going to happen," Royal said. "Whoever heard of storms lasting seven months? They'll get the trains running again."

"They better," said Almanzo, turning the pancakes. He thought of the old Indian, and he looked at his sacks of seed wheat. They were stacked along the end of the room and some were under the bed. The seed wheat did not belong to Royal; it belonged to him. He had raised it in Minnesota. He had plowed and harrowed the ground and sowed the grain. He had cut it and bound it, threshed and sacked it, and hauled it a hundred miles in his wagon.

If storms like this storm delayed the trains so that no more seed came from the East until after sowing time, his crop for next year, his homestead would depend on his having that seed wheat to sow. He would not sell it for any money. It was seed that made crops. You could not sow silver dollars.

"I'm not going to sell so much as a peck of my seed wheat," he said.

"All right, all right, nobody's bothering your wheat," Royal answered. "How about some pancakes?"

"This makes twenty-one," Almanzo said, putting them on Royal's plate.

"How many did you eat while I was doing the chores?" Royal asked him.

"I didn't count 'em," Almanzo grinned. "But gosh, I'm working up an appetite, feeding you."

"So long as we keep on eating, we don't have to wash the dishes," said Royal.

CHAPTER II

Pa Goes to Volga

AT NOON on Tuesday the blizzard ended. Then the wind died down and in the clear sky the sun shone brightly.

"Well, that's over," Pa said cheerfully. "Now maybe we'll have a spell of good weather."

Ma sighed comfortably. "It's good to see the sun again."

"And to hear the stillness," Mary added.

They could hear again the small sounds of the town. Now and then a store door slammed. Ben and Arthur went by, talking, and Cap Garland came whistling down Second Street. The only usual sound that they did not hear was the train's whistle.

At supper Pa said that the train was stopped by the snow-filled big cut near Tracy. "But they'll shovel through it in a couple of days," he said. "In weather like this, who cares about trains?"

Early next morning he went across the street to Fuller's store, hurrying back. He told Ma that some of the men were going to take the handcar from the depot and go meet the train at Volga, clearing the track as they went. Mr. Foster had agreed to do Pa's chores if Pa went along.

"I have been in one place so long, I would like to travel a little," Pa said.

"Go along, Charles, you might as well," Ma agreed. "But can you clear the track so far in one day?"

"We think so," said Pa. "The cuts are small from here to Volga and it's only about fifty miles. The worst stretch is east of Volga and the train crews are working at that. If we clear the rest of the way for them, we ought to come back with the regular train day after tomorrow."

He was putting on an extra pair of woolen socks while he talked. He wound the wide muffler around his neck, crossed it on his chest, and buttoned his overcoat snugly over it. He fastened his ear muffs, put on his warmest mittens, and then with his shovel on his shoulder he went to the depot.

It was almost schooltime but, instead of hurrying to school,

Laura and Carrie stood in Second Street watching Pa set out on his trip.

The handcar was standing on the track by the depot and men were climbing onto it as Pa came up.

"All ready, Ingalls! All aboard!" they called. The north wind blowing over the dazzling snow brought every word to Laura and Carrie.

Pa was on the car in a moment. "Let's go, boys!" he gave the word as he gripped a handbar.

Mr. Fuller and Mr. Mead and Mr. Hinz took their places in a row, facing Pa and Mr. Wilmarth and Royal Wilder. All their mittened hands were on the two long wooden handlebars that crossed the handcar, with the pump between them.

"All ready, boys! Let 'er go gallagher!" Mr. Fuller sang out and he and Mr. Mead and Mr. Hinz bent low, pushing down their handlebar. Then as their heads and their handlebar came up, Pa and the other two bent down, pushing their handlebar. Down and up, down and up, the rows of men bent and straightened as if they were bowing low to each other in turn, and the handcar's wheels began slowly to turn and then to roll rapidly along the track toward Volga. And as they pumped, Pa began to sing and all the others joined in.

"We'll *ROLL* the O-old *CHAR*iot a*LONG*,
We'll *ROLL* the O-old *CHAR*iot a*LONG*,
We'll *ROLL* the O-old *CHAR*iot a*LONG*.
And we *WON'T* drag *ON* be*HIND!*"

Up and down, up and down, all the backs moved evenly with the song and smoothly rolled the wheels, faster and faster.

"If the sinner's in the way,
We will stop and take him in,
And we *WON'T* drag *ON* be*HIND!*

We'll *ROLL* the O-old *CHAR*iot a*LONG*,
We'll *ROLL* the O-old *CHAR*——"

Bump! and the handcar was stuck fast in a snowbank.

"All off!" Mr. Fuller sang out. "Not this time, we don't roll it over!"

Picking up their shovels, all the men stepped down from the handcar. Bright snow dust flew in the wind from chunks of snow flung away by their busy shovels.

"We ought to be getting to school," Laura said to Carrie.

"Oh please, let's wait just a minute more and see . . ." Carrie said, gazing with squinting eyes across the glittering snow at Pa hard at work in front of the handcar.

In a moment or two all the men stepped onto it again, laying down their shovels and bending to the handlebars.

"If the Devil's in the way,
We will roll it over him,
And we *WON'T* drag *ON* be*HIND!*"

Smaller and smaller grew the dark handcar and the two rows of men bowing in turn to each other, and fainter and fainter the song came back over the glittering snow fields.

"We'll roll—the o-old—chariot along,
We'll roll—the o-old—chariot along,
We'll roll—the o-old—chariot along,
And we won't drag on behind. . . ."

Singing and pumping, rolling the car along, shoveling its way through snowbanks and cuts, Pa went away to Volga.

All the rest of the day and all the next day there was an emptiness in the house. Morning and evening Mr. Foster did the chores and, after he had left the stable, Ma sent Laura to make sure that he had done them properly. "Surely Pa will be home tomorrow," Ma said on Thursday night.

At noon the next day the long, clear train whistle sounded over the snow-covered prairie, and from the kitchen window Laura and Carrie saw the black smoke billowing on the sky and the roaring train coming beneath it. It was the work-train, crowded with singing, cheering men.

"Help me get the dinner on, Laura," Ma said. "Pa will be hungry."

Laura was taking up the biscuits when the front door opened and Pa called, "Look, Caroline! See who's come home with me?"

Grace stopped her headlong rush toward Pa and backed, staring, her fingers in her mouth. Ma put her gently aside as she stepped to the doorway with the dish of mashed potatoes in her hand.

"Why, Mr. Edwards!" Ma said.

"I told you we'd see him again, after he saved our homestead for us," said Pa.

Ma set the potatoes on the table. "I have wanted so much to thank you for helping Mr. Ingalls file on his claim," she said to Mr. Edwards.

Laura would have known him anywhere. He was the same tall, lean, lounging wildcat from Tennessee. The laughing lines in his leather-brown face were deeper, a knife scar was on his cheek that had not been there before, but his eyes were as laughing and lazy and keen as she remembered them. "Oh, Mr. Edwards!" she cried out.

"You brought our presents from Santa Claus," Mary remembered.

"You swam the creek," Laura said. "And you went away down the Verdigris river . . ."

Mr. Edwards scraped his foot on the floor and bowed low. "Mrs. Ingalls and girls, I surely am glad to see you all again."

He looked into Mary's eyes that did not see him and his voice was gentle when he said, "Are these two handsome young ladies your small little girls that I dandled on my knee, Ingalls, down on the Verdigris?"

Mary and Laura said that they were and that Carrie had been the baby then.

"Grace is our baby now," Ma said, but Grace would not go to meet Mr. Edwards. She would only stare at him and hang onto Ma's skirts.

"You're just in time, Mr. Edwards," Ma said hospitably. "I'll have dinner on the table in one minute," and Pa urged, "Sit right up, Edwards, and don't be bashful! There's plenty of it, such as it is!"

Mr. Edwards admired the well-built, pleasant house and heartily enjoyed the good dinner. But he said he was going on West with the train when it pulled out. Pa could not persuade him to stay longer.

"I'm aiming to go far West in the spring," he said. "This here country, it's too settled-up for me. The politicians are a-swarming in already, and ma'am if'n there's any worst pest than grasshoppers it surely is politicians. Why, they'll tax the lining out'n a man's pockets to keep up these here county-seat towns! I don't see nary use for a county, nohow. We all got along happy and content without 'em.

"Feller come along and taxed me last summer. Told me I got to put in every last least thing I had. So I put in Tom and Jerry, my horses, at fifty dollars apiece, and my oxen yoke, Buck and Bright, I put in at fifty, and my cow at thirty-five.

" 'Is that all you got?' he says. Well, I told him I'd put in five children I reckoned was worth a dollar apiece.

" 'Is that all?' he says. 'How about your wife?' he says.

" 'By Mighty!' I says to him. 'She says I don't own her and I don't aim to pay no taxes on her,' I says. And I didn't."

"Why, Mr. Edwards, it is news to us that you have a family," said Ma. "Mr. Ingalls said nothing of it."

"I didn't know it myself," Pa explained. "Anyway, Edwards, you don't have to pay taxes on your wife and children."

"He wanted a big tax list," said Mr. Edwards. "Politicians, they take pleasure a-prying into a man's affairs and I aimed to please 'em. It makes no matter. I don't aim to pay taxes. I sold the relinquishment on my claim and in the spring when the collector comes around I'll be gone from there. Got no children and no wife, nohow."

Before Pa or Ma could speak, the train whistle blew loud and long. "There's the call," said Mr. Edwards, and got up from the table.

"Change your mind and stay awhile, Edwards," Pa urged him. "You always brought us luck."

But Mr. Edwards shook hands all around and last with Mary who sat beside him.

"Good-by all!" he said, and going quickly out of the door he ran toward the depot.

Grace had looked and listened wide-eyed all the time without trying to say a word. Now that Mr. Edwards had vanished so suddenly, she took a deep breath and asked, "Mary, was that the man who saw Santa Claus?"

"Yes," Mary said. "That was the man who walked to Independence, forty miles, in the rain and saw Santa Claus there and brought back the Christmas presents for Laura and me when we were little girls."

"He has a heart of gold," said Ma.

"He brought us each a tin cup and a stick of candy," Laura remembered. She got up slowly and began to help Ma and Carrie clear the table. Pa went to his big chair by the stove.

Mary lifted her handkerchief from her lap, as she started to leave the table, and something fluttered to the floor. Ma stooped to pick it up. She stood holding it, speechless, and Laura cried, "Mary! A twenty dollar— You dropped a *twenty dollar bill!*"

"I couldn't!" Mary exclaimed.

"That Edwards," said Pa.

"We can't keep it," Ma said. But clear and long came the last farewell whistle of the train.

"What will you do with it, then?" Pa asked. "Edwards is gone and we likely won't see him again for years, if ever. He is going to Oregon in the spring."

"But, Charles . . . Oh, why did he do it?" Ma softly cried out in distress.

"He gave it to Mary," said Pa. "Let Mary keep it. It will help her go to college."

Ma thought for a moment, then said, "Very well," and she gave the bill to Mary.

Mary held it carefully, touching it with her fingertips, and her face shone. "Oh, I do *thank* Mr. Edwards."

"I hope he never has need of it himself, wherever he goes," said Ma.

"Trust Edwards to look out for himself," Pa assured her.

Mary's face was dreamy with the look it had when she was thinking of the college for the blind. "Ma," she said, "with the money you made keeping boarders last year, this makes thirty-five dollars and twenty-five cents."

CHAPTER 12

Alone

On Saturday the sun was shining and the wind was blowing softly from the south. Pa was hauling hay from the homestead, for the cow and the horses must eat a great deal of hay to keep themselves warm in cold weather.

In the sunshine from the western windows Mary rocked gently, and Laura's steel knitting needles flashed. Laura was knitting lace, of fine white thread, to trim a petticoat. She sat close to the window and watched the street, for she was expecting Mary Power and Minnie Johnson. They were coming to spend the afternoon, bringing their crocheting.

Mary was talking about the college that perhaps someday she could go to.

"I am keeping up with you in your lessons, Laura," she said. "I do wish, if I do go to college, that you could go, too."

"I suppose I'll be teaching school," Laura said, "so I couldn't go anyway. And I guess you care more about it than I do."

"Oh, I do care about it!" Mary softly exclaimed. "I want it more than *anything*. There's so much to learn, I always wanted to go studying on and on. And to think that I can, if we can save the money, even now that I'm blind. Isn't it wonderful?"

"Yes, it is," Laura agreed soberly. She did hope that somehow Mary could go. "Oh, bother! I've miscounted the stitches!" she exclaimed. She unraveled the row and began to pick the tiny stitches up again on the fine needle.

"Well," she said, " 'The Lord helps them that help themselves' and you surely will go to college, Mary, if . . ." She forgot what she was saying. The little loops of thread were dimming before her eyes as if she were going blind. She could not see them. The spool of thread dropped from her lap and rolled away on the floor as she jumped up.

"What's the matter?" Mary cried out.

"The light's gone!" Laura said. There was no sunshine. The air was gray and the note of the wind was rising. Ma came hurrying in from the kitchen.

"It's storming, girls!" she had time to say, then the house shook as the storm struck it. The darkening store fronts across the street disappeared in a whirl of snow. "Oh, I wish Charles had got home!" Ma said.

Laura turned from the window. She drew Mary's chair over to the heater, and from the coal hod she shoveled more coal on the fire. Suddenly the storm wind howled into the kitchen. The back door slammed hard and Pa came in, snowy and laughing.

"I beat the blizzard to the stable by the width of a gnat's eyebrow!" he laughed. "Sam and David stretched out and came lickety-split! We made it just in the nick of time! This is one blizzard that got fooled!"

Ma took his coat and folded it to carry the snow out to the lean-to. "Just so you're here, Charles," she murmured.

Pa sat down and leaned to the heater, holding out his hands to warm them. But he was uneasily listening to the wind. Before long he started up from his chair.

"I'm going to do the chores before this gets any worse," he said. "It may take me some time but don't worry, Caroline. Your clothesline'll hold and get me back all right."

He was gone till dark and longer. Supper was waiting when he came in, stamping his feet and rubbing his ears.

"Gosh all hemlock! but it's growing cold fast!" he exclaimed. "The snow strikes like buckshot. And listen to that wind howl!"

"I suppose this is blocking the trains?" Ma said.

"Well, we've lived without a railroad," Pa answered cheerfully, but he gave Ma the look that warned her to say no more about it while the girls were listening. "We're snug and warm, as we've been before without even the people and the stores," he went on. "Now let's have that hot supper!"

"And after supper, Pa, you'll play the fiddle, won't you?" Laura said. "Please."

So after supper Pa called for his fiddle and Laura brought it to him. But when he had tuned the strings and rosined the bow he played a strange melody. The fiddle moaned a deep, rushing undertone and wild notes flickered high above it, rising until they thinned away in nothingness, only to come wailing back, the same notes but not quite the same, as if they had been changed while out of hearing.

Queer shivers tingled up Laura's backbone and prickled over her scalp, and still the wild, changing melody came from the fiddle till she couldn't bear it and cried, "What is it, Pa? Oh, what is that tune?"

"Listen." Pa stopped playing and held his bow still, above the strings. "The tune is outdoors. I was only following it."

They all listened to the winds playing that tune until Ma said, "We will likely hear enough of that without your playing it, Charles."

"We'll have something different, then," Pa agreed. "What'll it be?"

"Something to warm us up," Laura asked, and the fiddle, gay and bright, began to warm them up. Pa played and sang, "Little Annie Rooney is My Sweetheart!" and "The Old Gray Mare, She Ain't what She Used to Be," till even Ma's toes were keeping time to it. He played the Highland Fling, and Irish jigs, and out on the clickety-clattering floor Laura and Carrie danced till their breath was gone.

When Pa laid the fiddle in the box he meant that now was bedtime.

It was hard to leave the warm room and go upstairs. Laura knew that in the cold up there every nail-point that came through the roof was fuzzy with frost. The downstairs windows were thickly covered with it, but somehow those frosty nails made her feel much colder.

She wrapped the two hot flatirons in their flannels and led the way. Mary and Carrie followed. Upstairs the air was so cold that it shriveled the insides of their noses, while they unbuttoned and dropped their shoes and shivered out of their dresses.

"God will hear us if we say our prayers under the covers," Mary chattered, and she crawled between the cold blankets. There had not been time for the hot irons to warm the beds. In the still cold under the frosty-nailed roof, Laura could feel the quivering of the bedsteads that Mary and Carrie were shaking in. The deep roar and the shrill wild cries of the winds were all around that little space of stillness.

"What in the world are you doing, Laura?" Mary called. "Hurry and come help warm the bed!"

Laura could not answer without unclenching her teeth to rattle. She stood at the window in her nightdress and stocking-feet.

She had scraped away the frost from a place on the glass and she was trying to look through it. She cupped her hands beside her eyes to shield them from the glimmer of lamplight that came up from the stairway. But still she could see nothing. In the roaring night outside, there was not one speck of light.

At last she crawled in beside Mary and curled up tightly, pressing her feet against the warm flatiron.

"I was trying to see a light," she explained. "There must be a light in some house."

"Didn't you?" Mary asked.

"No," Laura said. She had not been able even to see the light from the window downstairs where she knew the lamp was shining.

Carrie was quiet in her bed by the stovepipe that came up from the hot stove below. It helped to warm her and she had a hot flatiron too. She was fast asleep when Ma came up to tuck Grace in beside her.

"Are you warm enough, girls?" Ma whispered, bending over the bed and snuggling the covers more closely around them.

"We're getting warm, Ma," Laura answered.

"Then goodnight and sweet dreams."

But even after Laura was warm she lay awake listening to the wind's wild tune and thinking of each little house, in town, alone in the whirling snow with not even a light from the next house shining through. And the little town was alone on the wide prairie. Town and prairie were lost in the wild storm which was neither earth nor sky, nothing but fierce winds and a blank whiteness.

For the storm was white. In the night, long after the sun had gone and the last daylight could not possibly be there, the blizzard was whirling white.

A lamp could shine out through the blackest darkness and a shout could be heard a long way, but no light and no cry could reach through a storm that had wild voices and an unnatural light of its own.

The blankets were warm and Laura was no longer cold but she shivered.

CHAPTER 13

We'll Weather the Blast

MIXED with those wild voices, Laura heard the clatter of stove lids and Pa's singing, "Oh, I am as happy as a big sunflower that nods and bends in the breezes, Oh!"

"Caroline!" Pa called up the stairs, "the fires will be going good by the time you get down here. I'm going to the stable."

Laura heard Ma stirring. "Lie still, girls," she said. "No need for you to get up till the house is warmer."

It was terribly cold outside the bedcovers. But the roaring and shrilling of the storm would not let Laura sleep again. The frosted nails in the roof above her were like white teeth. She lay under them only a few minutes before she followed Ma downstairs.

The fire was burning brightly in the cookstove, and in the front room the heater's side was red-hot, but still the rooms were cold and so dark that it did not seem to be daytime.

Laura broke the ice on the water in the water pail. She filled the washbasin and set it on the stove. Then she and Ma waited, shivering, for the water to warm so that they could wash their faces. Laura had begun to like living in town but this was the same old wintertime.

When Pa came in, his whiskers were blown full of snow and his nose and ears were cherry-red.

"Jerusalem crickets! This is a humdinger!" he exclaimed. "Good thing the stable is tight. I had to dig my way into it. Snow was packed as high as the door. Lucky I put your clothesline where I did, Caroline. I had to come back to the lean-to to get the shovel, but there was the clothesline to hang onto. Hot pancakes and fried pork look good to me! I'm hungry as a wolf."

The water was warm in the washbasin for him, and while he washed and combed his hair at the bench by the door, Laura set the chairs to the table and Ma poured the fragrant tea.

The hot cakes were good, with crisped slices of fat pork and the brown-and-amber grease from the pan, and dried-apple sauce and sugar syrup besides. There was no butter, for Ellen was nearly dry, and Ma divided last night's milk between Grace's cup and Carrie's.

"Let's be thankful for the little milk we have," she said, "because there'll be less before there's more."

They were chilly at the table so, after breakfast, they all gathered around the heater. In silence they listened to the winds and the sound of snow driven against the walls and the windows. Ma roused herself with a little shake.

"Come, Laura. Let's get the work done. Then we can sit by the fire with an easy conscience."

In that well-built house it was strange that the fire did not warm the kitchen. While Ma put the beans to parboil and Laura washed the dishes, they wondered how cold it was now in the claim shanty. Ma put more coal on the fire and took the broom and Laura shivered at the foot of the stairs. She must go up to make the beds, but the cold came down the stairs and went through her woolen dress and petticoats and red flannels as if she were standing there in her bare skin.

"We'll leave the beds open to air, Laura," said Ma. "They're upstairs out of sight and you can do them when the house warms up."

She finished sweeping and the kitchen work was done. They went back to the front room and sitting down they put their cold feet on the footrest of the heater to warm.

Pa went into the kitchen and came back in his big coat and muffler, his cap in his hand.

"I'm going across the street to Fuller's to hear the news," he said.

"Must you, Charles?" Ma asked him.

"Somebody may be lost," he answered. Putting on his cap he went to the door, but paused to say, "Don't worry about me! I know how many steps it takes to cross the street, and if I don't strike a building then, I'll go no farther away till I do find one." He shut the door behind him.

Laura stood at the window. She had cleared a peephole through the frost but she saw only blank whiteness. She could not see Pa at the door nor tell when he left it. She went slowly back to the heater. Mary sat silently rocking Grace. Laura and Carrie just sat.

"Now, girls!" Ma said. "A storm outdoors is no reason for gloom in the house."

"What good is it to be in town?" Laura said. "We're just as much by ourselves as if there wasn't any town."

"I hope you don't expect to depend on anybody else, Laura." Ma was shocked. "A body can't do that."

"But if we weren't in town Pa wouldn't have to go out in this blizzard to find out if somebody else is lost."

"Be that as it may be," Ma said firmly, "it is time for our Sunday school lessons. We will each say the verse we learned this week and then we'll see how many of the old lessons we remember."

First Grace, then Carrie, then Laura and Mary, and Ma repeated their verses.

"Now Mary," Ma said, "you tell us a verse, then Laura will do the same, and then Carrie. See which one can keep on longest."

"Oh, Mary will beat," Carrie said, discouraged before she began.

"Come on! I'll help you," Laura urged.

"Two against one isn't fair," Mary objected.

"It is too fair!" Laura contradicted. "Isn't it, Ma? When Mary's been learning Bible verses so much longer than Carrie has."

"Yes," Ma decided. "I think it is fair enough but Laura must only prompt Carrie."

So they began, went on and on until Carrie could remember no more even when Laura prompted her. Then Mary and Laura went on, against each other, until at last Laura had to give up.

She hated to admit that she was beaten, but she had to. "You beat me, Mary. I can't remember another one."

"Mary beat! Mary beat!" Grace cried, clapping her hands and Ma said, smiling, to Mary, "That's my bright girl."

They all looked at Mary who was looking at nothing with her large, beautiful blue eyes that had no sight in them. She smiled with joy when Ma praised her and then her face changed as the light does when a blizzard comes. For a minute she looked as she used to look when she could see, and she and

Laura were quarreling. She never would give up to Laura because she was the older and the boss.

Then her whole face blushed pink and in a low voice she said, "I didn't beat you, Laura. We're even. I can't remember another verse, either."

Laura was ashamed. She had tried so hard to beat Mary at a game, but no matter how hard she tried she could never be as good as Mary was. Mary was truly good. Then for the first time Laura wanted to be a schoolteacher so that she could make the money to send Mary to college. She thought, "Mary is going to college, no matter how hard I have to work to send her."

At that moment the clock struck eleven times.

"My goodness, the dinner!" Ma exclaimed. She hurried into the kitchen to stir up the fire and season the bean soup. "Better put more coal in the heater, Laura," she called. "Seems like the house hasn't warmed up like it should have."

It was noon when Pa came in. He came in quietly and went to the heater where he took off his coat and cap. "Hang these up for me, will you, Laura? I'm pretty cold."

"I'm sorry, Charles," Ma said from the kitchen. "I can't seem to get the house warm."

"No wonder," Pa answered. "It's forty degrees below zero and this wind is driving the cold in. This is the worst storm yet, but luckily everyone is accounted for. Nobody's lost from town."

After dinner Pa played hymn tunes on his fiddle, and all the afternoon they sang. They sang:

> "There's a land that is fairer than day,
> And by faith we can see it afar. . . ."

And:

> "Jesus is a rock in a weary land,
> A weary land, a weary land,
> Jesus is a rock in a weary land,
> A shelter in the time of storm."

They sang Ma's favorite, "There is a Happy Land, Far, Far Away." And just before Pa laid the fiddle in its box because the time had come when he must get to the stable and take care of the stock, he played a gallant, challenging tune that brought them all to their feet, and they all sang lustily,

"Then let the hurricane roar!
It will the sooner be o'er.
We'll weather the blast
And land at last
On Canaan's happy shore!"

The hurricane was roaring, the icy snow as hard as buckshot and fine as sand was whirling, swirling, beating upon the house.

CHAPTER 14

One Bright Day

THAT blizzard lasted only two days. Tuesday morning Laura woke up suddenly. She lay with her eyes wide open, listening to hear again what had awakened her. There was no sound at all. Then she knew. The stillness had startled her awake. There was no noise of winds, no swish! swish! of icy snow scouring the walls and roof and window.

The sun was glowing bright through the frost on the window at the top of the stairs, and downstairs Ma's smile was like sunshine.

"The blizzard's over," she said. "It was only a two days' blizzard."

"You never can tell what a blizzard will do," Pa agreed.

"It may be that your hard winter won't prove to be so hard after all," Ma said happily. "Now the sun is shining, they should have the trains running again in no time, and, Laura, I'm sure there will be school today. Better get yourself ready for it while I get breakfast."

Laura went upstairs to tell Carrie and to put on her school dress. In the warm kitchen again she scrubbed her face and neck well with soap and pinned up her braids. Pa breezed in gaily from doing the chores.

"Old Sol's bright and shining this morning!" he told them. "Looks like his face was well washed in snow."

Hashed brown potatoes were on the table and Ma's wild ground-cherry preserves shone golden in a glass bowl. Ma stacked a platter with toast browned in the oven, and then took from the oven a small dish of butter.

"I had to warm the butter," she said. "It was frozen as hard as a rock. I could not cut it. I hope Mr. Boast brings us some more soon. This is what the cobbler threw at his wife."

Grace and Carrie were puzzled, while all the others laughed. It showed how happy Ma was that she would make jokes.

"That was his awl," Mary said. And Laura exclaimed, "Oh, no! It was the last. That was all he had."

"Girls, girls," Ma said gently because they were laughing too much at the table. Then Laura said, "But I thought we were out of butter when we didn't have any yesterday."

"Pancakes were good with salt pork," said Ma. "I saved the butter for toast." There was just enough butter for a scraping on every slice.

Breakfast was so merry in the warmth and stillness and light that the clock was striking half past eight before they finished, and Ma said, "Run along, girls. This one time I'll do your housework."

The whole outdoors was dazzling, sparkling brightly in bright sunshine. All the length of Main Street was a high drift of snow, a ridge taller than Laura. She and Carrie had to climb to its top and get carefully down its other side. The snow was packed so hard that their shoes made no marks on it and their heels could dig no dents to keep them from slipping.

In the schoolyard was another glittering drift almost as high as the schoolhouse. Cap Garland and Ben and Arthur and the little Wilmarth boys were skating down it on their shoes, as Laura used to slide on Silver Lake, and Mary Power and Minnie were standing out in the cold sunshine by the door watching the fun the boys were having.

"Hello, Laura!" Mary Power said gladly, and she tucked her mittened hand under Laura's arm and squeezed it. They were pleased to see each other again. It seemed a long time since Friday, and even since the Saturday afternoon that they had meant to spend together. But there was no time to talk, for Teacher came to the door and girls and boys must go in to their lessons.

At recess Mary Power and Laura and Minnie stood at the window and watched the boys sliding down the snowdrift. Laura wished she could go outdoors to play too.

"I wish we weren't too big now," she said. "I don't think it's any fun being a young lady."

"Well, we can't help growing up," Mary Power said.

"What would you do if you were caught in a blizzard, Mary?" Minnie Johnson was asking.

"I guess I would just keep on walking. You wouldn't freeze if you kept on walking," Mary answered.

"But you'd tire yourself out. You'd get so tired you'd die," said Minnie.

"Well, what would you do?" Mary Power asked her.

"I'd dig into a snowbank and let the snow cover me up. I don't think you'd freeze to death in a snowbank. Would you, Laura?"

"I don't know," Laura said.

"Well, what would you do, Laura, if you got caught in a blizzard?" Minnie insisted.

"I wouldn't get caught," Laura answered. She did not like to think about it. She would rather talk with Mary Power about other things. But Miss Garland rang the bell and the boys came trooping in, red with the cold and grinning.

That whole day long everyone was as cheerful as the sunshine. At noon Laura and Mary Power and Carrie, with the Beardsley girls, raced in the shouting crowd over the big snowdrifts home to dinner. On top of the high drift that was Main Street, some went north and some went south and Laura and Carrie slid down its east side to their own front door.

Pa was already in his place at the table, Mary was lifting Grace onto the pile of books in her chair, and Ma was setting a dish of steaming baked potatoes before Pa. "I do wish we had some butter for them," she said.

"Salt brings out the flavor," Pa was saying, when a loud knocking sounded on the kitchen door. Carrie ran to open it and, big and furry as a bear in his buffalo coat, Mr. Boast came in.

"Come in, Boast! Come in, come in!" Pa kept saying. They were so glad to see him. "Come in and put your feet under the table. You're just in time!"

"Where is Mrs. Boast?" Mary inquired.

"Yes, indeed! Didn't she come with you?" Ma said eagerly.

Mr. Boast was getting out of his wraps. "Well, no. You see, Ellie thought she must do the washing while the sun shone. I told her we'll have more good days but she said then she'd come to town on one of *them*. She sent you some butter. It's from our last churning. My cows are going dry. The weather we've been having, I couldn't take care of them."

Mr. Boast sat up to the table and they all began on the good baked potatoes, with butter, after all.

"Glad to know you came through the storm all right," Pa said.

"Yes, we were lucky. I was watering the stock at the well when the cloud came up. I hurried them in, had them all snug in the stable and got halfway to the house before the storm struck," Mr. Boast told them.

The baked potatoes and hot biscuits with butter were delicious, and to finish the dinner there were more biscuits with some of Ma's rich tomato preserves.

"There's no more salt pork in town," Pa said. "Getting all our supplies from the East, this way, we run a little short when the trains don't get through."

"What do you hear about the train?" Mr. Boast asked him.

"They've put extra gangs to work on the Tracy cut, Woodworth says," Pa replied. "And they're bringing out snowplows. We can look for a train before the end of the week."

"Ellie's counting on my getting some tea and sugar and flour," said Mr. Boast. "The storekeepers raising prices any?"

"Not that I know of," Pa reassured him. "Nothing's running short but meat."

Dinner was eaten and Mr. Boast said he must be getting along to reach home before night. He promised to bring Mrs. Boast in to see them all one day soon. Then he and Pa went up Main Street to Harthorn's grocery and Laura and Carrie, hand in hand, went joyously climbing up the drifts and sliding down them, back to school.

All that happy afternoon they were full of the clear, cold air and as bright as the sunshine. They knew their lessons perfectly, they enjoyed reciting them. Every face in school was smiling, and Cap Garland's flashing grin included them all.

It was good to see the town alive again and to know that again all the weekdays would be school days.

But in the night Laura dreamed that Pa was playing the wild storm-tune on his fiddle and when she screamed to him to stop, the tune was a blinding blizzard swirling around her and it had frozen her to solid ice.

Then she was staring at the dark, but for a long time that nightmare held her stiff and cold. It was not Pa's fiddle she heard, but the stormwind itself and the swish! swish! of icy snow on the walls and the roof. At last she was able to move. So cold that the dream still seemed half real, she snuggled close to Mary and pulled the quilts over their heads.

"What is it?" Mary murmured in her sleep.

"A blizzard," Laura answered.

CHAPTER 15

No Trains

IT WAS not worth while to get up in the morning. The daylight was dim, the windows were white and so were the nails in the roof. Another blizzard was roaring, screaming, and swishing around the house. There would be no school.

Laura lay sluggish and half awake. She would rather sleep than wake up to such a day. But Ma called, "Good morning, girls! Time to get up!"

Quickly, because of the cold, Laura put on her dress and her shoes and went downstairs.

"Why, what is the trouble, Laura?" Ma asked, looking up from the stove.

Laura almost wailed, "Oh Ma! How can I ever teach school and help send Mary to college? How can I ever amount to anything when I can get only one day of school at a time?"

"Now Laura," Ma said kindly. "You must not be so easily discouraged. A few blizzards more or less can make no great difference. We will hurry and get the work done, then you can study. There is enough figuring in your arithmetic to keep you busy for a good many days, and you can do as much of it as you want to. Nothing keeps you from learning."

Laura asked, "Why is the table here in the kitchen?" The table left hardly room to move about.

"Pa didn't build the fire in the heater this morning," Ma answered.

They heard Pa stamping in the lean-to and Laura opened the door for him. He looked sober. The little milk in the pail was frozen solid.

"This is the worst yet, I do believe," Pa said while he held his stiff hands over the stove. "I didn't start a fire in the heater, Caroline. Our coal is running low, and this storm will likely block the trains for some time."

"I thought as much when I saw you hadn't built the fire," Ma answered. "So I moved the table in here. We'll keep the middle door shut and the cookstove warms this room nicely."

"I'll go over to Fuller's right after breakfast," said Pa. He ate quickly and while he was putting on his wraps again Ma went upstairs. She brought down her little red Morocco pocketbook, with the shining, smooth mother-of-pearl sides and the steel clasps, in which she kept Mary's college money.

Pa slowly put out his hand and took it. Then he cleared his throat and said, "Mary, it may be the town's running short of supplies. If the lumberyard and the stores are putting up prices too high . . ."

He did not go on and Mary said, "Ma has my college money put away. You could spend that."

"If I do have to, Mary, you can depend on me paying it back," Pa promised.

After he had gone, Laura brought Mary's rocking chair from the cold front room and set it to warm before the open oven. As soon as Mary sat in it Grace climbed into her lap.

"I'll be warm, too," Grace said.

"You're a big girl now and too heavy," Ma objected, but Mary said quickly, "Oh no, Grace! I like to hold you, even if you are a big three-year-old girl."

The room was so crowded that Laura could hardly wash the dishes without bumping into some sharp edge. While Ma was making the beds in the upstairs cold, Laura polished the stove and cleaned the lamp chimney. Then she unscrewed the brass chimney holder and filled the lamp carefully with kerosene. The last clear drop poured out from the spout of the kerosene can.

"Oh! we didn't tell Pa to get kerosene!" Laura exclaimed before she thought.

"Don't we have kerosene?" Carrie gasped, turning around quickly from the cupboard where she was putting away the dishes. Her eyes were frightened.

"My goodness, yes, I've filled the lamp brimful," Laura answered. "Now I'll sweep the floor and you dust."

All the work was done when Ma came downstairs. "The wind is fairly rocking the house up there," she told them, shivering by the stove. "How nicely you have done everything, Laura and Carrie," she smiled.

Pa had not come back, but surely he could not be lost, in town.

Laura brought her books and slate to the table, close to Mary in her rocking chair. The light was poor but Ma did not light a lamp. Laura read the arithmetic problems one by one to Mary, and did them on the slate while Mary solved them in her head. They worked each problem backward to make sure that they had the correct answer. Slowly they worked lesson after lesson and as Ma had said, there were many more to come.

At last they heard Pa coming through the front room. His overcoat and cap were frozen white with snow and he carried a snowy package. He thawed by the stove and when he could speak, he said, "I didn't use your college money, Mary.

"There's no coal at the lumberyard," he went on. "People burned so much in this cold weather and Ely didn't have much on hand. He's selling lumber to burn now, but we can't afford to burn lumber at fifty dollars a thousand."

"People are foolish to pay it," Ma said gently. "Trains are bound to get through before long."

"There is no more kerosene in town," Pa said. "And no meat. The stores are sold out of pretty nearly everything. I got two pounds of tea, Caroline, before they ran out of that. So we'll have our bit of tea till the trains come through."

"There's nothing like a good cup of tea in cold weather," said Ma. "And the lamp is full. That's enough kerosene to last quite awhile if we go to bed early to save coal. I am so glad you thought to get the tea. We would miss that!"

Slowly Pa grew warm and without saying anything more he sat down by the window to read the *Chicago Inter-Ocean* that had come in the last mail.

"By the way," he said, looking up, "school is closed until coal comes."

"We can study by ourselves," Laura said stoutly. She and Mary murmured to each other over the arithmetic problems, Carrie studied the speller, while Ma worked at her mending and Pa silently read the paper. The blizzard grew worse. It was by far the most violent blizzard that they had ever heard.

The room grew colder. There was no heat from the front room to help the cookstove. The cold had crept into the front room and was sneaking in under the door. Beneath the lean-to door it was crawling in too. Ma brought the braided rugs from the front room and laid them, folded, tightly against the bottoms of the doors.

At noon Pa went to the stable. The stock did not need feeding at noon, but he went to see that the horses and the cow and the big calf were still safely sheltered.

He went out again in midafternoon. "Animals need a lot of feed to keep them warm in such cold," he explained to Ma. "The blizzard is worse than it was, and I had a hard tussle this morning to get hay into the stable in these winds. I couldn't do it if the haystack wasn't right at the door. Another good thing, the snowdrifts are gone. They've been scoured away, down to the bare ground."

The storm howled even louder when he went out into it, and a blast of cold came through the lean-to though Ma had pushed the folded rug against the inner door as soon as Pa shut it.

Mary was braiding a new rug. She had cut worn-out woolen clothes in strips, and Ma had put each color in a separate box. Mary kept the boxes in order and remembered where each color was. She was braiding the rag-strips together in a long braid that coiled down in a pile beside her chair. When she came to the end of a strip, she chose the color she wanted and sewed it on. Now and then she felt of the growing pile.

"I do believe I have nearly enough done," she said. "I'll be ready for you to sew the rug tomorrow, Laura."

"I wanted to finish this lace first," Laura objected. "And these storms keep making it so dark I can hardly see to count the stitches."

"The dark doesn't bother me," Mary answered cheerfully. "I can see with my fingers."

Laura was ashamed of being impatient. "I'll sew your rug whenever you're ready," she said willingly.

Pa was gone a long time. Ma set the supper back to keep warm. She did not light the lamp, and they all sat thinking that the clothesline would guide Pa through the blinding blizzard.

"Come, come, girls!" Ma said, rousing herself. "Mary, you start a song. We'll sing away the time until Pa comes." So they sang together in the dark until Pa came.

There was lamplight at supper, but Ma told Laura to leave

the dishes unwashed. They must all go to bed quickly, to save the kerosene and the coal.

Only Pa and Ma got up next morning at chore time. "You girls stay in bed and keep warm as long as you like," Ma said, and Laura did not get up until nine o'clock. The cold was pressing on the house and seeping in, rising higher and higher, and the ceaseless noise and the dusk seemed to hold time still.

Laura and Mary and Carrie studied their lessons. Laura sewed the rag braid into a round rug and laid it heavy over Mary's lap so that Mary could see it with her fingers. The rug made this day different from the day before, but Laura felt that it was the same day over again when they sang again in the dark until Pa came and ate the same supper of potatoes and bread with dried-apple sauce and tea and left the dishes unwashed and went to bed at once to save kerosene and coal.

Another day was the same. The blizzard winds did not stop roaring and shrieking, the swishing snow did not stop swishing, the noise and the dark and the cold would never end.

Suddenly they ended. The blizzard winds stopped. It was late in the third afternoon. Laura blew and scraped at the frost on a windowpane till through the peephole she could see snow scudding down Main Street low to the ground before a straight wind. A reddish light shone on the blowing snow from the setting sun. The sky was clear and cold. Then the rosy light faded, the snow was blowing gray-white, and the steady wind blew harder. Pa came in from doing the chores.

"Tomorrow I must haul some hay," he said. "But now I'm going across to Fuller's to find out if anybody but us is alive in this blame town. Here for three whole days we haven't been able to see a light, nor smoke, nor any sign of a living soul. What's the good of a town if a fellow can't get any good of it?"

"Supper's almost ready, Charles," Ma said.

"I'll be back in a jiffy!" Pa told her.

He came back in a few minutes asking, "Supper ready?" Ma was dishing it up and Laura setting the chairs to the table.

"Everything's all right in town," Pa said, "and word from the depot is that they'll start work tomorrow morning on that big cut this side of Tracy."

"How long will it take to get a train through?" Ma asked.

"Can't tell," Pa replied. "That one clear day we had, they

cleaned it out, ready to come through next day. But they shoveled the snow up, both sides of the cut, and now it's packed full, clear to the top of the banks. Something like thirty feet deep of snow, frozen solid, they've got to dig out now."

"That won't take very long in pleasant weather," Ma said. "Surely we're bound to have that. We've already had more, and worse, storms than we had all last winter."

CHAPTER 16

Fair Weather

MORNING was bright and clear but there was no school. There would be no more school until the train came bringing coal.

Outdoors the sun was shining but frost was still on the window and the kitchen seemed stale and dull. Carrie gazed out through the peephole in the frost while she wiped the breakfast dishes, and drearily Laura sloshed the cooling water in the dishpan.

"I want to go somewhere!" Carrie said fretfully. "I'm tired of staying in this old kitchen!"

"We were thankful enough for this warm kitchen yesterday," Mary gently reminded her. "And now we may be thankful the blizzard's over."

"You wouldn't go to school, anyway," Laura said crossly. She was ashamed as soon as she heard the words, but when Ma said reproachfully, "Laura," she felt more cross than before.

"When you girls have finished your work," Ma went on, covering the well-kneaded bread and setting it before the oven to rise, "you may put on your wraps, and Mary may, too, and all go out in the yard for a breath of fresh air."

That cheered them. Laura and Carrie worked quickly now, and in a little while they were hurrying into their coats and shawls and hoods, mufflers and mittens. Laura guided Mary through the lean-to, and they all burst out into the glittering cold. The sun glare blinded them and the cold took their breath away.

"Throw back your arms and breathe deep, deep!" Laura cried. She knew that cold is not so cold if you are not afraid of it. They threw back their arms and breathed the cold in, and through their cringing noses it rushed deep into their chests and warmed them all over. Even Mary laughed aloud.

"I can smell the snow!" she said. "So fresh and clean!"

"The sky is bright blue and the whole world is sparkling white,"

Laura told her. "Only the houses stick up out of the snow and spoil it. I wish we were where there aren't any houses."

"What a dreadful idea," said Mary. "We'd freeze to death."

"I'd build us an igloo," Laura declared, "and we'd live like Eskimos."

"Ugh, on raw fish," Mary shuddered. "I wouldn't."

The snow crunched and creaked under their feet. It was packed so hard that Laura could not scoop up a handful to make a snowball. She was telling Carrie how soft the snow used to be in the Big Woods of Wisconsin when Mary said, "Who's that coming? It sounds like our horses."

Pa came riding up to the stable. He was standing on a queer kind of sled. It was a low platform made of new boards and it was as long as a wagon and twice as wide. It had no tongue, but a long loop of chain was fastened to the wide-apart runners and the whiffletrees were fastened to the chain.

"Where did you get that funny sled, Pa?" Laura asked.

"I made it," Pa said. "At the lumberyard." He got his pitchfork from the stable. "It does look funny," he admitted. "But it would hold a whole haystack if the horses could pull it. I don't want to lose any time getting some hay here to feed the stock."

Laura wanted to ask him if he had any news of the train, but the question would remind Carrie that there was no more coal or kerosene and no meat until a train could come. She did not want to worry Carrie. They were all so brisk and cheery in this bright weather, and if sunny weather lasted for a while the train would come and there would be nothing to worry about.

While she was thinking this, Pa stepped onto the low, big sled.

"Tell your Ma they've brought a snowplow and a full work train out from the East and put them to work at the Tracy cut, Laura," he said. "A few days of this fine weather and they'll have the train running all right."

"Yes, Pa, I'll tell her," Laura said thankfully, and Pa drove away, around the street corner and out along Main Street toward the homestead.

Carrie sighed a long sigh and cried, "Let's tell her right away!" From the way she said it, Laura knew that Carrie had been wanting to ask Pa about the train too.

"My, what rosy cheeks!" Ma said when they went into the dusky, warm kitchen. The cold, fresh air shook out of their wraps while they took them off. The heat above the stove made their cold fingers tingle pleasantly, and Ma was glad to hear about the work train and the snowplow.

"This good weather will likely last for some time now, we have had so many storms," Ma said.

The frost was melting on the window and freezing into thin sheets of ice over the cold glass. With little trouble Laura pried it off and wiped the panes dry. She settled herself in the bright daylight and knitted her lace, looking out now and then at the sunshine on the snow. There was not a cloud in the sky and no reason to worry about Pa though he did not come back as soon as should be expected.

At ten o'clock he had not come. At eleven there was still no sign of him. It was only two miles to the homestead and back, and half an hour should load the shed with hay.

"I wonder what's keeping Pa?" Mary said finally.

"Likely he's found something to do at the claim," Ma said. She came to the window then and looked at the northwestern sky. There was no cloud in it.

"There's no cause to worry," Ma went on. "It may be the storms have done some damage to the shanty, but that's soon mended."

At noon the Saturday baking of bread was out of the oven, three crusty golden hot loaves, and the boiled potatoes were steaming dry and the tea was brewed, and still Pa had not returned.

They were all sure that something had happened to him, though no one said so and no one could think what it might be. The steady old horses would surely not run away. Laura thought of claim jumpers. Pa had no gun if claim jumpers were in the deserted shanty. But claim jumpers could not have come through the blizzards. There were no bears or panthers or wolves or Indians. There was no river to ford.

What could happen to hinder or hurt a man driving gentle horses, in good weather, only a mile in a sled over the snow to the homestead and the same way back again with a load of hay?

Then Pa came driving around the corner of Second Street and by the window. Laura saw him going by, snowy on the mound of snowy hay that hid the sled and seemed to be dragging on the snow. He stopped by the stable, unhitched the horses and put them in their stalls and then came stamping into the lean-to. Laura and Ma had put the dinner on the table.

"By George! that dinner looks good!" said Pa. "I could eat a raw bear without salt!"

Laura poured hot water from the teakettle into the washbasin for him. Ma said gently, "Whatever kept you so long, Charles?"

"Grass," said Pa. He buried his face in his hands full of soapy water and Laura and Ma looked at each other amazed. What did Pa mean? In a minute he reached for the roller towel and went on, "That confounded grass under the snow.

"You can't follow the road," Pa went on, wiping his hands. "There's nothing to go by, no fences or trees. As soon as you get out of town there's nothing but snowdrifts in all directions. Even the lake's covered up. The drifts are packed hard by the wind, and frozen, so the sled slides right along over them and you'd think you could make a beeline to wherever you wanted to go.

"Well, first thing I knew, the team went down to their chins in that hard snow. I'd hit the slough, and the snow looks as hard there as anywhere, but underneath it there's grass. The slough grass holds up that crust of snow on nothing but grass stems and air. As soon as the horses get onto it, down they go.

"I've spent this whole morning rassling with that dumb horse, Sam . . ."

"Charles," Ma said.

"Caroline," Pa answered, "it's enough to make a saint swear. David was all right, he's got horse sense, but Sam went plumb crazy. There those two horses are, down to their backs in snow, and every try they make to get out only makes the hole bigger. If they drag the sled down into it, I never will get it out. So I unhitch the sled. Then I try to get the team up onto hard going again, and there's Sam gone crazy-wild, plunging and snorting and jumping and wallowing all the time deeper into that confounded snow."

"It must have been a job," Ma agreed.

"He was threshing around so, I was afraid he'd hurt David," said Pa. "So I got down into it and unhitched them from each other. I held onto Sam and I tramped the snow down as well as I could, trying to make a hard enough path for him to walk on, up onto the top of the drifts. But he'd rear and plunge and break it down till I tell you it'd wear out any man's patience."

"Whatever did you do, Charles?" Ma asked.

"Oh, I got him out finally," said Pa. "David followed me as gentle as a lamb, stepping carefully and coming right on up. So I hitched him onto the sled and he dragged it around the hole. But I had to hang onto Sam all the time. There was nothing to tie him to. Then I hitched them both up together again and started on. We went about a hundred feet and down they went again."

"Mercy!" Ma exclaimed.

"So that's the way it was," said Pa. "The whole morning. Took me the whole half a day to go a couple of miles and get back with one load of hay, and I'm tireder than if I'd done a hard day's work. I'm going to drive David single this afternoon. He can't haul so big a load but it'll be easier on both of us."

He ate dinner in a hurry and hurried out to hitch David to the sled alone. Now they knew what Pa was doing and they were not worried, but they were sorry for David, falling through the deceitful snowdrifts, and for Pa, unhitching and helping the horse out and hitching him to the sled again.

Still, the whole afternoon was sunny, without a cloud in the sky, and before dark Pa had hauled two small loads of hay.

"David follows me like a dog," Pa told them all at supper. "When he breaks through the snow he stands still until I trample a solid path up. Then he follows me up out of the hole as carefully as if he understood all about it and I bet he does. Tomorrow I'm going to hitch him onto the sled by a long rope, so I won't have to unhitch him when he falls in. I'll only have to help him out and then, on the long rope, he can haul the sled around the hole."

After supper Pa went to Fuller's Hardware to buy the rope. He came back soon with news. The work train with the snowplow had got halfway through the Tracy cut that day.

"It takes longer this time to get through," he said, "because every time they cleared the track they threw the snow up on both sides, making the cut that much deeper. But Woodworth at the depot says they'll likely get a train through by day after tomorrow."

"That's good news," said Ma. "I'll be thankful to have some meat again."

"That's not all," Pa went on. "We're going to get the mail, train or no train. They're sending it through by team, and Gilbert, the mail carrier, is leaving here for Preston in the morning. He's making a sled now. So if you want to send a letter, you can."

"There is that letter I've been writing to the folks in Wisconsin," said Ma. "I wasn't intending to finish it so soon, but perhaps I may as well."

So she brought the letter to the tablecloth under the lamp, and after she had thawed the ink bottle they all sat around the table thinking of last things to say while Ma wrote them down with her little red pen that had a mother-of-pearl handle shaped like a feather. When her neat, clear writing filled the paper she turned it and filled it again crosswise. On the other side of the paper she did the same so that every inch of paper held all the words that it possibly could.

Carrie had been only a baby in Wisconsin. She did not remember the aunts and uncles and the cousins Alice and Ella and Peter, and Grace had never seen them. But Laura and Mary remembered them perfectly.

"Tell them I still have my doll, Charlotte," said Laura, "And I wish we had one of black Susan's great-great-great-grand kittens."

"'Descendants' takes less space," said Ma. "I'm afraid this letter will be overweight."

"Tell them there isn't a cat in this whole country," said Pa.

"I wish to goodness there was," said Ma. "We need one for the mice."

"Tell them we wish they could come spend Christmas with us this year like they did in the Big Woods," said Mary.

"'*As* they did,' Mary," said Ma.

"My goodness!" Laura exclaimed. "When *is* Christmas? I'd forgotten all about it. It's almost here."

Grace bounced on Mary's lap and cried, "When is Christmas coming? When is Santa Claus?"

Mary and Carrie had told her all about Santa Claus. Now Mary did not know what to say to her and neither did Laura. But Carrie spoke up.

"Maybe Santa Claus can't get here this winter, Grace, on account of the storms and the snow," Carrie said. "You see, even the train can't."

"Santa Claus comes on a sled," Grace said anxiously, looking at them with wide blue eyes. "He can come, can't he, Pa? Can't he, Ma?"

"Of course he can, Grace," said Ma. Then Laura said stoutly, "Santa Claus can come anywhere."

"Maybe he'll bring us the train," said Pa.

In the morning he took the letter to the post office and there he saw Mr. Gilbert put the mailbag into the sled and drive away, well wrapped in buffalo robes. He had twelve miles to go to Preston.

"He'll meet another team there with mail from the East and bring it back," Pa explained to Ma. "He ought to get back to-night, if he doesn't have too much trouble crossing the sloughs."

"He has good weather for the trip," Ma said.

"I'd better be taking advantage of it myself," said Pa.

He went out to harness David to the sled by the long rope. He hauled one load of hay that morning. At noon, while they sat at table, the light darkened and the wind began to howl.

"Here she comes!" Pa said. "I hope Gilbert has made it safe to Preston."

CHAPTER 17

Seed Wheat

THE cold and the dark had come again. The nails in the roof were white with frost, the windowpanes were gray. Scraping a peephole only showed the blank, whirling whiteness against the other side of the glass. The stout house quivered and shook; the wind roared and howled. Ma kept the rag rugs tightly against the bottom of the doors, and the cold came crawling in.

It was hard to be cheerful. Morning and afternoon, holding the clothesline, Pa went to the stable to feed the horses, the cow, and the heifer. He had to be sparing of the hay. He came in so cold that he could hardly get warm. Sitting before the oven, he took Grace on his knee and hugged Carrie close to him, and he told them the stories of bears and panthers that he used to tell Mary and Laura. Then in the evening he took his fiddle and played the merry tunes.

When it was bedtime, and the cold upstairs must be faced, Pa played them up to bed.

"Ready now, all together!" he said. "Right, left, right, left—March!"

Laura went first, carrying the wrapped hot flatiron, Mary came behind with her hand on Laura's shoulder. Last marched Carrie with the other flatiron and the music went with them up the stairs.

"March! March! Eskdale and Liddesdale!
All the blue bonnets are over the border!
Many a banner spread flutters about your head
Many a crest that is famous in story.
Mount, and make ready then,
Sons of the mountain glen!
Fight for your homes and the old Scottish glory!"

It helped some. Laura hoped that she seemed cheerful enough to encourage the others. But all the time she knew that this storm had blocked the train again. She knew that almost all the coal was gone from the pile in the lean-to. There was no more coal in town. The kerosene was low in the lamp though Ma lighted it only while they ate supper. There would be no meat until the train came. There was no butter and only a little fat-meat dripping was left to spread on bread. There were still potatoes, but no more than flour enough for one more bread baking.

When Laura had thought all this, she thought that surely a train must come before the last bread was gone. Then she began to think again about the coal, the kerosene, the little bit of dripping left, and the flour in the bottom of the flour sack. But surely, surely, the train must come.

All day and all night, the house trembled, the winds roared and screamed, the snow scoured against the walls and over the roof where the frosty nails came through. In the other houses there were people, there must be lights, but they were too far away to seem real.

In the back room behind the feed store, Almanzo was busy. He had taken saddles, harness, and clothes from the end wall and piled them on the bed. He had pushed the table against the cupboard and in the cleared space he had set a chair for a sawhorse.

He had set a frame of two-by-fours a foot from the end wall. Now he was sawing boards one by one and nailing them on the frame. The rasping of the saw and the hammering were hardly louder than the blizzard's noise.

When he had built the inner wall up halfway, he took out his jackknife and ripped open a sack of his seed wheat. He lifted up the hundred-and-twenty-five-pound sack and carefully let the wheat pour into the space between the new wall and the old one.

"I figure she'll hold it all," he said to Royal who sat whittling by the stove. "When I build all the way up so the bin won't show."

"It's your funeral," said Royal. "It's your wheat."

"You bet your life it's my wheat!" Almanzo replied. "And it's going into my ground, come spring."

"What makes you think I'd sell your wheat?" Royal demanded.

"You're pretty near sold out of grain already," Almanzo answered. "This blizzard'll let up sometime, or it'll be the first one that didn't, and soon as it does the whole town'll come piling in here to buy wheat. Harthorn and Loftus have got just three sacks of flour left between 'em, and this storm'll hold up the train till after Christmas at best."

"All that don't mean I'd sell your wheat," Royal insisted.

"Maybe not, but I know you, Roy. You're not a farmer, you're a storekeeper. A fellow comes in here and looks around and says, 'What's the price of your wheat?' You say, 'I'm sold out of wheat.' He says, 'What's that in those sacks?' You tell him, 'That's not my wheat, it's Manzo's.' So the fellow says, 'What'll you boys sell it for?' And don't try to tell me you'll say, 'We won't sell it.' No siree, Roy, you're a storekeeper. You'll say to him, 'What'll you give?' "

"Well, maybe I would," Royal admitted. "What's the harm in that?"

"The harm is that they'll bid up prices sky-high before a train gets through. I'll be out hauling hay or somewhere and you'll figure that I wouldn't refuse such a price, or you'll think you know better than I do what's for my best interests. You never would believe I mean what I say when I say it, Royal Wilder."

"Well, well, keep your shirt on, Manzo," said Royal. "I am considerable older than you be and maybe I do know best."

"Maybe you do and maybe you don't. Be that as it may be, I'm going to run my own business my own way. I'm nailing up my seed wheat so nobody'll see it and nobody'll bring up any question about it and it'll be right here when seedtime comes."

"All right, all right," Royal said. He went on carefully whittling a linked chain out of a stick of pine and Almanzo, bracing his legs, lifted the sacks one by one to his shoulder and let the wheat pour into its hiding place. Now and then a heavier blow of the winds shook the walls and now and then the red-hot stove puffed out smoke. A louder roar of the storm made them both listen and Almanzo said, "Golly, this one's a daisy!"

"Roy," he said after a while, "whittle me a plug to fit this knothole, will you? I want to get this job done before chore time."

Royal came to look at the knothole. He rounded it with his knife and chose a piece of wood that would make a plug to fit.

"If prices go up like you say, you're a fool not to sell your wheat," he remarked. "They'll have the train running before spring. You can buy your seed back and make a profit like I'm figuring on doing."

"You said that before," Almanzo reminded him. "I'd rather be sure than sorry. You don't know when the train'll be running and you don't know they'll ship in seed wheat before April."

"Nothing's sure but death and taxes," said Royal.

"Seedtime's pretty sure to come around," Almanzo said. "And good seed makes a good crop."

"You talk like Father," Royal mentioned. He tried the plug against the knothole and set to whittling it again. "If the train don't get through in a couple of weeks or so, I wonder how this town'll hold out. There's not much left in the grocery stores."

"Folks manage to get along when they've got to," said Almanzo. "Pretty near everybody brought out supplies last summer like we did. And we can make ours stretch till warm weather if we must."

CHAPTER 18

Merry Christmas

THE blizzard stopped at last. After three days of its ceaseless noise, the stillness rang in Laura's ears.

Pa hurried away to get a load of hay and when he came back he put David in the stable. The sun was still glittering on the snow, there was no cloud in the northwest, and Laura wondered why he stopped hauling hay.

"What's wrong, Charles?" Ma asked quietly when Pa came in.

Pa answered, "Gilbert made it to Preston and back. He's brought the mail!"

It was as if Christmas had happened unexpectedly. Ma hoped for the church paper. Laura and Mary and Carrie hoped that Reverend Alden had sent them something to read; sometimes he did. Grace was excited because they were excited. It was hard to wait for Pa to come back from the post office.

He was gone a long time. As Ma said, it did no good to be impatient. Every man in town was at the post office and Pa must wait his turn.

When at last he came, his hands were full. Ma reached eagerly for the church papers and Laura and Carrie both tried to take the bundle of *Youth's Companions*. There were newspapers too.

"Here! Here!" Pa laughed. "Don't mob a fellow! And that's not the whole of it. Guess what I got!"

"A letter? Oh Pa, did you get a letter?" Laura cried.

"Who is it from?" Ma asked.

"You've got the *Advances*, Caroline," Pa replied. "And Laura and Carrie've got the *Youth's Companions*. I've got the *Inter-Ocean* and the *Pioneer Press*. Mary gets the letter."

Mary's face shone. She felt the letter's size and thickness. "A big, fat letter! Please read it, Ma."

So Ma opened the letter and read it aloud.

The letter was from Reverend Alden. He was sorry that he had not been able to come back and help organize a church last spring, but he had been sent farther north. He hoped to be with them when spring came again. The children of the Sunday School in Minnesota were sending a bundle of *Youth's Companions* to the girls, and would send another bundle next year. His church had shipped them a Christmas barrel and he hoped the clothing would fit. As his own Christmas gift and some slight return for their hospitality to him and to Reverend Stuart last winter at Silver Lake, he had put in a Christmas turkey. He wished them all a Merry Christmas and a Happy New Year.

There was a little silence when Ma had finished reading. Then she said, "We have this good letter, anyway."

"Gilbert brought word that they're putting on a double work crew and two snowplows at the Tracy cut," Pa told them. "We may get the barrel by Christmas."

"It's only a few days," Ma said.

"A lot can be done in a few days," said Pa. "If this spell of clear weather holds out, no reason they can't get the train through."

"Oh, I hope the Christmas barrel comes," Carrie said.

"The hotels have shut down," Pa told Ma the news. "They've been burning lumber and now Banker Ruth has bought out the lumberyard, down to the last shingle."

"We couldn't afford to burn lumber anyway," said Ma. "But Charles, we are almost out of coal."

"We'll burn hay," Pa answered cheerfully.

"Hay?" Ma said, and Laura asked, "How can we burn hay, Pa?"

She thought of how quickly the prairie fires swept through dry grass. Flame licks through the light, thin stems and is gone before the frail ashes can fall. How could a room be kept warm by a fire so quickly burning out, when even the steady glow of hard coal could not keep out the cold?

"We will have to contrive," Pa told her. "We'll manage it! Needs must, when the devil drives."

"Likely the train will get through in time," Ma said.

Pa put on his cap again and asked Ma to make dinner a little late. He had time to haul another load of hay if he hustled. He went out and Ma said, "Come, girls, put the bundle of *Youth's Companions* away. We must get out the washing while the weather's clear so we can."

All that day Laura and Carrie and Mary looked forward to the *Youth's Companions* and often they spoke of them. But the bright day was short. They stirred and punched the clothes boiling on the stove; they lifted them on the broom handle into the tub where Ma soaped and rubbed them. Laura rinsed them, Carrie stirred the blueing bag in the second rinse-water until it was blue enough. Laura made the boiled starch. And when for the last time Ma went out into the cold to hang the freezing wash on the line, Pa had come for dinner.

Then they washed the dishes, they scrubbed the floor and blacked the stove, and washed the inside of the windowpanes. Ma brought in the frozen-dry clothes and they sorted them and sprinkled them and rolled them tightly, ready for ironing. Twilight had come. It was too late to read that day and after supper there was no lamplight because they must save the last of the kerosene.

"Work comes before pleasure," Ma always said. She smiled her gentle smile for Laura and Carrie and said now, "My girls have helped me do a good day's work," and they were rewarded.

"Tomorrow we'll read a story," Carrie said happily.

"Tomorrow we have to do the ironing," Laura reminded her.

"Yes, and we should air the bedding and give the upstairs a thorough cleaning, in this good weather," said Ma.

Pa came in and heard them. "Tomorrow I'm going to work on the railroad," he said.

Mr. Woodworth had word to put at work on the tracks all the men he could get. The superintendent at the Tracy cut was driving the work there and shovel gangs were shoveling eastward from Huron.

"If muscle and will-power can do it, we'll have a train through by Christmas!" Pa declared.

That night he came back from work with a broad smile on his sun-red face. "Good news!" he called out. "The work train will come through sometime tomorrow! The regular train'll come next, day after tomorrow probably."

"Oh, good! Good! Goody!" Laura and Carrie exclaimed together, and Ma said, "That is good news, indeed. What is wrong with your eyes, Charles?"

His eyes were red and puffed. He answered cheerfully,

"Shoveling snow in the sunshine is hard on eyes. Some of the men are snow-blind. Fix me up a little weak salt-water, will you, Caroline? And I'll bathe them after I do the chores."

When he had gone to the stable, Ma dropped into a chair near Mary. "I'm afraid, girls, this will be a poor Christmas," she said. "What with these awful storms and trying to keep warm, we've had no time to plan for it."

"Maybe the Christmas barrel . . ." Carrie began.

"We mustn't count on it," said Mary.

"We could wait for Christmas till it comes," Laura suggested. "All but . . ." and she picked up Grace who was listening wide-eyed.

"Can't Santa Claus come?" Grace asked, and her lower lip began to tremble.

Laura hugged her and looked over her golden head at Ma.

Ma said firmly, "Santa Claus always comes to good little girls, Grace. But girls," she went on, "I have an idea. What do you think of saving my church papers and your bundle of *Youth's Companions* to open on Christmas day?"

After a moment Mary said, "I think it is a good idea. It will help us to learn self-denial."

"I don't want to," Laura said.

"Nobody does," said Mary. "But it's good for us."

Sometimes Laura did not even want to be good. But after another silent moment she said, "Well, if you and Mary want to, Ma, I will. It will give us something to look forward to for Christmas."

"What do you say about it, Carrie?" Ma asked, and in a small voice Carrie said, "I will, too, Ma."

"That's my good girls," Ma approved them. She went on. "We can find a little something in the stores for . . ." and she glanced at Grace. "But you older girls know, Pa hasn't been able to get any work for wages this year. We can't spare money for presents, but we can have a happy Christmas just the same. I'll try to contrive something extra for dinner and then we'll all open our papers and read them, and when it's too dark to read, Pa will play the fiddle."

"We haven't much flour left, Ma," Laura said.

"The storekeepers are asking twenty-five cents a pound for flour so Pa's waiting for the train," Ma replied. "There's nothing to make a pie, anyway, and no butter or eggs for a cake and no more sugar in town. But we'll think of something for Christmas dinner."

Laura sat thinking. She was making a little picture frame of cross-stitch in wools on thin, silver-colored cardboard. Up the sides and across the top she had made a pattern of small blue flowers and green leaves. Now she was outlining the picture-opening in blue. While she put the tiny needle through the perforations in the cardboard and drew the fine, colored wool carefully after it, she was thinking how wistfully Carrie had looked at the beautiful thing. She decided to give it to Carrie for Christmas. Someday, perhaps, she could make another for herself.

How fortunate it was that she had finished knitting the lace for her petticoat. She would give that to Mary. And to Ma she would give the cardboard hair receiver that she had already embroidered to match the picture frame. Ma could hang it on the corner of her looking glass, and when she combed her hair she would put the combings in it to use later in the hair-switch she was making.

"But what can we do for Pa?" she asked.

"I declare I don't know," Ma worried. "I can't think of a thing."

"I've got some pennies," Carrie said.

"There's my college money," Mary began, but Ma said, "No, Mary, we won't touch that."

"I have ten cents," Laura said thoughtfully. "How many pennies have you, Carrie?"

"I have five," Carrie told her.

"We'd need twenty-five to get Pa a pair of suspenders," Laura said. "He needs a new pair."

"I have a dime," said Ma. "So that is settled. Laura, you and Carrie had better go and buy them as soon as Pa has gone to work tomorrow morning."

Next day, when their morning work was done, Laura and Carrie crossed the snowy street to Mr. Harthorn's store. Mr. Harthorn was there alone and the shelves were bare. On both long walls there were only a few pairs of men's boots and women's shoes and some bolts of calico.

The bean barrel was empty. The cracker barrel was empty.

The little brine in the bottom of the pork barrel had no pork in it. The long, flat codfish box held only a little salt scattered on its bottom. The dried-apple box and the dried-blackberry box were empty.

"I'm sold out of groceries till the train gets here," Mr. Harthorn said. "I was expecting a bill of groceries when the train stopped."

Some pretty handkerchiefs, combs, and hairpins, and two pairs of suspenders were in the showcase. Laura and Carrie looked at the suspenders. They were plain, dull gray.

"Shall I do them up for you?" Mr. Harthorn asked.

Laura did not like to say no, but she looked at Carrie and saw that Carrie hoped she would.

"No, thank you, Mr. Harthorn," Laura said. "We will not take them now."

Out in the glittering cold again, she said to Carrie, "Let's go to Loftus' store and see if we can't find prettier ones."

They bent their heads against the strong, cold wind and struggled along the icy path on the store porches till they reached the other Dry Goods and Groceries.

That store was bare and echoing, too. Every barrel and box was empty, and where the canned goods had been there were only two flat cans of oysters.

"I'm expecting a stock of groceries when the train comes tomorrow," Mr. Loftus told them. "It won't get here any too soon either."

In his showcase was a pair of blue suspenders, with small red flowers beautifully machine-woven along them and bright brass buckles. Laura had never seen such pretty suspenders. They were just right for Pa.

"How much are they?" she asked, almost sure that they would cost too much. But the price was twenty-five cents. Laura gave Mr. Loftus her own two five-cent pieces, Carrie's five pennies, and Ma's thin silver ten-cent piece. She took the slim package and the wind blew her and Carrie breathlessly home.

At bedtime that night no one spoke of hanging up stockings. Grace was too young to know about hanging stockings on Christmas eve and no one else expected a present. But they had never been so eager for Christmas day, because the tracks were clear now and the train would come tomorrow.

Laura's first thought in the morning was, "The train is coming today!" The window was not frosted, the sky was clear, the snowy prairie was turning rosy in early sunshine. The train would surely come and joyfully Laura thought about her Christmas surprises.

She slid out of bed without waking Mary and quickly pulled on her dress in the cold. She opened the box where she kept her own things. She took out the roll of knitted lace, already wrapped carefully in tissue paper. Then she found the prettiest card she had ever been given in Sunday school and she took the little embroidered picture frame and the cardboard hair receiver. With these in her hands, she hurried tiptoe downstairs.

Ma looked up in surprise. The table was set and Ma was putting on each plate a little package wrapped in red-and-white striped paper.

"Merry Christmas, Ma!" Laura whispered. "Oh, what are they?"

"Christmas presents," Ma whispered. "Whatever have you got there?"

Laura only smiled. She put her packages at Ma's plate and Mary's. Then she slipped the Sunday school card into the embroidered frame. "For Carrie," she whispered. She and Ma looked at it; it was beautiful. Then Ma found a piece of tissue paper to wrap it in.

Carrie and Grace and Mary were already clambering down the stairs, calling, "Merry Christmas! Merry Christmas!"

"Oo-oo!" Carrie squealed. "I thought we were waiting for Christmas till the Christmas barrel came on the train! Oo-oo, look! look!"

"What is it?" Mary asked.

"There are presents at every plate on the table!" Carrie told her.

"No, no, Grace, mustn't touch," Ma said. "We will all wait for Pa." So Grace ran around the table, looking but not touching.

Pa came with the milk and Ma strained it. Then Pa stepped into the lean-to and came back grinning broadly. He handed Ma the two cans of oysters from Loftus' store.

"Charles!" Ma said.

"Make us an oyster soup for Christmas dinner, Caroline!" Pa told her. "I got some milk from Ellen, not much, and it's the last; she's as good as dry. But maybe you can make it do."

"I'll thin it out with water," said Ma. "We'll have oyster soup for Christmas dinner!"

Then Pa saw the table. Laura and Carrie laughed aloud, shouting, "Merry Christmas, Merry Christmas, Pa!" and Laura told Mary, "Pa's surprised!"

"Hurrah for Santa Claus!" Pa sang out. "The old fellow made it in, if the train didn't!"

They all sat down at their places, and Ma gently held back Grace's hands. "Pa opens his first, Grace," she said.

Pa picked up his package. "Now what can this be, and who gave it to me?" He untied the string, unfolded the paper, and held up the new red-flowered suspenders.

"Whew!" he exclaimed. "Now how am I ever going to wear my coat? These are too fine to cover up." He looked around at all the faces. "All of you did this," he said. "Well, I'll be proud to wear them!"

"Not yet, Grace," Ma said. "Mary is next."

Mary unwrapped the yards of fine knitted lace. She fingered it lovingly and her face was shining with delight. "I'll save it to wear when I go to college," she said. "It's another thing to help me to go. It will be so pretty on a white petticoat."

Carrie was looking at her present. The picture was of the Good Shepherd in His blue and white robes, holding in His arms a snow-white lamb. The silvery cardboard embroidered in blue flowers made a perfect frame for it.

"Oh, how lovely. How lovely," Carrie whispered.

Ma said the hair receiver was just what she had been needing.

Then Grace tore the paper from her gift and gave a gurgle of joy. Two little, flat wooden men stood on a platform between two flat red posts. Their hands held onto two strings twisted tightly together above their heads. They wore peaked red caps and blue coats with gold buttons. Their trousers were red-and-green stripes. Their boots were black with turned-up toes.

Ma gently pressed the bottoms of the posts inward. One of the men somersaulted up and the other swung into his place. Then the first came down while the second went up and they nodded their heads and jerked their arms and swung their legs, dancing and somersaulting.

"Oh, look! Oh, look!" Grace shouted. She could never have enough of watching the funny little men dancing.

The small striped packages at each place held Christmas candy.

"Wherever did you get candy, Pa?" Laura wondered.

"I got it some time ago. It was the last bit of sugar in town," said Pa. "Some folks said they'd use it for sugar, but I made sure of our Christmas candy."

"Oh, what a lovely Christmas," Carrie sighed. Laura thought so too. Whatever happened, they could always have a merry Christmas. And the sun was shining, the sky was blue, the railroad tracks were clear, and the train was coming. The train had come through the Tracy cut that morning. Sometime that day they would hear its whistle and see it stopping by the depot.

At noon Ma was making the oyster soup. Laura was setting the table, Carrie and Grace were playing with the jumping-jack. Ma tasted the soup and set the kettle back on the stove. "The oysters are ready," she said, and stooping she looked at the slices of bread toasting in the oven. "And the bread is toasted. Whatever is Pa doing?"

"He's bringing in hay," said Laura.

Pa opened the door. Behind him the lean-to was almost full of slough hay. He asked, "Is the oyster soup ready?"

"I'm taking it up," Ma replied. "I'm glad the train is coming, this is the last of the coal." Then she looked at Pa and asked, "What is wrong, Charles?"

Pa said slowly. "There is a cloud in the northwest."

"Oh, not another blizzard!" Ma cried.

"I'm afraid so," Pa answered. "But it needn't spoil our dinner." He drew his chair up to the table. "I've packed plenty of hay into the stable and filled the lean-to. Now for our oyster soup!"

The sun kept on shining while they ate. The hot soup was good, even though the milk was mostly water. Pa crumbled the toast into his soup plate. "This toasted bread is every bit as good as crackers," he told Ma. "I don't know but better."

Laura enjoyed the good soup, but she could not stop thinking of that dark cloud coming up. She could not stop listening for the wind that she knew would soon come.

It came with a shriek. The windows rattled and the house shook.

"She must be a daisy!" Pa said. He went to the window but he could not see out. Snow came on the wind from the sky. Snow rose from the hard drifts as the wind cut them away. It all met in the whirling air and swirled madly. The sky, the sunshine, the town, were gone, lost in that blinding dance of snow. The house was alone again.

Laura thought, "The train can't come now."

"Come, girls," Ma said. "We'll get these dishes out of the way, and then we'll open our papers and have a cosy afternoon."

"Is there coal enough, Ma?" Laura asked.

Pa looked at the fire. "It will last till suppertime," he said. "And then we'll burn hay."

Frost was freezing up the windowpanes and the room was cold near the walls. Near the stove, the light was too dim for reading. When the dishes were washed and put away, Ma set the lamp on the red-checked tablecloth and lighted it. There was only a little kerosene in the bowl where the wick coiled, but it gave a warm and cheery light. Laura opened the bundle of *Youth's Companions* and she and Carrie looked eagerly at the wealth of stories printed on the smooth, white paper.

"You girls choose a story," Ma said. "And I will read it out loud, so we can all enjoy it together."

So, close together between the stove and the bright table, they listened to Ma's reading the story in her soft, clear voice. The story took them all far away from the stormy cold and dark. When she had finished that one, Ma read a second and a third. That was enough for one day; they must save some for another time.

"Aren't you glad we saved those wonderful stories for Christmas day?" Mary sighed happily. And they were. The whole afternoon had gone so quickly. Already it was chore time.

When Pa came back from the stable, he stayed some time in the lean-to and came in at last with his arms full of sticks.

"Here is your breakfast fuel, Caroline," he said, laying his armful down by the stove. "Good hard sticks of hay. I guess they will burn all right."

"Sticks of hay?" Laura exclaimed.

"That's right, Laura." Pa spread his hands in the warmth

above the stove. "I'm glad that hay's in the lean-to. I couldn't carry it in through the wind that's blowing now, unless I brought it one blade at a time, in my teeth."

The hay *was* in sticks. Pa had somehow twisted and knotted it tightly till each stick was almost as hard as wood.

"Sticks of hay!" Ma laughed. "What won't you think of next? Trust you, Charles, to find a way."

"You are good at that yourself," Pa smiled at her.

For supper there were hot boiled potatoes and a slice of bread apiece, with salt. That was the last baking of bread, but there were still beans in the sack and a few turnips. There was still hot tea with sugar, and Grace had her cup of cambric tea made with hot water because there was no more milk. While they were eating, the lamp began to flicker. With all its might the flame pulled itself up, drawing the last drops of kerosene up the wick. Then it fainted down and desperately tried again. Ma leaned over and blew it out. The dark came in, loud with the roar and the shrieking of the storm.

"The fire is dying, anyway, so we may as well go to bed," Ma said gently. Christmas Day was over.

Laura lay in bed and listened to the winds blowing, louder and louder. They sounded like the pack of wolves howling around the little house on the prairie long ago, when she was small and Pa had carried her in his arms. And there was the deeper howl of the great buffalo wolf that she and Carrie had met on the bank of Silver Lake.

She started trembling, when she heard the scream of the panther in the creek bed, in Indian Territory. But she knew it was only the wind. Now she heard the Indian war whoops when the Indians were dancing their war dances all through the horrible nights by the Verdigris river.

The war whoops died away and she heard crowds of people muttering, then shrieking and fleeing screaming away from fierce yells chasing them. But she knew she heard only the voices of the blizzard winds. She pulled the bedcovers over her head and covered her ears tightly to shut out the sounds, but still she heard them.

CHAPTER 19

Where There's a Will

THE hay made a quick, hot fire, but it burned away more swiftly than kindling. Ma kept the stove's drafts closed and all day long she was feeding the fire. All day long, except when he went through the storm to do the chores, Pa was twisting more sticks of hay in the lean-to. The storm grew fiercer and the cold more cruel.

Often Pa came to the stove to warm his hands. "My fingers get so numb," he said, "I can't make a good twist.'

"Let me help you, Pa," Laura begged.

He did not want to let her. "Your hands are too small for such work," he told her. Then he admitted, "But somebody's got to help. It is going to be more than one person can do, to keep this stove going and haul hay for it." Finally he decided, "Come along. I'll show you how."

Laura put on Pa's old coat and her hood and muffler and went into the lean-to with Pa.

The lean-to was not ceiled inside. The wind was blowing snow through all the cracks of the board walls. Snow traveled in little drifts across the floor and sifted over the hay.

Pa picked up a double handful of hay and shook the snow from it.

"Shake off all the snow," he told Laura. "If you leave it on, it will melt when you take the sticks in and make them too wet to burn."

Laura picked up all the hay her hands could hold and shook the snow from it. Then, watching Pa, she followed his motions in twisting the hay. First he twisted the long strand as far as his two hands could do it. Then he put the right-hand end of it under his left elbow and held it there, tight against his side, so that it could not untwist. Then his right hand took the other end from his left hand. His left hand slid down as near as it could get to the end under his left elbow and took hold of it. Pa twisted the strand again. This time he put its other end under his left elbow. He repeated these motions, again and again and again, till the whole strand of hay was twisted tight and kinking in the middle. Each time he twisted and tucked the end under his left arm, the tight twist coiled around itself.

When the whole length of the twist had wound itself tight, Pa bent the ends of hay together and tucked them into the last kink. He dropped the hard stick of hay on the floor and looked at Laura.

She was trying to tuck in the ends as Pa had done. The hay was twisted so tightly that she couldn't push them in.

"Bend your twist a little to loosen it," said Pa. "Then slip the ends in between the kinks and let it twist itself back tight. That's the way!"

Laura's stick of hay was uneven and raggedy, not smooth and hard like Pa's. But Pa told her that it was well done for the first one; she would do better next time.

She made six sticks of hay, each better than the one before till the sixth one was as it should be. But now she was so cold that her hands could not feel the hay.

"That's enough!" Pa told her. "Gather them up, and we'll go warm ourselves."

They carried the sticks of hay into the kitchen. Laura's feet were numb from cold; they felt like wooden feet. Her hands were red and when she held them in the warm air above the stove they tingled and stung and smarted where the sharp blades of the grass had cut them. But she had helped Pa. The sticks of hay that she had made gave him time enough to get thoroughly warm before they must go into the cold to twist more hay.

All that day and all the next day, Laura helped Pa twist hay while Ma kept the fire going and Carrie helped her take care of Grace and of the housework. For dinner they had baked potatoes and mashed turnips with pepper and salt, and for supper Ma chopped the potatoes and heated them in the oven because there was no fat to fry them in. But the food was hot and good, and there was plenty of tea and still some sugar.

"This is the last loaf of bread," Ma said, the second night at supper. "We really must have some flour, Charles."

"I'll buy some as soon as this storm lets up," Pa said. "No matter what it costs."

"Use my college money, Pa," Mary said. "Thirty-five dollars and twenty-five cents will buy all the flour we could want."

"That's our good girl, Mary," said Ma. "But I hope we won't have to spend your college money. I suppose prices depend on when they can get the train through?" she said to Pa.

"Yes," Pa said. "That's what they depend on."

Ma got up and put another stick of hay on the fire. When she lifted the stove lid, a reddish-yellow smoky light flared up and drove back the dark for a moment. Then the dark came back again. The wild screaming of the storm seemed louder and nearer in the dark.

"If only I had some grease I could fix some kind of a light," Ma considered. "We didn't lack for light when I was a girl, before this newfangled kerosene was ever heard of."

"That's so," said Pa. "These times are too progressive. Everything has changed too fast. Railroads and telegraph and kerosene and coal stoves—they're good things to have but the trouble is, folks get to depend on 'em."

In the morning the winds were still howling and outside the thick-frosted windows the snow was still whirling. But by mid-morning a straight, strong wind was blowing from the south and the sun was shining. It was very cold, so cold that the snow squeaked under Laura's feet in the lean-to.

Pa went across the street to get the flour. He was gone some time, and when he came back he was carrying a grain sack on his shoulder. He let it slide to the floor with a thump.

"Here's your flour, Caroline, or what will have to take the place of it," he said. "It is wheat, the last that's left of the Wilder boys' stock. There is no flour in the stores. Banker Ruth bought the last sack this morning. He paid fifty dollars for it, a dollar a pound."

"My goodness, Charles," Ma gasped.

"Yes. We couldn't buy much flour at that price, so I guess it's just as well Ruth got it. We may as well learn now how to cook wheat. How will it be, boiled?"

"I don't know, Charles. It isn't as if we had anything to eat on it," said Ma.

"It's a pity there isn't a grist mill in town," Pa said.

"We have a mill," Ma replied. She reached to the top of the cupboard and took down the coffee mill.

"So we have," said Pa. "Let's see how it works."

Ma set the little brown wooden box on the table. She turned the handle for a moment, to loosen every last grain of coffee from the grinders. Then she pulled out the little drawer, emptied it, and wiped it carefully. Pa opened the sack of wheat.

The black iron hopper in the top of the mill held half a cupful of the grain. Ma shut its top. Then she sat down, placed the square box between her knees to hold it firmly, and began turning the handle around and around. The mill gave out its grinding noise.

"Wheat will grind just like coffee," Ma said. She looked into the little drawer. The broken bits of wheat were crushed out flat. "Not like coffee, either," Ma said. "The wheat hasn't been roasted and has more moisture in it."

"Can you make bread of that?" Pa asked.

"Of course I can," Ma replied. "But we must keep the mill grinding if I'm to have enough to make a loaf for dinner."

"And I must go haul some hay to bake it with," said Pa. He took a round, flat wooden box from his pocket and handed it to Ma. "Here's something you can maybe use to make a light."

"Is there any word of the train, Charles?" Ma asked him.

"They're working again at that Tracy cut," said Pa. "It's packed full of snow again, to the top of the snowbanks they threw up on both sides when they cleared it last time."

He went to the stable to hitch David to the sled. Ma looked into the box. It was full of yellow axle grease. But there was no time then to think about making a light. The fire was dying and Ma put the last stick of hay on it. Laura hurried into the lean-to to twist more hay.

In a few minutes Ma came to help her. "Mary is grinding the wheat," Ma said. "We must twist a lot of hay to keep the fire going. We must have a good warm fire when Pa comes back. He will be almost frozen."

It was late afternoon before Pa came back. He unhitched the sled near the back door and put David in the stable. Then he pitched the hay into the lean-to until there was hardly space to squeeze through from door to door. When that was done, he came in to the stove. He was so cold that it was some time before he was warm enough to speak.

"I'm sorry to be so late, Caroline," he made excuse. "The

snow is much deeper than it was. I had a hard time digging the hay out of the drift."

"I think we may as well have dinner at this time every day," Ma answered. "What with saving fire and light, the days are so short that there's hardly time for three meals. A late dinner will serve for supper as well."

The brown bread that Ma had made from the ground wheat was very good. It had a fresh, nutty flavor that seemed almost to take the place of butter.

"I see you've got your sourdough working again," Pa remarked.

"Yes," Ma answered. "We don't need yeast or milk to make good bread."

"'Where there's a will there's a way,'" said Pa. He helped himself to another potato and sprinkled it with salt. "Potatoes and salt aren't to be sneezed at either. Salt brings out the full flavor of a potato; it's not all hidden with butter and gravy."

"Don't put sugar in your tea, Pa, and you'll get the full flavor of the tea," Laura said naughtily.

Pa's eyes twinkled at her. "A good hot cup of tea brings out the flavor of the sugar, Half-Pint," he answered. Then he asked Ma, "How did you make out with the axle grease, for a light?"

"I haven't had time yet," Ma told him. "But as soon as we finish eating I'm going to make a button lamp."

"What's a button lamp?" Pa asked.

"Wait and see," said Ma.

When he had gone to do the chores for the night Ma told Carrie to bring her the rag bag. She took some of the axle grease from the box and spread it in an old saucer. Then she cut a small square of calico. "Now find me a button in the button bag, Carrie."

"What kind of button, Ma?" Carrie asked, bringing the button bag from the cold front room.

"Oh, one of Pa's old overcoat buttons," said Ma.

She put the button in the center of the square of calico. She drew the cloth together over the button and wound a thread tightly around it and twisted the corners of calico straight upward in a tapering bunch. Then she rubbed a little axle grease up the calico and set the button into the axle grease in the saucer.

"Now we'll wait till Pa comes," she said.

Laura and Carrie hurried to finish washing the dishes in the gathering dusk. It was dark when Pa came in.

"Give me a match, Charles, please," Ma said. She lighted the taper tip of the button lamp. A tiny flame flickered and grew stronger. It burned steadily, melting the axle grease and drawing it up through the cloth into itself, keeping itself alight by burning. The little flame was like the flame of a candle in the dark.

"You're a wonder, Caroline," said Pa. "It's only a little light, but it makes all the difference."

Warming his hands above the stove, he looked down at the little pile of twisted hay. "But I don't need a light to twist hay," he said. "And we must have more now. There's not enough here for morning."

He went out to twist hay and Laura took the coffee mill from Mary. Turning the little handle around and around made the arm and shoulder ache so badly that they must take turns at the grinding. The little mill ground wheat so slowly that they had to keep it grinding all the time to make flour enough to bake for each meal.

Ma took off Grace's shoes and warmed her feet by the oven door while she slipped off her little dress, pulled on her nightgown, and wrapped her in the shawl that was warming over a chair by the stove.

"Come, Carrie, if you're good and warm," she said. "I'll put Grace in bed with you now."

When Grace and Carrie were tucked in bed with the warm shawl and the hot flatiron Ma came downstairs.

"I'll grind wheat now, Laura," she said. "You and Mary go to bed. As soon as Pa comes in we'll go to bed, too, to save this hay that is so hard to get and to twist."

CHAPTER 20

Antelope!

THERE came a sunny day when the loose snow was rolling like drifts of smoke across the frozen white prairie.

Pa came hurrying into the house. "There's a herd of antelope west of town!" he said, as he took his shotgun down from its hooks and filled his pockets with cartridges.

Laura threw Ma's shawl around her and ran into the cold front room. She scratched a peephole through the frost on the window and she saw a crowd of men gathering in the street. Several were on horseback. Mr. Foster and Almanzo Wilder were riding the beautiful Morgan horses. Cap Garland came running and joined the men on foot who were listening to Pa. They all carried guns. They looked excited and their voices sounded excited and loud.

"Come back where it's warm, Laura," Ma called.

"Think of venison!" Laura said, hanging up the shawl. "I hope Pa gets *two* antelopes!"

"I will be glad to have some meat to go with the brown bread," Ma said. "But we must not count chickens before they are hatched."

"Why, Ma, Pa will get an antelope, if there are any antelopes," said Laura.

Carrie brought a dish of wheat to fill the hopper of the coffee mill that Mary was grinding. "Roast venison," Carrie said. "With gravy, gravy on the potatoes and the brown bread!"

"Wait a minute, Mary!" Laura exclaimed. "Listen. There they go!"

The steady wind rushed by the house and whistled shrill along the eaves, but they could dimly hear the voices and the feet of men and horses moving away along Main Street.

At the end of the street they paused. They could see, a mile away across the snowdrifts and the blowing snow, the gray herd of antelope drifting southward.

"Slow and easy does it," said Pa. "Give us time to work around 'em to the north before you boys close in from the south.

Come in slow and herd 'em toward us without scaring 'em, if you can, till they're in gunshot. There's no hurry, we've got the day before us and if we work it right we ought to get us one apiece."

"Maybe we'd better ride to the north and you fellows on foot surround 'em from the south," Mr. Foster said.

"No, let it go as Ingalls said," Mr. Harthorn told him. "Come on, boys!"

"String out," Pa called. "And go slow and easy. Don't scare 'em!"

On the Morgans, Almanzo and Mr. Foster took the lead. The cold wind made the horses eager to go. They pricked their ears forward and back and tossed their heads, jingling the bits and pretending to shy a little at their own shadows. They stretched their noses forward, pulling on the bits and prancing to go faster.

"Hold her steady," Almanzo said to Mr. Foster. "Don't saw on the bits, she's tender-mouthed."

Mr. Foster did not know how to ride. He was as nervous as Lady and he was making her more nervous. He bounced in the saddle and did not hold the reins steadily. Almanzo was sorry he had let him ride Lady.

"Careful, Foster," Almanzo said. "That mare will jump out from under you."

"What's the matter with her? What's the matter with her?" Mr. Foster chattered in the cold wind. "Oh, there they are!"

In the clear air the antelope seemed nearer than they were. Beyond the drifting herd the men on foot were working westward. Almanzo saw Mr. Ingalls at the head of the line. In a few more minutes they would have the herd surrounded.

He turned to speak to Mr. Foster and he saw Lady's saddle empty. At that instant a shot deafened him and both horses jumped high and far. Almanzo reined Prince down, as Lady streaked away.

Mr. Foster was jumping up and down, waving his gun and yelling. Crazy with excitement, he had jumped off Lady, let go her reins, and fired at the antelope that were too far away to hit.

Heads and tails up, the antelope were skimming away as if the wind were blowing them above the snowdrifts. Brown Lady overtook the gray herd and reached its middle, running with them.

"Don't shoot! Don't shoot!" Almanzo yelled, though he knew that his yells were useless against the wind. The antelope were already passing through the line of men on foot, but no one fired at them for fear of hitting the mare. The glossy brown Morgan, head up and black mane and tail flying, went over a prairie swell in the midst of the gray, low cloud of antelope and vanished. In a moment the horse and the herd passed over another white curve, then, growing smaller, they appeared again and again the prairie swallowed them.

"Looks like you've lost her, Wilder," Mr. Harthorn said. "Too bad."

The other riders had come up. They sat still, on their horses, watching the distant prairie. The antelope herd, with Lady small and dark in it, appeared once more as a flying gray smudge that quickly vanished.

Mr. Ingalls came and the other men on foot. Cap Garland said, "Tough luck, Wilder. Guess we might as well have risked a shot."

"You're a mighty hunter before the Lord, Foster," Gerald Fuller said.

"He's the only man that got a shot," said Cap Garland. "And what a shot!"

"I'm sorry. I must have let the mare go," Mr. Foster said. "I was so excited, I didn't think. I thought the horse would stand. I never saw an antelope before."

"Next time you take a shot at one, Foster, wait till you're within range," Gerald Fuller told him.

No one else said anything. Almanzo sat in the saddle while Prince fought the bit, trying to get free to follow his mate. Frightened as Lady was, and racing with the herd, the danger was that she would run herself to death. Trying to catch her would do no good; chasing the herd would only make it run faster.

Judging by the landmarks, the antelope were five or six miles to the west when they turned northward.

"They're making for Spirit Lake," Mr. Ingalls said. "They'll shelter there in the brush and then they'll range back into the bluffs of the river. We'll not see them again."

"What about Wilder's horse, Mr. Ingalls?" Cap Garland asked.

Pa looked at Almanzo and then he looked again at the northwest. There was no cloud there but the wind blew strongly and bitter cold.

"That's the only horse in this country that can race an antelope, unless it's her mate here, and you'd kill him trying to catch them," Pa said. "It's a day's journey to Spirit Lake, at best, and no one knows when a blizzard'll hit. I wouldn't risk it myself, not this winter."

"I don't intend to," said Almanzo. "But I'll just circle around and come into town from the north. Maybe I'll catch sight of the mare. If not, maybe she'll find her own way back. So long! See you in town!"

He let Prince go into a canter and set off toward the north, while the others shouldered their guns and turned straight toward town.

He rode with his head bowed against the wind but on each prairie swell or high snowbank he looked over the land before him. There was nothing to be seen but gentle slopes of snow and the snow-spray blown from their tops by the cutting wind. The loss of Lady made him sick at heart, but he did not intend to risk his life for a horse. The matched team was ruined without her. In a lifetime he would not find another perfect match for Prince. He thought what a fool he had been to lend a horse to a stranger.

Prince went on smoothly, head up to the wind, galloping up the slopes and cantering down them. Almanzo did not intend to go far from the town, but the sky remained clear in the northwest and there was always another slope ahead of him, from which he might see farther north.

Lady, he thought, might have grown tired and dropped behind the antelope herd. She might be wandering, lost and bewildered. She might be in sight from the top of the next prairie swell.

When he reached it, there was only the white land beyond. Prince went smoothly down the slope and another one rose before him.

He looked back to see the town and there was no town. The huddle of tall false fronts and the thin smoke blowing from their stovepipes had vanished. Under the whole sky there was nothing but the white land, the snow blowing, and the wind and the cold.

He was not afraid. He knew where the town was and as long as the sun was in the sky or the moon or stars he could not be lost. But he had a feeling colder than the wind. He felt that he was the only life on the cold earth, under the cold sky; he and his horse alone in an enormous coldness.

"Hi-yup, Prince!" he said, but the wind carried away the sound in the ceaseless rush of its blowing. Then he was afraid of being afraid. He said to himself, "There's nothing to be afraid of." He thought, "I won't turn back now. I'll turn back from the top of that next slope," and he tightened the reins ever so little to hold the rhythm of Prince's galloping.

From the top of that slope he saw a low edge of cloud on the northwestern sky line. Then suddenly the whole great prairie seemed to be a trap that knew it had caught him. But he also saw Lady.

Far away and small, on a ridge of the rolling snow fields, the brown horse stood looking eastward. Almanzo tore off his glove and putting two fingers into his mouth he blew the piercing whistle used to call Lady across his father's pastures in Minnesota when she was a colt. But this prairie wind caught the shrill note at his lips and carried it soundlessly away. It carried away the long, whickering call from Prince's stretched throat. Lady still stood, looking away from them.

Then she turned to look southward and saw them. The wind brought her far, faint whinny. Her neck arched, her tail curved up, and she came galloping.

Almanzo waited until she topped a nearer rise and again her call came down the wind. He turned then and rode toward the town. The low cloud fell below the sky line as he rode, but again and again Lady appeared behind him.

In the stable behind the feed store he put Prince in his stall and rubbed him down. He filled the manger and held the water pail to let Prince drink a little.

There was a rattling at the stable door and he opened it to let Lady in. She was white with lather. A foam of sweat dripped from her and her sides were heaving.

Almanzo shut the stable door against the cold while Lady went into her stall. Then with the currycomb he scraped the foam from her panting sides and her flanks and covered her warmly with a blanket. He squeezed a wet cloth into her mouth to moisten her tongue. He rubbed her slender legs and dried them where the sweat still ran down.

"Well, Lady, so you can outrun an antelope! Made a fool of yourself, didn't you?" Almanzo talked to her while he worked. "It's the last time I'll let a fool ride you, anyway. Now you rest warm and quiet. I'll water and feed you after a while."

Pa had come quietly into the kitchen and without a word he laid his shotgun on its hooks. No one said anything; there was no need to. Carrie sighed. There would be no venison, no gravy on the brown bread. Pa sat down by the stove and spread his hands to the warmth.

After a little, he said, "Foster lost his head from excitement. He jumped off his horse and fired before he was anywhere near within gunshot. None of the rest of us had a chance. The whole herd's high-tailed it north."

Ma put a stick of hay in the stove. "They would have been poor eating anyway, this time of year," she said.

Laura knew that antelope had to paw away the deep snow to reach the dry grass that was their food. In a blizzard they couldn't do that, and now the snow was so deep that they must be starving. It was true that their meat would have been thin and tough. But it would have been meat. They were all so tired of nothing but potatoes and brown bread.

"The younger Wilder boy's horse got away, too," Pa said, and he told them how it had run with the antelope. He made a story for Carrie and Grace of the beautiful horse running free and far with the wild herd.

"And didn't it ever, ever come back, Pa?" Grace asked him, wide-eyed.

"I don't know," said Pa. "Almanzo Wilder rode off that way and I don't know whether he's come back or not. While you're getting dinner ready, Caroline, I'll step up to the feed store and find out."

The feed store was bare and empty, but Royal looked from the back room and said heartily, "Come on in, Mr. Ingalls! You're just in time to sample the pancakes and bacon!"

"I didn't know this was your dinnertime," Pa said. He looked at the platter of bacon keeping hot on the stove hearth. Three stacks of pancakes were tall on a plate, too, and Royal was frying more. There was molasses on the table and the coffeepot was boiling.

"We eat when we get hungry," said Royal. "That's the advantage of baching it. Where there's no womenfolks, there's no regular mealtimes."

"You boys are lucky to have brought in supplies," Pa said.

"Well, I was bringing out a carload of feed anyway and thought I might as well bring the stuff along," Royal replied. "I wish I'd brought a couple of carloads, now. I guess I could sell another carload before they get the train through."

"I guess you could," Pa agreed. He looked around the snug room, ran his eyes along the walls hung with clothes and harness, and noticed the empty spaces on the end wall. "Your brother not got back yet?"

"He just came into the stable," Royal answered. Then he exclaimed, "Jiminy crickets, look there!" They saw Lady, dripping with lather and empty-saddled, streaking past the window to the stable.

While they were talking about the hunt and Mr. Foster's crazy shot, Almanzo came in. He dumped the saddles in a corner to be cleaned before he hung them up and he warmed himself by the stove. Then he and Royal urged Pa to sit up to the table and eat with them.

"Royal don't make as good pancakes as I do," Almanzo said. "But nobody can beat this bacon. It's home-cured and hickory-smoked from corn-fattened young hogs raised on clover, back on the farm in Minnesota."

"Sit right up, Mr. Ingalls, and help yourself. There's plenty more down cellar in a teacup!" said Royal. So Pa did.

CHAPTER 21

The Hard Winter

THE sun shone again next morning and the winds were still. The day seemed warmer than it was, because the sunshine was so bright.

"This is a beautiful day," Ma said at breakfast, but Pa shook his head.

"The sun is too bright," he said. "I'll get a load of hay as soon as I can for we'll need plenty on hand if another storm comes." And he hurried away.

Anxiously from time to time Ma or Laura or Carrie peeped out through the frosty window to see the northwestern sky. The sun still was shining when Pa came safely back, and after the day's second meal of brown bread and potatoes he went across the street to hear the news.

In a little while he came gaily whistling through the front room and burst into the kitchen, singing out, "Guess what I got!"

Grace and Carrie ran to feel the package he carried. "It feels like . . . it feels like . . ." Carrie said, but she did not quite dare to say what it felt like for fear she was mistaken.

"It's beef!" Pa said. "Four pounds of beef! To go with our bread and potatoes." He handed the package to Ma.

"Charles! However did you get beef?" Ma asked, as if she could not believe it.

"Foster butchered his oxen," Pa answered. "I got there just in time. Every last bit, to bones and gristle, sold twenty-five cents a pound. But I got four pounds and here it is! Now we'll live like kings!"

Ma quickly took the paper off the meat. "I'll sear it all over well and pot-roast it," she said.

Looking at it made Laura's mouth water. She swallowed and asked, "Can you make a gravy, Ma, with water and brown flour?"

"Indeed I can," Ma smiled. "We can make this last a week,

for flavoring at least, and by that time the train will surely come, won't it?"

She looked smiling at Pa. Then she stopped smiling and quietly asked, "What is it, Charles?"

"Well," Pa answered reluctantly, "I hate to tell you." He cleared his throat. "The train isn't coming."

They all stood looking at him. He went on, "The railroad has stopped running trains, till spring."

Ma threw up her hands and dropped into a chair. "How can it, Charles? It can't. It can't do that. Till spring? This is only the first of January."

"They can't get the trains through," said Pa. "They no sooner get a train through a cut than a blizzard comes and snows it in again. They've got two trains between here and Tracy, snowed under between cuts. Every time they cleared a cut they threw up the snow on both sides, and now all the cuts are packed full of snow to the top of the snowbanks. And at Tracy the superintendent ran out of patience."

"Patience?" Ma exclaimed. "Patience! What's *his* patience got to do with it I'd like to know! He knows we are out here without supplies. How does he think we are going to live till spring? It isn't his business to be patient. It's his business to run the trains."

"Now, Caroline," Pa said. He put his hand on her shoulder and she stopped rocking and rolling her hands in her apron. "We haven't had a train for more than a month, and we are getting along all right," he told her.

"Yes," Ma said.

"There's only this month, then February is a short month, and March will be spring," Pa encouraged her.

Laura looked at the four pounds of beef. She thought of the few potatoes left and she saw the partly filled sack of wheat standing in the corner.

"Is there any more wheat, Pa?" she asked in a low voice.

"I don't know, Laura," Pa said strangely. "But don't worry. I bought a full bushel and it's by no means gone."

Laura could not help asking, "Pa, you couldn't shoot a rabbit?"

Pa sat down before the open oven and settled Grace on his

knee. "Come here, Half-Pint," he said, "and you, too, Carrie. I'm going to tell you a story."

He did not answer Laura's question. She knew what the answer was. There was not a rabbit left in all that country. They must have gone south when the birds went. Pa never took his gun with him when he was hauling hay, and he would have taken it if he had ever seen so much as one rabbit's track.

He put his arm around her as she stood close against Carrie on his knee. Grace cuddled in his other arm and laughed when his brown beard tickled her face as it used to tickle Laura's when she was little. They were all cosy in Pa's arms, with the warmth from the oven coming out pleasantly.

"Now listen, Grace and Carrie and Laura," said Pa. "And you, too, Mary and Ma. This is a funny story." And he told them the story of the superintendent.

The superintendent was an Eastern man. He sat in his offices in the East and ordered the train dispatchers to keep the trains running. But the engineers reported that storms and snow stopped the trains.

"Snowstorms don't stop us from running trains in the East," the superintendent said. "Keep the trains running in the Western end of the division. That's orders."

But in the West the trains kept stopping. He had reports that the cuts were full of snow.

"Clear the cuts," he ordered. "Put on extra men. Keep the trains running. Hang the costs!"

They put on extra men. The costs were enormous. But still the trains did not run.

Then the superintendent said, "I'll go out there and clear those tracks myself. What those men need is someone to show them how we do things in the East."

So he came out to Tracy, in his special car, and he got off there in his city clothes and his gloves and his fur-lined coat and this is what he said. "I've come out to take charge myself," he said. "I'll show you how to keep these trains running."

In spite of that, he was not a bad fellow when you knew him. He rode out in the work train to the big cut west of Tracy, and he piled out in the snow with the work crew and gave his orders like any good foreman. He moved that snow up out of the cut in double-quick time and in a couple of days the track was clear.

"That shows you how to do it," he said. "Now run the train through tomorrow and keep it running." But that night a blizzard hit Tracy. His special train couldn't run in that blizzard, and when it stopped blowing the cut was packed full of snow to the top of the snowbanks he'd had thrown up on both sides.

He got right out there with the men again, and again they cleared the cut. It took longer that time because they had to move more snow. But he got the work train through, just in time to be snowed under by the next blizzard.

You had to admit that the superintendent had stick-to-itiveness. He tackled the cut again and got it cleared again, and then he sat in Tracy through another blizzard. This time he ordered out two fresh work crews and two locomotives with a snowplow.

He rode out to the Tracy cut on the first locomotive. The cut rose up like a hill now. Between the snowbanks that he'd had thrown up on both sides of them, the blizzard had packed earth and snow, frozen solid, one hundred feet deep and tapering off for a quarter of a mile.

"All right, boys!" he said. "We'll clear her out with picks and shovels till we can run the snowplows through."

He kept them at it, double-quick and double pay, for two days. There was still about twelve feet of snow on the tracks, but he had learned something. He knew he would be lucky to get three clear days between blizzards. So on the third morning, he was going to run the snowplows through.

He gave his orders to the two locomotive engineers. They coupled the locomotives together with the snowplow in front and ran the work train out to the cut. The two work crews piled out and in a couple of hours of fast work they had moved another couple of feet of snow. Then the superintendent stopped the work.

"Now," he ordered the engineers, "you boys back down the track a full two miles, and come ahead from there with all the steam-pressure you've got. With two miles to get up speed you ought to hit this cut at forty miles an hour and go through her clean as a whistle."

The engineers climbed into their locomotives. Then the

man on the front engine got down again. The men of the work crews were standing around in the snow, stamping their feet and beating their hands to keep warm. They crowded in to hear what the engineer was going to say, but he walked up to the superintendent and said it just the same.

"I quit," he said. "I've been driving a locomotive for fifteen years and no man can call me a coward. But I'm not taking any orders to commit suicide. You want to send a locomotive up against ten foot of frozen snow at forty miles an hour, Mr. Superintendent; you can get some other man to drive it. I quit, right here and now."

Pa paused, and Carrie said, "I don't blame him."

"I do," said Laura. "He oughtn't to quit. He ought to figure out some other way to get through, if he thinks that way won't work. I think he was scared."

"Even if he was scared," Mary said, "he ought to do as he was told. The superintendent must know best what to do or how would he be the superintendent?"

"He doesn't know best," Laura contradicted. "Or he'd be keeping the train running."

"Go on, Pa, go on!" Grace begged.

" 'Please,' Grace," Ma said.

"Please," said Grace. "Go on, Pa! What happened next?"

"Yes, Pa, what did the superintendent do then?" Mary asked.

"He fired him," said Laura. "Didn't he, Pa?"

Pa went on.

"The superintendent looked at that engineer, and he looked at the men standing around listening, and he said, 'I've driven a locomotive in my time. And I don't order any man to do anything I won't do myself. I'll take that throttle.'

"He climbed up into the locomotive, and he set her in reverse, and the two locomotives backed off down the track.

"The superintendent kept them backing for a good long two miles, till they looked smaller than your thumb, far off down the track. Then he signaled with the whistle to the engineer behind and they both put on the steam-power.

"Those locomotives came charging down that two miles of straight track with wide-open throttles, full speed ahead and coming faster every second. Black plumes of coal smoke rolling away far behind them, headlights glaring bigger in the sunshine, wheels blurring faster, faster, roaring up to fifty miles an hour they hit that frozen snow."

"What . . . what happened . . . then, Pa?" Carrie asked, breathless.

"Then up rose a fountain of flying snow that fell in chunks for forty yards around. For a minute or two no one saw anything clear, nobody knew what had happened. But when the men came running to find out, there was the second locomotive buried halfway in the snow and the engineer crawling out of its hind end. He was considerably shaken up, but not hurt badly enough to mention.

" 'Where's the superintendent? What happened to him?' they asked the engineer. All he said was, 'How the dickens do I know? All I know is I'm not killed. I wouldn't do that again,' he said. 'Not for a million dollars in gold.'

"The foremen were shouting to the men to come on with their picks and shovels. They dug the snow loose from around the second engine and shoveled it away. The engineer backed it out and down the track out of the way, while the men dug furiously into the snow ahead, to come at the first engine and the superintendent. In hardly any time at all they struck solid ice.

"That first locomotive had run full speed, head-on into that snow, its full length. It was hot with speed and steam. It melted the snow all around it and the snow-water froze solid in the frozen snow. There sat the superintendent, madder than a hornet, inside the locomotive frozen solid in a cake of ice!"

Grace and Carrie and Laura laughed out loud. Even Ma smiled.

"The poor man," Mary said. "I don't think it's funny."

"I do," said Laura. "I guess now he doesn't think he knows so much."

" 'Pride goes before a fall,' " said Ma.

"Go on, Pa, please!" Carrie begged. "Did they dig him out?"

"Yes, they dug down and cracked the ice and broke a hole through it to the engine and they hauled him out. He was not hurt and neither was the locomotive. The snowplow had taken the brunt. The superintendent climbed out of the cut and walked back to the second engineer and said, 'Can you back her out?'

"The engineer said he thought so.

" 'All right, do it,' the superintendent said. He stood watching till they got the engine out. Then he said to the men, 'Pile in, we're going back to Tracy. Work's shut down till spring.'

"You see, girls," said Pa, "the trouble is, he didn't have enough patience."

"Nor perseverance," said Ma.

"Nor perseverance," Pa agreed. "Just because he couldn't get through with shovels or snowplows, he figured he couldn't get through at all and he quit trying. Well, he's an Easterner. It takes patience and perseverance to contend with things out here in the West."

"When did he quit, Pa?" Laura asked.

"This morning. The news came on the electric telegraph, and the operator at Tracy told Woodworth how it happened," Pa answered. "And now I must hustle to do the chores before it's too dark."

His arm tightened and gave Laura a little hugging shake, before he set Carrie and Grace down from his knees. Laura knew what he meant. She was old enough now to stand by him and Ma in hard times. She must not worry; she must be cheerful and help to keep up all their spirits.

So when Ma began to sing softly to Grace while she undressed her for bed, Laura joined in the song:

"Oh Canaan, bright Canaan,
I am bound for the . . ."

"Sing, Carrie!" Laura said hurriedly. So Carrie began to sing, then Mary's sweet soprano came in.

"On Jordan's stormy banks I stand
And cast a wishful eye
On Canaan's bright and shining strand
Where my possessions lie.
Oh Canaan, bright Canaan,
I am bound for the happy land of Canaan. . . ."

The sun was setting so red that it colored the frosted windowpanes. It gave a faintly rosy light to the kitchen where they all sat undressing and singing by the warm stove. But Laura thought there was a change in the sound of the wind, a wild and frightening note.

After Ma had seen them all tucked in bed and had gone downstairs, they heard and felt the blizzard strike the house. Huddled close together and shivering under the covers they listened to it. Laura thought of the lost and lonely houses, each one alone and blind and cowering in the fury of the storm. There were houses in town, but not even a light from one of them could reach another. And the town was all alone on the frozen, endless prairie, where snow drifted and winds howled and the whirling blizzard put out the stars and the sun.

Laura tried to think of the good brown smell and taste of the beef for dinner tomorrow, but she could not forget that now the houses and the town would be all alone till spring. There was half a bushel of wheat that they could grind to make flour, and there were the few potatoes, but nothing more to eat until the train came. The wheat and the potatoes were not enough.

CHAPTER 22

Cold and Dark

THAT blizzard seemed never to end. It paused sometimes, only to roar again quickly and more furiously out of the Northwest. Three days and nights of yelling shrill winds and roaring fury beat at the dark, cold house and ceaselessly scoured it with ice-sand. Then the sun shone out, from morning till noon perhaps, and the dark anger of winds and icy snow came again.

Sometimes in the night, half-awake and cold, Laura half-dreamed that the roof was scoured thin. Horribly the great blizzard, large as the sky, bent over it and scoured with an enormous invisible cloth, round and round on the paper-thin roof, till a hole wore through and squealing, chuckling, laughing a deep Ha! Ha! the blizzard whirled in. Barely in time to save herself, Laura jumped awake.

Then she did not dare to sleep again. She lay still and small in the dark, and all around her the black darkness of night, that had always been restful and kind to her, was now a horror. She had never been afraid of the dark. "I am not afraid of the dark," she said to herself over and over, but she felt that the dark would catch her with claws and teeth if it could hear her move or breathe. Inside the walls, under the roof where the nails were clumps of frost, even under the covers where she huddled, the dark was crouched and listening.

Daytimes were not so bad as the nights. The dark was thinner then and ordinary things were in it. A dark twilight filled the kitchen and the lean-to. Mary and Carrie took turns at the coffee mill that must never stop grinding. Ma made the bread and swept and cleaned and fed the fire. In the lean-to Laura and Pa twisted hay till their cold hands could not hold the hay to twist it and must be warmed at the stove.

The hay-fire could not keep the cold out of the kitchen, but close to the stove the air was warm. Mary's place was in front of the oven with Grace in her lap. Carrie stood behind the stovepipe and Ma's chair was on the other side of the stove. Pa and Laura leaned over the stove hearth into the warmth that rose upward.

Their hands were red and swollen, the skin was cold, and covered with cuts made by the sharp slough hay. The hay was cutting away the cloth of their coats on the left side and along the underneath of their left coat sleeves. Ma patched the worn places, but the hay cut away the patches.

For breakfast there was brown bread. Ma toasted it crisp and hot in the oven and she let them dip it in their tea.

"It was thoughtful of you, Charles, to lay in such a supply of tea," she said. There was still plenty of tea and there was still sugar for it.

For the second meal of the day she boiled twelve potatoes in their jackets. Little Grace needed only one, the others had two apiece, and Ma insisted that Pa take the extra one. "They're not big potatoes, Charles," she argued, "and you must keep up your strength. Anyway, eat it to save it. We don't want it, do we, girls?"

"No, Ma," they all said. "No, thank you, Pa, truly I don't want it." This was true. They were not really hungry. Pa was hungry. His eyes looked eagerly at the brown bread and the steaming potatoes when he came from struggling along the clothesline in the storm. But the others were only tired, tired of the winds and the cold and the dark, tired of brown bread and potatoes, tired and listless and dull.

Every day Laura found time to study a little. When enough hay was twisted to last for an hour, she sat down by Mary, between the stove and the table, and opened the school-books. But she felt dull and stupid. She could not remember history and she leaned her head on her hand and looked at a problem on her slate without seeing how to solve it or wanting to.

"Come, come, girls! We must not mope," Ma said. "Straighten up, Laura and Carrie! Do your lessons briskly and then we'll have an entertainment."

"How, Ma?" Carrie asked.

"Get your lessons first," said Ma.

When study time was over, Ma took the Independent Fifth Reader. "Now," she said, "let's see how much you can repeat from memory. You first, Mary. What shall it be?"

"The Speech of Regulus," said Mary. Ma turned the leaves until she found it and Mary began.

"'Ye doubtless thought—for ye judge of Roman virtue by your own—that I would break my plighted oath rather than, returning, brook your vengeance!'" Mary could repeat the whole of that splendid defiance. "'Here in your capital do I defy you! Have I not conquered your armies, fired your towns, and dragged your generals at my chariot wheels, since first my youthful arms could wield a spear?'"

The kitchen seemed to grow larger and warmer. The blizzard winds were not as strong as those words.

"You did that perfectly, Mary," Ma praised her. "Now, Laura?"

"Old Tubal Cain," Laura began, and the verses lifted her to her feet. You had to stand up and let your voice ring out with the hammer strokes of old Tubal Cain.

> "Old Tubal Cain was a man of might,
> In the days when the earth was young.
> By the fierce red light of his furnace bright,
> The strokes of his hammer rung . . ."

Pa came in before Laura reached the end. "Go on, go on," he said. "That warms me as much as the fire." So Laura went on, while Pa got out of his coat that was white and stiff with snow driven into it, and leaned over the fire to melt the snow frozen in his eyebrows.

> "And sang, 'Hurrah for Tubal Cain!
> Our staunch good friend is he;
> And for the plowshare and the plow
> To him our praise shall be.
> But while oppression lifts its head
> On a tyrant would be lord,
> Though we may thank him for the plow,
> We will not forget the sword.'"

"You remembered every word correctly, Laura," Ma said, shutting the book. "Carrie and Grace shall have their turns tomorrow."

It was time then to twist more hay but while Laura shivered and twisted the sharp stuff in the cold she thought of more verses. Tomorrow afternoon was something to look forward to. The Fifth Reader was full of beautiful speeches and poems and she wanted to remember perfectly as many of them as Mary remembered.

The blizzard stopped sometimes. The whirling winds straightened out and steadied, the air cleared above blowing snow, and Pa set out to haul hay.

Then Laura and Ma worked quickly to do the washing and hang it out in the cold to freeze dry. No one knew how soon the blizzard would come again. At any moment the cloud might rise and come faster than any horses could run. Pa was not safe out on the prairie away from the town.

Sometimes the blizzard stopped for half a day. Sometimes the sun shone from morning to sunset and the blizzard came back with the dark. On such days, Pa hauled three loads of hay. Until he came back and put David in the stable Laura and Ma worked hard and silently, looking often at the sky and listening to the wind, and Carrie silently watched the northwest through the peephole that she made on the window.

Pa often said that he could not have managed without David. "He is such a good horse," Pa said. "I did not know a horse could be so good and patient." When David fell through the snow, he always stood still until Pa shoveled him out. Then quietly and patiently he hauled the sled around the hole and went on until he fell through the snow crust again. "I wish I had some oats or corn to give him," Pa said.

When the roaring and shrieking winds came back and the scouring snow whirled again, Pa said, "Well, there's hay enough to last awhile, thanks to David."

The clothesline was there to guide him to the stable and back. There was hay and still some wheat and potatoes, and while the stormwinds blew Pa was safe at home. And in the afternoons Mary and Laura and Carrie recited. Even Grace knew "Mary's Little Lamb," and "Bo-peep Has Lost Her Sheep."

Laura liked to see Grace's blue eyes and Carrie's shine with excitement when she told them:

> Listen, my children, and you shall hear
> Of the midnight ride of Paul Revere.
> The eighteenth of April in Seventy-five,

Hardly a man is now alive
Who remembers that famous day and year. . . .

She and Carrie both loved to repeat, in concert, "The Swan's Nest":

Little Ellie sits alone
'Mid the beeches of a meadow,
By a stream side, on the grass,
And the trees are showering down
Doubles of their leaves in shadow
On her shining hair and face . . .

The air was warm and quiet there, the grass was warm in the sunshine, the clear water sang its song to itself, and the leaves softly murmured. The meadow's insects drowsily hummed. While they were there with little Ellie, Laura and Carrie almost forgot the cold. They hardly heard the winds and the whirling hard snow scouring the walls.

One still morning, Laura came downstairs to find Ma looking surprised and Pa laughing. "Go look out the back door!" he told Laura.

She ran through the lean-to and opened the back door. There was a rough, low tunnel going into shadows in gray-white snow. Its walls and its floor were snow and its snow roof solidly filled the top of the doorway.

"I had to gopher my way to the stable this morning," Pa explained.

"But what did you do with the snow?" Laura asked.

"Oh, I made the tunnel as low as I could get through. I dug the snow out and pushed it back of me and up through a hole that I blocked with the last of it. There's nothing like snow for keeping out wind!" Pa rejoiced. "As long as that snowbank stands, I can do my chores in comfort."

"How deep is the snow?" Ma wanted to know.

"I can't say. It's piled up considerably deeper than the lean-to roof," Pa answered.

"You don't mean to say this house is buried in snow!" Ma exclaimed.

"A good thing if it is," Pa replied. "You notice the kitchen is warmer than it has been this winter?"

Laura ran upstairs. She scratched a peephole on the window and put her eyes to it. She could hardly believe them. Main Street was level with her eyes. Across the glittering snow she could see the blank, square top of Harthorn's false front sticking up like a short piece of solid board fence.

She heard a gay shout and then she saw horses' hoofs trotting rapidly before her eyes. Eight gray hoofs, with slender brown ankles swiftly bending and straightening, passed quickly by, and then a long sled with two pairs of boots standing on it. She crouched down, to look upward through the peephole, but the sled was gone. She saw only the sky sharp with sunlight that stabbed her eyes. She ran down to the warm kitchen to tell what she had seen.

"The Wilder boys," Pa said. "They're hauling hay."

"How do you know, Pa?" Laura asked him. "I only saw the horses' feet, and boots."

"There's no one in town but those two, and me, that dares go out of town," said Pa. "Folks are afraid a blizzard'll come up. Those Wilder boys are hauling in all their slough hay from Big Slough and selling it for three dollars a load to burn."

"Three dollars!" Ma exclaimed.

"Yes, and fair enough for the risk they take. They're making a good thing out of it. Wish I could. But they've got coal to burn. I'll be glad if we have enough hay to last us through. I wasn't counting on it for our winter's fuel."

"They went by as high as the houses!" Laura exclaimed. She was still excited. It was strange to see horses' hoofs and a sled and boots in front of your eyes, as a little animal, a gopher, for instance, might see them.

"It's a wonder they don't sink in the drifts," Ma said.

"Oh, no." Pa was wolfing his toast and drinking his tea rapidly. "They won't sink. These winds pack the snow as hard as a rock. David's shoes don't even make tracks on it. The only trouble's where the grass is lodged and loose underneath."

He got into his wraps in a hurry. "Those boys have got the start of me this morning. I was digging the tunnel. Now I've got to dig David out of the stable. Got to haul hay while the sun shines!" he joked, as he shut the door behind him.

"He's feeling chipper because he's got that tunnel," said Ma.

"It's a blessing he can do the chores in some comfort, out of the wind."

That day they could not watch the sky from the kitchen window. So little cold came through the snow that Laura led Mary into the lean-to and taught her how to twist hay. Mary had wanted to learn but the lean-to had been too cold. It took her some time because she could not see how Laura twisted and held the strands and tucked in the ends, but at last she did it well. They stopped to warm themselves only a few times while they twisted the whole day's supply of hay sticks.

Then the kitchen was so warm that they need not crowd around the stove. The house was very still. The only sounds were the little sounds of Ma and Mary rocking, the slate pencil on the slate, the teakettle's pleasant hum, and their own low voices speaking.

"What a blessing this deep snowdrift is," Ma said.

But they could not watch the sky. Watching it did no good. If the low gray cloud was swiftly rising, they could not stop it. They could not help Pa. He would see the cloud and reach shelter as quickly as he could. Laura thought this many times, but just the same she hurried upstairs through the cold to peep from the window.

Ma and Carrie looked at her quickly when she came down, and she always answered them out loud so that Mary would know. "The sky's clear and not a thing is stirring but millions of glitters on the snow. I don't believe there's a breath of wind."

That afternoon Pa dragged hay through the tunnel to cram the lean-to full. He had dug the tunnel past the stable door so that David could get out, and beyond the stable he had turned the tunnel at an angle, to check the winds that might blow into it.

"I never saw such weather," he said. "It must be all of forty degrees below zero and not a breath of air stirring. The whole world seems frozen solid. I hope this cold holds. Going through that tunnel it's no chore at all to do the chores."

Next day was exactly the same. The stillness and the dusk and the warmth seemed to be a changeless dream going on forever the same, like the clock's ticking. Laura jumped in her chair when the clock cleared its throat before it struck.

"Don't be so nervous, Laura," Ma murmured as if she were half-asleep. They did not recite that day. They did not do anything. They just sat.

The night was still, too. But morning woke them with a howling fury. The winds had come again and the lashing whirl of snow.

"Well, the tunnel's going fast," Pa said, when he came into breakfast. His eyebrows were frozen white with snow again and his wraps were stiff with it. Cold was pressing the warmth back again to the stove. "I did hope my tunnel would last through one of these onslaughts, anyway. Gosh dang this blizzard! It only lets go long enough to spit on its hands."

"Don't swear, Charles!" Ma snapped at him. She clapped her hand to her mouth in horror. "Oh, Charles, I'm sorry," she apologized. "I didn't mean to snap at you. But this wind, blowing and blowing . . ." Her voice died away and she stood listening.

"I know, Caroline," Pa answered. "I know just how it makes you feel. It tires you out. I'll tell you what, after breakfast we'll read for a while about Livingston's Africa."

"It's too bad I've burned so much hay this morning, Charles," Ma said. "I've had to burn more, trying to get the place warm."

"Never mind, it's no trick to twist more," Pa replied.

"I'll help, Pa," Laura offered.

"We've got all day for it," Pa said. "Everything is snug at the stable till night. We'll twist hay first, then we'll read."

Grace began to whimper. "My feet's cold."

"For shame, Grace! A big girl like you! Go warm your feet," Laura told her.

"Come sit on my lap and warm them," Mary said, feeling her way to her rocking chair before the oven.

After Laura and Pa had twisted a great pile of hay sticks and stacked them by the stove, Carrie brought Pa his big green book.

"Please read about the lions, Pa," she asked him. "We can play the wind is lions roaring."

"I'm afraid I'll have to have a light, Caroline," Pa said. "This print is small." Ma lighted the button lamp and set it by him. "Now," he said, "this is a jungle night in Africa. The flickering light here is from our campfire. Wild animals are all around us, yowling and squealing and roaring, lions and tigers and hyenas and I guess a hippopotamus or two. They won't come anywhere near us because they are afraid of the fire. You hear big leaves rasping, too, and queer birds squawking. It's a thick, black, hot night with big stars overhead. Now I'm going to read what happens." He began to read.

Laura tried to listen but she felt stupid and numb. Pa's voice slid away into the ceaseless noises of the storm. She felt that the blizzard must stop before she could do anything, before she could even listen or think, but it would never stop. It had been blowing forever.

She was tired. She was tired of the cold and the dark, tired of brown bread and potatoes, tired of twisting hay and grinding wheat, filling the stove and washing dishes and making beds and going to sleep and waking up. She was tired of the blizzard winds. There was no tune in them any more, only a confusion of sound beating on her ears.

"Pa," she spoke suddenly, interrupting his reading, "won't you play the fiddle?"

Pa looked at her in surprise. Then he laid down the book. "Why yes, Laura," he said. "If you want to hear the fiddle, I'll play it."

He opened and shut his hands and rubbed the fingers while Laura brought the fiddle-box from its warm shelter on the floor behind the stove.

Pa rosined the bow, tucked the fiddle under his chin, and touched the strings. He looked at Laura.

"Play 'Bonnie Doon,'" Laura said, and Pa played and sang:

> "Ye banks and braes of Bonnie Doon,
> How can ye bloom sae fresh and fair?"

But every note from the fiddle was a very little wrong. Pa's fingers were clumsy. The music dragged and a fiddle string snapped.

"My fingers are too stiff and thick from being out in the cold so much, I can't play," Pa spoke as if he were ashamed. He laid the fiddle in its box. "Put it away, Laura, until some other time," he said.

"I wish you'd help me, anyway, Charles," Ma said. She took the coffee mill from Mary and emptied the ground wheat from its little drawer. She filled the small hopper with kernels and handed the mill to Pa. "I'll need another grinding to make the bread for dinner," she told him.

Ma took the covered dish of souring from its warm place under the stove. She stirred it briskly, then measured two cupfuls into a pan, added salt and saleratus, and the flour that Mary and Carrie had ground. Then she took the mill from Pa and added the flour he had made.

"That's just enough," she said. "Thank you, Charles."

"I'd better be doing the chores now before it gets too dark," Pa said.

"I'll have a hot meal ready and waiting by the time you come in," Ma reminded him. He put on his wraps and went out into the storm.

Laura listened to the winds while she stared at the blank window without seeing it. The worst thing that had happened was that Pa could not play the fiddle. If she had not asked him to play it, he might not have known that he could not do it.

Ma, with Carrie crowded in beside her, sat in her rocking chair by the stove, opposite Mary. She held Grace in her arms and rocked slowly, softly singing to her:

> "I will sing you a song of that beautiful land,
> The far away home of the soul
> Where no storms ever beat on that glittering strand
> While the years of eternity roll."

The wailing hymn blended with the wail of the winds while night settled down, deepening the dusk of whirling snow.

CHAPTER 23

The Wheat in the Wall

IN THE morning the snowdrift was gone. When Laura made a peephole on the upstairs window and looked through it she saw bare ground. Blown snow was driving over it in low clouds, but the street was hard, brown earth.

"Ma! Ma!" she cried. "I can see the ground!"

"I know," Ma answered. "The winds blew all the snow away last night."

"What time is it? I mean, what month is it?" Laura asked stupidly.

"It is the middle of February," Ma answered.

Then spring was nearer than Laura had thought. February was a short month and March would be spring. The train would come again and they would have white bread and meat.

"I am so tired of brown bread with nothing on it," Laura said.

"Don't complain, Laura!" Ma told her quickly. "Never complain of what you have. Always remember you are fortunate to have it."

Laura had not meant to complain but she did not know how to explain what she had meant. She answered meekly, "Yes, Ma." Then, startled, she looked at the wheat sack in the corner. There was so little wheat left in it that it lay folded like an empty sack.

"Ma!" she exclaimed, "Did you mean . . ." Pa had always said that she must never be afraid. She must never be afraid of anything. She asked, "How much more wheat is there?"

"I think enough for today's grinding," Ma answered.

"Pa can't buy any more, can he?" Laura said.

"No, Laura. There's no more in town." Ma laid the slices of brown bread carefully on the oven grate to toast for breakfast.

Then Laura braced herself, she steadied herself, and she said, "Ma. Will we starve?"

"We won't starve, no," Ma replied. "If Pa must, he will kill Ellen and the heifer calf."

"Oh, no! No!" Laura cried.

"Be quiet, Laura," Ma said. Carrie and Mary were coming downstairs to dress by the stove, and Ma went up to carry Grace down.

Pa hauled hay all day, and came into the house only to say that he was going to Fuller's store for a minute before supper. When he came back he brought news.

"There's a rumor in town that some settler, eighteen or twenty miles south or southeast of here, raised some wheat last summer," he said. "They say he's wintering in his claim shanty."

"Who says so?" Ma asked.

"It's a rumor," Pa said again. "Nearly everybody says so. Nearest I can find out, Foster is the man that started it. He says he heard it from somebody working on the railroad. Some fellow that was passing through last fall, he says, was telling about the crop of wheat this settler raised, said he had a ten-acre patch that must run thirty or forty bushels to the acre. Say three hundred bushels of wheat, within about twenty miles of here."

"I trust you aren't thinking of starting out on such a wild-goose chase, Charles," Ma said gently.

"A fellow might do it," Pa remarked. "With a couple of days of clear weather and a snowfall to hold up the sled, he ought to be able to make it all ri . . ."

"No!" said Ma.

Pa looked at her, startled. They all stared at her. They had never seen Ma look like that. She was quiet but she was terrible.

Quietly she told Pa, "I say, No. You don't take such a chance."

"Why . . . Caroline!" Pa said.

"Your hauling hay is bad enough," Ma told him. "*You don't go hunting for that wheat.*"

Pa said mildly, "Not as long as you feel that way about it, I won't. But . . ."

"I won't hear any buts," Ma said, still terrible. "This time I put my foot down."

"All right, that settles it," Pa agreed.

Laura and Carrie looked at each other. They felt as if thunder and lightning had come down on them suddenly, and suddenly gone. Ma poured the tea with a trembling hand.

"Oh Charles, I'm sorry, I spilled it," she said.

"Never mind," said Pa. He poured the spilled tea from his saucer into the cup. "A long time since I had to pour my tea into the saucer to cool it," he mentioned.

"I'm afraid the fire's going down," said Ma.

"It isn't the fire. The weather's turning colder," said Pa.

"You couldn't go, anyway," Ma said. "There'd be nobody to do the chores and nobody to haul hay."

"You're right, Caroline, you always are," Pa assured her. "We'll make out with what we have." Then he glanced at the corner where the wheat sack had been. But he said nothing about it until he had done the chores and twisted some hay. He laid down the armful of hay sticks by the stove and spread his hands to warm.

"Out of wheat, Caroline?" he asked.

"Yes, Charles," Ma said. "There's bread for breakfast."

"Running out of potatoes?"

"It seems as though everything is giving out at once," Ma answered. "But I have six potatoes for tomorrow."

"Where is the milk pail?" Pa asked.

"The milk pail?" Ma repeated.

"I'm going up the street a few minutes and I want the milk pail," Pa said.

Laura brought him the milk pail. She could not help asking, "Is there a milch cow in town, Pa?"

"No, Laura," he said. He went through the front room and they heard the front door shut.

Almanzo and Royal were eating supper. Almanzo had stacked the pancakes with brown sugar and he had made plenty of them. Royal had eaten halfway down his stack, Almanzo was nearing the bottom of his, and one tall stack of two dozen pancakes, dripping melted brown sugar, was standing untouched when Pa knocked at the door. Royal opened it.

"Come in, Mr. Ingalls! Sit up and have some pancakes with us!" Royal invited him.

"Thank you just the same. Could you be persuaded to sell me some wheat?" Pa asked, stepping in.

"Sorry," Royal said. "We have no more to sell."

"Clean sold out, uh?" said Pa.

"Clean sold out!" said Royal.

"I'd be willing to pay pretty high for some wheat," Pa said.

"I wish I'd brought out another carload," Royal replied. "Sit up and have some supper with us anyway. Manzo brags on his pancakes."

Pa did not answer. He walked to the end wall and lifted one of the saddles from its peg. Almanzo exclaimed, "Hey, what are you doing?"

Pa held the milk pail's rim firmly against the wall. He pulled the plug out of the knothole. A round stream of wheat, as large as the hole, poured rattling into the pail.

"I'm buying some wheat from you boys," Pa answered Almanzo.

"Say, that's my seed wheat; and I'm not selling it!" Almanzo declared.

"We're out of wheat at my house and I am buying some," Pa replied. The wheat kept on pouring into the pail, sliding down the climbing pile and tinkling a little against the tin. Almanzo stood watching him, but after a minute Royal sat down. He tipped his chair back against the wall, put his hands in his pockets, and grinned at Almanzo.

When the pail was full, Pa thrust the plug into the hole. He tapped it firm with his fist and then tapped lightly up the wall and across it.

"You've got plenty of wheat there," he said. "Now we'll talk price. What do you figure this pailful's worth?"

"How did you know it was there?" Almanzo wanted to know.

"The inside of this room doesn't fit the outside," said Pa. "It's a good foot short, allowing for two by four studding besides. Gives you a sixteen-inch space there. Any man with an eye can see it."

"I'll be darned," said Almanzo.

"I noticed that plug in the knothole, the day you had the saddles off on that antelope hunt," Pa added. "So I figured you had grain there. It's the only thing likely to run out of a knothole."

"Anybody else in town know it?" Almanzo asked.

"Not that I know of," Pa said.

"See here," Royal put in, "We didn't know you were out of wheat. That's Almanzo's wheat, it's not mine, but he wouldn't hang onto it and see anybody starve."

"It's my seed wheat," Almanzo explained. "Extra good seed, too. And no telling either if seed will be shipped in here in time for spring planting. Of course I won't see anybody starve, but somebody can go after that wheat that was raised south of town."

"Southeast, I heard," Pa said. "I did think of going myself, but . . ."

"You can't go," Royal interrupted. "Who'd take care of your folks if you got caught in a storm and . . . got delayed or anything?"

"This isn't settling what I'm to pay for this wheat," Pa reminded them.

Almanzo waved that away, "What's a little wheat between neighbors? You're welcome to it, Mr. Ingalls. Draw up a chair and sample these pancakes before they get cold."

But Pa insisted on paying for the wheat. After some talk about it, Almanzo charged a quarter and Pa paid it. Then he did sit down, as they urged him, and lifting the blanket cake on the untouched pile, he slipped from under it a section of the stack of hot, syrupy pancakes. Royal forked a brown slice of ham from the frying pan onto Pa's plate and Almanzo filled his coffee cup.

"You boys certainly live in the lap of luxury," Pa remarked. The pancakes were no ordinary buckwheat pancakes. Almanzo followed his mother's pancake rule and the cakes were light as foam, soaked through with melted brown sugar. The ham was sugar-cured and hickory-smoked, from the Wilder farm in Minnesota. "I don't know when I've eaten a tastier meal," said Pa.

They talked about weather and hunting and politics, railroads and farming, and when Pa left both Royal and Almanzo urged him to drop in often. Neither of them played checkers, so they did not spend much time in the stores. Their own place was warmer.

"Now you've found the way, Mr. Ingalls, come back!" Royal said heartily. "Be glad to see you any time; Manzo and I get tired of each other's company. Drop in any time, the latchstring is always out!"

"I'll be glad to!" Pa was answering; he broke off and listened. Almanzo stepped out with him into the freezing wind. Stars glittered overhead, but in the northwest sky they were going out rapidly as solid darkness swept up over them. "Here she comes!" said Pa. "I guess nobody'll do any visiting for a spell. I'll just about make it home if I hurry."

The blizzard struck the house when he was at the door so no one heard him come in. But they had little time to worry, for almost at once he came into the kitchen where they were all sitting in the dark. They were close to the stove and warm enough, but Laura was shivering, hearing the blizzard again and thinking that Pa was out in it.

"Here's some wheat to go on with, Caroline," Pa said, setting the pail down beside her. She reached down to it and felt the kernels.

"Oh, Charles. Oh, Charles," she said, rocking, "I might have known you'd provide for us, but wherever did you get it? I thought there was no wheat left in town."

"I wasn't sure there was or I'd have told you. But I didn't want to raise hopes to be disappointed," Pa explained. "I agreed not to tell where I got it, but don't worry, Caroline. There's more where that came from."

"Come, Carrie, I'm going to put you and Grace to bed now," Ma said with new energy. When she came downstairs she lighted the button lamp and filled the coffee mill. The sound of the grinding began again, and it followed Laura and Mary up the cold stairs until it was lost in the blizzard's howling.

CHAPTER 24

Not Really Hungry

"It's remarkable how the potatoes came out exactly even," said Pa.

Slowly they ate the last potatoes, skins and all. The blizzard was beating and scouring at the house, the winds were roaring and shrieking. The window was pale in the twilight and the stove pressed out its feeble heat against the cold.

"I'm not hungry, honest, Pa," Laura said. "I wish you'd finish mine."

"Eat it, Laura," Pa told her, kindly but firmly. Laura had to choke down mouthfuls of the potato that had grown cold on the cold plate. She broke a little piece from her slice of brown bread and left the rest. Only the hot, sweet tea was good. She felt numb and half-asleep.

Pa put on his overcoat and cap again and went into the lean-to to twist hay. Ma roused herself. "Come, girls! Wash up the dishes and wipe the stove and sweep while I make the beds, and then settle down to your studies. When they're done I'll hear your recitations, and then I have a surprise for supper!"

No one really cared but Laura tried to answer Ma.

"Have you, Ma? That's nice," she said. She washed the dishes and swept the floor, and getting into her patched coat she went into the lean-to to help Pa twist hay. Nothing seemed real but the blizzard that never stopped.

That afternoon she began:

"Old Tubal Cain was a mighty man, a mighty man was he,
He called for his pipe and he called for his bowl
And he called for his fiddlers three . . ."

"Oh, Ma, I don't know what's the matter with me! I can't think!" she almost wailed.

"It's this storm. I believe we are all half-asleep," Ma said. After some time she went on, "We must stop listening to it."

Everything was very slow. Mary asked after a while, "How can we stop listening to it?"

Ma slowly let the book close. At last she got up. "I will get the surprise," she said.

She brought it from the front room. It was a part of a salt codfish, frozen solidly, that she had been keeping there. "We'll have codfish gravy on our bread, for dinner!" she told them.

"By George, Caroline, nothing can beat the Scotch!" Pa exclaimed.

Ma put the codfish in the open oven to thaw, and took the coffee mill from him. "The girls and I will finish the grinding. I'm sorry, Charles, but I'll need more hay, and you must have time to warm before you do the chores."

Laura went to help him. When they brought in the armfuls of hay sticks, Carrie was wearily grinding at the coffee mill and Ma was flaking the codfish.

"Just the smell of it chirks a fellow up," Pa said. "Caroline, you are a wonder."

"I think it will be tasty for a change," Ma admitted. "But the bread's what we have to be thankful for, Charles." She saw him looking at the wheat in the milk pail and she told him, "There's enough to outlast this storm, if it's no longer than usual."

Laura took the coffee mill from Carrie. It worried her to see how thin and white Carrie was, and so exhausted from grinding. But even worry was dull and farther away than the hateful ceaseless pounding of the storm. The coffee mill's handle ground round and round, it must not stop. It seemed to make her part of the whirling winds driving the snow round and round over the earth and in the air, whirling and beating at Pa on his way to the stable, whirling and shrieking at the lonely houses, whirling the snow between them and up to the sky and far away, whirling forever over the endless prairie.

CHAPTER 25

Free and Independent

ALL the days of that storm Almanzo was thinking. He did not crack jokes as usual, and when doing the chores he curried and brushed his horses mechanically. He even sat thoughtfully whittling and let Royal make the supper pancakes.

"You know what I think, Roy?" he asked at last.

"It ought to be something worth while, the time you've been spending on it," Royal replied.

"I think there's folks in this town that are starving," Almanzo stated.

"Some are getting pretty hungry, maybe," Royal admitted, turning the pancakes.

"I said starving," Almanzo repeated. "Take Ingalls, there's six in his family. You notice his eyes and how thin he was? He said he was out of wheat. Well, take a peck, say a peck and a quarter, of wheat, how long will it last a family of six? Figure it out for yourself."

"He must have other provisions," said Royal.

"They came out here summer before last and they didn't go West with the railroad jobs. He took a homestead. You know yourself how much a man can raise the first summer on sod. And there's been no work around here for wages."

"What are you getting at?" Royal asked. "Going to sell your seed wheat?"

"Not on your tintype! Not if there's any way to save it," Almanzo declared.

"Well, then what?" Royal demanded.

Almanzo paid no attention to the question. "I figure Ingalls isn't the only man in about the same fix," he continued. Slowly and methodically he reckoned up the supply of provisions in town when the train stopped running, and named the families that he had reason to believe were already running short. He estimated the time it would take to clear the railroad cuts of snow, after the blizzard stopped.

"Say they stop in March," he concluded, "I've proved that

folks will have to eat up my wheat or starve before provisions can be shipped in, haven't I?"

"I guess you have, for a fact," Royal admitted soberly.

"On the other hand, suppose this weather keeps up till April. That old Indian predicted seven months of it, don't forget. If trains aren't running before April, or if they don't bring in seed wheat before then, I've got to save my seed wheat, or lose a year's crop."

"Looks that way," Royal agreed.

"And to top that, if trains don't run early in April folks will starve anyway. Even if they have eaten up my wheat."

"Well, come to the point," said Royal.

"This is the point. Somebody's got to go get that wheat that was raised south of town."

Royal slowly shook his head. "Nobody'll do it. It's as much as a man's life is worth."

All at once, Almanzo was cheerful again. He pulled up to the table, lifted a stack of pancakes onto his plate. "Oh well, why not take a chance?" he asked gaily, pouring molasses over the steaming pile. "You can't sometimes 'most always tell!"

"Forty miles?" Royal said. "Go out on these prairies looking for a needle in a haystack—twenty miles and back? Man alive, you know yourself nobody can tell when a blizzard will hit you. We haven't had more than one clear day at a time since this thing started. More often, half a day. It can't be done, Manzo. A fellow wouldn't have the chance of a snowball in hades."

"Somebody's got to do it," Almanzo replied reasonably. "I proved that."

"Yes, but, gee whillikins!" said Royal.

"'Be sure you're right, then go ahead,'" Almanzo quoted their father.

"'Better be safe than sorry,'" Royal retorted with their mother's saying.

"Oh well, you're a storekeeper, Roy," Almanzo returned. "A farmer takes chances. He has to."

"Almanzo," Royal said solemnly, "if I let you lose your fool self out on these prairies, what'll I say to Father and Mother?"

"You tell 'em you had nothing to say about it, Roy," Almanzo answered. "I'm free, white, and twenty-one . . . or as good as. Anyway, this is a free country and I'm free and independent. I do as I please."

"Don't go off half-cocked, Manzo," Royal urged him. "Think it over."

"I been thinking it over," said Almanzo.

Royal was silent. They sat quietly eating in the steady warmth of the coal fire and the strong light shining from the lamp and its bright tin reflector. The walls trembled a little and the shadows on them slightly quivered under the blows of winds that squealed along the eaves, split shrieking at the corners, and always roared like a waterfall. Almanzo took another stack of pancakes.

Suddenly Royal laid down his knife and pushed back his plate.

"One thing's sure," he said. "You're not going to tackle any such foolhardy trip alone. If you're bound and determined to do it, I'm going along with you."

"See here!" Almanzo exclaimed. "We *can't* both of us go!"

CHAPTER 26

Breathing Spell

NEXT morning was still. The sun shone bright and cold and only the round-and-round growl of the coffee grinder, the rush of a steady wind, and the crackling of the hay sounded in the lean-to where Laura and Mary worked. They were very cold. Neither could twist more than two or three sticks of hay without going to thaw their hands over the stove.

They could barely keep the fire alive; they could not pile up a store of sticks and get time to help with the washing. So Ma put the washing by till later. "Perhaps it will be warmer tomorrow," she said, and she helped twist hay. She spelled Mary and Laura in turns so that they could spell Carrie at the coffee grinder.

Pa did not come home until late afternoon. The afternoon meal of bread and tea was waiting when he came at last.

"Gee whillikins, it's a cold day," he said.

He had been able to haul only one load of hay that day. The haystacks were buried in snow. He had to dig the hay out of enormous drifts. Fresh snow had covered the sled's old tracks and changed the look of the slough. David had continually fallen deep into hidden pockets of slough grass.

"Did your nose freeze, Pa?" Grace asked him anxiously. Of course in this weather Pa's ears and his nose froze so that he had to rub them with snow to thaw them. He pretended to Grace that his nose grew longer every time it froze, and Grace pretended to believe that it did. This was their own special joke.

"Froze it five or six times today," Pa answered her, tenderly feeling his red, swollen nose.

"If spring doesn't come soon, I'm going to have a nose as long as an elephant's. Ears like an elephant's, too." That made Grace laugh.

After they had eaten the daily bread, Pa twisted hay enough to last till bedtime. He had done the chores when he put David in the stable. There was still a little daylight left, and he said, "I believe I'll go over to Bradley's drugstore and watch the checker game awhile."

"Do, Charles," Ma said. "Why don't you play some checkers yourself?"

"Well, you see, those bachelors spend all their time this winter at checkers and cards," Pa answered. "They are good checker players, having nothing else to do. Too good for me. So I'll just look on but I don't know's there's anything more enjoyable than watching a good game of checkers."

He was not gone long. The drugstore was so cold, he said, that there was no game of checkers that day. But there was news.

"Almanzo Wilder and Cap Garland are going after that wheat south of town."

Ma's face went still and her eyes opened as if she saw something frightening. "How far did you say it was?"

"No one knows exactly," Pa said. "Nor exactly where it is. There's only a rumor that a settler around there somewhere raised wheat last year. Nobody around here sold wheat to anybody in town, so it must be there, if he is, and if he raised wheat. Foster says somebody told him the settler was wintering on his claim. The boys are going to try to find it. Loftus has put up the money for them to buy all that they can haul."

Grace began to clamor at his knee, trying to climb up to measure his nose with her finger. He lifted her absently. Even Grace, little as she was, saw that this was no time for a joke. She looked anxiously up at him and then at Ma, and sat still on Pa's knee.

"When are they starting?" Ma asked.

"First thing tomorrow morning. They built a sled for Cap Garland today. Both Wilders were going but they decided that one of them ought to stay in case the one who goes gets caught in a blizzard."

No one said anything for a moment.

"They may make it all right," Pa said. "So long as this clear weather holds, they'll be able to travel. It may hold for two or three days. You can't tell."

"That's the trouble," said Ma. "You can't tell."

"If they do make it," Pa pointed out, "we'll have wheat enough to last us till spring. If the wheat's there and they find it."

In the night Laura felt the shock and heard the howls of the blizzard winds. There had been only one short day of rest. The blizzard would let nobody start out tomorrow to look for wheat.

CHAPTER 27

For Daily Bread

IN THE third night of that storm a stillness woke Almanzo. The blizzard had stopped. He reached out through the cold to his vest hanging on a chair, got out his watch and a match, and saw that the time was nearly three o'clock.

In winter's dark, cold mornings he still missed his father's routing him out of bed. Now he had to rout himself out of warm blankets into the cold. He must light the lantern, stir up the fire, and break the ice in the water pail himself, and he could choose between getting his own breakfast and going hungry. Three o'clock on winter mornings was the only time that he was not glad to be free and independent.

Once out of bed and into his clothes, though, he liked early morning better than any other part of the day. The air was fresher then than at any other time. Low in the eastern sky hung the morning star. The temperature was ten below zero, the wind blew steadily. The day promised to be fair.

When he rode down Main Street on the hay-sled, the sun had not yet risen but the morning star had melted in an upward rush of light. The Ingalls' building stood solid black against the endless eastern prairie covered with snow. Down Second Street, beyond it, the two stables with their haystacks looked small, and beyond them Garland's little house had a speck of light in its kitchen. Cap Garland came riding up on his sled, driving his buckskin gelding.

He waved to Almanzo and Almanzo lifted his own arms, stiff in the weight of woolen sleeves. Their faces were wrapped in mufflers and there was no need to say anything. Three days ago, before the last blizzard struck, they had made their plan. Almanzo drove on without stopping and Cap Garland swung the buckskin into Main Street behind him.

At the end of the short street Almanzo turned southeast to cross the neck of Big Slough at its narrowest place. The sun was rising. The sky was a thin, cold blue and the earth to its far horizon was covered with snowdrifts, flushed pink and faintly shadowed with blue. The horse's breath made a white cloud about his head.

The only sounds were the clumping of Prince's hoofs on the hard snow and the rasp of the sled's runners. There was not a track on the waves of snow, not a print of rabbit's paw or bird's claws. There was no trace of a road, no sign that any living thing had ever been on the frozen snow fields where every curve was changed and unknown. Only the wind had furrowed them in tiny wavelets, each holding its own faint line of blue shadow, and the wind was blowing a spray of snow from every smooth, hard crest.

There was something mocking in the glitter of that trackless sea where every shadow moved a little and the blown snow spray confused the eyes searching for lost landmarks. Almanzo judged directions and distance as well as he could, where everything was changed and uncertain, and he thought, "Well, we'll have to make it by guess and by golly!"

He guessed that he had struck the neck of the buried Big Slough somewhere near the place where he crossed to haul hay. If he was right, the snow underneath the sled would be packed hard and in five minutes or less he would be safe on upland again. He glanced back. Cap had slowed the buckskin and was following at a cautious distance. With no warning, Prince went down.

"Whoa-oa, steady!" Almanzo shouted through his muffler but he shouted calmly and soothingly. Only the horse's snorting head stuck up from the grassy air-pocket in front of the sled. The sled ran on, sliding forward; there is no way to put brakes on a sled, but it stopped in time.

"Whoa, Prince. Steady now," Almanzo said, drawing the reins firmly. "Steady, steady." Buried deep in snow, Prince stood still.

Almanzo jumped off the sled. He unhitched the whiffletree from the chain fastened to the sled's runners. Cap Garland drove around him and stopped. Almanzo went to Prince's head and wallowing down into the broken snow and tangling dead grass he took hold of the reins under the bits. "Steady, Prince old fellow, steady, steady," he said, for his own flounderings were frightening Prince again.

Then he trampled down the snow until he could persuade Prince that it was firm enough to step on. Holding Prince by the bits again he urged him forward till with a mighty heave he burst up out of the hole and Almanzo led him rapidly climbing up out of the hole to the solid snow again. He led him on to Cap Garland's sled and handed over the reins to Cap.

Cap's light eyes showed that he was cheerfully grinning under the muffler. "So that's the way you do it!" he said.

"Nothing much to it," Almanzo replied.

"Fine day for a trip," Cap remarked.

"Yep, it's a fine, large morning!" Almanzo agreed.

Almanzo went to pull his empty sled sidewise behind the large hole that Prince and he had made in the snow. He liked Cap Garland. Cap was lighthearted and merry but he would fight his weight in wildcats. When Cap Garland had reason to lose his temper his eyes narrowed and glittered with a look that no man cared to stand up to. Almanzo had seen him make the toughest railroader back down.

Taking a coiled rope from his sled Almanzo tied one end of the sled's chain. The other end he tied to Prince's whiffletree, and with Prince helping him pull he guided the sled around the hole. Then he hitched Prince to the sled, coiled the long rope again, and drove on.

Cap Garland fell in behind him once more. He was really only a month younger than Almanzo. They were both nineteen. But because Almanzo had a homestead claim, Cap supposed that he was older than twenty-one. Partly for that reason, Cap treated Almanzo with respect. Almanzo made no objection to that.

Leading the way, he drove toward the sun until he was sure he had crossed Big Slough. Then he headed southward toward the twin lakes, Henry and Thompson.

The only color now on the endless snow-fields was a pale reflection of the blue sky. Everywhere tiny glints sparkled sharply. The glitter stabbed Almanzo's eyes, screwed almost shut in the slot between his cap and muffler. The icy wool blew out and sucked back against his nose and mouth with every breath.

His hands grew too cold to feel the reins, so he shifted the reins from hand to hand, beating the free arm against his chest to make the blood flow warm in it.

When his feet grew numb he stepped off the sled and ran beside it. His heart, pumping fast, forced warmth to his feet until they tingled and itched and burned, and he jumped onto the sled again.

"Nothing like exercise to warm you up!" he shouted back to Cap.

"Let me in by the stove!" Cap shouted, and he jumped off his sled and ran beside it.

So they went on, running, riding, and thumping their chests, then running again, while the horses briskly trotted. "Say, how long do we keep this up?" Cap shouted once, joking. "Till we find wheat, or hell freezes!" Almanzo answered.

"You can skate on it now!" Cap shouted back.

They went on. The rising sun poured down sunshine that seemed colder than the wind. There was no cloud in the sky, but the cold steadily grew more intense.

Prince went down again in some unknown little slough. Cap drove up and stopped. Almanzo unhitched Prince, got him up on the firm snow, hauled the sled around the hole, hitched up again.

"See the Lone Cottonwood anywhere ahead?" he asked Cap.

"Nope. But I can't depend on my eyes," Cap answered. The sun-glare made them see black spots everywhere.

They rewound their mufflers, shifting the ice-patches away from their raw faces. To the far horizon all around them, there was nothing but glittering snow and the cruel wind blowing.

"Lucky so far," Almanzo said. "Gone down only twice."

He stepped onto his sled and started and heard Cap shout. Swinging in to follow, the buckskin had gone down.

Cap dug him out, hauled the sled around the hole, and hitched up again.

"Nothing like exercise to keep a fellow warm!" he reminded Almanzo.

From the top of the next low swell they saw the Lone Cottonwood, bare and gaunt. Snow covered the twin lakes and the low bushes that grew between them. Only the lonely tree's bare top rose up from the endless whiteness.

As soon as he saw it, Almanzo turned westward quickly to keep well away from the sloughs around the lakes. On the upland grass the snow was solid.

The Lone Tree was the last landmark. It was soon lost again in the trackless waves of snow. There was no road, no trace nor track of any kind to be seen anywhere. No one knew where the settler lived who had raised wheat. No one was even sure that he was still in that country. It might be that he had gone out for the winter. It might be that there had never been such a man. There was only a rumor that someone had told somebody that a man living somewhere in that region had raised wheat.

One wave of the endless frozen snow-sea was like another. Beneath the snow-spray blown from their crests, the low prairie swells seemed to come on forever, all the same. The sun slowly rose higher and the cold increased.

There was no sound but the horses' hoofs and the rasp of the sled runners that made no tracks on the ice-hard snow, and the rushing sound of the wind that faintly whistled against the sled.

From time to time Almanzo looked back and Cap shook his head. Neither of them saw any wisp of smoke against the cold sky. The small, cold sun seemed to hang motionless but it was climbing. The shadows narrowed, the waves of snow and the prairie's curves seemed to flatten. The white wilderness leveled out, bleak and empty.

"How far we going?" Cap shouted.

"Till we find that wheat!" Almanzo called back. But he, too, was wondering whether there was any wheat in that endless emptiness. The sun was in the zenith now, the day half gone. There was still no threat in the northwestern sky, but it would be unusual to have more than this one clear day between blizzards.

Almanzo knew they should turn back toward town. Numb from cold, he stumbled off the sled and ran on beside it. He did not want to go back to the hungry town and say that he had turned back with an empty sled.

"How far you figure we've come?" Cap asked.

"About twenty miles," Almanzo guessed. "Think we better go back?"

"Never give up till you're licked!" Cap said cheerfully.

They looked around. They were on an upland. If the lower air had not been a little hazy with a glitter of blowing snow, they could have seen perhaps twenty miles. But the prairie swells, that seemed level under the high sun, hid the town to the northwest. The northwest sky was still clear.

Stamping their feet and beating their arms on their chests they searched the white land from west to east, as far south as they could see. There was not a wisp of smoke anywhere.

"Which way'll we go?" Cap asked.

"Any way's as good as any other," Almanzo said. They rewound their mufflers again. Their breath had filled the mufflers with ice. They could hardly find a spot of wool to relieve the pain of ice on skin that it had chafed raw. "How are your feet?" he asked Cap.

"They don't say," Cap replied. "They'll be all right, I guess. I'm going on running."

"So am I," Almanzo said. "If they don't warm up pretty soon, we better stop and rub them with snow. Let's follow this swell west a ways. If we don't find anything that way we can circle back, farther south."

"Suits me," Cap agreed. Their good horses went willingly into a trot again and they ran on beside the sleds.

The upland ended sooner than they had expected. The snow-field sloped downward and spread into a flat hollow that the upland had hidden. It looked like a slough. Almanzo pulled Prince to a walk and got onto the sled to look the land over. The flat hollow ran on toward the west; he saw no way to get around it without turning back along the upland. Then he saw, ahead and across the slough, a smear of gray-brown in the snow blowing from a drift. He stopped Prince and yelled, "Hi, Cap! That look like smoke ahead there?"

Cap was looking at it. "Looks like it comes out of a snowbank!" he shouted.

Almanzo drove on down the slope. After a few minutes he called back, "It's smoke all right! There's some kind of house there!"

They had to cross the slough to reach it. In their hurry, Cap drove alongside Almanzo and the buckskin went down. This was the deepest hole they had got a horse out of yet, and all around it the snow broke down into air-pockets under the surface till there seemed no end to their floundering. Shadows were beginning to creep eastward before they got the buckskin to solid footing and began cautiously to go on.

The thin smoke did rise from a long snowbank, and there was not a track on the snow. But when they circled and came back on the southern side, they saw that the snow had been shoveled away from before a door in the snowbank. They pulled up their sleds and shouted.

The door opened and a man stood there, astonished. His hair was long and his unshaven beard grew up to his cheekbones.

"Hello! Hello!" he cried. "Come in! Come in! Where did you come from? Where are you going? Come in! How long can you stay? Come right in!" He was so excited that he did not wait for answers.

"We've got to take care of our horses first," Almanzo answered.

The man snatched on a coat and came out, saying, "Come along, right over this way, follow me. Where did you fellows come from?"

"We just drove out from town," Cap said. The man led the way to a door in another snowbank. They told him their names while they unhitched, and he said his name was Anderson. They led the horses into a warm, sod stable, snug under the snowbank.

The end of the stable was partitioned off with poles and a rough door, and grains of wheat had trickled through a crack. Almanzo and Cap looked at it and grinned to each other.

They watered Prince and the buckskin from the well at the door, fed them oats, and left them tied to a mangerful of hay beside Anderson's team of black horses. Then they followed Anderson to the house under the snowbank.

The one room's low ceiling was made of poles covered with hay and sagging under the weight of snow. The walls were sods. Anderson left the door ajar to let in a little light.

"I haven't got my window shoveled out since the last blow," he said. "The snow piles over that little rise to the northwest and covers me up. Keeps the place so warm I don't need much fuel. Sod houses are the warmest there are, anyway."

The room was warm, and steamy from a kettle boiling on the stove. Anderson's dinner was on a rough table built against the wall. He urged them to draw up and eat with him. He had not seen a soul since last October, when he had gone to town and brought home his winter's supplies.

Almanzo and Cap sat down with him and ate heartily of the

boiled beans, sourdough biscuit and dried-apple sauce. The hot food and coffee warmed them, and their thawing feet burned so painfully that they knew they were not frozen. Almanzo mentioned to Mr. Anderson that he and Cap might buy some wheat.

"I'm not selling any," Mr. Anderson said flatly. "All I raised, I'm keeping for seed. What are you buying wheat for, this time of year?" he wanted to know.

They had to tell him that the trains had stopped running, and the people in town were hungry.

"There's women and children that haven't had a square meal since before Christmas," Almanzo put it to him. "They've got to get something to eat or they'll starve to death before spring."

"That's not my lookout," said Mr. Anderson. "Nobody's responsible for other folks that haven't got enough forethought to take care of themselves."

"Nobody thinks you are," Almanzo retorted. "And nobody's asking you to give them anything. We'll pay you the full elevator price of eighty-two cents a bushel, and save you hauling it to town into the bargain."

"I've got no wheat to sell," Mr. Anderson answered, and Almanzo knew he meant what he said.

Cap came in then, his smile flashing in his raw-red face chapped by the icy wind. "We're open and aboveboard with you, Mr. Anderson. We've put our cards on the table. The folks in town have got to have some of your wheat or starve. All right, they've got to pay for it. What'll you take?"

"I'm not trying to take advantage of you boys," Mr. Anderson said. "I don't want to sell. That's my seed wheat. It's my next year's crop. I could have sold it last fall if I was going to sell it."

Almanzo quickly decided. "We'll make it a dollar a bushel," he said. "Eighteen cents a bushel above market price. And don't forget we do the hauling to boot."

"I'm not selling my seed," said Mr. Anderson. "I got to make a crop next summer."

Almanzo said meditatively, "A man can always buy seed. Most folks out here are going to. You're throwing away a clear profit of eighteen cents a bushel above market price, Mr. Anderson."

"How do I know they'll ship in seed wheat in time for sowing?" Mr. Anderson demanded.

Cap asked him reasonably, "Well, for that matter, how do you know you'll make a crop? Say you turn down this cash offer and sow your wheat. Hailstorm's liable to hit it, or grasshoppers."

"That's true enough," Mr. Anderson admitted.

"The one thing you're sure of is cash in your pocket," said Almanzo.

Mr. Anderson slowly shook his head. "No, I'm not selling. I like to killed myself breaking forty acres last summer. I got to keep the seed to sow it."

Almanzo and Cap looked at each other. Almanzo took out his wallet. "We'll give you a dollar and twenty-five cents a bushel. Cash." He laid the stack of bills on the table.

Mr. Anderson hesitated. Then he took his gaze away from the money.

"'A bird in the hand is worth two in the bush,'" Cap said.

Mr. Anderson glanced again at the bills in spite of himself. Then he leaned back and considered. He scratched his head. "Well," he said finally, "I might sow some oats."

Neither Almanzo nor Cap said anything. They knew his mind was quivering in the balance and if he decided now against selling, he would not change. At last he decided, "I guess I could let you have around sixty bushels at that price."

Almanzo and Cap rose quickly from the table.

"Come on, let's get it loaded!" said Cap. "We're a long way from home."

Mr. Anderson urged them to stay all night but Almanzo agreed with Cap. "Thanks just the same," he said hurriedly, "but one day is all we have between blizzards lately, and it's past noon now. We're already late getting started back."

"The wheat's not sacked," Mr. Anderson pointed out, but Almanzo said, "We brought sacks."

They hurried to the stable. Mr. Anderson helped them shovel the wheat from the bin into the two-bushel sacks, and they loaded the sleds. While they hitched up they asked Mr. Anderson how best to get across the slough, but he had not crossed it that winter, and for lack of landmarks he could not show them exactly where he had driven through the grass last summer.

"You boys better spend the night here," he urged them again, but they told him good-by and started home.

They drove from the shelter of the big snowbanks into the piercing cold wind, and they had hardly begun to cross the flat valley when Prince broke down into an airpocket. Swinging out to circle the dangerous place, Cap's buckskin felt the snow give way under him so suddenly that he screamed as he went plunging down.

The horse's scream was horrible. For a moment Almanzo had all he could do to keep Prince quiet. Then he saw Cap down in the snow, hanging onto the frantic buckskin by the bits. Plunging and rearing, the buckskin almost jerked Cap's sled into the hole. It tipped on the very edge and the load of wheat slid partly off it.

"All right?" Almanzo asked when the buckskin seemed quiet.

"Yep!" Cap answered. Then for some time they worked, each unhitching his own horse down in the broken snow and wiry grass, and floundering about in it, trampling and stamping to make a solid footing for the horse. They came up chilled to the bone and covered with snow.

They tied both horses to Almanzo's sled, then unloaded Cap's sled, dragged it back from the hole, and piled the snowy, hundred and twenty-five pound sacks onto it again. They hitched up again. It was hard to make their numb fingers buckle the stiff, cold straps. And gingerly once more Almanzo drove on across the treacherous slough.

Prince went down again but fortunately the buckskin did not. With Cap to help, it did not take so long to get Prince out once more. And with no further trouble they reached the upland.

Almanzo stopped there and called to Cap, "Think we better try to pick up our trail back?"

"Nope!" Cap answered. "Better hit out for town. We've got no time to lose." The horses' hoofs and the sleds had made no tracks on the hard snowcrust. The only marks were the scattered holes where they had floundered in the sloughs and these lay east of the way home.

Almanzo headed toward the northwest, across the wide prairie white in its covering of snow. His shadow was his only guide. One prairie swell was like another, one snow-covered slough differed from the next only in size. To cross the lowland meant taking the risk of breaking down and losing time. To follow the ridges of higher ground meant more miles to travel. The horses were growing tired. They were afraid of falling into hidden holes in the snow and this fear added to their tiredness.

Time after time they did fall through a thin snowcrust. Cap and Almanzo had to unhitch them, get them out, hitch up again.

They plodded on, into the sharp cold of the wind. Too tired now to trot with their heavy loads, the horses did not go fast enough so that Almanzo and Cap could run by the sleds. They could only stamp their feet hard as they walked to keep them from freezing, and beat their arms against their chests.

They grew colder. Almanzo's feet no longer felt the shock when he stamped them. The hand that held the lines was so stiff that the fingers would not unclasp. He put the lines around his shoulders to leave both hands free, and with every step he whipped his hands across his chest to keep the blood moving in them.

"Hey, Wilder!" Cap called. "Aren't we heading too straight north?"

"How do I know?" Almanzo called back.

They plodded on. Prince went down again and stood with drooping head while Almanzo unhitched him and trampled the snow, led him out and hitched him again. They climbed to an upland, followed it around a slough, went down to cross another slough. Prince went down.

"You want me to take the lead awhile?" Cap asked, when Almanzo had hitched up again. "Save you and Prince the brunt of it."

"Suits me," said Almanzo. "We'll take turns."

After that, when a horse went down, the other took the lead until he went down. The sun was low and a haze was thickening in the northwest.

"We ought to see the Lone Cottonwood from that rise ahead," Almanzo said to Cap.

After a moment Cap answered, "Yes, I think we will."

But when they topped the rise there was nothing but the same endless, empty waves of snow beyond it and the thick haze low in the northwest. Almanzo and Cap looked at it, then spoke to their horses and went on. But they kept the sleds closer together.

The sun was setting red in the cold sky when they saw the bare top of the Lone Cottonwood away to the northeast. And in the northwest the blizzard cloud was plain to be seen, low along the horizon.

"It seems to be hanging off," Almanzo said. "I've been watching it from away back."

"So have I," said Cap. "But we better forget about being cold and *drive.* Let's ride awhile."

"You bet you," Almanzo agreed. "I could do with a few minutes' rest."

They said nothing more except to urge the tired horses to a faster walk. Cap led the way straight over the rises and straight across the hollows, into the teeth of the wind. Heads bent against it, they kept going till the buckskin broke through a snowcrust.

Almanzo was so close behind that he could not avoid the hidden airhole. He turned quickly aside but Prince went down near the buckskin. Between them the whole snowcrust gave way and Almanzo's sled tipped, load and all, into the broken snow and grass.

Darkness slowly settled down while Cap helped Almanzo drag back the sled and dig out and carry the heavy sacks of wheat. The snow was palely luminous. The wind had died, not a breath of air moved in the darkening stillness. Stars shone in the sky overhead and to the south and the east, but low in the north and the west the sky was black. And the blackness rose, blotting out the stars above it one by one.

"We're in for it, I guess," Cap said.

"We must be nearly there," Almanzo answered. He spoke to Prince and moved on ahead. Cap followed, he and the sled a bulky shadow moving over the dim whiteness of snow.

Before them in the sky, star after star went out as the black cloud rose.

Quietly Almanzo and Cap spoke to the tired horses, urging them on. There was still the neck of Big Slough to cross. They could not see the swells or the hollows now. They could see only a little way by the paleness of the snow and the faint starshine.

CHAPTER 28

Four Days' Blizzard

ALL day, while Laura turned the coffee mill or twisted hay, she remembered that Cap Garland and the younger Wilder brother were driving across the trackless snow-fields, going in search of wheat to bring to town.

That afternoon she and Mary went out in the back yard for a breath of air and Laura looked fearfully to the northwest, dreading to see the low-lying rim of darkness that was the sure sign of a coming blizzard. There was no cloud but still she distrusted the bright sunshine. It was too bright and the snow-covered prairie, glittering as far as eye could see, seemed menacing. She shivered.

"Let's go in, Laura," Mary said. "The sunshine is too cold. Do you see the cloud?"

"There is no cloud," Laura assured her. "But I don't like the weather. The air feels savage, somehow."

"The air is only air," Mary replied. "You mean it is cold."

"I don't either mean it's cold. I mean it's savage!" Laura snapped.

They went back into the kitchen through the lean-to entryway.

Ma looked up from Pa's sock that she was darning. "You didn't stay out long, girls," she said. "You should get what fresh air you can, before the next storm."

Pa came into the entry. Ma put away her work and took from the oven the loaf of sourdough brown bread, while Laura poured the thin codfish gravy into a bowl.

"Gravy again. Good!" Pa said, sitting down to eat. The cold and the hard work of hauling hay had made him hungry. His eyes glittered at sight of the food. Nobody, he said, could beat Ma at making good bread, and nothing was better on bread than codfish gravy. He made the coarse bread and the gruel of groundwheat flour with a bit of salt fish in it seem almost a treat.

"The boys have a fine day for their trip," he said. "I saw

where one of the horses went down in Big Slough, but they got him out with no trouble."

"Do you think they will get back all right, Pa?" Carrie asked timidly, and Pa said, "No reason why not, if this clear weather holds."

He went out to do the chores. The sun had set and the light was growing dim when he came back. He came through the front room so they knew that he had gone across the street to get the news. They knew when they saw him that it was not good news.

"We're in for it again," he said, as he hung his coat and cap on the nail behind the door. "There's a cloud coming fast."

"They didn't get back?" Ma asked him.

"No," Pa said.

Ma silently rocked and they all sat silent while the dusk deepened. Grace was asleep in Mary's lap. The others drew their chairs closer to the stove, but they were still silent, just waiting, when the jar of the house came and the roar and howl of the wind.

Pa rose with a deep breath. "Well, here it is again."

Then suddenly he shook his clenched fist at the northwest. "Howl! blast you! howl!" he shouted. "We're all here safe! You can't get at us! You've tried all winter but we'll beat you yet! We'll be right here when spring comes!"

"Charles, Charles," Ma said soothingly. "It is only a blizzard. We're used to them."

Pa dropped back in his chair. After a minute he said, "That was foolish, Caroline. Seemed for a minute like that wind was something alive, trying to get at us."

"It does seem so, sometimes," Ma went on soothing him.

"I wouldn't mind so much if I could only play the fiddle," Pa muttered, looking down at his cracked and stiffened hands that could be seen in the glow of fire from the cracks of the stove.

In all the hard times before, Pa had made music for them all. Now no one could make music for him. Laura tried to cheer herself by remembering what Pa had said; they were all there, safe. But she wanted to do something for Pa. Then suddenly she remembered. "We're all here!" It was the chorus of the "Song of the Freed Men."

"We can sing!" she exclaimed, and she began to hum the tune.

Pa looked up quickly. "You've got it, Laura, but you are a little high. Try it in B flat," he said.

Laura started the tune again. First Pa, then the others, joined in, and they sang:

"When Paul and Silas were bound in jail,
Do thy-self-a no harm,
One did sing and the other did pray,
Do thy-self-a no harm.

"We're all here, we're all here,
Do thy-self-a no harm,
We're all here, we're all here,
Do thy-self-a no harm.

"If religion was a thing that money could buy,
Do thy-self-a no harm,
The rich would live and the poor would die,
Do thy-self-a no harm."

Laura was standing up now and so was Carrie, and Grace was awake and singing with all her might:

"We're all here, we're all here!
Do thy-self-a no harm.
We're all here, we're all here!
Do thy-self-a no harm!"

"That was fine!" Pa said. Then he sounded a low note and began:

"De old Jim riber, I float down,
I ran my boat upon de groun'
De drif' log come with a rushin' din,
An' stove both ends of my ol' boat in."

"Now, all together on the chorus!" And they all sang:

"It will neber do to gib it up so,
It will neber do to gib it up so,
It will neber do to gib it up so, Mr. Brown!
It will neber do to gib it up so!"

When they stopped singing, the storm seemed louder than ever. It was truly like a great beast worrying the house, shaking it, growling and snarling and whining and roaring at the trembling walls that stood against it.

After a moment Pa sang again, and the stately measures were suited to the thankfulness they were all feeling:

"Great is the Lord
And greatly to be prais-ed
In the city of our God,
In the mountain of His holiness."

Then Ma began:

"When I can read my title clear
To mansions in the skies,
I'll bid farewell to every fear
And wipe my weeping eyes."

The storm raged outside, screaming and hammering at walls and window, but they were safely sheltered, and huddled in the warmth of the hay fire they went on singing.

It was past bedtime when the warmth died from the stove, and because they could not waste hay they crept from the dark, cold kitchen through the colder darkness upstairs and to the beds.

Under the quilts, Laura and Mary silently said their prayers, and Mary whispered, "Laura."

"What?" Laura whispered.

"Did you pray for them?"

"Yes," Laura answered. "Do you think we ought to?"

"It isn't like asking for anything for ourselves," Mary replied. "I didn't say anything about the wheat. I only said please to save their lives if it's God's will."

"I think it ought to be," Laura said. "They were doing their best. And Pa lived three days in that Christmas blizzard when we lived on Plum Creek."

All the days of that blizzard nothing more was said about Cap Garland and the young Wilder brother. If they had found shelter they might live through the storm. If not, nothing could be done for them. It would do no good to talk.

The constant beating of the winds against the house, the

roaring, shrieking, howling of the storm, made it hard even to think. It was possible only to wait for the storm to stop. All the time, while they ground wheat, twisted hay, kept the fire burning in the stove, and huddled over it to thaw their chapped, numb hands and their itching, burning, chilblained feet, and while they chewed and swallowed the coarse bread, they were all waiting until the storm stopped.

It did not stop during the third day or the third night. In the fourth morning it was still blowing fiercely.

"No sign of a letup," Pa said when he came in from the stable. "This is the worst yet."

After a while, when they were all eating their morning bread, Ma roused herself and answered, "I hope everyone is all right in town."

There was no way to find out. Laura thought of the other houses, only across the street, that they could not even see. For some reason she remembered Mrs. Boast. They had not seen her since last summer, nor Mr. Boast since the long-ago time when he brought the last butter.

"But we might as well be out on a claim too," she said. Ma looked at her, wondering what she meant, but did not ask. All of them were only waiting for the blizzard noises to stop.

That morning Ma carefully poured the last kernels of wheat into the coffee mill.

There was enough to make one last small loaf of bread. Ma scraped the bowl with the spoon and then with her finger to get every bit of dough into the baking pan.

"This is the last, Charles," she said.

"I can get more," Pa told her. "Almanzo Wilder was saving some seed wheat. I can get to it through the blizzard if I have to."

Late that day, when the bread was on the table, the walls stopped shaking. The howling shrillness went away and only a rushing wind whistled under the eaves. Pa got up quickly, saying, "I believe it's stopping!"

He put on his coat and cap and muffler and told Ma that he was going across the street to Fuller's store. Looking through peepholes that they scratched in the frost, Laura and Carrie saw snow blowing by on the straight wind.

Ma relaxed in her chair and sighed, "What a merciful quiet."

The snow was settling. After a while Carrie saw the sky and called Laura to see it. They looked at the cold, thin blue overhead and at the warm light of sunset on the low-blowing snow. The blizzard really was ended. And the northwest sky was empty.

"I hope Cap Garland and young Mr. Wilder are somewhere safe," Carrie said. So did Laura, but she knew that saying so would not make any difference.

CHAPTER 29

The Last Mile

ALMANZO thought that perhaps they had crossed the neck of Big Slough. He could not be sure where they were. He could see Prince and the slowly moving bulk of the loaded sled. Beyond them the darkness was like a mist thickening over a flat, white world. Stars twinkled far away around part of its rim. Before him, the black storm climbed rapidly up the sky and in silence destroyed the stars.

He shouted to Cap, "Think we've crossed Big Slough?"

He had forgotten that they need not shout since the wind had stopped. Cap said, "Don't know. You think so?"

"We haven't broken down," Almanzo said.

"She's coming fast," Cap said. He meant the rising black storm.

There was nothing to say to that. Almanzo spoke encouragingly to Prince again and trudged on. He stamped his feet as he walked but he could hardly feel the shock; his legs were like wood from the knees down. Every muscle in his body was drawn tight against the cold. He could not relax the tightness and it hurt his jaws and ached in his middle. He beat his numb hands together.

Prince was pulling harder. Though the snow underfoot looked level, it was an upward slope. They had not seen the hole where Prince had broken down in Big Slough that morning, but they must somehow have crossed the slough.

Yet everything seemed unfamiliar. The darkness mixed with faint starshine coming up from the snow made the way strange. In the blackness ahead there was no star to steer by.

"Guess we've crossed it!" Almanzo called back. Cap's sled came on behind him and after a while Cap answered, "Looks that way."

But Prince still pulled hesitatingly, trembling not only from cold and tiredness but from fear that his footing would give way.

"Yep! We're across!" Almanzo sang out. He was sure of it now. "We're on the upland, all right!"

"Where's town?" Cap called.

"We must be pretty near there," Almanzo answered.

"It'll take fast driving," Cap said.

Almanzo knew that. He slapped Prince's flank. "Get up, Prince! Get up!" But Prince quickened only one step, then plodded again. The horse was tired out and he did not want to go toward the storm. It was rising fast now; almost half the sky was blotted out and the dark air was stirring.

"Get on and drive or we won't make it!" Cap said. Almanzo hated to do it, but he stepped onto the sled and taking the stiff lines from his shoulders he beat Prince with the knotted ends.

"Get up there, Prince! Get up!" Prince was startled and frightened; Almanzo had never beaten him before. He lunged against the neckyoke and jerked the sled forward, then on a downward slope he trotted. Cap was beating the buckskin, too. But they were not sure where the town was.

Almanzo headed for it as well as he could. It was somewhere in the thick darkness ahead.

"See anything?" Almanzo called.

"Nope. We're in for it, I guess," Cap answered.

"Town can't be far ahead," Almanzo told him.

The corner of his eye caught a gleam of light. He looked toward it and saw nothing in the storm-dark. Then he saw it again—a glow that shone bright, then abruptly went out. He knew what it was; light was shining out from a door opened and shut. Near where it had been, he thought he saw now the faint glow of a frost-covered window, and he yelled to Cap.

"See that light? Come on!"

They had been going a little too far to the west. Now, headed straight north, Almanzo felt that he knew the way. Prince, too, went more eagerly and the buckskin came trotting behind. Once more Almanzo saw the glow flash out across the street, and now the dim blur of the window was steady. It was the window of Loftus' store.

As they pulled up in front of it, the winds struck them with a whirl of snow.

"Unhitch and run for it!" Almanzo told Cap. "I'll take care of the wheat."

Cap unfastened the tugs and swung onto the buckskin.

"Think you can make it?" Almanzo asked him through the storm.

"Can I? I got to," Cap shouted as he started the buckskin on a run across the vacant lots toward his stable.

Almanzo clumped into the warm store. Mr. Loftus got up from his chair by the stove. No one else was there. Mr. Loftus said, "So you boys made it. We figured you hadn't."

"Cap and I figure we'll do what we set out to do," Almanzo said.

"Find that fellow that raised wheat?" Mr. Loftus asked.

"And bought sixty bushels. Want to help bring it in?" Almanzo answered.

They lugged in the sacks of wheat and stacked them by the wall. The storm was blowing fiercely. When the last sack was on the pile, Almanzo gave Mr. Loftus the receipt that Mr. Anderson had signed and handed over the balance in change.

"You gave me eighty dollars to buy wheat with, and here's what's left, just five dollars even."

"A dollar and twenty-five cents a bushel. That's the best you could do?" Mr. Loftus said, looking at the receipt.

"Any time you say, I'll take it off your hands at that price," Almanzo retorted.

"I don't go back on a bargain," the storekeeper hastily replied. "How much do I owe you for hauling?"

"Not a red cent," Almanzo told him, leaving.

"Hey, aren't you going to stay and thaw out?" Mr. Loftus called after him.

"And let my horse stand in this storm?" Almanzo slammed the door.

He took Prince by the bridle bits and led him up the straight street, along the row of hitching posts and the porch edges in front of the stores. By the long side wall of the feed store they plodded to the stable. Almanzo unhitched and led Prince into the stable's quiet where Lady whinnied a welcome. He barred the door against the storm, then pulled off a mitten and warmed his right hand in his armpit until the fingers were supple enough to light the lantern.

He put Prince in his stall, watered him, and fed him, then curried and brushed him well. That done, he spread for the tired horse a soft, deep bed of clean hay.

"You saved the seed wheat, old boy," he told Prince, giving him a gentle slap.

He took the water pail on his arm and struggled through the blizzard. Just outside the door of the back room he filled the pail with snow. When he stumbled in, Royal was coming from the empty feed store in front.

"Well. Here you are," Royal said. "I was trying to see down the street, looking for you, but you can't see a foot into this blizzard. Listen to it howl! Lucky you got in when you did."

"We brought sixty bushels of wheat," Almanzo told him.

"You don't say! And I thought it was a wild-goose chase." Royal put coal on the fire. "How much did you pay for it?"

"A dollar and a quarter." Almanzo had got his boots off.

"Whew!" Royal whistled. "That the best you could do?"

"Yes," Almanzo said shortly, peeling down layers of socks.

Then Royal noticed what he was doing and saw the pail full of snow. He exclaimed, "What's that snow for?"

"What do you suppose?" Almanzo snorted. "To thaw my feet."

His feet were bloodless-white and dead to the touch. Royal helped him rub them with snow, in the coldest corner of the room, until they began to tingle with a pain that made his stomach sick. Tired as he was, he could not sleep that night with the feverish pain of his feet and he was glad because the pain meant that they were not dangerously frozen.

All the days and nights of that blizzard his feet were so swollen and painful that he had to borrow Royal's boots when it was his turn to do the chores. But when the blizzard stopped, in the late afternoon of the fourth day, he was able to get into his own boots and go down the street.

It was good to be out in the fresh, clean cold, to see sunshine and hear only the straight wind after hearing the storm so long. But the strength of that wind would wear a man out, and before he had gone a block he was so chilled that he was glad enough to blow into Fuller's Hardware store.

The place was crowded. Nearly every man in town was there and they were talking angrily in growing excitement.

"Hello, what's up?" Almanzo asked.

Mr. Harthorn turned round to him. "Say, you charge Loftus

anything for hauling that wheat? Cap Garland, here, says he didn't."

Cap's grin lighted up his face. "Hello, Wilder! You soak it to that skinflint, why don't you? I was fool enough to tell him we made that trip for the fun of it. I wish now I'd charged him all he's got."

"What's all this about?" Almanzo demanded. "No, I'm not charging a red cent. Who says we took that trip for pay?"

Gerald Fuller told him, "Loftus is charging three dollars a bushel for that wheat."

They all began to talk again, but Mr. Ingalls rose up thin and tall from the box by the stove. His face had shrunken to hollows and jutting cheekbones above his brown beard, and his blue eyes glittered bright.

"We aren't getting anywhere with all this talk," he said. "I say, let's all go reason with Loftus."

"Now you're talking!" another man sang out. "Come on, boys! We'll help ourselves to that wheat!"

"Reason with him, I said," Mr. Ingalls objected to that. "I'm talking about reason and justice."

"Maybe *you* are," someone shouted. "I'm talking about something to eat, and by the Almighty! I'm not going back to my youngsters without it! Are the rest of you fellows?"

"No! No!" several agreed with him. Then Cap spoke up.

"Wilder and I have got something to say about this. We brought in the wheat. We didn't haul it in to make trouble."

"That's so," Gerald Fuller said. "See here, boys, we don't want any trouble in town."

"I don't see any sense of flying off the handle," said Almanzo. He was going on, but one of the men interrupted him.

"Yes, and you've got plenty to eat! Both you and Fuller. I'm not going home without—"

"How much you got to eat at your house, Mr. Ingalls?" Cap interrupted him.

"Not a thing," Mr. Ingalls answered. "We ground up the last wheat we had, yesterday. Ate it this morning."

"There you are!" said Almanzo. "Let Mr. Ingalls engineer this."

"All right, I'll take the lead," Mr. Ingalls agreed. "The rest of you boys come along and we'll see what Loftus has to say."

They all tramped along after him single file over the snowdrifts. They crowded into the store where Loftus, when they began coming in, went behind his counter. There was no wheat in sight. Loftus had moved the sacks into his back room.

Mr. Ingalls told him that they thought he was charging too much for the wheat.

"That's my business," said Loftus. "It's my wheat, isn't it? I paid good hard money for it."

"A dollar and a quarter a bushel, we understand," Mr. Ingalls said.

"That's my business," Mr. Loftus repeated.

"We'll show you whose business it is!" the angry man shouted.

"You fellows so much as touch my property and I'll have the law on you!" Mr. Loftus answered. Some of them laughed snarlingly. But Loftus was not going to back down. He banged his fist on the counter and told them, "That wheat's mine and I've got a right to charge any price I want to for it."

"That's so, Loftus, you have," Mr. Ingalls agreed with him. "This is a free country and every man's got a right to do as he pleases with his own property." He said to the crowd, "You know that's a fact, boys," and he went on, "Don't forget every one of us is free and independent, Loftus. This winter won't last forever and maybe you want to go on doing business after it's over."

"Threatening me, are you?" Mr. Loftus demanded.

"We don't need to," Mr. Ingalls replied. "It's a plain fact. If you've got a right to do as you please, we've got a right to do as we please. It works both ways. You've got us down now. That's your business, as you say. But your business depends on our good will. You maybe don't notice that now, but along next summer you'll likely notice it."

"That's so, Loftus," Gerald Fuller said. "You got to treat folks right or you don't last long in business, not in this country."

The angry man said, "We're not here to palaver. Where's that wheat?"

"Don't be a fool, Loftus," Mr. Harthorn said.

"The money wasn't out of your till more than a day," Mr. Ingalls said. "And the boys didn't charge you a cent for hauling it. Charge a fair profit and you'll have the cash back inside of an hour."

"What do you call a fair profit?" Mr. Loftus asked. "I buy as low as I can and sell as high as I can; that's good business."

"That's not my idea," said Gerald Fuller. "I say it's good business to treat people right."

"We wouldn't object to your price, if Wilder and Garland here had charged you what it was worth to go after that wheat," Mr. Ingalls told Loftus.

"Well, why didn't you?" Mr. Loftus asked them. "I stood ready to pay any reasonable charge for hauling."

Cap Garland spoke up. He was not grinning. He had the look that had made the railroader back down. "Don't offer us any of your filthy cash. Wilder and I didn't make that trip to skin a profit off folks that are hungry."

Almanzo was angry, too. "Get it through your head if you can, there's not money enough in the mint to pay for that trip. We didn't make it for you and you can't pay us for it."

Mr. Loftus looked from Cap to Almanzo and then around at the other faces. They all despised him. He opened his mouth and shut it. He looked beaten. Then he said, "I'll tell you what I'll do, boys. You can buy the wheat for just what it cost me, a dollar twenty-five cents a bushel."

"We don't object to your making a fair profit, Loftus," Mr. Ingalls said, but Loftus shook his head.

"No, I'll let it go for what it cost me."

This was so unexpected that for a moment no one knew exactly how to take it. Then Mr. Ingalls suggested, "What do you say we all get together and kind of ration it out, on a basis of how much our families need to last through till spring?"

They did this. It seemed that there was wheat enough to keep every family going for eight to ten weeks. Some had a few potatoes left and some even had crackers. One man had molasses. They bought less wheat. Almanzo bought none. Cap Garland bought half a bushel and Mr. Ingalls paid for a two-bushel sack.

Almanzo noticed that he did not swing it onto his shoulder as a man naturally would. "That's quite a load to handle," Almanzo said, and helped him lift and balance it. He would have carried it across the street for him, but a man does not like to admit that he cannot carry a hundred and twenty-five pounds.

"Bet you a cigar I can beat you at a game of checkers," Almanzo then said to Cap, and they went up the street to the drugstore. Mr. Ingalls was going into his store building as they passed by in the blowing snow.

Laura heard the front door open and shut. They all sat still in the dark and, as if in a dream, they heard Pa's steps coming heavily the length of the front room, and the kitchen door opening. Pa let a heavy weight come down on the floor with a thud that painfully shook it. Then he shut the door against the solid cold coming in with him.

"The boys got back!" he said, breathing hard. "Here's some of the wheat they brought, Caroline!"

CHAPTER 30

It Can't Beat Us

WINTER had lasted so long that it seemed it would never end. It seemed that they would never really wake up.

In the morning Laura got out of bed into the cold. She dressed downstairs by the fire that Pa had kindled before he went to the stable. They ate their coarse brown bread. Then all day long she and Ma and Mary ground wheat and twisted hay as fast as they could. The fire must not go out; it was very cold. They ate some coarse brown bread. Then Laura crawled into the cold bed and shivered until she grew warm enough to sleep.

Next morning she got out of bed into the cold. She dressed in the chilly kitchen by the fire. She ate her coarse brown bread. She took her turns at grinding wheat and twisting hay. But she did not ever feel awake. She felt beaten by the cold and the storms. She knew she was dull and stupid but she could not wake up.

There were no more lessons. There was nothing in the world but cold and dark and work and coarse brown bread and winds blowing. The storm was always there, outside the walls, waiting sometimes, then pouncing, shaking the house, roaring, snarling, and screaming in rage.

Out of bed in the morning to hurry down and dress by the fire. Then work all day to crawl into a cold bed at night and fall asleep as soon as she grew warm. The winter had lasted so long. It would never end.

Pa did not sing his trouble song in the mornings any more.

On clear days he hauled hay. Sometimes a blizzard lasted only two days. There might be three days of clear cold, or even four days, before the blizzard struck again. "We're outwearing it," Pa said. "It hasn't got much more time. March is nearly gone. We can last longer than it can."

"The wheat is holding out," Ma said. "I'm thankful for that."

The end of March came. April began. Still the storm was there, waiting a little longer now perhaps but striking even more furiously. There was the bitter cold still, and the dark storm days, the wheat to be ground, the hay to be twisted. Laura seemed to have forgotten summer; she could not believe it would ever come again. April was going by.

"Is the hay holding out, Charles?" Ma asked.

"Yes, thanks to Laura," Pa said. "If you hadn't helped me in the haying, little Half-Pint, I'd not have put up enough hay. We would have run short before this."

Those hot days of haying were very far away and long ago. Laura's gladness because Pa said that seemed far away too. Only the blizzard and the coffee mill's grinding, the cold and the dusk darkening to night again, were real. Laura and Pa were holding their stiff, swollen red hands over the stove, Ma was cutting the coarse brown bread for supper. The blizzard was loud and furious.

"It can't beat us!" Pa said.

"Can't it, Pa?" Laura asked stupidly.

"No," said Pa. "It's got to quit sometime and we don't. It can't lick us. We won't give up."

Then Laura felt a warmth inside her. It was very small but it was strong. It was steady, like a tiny light in the dark, and it burned very low but no winds could make it flicker because it would not give up.

They ate the coarse brown bread and went through the dark and cold upstairs to bed. Shivering in the cold bed Laura and Mary silently said their prayers and slowly grew warm enough to sleep.

Sometime in the night Laura heard the wind. It was still blowing furiously but there were no voices, no howls or shrieks in it. And with it there was another sound, a tiny, uncertain, liquid sound that she could not understand.

She listened as hard as she could. She uncovered her ear to listen and the cold did not bite her cheek. The dark was warmer. She put out her hand and felt only a coolness. The little sound that she heard was a trickling of waterdrops. The eaves were dripping. Then she knew.

She sprang up in bed and called aloud, "Pa! Pa! The Chinook is blowing!"

"I hear it, Laura," Pa answered from the other room. "Spring has come. Go back to sleep."

The Chinook was blowing. Spring had come. The blizzard had

given up; it was driven back to the north. Blissfully Laura stretched out in bed; she put both arms on top of the quilts and they were not very cold. She listened to the blowing wind and dripping eaves and she knew that in the other room Pa was lying awake, too, listening and glad. The Chinook, the wind of spring, was blowing. Winter was ended.

In the morning the snow was nearly gone. The frost was melted from the windows, and outdoors the air was soft and warm.

Pa was whistling as he came from doing the chores.

"Well, girls," he said gaily. "We beat old Winter at last! Here it is spring, and none of us lost or starved or frozen! Anyway, not *much* frozen," and he felt tenderly of his nose. "I do believe it is longer," he said anxiously to Grace, and his eyes twinkled. He looked in the glass. "It is longer, and red, too."

"Stop worrying about your looks, Charles," Ma told him. " 'Beauty is only skin deep.' Come eat your breakfast."

She was smiling and Pa chucked her under the chin as he went to the table. Grace scampered to her chair and climbed into it laughing.

Mary pushed her chair back from the stove. "It is really too warm, so close to the fire," she said.

How marvelous it was that anyone could be too warm.

Carrie would hardly leave the window. "I like to see the water run," she explained.

Laura said nothing; she was too happy. She could hardly believe that the winter was gone, that spring had come. When Pa asked her why she was so silent, she answered soberly, "I said it all in the night."

"I should say you did! Waking us all from a sound sleep to tell us the wind was blowing!" Pa teased her. "As if the wind hadn't blown for months!"

"I said the Chinook," Laura reminded him. "That makes all the difference."

CHAPTER 31

Waiting for the Train

"WE'VE got to wait for the train," Pa said. "We can't move to the claim till it comes."

Tightly as he had nailed and battened the tar-paper to the shanty, blizzard winds had torn it loose and whipped it to shreds, letting in the snow at sides and roof. And now the spring rains were beating in through the cracks. The shanty must be repaired before anyone could live in it and Pa could not repair it until the train came, for there was no tar-paper at the lumberyard.

The snow had all disappeared from the prairie. In its place was the soft green of new grass. All the sloughs brimmed with water that had run into them when the deep snow melted. Big Slough had spread until it was a part of Silver Lake and Pa must drive miles around it to reach the homestead from the south.

One day Mr. Boast came walking into town. He explained that he could not drive in, because much of the road was under water. He had walked the railroad track on the long fill that crossed the slough.

Mrs. Boast was well, he told them. She had not come with him because of the slough-lakes spreading everywhere. He had not known whether he could reach town by the railroad track. He promised that Mrs. Boast would walk in with him some day soon.

One afternoon Mary Power came, and she and Laura took Mary walking on the high prairie west of town. It was so long since Laura had seen Mary Power that they felt like strangers again, beginning to get acquainted.

All over the softly green prairie the sloughs were a broken network of water, reflecting the warm, blue sky. Wild geese and ducks were flying high overhead, their clamoring calls coming faintly down. None of them stopped at Silver Lake. They were hurrying, late, to their nesting grounds in the North.

Soft spring rains fell all day long from harmless gray skies and swelled still wider the brimming sloughs. Days of sunshine came and then again rain. The feed store was locked and vacant. The Wilder brothers had hauled the seed wheat around the slough north of town to their claims. Pa said that they were sowing the wheat on their big fields.

And still the train did not come. Still, day after day, Laura and Mary and Carrie took turns at the endless grind of the coffee mill, and morning and evening they ate the coarse brown bread. The wheat was low in the sack. And the train did not come.

The blizzard winds had blown earth from the fields where the sod was broken, and had mixed it with snow packed so tightly in the railroad cuts that snowplows could not move it. The icy snow could not melt because of the earth mixed with it, and men with picks were digging it out inch by inch. It was slow work because in many big cuts they must dig down twenty feet to the steel rails.

April went slowly by. There was no food in the town except the little wheat left from the sixty bushels that young Mr. Wilder and Cap had brought in the last week of February. Every day Ma made a smaller loaf and still the train did not come.

"Could something be hauled in, Charles?" Ma asked.

"We've talked that over, Caroline. None of us see how," Pa answered. He was tired from working all day with a pick. The men from town were digging away at the cut to the west, for the stranded work train must go on to Huron before a freight train could come on the single track.

"There's no way to get a team and wagon out to the east," Pa said. "All the roads are under water, the sloughs are lakes in every direction, and even on the uplands a wagon would mire down in the mud. If worst comes to worst, a man can walk out on the railroad ties, but it's more than a hundred miles to Brookings and back. He couldn't carry much and he'd have to eat some of that while he was getting here."

"I've thought of greens," Ma said. "But I can't find any weeds in the yard that are big enough to pick yet."

"Could we eat grass?" Carrie asked.

"No, Nebuchadnezzar," Pa laughed. "You don't have to eat grass! The work crews at Tracy are more than half way through the big cut already. They ought to get the train here inside of a week."

"We can make the wheat last that long," said Ma. "But I wish you wouldn't work so hard, Charles."

Pa's hands were shaking. He was very tired from working all day with pick and shovel. But he said that a good night's sleep was all he needed. "The main thing is to get the cut clear," he said.

On the last day of April the work train went through to Huron. It seemed to wake the whole town up to hear the train whistle again and see the smoke on the sky. Puffing and steaming and clanging its bell, it stopped at the depot, then pulled out, whistling loud and clear again. It was only a passing train that brought nothing, but a freight train was coming tomorrow.

In the morning Laura woke thinking, "The train is coming!" The sun was shining brightly; she had overslept, and Ma had not called her. She jumped out of bed and hurried to dress.

"Wait for me, Laura!" Mary begged. "Don't be in such a hurry, I can't find my stockings."

Laura looked for them. "Here they are. I'm sorry, I pushed them out of the way when I jumped out of bed. Now hurry! Come on, Grace!"

"When will it get here?" Carrie asked breathless.

"Any minute. Nobody knows when," Laura answered, and she ran downstairs singing:

"If you're waking call me early,
Call me early, mother dear."

Pa was at the table. He looked up and laughed at her. "Well, Flutterbudget! you're to be Queen of the May, are you? And late to breakfast!"

"Ma didn't call me," Laura made excuse.

"I didn't need help to cook this little bit of breakfast," Ma said. "Only one biscuit apiece, and small ones at that. It took the last bit of the wheat to make them."

"I don't want even one," Laura said. "The rest of you can divide mine. I won't be hungry till the train comes in."

"You will eat your share," Pa told her. "Then we'll all wait till the train brings more."

They were all merry over the biscuits. Ma said that Pa must have the biggest one. When Pa agreed to that, he insisted that

Ma take the next size. Mary's of course came next. Then there was some doubt about Laura and Carrie; they had to have the two most nearly alike. And the smallest one was for Grace.

"I thought I made them all the same size," Ma protested.

"Trust a Scotchwoman to manage," Pa teased her. "You not only make the wheat come out even with the very last meal before the train comes, but you make the biscuits in sizes to fit the six of us."

"It is a wonder, how evenly it comes out," Ma admitted.

"You are the wonder, Caroline," Pa smiled at her. He got up and put on his hat. "I feel good!" he declared. "We really got winter licked now! with the last of the blizzards thrown out of the cuts and the train coming in!"

Ma left the doors open that morning to let in the spring air, moist from the sloughs. The house was fresh and fragrant, the sun was shining, and the town astir with men going toward the depot. Clear and long across the prairie, the train whistle sounded and Laura and Carrie ran to the kitchen window. Ma and Grace came, too.

They saw the smoke from the smokestack rolling up black against the sky. Then puffing and chuffing the engine came hauling the line of freight cars toward the depot. A little crowd of men on the depot platform stood watching the engine go by. White steam puffed up through its smoke and its clear whistle came after every puff. Brakemen along the top of the train were jumping from car to car and setting the brakes.

The train stopped. It was really there, a train at last.

"Oh, I do hope that Harthorn and Wilmarth both get all the groceries they ordered last fall," said Ma.

After a few moments the engine whistled, the brakemen ran along the tops of the cars loosening the brakes. Clanging its bell, the engine went ahead, then backed, then went ahead again and rushed on away to the west, trailing its smoke and its last long whistle. It left behind it three freight cars standing on the sidetrack.

Ma drew a deep breath. "It will be so good to have enough of everything to cook with again."

"I hope I never see another bite of brown bread," Laura declared.

"When is Pa coming? I want Pa to come!" Grace insisted. "I want Pa to come now!"

"Grace," Ma reproved her, gently but firmly, and Mary took Grace into her lap while Ma added, "Come, girls, we must finish airing the bedding."

It was almost an hour before Pa came. At last even Ma wondered aloud what could be keeping him. They were all impatiently waiting before he came. His arms were filled with a large package and two smaller ones. He laid them on the table before he spoke.

"We forgot the train that was snowed in all winter," he said. "It came through, and what do you suppose it left for De Smet?" He answered his own question, "One carload of telegraph poles, one carload of farm machinery, and one emigrant car."

"No groceries?" Ma almost wailed.

"No. Nothing," Pa said.

"Then what is this?" Ma touched the large package.

"That is potatoes. The small one is flour and the smallest is fat salt pork. Woodworth broke into the emigrant car and shared out what eatables he could find," said Pa.

"Charles! He ought not to do that," Ma said in dismay.

"I'm past caring what he ought to do!" Pa said savagely. "Let the railroad stand some damages! This isn't the only family in town that's got nothing to eat. We told Woodworth to open up that car or we'd do it. He tried to argue that there'll be another train tomorrow, but we didn't feel like waiting. Now if you'll boil some potatoes and fry some meat, we'll have us a dinner."

Ma began to untie the packages. "Put some hay in the stove, Carrie, to make the oven hot. I'll mix up some white-flour biscuits, too," she said.

CHAPTER 32

The Christmas Barrel

NEXT day the second train came. After its departing whistle had died away, Pa and Mr. Boast came down the street carrying a barrel between them. They upended it through the doorway and stood it in the middle of the front room.

"Here's that Christmas barrel!" Pa called to Ma.

He brought his hammer and began pulling nails out of the barrel-head, while they all stood around it waiting to see what was in it. Pa took off the barrel-head. Then he lifted away some thick brown paper that covered everything beneath.

Clothes were on top. First Pa drew out a dress of beautifully fine, dark-blue flannel. The skirt was full pleated and the neat, whaleboned basque was buttoned down the front with cut-steel buttons.

"This is about your size, Caroline," Pa beamed. "Here, take it!" and he reached again into the barrel.

He took out a fluffy, light-blue fascinator for Mary, and some warm flannel underthings. He took out a pair of black leather shoes that exactly fitted Laura. He took out five pairs of white woolen stockings, machine-knit. They were much finer and thinner than home-knit ones.

Then he took out a warm, brown coat, a little large for Carrie, but it would fit her next winter. And he took out a red hood and mittens to go with it.

Next came a silk shawl!

"Oh, Mary!" Laura said. "The most beautiful thing—a shawl made of silk! It is dove-colored, with fine stripes of green and rose and black and the richest, deep fringe with all those colors shimmering in it. Feel how soft and rich and heavy the silk is," and she put a corner of the shawl in Mary's hand.

"Oh, lovely!" Mary breathed.

"Who gets this shawl?" Pa asked, and they all said, "Ma!" Such a beautiful shawl was for Ma, of course. Pa laid it on her arm, and it was like her, so soft and yet firm and well-wearing, with the fine, bright colors in it.

"We will all take turns wearing it," Ma said. "And Mary shall take it with her when she goes to college."

"What is there for you, Pa?" Laura asked jealously. For Pa there were two fine, white shirts, and a dark brown plush cap.

"That isn't all," said Pa, and he lifted out of the barrel one, two little dresses. One was blue flannel, one was green-and-rose plaid. They were too small for Carrie and too big for Grace, but Grace would grow to fit them. Then there was an A-B-C book printed on cloth, and a small, shiny Mother Goose book of the smoothest paper, with a colored picture on the cover.

There was a pasteboard box full of bright-colored yarns and another box filled with embroidery silks and sheets of perforated thin cardboard, silver-colored and gold-colored. Ma gave both boxes to Laura, saying, "You gave away the pretty things you had made. Now here are some lovely things for you to work with."

Laura was so happy that she couldn't say a word. The delicate silks caught on the roughness of her fingers, scarred from twisting hay, but the beautiful colors sang together like music, and her fingers would grow smooth again so that she could embroider on the fine, thin silver and gold.

"Now I wonder what this can be?" Pa said, as he lifted from the very bottom of the barrel something bulky and lumpy that was wrapped around and around with thick brown paper.

"Je-ru-salem crickets!" he exclaimed. "If it isn't our Christmas turkey, still frozen solid!"

He held the great turkey up where all could see. "And fat! Fifteen pounds or I miss my guess." And as he let the mass of brown paper fall, it thumped on the floor and out of it rolled several cranberries.

"And if here isn't a package of cranberries to go with it!" said Pa.

Carrie shrieked with delight. Mary clasped her hands and said, "Oh my!" But Ma asked, "Did the groceries come for the stores, Charles?"

"Yes, sugar and flour and dried fruit and meat— Oh, everything anybody needs," Pa answered.

"Well, then, Mr. Boast, you bring Mrs. Boast day after tomorrow," Ma said. "Come as early as you can and we will celebrate the springtime with a Christmas dinner."

"That's the ticket!" Pa shouted, while Mr. Boast threw back his head and the room filled with his ringing laugh. They all joined in, for no one could help laughing when Mr. Boast did.

"We'll come! You bet we'll come!" Mr. Boast chortled. "Christmas dinner in May! That will be great, to feast after a winter of darn near fasting! I'll hurry home and tell Ellie."

CHAPTER 33

Christmas in May

PA BOUGHT groceries that afternoon. It was wonderful to see him coming in with armfuls of packages, wonderful to see a whole sack of white flour, sugar, dried apples, soda crackers, and cheese. The kerosene can was full. How happy Laura was to fill the lamp, polish the chimney, and trim the wick. At suppertime the light shone through the clear glass onto the red-checked tablecloth and the white biscuits, the warmed up potatoes, and the platter of fried salt pork.

With yeast cakes, Ma set the sponge for light bread that night, and she put the dried apples to soak for pies.

Laura did not need to be called next morning. She was up at dawn, and all day she helped Ma bake and stew and boil the good things for next day's Christmas dinner.

Early that morning Ma added water and flour to the bread sponge and set it to rise again. Laura and Carrie picked over the cranberries and washed them. Ma stewed them with sugar until they were a mass of crimson jelly.

Laura and Carrie carefully picked dried raisins from their long stems and carefully took the seeds out of each one. Ma stewed the dried apples, mixed the raisins with them, and made pies.

"It seems strange to have everything one could want to work with," said Ma. "Now I have cream of tartar and plenty of saleratus, I shall make a cake."

All day long the kitchen smelled of good things, and when night came the cupboard held large brown-crusted loaves of white bread, a sugar-frosted loaf of cake, three crisp-crusted pies, and the jellied cranberries.

"I wish we could eat them now," Mary said. "Seems like I can't wait till tomorrow."

"I'm waiting for the turkey first," said Laura, "and you may have sage in the stuffing, Mary."

She sounded generous but Mary laughed at her. "That's only because there aren't any onions for you to use!"

"Now, girls, don't get impatient," Ma begged them. "We will have a loaf of light bread and some of the cranberry sauce for supper."

So the Christmas feasting was begun the night before.

It seemed too bad to lose any of that happy time in sleep. Still, sleeping was the quickest way to tomorrow morning. It was no time at all, after Laura's eyes closed, till Ma was calling her and tomorrow was today.

What a hurrying there was! Breakfast was soon over, then while Laura and Carrie cleared the table and washed the dishes, Ma prepared the big turkey for roasting and mixed the bread-stuffing for it.

The May morning was warm and the wind from the prairie smelled of springtime. Doors were open and both rooms could be used once more. Going in and out of the large front room whenever she wanted to, gave Laura a spacious and rested feeling, as if she could never be cross again.

Ma had already put the rocking chairs by the front windows to get them out of her way in the kitchen. Now the turkey was in the oven, and Mary helped Laura draw the table into the middle of the front room. Mary raised its drop-leaves and spread smoothly over it the white tablecloth that Laura brought her. Then Laura brought the dishes from the cupboard and Mary placed them around the table.

Carrie was peeling potatoes and Grace was running races with herself the length of both rooms.

Ma brought the glass bowl filled with glowing cranberry jelly. She set it in the middle of the white tablecloth and they all admired the effect.

"We do need some butter to go with the light bread, though," Ma said.

"Never mind, Caroline," said Pa. "There's tar-paper at the lumberyard now. I'll soon fix up the shanty and we'll move out to the homestead in a few days."

The roasting turkey was filling the house with scents that made their mouths water. The potatoes were boiling and Ma was putting the coffee on when Mr. and Mrs. Boast came walking in.

"For the last mile, I've been following my nose to that turkey!" Mr. Boast declared.

"I was thinking more of seeing the folks, Robert, than of anything to eat," Mrs. Boast chided him. She was thin and the lovely rosy color was gone from her cheeks, but she was the same darling Mrs. Boast, with the same laughing black-fringed blue eyes and the same dark hair curling under the same brown hood. She shook hands warmly with Ma and Mary and Laura and stooped down to draw Carrie and Grace close in her arms while she spoke to them.

"Come into the front room and take off your things, Mrs. Boast," Ma urged her. "It is good to see you again after so long. Now you rest in the rocking chair and visit with Mary while I finish up dinner."

"Let me help you," Mrs. Boast asked, but Ma said she must be tired after her long walk and everything was nearly ready.

"Laura and I will soon have dinner on the table," said Ma, turning quickly back to the kitchen. She ran against Pa in her haste.

"We better make ourselves scarce, Boast," said Pa. "Come along, and I'll show you the *Pioneer Press* I got this morning."

"It will be good to see a newspaper again," Mr. Boast agreed eagerly. So the kitchen was left to the cooks.

"Get the big platter to put the turkey on," Ma said, as she lifted the heavy dripping-pan out of the oven.

Laura turned to the cupboard and saw on the shelf a package that had not been there before.

"What's that, Ma?" she asked.

"I don't know. Look and see," Ma told her, and Laura undid the paper. There on a small plate was a ball of butter.

"Butter! It's butter!" she almost shouted.

They heard Mrs. Boast laugh. "Just a little Christmas present!" she called.

Pa and Mary and Carrie exclaimed aloud in delight and Grace squealed long and shrill while Laura carried the butter to the table. Then she hurried back to slide the big platter carefully beneath the turkey as Ma raised it from the dripping-pan.

While Ma made the gravy Laura mashed the potatoes. There was no milk, but Ma said, "Leave a very little of the boiling water in, and after you mash them beat them extra hard with the big spoon."

The potatoes turned out white and fluffy, though not with the flavor that plenty of hot milk and butter would have given them.

When all the chairs were drawn up to the well-filled table, Ma looked at Pa and every head bowed.

"Lord, we thank Thee for all Thy bounty." That was all Pa said, but it seemed to say everything.

"The table looks some different from what it did a few days ago," Pa said as he heaped Mrs. Boast's plate with turkey and stuffing and potatoes and a large spoonful of cranberries. And as he went on filling the plates he added, "It has been a long winter."

"And a hard one," said Mr. Boast.

"It is a wonder how we all kept well and came through it," Mrs. Boast said.

While Mr. and Mrs. Boast told how they had worked and contrived through that long winter, all alone in the blizzard-bound shanty on their claim, Ma poured the coffee and Pa's tea. She passed the bread and the butter and the gravy and reminded Pa to refill the plates.

When every plate had been emptied a second time Ma refilled the cups and Laura brought on the pies and the cake.

They sat a long time at the table, talking of the winter that was past and the summer to come. Ma said she could hardly wait to get back to the homestead. The wet, muddy roads were the difficulty now, but Pa and Mr. Boast agreed that they would dry out before long. The Boasts were glad that they had wintered on their claim and didn't have to move back to it now.

At last they all left the table. Laura brought the red-bordered table cover and Carrie helped her to spread it to cover neatly out of sight the food and the empty dishes. Then they joined the others by the sunny window.

Pa stretched his arms above his head. He opened and closed his hands and stretched his fingers wide, then ran them through his hair till it all stood on end.

"I believe this warm weather has taken the stiffness out of my fingers," he said. "If you will bring me the fiddle, Laura, I'll see what I can do."

Laura brought the fiddle-box and stood close by while Pa

lifted the fiddle out of its nest. He thumbed the strings and tightened the keys as he listened. Then he rosined the bow and drew it across the strings.

A few clear, true notes softly sounded. The lump in Laura's throat almost choked her.

Pa played a few bars and said, "This is a new song I learned last fall, the time we went to Volga to clear the tracks. You hum the tenor along with the fiddle, Boast, while I sing it through the first time. A few times over, and you'll all pick up the words."

They all gathered around him to listen while he played again the opening bars. Then Mr. Boast's tenor joined the fiddle's voice and Pa's voice singing:

"This life is a difficult riddle,
For how many people we see
With faces as long as a fiddle
That ought to be shining with glee.
I am sure in this world there are plenty
Of good things enough for us all,
And yet there's not one out of twenty
But thinks that his share is too small.

"Then what is the use of repining,
For where there's a will, there's a way,
And tomorrow the sun may be shining,
Although it is cloudy today.

"Do you think that by sitting and sighing
You'll ever obtain all you want?
It's cowards alone that are crying
And foolishly saying, 'I can't!'
It is only by plodding and striving
And laboring up the steep hill
Of life, that you'll ever be thriving,
Which you'll do if you've only the will."

They were all humming the melody now and when the chorus came again, Mrs. Boast's alto, Ma's contralto, and Mary's sweet soprano joined Mr. Boast's tenor and Pa's rich bass, singing the words, and Laura sang, too, soprano:

"Then what is the use of repining,
For where there's a will, there's a way,
And tomorrow the sun may be shining,
Although it is cloudy today."

And as they sang, the fear and the suffering of the long winter seemed to rise like a dark cloud and float away on the music. Spring had come. The sun was shining warm, the winds were soft, and the green grass growing.

LITTLE TOWN ON THE PRAIRIE

CONTENTS

CHAPTER I

Surprise

ONE evening at supper, Pa asked, "How would you like to work in town, Laura?"

Laura could not say a word. Neither could any of the others. They all sat as if they were frozen. Grace's blue eyes stared over the rim of her tin cup, Carrie's teeth stayed bitten into a slice of bread, and Mary's hand held her fork stopped in the air. Ma let tea go pouring from the teapot's spout into Pa's brimming cup. Just in time, she quickly set down the teapot.

"What did you say, Charles?" she asked.

"I asked Laura how she'd like to take a job in town," Pa replied.

"A job? For a girl? In town?" Ma said "Why, what kind of a job—" Then quickly she said, "No, Charles, I won't have Laura working out in a hotel among all kinds of strangers."

"Who said such a thing?" Pa demanded. "No girl of ours'll do that, not while I'm alive and kicking."

"Of course not," Ma apologized. "You took me so by surprise. What other kind of work can there be? and Laura not old enough to teach school yet."

All in the minute before Pa began to explain, Laura thought of the town, and of the homestead claim where they were all so busy and happy now in the springtime, and she did not want anything changed. She did not want to work in town.

CHAPTER 2

Springtime on the Claim

AFTER the October Blizzard last fall, they had all moved to town and for a little while Laura had gone to school there. Then the storms had stopped school, and all through that long winter the blizzards had howled between the houses, shutting them off from each other so that day after day and night after night not a voice could be heard and not a light could be seen through the whirling snow.

All winter long, they had been crowded in the little kitchen, cold and hungry and working hard in the dark and the cold to twist enough hay to keep the fire going and to grind wheat in the coffee mill for the day's bread.

All that long, long winter, the only hope had been that sometime winter must end, sometime blizzards must stop, the sun would shine warm again and they could all get away from the town and go back to the homestead claim.

Now it was springtime. The Dakota prairie lay so warm and bright under the shining sun that it did not seem possible that it had ever been swept by the winds and snows of that hard winter. How wonderful it was, to be on the claim again! Laura wanted nothing more than just being outdoors. She felt she never could get enough sunshine soaked into her bones.

In the dawns when she went to the well at the edge of the slough to fetch the morning pail of fresh water, the sun was rising in a glory of colors. Meadow larks were flying, singing, up from the dew-wet grass. Jack rabbits hopped beside the path, their bright eyes watching and their long ears twitching as they daintily nibbled their breakfast of tender grass tips.

Laura was in the shanty only long enough to set down the water and snatch the milk pail. She ran out to the slope where Ellen, the cow, was cropping the sweet young grass. Quietly Ellen stood chewing her cud while Laura milked.

Warm and sweet, the scent of new milk came up from the streams hissing into the rising foam, and it mixed with the scents of springtime. Laura's bare feet were wet and cool in the dewy grass, the sunshine was warm on her neck, and Ellen's flank was warmer against her cheek. On its own little picket rope, Ellen's baby calf bawled anxiously, and Ellen answered with a soothing moo.

When Laura had stripped the last creamy drops of milk, she lugged the pail to the shanty. Ma poured some of the warm new milk into the calf's pail. The rest she strained through a clean white cloth into tin milk pans, and Laura carefully carried them down cellar while Ma skimmed thick cream from last night's milk. Then she poured the skimmed milk into the calf's pail, and Laura carried it to the hungry calf.

Teaching the calf to drink was not easy, but always interesting. The wobbly-legged baby calf had been born believing that it must butt hard with its little red poll, to get milk. So when it smelled the milk in the pail, it tried to butt the pail.

Laura must keep it from spilling the milk, if she could, and she had to teach it how to drink, because it didn't know. She dipped her fingers into the milk and let the calf's rough tongue suck them, and gently she led its nose down to the milk in the pail. The calf suddenly snorted milk into its nose, sneezed it out with a whoosh that splashed milk out of the pail, and then with all its might it butted into the milk. It butted so hard that Laura almost lost hold of the pail. A wave of milk went over the calf's head and a splash wet the front of Laura's dress.

So, patiently she began again, dipping her fingers for the calf to suck, trying to keep the milk in the pail and to teach the calf to drink it. In the end, some of the milk was inside the calf.

Then Laura pulled up the picket pins. One by one, she led Ellen, the baby calf and the yearling calf to fresh places in the soft, cool grass. She drove the iron pins deep into the ground. The sun was fully up now, the whole sky was blue, and the whole earth was waves of grass flowing in the wind. And Ma was calling.

"Hurry, Laura! Breakfast's waiting!"

In the shanty, Laura quickly washed her face and hands at the washbasin. She threw out the water in a sparkling curve falling on grass where the sun would swiftly dry it. She ran the comb through her hair, over her head to the dangling braid.

There was never time before breakfast to undo the long braid, brush her hair properly, and plait it again. She would do that after the morning's work was done.

Sitting in her place beside Mary, she looked across the clean, red-checked tablecloth and the glinting dishes at little sister Carrie and baby sister Grace, with their soap-shining morning faces and bright eyes. She looked at Pa and Ma so cheerful and smiling. She felt the sweet morning wind from the wide-open door and window, and she gave a little sigh.

Pa looked at her. He knew how she felt. "I think, myself, it's pretty nice," he said.

"It's a beautiful morning," Ma agreed.

Then after breakfast Pa hitched up the horses, Sam and David, and drove them out on the prairie east of the shanty, where he was breaking ground for sod corn. Ma took charge of the day's work for the rest of them, and best of all Laura liked the days when she said, "I must work in the garden."

Mary eagerly offered to do all the housework, so that Laura could help Ma. Mary was blind. Even in the days before scarlet fever had taken the sight from her clear blue eyes, she had never liked to work outdoors in the sun and wind. Now she was happy to be useful indoors. Cheerfully she said, "I must work where I can see with my fingers. I couldn't tell the difference between a pea vine and a weed at the end of a hoe, but I can wash dishes and make beds and take care of Grace."

Carrie was proud, too, because although she was small she was ten years old and could help Mary do all the housework. So Ma and Laura went out to work in the garden.

People were coming from the East now, to settle all over the prairie. They were building new claim shanties to the east and to the south, and west beyond Big Slough. Every few days a wagon went by, driven by strangers going across the neck of the slough and northward to town, and coming back. Ma said there would be time to get acquainted when the spring work was done. There is no time for visiting in the spring.

Pa had a new plow, a breaking plow. It was wonderful for breaking the prairie sod. It had a sharp-edged wheel, called a rolling coulter, that ran rolling and cutting through the sod ahead of the plowshare. The sharp steel plowshare followed it, slicing underneath the matted grass roots, and the moldboard lifted the long, straight-edged strip of sod and turned it upside down. The strip of sod was exactly twelve inches wide, and as straight as if it had been cut by hand.

They were all so happy about that new plow. Now, after a whole day's work, Sam and David gaily lay down and rolled, and pricked their ears and looked about the prairie before they fell to cropping grass. They were not being worn down, sad and gaunt, by breaking sod that spring. And at supper, Pa was not too tired to joke.

"By jingo, that plow can handle the work by itself," he said. "With all these new inventions nowadays, there's no use for a man's muscle. One of these nights that plow'll take a notion to keep on going, and we'll look out in the morning and see that it's turned over an acre or two after the team and I quit for the night."

The strips of sod lay bottom-side-up over the furrows, with all the cut-off grass roots showing speckled in the earth. The fresh furrow was delightfully cool and soft to bare feet, and often Carrie and Grace followed behind the plow, playing. Laura would have liked to, but she was going on fifteen years old now, too old to play in the fresh, clean-smelling dirt. Besides, in the afternoons Mary must go for a walk to get some sunshine.

So when the morning's work was done, Laura took Mary walking over the prairie. Spring flowers were blossoming and cloud-shadows were trailing over the grassy slopes.

It was odd that when they were little, Mary had been the older and often bossy, but now that they were older they seemed to be the same age. They liked the long walks together in the wind and sunshine, picking violets and buttercups and eating sheep sorrel. The sheep sorrel's lovely curled lavender blossoms, the clover-shaped leaves and thin stems had a tangy taste.

"Sheep sorrel tastes like springtime," Laura said.

"It really tastes a little like lemon flavoring, Laura," Mary gently corrected her. Before she ate sheep sorrel she always asked, "Did you look carefully? You're sure there isn't a bug on it?"

"There never are any bugs," Laura protested. "These prairies are so *clean!* There never was such a clean place."

"You look, just the same," said Mary. "I don't want to eat the only bug in the whole of Dakota Territory."

They laughed together. Mary was so light-hearted now that she often made such little jokes. Her face was so serene in her sunbonnet, her blue eyes were so clear and her voice so gay that she did not seem to be walking in darkness.

Mary had always been good. Sometimes she had been so good that Laura could hardly bear it. But now she seemed different. Once Laura asked her about it.

"You used to try all the time to be good," Laura said. "And you always were good. It made me so mad sometimes, I wanted to slap you. But now you are good without even trying."

Mary stopped still. "Oh, Laura, how awful! Do you ever want to slap me now?"

"No, never," Laura answered honestly.

"You honestly don't? You aren't just being gentle to me because I'm blind?"

"No! Really and honestly, no, Mary. I hardly think about your being blind. I—I'm just glad you're my sister. I wish I could be like you. But I guess I never can be," Laura sighed. "I don't know how you can be so good."

"I'm not really," Mary told her. "I do try, but if you could see how rebellious and mean I feel sometimes, if you could see what I really am, inside, you wouldn't want to be like me."

"I *can* see what you're like inside," Laura contradicted. "It shows all the time. You're always perfectly patient and never the least bit mean."

"I know why you wanted to slap me," Mary said. "It was because I was showing off. I wasn't really wanting to be good. I was showing off to myself, what a good little girl I was, and being vain and proud, and I deserved to be slapped for it."

Laura was shocked. Then suddenly she felt that she had known that, all the time. But, nevertheless, it was not true of Mary. She said, "Oh no, you're not like that, not really. You *are* good."

"We are all desperately wicked and inclined to evil as the sparks fly upwards," said Mary, using the Bible words. "But that doesn't matter."

"What!" cried Laura.

"I mean I don't believe we ought to think so much about

ourselves, about whether we are bad or good," Mary explained.

"But, my goodness! How can anybody be good without thinking about it?" Laura demanded.

"I don't know, I guess we couldn't," Mary admitted. "I don't know how to say what I mean very well. But—it isn't so much thinking, as—as just knowing. Just being sure of the goodness of God."

Laura stood still, and so did Mary, because she dared not step without Laura's arm in hers guiding her. There Mary stood in the midst of the green and flowery miles of grass rippling in the wind, under the great blue sky and white clouds sailing, and she could not see.

Everyone knows that God is good. But it seemed to Laura then that Mary must be sure of it in some special way.

"You are sure, aren't you?" Laura said.

"Yes, I am sure of it now all the time," Mary answered. "The Lord is my shepherd, I shall not want. He maketh me to lie down in green pastures, He leadeth me beside the still waters. I think that's the loveliest Psalm of all. Why are we stopping here? I don't smell the violets."

"We came by the buffalo wallow, talking," said Laura. "We'll go back that way."

When they turned back, Laura could see the low swell of land sloping up from the coarse grasses of Big Slough to the little claim shanty. It looked hardly larger than a hen coop, with its half-roof slanting up and stopping. The sod stable hardly showed in the wild grasses. Beyond them Ellen and the two calves were grazing, and to the east Pa was planting corn in the newly broken sod.

He had broken all the sod he had time to, before the ground grew too dry. He had harrowed the ground he had broken last year, and sowed it to oats. Now with a sack of seed corn fastened to a shoulder harness, and the hoe in his hand, he was going slowly across the sod field.

"Pa is planting the corn," Laura told Mary. "Let's go by that way. Here's the buffalo wallow now."

"I know," said Mary. They stood a moment, breathing in deeply the perfume of warm violets that came up as thick as honey. The buffalo wallow, perfectly round and set down into the prairie like a dish three or four feet deep, was solidly paved with violets. Thousands, millions, crowded so thickly that they hid their own leaves.

Mary sank down among them. "Mmmmmm!" she breathed. Her fingers delicately felt over the masses of petals, and down the thin stems to pick them.

When they passed by the sod field Pa breathed in a deep smell of the violets, too. "Had a nice walk, girls?" he smiled at them, but he did not stop working. He mellowed a spot of earth with the hoe, dug a tiny hollow in it, dropped four kernels of corn in the hollow, covered them with the hoe, pressed the spot firm with his boot, then stepped on to plant the next hill.

Carrie came hurrying to bury her nose in the violets.

She was minding Grace, and Grace would play nowhere but in the field where Pa was. Angleworms fascinated Grace. Every time Pa struck the hoe into the ground she watched for one, and chuckled to see the thin, long worm make itself fat and short, pushing itself quickly into the earth again.

"Even when it's cut in two, both halves do that," she said. "Why, Pa?"

"They want to get into the ground, I guess," said Pa.

"Why, Pa?" Grace asked him.

"Oh, they just want to," said Pa.

"Why do they want to, Pa?"

"Why do you like to play in the dirt?" Pa asked her.

"Why, Pa?" Grace said. "How many corns do you drop, Pa?"

"Kernels," said Pa. "Four kernels. One, two, three, four."

"One, two, four," Grace said. "Why, Pa?"

"That's an easy one," said Pa.

One for the blackbird,
One for the crow,
And that will leave
Just two to grow.

The garden was growing now. In tiny rows of different greens, the radishes, lettuce, onions, were up. The first crumpled leaves of peas were pushing upward. The young tomatoes stood on thin stems, spreading out their first lacy foliage.

"I've been looking at the garden, it needs hoeing," Ma said, while Laura set the violets in water to perfume the supper table. "And I do believe the beans will be up any day now, it's turned so warm."

All one hot morning, the beans were popping out of the ground. Grace discovered them and came shrieking with excitement to tell Ma. All that morning she could not be coaxed away from watching them. Up from the bare earth, bean after bean was popping, its stem uncoiling like a steel spring, and up in the sunshine the halves of the split bean still clutched two pale twin-leaves. Every time a bean popped up, Grace squealed again.

Now that the corn was planted, Pa built the missing half of the claim shanty. One morning he laid the floor joists. Then he made the frame, and Laura helped him raise it and hold it straight to the plumb line while he nailed it. He put in the studding, and the frames for two windows. Then he laid the rafters, to make the other slant of the roof that had not been there before.

Laura helped him all the time, Carrie and Grace watched, and picked up every nail that Pa dropped by mistake. Even Ma often spent minutes in idleness, looking on. It was exciting to see the shanty being made into a house.

When it was done, they had three rooms. The new part was two tiny bedrooms, each with a window. Now the beds would not be in the front room any more.

"Here's where we kill two birds with one stone," said Ma. "We'll combine spring housecleaning and moving."

They washed the window curtains and all the quilts and hung them out to dry. Then they washed the new windows till they shone, and hung on them new curtains made of old sheets and beautifully hemmed with Mary's tiny stitches. Ma and Laura set up the bedsteads in the new rooms all made of fresh, clean-smelling boards. Laura and Carrie filled the straw ticks with the brightest hay from the middle of a haystack, and they made up the beds with sheets still warm from Ma's ironing and with the clean quilts smelling of the prairie air.

Then Ma and Laura scrubbed and scoured every inch of the old shanty, that was now the front room. It was spacious now, with no beds in it, only the cookstove and cupboards and table and chairs and the whatnot. When it was perfectly clean, and everything in place, they all stood and admired it.

"You needn't see it for me, Laura," Mary said. "I can feel how large and fresh and pretty it is."

The fresh, starched white curtains moved softly in the wind at the open window. The scrubbed board walls and the floor were a soft yellow-gray. A bouquet of grass flowers and windflowers that Carrie had picked and put in the blue bowl on the table, seemed to bring springtime in. In the corner the varnished brown whatnot stood stylish and handsome.

The afternoon light made plain the gilded titles of the books on the whatnot's lower shelf, and glittered in the three glass boxes on the shelf above, each with tiny flowers painted on it. Above them, on the next shelf, the gilt flowers shone on the glass face of the clock and its brass pendulum glinted, swinging to and fro. Higher still, on the very top shelf, was Laura's white china jewel box with the wee gold cup and saucer on its lid, and beside it, watching over it, sat Carrie's brown and white china dog.

On the wall between the doors of the new bedrooms, Ma hung the wooden bracket that Pa had carved for her Christmas present, long ago in the Big Woods of Wisconsin. Every little flower and leaf, the small vine on the edge of the little shelf, and the larger vines climbing to the large star at the top, were still as perfect as when he had carved them with his jackknife. Older still, older than Laura could remember, Ma's china shepherdess stood pink and white and smiling on the shelf.

It was a beautiful room.

CHAPTER 3

The Necessary Cat

Now the first yellow-green spears of corn were dotted like fluttering ribbon-ends along the furrows of broken sod. One evening Pa walked across the field to look at them. He came back tired and exasperated.

"I've got to replant more than half the cornfield," he said.

"Oh, Pa. Why?" Laura asked.

"Gophers," said Pa. "Well, this is what a man gets for putting in the first corn in a new country."

Grace was hugging his legs. He picked her up and tickled her cheek with his beard to make her laugh. She remembered the planting rhyme, and sitting on his knee she chanted it proudly.

One for the blackbird,
One for the crow,
And that will leave
Just two to grow.

"The man that made that up was an Easterner," Pa told her. "Out here in the Territory we'll have to make our own rhyme, Grace. How's this for a try?

One for a gopher,
Two for a gopher,
Three for a gopher,
Four don't go fur.

"Oh, Charles," Ma protested, laughing. She did not think puns were funny, but she could not help laughing at the naughty look Pa gave her when he made one.

He had no sooner planted the seed corn than the striped gophers found it. All over the field they had been scampering, and stopping to dig into the little spots of fine soil with their tiny paws. It was a wonder that they knew exactly where the kernels were buried.

It was amazing that those little gophers, scampering, digging, sitting up straight and nibbling, each one, at one kernel of corn held in its paws, had eaten more than half of that whole field of corn.

"They are pests!" said Pa. "I wish we had a cat like old Black Susan used to be. She'd have thinned 'em out."

"I need a cat in the house, too," Ma agreed. "I declare the mice are getting so thick I can't leave food uncovered in the cupboard. Is there a cat to be had, Charles?"

"There's not a cat in this whole country, that I know of," Pa answered. "The storekeepers in town are complaining, too. Wilmarth's talking of getting a cat shipped out from the East."

That very night, Laura was startled out of a sound sleep. Through the partition between the bedrooms she heard a gasp, a grunt, and a sudden thud of something small and squashing. She heard Ma say, "Charles! What is it?"

"I dreamed it," Pa said, low. "I dreamed a barber was cutting my hair."

Ma spoke low, too, because this was the middle of the night and the house was asleep. "It was only a dream. Lie down again and let me have some of the covers back."

"I heard the barber's shears go snip, snip," said Pa.

"Well, lie down and go to sleep," Ma yawned.

"My hair *was* being cut," said Pa.

"I never knew you to be upset by a dream before." Ma yawned again. "Lie down and turn over and you won't go on dreaming it."

"Caroline, my hair was being cut," Pa repeated.

"What do you mean?" Ma asked, more awake now.

"I am telling you," Pa said. "In my sleep I put up my hand and— Here. Feel my head."

"*Charles!* Your hair's been *cut!*" Ma exclaimed. Laura heard her sit up in bed. "I can feel it, there's a place on your head——"

"Yes, that's the spot," said Pa. "I put up my hand——"

Ma interrupted. "A place as big as my hand, shorn clean off."

"I put up my hand," said Pa, "and I took hold of—something——"

"What? What was it?" Ma asked.

"I think," said Pa, "I think it was a mouse."

"*Where is it?*" Ma cried out.

"I don't know. I threw it away, as hard as I could," said Pa.

"My goodness!" Ma said weakly. "It must have been a mouse. Cutting off your hair to make itself a nest."

After a minute Pa said, "Caroline, I swear——"

"No, Charles," Ma murmured.

"Well, I would swear, if I did, that I can't lie awake nights to keep mice out of my hair."

"I do wish we had a cat," Ma wished hopelessly.

Sure enough, in the morning a mouse lay dead by the bedroom wall where Pa had thrown it. And Pa appeared at breakfast with an almost bare spot on the back of his head, where the mouse had shorn his hair away.

He would not have minded so much, but there was not time for the hair to grow before he must go to a meeting of county commissioners. The country was settling so rapidly that already a county was being organized, and Pa must help. As the oldest settler, he could not shirk his duty.

The meeting was to be held at Whiting's homestead claim, four miles northeast of town. No doubt Mrs. Whiting would be there, and Pa could not keep his hat on.

"Never mind," Ma consoled him. "Just tell them how it happened. Likely they have mice."

"There'll be more important things to talk about," said Pa. "No, better just let them think this is the way my wife cuts my hair."

"Charles, you wouldn't!" Ma exclaimed, before she saw that he was teasing her.

When he drove away in the wagon that morning, he told Ma not to expect him for dinner. He had a ten-mile drive to make, on top of the time spent at the meeting.

It was supper time when he came driving to the stable. He unhitched and came hurrying to the house so quickly that he met Carrie and Grace running out.

"Girls! Caroline!" he called. "Guess what I've brought you!" His hand was in his pocket and his eyes were twinkling.

"Candy!" Carrie and Grace answered together.

"Better than that!" said Pa.

"A letter?" Ma asked.

"A paper," Mary guessed. "Maybe *The Advance*."

Laura was watching Pa's pocket. She was certain that something, not Pa's hand, was moving inside it.

"Let Mary see it first," Pa warned the others. He took his hand from his pocket. There on his palm lay a tiny blue and white kitten.

He laid it carefully in Mary's hand. She stroked its soft fur with a finger tip. Gently she touched its tiny ears and its nose and its wee paws.

"A kitten," she said wonderingly. "Such a very little kitten."

"Its eyes aren't open yet," Laura told her. "Its baby fur is as blue as tobacco smoke, and its face and its breast and its paws and the very tip of its tail are white. Its claws are the tiniest wee white things."

They all bent over the soft, blind little kitten in Mary's hand. It opened its pink mouth in a silent mew.

"It's too small to take from its mother," Pa said. "But I had to take it while I had the chance, before somebody else did. Whiting had the cat sent out to them from the East. She had five kittens, and they sold four of them today for fifty cents apiece."

"You didn't pay fifty cents for this kitten, Pa?" Laura asked him, wide-eyed.

"Yes, I did," said Pa.

Quickly Ma said, "I don't blame you, Charles. A cat in this house will be well worth it."

"Can we raise such a little kitten?" Mary asked anxiously.

"Oh, yes," Ma assured them. "We will have to feed it often, wash its eyes carefully, and keep it warm. Laura, find a small box and pick out the softest, warmest scraps from the scrap bag."

Laura made a snug, soft nest for the kitten in a pasteboard box, while Ma warmed some milk. They all watched while Ma took the kitten in her hand and fed it, a drop of milk at a time, from a teaspoon. The kitten's wee paws clutched at the spoon and its pink mouth tried to suck, and drop by drop it sucked in the warm milk, though some ran down its chin. Then they put it in its nest, and under Mary's warm hand it snuggled down to sleep.

"It has nine lives like any cat, and it will live all right," said Ma. "You'll see."

CHAPTER 4

The Happy Days

PA SAID that the town was growing fast. New settlers were crowding in, hurrying to put up buildings to shelter them. One evening Pa and Ma walked to town to help organize a church, and soon a foundation was laid for a church building. There were not carpenters enough to do all the building that was wanted, so Pa got carpenter work to do.

Every morning he did the chores and walked to town, taking a lunch in a tin pail. He began working promptly at seven o'clock, and by taking only a short nooning he was through work at half past six, and home again for a late supper. And every week he was earning fifteen dollars.

That was a happy time, for the garden was growing well, the corn and oats were thriving, the calf was weaned so that now there was skim-milk for cottage cheese and there was cream to make butter and buttermilk, and best of all, Pa was earning so much money.

Often while Laura worked in the garden, she thought of Mary's going to college. It was nearly two years since they had heard that there was a college for the blind in Iowa. Every day they had thought of that, and every night they prayed that Mary might go. The sorest grief in Mary's blindness was that it hindered her studying. She liked so much to read and learn, and she had always wanted to be a schoolteacher. Now she could never teach school. Laura did not want to, but now she must; she had to be able to teach school as soon as she grew old enough, to earn money for Mary's college education.

"Never mind," she thought, while she hoed, "I can see."

She saw the hoe, and the colors of the earth, and all the leafy little lights and shadows of the pea vines. She had only to glance up, and she saw miles of blowing grasses, the far blue skyline, the birds flying, Ellen and the calves on the green slope, and the different blues of the sky, the snowy piles of huge summer clouds. She had so much, and Mary saw only darkness.

She hoped, though she hardly dared to, that perhaps Mary

might go to college that fall. Pa was making so much money. If Mary could only go now, Laura would study with all her might, she would work so hard that surely she could teach school as soon as she was sixteen years old, and then her earnings would keep Mary in college.

They all needed dresses and they all needed shoes, and Pa always had to buy flour and sugar and tea and salt meat. There was the lumber bill for the new half of the house, and coal must be bought for winter, and there were taxes. But this year there was the garden, and the corn and oats. By year after next, almost all they ate could be raised from the land.

If they had hens and a pig, they would even have meat. This was settled country now, hardly any game was left, and they must buy meat or raise it. Perhaps next year Pa could buy hens and a pig. Some settlers were bringing them in.

One evening Pa came home beaming.

"Guess what, Caroline and girls!" he sang out. "I saw Boast in town today, and he sent word from Mrs. Boast. *She's setting a hen for us!*"

"Oh, Charles!" Ma said.

"As soon as the chicks are big enough to scratch for themselves, he's going to bring us the whole batch," said Pa.

"Oh, Charles, this *is* good news. It's just like Mrs. Boast to do it, too," Ma said thankfully. "How is she, did he say?"

"Said they're getting along fine. She's so busy, she hasn't been able to get to town this spring, but she's certainly keeping you in mind."

"A whole setting of eggs, likely twelve or more young chicks," said Ma. "There's not many that would do it."

"They don't forget how you took them in when they came out here, just married, and got lost in a snowstorm, and we were the only settlers in forty miles," Pa reminded her. "Boast often speaks of it."

"Pshaw," said Ma. "That was nothing. But a whole setting of eggs— It saves us a year in starting a flock."

If they could raise the chicks, if hawks or weasels or foxes did not get them, some would be pullets that summer. Next year the pullets would begin laying, then there would be eggs to set. Year after next, there would be cockerels to fry, and more pullets to increase the flock. Then there would be eggs to eat, and when the hens grew too old to lay eggs, Ma could make them into chicken pie.

"And if next spring Pa can buy a young pig," said Mary, "then in a couple of years we'll have fried ham and eggs. And lard and sausages and spareribs and headcheese!"

"And Grace can roast the pig's tail!" Carrie chimed in.

"Why?" Grace wanted to know. "What is a pig's tail?"

Carrie could remember butchering time, but Grace had never held a pig's skinned tail in front of the cookstove grate and watched it sizzling brown. She had never seen Ma take from the oven the dripping pan full of brown, crackling, juicy spareribs. She had never seen the blue platter heaped with fragrant sausage-cakes, nor spooned their red-brown gravy onto pancakes. She remembered only Dakota Territory, and the meat she knew was the salt, white, fat pork that Pa bought sometimes.

But someday they would have all the good things to eat again, for better times were coming. With so much work to do now, and everything to look forward to, the days were flying by. They were all so busy that they hardly missed Pa during the day. Then every night there was his coming home, when he brought news of the town, and they always had so much to tell him.

All day they had been saving a most exciting thing to tell him. They could hardly expect him to believe it, for this was what had happened:

While Ma was making the beds and Laura and Carrie were washing the breakfast dishes, they all heard the kitten cry out piteously. Kitty's eyes were open now and she could scamper across the floor, chasing a scrap of paper that Grace drew on a string.

"Grace, be careful!" Mary exclaimed. "Don't hurt the kitty."

"I'm not hurting the kitty," Grace answered earnestly.

Before Mary could speak, the kitten squalled again.

"Don't, Grace!" Ma said from the bedroom. "Did you step on it?"

"No, Ma," Grace answered. The kitten cried desperately, and Laura turned around from the dishpan.

"Stop it, Grace! What are you doing to the kitty?"

"I'm not doing anything to the kitty!" Grace wailed. "I can't find it!"

The kitten was nowhere to be seen. Carrie looked under the stove and behind the woodbox. Grace crawled under the table-cloth to see beneath the table. Ma looked under the whatnot's bottom shelf and Laura hunted through both bedrooms.

Then the kitten squalled again, and Ma found it behind the opened door. There, between the door and the wall, the tiny kitten was holding fast to a mouse. The mouse was full-grown and strong, nearly as big as the wobbling little kitten, and it was fighting. It squirmed and bit. The kitten cried when the mouse bit her, but she would not let go. She braced her little legs and kept her teeth set in a mouthful of the mouse's loose skin. Her baby legs were so weak that she almost fell over. The mouse bit her again and again.

Ma quickly got the broom. "Pick up the kitten, Laura, I'll deal with the mouse."

Laura was obeying, of course, but she couldn't help saying, "Oh, I hate to, Ma! She's hanging on. It's her fight."

Right under Laura's grasping hand the tiny kitten made one great effort. She leaped onto the mouse. She held it down under both her front legs and screamed again as its teeth bit into her. Then her own little teeth snapped hard, into the mouse's neck. The mouse squeaked shrilly and went limp. All by herself, the kitten had killed it; her first mouse.

"I declare," Ma said. "Whoever heard of a cat-and-mouse *fight!*"

The baby kitten should have had its mother to lick its wounds and purr proudly over it. Ma carefully washed the bites and fed her warmed milk, Carrie and Grace stroked her wee nose and fuzzy soft head, and under Mary's warm hand she cuddled to sleep. Grace carried the dead mouse out by the tail and threw it far away. And all the rest of that day they often said, What a tale they had to tell Pa when he came home!

They waited until he had washed, and combed his hair, and sat down to supper. Laura answered his question about the chores; she had watered the horses and Ellen and the calves, and moved their picket pins. The nights were so pleasant now that she need not put them in the stable. They slept under the stars, and woke and grazed whenever they liked.

Then came the time to tell Pa what the kitten had done.

He said he had never heard anything like it. He looked at

the little blue and white kitty, walking carefully across the floor with her thin tail standing straight up, and he said, "That kitten will be the best hunter in the county."

The day was ending in perfect satisfaction. They were all there together. All the work, except the supper dishes, was done until tomorrow. They were all enjoying good bread and butter, fried potatoes, cottage cheese, and lettuce leaves sprinkled with vinegar and sugar.

Beyond the open door and window the prairie was dusky but the sky was still pale, with the first stars beginning to quiver in it. The wind went by, and in the house the air stirred, pleasantly warmed by the cookstove and scented with prairie freshness and food and tea and a cleanness of soap and a faint lingering smell of the new boards that made the new bedrooms.

In all that satisfaction, perhaps the best part was knowing that tomorrow would be like today, the same and yet a little different from all other days, as this one had been. But Laura did not know this, until Pa asked her, "How would you like to work in town?"

CHAPTER 5

Working in Town

NO ONE could imagine what work there could be for a girl in town, if it wasn't working as a hired girl in the hotel.

"It's a new idea of Clancy's," Pa said. Mr. Clancy was one of the new merchants. Pa was working on his store building. "We've got the store pretty near finished, and he's moving in his dry goods. His wife's mother's come West with them, and she's going to make shirts."

"Make shirts?" said Ma.

"Yes. So many men are baching on their claims around here that Clancy figures he'll get most of the trade in yard goods, with somebody there in the store making them up into shirts, for men that haven't got any womenfolks to do their sewing."

"That is a good idea," Ma had to admit.

"You bet! There's no flies on Clancy," said Pa. "He's got a machine to sew the shirts."

Ma was interested. "A sewing machine. Is it like that picture we saw in the *Inter-Ocean*? How does it work?"

"About like I figured out it would," Pa answered. "You work the pedal with your feet, and that turns the wheel and works the needle up and down. There's a little contraption underneath the needle that's wound full of thread, too. Clancy was showing some of us. It goes like greased lightning, and makes as neat a seam as you'd want to see."

"I wonder how much it costs," said Ma.

"'Way too much for ordinary folks," said Pa. "But Clancy looks on it as an investment; he'll get his money back in profits."

"Yes, of course," Ma said. Laura knew she was thinking how much work such a machine would save, but even if they could afford it, it would be foolish to buy one only for family sewing. "Does he expect Laura to learn how to run it?"

Laura was alarmed. She could not be responsible for some accident to such a costly machine.

"Oh, no, Mrs. White's going to run it," Pa replied. "She wants a good handy girl to help with the hand sewing."

He said to Laura: "She was asking me if I knew such a girl. I told her you're a good sewer, and she wants you to come in and help her. Clancy's got more orders for shirts than she can handle by herself. She says she'll pay a good willing worker twenty-five cents a day and dinner."

Quickly Laura multiplied in her head. That was a dollar and a half a week, a little more than six dollars a month. If she worked hard and pleased Mrs. White, maybe she could work all summer. She might earn fifteen dollars, maybe even twenty, to help send Mary to college.

She did not want to work in town, among strangers. But she couldn't refuse a chance to earn maybe fifteen dollars, or ten, or five. She swallowed, and asked, "May I go, Ma?"

Ma sighed. "I don't like it much, but it isn't as if you had to go alone. Your Pa will be there in town. Yes, if you want to, you may."

"I—don't want to leave you all the work to do," Laura faltered.

Carrie eagerly offered to help. She could make beds, and sweep, and do the dishes by herself, and weed in the garden. Ma said that Mary was a great help in the house, too, and now that the stock was picketed out, the evening's chores were not so much to do. She said, "We'll miss you, Laura, but we can manage."

There was no time to waste next morning. Laura brought the water and milked Ellen, she hurried to wash and to brush and braid her hair and pin it up. She put on her newest calico dress, and stockings and shoes. She rolled up her thimble in a freshly ironed apron.

The little breakfast that she had time to swallow had no taste. She tied on her sunbonnet and hurried away with Pa. They must be at work in town by seven o'clock.

Morning freshness was in the air. Meadow larks were singing, and up from Big Slough rose the thunder-pumps with long legs dangling and long necks outstretched, giving their short, booming cry. It was a beautiful, lively morning, but Pa and Laura were too hurried. They were running a race with the sun.

Up rose the sun with no effort at all, while they kept walking as fast as they could, north on the prairie road toward the south end of Main Street.

The town was so changed that it seemed like a new place. Two whole blocks on the west side of Main Street were solidly filled with new, yellow-pine buildings. A new board sidewalk was in front of them. Pa and Laura did not have time to cross the street to it. They hurried, Indian file, along the narrow dusty path on the other side of the street.

On this side, the prairie still covered all the vacant lots, right up to Pa's stable and his office-building at the corner of Main and Second Streets. But beyond them, on the other side of Second Street, the studding of a new building stood on the corner lot. Beyond it, the path hurried past vacant lots again till it came to Clancy's new store.

The inside of the store was all new, and still smelled of pine shavings. It had, too, the faint starchy smell of bolts of new cloth. Behind two long counters, all along both walls ran long shelves, stacked to the ceiling with bolts of muslin and calicoes and lawns, challis and cashmeres and flannels and even silks.

There were no groceries, and no hardware, no shoes or tools. In the whole store there was nothing but dry goods. Laura had never before seen a store where nothing was sold but dry goods.

At her right hand was a short counter-top of glass, and inside it were cards of all kinds of buttons, and papers of needles and pins. On the counter beside it, a rack was full of spools of thread of every color. Those colored threads were beautiful in the light from the windows.

The sewing machine stood just behind the front end of the other counter, near that window. Its nickel parts and its long needle glittered and its varnished wood shone. A spool of white thread stood up on its thin black ridge. Laura would not have touched it for anything.

Mr. Clancy was unrolling bolts of calico before two customers, men in very dirty shirts. A large, fat woman with tight-combed black hair was pinning pattern-pieces of newspaper to a length of checked calico spread on the counter near the sewing machine. Pa took off his hat and said good morning to her.

He said, "Mrs. White, here's my girl, Laura."

Mrs. White took the pins out of her mouth and said, "I hope you're a fast, neat sewer. Can you baste bias facings and make good firm buttonholes?"

"Yes, ma'am," Laura said.

"Well, you can hang your bonnet on that nail there, and I'll get you started," said Mrs. White.

Pa gave Laura a helping smile, and then he was gone.

Laura hoped that her trembly feeling would wear off, in time. She hung up her bonnet, tied on her apron, and put her finger into the thimble. Mrs. White handed her pieces of a shirt to baste together, and told her to take the chair in the window by the sewing machine.

Quickly Laura drew the straight-backed chair back a little way, so that the sewing machine partly hid her from the street. She bent her head over her work and basted rapidly.

Mrs. White did not say a word. Anxiously and nervously she kept fitting the pattern-pieces to the goods and cutting out shirt after shirt with long shears. As soon as Laura finished basting a shirt, Mrs. White took it from her and gave her another to baste.

After a time, she sat down at the machine. She whirled its wheel with her hand, and then her feet working fast on the pedal underneath kept the wheel whirring. The racketing hum of the machine filled Laura's head like the buzzing of a gigantic bumblebee. The wheel was a blur and the needle was a streak of light. Mrs. White's plump hands scrambled on the cloth, feeding it rapidly under the needle.

Laura basted as fast as she could. She put the basted shirt on the shrinking pile at Mrs. White's left hand, seized pieces of the next one from the counter and basted it. Mrs. White took basted shirts from the pile, sewed them on the machine and piled them at her right hand.

There was a pattern in the way the shirts went, from the counter to Laura to a pile, from the pile to Mrs. White and through the machine to another pile. It was something like the circles that men and teams had made on the prairie, building the railroad. But only Laura's hands moved, driving the needle as fast as they could along the seams.

Her shoulders began to ache, and the back of her neck. Her chest was cramped and her legs felt tired and heavy. The loud machine buzzed in her head.

Suddenly the machine stopped, still. "There!" Mrs. White said. She had sewed the last basted shirt.

Laura still had to gather a sleeve and to baste the armhole and underarm seam. And the pieces of one more shirt lay waiting on the counter.

"I'll baste that one," Mrs. White said, snatching it up. "We're behindhand."

"Yes, ma'am," Laura said. She felt she should have worked faster, but she had done the best she could.

A big man looked in at the door. His dusty face was covered with an unshaved stubble of red beard. He called, "My shirts ready, Clancy?"

"Be ready right after noon," Mr. Clancy answered.

When the big man had gone on, Mr. Clancy asked Mrs. White when his shirts would be done. Mrs. White said she did not know which shirts they were. Then Mr. Clancy swore.

Laura scrooged small in her chair, basting as fast as she could. Mr. Clancy snatched shirts from the pile and almost threw them at Mrs. White. Still shouting and swearing, he said she'd get them done before dinner or he'd know the reason why.

"I'll not be driven and hounded!" Mrs. White blazed. "Not by you nor any other shanty Irishman!"

Laura hardly heard what Mr. Clancy said then. She wanted desperately to be somewhere else. But Mrs. White told her to come along to dinner. They went into the kitchen behind the store, and Mr. Clancy came raging after them.

The kitchen was hot and crowded and cluttered. Mrs. Clancy was putting dinner on the table, and three little girls and a boy were pushing each other off their chairs. Mr. and Mrs. Clancy and Mrs. White, all quarreling at the top of their voices, sat down and ate heartily. Laura could not even understand what they were quarreling about. She could not tell whether Mr. Clancy was quarreling with his wife or her mother, nor whether they were quarreling with him or with each other.

They seemed so angry that she was afraid they would strike each other. Then Mr. Clancy would say, "Pass the bread," or, "Fill up this cup, will you?" Mrs. Clancy would do it, while they went on calling each other names, yelling them. The children paid no attention. Laura was so upset that she could not eat, she wanted only to get away. She went back to her work as soon as she could.

Mr. Clancy came from the kitchen whistling a tune, as if he

had just had a nice, quiet dinner with his family. He asked Mrs. White cheerfully, "How long'll it take to finish those shirts?"

"Not more than a couple of hours," Mrs. White promised. "We'll both work on them."

Laura thought of Ma's saying, "It takes all kinds of people to make a world."

In two hours they finished the four shirts. Laura basted the collars carefully; collars are hard to set properly onto a shirt. Mrs. White sewed them on the machine. Then there were the cuffs to set on the sleeves, and the narrow hems all around the shirt bottoms to be done. Then the fronts, and the cuff openings, were to be faced. There were all the small buttons to sew firmly on, and the buttonholes to be made.

It is not easy to space buttonholes exactly the same distance apart, and it is very difficult to cut them precisely the right size. The tiniest slip of the scissors will make the hole too large, and even one thread uncut will leave it too small.

When she had cut the buttonholes, Laura whipped the cut edges swiftly, and swiftly covered them with the small, knotted stitches, all precisely the same length and closely set together. She so hated making buttonholes that she had learned to do them quickly, and get it over with. Mrs. White noticed her work, and said, "You can beat me making buttonholes."

After those four shirts were done, there were only three more hours of work that day. Laura went on finishing shirts, while Mrs. White cut out more.

Laura had never sat still so long. Her shoulders ached, her neck ached, her fingers were roughened by needle pricks and her eyes were hot and blurry. Twice she had to take out bastings and do them over. She was glad to stand up and fold her work when Pa came in.

They walked briskly home together. The whole day had gone and now the sun was setting.

"How did you like your first day of working for pay Half-Pint?" Pa asked her. "You make out all right?"

"I think so," she answered. "Mrs. White spoke well of my buttonholes."

CHAPTER 6

The Month of Roses

ALL through that lovely month of June, Laura sewed shirts. Wild roses were blooming in great sweeps of pink through the prairie grasses, but Laura saw them only in the early mornings when she and Pa were hurrying to work.

The soft morning sky was changing to a clearer blue, and already a few wisps of summer cloud were trailing across it. The roses scented the wind, and along the road the fresh blossoms, with their new petals and golden centers, looked up like little faces.

At noon, she knew, great white cloud-puffs would be sailing in sparkling blue. Their shadows would drift across blowing grasses and fluttering roses. But at noon she would be in the noisy kitchen.

At night when she came home, the morning's roses were faded and their petals were scattering on the wind.

Still, she was too old now to play any more. And it was wonderful to think that already she was earning good wages. Every Saturday night Mrs. White counted out a dollar and a half, and Laura took it home to Ma.

"I don't like to take all your money, Laura," Ma said once. "It does seem that you should keep some for yourself."

"Why, Ma, what for?" Laura asked. "I don't need anything."

Her shoes were still good; she had stockings and underwear and her calico dress was almost new. All the week, she looked forward to the pleasure of bringing home her wages to Ma. Often she thought, too, that this was only the beginning.

In two more years she would be sixteen, old enough to teach school. If she studied hard and faithfully, and got a teacher's certificate, and then got a school to teach, she would be a real help to Pa and Ma. Then she could begin to repay them for all that it had cost to provide for her since she was a baby. Then, surely, they could send Mary to college.

Sometimes she almost asked Ma if they could not somehow manage to send Mary to college now, counting on her earnings later to help keep Mary there. She never quite spoke of it, for fear that Ma would say it was too great a chance to take.

Still, the faint hope kept her going more cheerfully to town to work. Her wages were a help. She knew that Ma saved every penny that could be saved, and Mary would go to college as soon as Pa and Ma could possibly send her.

The town was like a sore on the beautiful, wild prairie. Old haystacks and manure piles were rotting around the stables, the backs of the stores' false fronts were rough and ugly. The grass was worn now even from Second Street, and gritty dust blew between the buildings. The town smelled of staleness and dust and smoke and a fatty odor of cooking. A dank smell came from the saloons and a musty sourness from the ground by back doors where the dishwater was thrown out. But after you had been in town a little while you did not smell its smells, and there was some interest in seeing strangers go by.

The boys and girls that Laura had met in town last winter were not there now. They had gone out to stay on homestead claims. The storekeepers stayed in town to run their stores and bach in the rooms behind them, while wives and children lived all summer out on the prairie in claim shanties. For the law was that a man could not keep a homestead claim unless his family lived on it, six months of every year for five years. Also he must keep ten acres of the sod broken up and planted to crops for five years, before the Government would give him a title to the land. But nobody could make a living from that wild land. So the women and girls stayed all summer in claim shanties to satisfy the law, and the boys broke the sod and planted crops, while the fathers built the town and tried to make money enough to buy food and tools from the East.

The more Laura saw of the town, the more she realized how well off her own family was. That was because Pa had got a whole year's start ahead of the others. He had broken sod last year. Now they had the garden, and the oatfield, and the second planting of corn was growing quite well in the sod. Hay would feed the stock through the winter, and Pa could sell the corn and oats, to buy coal. All the new settlers were beginning now where Pa had begun a year ago.

When Laura looked up from her work she could see almost

the whole town, because nearly all the buildings were in the two blocks across the street. All their false fronts stood up, square-cornered at different heights, trying to make believe that the buildings were two stories high.

Mead's Hotel at the end of the street, and Beardsley's Hotel almost opposite Laura, and Tinkham's Furniture Store near the middle of the next block, really did have two stories. Curtains fluttered at their upstairs windows and showed how honest those buildings were, in that row of false fronts.

That was the only difference between them and the other buildings. They were all of pine lumber beginning to weather gray. Each building had two tall glass windows in its front, and a door between them. Every door was open now to the warm weather, and every doorway was filled with a strip of faded pink mosquito netting tacked onto a framework to make a screen door.

In front of them all ran the level board sidewalk, and all along its edge were hitching posts. There were always a few horses in sight, tied here and there to the posts, and sometimes a wagon with a team of horses or oxen.

Once in a while, when she bit off a thread, Laura saw a man cross the sidewalk, untie his horse, swing onto it and ride away. Sometimes she heard a team and wagon, and when the sounds were loudest she glanced up and saw it passing by.

One day an outburst of confused shouting startled her. She saw a tall man come bursting out of Brown's saloon. The screen door loudly slammed shut behind him.

With great dignity the man turned about. He looked haughtily at the screen door, and lifting one long leg he thrust his foot contemptuously through the pink mosquito netting. It tore jaggedly from top to bottom. A yell of protest came out of the saloon.

The tall man paid no attention whatever to the yell. He turned haughtily away, and saw in front of him a round little short man. The short man wanted to go into the saloon. The tall man wanted to walk away. But each was in front of the other.

The tall man stood very tall and dignified. The short man stood puffed out with dignity.

In the doorway the saloonkeeper complained about the torn

screen door. Neither of them paid any attention to him. They looked at each other and grew more and more dignified.

Suddenly the tall man knew what to do. He linked his long arm in the little man's fat arm, and they came down the sidewalk together, singing.

> Pull for the shore, sailor!
> Pull for the shore!
> Heed not the stormy winds—

The tall man solemnly lifted his long leg and thrust his foot through Harthorn's screen door. A yell came out. "Hey, there! What the——"

The two men came on, singing.

> Though loudly they roar!
> Pull for the shore, sailor—

They were as dignified as could be. The tall man's long legs made the longest possible steps. The puffed-out little man tried with dignity to stretch his short legs to steps as long.

> Heed not the stormy winds—

The tall man gravely thrust his foot through the mosquito-netting door of Beardsley's Hotel. Mr. Beardsley came boiling out. The man marched solemnly on.

> Though loudly they roar!

Laura was laughing so that tears ran out of her eyes. She saw the long, solemn leg rip the mosquito netting in the door of Barker's grocery. Mr. Barker popped out, protesting. The long legs stalking and the fat short legs gravely stretching went away from him haughtily.

> Pull for the shore!

The tall man's foot pushed through the screen door of Wilder's Feed Store. Royal Wilder yanked it open and said what he thought.

The two men stood listening gravely until he stopped for breath. Then the fat little man said with great dignity, "My name is Tay Pay Pryor and I'm drunk."

They went on, arm in arm, chanting those words. First the pudgy little man,

My name is Tay Pay Pryor—

Then both together, like bullfrogs,

—and I'm drunk!

The tall man would not say that his name was T. P. Pryor, but he always came in solemnly, "—and I'm *DRUNK!*"

They wheeled square about and marched into the other saloon. Its screen door slammed loudly behind them. Laura held her breath, but that one door's mosquito netting stayed smooth and whole.

Laura laughed till her sides ached. She could not stop when Mrs. White snapped out that it was a disgrace to snakes, what men would do with liquor in them.

"Think of the cost of all those screen doors," Mrs. White said. "I'm surprised at you. Young folks nowadays seem to have no realizing sense."

That evening when Laura tried to describe those two men so that Mary could see them, no one laughed.

"Goodness gracious, Laura. How could you laugh at drunken men?" Ma wanted to know.

"I think it is dreadful," Mary added.

Pa said, "The tall one was Bill O'Dowd. I know for a fact that his brother brought him to a claim out here, to keep him from drinking. Two saloons in this town are just two saloons too many."

"It's a pity more men don't say the same," said Ma. "I begin to believe that if there isn't a stop put to the liquor traffic, women must bestir themselves and have something to say about it."

Pa twinkled at her. "Seems to me you have plenty to say, Caroline. Ma never left me in doubt as to the evil of drink, nor you either."

"Be that as it may be," said Ma. "It's a crying shame that such things can happen before Laura's very eyes."

Pa looked at Laura, and his eyes were still twinkling. Laura knew that he didn't blame her for laughing.

CHAPTER 7

Nine Dollars

Mr. Clancy was not getting so many orders for shirts. It seemed that most of the men who could buy shirts that year had bought them. One Saturday evening Mrs. White said, "The spring rush seems to be over."

"Yes, ma'am," said Laura.

Mrs. White counted out a dollar and fifty cents and gave it to her. "I won't be needing you any more, so you needn't come in Monday morning," she said. "Good-by."

"Good-by," Laura said.

She had worked six weeks and earned nine dollars. One dollar had seemed a great deal of money only six weeks ago, but now nine dollars was not enough. If she could have earned only one more week's wages, that would have made ten dollars and a half, or two weeks would have made a whole twelve dollars.

She knew how good it would be to stay at home again, to help with the housework and do the chores and work in the garden, to go walking with Mary and gather wild flowers, and to look forward to Pa's homecoming at night. But somehow she felt cast out, and hollow inside.

Slowly she went along the path beside Main Street. Pa was working now on the building at the corner of Second. He stood by a stack of shingles, waiting for Laura, and when he saw her he sang out, "Look what we've got, to take home to your Ma!"

In the shade of the shingles stood a bushel basket covered with a grain sack. Inside it there was a small rasping of claws, and a cheeping chorus. The chickens!

"Boast brought 'em in today," said Pa. "Fourteen of 'em, all healthy and thriving." His whole face was beaming with anticipation of Ma's delight.

He told Laura, "The basket's not heavy. You take one handle and I'll take the other, and we'll carry them level, between us."

They went down Main Street and out on the road toward

home, carrying the basket carefully between them. Sunset was flaming in crimson and burning gold over the whole sky. The air was filled with golden light and Silver Lake to the east was blazing like fire. Up from the basket came the chickens' wondering and anxious cheeping.

"Pa, Mrs. White doesn't want me any more," Laura said.

"Yes, I guess the spring rush is about over," said Pa.

Laura had not thought that Pa's job might end.

"Oh, Pa, won't there be any more carpentering, either?" she asked.

"We couldn't expect it to last all summer," said Pa. "Anyway, I'll have to be making hay pretty soon."

After a while Laura said, "I only earned nine dollars, Pa."

"Nine dollars is nothing to sneeze at," said Pa. "You've done good work, too, and fully satisfied Mrs. White, haven't you?"

"Yes," Laura answered honestly.

"Then it's a good job well done," said Pa.

It was true that that was some satisfaction. Laura felt a little better. Besides, they were taking the chickens to Ma.

Ma was delighted when she saw them. Carrie and Grace crowded to peep at them in the basket, and Laura told Mary about them. They were healthy, lively chicks, with bright black eyes and bright yellow claws. Already the down was coming off them, leaving naked patches on their necks, and the sprouting feathers were showing on their wings and tails. They were every color that chickens are, and some were spotted.

Ma lifted each one carefully into her apron. "Mrs. Boast can't have got these all from one hatching," she said. "I do believe there's not more than two cockerels among them."

"The Boasts have got such a head-start with chickens, likely they're planning to eat friers this summer," said Pa. "It may be she took a few cockerels out of this flock, looking on them as meat."

"Yes, and replaced them with pullets that will be layers," Ma guessed. "It would be Mrs. Boast all over. A more generous woman never lived."

She carried the chicks in her apron, to set them one by one into the coop that Pa had already made. It had a front of laths, to let in air and sun, and a little door with a wooden button to fasten it. It had no floor, but was set on clean grass that the chicks could eat, and when the grass grew trampled and dirty, the coop could be moved to fresh grass.

In an old pie pan Ma mixed a crumbly bran mash, well peppered. She set it in the coop, and the chicks crowded onto it, gobbling up the bran mash so greedily that sometimes they tried to swallow their own toes by mistake. When they could eat no more, they perched on the edge of the water pan, and scooping up water in their beaks they stretched up their necks and tilted back their heads, to swallow it.

Ma said it would be Carrie's task to feed them often and to keep their water pan filled with cool, fresh water. Tomorrow she would let the chicks out to run, and it would be Grace's part to keep a sharp lookout for hawks.

After supper that evening she sent Laura to make sure that the chicks were sleeping safely. All the stars were shining over the dark prairie and a sickle moon was low in the west. The grasses were breathing softly, asleep in the quiet night.

Laura's hand felt gently over the sleeping chicks, huddled warm together in a corner of the coop. Then she stood looking at the summer night. She did not know how long she had stood there, until she saw Ma coming from the house.

"Oh, there you are, Laura," Ma softly said. As Laura had done, she knelt and put her hand through the coop's door to feel the huddled chicks. Then she, too, stood looking.

"The place begins to look like a farm," she said. The oatfield and the cornfield were shadowy pale in the darkness, and the garden was bumpy with lumps of dark leaves. Like pools of faint star-shine among them spread the cucumber vines and the pumpkins. The low sod stable could hardly be seen, but from the house window a warm yellow light shone out.

Suddenly, without thinking at all, Laura said, "Oh Ma, I do wish Mary could go to college this fall."

Unexpectedly Ma replied, "It may be that she can. Your Pa and I have been talking of it."

Laura could not speak for a minute. Then she asked, "Have you—have you said anything to her?"

"Not yet," said Ma. "We must not raise hopes only to be disappointed. But with Pa's wages, and the oats and the corn, if nothing goes wrong, we think she can go this fall. We must trust to ourselves to contrive to keep her there till she finishes the full seven years' course, both college and manual training."

Then for the first time Laura realized that when Mary went to college, she would go away. Mary would be gone. All day long, Mary would not be there. Laura could not think what living would be, without Mary.

"Oh, I wish—" she began, and stopped. She had been so eagerly hoping that Mary could go to college.

"Yes, we will miss her," Ma said steadily. "But we must think what a great opportunity it will be for her."

"I know, Ma," Laura said miserably.

The night was large and empty now. The light shining from the house was warm and steady, but even home would not be the same when Mary was not there.

Then Ma said, "Your nine dollars are a great help, Laura. I have been planning, and I do believe that with nine dollars I can buy the goods for Mary's best dress, and perhaps the velvet to make her a hat."

CHAPTER 8

Fourth of July

BOOM!

Laura was jerked out of sleep. The bedroom was dark. Carrie asked in a thin, scared whisper, "What was that?"

"Don't be scared," Laura answered. They listened. The window was hardly gray in the dark, but Laura could feel that the middle of the night was past.

BOOM! The air seemed to shake.

"Great guns!" Pa exclaimed sleepily.

"Why? Why?" Grace demanded. "Pa, Ma, why?"

Carrie asked, "Who is it? What are they shooting?"

"What time is it?" Ma wanted to know.

Through the partition Pa answered, "It's Fourth of July, Carrie." The air shook again. BOOM!

It was not great guns. It was gunpowder exploded under the blacksmith's anvil, in town. The noise was like the noise of battles that Americans fought for independence. Fourth of July was the day when the first Americans declared that all men are born free and equal. BOOM!

"Come, girls, we might as well get up!" Ma called.

Pa sang, " 'Oh, say, can you see, by the dawn's early light?' "

"Charles!" Ma protested, but she was laughing, because it really was too dark to see.

"It's nothing to be solemn about!" Pa jumped out of bed. "Hurray! we're Americans!" He sang,

> Hurray! Hurray! We'll sing the jubilee!
> Hurray! Hurray! The flag that sets men free!

Even the sun, as it rose shining into the clearest of skies, seemed to know this day was the glorious Fourth. At breakfast Ma said, "This would be a perfect day for a Fourth of July picnic."

"Maybe the town'll be far enough along to have one, come next July," said Pa.

"We couldn't hardly have a picnic this year, anyway," Ma

admitted. "It wouldn't seem like a picnic, without fried chicken."

After such a rousing beginning, the day did seem empty. Such a special day seemed to expect some special happening, but nothing special could happen.

"I feel like dressing up," Carrie said while they did the dishes.

"So do I, but there's nothing to dress up for," Laura replied.

When she carried out the dishwater to throw it far from the house, she saw Pa looking at the oats. They were growing thick and tall, gray-green and smoothly rippling in the wind. The corn was growing lustily, too. Its long, yellow-green, fluttering leaves almost hid the broken sod. In the garden the cucumber vines were reaching out, their crawling tips uncurling beyond patches of spreading big leaves. The rows of peas and beans were rounding up, the carrot rows were feathery green and the beets were thrusting up long, dark leaves on red stems. The ground-cherries were already small bushes. Through the wild grasses the chickens were scattered, chasing insects to eat.

All this was satisfaction enough for an ordinary day, but for Fourth of July there should be something more.

Pa felt the same way. He had nothing to do, for on Fourth of July no work could be done except the chores and housework. In a little while he came into the house and said to Ma, "There's a kind of a celebration in town today, would you like to go?"

"What kind of celebration?" Ma asked.

"Well, mostly horse racing, but they took up a collection for lemonade," Pa replied.

"Women are not likely to be at a horse race," Ma said. "And I couldn't go calling, uninvited, on Fourth of July."

Laura and Carrie stood almost bursting with eagerness while Ma considered, and shook her head. "You go along, Charles. It would be too much for Grace, anyway."

"It is much nicer at home," said Mary.

Then Laura spoke. "Oh Pa, if you go, can't Carrie and I?"

Pa's doubtful eyes brightened, and twinkled at her and Carrie. Ma smiled on them.

"Yes, Charles, it will be a nice outing for you all," she said. "Run down cellar and bring up the butter, Carrie, and while you're dressing I'll put up some bread-and-butter for you to take along."

Suddenly the day seemed really Fourth of July. Ma made sandwiches, Pa blacked his boots, Laura and Carrie hurriedly dressed up. Luckily Laura's sprigged calico was freshly washed and ironed. She and Carrie took turns at the washbasin, scrubbing their faces and necks and ears pink. Over their unbleached muslin union suits they put on crackling stiff petticoats of bleached muslin. They brushed and braided their hair. Laura wound her heavy braids around her head and pinned them. She tied the Sunday hair ribbon on the ends of Carrie's braids. Then she put on her fresh sprigged calico and buttoned it up the back. The full ruffle on the bottom of the full skirt came down to the tops of her shoes.

"Please button me up," Carrie asked. In the middle of her back there were two buttons that she couldn't reach. She had buttoned all the others outside-in.

"You can't wear your buttons turned inside, at a Fourth of July celebration," said Laura, unbuttoning them all and buttoning them again properly.

"If they're outside, they keep pulling my hair," Carrie protested. "My braids catch on them."

"I know. Mine always did," said Laura. "But you just have to stand it till you're big enough to put your hair up."

They put on their sunbonnets. Pa was waiting, holding the brown-paper packet of sandwiches. Ma looked at them carefully and said, "You look very nice."

"It's a treat to me, to be stepping out with my two good-looking girls," said Pa.

"You look nice, too, Pa," Laura told him. His boots were glossily polished, his beard was trimmed, and he was wearing his Sunday suit and broad-brimmed felt hat.

"I want to go!" Grace demanded. Even when Ma said, "No, Grace," she repeated two or three times, "I want to!" Because she was the baby, they had almost spoiled her. Now her unruliness must be nipped in the bud. Pa had to set her sternly in a chair and tell her, "You heard your Ma speak."

They set out soberly, unhappy about Grace. But she must be taught to mind. Perhaps next year she could go, if there were a big celebration and they all rode in the wagon. Now they were walking, to let the horses stay on their picket ropes and eat grass. Horses grow tired, standing all day at hitching posts in dust and heat. Grace was too little to walk the mile and back, and she was too big to be carried.

Even before they reached town, they could hear a sound like corn popping. Carrie asked what it was, and Pa said it was firecrackers.

Horses were tied along the whole length of Main Street. Men and boys were so thick on the sidewalk that in places they almost touched each other. Boys were throwing lighted firecrackers into the dusty street, where they sizzled and exploded. The noise was startling.

"I didn't know it would be like this," Carrie murmured. Laura did not like it, either. They had never been in such a crowd before. There was nothing to do but keep on walking up and down in it, and to be among so many strangers made them uncomfortable.

Twice they walked the two blocks with Pa, and then Laura asked him if she and Carrie could not stay in his store building. Pa said that was a fine idea. They could watch the crowd while he circulated a little; then they would eat their lunch and see the races. He let them into the empty building and Laura shut the door.

It was pleasant to be alone in the echoing bare place. They looked at the empty kitchen behind it, where they had all lived huddled during the long hard winter. They tiptoed upstairs to the hollow, hot bedrooms under the eaves of the shingle roof, and stood looking down from the front window at the crowd, and at firecrackers squirming and popping in the dust.

"I wish we had some firecrackers," Carrie said.

"They're guns," Laura pretended. "We're in Fort Ticonderoga, and those are British and Indians. We're Americans, fighting for independence."

"It was the British in Fort Ticonderoga, and the Green Mountain boys took it," Carrie objected.

"Then I guess we're with Daniel Boone in Kentucky, and this is a log stockade," said Laura. "Only the British and Indians captured him," she had to admit.

"How much do firecrackers cost?" Carrie asked.

"Even if Pa could afford them, it's foolish to spend money just to make a little noise," Laura said. "Look at that little bay pony. Let's pick out the horses we like best; you can have first choice."

There was so much to see that they could hardly believe it was noon when Pa's boots sounded downstairs and he called, "Girls! Where are you?"

They rushed down. He was having a good time, his eyes were twinkling bright. He sang out, "I've brought us a treat! Smoked herring, to go with our bread and butter! And look what else!" He showed them a bunch of firecrackers.

"Oh, Pa!" Carrie cried. "How much did they cost?"

"Didn't cost me a cent," said Pa. "Lawyer Barnes handed them to me, said to give them to you girls."

"Why on earth did he do that?" Laura asked. She had never heard of Lawyer Barnes before.

"Oh, he's going in for politics, I guess," said Pa. "He acts that way, affable and agreeable to everybody. You want me to set these off for you now, or after we eat?"

Laura and Carrie were thinking the same thing. They knew it when they looked at each other, and Carrie said it. "Let's save them, Pa, to take home to Grace."

"All right," said Pa. He put them in his pocket and undid the smoked herring while Laura opened the packet of sandwiches. The herring was delicious. They saved some to take home to Ma. When they had eaten the last bit of bread and butter they went out to the well and drank, long and deep, from the edge of the pail that Pa drew dripping up. Then they washed their hands and their hot faces and dried them on Pa's handkerchief.

It was time to go to the races. The whole crowd was moving across the railroad tracks and out on the prairie. On a pole set up there, the American flag fluttered against the sky. The sun was shining warm and a cool breeze was blowing.

Beside the flagpole a man rose up tall above the crowd. He was standing on something. The sound of talking died down, and he could be heard speaking.

"Well, boys," he said, "I'm not much good at public speaking, but today's the glorious Fourth. This is the day and date when our forefathers cut loose from the despots of Europe.

There wasn't many Americans at that time, but they wouldn't stand for any monarch tyrannizing over them. They had to fight the British regulars and their hired Hessians and the murdering scalping red-skinned savages that those fine gold-laced aristocrats turned loose on our settlements and paid for murdering and burning and scalping women and children. A few barefoot Americans had to fight the whole of them and lick 'em, and they did fight them and they did lick them. Yes sir! We licked the British in 1776 and we licked 'em again in 1812, and we backed all the monarchies of Europe out of Mexico and off this continent less than twenty years ago, and by glory! Yessir, by Old Glory right here, waving over my head, any time the despots of Europe try to step on America's toes, we'll lick 'em again!"

"Hurray! Hurray!" everybody shouted. Laura and Carrie and Pa yelled, too, "Hurray! Hurray!"

"Well, so here we are today," the man went on. "Every man Jack of us a free and independent citizen of God's country, the only country on earth where a man is free and independent. Today's the Fourth of July, when this whole thing was started, and it ought to have a bigger, better celebration than this. We can't do much this year. Most of us are out here trying to pull ourselves up by our own boot straps. By next year, likely some of us will be better off, and able to chip in for a real big rousing celebration of Independence Day. Meantime, here we are. It's Fourth of July, and on this day somebody's got to read the Declaration of Independence. It looks like I'm elected, so hold your hats, boys; I'm going to read it."

Laura and Carrie knew the Declaration by heart, of course, but it gave them a solemn, glorious feeling to hear the words. They took hold of hands and stood listening in the solemnly listening crowd. The Stars and Stripes were fluttering bright against the thin, clear blue overhead, and their minds were saying the words before their ears heard them.

"When in the course of human events it becomes necessary for one people to dissolve the political bonds which have connected them with another, and to assume among the powers of the earth the separate and equal station to which the laws of Nature and of Nature's God entitle them, a decent respect to the opinions of mankind requires that they should declare the causes which impell them to the separation.

"We hold these truths to be self-evident, that all men are created equal, that they are endowed by their Creator with certain inalienable rights, that among these are Life, Liberty, and the pursuit of Happiness. . . ."

Then came the long and terrible list of the crimes of the King.

"He has endeavored to prevent the population of these States.

"He has obstructed the administration of Justice.

"He has made Judges dependent on his will alone.

"He has erected a multitude of new offices, and sent hither swarms of officers to harass our people and to eat out their substance.

"He has plundered our seas, ravaged our coasts, burnt our towns, and destroyed the lives of our people . . .

"He is at this time transporting large Armies of foreign Mercenaries to complete the works of death, destruction and tyranny, already begun with circumstances of cruelty and perfidy scarcely paralleled in the most barbarous ages, and totally unworthy the head of a civilized nation. . . .

"We, therefore, the Representatives of the United States of America, in General Congress assembled, appealing to the Supreme Judge of the world for the rectitude of our intentions, do, in the name and by the authority of the good People of these Colonies, solemnly publish and declare,

"That these United Colonies are, and of right ought to be, Free and Independent States, that they are absolved from all allegiance to the British Crown, and that all political connection between them and the State of Great Britain is and ought to be totally dissolved; and that as Free and Independent States, they have full right to levy War . . .

"And for the support of this Declaration, with a firm reliance on the protection of Divine Providence, we mutually pledge to each other our Lives, our Fortunes, and our sacred Honor."

No one cheered. It was more like a moment to say, "Amen." But no one quite knew what to do.

Then Pa began to sing. All at once everyone was singing,

My country, 'tis of thee,
Sweet land of liberty,
Of thee I sing. . . .

Long may our land be bright
With Freedom's holy light.
Protect us by Thy might,
Great God, our King!

The crowd was scattering away then, but Laura stood stock still. Suddenly she had a completely new thought. The Declaration and the song came together in her mind, and she thought: God is America's king.

She thought: Americans won't obey any king on earth. Americans are free. That means they have to obey their own consciences. No king bosses Pa; he has to boss himself. Why (she thought), when I am a little older, Pa and Ma will stop telling me what to do, and there isn't anyone else who has a right to give me orders. I will have to make myself be good.

Her whole mind seemed to be lighted up by that thought. This is what it means to be free. It means, you have to be good. "Our father's God, author of liberty—" The laws of Nature and of Nature's God endow you with a right to life and liberty. Then you have to keep the laws of God, for God's law is the only thing that gives you a right to be free.

Laura had no time then to think any further. Carrie was wondering why she stood so still, and Pa was saying, "This way, girls! There's the free lemonade!"

The barrels stood in the grass by the flagpole. A few men were waiting for their turns to drink from the tin dipper. As each finished drinking, he handed the dipper on, and then strolled away toward the horses and buggies by the race track.

Laura and Carrie hung back a little, but the man who had the dipper saw them and handed the dipper to Pa. He filled it from the barrel and gave it to Carrie. The barrel was almost full, and slices of lemon floated thick on the lemonade.

"I see they put in plenty of lemons, so it ought to be good," Pa said, while Carrie slowly drank. Her eyes grew round with delight; she had never tasted lemonade before.

"They've just mixed it," one of the waiting men told Pa. "The water is fresh from the hotel well, so it's cold."

Another man who was waiting said, "It depends, some, on how much sugar they put in."

Pa filled the dipper again and gave it to Laura. She had once tasted lemonade, at Nellie Oleson's party, when she was a little girl in Minnesota. This lemonade was even more delicious. She drank the last drop from the dipper and thanked Pa. It would not be polite to ask for more.

When Pa had drunk, they went across the trampled grass to the crowd by the race track. A great ring of sod had been broken, and the sod carried off. The breaking plow with its coulter had left the black earth smooth and level. In the middle of the ring and all around it the prairie grasses were waving, except where men and buggies had made trampled tracks.

"Why, hello, Boast!" Pa called, and Mr. Boast came through the crowd. He had just got to town in time for the races. Mrs. Boast, like Ma, had preferred to stay at home.

Four ponies came out on the track. There were two bay ponies, one gray, and one black. The boys who were riding them lined them up in a straight row.

"Which'd you bet on, if you were betting?" Mr. Boast asked.

"Oh, the black one!" Laura cried. The black pony's coat shone in the sunlight and its long mane and tail blew silky on the breeze. It tossed its slender head and picked up its feet daintily.

At the word, "Go!" all the ponies leaped into a run. The crowd yelled. Stretched out low and fast, the black pony went by, the others behind it. All their pounding feet raised a cloud of dust that hid them. Then around the far side of the track they went, running with all their might. The gray pony crept up beside the black. Neck and neck they were running, then the gray pulled a little ahead and the crowd yelled again. Laura still hoped for the black. It was doing its best. Little by little it gained on the gray. Its head passed the gray's neck, its outstretched nose was almost even with the gray's nose. Suddenly all four ponies were coming head-on down the track, quickly growing larger and larger in front of the oncoming dust. The bay pony with the white nose came skimming past the black and the gray, across the line ahead of them both while the crowd cheered.

"If you'd bet on the black, Laura, you'd 've lost," said Pa.

"It's the prettiest, though," Laura answered. She had never been so excited. Carrie's eyes shone, her cheeks were pink with excitement; her braid was snared on a button and recklessly she yanked it loose.

"Are there any more, Pa? more races?" Carrie cried.

"Sure, here they come for the buggy race," Pa answered. Mr. Boast joked, "Pick the winning team, Laura!"

Through the crowd and out onto the track came first a bay team hitched to a light buggy. The bays were perfectly matched and they stepped as though the buggy weighed nothing at all. Then came other teams, other buggies, but Laura hardly saw them, for there was a team of brown horses that she knew. She knew their proud, gay heads and arching necks, the shine of light on their satiny shoulders, the black manes blowing and the forelocks tossing above their quick, bright, gentle eyes.

"Oh, look, Carrie, look! It's the brown Morgans!" she cried.

"That's Almanzo Wilder's team, Boast," said Pa. "What in creation has he got 'em hitched to?"

High up above the horses, Almanzo Wilder was sitting. His hat was pushed back on his head and he looked cheerful and confident.

He turned the team toward its place in line, and they saw that he was sitting on a high seat, on top of a long, high, heavy wagon, with a door in its side.

"It's his brother Royal's peddler's wagon," said a man standing near by.

"He don't have a chance, with that weight, against all those light buggies," said another. Everyone was looking at the Morgans and the wagon and talking about them.

"The off horse, Prince, is the one he drove last winter, that forty-mile trip that he and Cap Garland made, and brought in the wheat that kept us all from starving to death," Pa told Mr. Boast. "The other one's Lady, that ran off with the antelope herd that time. They've both got good action, and speed."

"I see that," Mr. Boast agreed. "But no team can haul that heavy cart and beat Sam Owen's bays on his light buggy. Seems like the young fellow might have rousted out a buggy somewheres in this country."

"He's an independent kind of a young cuss," someone said. "He'd rather lose with what he's got than win with a borrowed buggy."

"Too bad he don't own a buggy," Mr. Boast said.

The brown horses were by far the most beautiful on the track, and so proud. They did not seem to mind the heavy wagon at all, but tossed their heads, pricked their ears, and lifted their feet as if the ground were not quite good enough for them to step on.

"Oh, what a shame, what a *shame* they haven't a fair chance," Laura was thinking. Her hands were clenched. She wished so much that those proud, fine horses might only have a fair chance. Hitched to that heavy wagon, they could not win. She cried out, "Oh, it isn't *fair!*"

The race started. Fast came the bays, leading all the others. The shining legs trotting and the wheels whirling hardly seemed to touch the ground. Every buggy rushing by was a light, one-seated buggy. Not a team drew even the weight of a two-seated buggy, except the beautiful brown horses who came last, pulling the high, heavy peddler's cart.

"Best team in the country," Laura heard a man say, "but not a chance."

"Nope," said another. "That wagon's too heavy for them to pull. Sure as shooting, they'll break their trot."

But they were pulling it, and they were trotting. Evenly, without a break, the eight brown legs kept moving in a perfect trot. The dust-cloud rose up and hid them. Then bursting out of it, up the other side of the track the teams and buggies were speeding. One buggy— No, two buggies! were behind the peddler's cart. Three buggies were behind it. Only the bays were ahead of it.

"Oh, come on! Come on! Win Win!" Laura was begging the brown horses. She so wanted them to trot faster that it seemed her wishing was pulling them.

They were almost around the track. They were coming now around the turn and on toward the line. The bays were ahead. The Morgans could not do it, they could not win, the weight was too much for them, but still Laura kept on wishing with all of her. "Faster, faster, only a little faster. Oh, come on, come *on!*"

Almanzo leaned forward from the high seat and seemed to speak to them. Still smoothly trotting, they came faster. Their heads reached Mr. Owen's buggy and slowly, smoothly crept by it. All the legs were moving fast, fast, while so slowly the brown heads came up, even with the bays'. All four horses were coming now in a line, faster, faster.

"A tie. By gosh, it's a tie," a man said.

Then Mr. Owen's buggy whip flashed out. It swished down, once, twice, as he shouted. The bays leaped ahead. Almanzo had no whip. He was leaning forward, lightly holding the reins firm. Once more he seemed to speak. Fast and smooth as swallows flying, the brown Morgans passed the bays and crossed the line. They'd won!

The whole crowd shouted. It surged to surround the brown horses and Almanzo high on the cart. Laura found that she had been holding her breath. Her knees were wobbly. She wanted to yell and to laugh and to cry and to sit down and rest.

"Oh, they won! they won! they won!" Carrie kept saying, clapping her hands. Laura did not say anything.

"He earned that five dollars," said Mr. Boast.

"What five dollars?" Carrie asked.

"Some men in town put up five dollars for the best trotting team," Pa explained. "Almanzo Wilder's won it."

Laura was glad she had not known. She could not have borne it if she had known that the brown horses were running for a five-dollar prize.

"He has it coming to him," said Pa. "That young man knows how to handle horses."

There were no more races. There was nothing more to do but stand around and listen to the talking. The lemonade was low in the barrel. Mr. Boast brought Laura and Carrie a dipperful and they divided it. It was sweeter than before, but not so cold. The teams and buggies were going away. Then Pa came from the dwindling crowd and said it was time to go home.

Mr. Boast walked with them along Main Street. Pa said to him that the Wilders had a sister who was a schoolteacher back East in Minnesota. "She's taken a claim half a mile west of town here," said Pa, "and she wants Almanzo to find out if she can get this school to teach next winter. I told him to tell her to send in her application to the school board. Other things being equal, I don't know why she can't as well have it."

Laura and Carrie looked at each other. Pa was on the school board, and no doubt the others would feel as he did. Laura thought, "Maybe, if I am a very good scholar and if she likes me, maybe she might take me driving behind those beautiful horses."

CHAPTER 9

Blackbirds

In August, the days were so hot that Laura and Mary took their walks in the early mornings before the sun had risen far. The air still had some freshness then and it was not too hot to be pleasant. But every walk seemed like a little bit of the last walk they would have together, for soon Mary was going away.

She was really going to college, that fall. They had looked forward so long to her going, that now when she really was going, it did not seem possible. It was hard to imagine, too, because none of them knew what college would be like; they had never seen one. But Pa had earned nearly a hundred dollars that spring; the garden and the oats and the corn were growing marvelously; and Mary really could go to college.

Coming back from their walk one morning, Laura noticed several grasses sticking to Mary's skirt. She tried to pull them off, but they would not come loose.

"Ma!" she called. "Come look at this funny grass." Ma had never seen a grass like it. The grass heads were like barley beards, except that they were twisted, and they ended in a seed pod an inch long, with a point as fine and hard as a needle, and a shaft covered with stiff hairs pointing backward. Like real needles, the points had sewed themselves into Mary's dress. The stiff hair followed the needle-point easily, but kept it from being pulled back, and the four-inch-long, screw-like beard followed, twisting and pushing the needle-point farther in.

"Ouch! something bit me!" Mary exclaimed. Just above her shoetop, one of the strange grasses had pierced her stocking and was screwing itself into her flesh.

"I declare this beats all," said Ma. "What next will we encounter on this homestead?"

When Pa came in at noon, they showed him the strange grass. He said it was Spanish needle grass. When it got into the mouths of horses or cattle, it must be cut out of their lips and tongues. It worked through sheep's wool and into the sheep's bodies, often killing them.

"Where did you girls find it?" he asked, and he was glad that Laura could not tell him. "If you didn't notice it, there can't be much of it. It grows in patches, and spreads. Exactly where did you go walking?"

Laura could tell him that. He said he would attend to that grass. "Some say it can be killed by burning it over, green," he told them. "I'll burn it now, to kill as many seeds as I can, and next spring I'll be on the lookout and burn it, green."

There were little new potatoes for dinner, creamed with green peas, and there were string beans and green onions. And by every plate was a saucer full of sliced ripe tomatoes, to be eaten with sugar and cream.

"Well, we've got good things to eat, and plenty of them," said Pa, taking a second helping of potatoes and peas.

"Yes," Ma said happily; "nowadays we can all eat enough to make up for what we couldn't have last winter."

She was proud of the garden; it was growing so well. "I shall begin salting down cucumbers tomorrow, little ones are thick under all those vines. And the potato tops are thriving so, I can hardly find the hills underneath them, to scrabble."

"If nothing happens to them, we'll have plenty of potatoes *this* winter!" Pa rejoiced.

"We'll have roasting ears soon, too," Ma announced. "I noticed, this morning, some of the corn silks are beginning to darken."

"I never saw a better corn crop," said Pa. "We've got that to depend on."

"And the oats," said Ma. Then she asked, "What's wrong with the oats, Charles?"

"Well, blackbirds are getting most of them," Pa told her. "I no sooner set up a shock than it's covered thick with the pests. They're eating all the grain they can get at, and not leaving much but the straw."

Ma's cheerful face dimmed, but Pa went on. "Never mind, there's a good crop of straw, and soon as I get the oats cut and shocked I'll clear out the blackbirds with a shotgun."

That afternoon, looking up from her sewing to thread her

needle, Laura saw a wisp of smoke wavering in the heat waves from the prairie. Pa had taken time from his work in the oat-field to cut a swath around the patch of Spanish needles and set fire to those vicious grasses.

"The prairie looks so beautiful and gentle," she said. "But I wonder what it will do next. Seems like we have to fight it all the time."

"This earthly life is a battle," said Ma. "If it isn't one thing to contend with, it's another. It always has been so, and it always will be. The sooner you make up your mind to that, the better off you are, and the more thankful for your pleasures. Now Mary, I'm ready to fit the bodice."

They were making Mary's best winter dress, for college. In the hot room, with the sun blazing on the thin board walls and roof, the lapfuls of wool cashmere almost smothered them. Ma was nervous about this best dress. She had made the summer dresses first, for practice with the patterns.

She had cut the patterns from newspaper, using her dress-maker's chart of thin cardboard as a guide. Lines and figures for all different sizes were printed on it. The trouble was that nobody was exactly any of the sizes on the chart. After Ma had measured Mary, and figured and marked the size of every sleeve and skirt and bodice piece on the chart, and cut the patterns, and cut and basted the dress lining, then when she tried the lining on Mary she had to make changes all along the seams.

Laura had never before known that Ma hated sewing. Her gentle face did not show it now, and her voice was never exasperated. But her patience was so tight around her mouth that Laura knew she hated sewing as much as Laura did.

They were worried, too, because while they were buying the dress goods Mrs. White had told them that she had heard from her sister in Iowa that hoop skirts were coming back, in New York. There were no hoops yet to be bought in town, but Mr. Clancy was thinking of ordering some.

"I declare, I don't know," Ma said, worrying about hoop skirts. Mrs. Boast had had a *Godey's Lady's Book* last year. If she had one now, it would decide the question. But Pa must cut the oats and the hay; they were all too tired on Sundays to make the long, hot trip to the Boasts' claim. When at last Pa saw Mr.

Boast in town one Saturday, he said that Mrs. Boast did not have a new *Godey's Lady's Book.*

"We'll just make the skirts wide enough, so if hoops do come back, Mary can buy some in Iowa and wear them," Ma decided. "Meanwhile, her petticoats can hold the skirts out full."

They had made four new petticoats for Mary, two of unbleached muslin, one of bleached muslin, and one of fine white cambric. Around the bottom of the fine cambric one, Laura had sewed with careful, tiny stitches the six yards of knitted lace that she had given Mary for Christmas.

They had made for her two gray flannel petticoats and three red flannel union suits. Around the top of the petticoats' hems, Laura made a row of catch-stitching in bright, red yarn. It was pretty on the gray flannel. She back-stitched all the seams of the petticoats and the long red flannel union suits, and around the necks and the wrists of the long red sleeves she catch-stitched a trimming of blue yarn.

She was using all the pretty yarns that had come in last winter's Christmas barrel, but she was glad to do it. Not one of the girls in college would have prettier underwear than Mary's.

When Ma had back-stitched the seams of Mary's dresses and carefully ironed them flat, Laura sewed the whalebone stays onto the underarm seams and dart-seams of the basques. She took great pains to sew them evenly on both edges without making the tiniest wrinkle in the seams, so that the basque would fit trimly and smoothly on the outside. This was such anxious work that it made the back of her neck ache.

Now the basque of Mary's best dress was ready to try on for the last time. It was brown cashmere, lined with brown cambric. Small brown buttons buttoned it down the front, and on either side of the buttons and around the bottom Ma had trimmed it with a narrow, shirred strip of brown-and-blue plaid, with red threads and golden threads running through it. A high collar of the plaid was sewed on, and Ma held in her hand a gathered length of white machine-made lace. The lace was to be fitted inside the collar, so that it would fall a little over the top.

"Oh, Mary, it's beautiful. The back fits without a wrinkle,

and so do the shoulders," Laura told her. "And the sleeves look absolutely skin-tight to the elbows."

"They are," Mary said. "I don't know if I can button——"

Laura went around in front. "Hold your breath, Mary. Breathe out, and hold it," she advised anxiously.

"It's too tight," Ma said in despair. Some of the buttons strained in the buttonholes, some could not be buttoned at all.

"Don't breathe, Mary! Don't breathe!" Laura said frantically, and quickly she unbuttoned the straining buttons. "Now you can." Mary breathed, outbursting from the open bodice.

"Oh, how ever did I make such a mistake," Ma said. "That bodice fitted well enough last week."

Laura had a sudden thought. "It's Mary's corsets! It must be. The corset strings must have stretched."

It was so. When Mary held her breath again and Laura pulled tight the corset strings, the bodice buttoned, and it fitted beautifully.

"I'm glad I don't have to wear corsets yet," said Carrie.

"Be glad while you can be," said Laura. "You'll have to wear them pretty soon." Her corsets were a sad affliction to her, from the time she put them on in the morning until she took them off at night. But when girls pinned up their hair and wore skirts down to their shoe-tops, they must wear corsets.

"You should wear them all night," Ma said. Mary did, but Laura could not bear at night the torment of the steels that would not let her draw a deep breath. Always before she could get to sleep, she had to take off her corsets.

"What your figure will be, goodness knows," Ma warned her. "When I was married, your Pa could span my waist with his two hands."

"He can't now," Laura answered, a little saucily. "And he seems to like you."

"You must not be saucy, Laura," Ma reproved her, but Ma's cheeks flushed pink and she could not help smiling.

Now she fitted the white lace into Mary's collar and pinned it so that it fell gracefully over the collar's edge and made a full cascade between the collar's ends in front.

They all stood back to admire. The gored skirt of brown cashmere was smooth and rather tight in front, but gathered full around the sides and back, so that it would be ample for hoops. In front it touched the floor evenly, in back it swept into a graceful short train that swished when Mary turned. All around the bottom was a pleated flounce.

The overskirt was of the brown-and-blue plaid. It was shirred in front, it was draped up at the sides to show more of the skirt beneath, and at the back it fell in rich, full puffs, caught up above the flounced train.

Above all this, Mary's waist rose slim in the tight, smooth bodice. The neat little buttons ran up to the soft white lace cascading under Mary's chin. The brown cashmere was smooth as paint over her sloping shoulders and down to her elbows; then the sleeves widened. A shirring of the plaid curved around them, and the wide wrists fell open, showing a lining of white lace ruffles that set off Mary's slender hands.

Mary was beautiful in that beautiful dress. Her hair was silkier and more golden than the golden silk threads in the plaid. Her blind eyes were bluer than the blue in it. Her cheeks were pink, and her figure was so stylish.

"Oh, Mary," Laura said. "You look exactly as if you'd stepped out of a fashion plate. There won't be, there just can't be, one single girl in college who can hold a candle to you."

"Do I really look so well, Ma?" Mary asked timidly, and she flushed pinker.

For once Ma did not guard against vanity. "Yes, Mary, you do," she said. "You are not only as stylish as can be, you are beautiful. No matter where you go, you will be a pleasure to every eye that sees you. And, I am thankful to say, you may be sure your clothes are equal to any occasion."

They could not look at her longer. She was almost fainting from the heat, in that woolen dress. They laid it carefully away, done at last, and a great success. There were only a few more things to be done now. Ma must make Mary a winter hat of velvet, and knit some stockings for her, and Laura was knitting her a pair of mitts, of brown silk thread.

"I can finish them in spare time," Laura said. "We're through with the sewing, in time for me to help Pa make hay."

She liked working with Pa, and she liked working outdoors in the sun and wind. Besides, secretly she was hoping to leave off her corsets while she worked in the haying.

"I suppose you may help to load the hay," Ma agreed reluctantly, "but it will be stacked in town."

"Oh, Ma, *no!* Do we have to move to town again?" Laura cried.

"Modulate your voice, Laura," Ma said gently. "Remember, 'Her voice was ever gentle, low, and soft, an excellent thing in woman.' "

"Do we have to go to town?" Laura murmured.

"Your Pa and I think best not to risk a winter in this house until he can make it more weatherproof," said Ma. "You know that we could not have lived through last winter here."

"Maybe this winter won't be so bad," Laura pleaded.

"We must not tempt Providence," Ma said firmly. Laura knew it was decided; they had to live in town again next winter, and she must make the best of it.

That evening when the flock of happy blackbirds was swirling at play in the sunset air above the oatfield, Pa took out his shotgun and shot them. He did not like to do it, and in the house no one liked to hear the shots, but they knew it must be done. Pa must protect the crops. The horses and Ellen and her calves would live on hay that winter, but the oats and the corn were cash crops. They would sell for money to pay taxes and buy coal.

As soon as the dew was off the grass next morning, Pa went out to cut it with the mowing machine. In the house Ma began to make Mary's velvet hat, and Laura busily knitted a brown silk mitt. At eleven o'clock Ma said, "Mercy, it's time to start dinner already. Run out, Laura, and see if you can find a mess of roasting ears to boil."

The corn was taller than Laura now, a lavish sight to see, with its long leaves rustling thickly and its nodding tasseled tops. As Laura went in between the rows, a great black swirl of birds rose up and whirled above her. The noise of their wings was louder than the rustling of all the long leaves. The birds were so many that they made a shadow like a cloud. It passed swiftly over the corn tops and the crowd of birds settled again.

The ears of corn were plentiful. Nearly every stalk had two ears on it, some had three. The tassels were dry, only a little pollen was still flying, and the cornsilks hung like thick, green hair from the tips of the green cornhusks. Here and there a tuft of cornsilk was turning brown, and the ear felt full in the husk when Laura gently pinched it. To make sure, before she tore it from the stalk, she parted the husks to see the rows of milky kernels.

Blackbirds kept flying up around her. Suddenly she stood stock-still. The blackbirds were eating the corn!

Here and there she saw bare tips of ears. The husks were stripped back, and kernels were gone from the cobs. While she stood there, blackbirds settled around her. Their claws clung to the ears, their sharp beaks ripped away the husks, and quickly pecking they swallowed the kernels.

Silently, desperately, Laura ran at them. She felt as if she were screaming. She beat at the birds with her sunbonnet. They rose up swirling on noisy wings and settled again to the corn, before her, behind her, all around her. They swung clinging to the ears, ripping away the husks, swallowing the corn crop. She could do nothing against so many.

She took a few ears in her apron and went to the house. Her heart was beating fast and her wrists and knees trembled. When Ma asked what was the matter, she did not like to answer.

"The blackbirds are in the corn," she said. "Oughtn't I to tell Pa?"

"Blackbirds always eat a little corn, I wouldn't worry about it," said Ma. "You might take him a cold drink."

In the hayfield, Pa was not much troubled about the blackbirds. He said he had about cleaned them out of the oats, he had shot a hundred or more. "Likely they'll do some harm to the corn, but that can't be helped," he said.

"There are so many of them," Laura said. "Pa, if you don't get a corn crop, can—can Mary go to college?"

Pa looked bleak. "You think it's as bad as that?"

"There's so many of them," said Laura.

Pa glanced at the sun. "Well, another hour can't make much difference. I'll see about it when I come to dinner."

At noon he took his shotgun to the cornfield. He walked between the corn rows and shot into the cloud of blackbirds as it rose. Every shot brought down a hail of dead birds, but the black cloud settled into the corn again. When he had shot away all his cartridges, the swirl of wings seemed no thinner.

There was not a blackbird in the oatfield. They had left it. But they had eaten every kernel of oats that could be dug out of the shocks. Only straw was left.

Ma thought that she and the girls could keep them away from the corn. They tried to do it. Even Grace ran up and down the rows, screeching and waving her little sunbonnet. The blackbirds only swirled around them and settled again to the ears of corn, tearing the husks and pecking away the kernels.

"You'll wear yourselves out for nothing, Caroline," said Pa. "I'll go to town and buy more cartridges."

When he had gone, Ma said, "Let's see if we can't keep them off till he gets back."

They ran up and down, in the sun and heat, stumbling over the rough sods, screeching and shouting and waving their arms. Sweat ran down their faces and their backs, the sharp corn-leaves cut their hands and cheeks. Their throats ached from yelling. And always the swirling wings rose and settled again. Always scores of blackbirds were clinging to the ears, and sharp beaks were tearing and pecking.

At last Ma stopped. "It's no use, girls," she said.

Pa came with more cartridges. All that afternoon he shot blackbirds. They were so thick that every pellet of shot brought down a bird. It seemed that the more he shot, the more there were. It seemed that all the blackbirds in the Territory were hurrying to that feast of corn.

At first there were only common blackbirds. Then came larger, yellow-headed blackbirds, and blackbirds with red heads and a spot of red on each wing. Hundreds of them came.

In the morning a dark spray of blackbirds rose and fell above the cornfield. After breakfast Pa came to the house, bringing both hands full of birds he had shot.

"I never heard of anyone's eating blackbirds," he said, "but these must be good meat, and they're as fat as butter."

"Dress them, Laura, and we'll have them fried for dinner," said Ma. "There's no great loss without some small gain."

Laura dressed the birds, and at noon Ma heated the frying-pan and laid them in it. They fried in their own fat, and at dinner everyone agreed that they were the tenderest, most delicious meat that had ever been on that table.

After dinner, Pa brought another armful of blackbirds and an armful of corn.

"We might as well figure that the crop's gone," he said. "This corn's a little too green, but we'd better eat what we can of it before the blackbirds get it all."

"I don't know why I didn't think of it sooner!" Ma exclaimed. "Laura and Carrie, hurry and pick every ear that's possibly old enough to make dried corn. Surely we can save a little, to eat next winter."

Laura knew why Ma had not thought of that sooner; she was too distracted. The corn crop was gone. Pa would have to take from his savings to pay taxes and buy coal. Then how could they manage to send Mary to college this fall?

The blackbirds were so thick now that between the corn rows their wings beat rough against Laura's arms and battered her sunbonnet. She felt sharp little blows on her head, and Carrie cried out that the birds were pecking her. They seemed to feel that the corn was theirs, and to be fighting for it. They rose up harsh at Laura's face and Carrie's, and flew scolding and pecking at their sunbonnets.

Not much corn was left. Even the youngest ears, on which the kernels were hardly more than blisters, had been stripped and pecked at. But Laura and Carrie several times filled their aprons with ears only partly eaten.

When Laura looked for the blackbirds, to dress them for dinner, she could not find them and Ma would not say where they were.

"Wait and see," Ma answered mysteriously. "Meantime, we'll boil this corn, and cut it off the cobs, to dry."

There is a knack to cutting corn from a cob. The knife must slice evenly, the whole length of the rows, cutting deep enough to get almost the whole kernel, but not so deep as to cut even an edge from the sharp pocket in which each kernel grows. The kernels fall away in milky slabs, moist and sticky.

Ma spread these on a clean, old tablecloth laid outdoors in the sunshine, and she covered them with another cloth, to keep away the blackbirds and the chickens and the flies. The hot sun would dry the corn, and next winter, soaked and boiled, it would be good eating.

"That's an Indian idea," Pa remarked, when he came to dinner. "You'll admit yet, Caroline, there's something to be said for Indians."

"If there is," Ma replied, "you've already said it, many's the time, so I needn't." Ma hated Indians, but now she was brimming with some secret. Laura guessed that it must be the missing blackbirds. "Comb your hair and sit up to the table, Charles," Ma said.

She opened the oven door, and took out the tin milk pan. It was full of something covered thickly over with delicately browned biscuit crust. She set it before Pa and he looked at it amazed. "Chicken pie!"

" 'Sing a song of sixpence—' " said Ma.

Laura went on from there, and so did Carrie and Mary and even Grace.

A pocket full of rye,
Four and twenty blackbirds,
Baked in a pie!
When the pie was opened
The birds began to sing.
Was not that a dainty dish
To set before the king?

"Well, I'll be switched!" said Pa. He cut into the pie's crust with a big spoon, and turned over a big chunk of it onto a plate. The underside was steamed and fluffy. Over it he poured spoonfuls of thin brown gravy, and beside it he laid half a blackbird, browned, and so tender that the meat was slipping from the bones. He handed that first plate across the table to Ma.

The scent of that opened pie was making all their mouths water so that they had to swallow again and again while they waited for their portions, and under the table the kitty curved against their legs, her hungry purring running into anxious miows.

"The pan held twelve birds," said Ma. "Just two apiece, but one is all that Grace can possibly eat, so that leaves three for you, Charles."

"It takes you to think up a chicken pie, a year before there's chickens to make it with," Pa said. He ate a mouthful and said, "This beats a chicken pie all hollow."

They all agreed that blackbird pie was even better than chicken pie. There were, besides, new potatoes and peas, and sliced cucumbers, and young boiled carrots that Ma had thinned from the rows, and creamy cottage cheese. And the day was not even Sunday. As long as the blackbirds lasted, and the garden was green, they could eat like this every day.

Laura thought, "Ma is right, there is always something to be thankful for." Still, her heart was heavy. The oats and the corn crop were gone. She did not know how Mary could go to college now. The beautiful new dress, the two other new dresses, and the pretty underwear, must be laid away until next year. It was a cruel disappointment to Mary.

Pa ate the last spoonful of pink, sugary cream from his saucer of tomatoes, and drank his tea. Dinner was over. He got up and took his hat from its nail and he said to Ma, "Tomorrow's Saturday. If you'll plan to go to town with me, we can pick out Mary's trunk."

Mary gasped. Laura cried out, "Is Mary going to college?"

Pa was astonished. He asked, "What's the matter with you, Laura?"

"How can she?" Laura asked him. "There isn't any corn, or any oats."

"I didn't realize you're old enough to be worrying," said Pa. "I'm going to sell the heifer calf."

Mary cried out, "Oh *no!* Not the heifer!"

In another year the heifer would be a cow. Then they would have had two cows. Then they would have had milk and butter all the year around. Now, if Pa sold the heifer, they would have to wait two more years for the little calf to grow up.

"Selling her will help out," said Pa. "I ought to get all of fifteen dollars for her."

"Don't worry about it, girls," said Ma. "We must cut our coat to fit the cloth."

"Oh, Pa, it sets you back a whole year," Mary mourned.

"Never mind, Mary," said Pa. "It's time you were going to college, and now we've made up our minds you're going. A flock of pesky blackbirds can't stop us."

CHAPTER 10

Mary Goes to College

THE last day came. Tomorrow Mary was going away.

Pa and Ma had brought home her new trunk. It was covered outside with bright tin, pressed into little bumps that made a pattern. Strips of shiny varnished wood were riveted around its middle and up its corners, and three strips ran lengthwise of its curved lid. Short pieces of iron were screwed onto the corners, to protect the wooden strips. When the lid was shut down, two iron tongues fitted into two small iron pockets, and two pairs of iron rings came together so that the trunk could be locked with padlocks.

"It's a good, solid trunk," Pa said. "And I got fifty feet of stout new rope to rope it with."

Mary's face shone while she felt it over carefully with her sensitive fingers and Laura told her about the bright tin and shiny yellow wood. Ma said, "It is the very newest style in trunks, Mary, and it should last you a lifetime."

Inside, the trunk was smooth-polished wood. Ma lined it carefully with newspapers, and packed tightly into it all Mary's belongings. Every corner she crammed with wadded newspapers, so firmly that nothing could move during the rough journey on the train. She put in many layers of newspapers, too, for she feared that Mary did not have enough clothes to fill the trunk. But when everything was in and cram-jammed down as tightly as possible, the paper-covered mound rose up high enough to fill the curved lid, and Ma sat on it to hold it down while Pa snapped the padlocks.

Then, rolling the trunk end over end, and over and over, Pa tugged and strained loops of the new rope around it, and Laura helped hold the rope tight while he drew the knots fast.

"There," he said finally. "That's one job well done."

As long as they were busy, they could keep pushed deep down inside them the knowledge that Mary was going away. Now everything was done. It was not yet supper time, and the time was empty, for thinking.

Pa cleared his throat and went out of the house. Ma brought her darning basket, but she set it on the table and stood looking out of the window. Grace begged, "Don't go away, Mary, why? Don't go away, tell me a story."

This was the last time that Mary would hold Grace in her lap and tell the story of Grandpa and the panther in the Big Woods of Wisconsin. Grace would be a big girl before Mary came back.

"No, Grace, you must not tease," Ma said, when the story was finished. "What would you like for supper, Mary?" It would be Mary's last supper at home.

"Anything you put on the table is good, Ma," Mary answered.

"It is so hot," Ma said. "I believe I will have cottage cheese balls with onions in them, and the cold creamed peas. Suppose you bring some lettuce and tomatoes from the garden, Laura."

Suddenly Mary asked, "Could I come with you? I would like a little walk."

"You needn't hurry," Ma told them. "There is plenty of time before supper."

They went walking past the stable and up the low hill beyond. The sun was sinking to rest, like a king, Laura thought, drawing the gorgeous curtains of his great bed around him. But Mary was not pleased by such fancies. So Laura said, "The sun is sinking, Mary, into white downy clouds that spread to the edge of the world. All the tops of them are crimson, and streaming down from the top of the sky are great gorgeous curtains of rose and gold with pearly edges. They are a great canopy over the whole prairie. The little streaks of sky between them are clear, pure green."

Mary stood still. "I'll miss our walks," she said, her voice trembling a little.

"So will I." Laura swallowed, and said, "but only think, you are going to college."

"I couldn't have, without you," Mary said. "You have always helped me to study, and you gave Ma your nine dollars for me."

"It wasn't much," said Laura. "It wasn't anything like I wish I——".

"It was, too!" Mary contradicted. "It was a lot."

Laura's throat choked up. She winked her eyelids hard and

took a deep breath but her voice quivered. "I hope you like college, Mary."

"Oh, I will. I will!" Mary breathed. "Think of being able to study and learn— Oh, everything! Even to play the organ. I do owe it partly to you, Laura. Even if you aren't teaching school yet, you have helped me to go."

"I am going to teach school as soon as I am old enough," said Laura. "Then I can help more."

"I wish you didn't have to," Mary said.

"Well, I do have to," Laura replied. "But I can't, till I'm sixteen. That's the law, a teacher has to be sixteen years old."

"I won't be here then," said Mary. Then suddenly they felt as if she were going away forever. The years ahead of them were empty and frightening.

"Oh, Laura, I never have been away from home before. I don't know what I'll do," Mary confessed. She was trembling all over.

"It will be all right," Laura told her stoutly. "Ma and Pa are going with you, and I know you can pass the examinations. Don't be scared."

"I'm not scared. I won't *be* scared," Mary insisted. "I'll be lonesome. But that can't be helped."

"No," Laura said. After a minute she cleared her throat and told Mary, "The sun has gone through the white clouds. It is a huge, pulsing ball of liquid fire. The clouds above it are scarlet and crimson and gold and purple, and the great sweeps of cloud over the whole sky are burning flames."

"It seems to me I can feel their light on my face," Mary said. "I wonder if the sky and the sunsets are different in Iowa?"

Laura did not know. They came slowly down the low hill. This was the end of their last walk together, or at least, their last walk for such a long time that it seemed forever.

"I am sure I can pass the examinations, because you helped me so much," Mary said. "You went over every word of your lessons with me, until I do know everything in the school books. But Laura, what will you do? Pa is spending so much for me—the trunk, and a new coat, a new pair of shoes, the railroad fares, and all—it worries me. How can he ever manage school books and clothes for you and Carrie?"

"Never mind, Pa and Ma will manage," said Laura. "You know they always do."

Early next morning, even before Laura was dressed, Ma was scalding and plucking blackbirds that Pa had killed. She fried them after breakfast, and as soon as they were cool she packed in a shoe box the lunch to take on the train.

Pa and Ma and Mary had bathed the night before. Now Mary put on her best old calico dress and her second-best shoes. Ma dressed in her summer challis, and Pa put on his Sunday suit. A neighbor boy had agreed to drive them to the depot. Pa and Ma would be gone a week, and when they came home without Mary they could walk from town.

The wagon came. The freckled boy, with red hair sticking through a rent in his straw hat, helped Pa load Mary's trunk into the wagon. The sun was shining hot and the wind was blowing.

"Now, Carrie and Grace, be good girls and mind Laura," Ma said. "Remember to keep the chickens' water pan filled, Laura, and look out for hawks, and scald and sun the milk pans every day."

"Yes, Ma," they all answered.

"Good-by," Mary said. "Good-by, Laura. And Carrie. And Grace."

"Good-by," Laura and Carrie managed to say. Grace only stared round-eyed. Pa helped Mary to climb up the wagon-wheel to sit with Ma and the boy on the wagon seat. He took his seat on the trunk.

"All right, let's go," he said to the boy. "Good-by, girls."

The wagon started. Grace's mouth opened wide and she bawled.

"For shame, Grace! For *shame!* a big girl like you, *crying!*" Laura choked out. Her throat was swelling so that it hurt. Carrie looked as though she might cry in a moment. "*Shame* on you!" Laura said again, and Grace gulped down a last sob.

Pa and Ma and Mary did not look back. They had to go. The wagon taking them away left silence behind it. Laura had never felt such a stillness. It was not the happy stillness of the prairie. She felt it in the very pit of her stomach.

"Come," she said. "We'll go into the house."

That silence had settled into the house. It was so still that Laura felt she must whisper. Grace smothered a whimpering. They stood there in their own house and felt nothing around them but silence and emptiness. Mary was gone.

Grace began to cry again and two large tears stood in Carrie's eyes. This would never do. Right now, and for a whole week, everything was in Laura's charge, and Ma must be able to depend upon her.

"Listen to me, Carrie and Grace," she said briskly. "We are going to clean this house from top to bottom, and we'll begin right now! So when Ma comes home, she'll find the fall house-cleaning done."

There had never been such a busy time in all Laura's life. The work was hard, too. She had not realized how heavy a quilt is, to lift soaked and dripping from a tub, and to wring out, and to hang on a line. She had not known how hard it would be, sometimes, never to be cross with Grace who was always trying to help and only making more work. It was amazing, too, how dirty they all got, while cleaning a house that had seemed quite clean. The harder they worked, the dirtier everything became.

The worst day of all was very hot. They had tugged and lugged the straw ticks outdoors, and emptied them and washed them, and when they were dry they had filled them with sweet fresh hay. They had got the bedsprings off the bedsteads and leaned them against the walls, and Laura had jammed her finger. Now they were pulling the bedsteads apart. Laura jerked at one corner and Carrie jerked at the other. The corners came apart, and suddenly the headboard came down on Laura's head so that she saw stars.

"Oh, Laura! did it hurt you?" Carrie cried.

"Well, not very much," Laura said. She pushed the headboard against the wall, and it slid down swiftly and hit her anklebone. "Ouch!" she couldn't help yelling. Then she added, "Let it lie there if it wants to!"

"We have to scrub the floor," Carrie pointed out.

"I know we have to," Laura said grimly. She sat on the floor, gripping her ankle. Her straggling hair stuck to her sweating neck. Her dress was damp and hot and dirty, and her fingernails were positively black. Carrie's face was smudged with dust and sweat and there were bits of hay in her hair.

"We ought to have a bath," Laura murmured. Suddenly she cried out, "*Where's Grace?*"

They had not thought of Grace for some time. Grace had once been lost on the prairie. Two children at Brookings, lost on the prairie, had died before they could be found.

"Here I yam," Grace answered sweetly, coming in. "It's raining."

"No!" Laura exclaimed. Indeed, a shadow was over the house. A few large drops were falling. At that moment, thunder crashed. Laura screamed, "Carrie! The straw ticks! The bedding!"

They ran. The straw ticks were not very heavy, but they were stuffed fat with hay. They were hard to hold on to. The edge kept slipping out of Laura's grasp or Carrie's. When they got one to the house, they had to hold it up edgewise to get it through the doorway.

"We can hold it up or we can move it, we can't do both," Carrie panted. Already the swift thunderstorm was rolling overhead and rain was falling fast.

"Get out of the way!" Laura shouted. Somehow she pushed and carried the whole straw tick into the house. It was too late to bring in the other one, or the bedding from the line. Rain was pouring down.

The bedding would dry on the line, but the other straw tick must be emptied again, washed again, and filled again. Straw ticks must be perfectly dry, or the hay in them would smell musty.

"We can move everything out of the other bedroom into the front room, and go on scrubbing," said Laura. So they did that. For some time there was no sound but thunder and beating rain, and the swish of scrubbing cloths and the wringing out. Laura and Carrie had worked backward on hands and knees almost across the bedroom floor, when Grace called happily, "I'm helping!"

She was standing on a chair and blacking the stove. She was splashed from head to foot with blacking. On the floor all around the stove were dribbles and splotches of blacking.

Grace had filled the blacking box full of water. As she looked up beaming for Laura's approval, she gave the smeared stove top another swipe of the blacking cloth, and pushed the box of soft blacking off it.

Her blue eyes were filled with tears.

Laura gave one wild look at that awful house that Ma had left so neat and pretty. She just managed to say, "Never mind, Grace; don't cry. I'll clean it up." Then she sank down on the stacked pieces of the bedsteads and let her forehead sink to her pulled-up knees.

"Oh, Carrie, I just don't seem to know how to manage the way Ma does!" she almost wailed.

That was the worst day. On Friday the house was almost in order, and they worried lest Ma come home too soon. They worked far into the night that night, and on Saturday it was almost midnight before Laura and Carrie took their baths and collapsed to sleep. But for Sunday the house was immaculate.

The floor around the stove was scrubbed bone-white. Only faintest traces of the blacking remained. The beds were made up with clean, bright quilts and they smelled sweetly of fresh hay. The windowpanes glittered. Every shelf in the cupboards was scrubbed and every dish washed. "And we'll eat bread and drink milk from now on, and *keep* the dishes clean!" said Laura.

There remained only the curtains to be washed and ironed and hung, and of course the usual washing to do, on Monday. They were glad that Sunday is a day of rest.

Early Monday morning, Laura washed the curtains. They were dry when she and Carrie hung the rest of the washing on the line. They sprinkled the curtains and ironed them, and hung them at the windows. The house was perfect.

"We'll keep Grace out of it till Pa and Ma come home," Laura said privately to Carrie. Neither of them felt like even taking a walk. So they sat on the grass in the shade of the house and watched Grace run about, and watched for the smoke of the train.

They saw it rolling up from the prairie and fading slowly along the skyline like a line of writing that they could not read. They heard the train whistle. After a pause it whistled again, and the curling smoke began again to write low above the skyline. They had almost decided that Pa and Ma had not come yet, when they saw them small and far away, walking out on the road from town.

Then all the lonesomeness for Mary came back, as sharply as if she had just gone away.

They met Pa and Ma at the edge of Big Slough, and for a little while they all talked at once.

Pa and Ma were greatly pleased with the college. They said it was a fine place, a large brick building. Mary would be warm and comfortable in it when winter came. She would have good food, and she was with a crowd of pleasant girls. Ma liked her roommate very much. The teachers were kind. Mary had passed the examinations with flying colors. Ma had seen no clothes there nicer than hers. She was going to study political economy, and literature, and higher mathematics, and sewing, knitting, beadwork, and music. The college had a parlor organ.

Laura was so glad for Mary that she could almost forget the lonesome ache of missing her. Mary had always so loved to study. Now she could revel in studying so much that she had never before had a chance to learn.

"Oh, she must stay there, she *must*," Laura thought, and she renewed her vow to study hard, though she didn't like to, and get a teacher's certificate as soon as she was sixteen, so that she could earn the money to keep Mary in college.

She had forgotten that week of housecleaning, but as they came to the house Ma asked, "Carrie, what are you and Grace smiling about? You're keeping something up your sleeves!"

Then Grace jumped up and down and shouted, "I blacked the stove!"

"So you did," said Ma, going into the house. "It looks very nice, but Grace, I am sure that Laura helped you black it. You must not say—" Then she saw the curtains. "Why, Laura," she said, "did you wash the—and the windows—and— Why, I declare!"

"We did the fall housecleaning for you, Ma," said Laura, and Carrie chimed in, "We washed the bedding, and filled the straw ticks, and scrubbed the floors, and everything."

Ma lifted her hands in surprise, then she sat weakly down and let her hands fall. "My goodness!"

Next day, when she unpacked her valise, she surprised them. She came from the bedroom with three small flat packages, and gave one to Laura, one to Carrie, and one to Grace.

In Grace's package was a picture book. The colored pictures, on shiny paper, were pasted to cloth leaves of many pretty colors, and every leaf was pinked around its edges.

In Laura's package was a beautiful small book, too. It was thin, and wider than it was tall. On its red cover, embossed in gold, were the words,

Autograph Album

The pages, of different soft colors, were blank. Carrie had another exactly like it, except that the cover of hers was blue and gold.

"I found that autograph albums are all the fashion nowadays," said Ma. "All the most fashionable girls in Vinton have them."

"What are they, exactly?" Laura asked.

"You ask a friend to write a verse on one of the blank pages and sign her name to it," Ma explained. "If she has an autograph album, you do the same for her, and you keep the albums to remember each other by."

"I won't mind going to school so much now," said Carrie. "I will show my autograph album to all the strange girls, and if they are nice to me I will let them write in it."

Ma was glad that the autograph albums pleased them both. She said, "Your Pa and I wanted our other girls to have something from Vinton, Iowa, where Mary is going to college."

CHAPTER II

Miss Wilder Teaches School

EARLY on the First Day of School Laura and Carrie set out. They wore their best sprigged calico dresses, for Ma said they would outgrow them before next summer, anyway. They carried their school books under their arms, and Laura carried their tin dinner pail.

The coolness of night still lingered in the early sunlight. Under the high blue sky the green of the prairie was fading to soft brown and mauve. A little wind wandered over it carrying the fragrance of ripening grasses and the pungent smell of wild sunflowers. All along the road the yellow blossoms were nodding, and in its grassy middle they struck with soft thumps against the swinging dinner pail. Laura walked in one wheel track, and Carrie in the other.

"Oh, I do hope Miss Wilder will be a good teacher," said Carrie. "Do you think so?"

"Pa must think so, he's on the school board," Laura pointed out. "Though maybe they hired her because she's the Wilder boy's sister. Oh Carrie, remember those beautiful brown horses?"

"Just because he has those horses doesn't make his sister nice," Carrie argued. "But maybe she is."

"Anyway, she knows how to teach. She has a certificate," said Laura. She sighed, thinking how hard she must study. She must study to get her own certificate.

Main Street was growing longer. Now a new livery stable was on Pa's side of it, across from the bank. A new grain elevator stood tall beyond the far end of the street, across the railroad tracks.

"Why are all those lots vacant, between the livery stable and Pa's?" Carrie wondered.

Laura did not know. Anyway, she liked the wild prairie grasses there. Pa's new haystacks stood thick around his barn. He would not have to haul hay from the claim to burn this winter.

She and Carrie turned west on Second Street. Beyond the

schoolhouse, new little claim shanties were scattered now. A new flour mill was racketing by the railroad tracks, and across the vacant lots between Second Street and Third Street could be seen the skeleton of the new church building on Third Street. Men were working on it. A great many strangers were in the crowd of pupils gathered near the schoolhouse door.

Carrie timidly shrank back, and Laura's knees weakened, but she must be brave for Carrie, so she went on boldly. The palms of her hands grew moist with sweat when so many eyes looked at her. There must have been twenty boys and girls.

Taking firm grip on her courage, Laura walked up to them and Carrie went with her. The boys stood back a little on one side and the girls on the other. It seemed to Laura that she simply could not walk to the schoolhouse steps.

Then suddenly she saw on the steps Mary Power and Minnie Johnson. She knew them; they had been in school last fall, before the blizzards came. Mary Power said, "Hello, Laura Ingalls!"

Her dark eyes were glad to see Laura, and so was Minnie Johnson's freckled face. Laura felt all right then. She felt she would always be very fond of Mary Power.

"We've picked out our seats, we're going to sit together," said Minnie. "But why don't you sit across the aisle from us?"

They went into the schoolhouse together. Mary's books and Minnie's were on the back desk next the wall, on the girls' side. Laura laid hers on the desk across the aisle. Those two back seats were the very best seats. Carrie, of course, must sit nearer the teacher, with the smaller girls.

Miss Wilder was coming down the aisle, with the school bell in her hand. Her hair was dark and her eyes were gray. She seemed a very pleasant person. Her dark gray dress was stylishly made, like Mary's best one, tight and straight in the front, with a pleated ruffle just touching the floor, and an overskirt draped and puffed above a little train.

"You girls have chosen your seats, haven't you?" she said pleasantly.

"Yes, ma'am," Minnie Johnson said bashfully, but Mary Power smiled and said, "I am Mary Power, and this is Minnie Johnson, and Laura Ingalls. We would like to keep these seats if we may, please. We are the biggest girls in school."

"Yes, you may keep these seats," said Miss Wilder, very pleasantly.

She went to the door and rang the bell. Pupils came crowding in, till nearly all the seats were filled. On the girls' side, only one seat was left vacant. On the boys' side, all the back seats were empty because the big boys would not come to school until the winter term. They were still working on the claims now.

Laura saw that Carrie was sitting happily with Mamie Beardsley, near the front where younger girls should sit. Then suddenly she saw a strange girl hesitating in the aisle. She seemed about as old as Laura, and as shy. She was small and slim. Her soft brown eyes were large in a small round face. Her hair was black and softly wavy, and around her forehead the short hairs curled. She was flushing pink from nervousness. Timidly she glanced at Laura.

Unless Laura would take her as a seatmate, she must sit alone in the empty seat.

Quickly Laura smiled, and patted the seat beside her. The new girl's great brown eyes laughed joyously. She laid her books on the desk and sat down beside Laura.

When Miss Wilder had called the school to order, she took the record book and went from desk to desk, writing down the pupils' names. Laura's seatmate answered that her name was Ida Wright, but she was called Ida Brown. She was the adopted daughter of Reverend Brown and Mrs. Brown.

Rev. Brown was the new Congregational minister who had just come to town. Laura knew that Pa and Ma did not like him very much, but she was sure she liked Ida.

Miss Wilder had put the record book in her desk and was ready to begin school, when the door opened again. Everyone looked to see who had come tardily to school on this First Day.

Laura could not believe her eyes. The girl who came in was Nellie Oleson, from Plum Creek in Minnesota.

She had grown taller than Laura, and she was much slimmer. She was willowy, while Laura was still as round and dumpy as a little French horse. But Laura knew her at once, though it was two years since she had seen her. Nellie's nose was still held high and sniffing, her small eyes were still set close to it, and her mouth was prim and prissy.

Nellie was the girl who had made fun of Laura and Mary because they were only country girls, while her father was a storekeeper. She had spoken impudently to Ma. She had been mean to Jack, the good and faithful bulldog, who was dead now.

She had come late to school, yet she stood looking as if the school were not good enough for her. She wore a fawn-colored dress made with a polonaise. Deep pleated ruffles were around the bottom of the skirt, around her neck, and falling from the edges of the wide sleeves. At her throat was a full jabot of lace. Her fair, straight hair was drawn smoothly back from her sharp face, and twisted into a tall French knot. She held her head high and looked scornfully down her nose.

"I would like a back seat, if you please," she said to Miss Wilder. And she gave Laura a nudging look that said, "Get out and give me that seat."

Laura sat more solidly and firmly where she was, and looked back at Nellie through narrowed eyes.

Everyone else looked at Miss Wilder to see what she would do. Miss Wilder cleared her throat nervously. Laura kept on looking at Nellie, till Nellie looked away. She looked at Minnie Johnson and said, nodding toward Minnie's seat, "That place will do."

"Will you change, Minnie?" Miss Wilder asked. But she had promised that Minnie might sit there.

Slowly Minnie answered, "Yes, m'am." Slowly she picked up her books and went forward to the vacant seat. Mary Power did not move, and Nellie stood waiting in the aisle; she would not go around the seat to the place that Minnie had left.

"Now, Mary," Miss Wilder said, "if you will move over and make room for our new girl, we will all be settled."

Mary stood up. "I'll go with Minnie," she said shortly. "I'd rather."

Nellie sat down smiling. She had the best seat in the room, and the whole desk for her own use.

Laura was meanly glad to hear her tell Miss Wilder, for the record book, that her father was living on a claim north of town. So Nellie herself was a country girl now! Then suddenly Laura realized that Pa was moving to town for the winter; she and Carrie would be town girls.

Miss Wilder rapped the desk with her ruler, and said,

"Attention, boys and girls!" Then she made a little speech, smiling all the time.

She said, "Now we are all ready to begin the school term, and we're all going to do our best to make it a success, aren't we? You know you are all here to learn as much as you possibly can, and I am here to help you. You must not look upon me as a taskmistress, but as a friend. We are all going to be the very best of friends, I'm sure."

The small boys were squirming, and Laura wanted to. She could not look at Miss Wilder's smiling any more.

She only wished that Miss Wilder would stop talking. But Miss Wilder went on in her smiling voice: "None of us will ever be unkind or selfish, will we? I am sure that not one of you will ever be unruly, so there need be no thought of punishments here in our happy school. We shall all be friends together and love and help each other."

Then at last she said, "You may take your books."

There were no recitations that morning, for Miss Wilder was sorting the pupils into their classes. Laura and Ida, Mary Power and Minnie, and Nellie Oleson, were the only big girls. They were the most advanced class, and the whole class until the big boys would come to school.

At recess they stayed in a group, getting acquainted. Ida was as warm and friendly as she looked. "I'm only an adopted child," she said. "Mother Brown took me out of a Home, but she must have liked me to do that, don't you think so?"

"Of course she liked you, she couldn't have helped it," Laura said. She could imagine what a pretty baby Ida must have been, with her black curls and big, laughing brown eyes.

But Nellie wanted all attention for herself.

"I really don't know whether we'll like it out here," Nellie said. "We are from the East. We are not used to such a rough country and rough people."

"You come from western Minnesota, from the same place we did," said Laura.

"Oh, *that!*" Nellie brushed away Minnesota with her hand. "We were there only a little while. We come from the East, from New York State."

"We all come from the East," Mary Power told her shortly. "Come on, let's all go outdoors in the sunshine."

"My goodness, no!" said Nellie. "Why, this wind will tan your skin!"

They were all tanned but Nellie, and she went on airily, "I may have to live out in this rough country for a little while, but I shan't let it spoil my complexion. In the East, a lady always keeps her skin white and her hands smooth." Nellie's hands were white and slender.

There was no time to go outdoors, anyway. Recess was over. Miss Wilder went to the door and rang the bell.

At home that night, Carrie chattered about the day at school until Pa said she was as talkative as a bluejay. "Let Laura get a word in edgewise. Why are you so quiet, Laura? Anything go wrong?"

Then Laura told about Nellie Oleson and all she had said and done. She finished, "Miss Wilder shouldn't have let her take the seat away from Mary Power and Minnie."

"Nor should you ever criticize a teacher, Laura," Ma gently reminded her.

Laura felt her cheeks grow hot. She knew what a great opportunity it was, to go to school. Miss Wilder was there to help her learn, and she should be grateful, she should never impertinently criticize. She should only try to be perfect in her lessons and in deportment. Yet she could not help thinking, "Just the same, she shouldn't have! It was not fair."

"So the Olesons came from New York State, did they?" Pa was amused. "That's not so much to brag about."

Laura remembered then that Pa had lived in New York State when he was a boy.

He went on, "I don't know how it happened, but Oleson lost everything he had in Minnesota. He hasn't a thing in the world now but his homestead claim, and they tell me his folks back East are helping him out, or he couldn't hang on to that till he makes a crop. Maybe Nellie feels she's got to brag a little, to hold her own. I wouldn't let it worry me, Laura."

"But she had such pretty clothes," Laura protested. "And she can't do a bit of work, she keeps her face and her hands so white."

"You could wear your sunbonnet, you know," said Ma. "As for her pretty dresses, likely they come out of a barrel, and maybe she's like the girl in the song, who was so fine 'with a double ruffle around her neck and nary a shoe to wear.' "

Laura supposed she should be sorry for Nellie, but she wasn't. She wished that Nellie Oleson had stayed in Plum Creek.

Pa got up from the supper table and drew his chair near the open door. He said, "Bring me the fiddle, Laura. I want to try a song I heard a fellow singing the other day. He whistled the chorus. I believe the fiddle will beat his whistling."

Softly Laura and Carrie washed the dishes, not to miss a note of the music. Pa sang, low and longingly, with the sweet clear voice of the fiddle.

Then meet me—Oh, meet me,
When you hear
The first whip-poor-will call—

"Whip-poor-will," the fiddle called, and fluting, throbbing like the throat of the bird, "Whip-poor-will," the fiddle answered. Near and pleading, "Whip-poor-will," then far and soft but coming nearer, "Whip-poor-will," till all the gathering twilight was filled with the wooing of the birds.

Laura's thoughts untangled from their ugly snarls and became smooth and peaceful. She thought, "I will be good. It doesn't matter how hateful Nellie Oleson is, I will be good."

CHAPTER 12

Snug for Winter

ALL through the pleasant fall weather Laura and Carrie were busy girls. In the mornings they helped do the chores and get breakfast. Then they filled their dinner pail, dressed for school and hurried away on the mile walk to town. After school they hurried home, for there was work to do until darkness came.

Saturday was a whole day of busy working, in a hurry to be ready to move to town.

Laura and Carrie picked up potatoes while Pa dug them. They cut the tops from turnips and helped Pa pile them in the wagon. They pulled and topped the carrots, too, and the beets and onions. They gathered the tomatoes and the ground-cherries.

The ground-cherries grew on low leafy bushes. Thick on the stems under the large leaves hung the six-cornered bells, pale gray and thinner than paper, and inside each bell was a plump, golden, juicy round fruit.

The husk-tomatoes were covered with a smooth, dull-brown husk. When this was opened there lay the round, bright-purple tomato, larger than a ground-cherry but much smaller than the red tomatoes that openly flaunted their bright colors.

All day long while the girls were in school, Ma made preserves of the red tomatoes, of the purple husk-tomatoes, and of the golden ground-cherries. She made pickles of the green tomatoes that would not have time to ripen before it froze. The house was full of the sirupy scent of preserves and the spicy odor of pickles.

"We will take our provisions with us when we move to town this time," said Pa with satisfaction. "And we must go soon. I don't want another October blizzard to catch us in this thin-walled little house."

"This winter isn't going to be as hard as last winter," Laura said. "The weather doesn't feel the same."

"No," Pa agreed. "It isn't likely this winter will be as hard, nor come as soon, but this time I intend to be ready for it when it does come."

He hauled the oat straw and the corn fodder and stacked them near his haystacks in town. He hauled the potatoes and turnips, beets and carrots, and stored them in the cellar of his store building. Then busily all one Monday evening and far into the night, Laura and Carrie helped Ma pack clothes and dishes and books.

It was then that Laura discovered a secret. She was on her knees, lifting winter underwear out of Ma's bottom bureau drawer, and under the red flannels she felt something hard. She put in her hand and drew out a book.

It was a perfectly new book, beautifully bound in green cloth with a gilded pattern pressed into it. The smooth, straight, gilt edges of the pages looked like solid gold. On the cover two curving scrolls of lovely, fancy letters made the words,

TENNYSON'S
POEMS

Laura was so startled and so amazed by this rich and beautiful book, hidden there among the flannels, that she almost dropped it. It fell open on her hands. In the lamplight the fresh, untouched pages lay spread, each exciting with unread words printed upon it in clear, fine type. Straight, thin red lines enclosed each oblong of printing, like the treasure it was, and outside the red lines were the pages' pure margins.

Near the bottom of the left-hand page was a short line in larger type: THE LOTOS-EATERS.

"Courage!" was the first word under that, and breathlessly Laura read,

"Courage!" he said, and pointed to the land,
"This mounting wave will roll us shoreward soon."
In the afternoon they came unto a land
In which it seemed always afternoon.
All round the coast the languid air did swoon,

Breathing like one that hath a weary dream.
Full-faced above the valley stood the moon;
And, like a——

Laura stopped, aghast. Suddenly she had realized what she was doing. Ma must have hidden this book. Laura had no right to read it. Quickly she shut her eyes, and then she shut the book. It was almost more than she could do, not to read just one word more, just to the end of that one line. But she knew that she must not yield one tiny bit of temptation.

She put the book where it had been, between the red flannels. She put the flannels back into the drawer, shut the drawer, and opened the drawer above it. Then she did not know what to do.

She should confess to Ma what she had done. But instantly she knew that Ma must be keeping the book hidden, for a surprise. She thought swiftly, and her heart was pounding hard, that Pa and Ma must have bought that book in Vinton, Iowa; they must be saving it for a Christmas present. A book so rich and fine, a book of poems, could only be a Christmas present. And Laura was the oldest girl at home now; it must be a Christmas present for her!

If she confessed to Ma, she would spoil their Christmas pleasure, that they were looking forward to. Pa and Ma would be so disappointed.

It seemed a long time since she had found that book, but really it had only been a moment. Ma came in hurriedly and said, "I'll finish in here, Laura, you go to bed now, it's past your bedtime."

"Yes, Ma," Laura said. She knew that Ma had feared she would open that lower drawer and find the book. Never before had she kept a guilty secret from Ma, but now she did not say a word.

After school next day, she and Carrie did not take the long walk to the claim. Instead they stopped at Pa's store building at the corner of Second Street and Main. Pa and Ma had moved into town for the winter.

The stove and the cupboard were set up in the kitchen. Upstairs the bedsteads stood under the slanting shingle roof, the straw ticks lay plumply on them under heaped quilts and pillows. Making the beds was all that Ma had left for Laura and Carrie to do. And Laura was sure that the Christmas book, Tennyson's *Poems*, was hidden in Ma's bureau drawer. She would never look to see, of course.

Yet every time she saw the bureau she could not help thinking,

> Full-faced above the valley stood the moon;
> And, like a——

Like what? She would have to wait until Christmas to learn the rest of that lovely poem. "Courage!" he said, and pointed to the land. "This mounting wave will roll us shoreward soon." In the afternoon they came unto a land in which it seemed always afternoon. But it did not seem to Laura that Christmas was soon.

Downstairs Ma had already made the big storeroom neat and pleasant. The heater was polished, the curtains hung fresh at the windows, the clean little rag rugs lay on the swept floor. The two rocking chairs were in the sunny corner. Mary's was empty.

Often Laura missed Mary so much that she ached. But it would do no good to speak of it. Mary was in college, where she had so wanted to be. A teacher had written Pa that she was well and making rapid progress; soon she would be able to write a letter.

So no one spoke of the emptiness they all felt now. Quietly and cheerfully they went about getting supper and setting the table, and Ma did not know that she sighed when she said, "Well, we are all settled snug for the winter."

"Yes," Pa said. "This time we are well fixed for it."

They were not the only ones who were ready. Everyone in the town had been preparing. The lumberyard was stocked with coal, the merchants had stuffed their stores full of goods. There was flour at the mill, and wheat in its bins.

"We will have coal to burn and something to eat all winter, if the trains can't get through," Pa gloated. It was good to feel so safe and prospering, with food enough and fuel enough so that they need not dread hunger or cold.

Laura missed the pleasant long walks to school and back. She had delighted in them. But now there was no hurry in the mornings, since she had no chores to do. Pa did them all, now that he had no farm work. And the shorter walk was better for Carrie.

Pa and Ma and Laura were worried about Carrie. She had never been strong, and she was not recovering from the hard winter as she should. They spared her all but the lightest housework, and Ma coaxed her appetite with the best there was to eat. Still she was thin and pale, small for her age and spindly. Her eyes were too large in her peaked little face. Often in the mornings, though the walk was only a mile and Laura carried her books, Carrie grew tired before they reached the schoolhouse. Sometimes her head ached so badly that she failed in her recitations. Living in town was easier. It would be much better for Carrie.

CHAPTER 13

School Days

LAURA was enjoying school. She knew all the pupils now, and she and Ida, Mary Powers and Minnie, were becoming fast friends. At recess and noon they were always together.

In the crisp, sunny weather the boys played ante-over and catch, and sometimes they just threw the ball against the schoolhouse and ran jostling and bumping together to catch it in the wild prairie grasses. Often they coaxed Laura, "Come, play with us, Laura. Aw, come on!"

It was tomboyish to run and play, at her age. But she did so love to run and jump and catch the ball and throw it, that sometimes she did join in the games. The boys were only little boys. She liked them, and she never complained when the games grew rough now and then. One day she overheard Charley saying, "She isn't a sissy, even if she is a girl."

Hearing that made her feel glad and cozy. When even little boys like a big girl, she knows that everyone likes her.

The other girls knew that Laura was not really a tomboy, even when her face was hot from running and jumping, and the hairpins were coming loose in her hair. Ida sometimes played, too, and Mary Power and Minnie would look on, applauding. Only Nellie Oleson turned up her nose.

Nellie would not even go walking, though they asked her politely. It was all "too rough, really," she said.

"She's afraid of spoiling her New York State complexion," Ida laughed.

"I think she stays in the schoolhouse to make friends with Miss Wilder," said Mary Power. "She talks to her all the time."

"Well, let her. We have a much better time without her," Minnie said.

"Miss Wilder used to live in New York State, too. Likely that is what they talk about," Laura remarked.

Mary Power gave her a laughing, sidelong glance and squeezed her arm. No one called Nellie "teacher's pet," but that was what they were thinking. Laura did not care. She was at the head of the class in all their studies, and she need not be a teacher's pet to stay there.

Every evening after supper she studied till bedtime. It was then that she missed Mary most painfully. They had always gone over their lessons together. But she knew that far away in Iowa, Mary was studying, too, and if she were to stay in college and enjoy all its wonderful opportunities of learning, Laura must get a teacher's certificate.

All this went through her head in a flash, while she went walking, arm in arm with Mary Power and Ida.

"You know what I think?" Minnie asked.

"No, what?" they all asked her.

"I bet that's what Nellie's scheming about," Minnie said, and she nodded at a team that was coming toward them along the wagon tracks ahead. It was the brown Morgan horses.

All their slender legs were moving swiftly, their hoofs raising little explosions of dust. Their glossy shoulders glistened, their black manes and tails blew shining in the wind. Their ears pricked forward, and their glancing bright eyes saw everything gaily. Dancing little red tassels trimmed their bridles.

Sunlight ran glistening on the curve of their arched necks, straight along their smooth sides and curving again on their round haunches. And behind them ran a shining new buggy. Its dashboard glittered, its spotless black top curved over the seat on gleaming black spokes, its wheels were red. Laura had never seen such a buggy.

"Why didn't you bow, Laura?" Ida asked when it had sped by.

"Didn't you see him raise his hat to us?" said Mary Power. Laura had seen only the beautiful horses, till the buggy flashed before her eyes.

"Oh, I'm sorry. I didn't mean to be impolite," she said. "They are just like poetry, aren't they?"

"You don't mean she's setting her cap for him, Minnie," Mary Power said. "Why, he's a grown-up man, he's a homesteader."

"I've seen her looking at those horses," said Minnie. "I bet she's made up her mind to get a ride behind them. You know that kind of scheming look she has sometimes. And now that he's got such a buggy——"

"He didn't have any buggy last Fourth of July," said Laura.

"It's just come from the East," Minnie told them. "He ordered it after he sold his wheat crop. He had a wonderful wheat crop." Minnie always knew such news, because her brother Arthur told her.

Slowly Mary Power said, "I do believe you are right, I wouldn't put it past her."

Laura felt a little guilty. She wouldn't make up to Miss Wilder just to get a ride behind Almanzo Wilder's horses. Yet she had often thought that if Miss Wilder liked her, she might someday take her riding behind them.

Miss Wilder had taken a claim on this road, only a quarter of a mile beyond the schoolhouse. She lived there in a little claim shanty. Almanzo often brought her to the schoolhouse in the morning, or stopped after school to take her home. And always, when she saw those horses, Laura hoped that Miss Wilder might, perhaps, sometime, ask her for a ride. Could it be that she was as horrid as Nellie Oleson?

Now that she had seen that buggy, more than ever Laura wanted such a ride. How could she prevent such thoughts, when those horses were so beautiful and the buggy so swift?

"It's almost time for the bell," Ida said, and they all turned back to the schoolhouse. They must not be late. In the entry they drank from the dipper that floated in the water pail there. Then they went in, tanned and windblown, and hot and dusty. Nellie was neat and ladylike, her skin was white, and every hair of her head was in its place.

She looked down her nose at them, and smiled a lofty smile. Laura looked straight back at her, and Nellie gave a little flounce of her shoulder and chin.

"You needn't think you're so much, Laura Ingalls!" Nellie said. "Miss Wilder says your father has nothing much to say about this school, even if he is on the school board."

"Why!" Laura gasped.

"I guess he's got as much to say about this school as anybody, and maybe more!" Ida said stoutly. "Hasn't he, Laura?"

"He certainly has!" Laura cried.

"Yes," said Mary Power. "He has more, because Laura and Carrie are in this school and the others on the board haven't any children."

Laura was furious with rage, that Nellie dared to say anything against Pa. On the steps Miss Wilder was ringing the bell and its noise clanged in Laura's head. She said, "It's just too bad your folks are nothing but country folks, Nellie. If you lived in town, then maybe your father could be on the school board and have something to say about this school."

Nellie was going to slap her. Laura saw her hand rising, and she barely had time to think that she must not, *must not* slap Nellie, and to hope she wouldn't. Then Nellie's hand dropped quickly and she slid into her seat. Miss Wilder had come in.

All the pupils came clattering, and Laura sat down in her own seat. She was still so angry that she could hardly see. Under the desk-top Ida's hand gave her clenched fist a quick little squeeze that meant, "Good for you! You served her right!"

CHAPTER 14

Sent Home from School

MISS WILDER was puzzling everyone in school. From the first day, of course, the boys had been trying to find out how far they could go in naughtiness before she made them behave themselves, and no one could understand why she did not show them.

At first they fidgeted and then they began making little noises with their books and slates. Miss Wilder paid no attention until the noise was disturbing. Then she did not speak sharply to the noisiest boy, but smiled at them all and politely asked them to be quieter.

"I know you do not realize that you are disturbing others," she said.

They did not know what to make of this. When she turned to the blackboard, the noise would grow loud again. The boys even began to whisper.

Every day Miss Wilder asked everyone, several times, to be just a little quieter, please. This was not fair to those who were making no noise at all. Soon all the boys were whispering, nudging each other, and sometimes slyly scuffling in their seats. Some of the little girls wrote notes to each other on their slates.

Still Miss Wilder did not punish anyone. One afternoon she rapped on her desk to call the whole school to attention, and talked to them about how good she was sure they all meant to be. She said she did not believe in punishing children. She meant to rule them by love, not fear. She liked them all and she was sure that they liked her. Even the big girls were embarrassed by her way of talking.

"Birds in their little nests agree," she said, smiling, and Laura and Ida almost squirmed from embarrassment. Besides, that showed that she knew nothing at all about birds.

Miss Wilder kept on always smiling even when her eyes were worried. Only her smiles at Nellie Oleson seemed real. She seemed to feel that she could depend on Nellie Oleson.

"She's a—well, almost a hypocrite," Minnie said, low, one day at recess. They were standing at the window, watching the boys play ball. Miss Wilder and Nellie were chatting together by the stove. It was colder at the window, but the other girls would rather be there.

"I don't think she really is, quite," Mary Power answered. "Do you, Laura?"

"No-o," Laura said. "Not exactly. I think she just hasn't got very good judgment. But she does know everything in the books. She is a good scholar."

"Yes, she is," Mary Power agreed. "But can't a person know what is in books and still have more common sense? I wonder what is going to happen when the big boys come to school, if she can't control these little ones."

Minnie's eyes lighted up with excitement, and Ida laughed. Ida would be good and gay and laughing, no matter what happened, but Mary Power was sober and Laura was worried. She said, "Oh, we must not have trouble in school!" She must be able to study and get a teacher's certificate.

Now that Laura and Carrie were living in town, they went home at noon for a good, hot dinner. Surely the hot food was better for Carrie, though it seemed to make no difference. She was still pale and spindly, and always tired. Often her head ached so badly that she could not learn her spelling. Laura helped her with it. Carrie would know every word in the morning; then when she was called upon to recite, she would make a mistake.

Ida and Nellie still brought their dinners to school, and so did Miss Wilder. They ate together, cozily by the stove. When the other girls came back to school, Ida would join them, but Nellie often chatted with Miss Wilder through the whole noon hour.

Several times she said to the other girls, with a sly smile, "One of these days I'm going riding behind those Morgan horses, in that new buggy. You just wait and see!" They did not doubt it.

Coming in one day at noon, Laura took Carrie to the stove, to take off her wraps in the warmth. Miss Wilder and Nellie were there, talking earnestly together. Laura heard Miss Wilder say indignantly, "—school board!" Then they both saw her.

"I must ring the bell," Miss Wilder said hurriedly, and she

did not look at Laura as she passed by her. Perhaps Miss Wilder had some complaint against the school board, Laura thought, and she had remembered when she saw Laura, that Pa was on the board.

That afternoon, again, Carrie missed three words in her spelling lesson. Laura's heart ached. Carrie looked so white and pitiful, she tried so hard, but it was plain to be seen that her head was aching terribly. It would be a little comfort to her, Laura thought, that Mamie Beardsley made some mistakes, too.

Then Miss Wilder closed her speller, and said sadly that she was disappointed and grieved. "Go to your seat, Mamie, and study this same lesson again," she said. "Carrie, you may go to the blackboard. I want to see you write, 'cataract,' 'separate,' and 'exasperate,' on the board, correctly, fifty times each."

She said it with a kind of triumph in her voice.

Laura tried to control her temper, but she could not. She was furious. It was meant as a punishment for poor little Carrie, to make her stand ashamed before the whole school. It was not fair! Mamie had missed words, too. Miss Wilder let Mamie off, and punished Carrie. She must see that Carrie did her best, and was not strong. She was mean, mean and cruel, and she was not fair!

Laura had to sit helpless. Carrie went miserably but bravely to the blackboard. She was trembling and she had to wink back tears but she would not cry. Laura sat watching her thin hand slowly writing, one long line of words and then another. Carrie grew pale and paler, but she kept on writing. Suddenly her face went gray, and she hung on to the eraser trough.

Quickly Laura raised her hand, then she jumped up, and when Miss Wilder looked at her she spoke without waiting for permission. "Please! Carrie is going to faint."

Miss Wilder turned swiftly and saw Carrie.

"Carrie! You may sit down!" she said. Sweat came out on Carrie's face and it was not so deathly gray. Laura knew the worst was over. "Sit down on the front seat," Miss Wilder said, and Carrie was able to get to it.

Then Miss Wilder turned to Laura. "Since you do not want Carrie to write her misspelled words, Laura, you may go to the board and write them."

The whole school was frozen silent, looking at Laura. It was a disgrace for her, one of the big girls, to stand at the blackboard writing words as a punishment. Miss Wilder looked at Laura, too, and Laura looked straight back.

Then she went to the blackboard and took the chalk. She began to write. She felt her face grow flaming hot, but after a moment she knew that no one was jeering at her. She went on rapidly writing the words, all alike, one below another.

Several times she heard behind her a low, repeated, "Sssst! Sssst!" The whole room was noisy, as usual. Then she heard a whispered, "Laura! Sssst!"

Charley was signaling to her. He whispered, "Sssst! Don't do it! Tell her you won't do it! We'll all stand by you!"

Laura was warmed all through. But the one thing that must not happen was trouble in school. She smiled and frowned and shook her head at Charley. He sank back, disappointed but quiet. Then suddenly Laura's eye caught a furious glance from Miss Wilder. Miss Wilder had seen the whole thing.

Laura turned to the blackboard and went on writing. Miss Wilder said nothing to her or to Charley. Laura thought resentfully, "She has no right to be mad at me. She might have the grace to appreciate my trying to help keep order in school."

After school that evening Charley and his chums, Clarence and Alfred, walked close behind Laura and Mary Power and Minnie.

"I'll fix that old meanie tomorrow!" Clarence bragged, loudly, so that Laura would hear him. "I'm going to put a bent pin in her chair."

"I'll break her ruler beforehand," Charley promised him. "So she can't punish you if she catches you."

Laura turned around and walked backward. "Please don't do that, boys. Please," she asked them.

"Aw, why not? It'll be fun, and she won't do anything to us," Charley argued.

"But where is the fun?" Laura said. "That is no way for you boys to treat a woman, even if you don't like her. I do wish you wouldn't."

"We-e-ll," Clarence gave in. "Oh, all right. I won't, then."

"Then we won't, either," Alfred and Charley agreed. Laura knew they would keep their word, though they didn't want to.

Studying her lessons by the lamp that night, Laura looked

up to say, "Miss Wilder doesn't like Carrie nor me, and I don't know why."

Ma paused in her knitting. "You must imagine it, Laura," she said.

Pa looked over the edge of his paper. "See that you don't give her any reason, and you'll soon feel differently."

"I don't give her any reason not to like me, Pa," Laura said earnestly. "Maybe Nellie Oleson influences her," she added, bending her head again over her book, and to herself she thought, "She listens too much to Nellie Oleson."

Laura and Carrie were early at school next morning. Miss Wilder and Nellie were sitting together by the stove. No one else was there. Laura said good morning, and as she went into the warmth of the stove her skirt brushed against the coal hod and caught on its broken rim.

"Oh, bother!" Laura exclaimed as she stooped to loosen it.

"Did you tear your dress, Laura?" Miss Wilder asked acidly. "Why don't you get us a new coal hod, since your father is on the school board and you can have everything as you want it?"

Laura looked at her in amazement. "Why, no, I can't!" she exclaimed. "But likely you could have a new coal hod if you want one."

"Oh, thank you," said Miss Wilder.

Laura could not understand why Miss Wilder spoke to her in that way. Nellie pretended to be intent on a book, but a sly smile was at the corner of her mouth. Laura could not think what to say, so she said nothing.

All that morning the room was restless and noisy, but the boys kept their promise. They were no naughtier than usual. They did not know their lessons, for they would not study, and Miss Wilder was so harassed that Laura pitied her.

The afternoon began more quietly. Laura was intent on her geography lesson. Glancing up, while she memorized and thought about the exports of Brazil, she saw Carrie and Mamie Beardsley buried in study. Their heads were together over their spelling book, their eyes were fixed upon it, and their lips silently moved as they spelled the words to themselves. They did not know that they were swaying back and forth, and that their seat was swaying a little with them.

The bolts that should fasten the seat to the floor must be

loose, Laura thought. The movement of the seat made no sound, so it did not matter. Laura looked at her book again and thought about seaports.

Suddenly she heard Miss Wilder speak sharply. "Carrie and Mamie! You may put away your books, and just rock that seat!"

Laura looked up. Carrie's eyes and mouth were open in surprise. Her peaked little face was white from shock, then red with shame. She and Mamie put away their speller and rocked the seat, meekly and still quietly.

"We must have quiet in order to study," Miss Wilder explained sweetly. "Hereafter anyone who disturbs us may continue that disturbance until he or she is thoroughly tired of making it."

Mamie did not mind so much, but Carrie was so ashamed that she wanted to cry.

"Go on rocking that seat, girls, till I give you leave to stop," said Miss Wilder, with that queer triumphant tone in her voice again. She turned to the blackboard, where she was explaining an arithmetic problem to the boys, who paid no attention.

Laura tried again to think about Brazil, but she could not. After a moment, Mamie gave a little toss of her head and boldly moved across the aisle into another seat.

Carrie went on rocking, but the double seat was too heavy for one little girl to rock from one end. Slowly its motion stopped.

"Keep on rocking, Carrie," Miss Wilder said sweetly. She said nothing to Mamie.

Laura's face flushed hot with fury. She did not even try to control her temper. She hated Miss Wilder, for her unfairness and her meanness. There sat Mamie, refusing to take her share of the punishment, and Miss Wilder did not say a word to her. Carrie was not strong enough to rock the heavy seat alone. Laura could hardly control herself. She bit her lip hard, and sat still.

Surely, she thought, Carrie will be excused soon. Carrie was white. She was doing her best to keep the seat rocking, but it was too heavy. Its movement grew less, and less. At last with all her strength Carrie could hardly move it at all.

"Faster, Carrie! Faster!" Miss Wilder said. "You wanted to rock the seat. Now do it."

Laura was on her feet. Her fury took possession of her, she

did not try to resist it, she gave way completely. "Miss Wilder," she cried, "if you want that seat rocked faster, I'll rock it for you!"

Miss Wilder pounced on that gladly. "You may do just that! You needn't take your book, just rock that seat."

Laura hurried down the aisle. She whispered to Carrie, "Sit still and rest." She braced her feet solidly on the floor, and she rocked.

Not for nothing had Pa always said that she was as strong as a little French horse.

"THUMP!" went the back legs on the floor.
"THUMP!" the front legs came down.

All the bolts came quite loose, and

"THUMP, THUMP! THUMP, THUMP!"

the seat went in rhythm, while gladly Laura rocked and Carrie simply sat resting.

Not even the swinging weight eased Laura's fury. She grew angrier and angrier, while louder and faster she rocked.

"THUMP, THUMP! THUMP, THUMP!"

No one could study now.

"THUMP, THUMP! THUMP, THUMP!"

Miss Wilder could hardly hear her own voice. Loudly she called the Third Reader class.

"THUMP, THUMP! THUMP, THUMP!"

No one could recite, no one could even be heard.

"THUMP, THUMP! THUMP, THUMP! THUMP—"

Loudly Miss Wilder said, "Laura, you and Carrie are excused from school. You may go home for the rest of the day."

"THUMP!" Laura made the seat say. Then there was dead silence.

Everyone had heard of being sent home from school. No one there had seen it done before. It was a punishment worse than whipping with a whip. Only one punishment was more dreadful; that was to be expelled from school.

Laura held her head up, but she could hardly see. She gathered Carrie's books together. Carrie followed shrinking behind her and waited trembling by the door while Laura took her own books. There was not a sound in the room. From sympathy, Mary Power and Minnie did not look at Laura. Nellie Oleson, too, was intent on a book, but the sly smile quivered at the corner of her mouth. Ida gave Laura one stricken glance of sympathy.

Carrie had opened the door, Laura walked out, and shut it behind them.

In the entry, they put on their wraps. Outside the schoolhouse everything seemed strange and empty because no one else was there, no one was on the road to town. The time was about two o'clock, when they were not expected at home.

"Oh, Laura, what will we do?" Carrie asked forlornly.

"We'll go home, of course," Laura replied. They were going home; already the schoolhouse was some distance behind them.

"What will Pa and Ma say?" Carrie quavered.

"We'll know when they say it," said Laura. "They won't blame you, this isn't your fault. It's my fault because I rocked that seat so hard. I'm glad of it!" she added. "I'd do it again!"

Carrie did not care whose fault it was. There is no comfort anywhere for anyone who dreads to go home.

"Oh, Laura!" Carrie said. Her mittened hand slid into Laura's, and hand in hand they went on, not saying anything more. They crossed Main Street and walked up to the door. Laura opened it. They went in.

Pa turned from his desk where he was writing. Ma rose up from her chair and her ball of yarn rolled across the floor. Kitty pounced on it gaily.

"*What in the world?*" Ma exclaimed. "Girls, what is the matter? Is Carrie sick?"

"We were sent home from school," Laura said.

Ma sat down. She looked helplessly at Pa. After a dreadful stillness, Pa asked, "Why?" and his voice was stern.

"It was my fault, Pa," Carrie quickly answered. "I didn't mean to, but it was. Mamie and I began it."

"No, it's all my fault," Laura contradicted. She told what had happened. When she had finished, the stillness was dreadful again.

Then Pa spoke sternly. "You girls will go back to school tomorrow morning, and go on as though none of this had happened. Miss Wilder may have been wrong, but she is the teacher. I cannot have my girls making trouble in school."

"No, Pa. We won't," they promised.

"Now take off your school dresses and settle down to your books," said Ma. "You can study here, the rest of the afternoon. Tomorrow you'll do as Pa says, and likely it will all blow over."

CHAPTER 15

The School Board's Visit

LAURA thought that Nellie Oleson looked surprised and disappointed when she and Carrie came into the schoolhouse next morning. Nellie might have expected that they would not come back to school.

"Oh, I'm glad you've come back!" Mary Power said, and Ida gave Laura's arm a warm little squeeze.

"You wouldn't let her meanness keep you away from school, would you, Laura?" Ida said.

"I wouldn't let anything keep me from getting an education," Laura replied.

"I guess you wouldn't get an education if you were expelled from school," Nellie put in.

Laura looked at her. "I've done nothing to be expelled for, and I won't do anything."

"You couldn't be, anyway, could you, with your father on the school board," said Nellie.

"I wish you'd stop talking about Pa's being on the school board!" Laura burst out. "I don't know what business it is of yours if—" The bell began to ring then, and they all went to their seats.

Carrie was carefully good, and in obedience to Pa, Laura was well-behaved, too. She did not think then of the Bible verse that speaks of the cup and platter that were clean only on the outside, but the truth is that she was like that cup and platter. She hated Miss Wilder. She still felt a burning resentment against Miss Wilder's cruel unfairness to Carrie. She wanted to get even with her. Outside, she was shining clean with good behavior, but she made not the least effort to be truly good inside.

The school had never been so noisy. All over the room there was a clatter of books and feet and a rustle of whispering. Only the big girls and Carrie sat still and studied. Whichever way Miss Wilder turned, unruliness and noise swelled up behind her. Suddenly there was a piercing yell.

Charley had leaped to his feet. His hands were clapped to the seat of his trousers. "A pin!" he yelled. "A pin in my seat!"

He held up a bent pin for Miss Wilder to see.

Her lips pressed tight together. This time she did not smile. Sharply she said, "You may come here, Charley."

Charley winked at the room, and went trudging up to Miss Wilder's desk.

"Hold out your hand," she said, as she reached inside her desk for her ruler. For a moment she felt about for it, then she looked into the desk. Her ruler was not there. She asked, "Has anyone seen my ruler?"

Not a hand was raised. Miss Wilder's face went red with anger. She said to Charley, "Go stand in that corner. Face to the wall!"

Charley went to the corner, rubbing his behind as if he still felt the pin-prick. Clarence and Alfred laughed aloud. Miss Wilder turned toward them quickly, and even more quickly Charley looked over his shoulder and made such a face at her that all the boys burst out laughing. Charley was so quick that she saw only the back of his head when very quickly she turned to see what caused the laughter.

Three or four times she turned quickly this way and that, and Charley turned more quickly, making faces at her. The whole school was roaring. Only Laura and Carrie were able to keep their faces perfectly straight. Even the other big girls were strangling and choking in their handkerchiefs.

Miss Wilder rapped for order. She had to rap with her knuckles, she had no ruler. And she could not keep order. She could not watch Charley every minute, and whenever her head was turned, he made a face at her and laughter broke out.

The boys were not breaking their promise to Laura, but they were contriving to be even naughtier than they had promised not to be. And Laura did not care. Truth to tell, she was pleased with them.

When Clarence slid out of his seat and came up the aisle on all fours, she smiled at him.

At recess, she stayed in the schoolhouse. She was sure the boys were planning more mischief, and she meant to be where she could not hear them.

After recess, the disorder was worse. The boys kept paper wads and spitballs flying on their side of the room. All the smaller girls were whispering and passing notes. While Miss Wilder was at the blackboard, Clarence went down the aisle on hands and knees, Alfred followed him, and Charley, lightfooted as a cat, ran down the aisle and leap-frogged over their backs.

They looked for Laura's approval, and she smiled at them.

"What are you laughing at, Laura?" Miss Wilder asked sharply, turning from the blackboard.

"Why, was I laughing?" Laura looked up from her book and sounded surprised. The room was quiet, the boys were in their seats, everyone seemed to be busily studying.

"Well, see that you don't!" Miss Wilder snapped. She looked sharply at Laura, then turned to the blackboard, and almost everyone but Laura and Carrie burst out laughing.

All the rest of the morning, Laura was quiet and kept her eyes on her lessons, only stealing a glance at Carrie now and then. Once Carrie looked back at Laura. Laura put a finger to her lips, and Carrie bent again over her book.

With so much noise and confusion behind her whichever way she turned, Miss Wilder grew confused herself. At noon she dismissed school half an hour early, and again Laura and Carrie were asked to explain their early arrival at home.

They told of the disorder in school, and Pa looked serious. But all he said was, "You girls be very sure that you behave yourselves. Now remember what I say."

They did. Next day the disorder was worse. The whole school was almost openly jeering at Miss Wilder. Laura was appalled at what she had started, by only two smiles at naughtiness. Still she would not try to stop it. She would never forgive Miss Wilder's unfairness to Carrie. She did not want to forgive her.

Now that everyone was teasing, baiting, or at least giggling at Miss Wilder, Nellie joined in. She was still teacher's pet, but she repeated to the other girls everything that Miss Wilder said, and laughed at her. One day she told them that Miss Wilder's name was Eliza Jane.

"It's a secret," Nellie said. "She's told me a long time ago, but she doesn't want anyone else out here to know it."

"I don't see why," Ida wondered. "Eliza Jane is a nice name."

"I can tell you why," said Nellie. "When she was a little girl, in New York State, a dirty little girl came to school and Miss

Wilder had to sit with her, and"—Nellie drew the others close and whispered—"she got lice in her hair."

They all backed away, and Mary Power exclaimed, "You shouldn't tell such horrid things, Nellie!"

"I wouldn't, only Ida asked me," said Nellie.

"Why, Nellie Oleson, I did no such thing!" Ida declared.

"You did so! Listen," Nellie giggled. "That isn't all. Her mother sent a note to the teacher, and the teacher sent the dirty little girl home, so everyone knew about it. And Miss Wilder's mother kept her out of school a whole morning to fine-comb her hair. Miss Wilder cried and cried, and she dreaded so to go back to school that she walked slow and was late. At recess her whole class made a ring around her and kept yelling, 'Lazy, lousy, Lizy Jane!' And from that day to this, she just can't bear her name. As long as she was in that school, that's what anyone called her that got mad at her, 'Lazy, lousy, Lizy Jane!' "

She said it so comically that they laughed, though they were a little ashamed of doing so. Afterward, they agreed that they would never tell Nellie anything, because she was two-faced.

The school was so noisy now it was not really school any more. When Miss Wilder rang the bell, all the pupils joyfully trooped in to annoy her. She could not watch every one of them at once, she could hardly ever catch anyone. They banged their slates and their books, they threw paper wads and spitballs, they whistled between their teeth and scampered in the aisles. They were all together against Miss Wilder, they delighted in harassing and baffling and hounding her and jeering.

That feeling against Miss Wilder almost frightened Laura. No one could stop them now. The disorder was so great that Laura could not study. If she could not learn her lessons, she could not get a teacher's certificate soon enough to help keep Mary in college. Perhaps Mary must leave college, because Laura had twice smiled at naughtiness.

She knew now that she should not have done that. Yet she did not really repent. She did not forgive Miss Wilder. She felt hard and hot as a burning coal when she thought of Miss Wilder's treatment of Carrie.

One Friday morning Ida gave up trying to study in the

confusion, and began to draw on her slate. The whole First spelling class was making mistakes on purpose and laughing at them. Miss Wilder sent the class to the board to write the lesson. Then she was caught between the pupils at the board and those in the seats. Ida was busily drawing, swinging her feet and humming a little tune in her throat without knowing it, and Laura kept her fists clamped to her ears and tried to study.

When Miss Wilder dismissed school for recess, Ida showed Laura the picture she had drawn. It was a comic picture of Miss Wilder, so well done that it looked exactly like her, only more so. Under it Ida had written,

> We have lots of fun going to school,
> Laugh and grow fat is the only rule,
> Everyone laughs until their sides ache again
> At lazy, lousy, Lizy Jane.

"I can't get the verse just right, somehow," Ida said. Mary Power and Minnie were admiring the picture and laughing, and Mary Power said, "Why don't you get Laura to help you, she makes good verses."

"Oh, will you, Laura? Please," Ida asked. Laura took the slate and the pencil, and while the others waited she thought of a tune and fitted words to it. She meant only to please Ida, and perhaps, just a little, to show off what she could do. She wrote, in the place of the verse that Ida had erased,

> Going to school is lots of fun,
> From laughing we have gained a ton,
> We laugh until we have a pain,
> At lazy, lousy, Lizy Jane.

Ida was delighted, and so were the others. Mary Power said, "I told you Laura could do it." At that moment Miss Wilder rang the bell. The whole recess had gone, as quickly as that.

The boys came in, making all the noise they could, and as Charley passed by and caught sight of the slate, Ida laughed and let him take it.

"Oh, no!" Laura cried in a whisper, but she was too late. Until noon the boys were slipping that slate from one to another, and Laura feared that Miss Wilder would capture it, with Ida's drawing and her handwriting on it. Laura breathed a great sigh of relief when the slate came slipping back, and Ida quickly cleaned it with her slate-rag.

When they all went out to the crisp, sunny outdoors to go home for dinner, Laura heard the boys chanting all along the road to Main Street,

> Going to school is lots of fun,
> From laughing we have gained a ton,
> We laugh until we have a pain,
> At LAZY, LOUSY, LIZY JANE!

Laura gasped. She felt sick for a minute. She cried out, "They mustn't! We must stop them. Oh, Mary Power, Minnie, come on, hurry." She called, "Boys! Charley! Clarence!"

"They don't hear you," Minnie said. "We couldn't stop them, anyway."

Already the boys were separating at Main Street. They were only talking, but Laura had no more than sighed in relief when one began to chant again, and others joined in. "Going to school is lots of fun—" Both up and down Main Street they yelled;

"*LAZY, LOUSY, LIZY JANE!*"

"Oh, *why* haven't they better sense!" Laura said.

"Laura," said Mary Power, "there's just one thing to do. Don't tell who wrote that. Ida won't, I know. I won't, and Minnie won't, will you, Minnie?"

"Cross my heart," Minnie promised. "But what about Nellie Oleson?"

"She doesn't know. She was talking with Miss Wilder, the whole recess," Mary Power reminded them. "And you'll never tell, will you, Laura?"

"Not unless Pa or Ma asks me, straight out," said Laura.

"Likely they won't think to, and then nobody will ever know," Mary Power tried to comfort Laura.

While they were eating dinner, Charley and Clarence passed by, chanting that frightful verse, and Pa said, "That sounds like some song I don't know. You ever hear a song before about lazy, lousy, Lizy Jane?"

"I never did," said Ma. "It doesn't sound like a nice song."

Laura did not say a word. She thought she had never been so miserable.

Around the schoolhouse the boys were chanting that verse. Nellie's brother Willie was with them. Inside the schoolhouse Ida and Nellie were standing at the window farthest from Miss Wilder. She must have known that Nellie had told.

Nellie was furious. She wanted to know who had written that verse, but Ida had not told her and none of the others would. No doubt her brother Willie knew or would find out. He would tell her and then she would tell Miss Wilder.

After school that night, and again on Saturday, the boys could be heard chanting those words. In the bright, clear weather they were all outdoors. Laura could almost have welcomed a blizzard to shut them in. She had never felt so ashamed, for she had spread Nellie's mean tattle-telling farther than Nellie ever could have. She blamed herself, yet she still blamed Miss Wilder far more. If Miss Wilder had been only decently fair to Carrie, Laura never could have got into such trouble.

That afternoon Mary Power came to visit. Often on Saturday afternoons she and Laura visited and worked together. They sat in the pleasant, sunny, front room.

Laura was crocheting a nubia of soft white wool, for Mary's Christmas present in college, and Mary Power was knitting a silk necktie for her father's Christmas. Ma rocked and knitted, or sometimes read interesting bits to them from her church paper, *The Advance.* Grace played about, and Carrie sewed a nine-patch quilt block.

Those were such pleasant afternoons. The winter sunshine streamed in. The room was pleasantly warm from the coal heater. Kitty, grown now to a cat, stretched and lazily purred in the sunshine on the rag rug, or curved purring against the front door, asking with a mrrreow to be let out to watch for dogs.

Kitty had become famous in town. She was such a pretty cat, such a clean blue and white, with slender body and long tail, that everyone wanted to pet her. But she was a one-family cat. Only the family could touch her. When anyone else stooped to stroke her, she flew snarling and clawing into his face. Usually someone screeched, "Don't touch that cat!" in time to save him.

She liked to sit on the front doorstep and look about the

town. Boys, and sometimes the men, would set a new dog on her to see the fun. Kitty sat placidly while the dog growled and barked, but she was always ready. When the dog rushed, she rose in air with a heart-stopping yowl and landed squarely on the dog's back with all claws sunk into it. The dog went away from there.

They went in a streak, Kitty silently riding and the dog ki-yi-yowling. When Kitty thought she was far enough from home she dropped off, but the dog went on. Then Kitty walked home with proudly upright tail. Only a new dog could be set on Kitty.

Nothing could be a greater pleasure than those Saturday afternoons, when Mary Power's friendliness was added to the cosiness of home, and Kitty might furnish exciting entertainment. Now Laura could not truly enjoy even this. She sat dreading to hear the boys chanting that verse again, and in her chest was a gloomy weight.

"I should make a clean breast of it, to Pa and Ma," she thought. She felt again a scalding fury against Miss Wilder. She had not meant to do harm when she wrote that verse; she had written it at recess, not in school hours. It was all too difficult to explain. Perhaps, as Ma had said, it would blow over. Least said, soonest mended. Yet at that moment perhaps someone was telling Pa.

Mary Power was troubled, too. They both made mistakes and had to unravel stitches. Never had they accomplished so little in a Saturday afternoon. Neither of them said a word about school. All the pleasure was gone from school. They were not looking forward to Monday morning.

That Monday morning was the worst yet. There was no pretense of study. The boys whistled and cat-called, and scuffled in the aisles. All the little girls but Carrie were whispering and giggling and even moving from seat to seat. Miss Wilder's, "Quiet, please! Please be quiet!" could hardly be heard.

There was a knock at the door. Laura and Ida heard it; they sat nearest the door. They looked at each other, and when the knock came again, Ida raised her hand. Miss Wilder paid no attention.

Suddenly a loud knock sounded on the entry's inner door. Everyone heard that. The door opened, and the noise died away to silence. The room grew deathly still as Pa came in. Behind him came two other men whom Laura did not know.

"Good morning, Miss Wilder," said Pa. "The school board decided it was time to visit the school."

"It is about time that something was done," Miss Wilder returned. She flushed red and then went pale while she answered, "Good morning," to the other two men and welcomed them, with Pa, to the front of the room. They stood looking over it.

Every pupil was perfectly still, and Laura's heart pounded loud.

"We heard you have been having a little trouble," the tall, solemn man said gravely but kindly.

"Yes, and I am very glad of this opportunity to tell you gentlemen the facts of the case," Miss Wilder replied angrily. "It is Laura Ingalls who makes all the trouble in this school. She thinks she can run the school because her father is on the school board. Yes, Mr. Ingalls, that is the truth! She brags that she can run this school. She didn't think I would hear of it, but I did!" She flashed a glance of angry triumph at Laura.

Laura sat dumbfounded. She had never thought that Miss Wilder would tell a lie.

"I am sorry to hear this, Miss Wilder," said Pa. "I am sure that Laura did not intend to make trouble."

Laura raised her hand, but Pa slightly shook his head at her.

"She encourages the boys to be unruly, too. That is the whole trouble with them," Miss Wilder declared. "Laura Ingalls eggs them on, in every kind of mischief and disobedience."

Pa looked at Charley and his eyes were twinkling. He said, "Young man, I hear you got punished for sitting on a bent pin."

"Oh, no, sir!" Charley replied, a picture of innocence. "I was not punished for sitting on it, sir, but for getting up off it."

The jolly member of the school board suddenly choked a laugh into a cough. Even the solemn man's mustache twitched. Miss Wilder flushed dark red. Pa was perfectly sober. No one else even felt like smiling.

Slowly and weightily, Pa said, "Miss Wilder, we want you to know that the school board stands with you to keep order in this school." He looked sternly over the whole room. "All you scholars must obey Miss Wilder, behave yourselves, and learn your lessons. We want a good school, and we are going to have it."

When Pa spoke like that, he meant what he said, and it would happen.

The room was still. The stillness continued after the school board had said good day to Miss Wilder and gone. There was no fidgeting, no whispering. Quietly every pupil studied, and class after class recited diligently in the quiet.

At home Laura was quiet, too, wondering what Pa would say to her. It was not her place to speak of what had happened, until he did. He said nothing about it until the supper dishes were washed and they were all settled for the evening around the lamp.

Then laying down his paper he looked at Laura and said slowly, "It is time for you to explain what you said to anyone, that you could give Miss Wilder the idea you thought you could run the school because I am on the school board."

"I didn't say such a thing, and I did not think so, Pa," Laura said earnestly.

"I know you didn't," said Pa. "But there was something that gave her such an idea. Think what it could have been."

Laura tried to think. She was not prepared for this question, for she had been defending herself in her mind and declaring that Miss Wilder had told a lie. She had not looked for the reason why Miss Wilder told it.

"Did you speak to anyone about my being on the school board?" Pa prompted her.

Nellie Oleson had often spoken of that, but Laura had only wished that she wouldn't. Then she remembered the quarrel, when Nellie had almost slapped her. She said, "Nellie Oleson told me that Miss Wilder said you haven't much to say about the school, even if you are on the school board. And I said——"

She had been so angry that it was hard to remember exactly what she had said. "I said that you have as much to say about the school as anybody. Then I said, 'It's too bad your father doesn't own a place in town. Maybe if you weren't just country folks, your father could be on the school board.' "

"Oh, Laura," Ma said sorrowfully. "That made her angry."

"I wanted to," said Laura. "I meant to make her mad. When

we lived on Plum Creek she was always making fun of Mary and me because we were country girls. She can find out what it feels like, herself."

"Laura, Laura," Ma protested in distress. "How can you be so unforgiving? That was years ago."

"She was impudent to you, too. And mean to Jack," Laura said, and tears smarted in her eyes.

"Never mind," Pa said. "Jack was a good dog and he's gone to his reward. So Nellie twisted what you said and told it to Miss Wilder, and that's made all this trouble. I see." He took up his paper. "Well, Laura, maybe you have learned a lesson that is worth while. Just remember this, 'A dog that will fetch a bone, will carry a bone.' "

For a little while there was silence, and Carrie began again to study her spelling. Then Ma said, "If you will bring me your album, Laura, I would like to write in it."

Laura fetched her album from her box upstairs, and Ma sat at the desk and carefully wrote in it with her little pearl-handled pen. She dried the page carefully over the lamp, and returned the album to Laura.

On the smooth, cream-colored page, in Ma's fine handwriting, Laura read:

If wisdom's ways you wisely seek,
Five things observe with care,
To whom you speak,
Of whom you speak,
And how, and when, and where

Your loving mother
C L Ingalls

De Smet November 15th. 1881

CHAPTER 16

Name Cards

After all the preparation for winter, it seemed that there would be no winter. The days were clear and sunny. The frozen ground was bare of snow.

The fall term of school ended and Miss Wilder went back to Minnesota. The new teacher, Mr. Clewett, was quiet but firm, a good disciplinarian. There was not a sound in school now, except the low voices of classes reciting, and in the rows of seats every pupil diligently studied.

All the big boys were coming to school. Cap Garland was there, his face tanned dark red-brown and his pale hair and pale blue eyes seeming almost white. His smile still flashed quick as lightning and warmer than sunshine. Everyone remembered that he had made the terrible trip with Almanzo Wilder, last winter, to bring the wheat that saved them all from dying of hunger. Ben Woodworth came back to school, and Fred Gilbert, whose father had brought in the last mail after the trains stopped running, and Arthur Johnson, Minnie's brother.

Still there was no snow. At recess and at noon the boys played baseball, and the big girls did not play outdoors anymore.

Nellie worked at her crocheting. Ida and Minnie and Mary Power stood at the window, watching the ball games. Sometimes Laura stood with them, but usually she stayed at her desk and studied. She had a feeling of haste, almost of fear, that she would not be able to pass the examinations and get a teacher's certificate when she was sixteen. She was almost fifteen now.

"Oh, come on, Laura. Come watch this ball game," Ida coaxed one noon. "You have a whole year to study before you need to know so much."

Laura closed her book. She was happy that the girls wanted her. Nellie scornfully tossed her head. "I'm glad I don't have to be a teacher," she said. "My folks can get along without my having to work."

With an effort Laura held her voice low and answered sweetly.

"Of course you needn't, Nellie, but you see, we aren't poor relations being helped out by our folks back East."

Nellie was so angry that she stammered as she tried to speak, and Mary Power interrupted her coolly. "If Laura wants to teach school, I don't know that it's anybody's business. Laura is smart. She will be a good teacher."

"Yes," Ida said. "She's far ahead of—" She stopped because the door opened and Cap Garland came in. He had come straight from town and he had in his hand a small striped paper bag.

"Hello, girls," he said, looking at Mary Power, and his smile lighted up as he held out the bag to her. "Have some candy?"

Nellie was quick. "Oh, Cappie!" she cried, taking the bag. "How did you know that I like candy so much? The nicest candy in town, too!" She smiled up into his face with a look that Laura had never seen before. Cap seemed startled, then he looked sheepish.

"Would you girls like some?" Nellie went on generously, and quickly she offered each one the opened bag, then taking a piece herself, she put the bag in her skirt pocket.

Cap looked pleadingly at Mary Power, but she tossed her head and looked away. Uncertainly he said, "Well, I'm glad you like it," and he went out to the ball game.

The next day at noon he brought candy again. Again he tried to give it to Mary Power, and again Nellie was too quick.

"Oh, Cappie, you are such a dear boy to bring me more candy," she said, smiling up at him. This time she turned a little away from the others. She had no eyes for anyone but Cap. "I mustn't be a pig and eat it all myself, do have a piece, Cappie," she coaxed. He took a piece and she rapidly ate all the rest while she murmured to Cap how nice he was, and so tall and strong.

Cap looked helpless, yet pleased. He would never be able to cope with Nellie, Laura knew. Mary Power was too proud to enter into competition with her. Angrily Laura wondered, Must a girl like Nellie be able to grab what she wants? It was not only the candy.

Until Mr. Clewett rang the bell, Nellie kept Cap by her side and listening to her. The others pretended not to notice them.

Laura asked Mary Power to write in her autograph album. All the girls but Nellie were writing in each other's albums. Nellie did not have one.

Mary Power sat at her desk and carefully wrote, with ink, while the others waited to read the verse when she finished it. Her writing was beautiful, and so was the verse she had chosen.

The rose of the valley may wither,
The pleasures of youth pass away,
But friendship will blossom forever
While all other flowers decay.

Laura's album had many treasures in it now. There was the verse that Ma had written, and on the next page was Ida's.

In memory's golden casket,
Drop one pearl for me.
Your loving friend,
Ida B. Wright.

Every now and then Cap looked helplessly at them over Nellie's shoulder, but they paid no attention to him or Nellie. Minnie Johnson asked Laura to write in her album, and Laura said, "I will, if you'll write in mine."

"I'll do my best, but I can't write as beautifully as Mary does. Her writing is just like copper plate," Minnie said, and she sat down and wrote:

When the name that I write here
Is dim on the page
And the leaves of your album
Are yellow with age,
Still think of me kindly
And do not forget
That wherever I am
I remember you yet.
Minnie Johnson.

Then the bell rang, and they all went to their seats.

That afternoon at recess, Nellie sneered at autograph albums. "They're out of date," she said. "I used to have one, but

I wouldn't have one of the old things now." No one believed her. She said, "In the East, where I come from, it's name cards that are all the rage now."

"What are name cards?" Ida asked.

Nellie pretended to be surprised, then she smiled, "Well, of course you wouldn't know, I'll bring mine to school and show you, but I won't give you one, because you haven't one to give me. It's only proper to exchange name cards. Everybody's exchanging name cards now, in the East."

They did not believe her. Autograph albums could not be out of style, because theirs were almost new. Ma had brought Laura's from Vinton, Iowa, only last September. On the way home after school, Minnie Johnson said, "She's just bragging. I don't believe she had name cards, I don't believe there's any such a thing."

But next morning she and Mary Power were so eager to see Laura that they waited for her to come out of the house. Mary Power had found out about name cards. Jake Hopp, who ran the newspaper, had them at the newspaper office next to the bank. They were colored cards, with colored pictures of flowers and birds, and Mr. Hopp would print your name on them.

"I don't believe Nellie Oleson has any," Minnie still declared. "She only found out about them before we did, and she plans to get some and pretend they came from the East."

"How much do they cost?" Laura asked.

"That depends on the pictures, and the kind of printing," Mary told them. "I'm getting a dozen, with plain printing, for twenty-five cents."

Laura said no more. Mary Power's father was the tailor and he could work all winter, but now there was no carpentering work in town and would be none till spring. Pa had five to feed at home, and Mary to keep in college. It was folly even to think of spending twenty-five cents for mere pleasure.

Nellie had not brought her name cards that morning. Minnie asked her, as soon as they gathered around the stove where she was warming her hands after her long, chilly walk to school.

"My goodness, I forgot all about them!" she said. "I guess I'll have to tie a string on my finger to remind me." Minnie's look said to Mary Power and Laura, "I told you so."

At noon that day Cap did bring candy again, and as usual

Nellie was nearest the door. She began to coo, "Oo-oo, Cappie!" and just as she was grasping the bag of candy, Laura reached and whisked it from her surprised hand, and gave it to Mary Power.

Everyone was startled, even Laura. Then Cap's smile lighted his whole face, he glanced gratefully at Laura and looked at Mary.

"Thank you," Mary said to him. "We will all enjoy the candy so much." She offered it to the others, while as he went out to the ball game Cap gave one backward look, a grin of delight.

"Have a piece, Nellie," Mary Power invited.

"I will!" Nellie took the largest piece. "I do like Cap's candy, but as for him—pooh! you may have the greeny."

Mary Power flushed, but she did not answer. Laura felt her own face flame. "I guess you'd take him well enough if you could get him," she said. "You knew all the time he was bringing the candy to Mary."

"My goodness, I could twist him around my finger if I wanted to," Nellie bragged. "He isn't such a much. It's that chum of his I want to know, that young Mr. Wilder with the funny name. You'll see," she smiled to herself, "I'm going riding behind those horses of his."

Yes, she surely would, Laura thought. Nellie had been so friendly with Miss Wilder, it was a wonder that Miss Wilder's brother had not invited her for a drive before now. As for herself, Laura knew she had spoiled any chance of such a pleasure.

Mary Power's name cards were finished the next week, and she brought them to school. They were beautiful. The cards were palest green, and on each was a picture of a bobolink swaying and singing on a spray of goldenrod. Beneath it was printed in black letters, MARY POWER. She gave one to Minnie, one to Ida and one to Laura, though they had none to give her.

That same day, Nellie brought hers to school. They were pale yellow, with a bouquet of pansies and a scroll that said, "For Thoughts." Her name was printed in letters like handwriting. She traded one of her cards for one of Mary's.

Next day, Minnie said she was going to buy some. Her father had given her the money, and she would order them after school if the other girls would come with her. Ida could not go. She said cheerfully, "I ought not to waste time. Because

I'm an adopted child, you see, I have to hurry home to help with the housework as much as I can. I couldn't ask for name cards. Father Brown is a preacher and such things are a vanity. So I'll just enjoy looking at yours when you get them, Minnie."

"Isn't she a dear?" Mary Power said after Ida had left them. No one could help loving Ida. Laura wished to be like her, but she wasn't. Secretly she so wanted name cards that she almost felt envious of Mary Power and Minnie.

In the newspaper office Mr. Hopp in his ink-spotted apron spread the sample cards on the counter for them to see. Each card was more beautiful than the last. And Laura was mean enough to be pleased that Nellie's was among them; it proved that she had bought her cards there.

They were every pale, lovely color, some even had gilt edges. There was a choice of six different bouquets, and one had a birds' nest nestled among the flowers, two birds on its rim, and above them the word Love.

"That's a young man's card," Mr. Hopp told them. "Only a young fellow's brash enough to hand out a card with 'Love' on it."

"Of course," Minnie murmured, flushing.

It was so hard to choose among them that finally Mr. Hopp said, "Well, take your time. I'll go on getting out the paper."

He went back to inking the type and laying sheets of paper on it. He had lighted the lamp before Minnie finally decided to take the pale blue card. Then guiltily, because they were so late, they all hurried home.

Pa was washing his hands and Ma was putting supper on the table when Laura came in, breathless. Quietly Ma asked, "Where have you been, Laura?"

"I'm sorry, Ma. I only meant to take a minute," Laura apologized. She told them about name cards. Of course she did not say that she wanted some. Pa remarked that Jake was up-and-coming, bringing out such novelties.

"How much do they cost?" he asked, and Laura answered that the cheapest cost twenty-five cents a dozen.

It was almost bedtime, and Laura was staring at the wall, thinking about the War of 1812, when Pa folded his paper, laid it down, and said, "Laura."

"Yes, Pa?"

"You want some of these new-fangled name cards, don't you?" Pa asked.

"I was just thinking the same thing, Charles," said Ma.

"Well, yes, I do want them," Laura admitted. "But I don't *need* them."

Pa's eyes smiled twinkling at her as he took from his pocket some coins and counted out two dimes and a nickel. "I guess you can have them, Half-Pint," he said. "Here you are."

Laura hesitated. "Do you really think I ought to? Can we afford it?" she asked.

"Laura!" Ma said. She meant, "Are you questioning what your Pa does?" Quickly Laura said, "Oh, Pa, *thank you!*"

Then Ma said, "You are a good girl, Laura, and we want you to have the pleasures of other girls of your age. Before school tomorrow morning, if you hurry, you can run up the street and order your name cards."

In her lonely bed that night without Mary, Laura felt ashamed. She was not truly good, like Ma and Mary and Ida Brown. At that very minute she was so happy to think of having name cards, not only because they were beautiful, but partly to be meanly even with Nellie Oleson, and partly to have things as nice as Mary Power and Minnie had.

Mr. Hopp promised that the cards would be ready on Wednesday at noon, and that day Laura could hardly eat her dinner. Ma excused her from doing the dishes, and she hurried to the newspaper office. There they were, delicate pink cards, with a spray of pinker roses and blue cornflowers. Her name was printed in thin, clear type: Laura Elizabeth Ingalls.

She had hardly time to admire them, for she must not be late to school. A long block from Second Street, she was hurrying along the board sidewalk, when suddenly a shining buggy pulled up beside it.

Laura looked up, surprised to see the brown Morgans. Young Mr. Wilder stood by the buggy, his cap in one hand. He held out his other hand to her and said, "Like a ride to the schoolhouse? You'll get there quicker."

He took her hand, helped her into the buggy, and stepped in beside her. Laura was almost speechless with surprise and shyness and the delight of actually riding behind those beautiful horses. They trotted gaily but very slowly and their small ears twitched, listening for the word to go faster.

"I—I'm Laura Ingalls," Laura said. It was a silly thing to say. Of course he must know who she was.

"I know your father, and I've seen you around town for quite a while," he replied. "My sister often spoke of you."

"Such beautiful horses! What are their names?" she asked. She knew quite well, but she had to say something.

"The near one is Lady, and the other is Prince," he told her.

Laura wished he would let them go faster—as fast as they could go. But it would not be polite to ask.

She thought of speaking about the weather, but that seemed silly.

She could not think of anything to say, and in all this time they had gone only one block.

"I have been getting my name cards," she heard herself saying.

"That so?" he said. "Mine are just plain cards. I brought them out from Minnesota."

He took one from his pocket and handed it to her. He was driving with one capable hand, keeping the lines in play between his gloved fingers. The card was plain and white. Printed on it in Old English letters was, Almanzo James Wilder.

"It's kind of an outlandish name," he said.

Laura tried to think of something nice to say about it. She said, "It is quite unusual."

"It was wished on me," he said grimly. "My folks have got a notion there always has to be an Almanzo in the family, because 'way back in the time of the Crusades there was a Wilder went to them, and an Arab or somebody saved his life. El Manzoor, the name was. They changed it after a while in England, but I guess there's no way to improve it much."

"I think it is a very interesting name," said Laura honestly.

She did think so, but she did not know what to do with the card. It seemed rude to give it back to him, but perhaps he did not mean her to keep it. She held it so that he could take it back if he wanted to. The team turned the corner at Second Street. In a panic Laura wondered whether, if he did not take back his card, she should give him one of hers. Nellie had said it was proper to exchange name cards.

She held his card a little nearer him, so that he could see it plainly. He went on driving.

"Do you—do you want your card back?" Laura asked him.

"You can keep it if you want to," he replied.

"Then do you want one of mine?" She took one out of the package and gave it to him.

He looked at it and thanked her. "It is a very pretty card," he said as he put it in his pocket.

They were at the schoolhouse. He held the reins while he sprang out of the buggy, took off his cap and offered his hand to help her down. She did not need help; she barely touched his glove with her mitten-tip as she came lightly to the ground.

"Thank you for the ride," she said.

"Don't mention it," he answered. His hair was not black, as she had thought. It was dark brown, and his eyes were such a dark blue that they did not look pale in his darkly tanned face. He had a steady, dependable, yet light-hearted look.

"Hullo, Wilder!" Cap Garland greeted him, and he waved in answer as he drove away. Mr. Clewett was ringing the bell, and the boys were trooping in.

As Laura slipped into her seat, there was barely time for Ida to squeeze her arm delightedly and whisper, "Oh, I *wish* you could have seen her face! when you came driving up!"

Mary Power and Minnie were beaming at Laura across the aisle, but Nellie was looking intently away from her.

CHAPTER 17

The Sociable

ONE Saturday afternoon Mary Power came blowing in to see Laura. Her cheeks were pink with excitement. The Ladies' Aid Society was giving a dime sociable in Mrs. Tinkham's rooms over the furniture store, next Friday night.

"I'll go if you do, Laura," Mary Power said. "Oh, please may she, Mrs. Ingalls?"

Laura did not like to ask what a dime sociable was. Fond as she was of Mary Power, she felt at a slight disadvantage with her. Mary Power's clothes were so beautifully fitted because her father tailored them, and she did her hair in the stylish new way, with bangs.

Ma said that Laura might go to the sociable. She had not heard, until now, that a Ladies' Aid was organized.

To tell the truth, Pa and Ma were sadly disappointed that dear Rev. Alden from Plum Creek was not the preacher. He had wanted to be, and the church had sent him. But when he arrived, he found that Rev. Brown had established himself there. So dear Rev. Alden had gone on as a missionary to the unsettled West.

Pa and Ma could not lose interest in the church, of course, and Ma would work in the Ladies' Aid. Still, they could not feel as they would have felt had Rev. Alden been the preacher.

All next week Laura and Mary Power looked forward to the sociable. It cost a dime, so Minnie and Ida doubted that they could go, and Nellie said that, really, it didn't interest her.

Friday seemed long to Laura and Mary Power, they were so impatient for night to come. That night Laura did not take off her school dress, but put on a long apron and pinned its bib under her chin. Supper was early, and as soon as she had washed the dishes Laura began to get ready for the sociable.

Ma helped her carefully brush her dress. It was brown woolen, made in princess style. The collar was a high, tight band, close under Laura's chin, and the skirt came down to the tops of her high-buttoned shoes. It was a very pretty dress, with pipings of red around wrists and collar, and the buttons all down the front were of brown horn, with a tiny raised castle in the center of each one.

Standing before the looking glass in the front room, where the lamp was, Laura carefully brushed and braided her hair, and put it up and took it down again. She could not arrange it to suit her.

"Oh, Ma, I do wish you would let me cut bangs," she almost begged. "Mary Power wears them, and they are so stylish."

"Your hair looks nice the way it is," said Ma. "Mary Power is a nice girl, but I think the new hair style is well called a 'lunatic fringe.'"

"Your hair looks beautiful, Laura," Carrie consoled her. "It's such a pretty brown and so long and thick, and it shines in the light."

Laura still looked unhappily at her reflection. She thought of the short hairs always growing at the edge around her forehead. They did not show when they were brushed back, but now she combed them all out and downward. They made a thin little fringe.

"Oh, please, Ma," she coaxed. "I wouldn't cut a heavy bang like Mary Power's, but please let me cut just a little more, so I could curl it across my forehead."

"Very well, then," Ma gave her consent.

Laura took the shears from Ma's workbasket and standing before the glass she cut the hair above her forehead into a narrow fringe about two inches long. She laid her long slate pencil on the heater, and when it was heated she held it by the cool end and wound wisps of the short hair around the heated end. Holding each wisp tightly around the pencil, she curled all the bangs.

The rest of her hair she combed smoothly back and braided. She wound the long braid flatly around and around on the back of her head and snugly pinned it.

"Turn around and let me see you," Ma said.

Laura turned. "Do you like it, Ma?"

"It looks quite nice," Ma admitted. "Still, I liked it better before it was cut."

"Turn this way and let me see," said Pa. He looked at her a long minute and his eyes were pleased. "Well, if you must wear this 'lunatic fringe,' I think you've made a good job of it." And Pa turned again to his paper.

"I think it is pretty. You look very nice," Carrie said softly.

Laura put on her brown coat and set carefully over her head her peaked hood of brown woolen lined with blue. The brown and the blue edges of cloth were pinked, and the hood had long ends that wound around her neck like a muffler.

She took one more look in the glass. Her cheeks were pink with excitement, and the curled bangs were stylish under the hood's blue lining that made her eyes very blue.

Ma gave her a dime and said, "Have a pleasant time, Laura. I am sure you will remember your manners."

Pa asked, "Had I better go with her as far as the door, Caroline?"

"It's early yet, and only across the street, and she's going with Mary Power," Ma answered.

Laura went out into the dark and starry night. Her heart was beating fast with anticipation. Her breath puffed white in the frosty air. Lamplight made glowing patches on the sidewalk in front of the hardware store and the drugstore, and above the dark furniture store two windows shone bright. Mary Power came out of the tailor shop, and together they climbed the outdoor stairs between it and the furniture store.

Mary Power knocked on the door, and Mrs. Tinkham opened it. She was a tiny woman, in a black dress with white lace ruffles at throat and wrists. She said good evening, and took Mary Power's dime and Laura's. Then she said, "Come this way to leave your wraps."

All the week Laura had hardly been able to wait to see what a sociable was, and now she was here. Some people were sitting in a lighted room. She felt embarrassed as she hurriedly followed Mrs. Tinkham past them, into a small bedroom. She and Mary Power laid their coats and hoods on the bed. Then quietly they slipped into chairs in the larger room.

Mr. and Mrs. Johnson sat on either side of the window. The window had dotted-Swiss curtains, and before it stood a polished center table, holding a large glass lamp with a white china shade on which red roses were painted. Beside the lamp lay a green plush photograph album.

A bright flowered carpet covered the whole floor. A tall

shining heater with isinglass windows stood in its center. The chairs around the walls were all of polished woods. Mr. and Mrs. Woodworth were sitting on a sofa with shining high wooden back and ends and a glittering black haircloth seat.

Only the walls of boards were like those in the front room at home, and these were thickly hung with pictures of people and places that Laura did not know. Some had wide, heavy, gilded frames. Of course Mr. Tinkham owned the furniture store.

Cap Garland's older sister Florence was there, with their mother. Mrs. Beardsley was there, and Mrs. Bradley, the druggist's wife. They all sat dressed up and silent. Mary Power and Laura did not speak, either. They did not know what to say.

Someone knocked at the door. Mrs. Tinkham hurried to it, and Rev. and Mrs. Brown came in. His rumbling voice filled the room with greetings to everyone, and then he talked with Mrs. Tinkham about the home she had left in Massachusetts.

"Not much like this place," he said. "But we are all strange here."

He fascinated Laura. She did not like him. Pa said he claimed to be a cousin of John Brown of Osawatomie who had killed so many men in Kansas and finally succeeded in starting the Civil War. Rev. Brown did look just like the picture of John Brown in Laura's history book.

His face was large and bony. His eyes were sunk deep under shaggy white eyebrows and they shone hot and fierce even when he was smiling. His coat hung loose on his big body, his hands at the end of the sleeves were large and rough with big knuckles. He was untidy. Around his mouth his long white beard was stained yellow as if with dribbling tobacco juice.

He talked a great deal, and after he came the others talked some, except Mary Power and Laura. They tried to sit still politely, but now and then they did fidget. It was a long time before Mrs. Tinkham began to bring plates from the kitchen. On each plate was a small sauce dish of custard and a piece of cake.

When Laura had eaten hers, she murmured to Mary Power, "Let's go home," and Mary answered, "Come on, I'm going." They set their empty dishes on a small table near them, put on their coats and hoods, and said good-by to Mrs. Tinkham.

Down on the street once more, Laura drew a deep breath. "Whew! If that is a sociable, I don't like sociables."

"Neither do I," Mary Power agreed. "I wish I hadn't gone. I'd rather have the dime."

Pa and Ma looked up in surprise when Laura came in, and Carrie eagerly asked, "Did you have a good time, Laura?"

"Well, no, I didn't," Laura had to admit. "You should have gone, Ma, instead of me. Mary Power and I were the only girls there. We had no one to talk to."

"This is only the first sociable," Ma made excuse. "No doubt when folks here are better acquainted, the sociables will be more interesting. I know from reading *The Advance* that church sociables are greatly enjoyed."

CHAPTER 18

Literaries

CHRISTMAS was near, yet there was still no snow. There had not been a single blizzard. In the mornings the frozen ground was furry white with hoarfrost, but it vanished when the sun rose. Only the underneath of the sidewalk and the shadows of the stores were frosty when Laura and Carrie hurried to school. The wind nipped their noses and chilled their mittened hands and they did not try to talk through their mufflers.

The wind had a desolate sound. The sun was small and the sky was empty of birds. On the endless dull prairie the grasses lay worn-out and dead. The schoolhouse looked old and gray and tired.

It seemed that the winter would never begin and never end. Nothing would ever happen but going to school and going home, lessons at school and lessons at home. Tomorrow would be the same as today, and in all her life, Laura felt, there would never be anything but studying and teaching school. Even Christmas would not be a real Christmas without Mary.

The book of poems, Laura supposed, was still hidden in Ma's bureau drawer. Every time Laura passed the bureau at the head of the stairs in Ma's room, she thought of that book and the poem she had not finished reading. "Courage!" he said, and pointed to the land, "This mounting wave will roll us shoreward soon." She had thought the same thought so often that it was stale, and even looking forward to the book for Christmas was no longer exciting.

Friday night came again. Laura and Carrie washed the dishes as usual. As usual, they brought their books to the lamplit table. Pa was in his chair, reading the paper. Ma was gently rocking and her knitting needles were clicking as they always did. As usual, Laura opened her history book.

Suddenly she could not bear it all. She thrust back her chair, slammed her book shut and thumped it down on the table. Pa and Ma started, and looked at her in surprise.

"I don't care!" she cried out. "I don't want to study! I don't want to learn! I don't want to teach school, *ever!*"

Ma looked as stern as it was possible for her to look. "*Laura,*" she said, "I know you would not swear, but losing your temper and slamming things is as bad as saying the words. Let us have no more wooden swearing."

Laura did not answer.

"What is the matter, Laura?" Pa asked. "Why don't you want to learn, and to teach school?"

"Oh, I don't know!" Laura said in despair. "I am so tired of everything. I want—I want something to happen. I want to go West. I guess I want to just play, and I know I am too old," she almost sobbed, a thing she never did.

"Why, Laura!" Ma exclaimed.

"Never mind," Pa said soothingly. "You have been studying too hard, that is all."

"Yes, put away your books for this one evening," said Ma. "In the last bundle of *Youth's Companions*, there are still some stories that we have not read. You may read one to us, Laura, wouldn't you like that?"

"Yes, Ma," Laura answered hopelessly. Even reading a story was not what she wanted. She did not know what she wanted, but she knew she could not have it, whatever it was. She got the *Youth's Companions* and pulled her chair to the table again. "You choose the story you want, Carrie," she said.

Patiently she read aloud, while Carrie and Grace listened wide-eyed and Ma's rocker swayed and her knitting needles clicked. Pa had gone across the street, to spend an evening talking with the men around the stove in Fuller's hardware store.

Suddenly the door opened and Pa burst in, saying, "Put on your bonnets, Caroline and girls! There's a meeting at the schoolhouse!"

"Whatever in the world—" Ma said.

"Everybody's going!" said Pa. "We are starting a literary society."

Ma laid aside her knitting. "Laura and Carrie, get your wraps on while I bundle up Grace."

Quickly they were ready to follow Pa's lighted lantern. When Ma blew out the lamp, Pa picked it up. "Better take it along, we'll want lights in the schoolhouse," he explained.

Other lanterns were coming along Main Street, and bobbing into the darkness of Second Street ahead. Pa called for Mr. Clewett, who was there and had brought the schoolhouse key. The desks looked weird in flickering lantern light. Others had brought lamps, too. Mr. Clewett lighted a large one on his desk, and Gerald Fuller drove a nail into the wall and hung up a lamp with a tin reflector. He had closed his store for the meeting. All the storekeepers were closing their stores and coming. Almost everyone in town was coming. Pa's lamp helped the lanterns to make the schoolhouse quite light.

The seats were filled and men were standing thick behind them, when Mr. Clewett called the room to order. He said that the purpose of this meeting was to organize a literary society.

"The first thing in order," he said, "will be a roll call of members. I will then hear nominations for temporary chairman. The temporary chairman will take charge, and we will then proceed to nominate and ballot for permanent officers."

Everyone was a little taken aback, and felt less jolly, but it was an interesting question, who could be elected President. Then Pa stood up by his seat, and said, "Mr. Clewett and townfolks, what we've come here for is some fun to liven us up. It does not seem necessary to organize anything.

"From what I've seen," Pa went on, "the trouble with organizing a thing is that pretty soon folks get to paying more attention to the organization than to what they're organized for. I take it we're pretty well agreed right now on what we want. If we start organizing and electing, the chances are we won't be as well agreed on who's to be elected to fill office. So I suggest, let's just go straight ahead and do what we want to do, without any officers. We've got the schoolteacher, Mr. Clewett, to act as leader. Let him give out a program, every meeting, for the next meeting. Anybody that gets a good idea can speak up for it, and anybody that's called on will pitch in and do his share in the programs the best he can, to give everybody a good time."

"That's the ticket, Ingalls!" Mr. Clancy sang out, and as Pa sat down, a good many began to clap. Mr. Clewett said, "All in favor, say 'Aye!'" A loud chorus of "Ayes" voted that it should be so.

Then for a minute, no one knew what to do next. Mr. Clewett said, "We haven't any program for this meeting." Some man answered, "Shucks, we aren't going home yet!" The barber suggested singing, and someone said, "You got some pupils that can speak pieces? How about it, Clewett?" Then a voice said, "How about a spelling match?" Several chimed in to that, "That's the notion!" "That's the idea! Let's have a spelling match!"

Mr. Clewett appointed Pa and Gerald Fuller as leaders. There was a good deal of joking as they took their places in the front corners of the room and began to call out names.

Laura sat anxiously waiting. The grown-ups were chosen first, of course. One by one they went up, and as the two lines grew longer, Laura grew more afraid that Gerald Fuller might call her before Pa did. She did not want to spell against Pa. At last there was the most anxious pause. It was Pa's turn to choose, and though he made a joke that set everyone laughing, Laura could see that he was hesitating. He decided, and called, "Laura Ingalls."

She hurried to take the next place in his line. Ma was already in it, above her. Gerald Fuller called then, "Foster!" Last of the grown-ups, Mr. Foster took the place opposite Laura. Perhaps Pa should have chosen him because he was grown-up, but Pa had wanted Laura. Surely, Laura thought, Mr. Foster could not be much of a speller. He was one of the homesteaders who drove oxen, and last winter he had stupidly jumped off Almanzo Wilder's horse, Lady, and let her run away while he fired at the antelope herd, though he was not within range.

Rapidly now all the school pupils were chosen, even the smallest. The two lines went from the teacher's desk all around the walls to the door. Then Mr. Clewett opened the speller.

First he gave out the primer words. "Foe, low, woe, roe, row, hero—" and he caught Mr. Barclay! Confused, Mr. Barclay spelled, "Hero; h-e-, he, r-o-e, ro, hero," and the roar of laughter surprised him. He joined in it as he went to a seat, the first one down.

The words grew longer. More and more spellers went down. First Gerald Fuller's side was shorter, then Pa's, then Gerald Fuller's again. Everyone grew warm from laughter and excitement. Laura was in her element. She loved to spell. Her toes on a crack in the floor and her hands behind her, she spelled every word that came to her. Down went four from the enemy's side, and three from Pa's, then the word came to Laura. She took a deep breath and glibly spelled, "Differentiation: d-i-f, dif; f-e-r, fer, differ; e-n-t, ent, different; i, differenti; a-t-i-o-n, ashun; differentiation!"

Slowly almost all the seats filled with breathless, laughing folks who had been spelled down. Six remained in Gerald Fuller's line, and only five in Pa's—Pa and Ma and Florence Garland and Ben Woodworth and Laura.

"Repetitious," said Mr. Clewett. Down went one from the other side, leaving the lines even. Ma's gentle voice spelled, "Repetitious: r-e, re; p-e-t, pet, repet; i, repeti; t-i-o-u-s, shius, repetitious."

"Mimosaceous," said Mr. Clewett. Gerald Fuller spelled, "Mimosaceous; m-i-m, mim; o-s-a, mimosa; t-i-—" He was watching Mr. Clewett. "No, s-i-," he began again. "That's got me beat," he said, and sat down.

"Mimosaceous," said Florence Garland. "M-i-m, mim; o-s-a, mimosa; t-e-—" And she had been a schoolteacher!

The next one on Gerald Fuller's side went down, then Ben shook his head and quit without trying. Laura stood straighter, waiting to spell the word. Now at the head of the other line, Mr. Foster began. "Mimosaceous: m-i, mi; m-o, mo, mimo; s-a, sa, mimosa; c-e-o-u-s, sius, mimosaceous."

A great burst of applause rose up, and some man shouted, "Good for you, Foster!" Mr. Foster had taken off his thick jacket and he stood in his checked shirt, smiling sheepishly. But there was a glint in his eye. No one had guessed that he was a brilliant speller.

Fast and hard the words came pelting then, the tricky words from the very back of the spelling book. On the other line, everyone went down but Mr. Foster. Ma went down. Only Pa and Laura were left, to down Mr. Foster.

Not one of them missed a word. In breathless silence, Pa spelled, Mr. Foster spelled, Laura spelled, then Mr. Foster again. He was one against two. It seemed that they could not beat him.

Then, "Xanthophyll," said Mr. Clewett. It was Laura's turn.

"Xanthophyll," she said. To her surprise, she was suddenly

confused. Her eyes shut. She could almost see the word on the speller's last page, but she could not think. It seemed that she stood a long time in a dreadful silence full of watching eyes.

"Xanthophyll," she said again desperately, and she spelled quickly, "X-a-n, zan; t-h-o, tho, zantho; p-h—" Wildly she thought, "Grecophil," and in a rush she ended, "-i-l-?" Mr. Clewett shook his head.

Trembling, Laura sat down. Now there was only Pa left.

Mr. Foster cleared his throat. "Xanthophyll," he said. "X-a-n, zan; t-h-o, tho zantho; p-h-y—" Laura could not breathe. No one breathed. "-l," said Mr. Foster.

Mr. Clewett waited. Mr. Foster waited, too. It seemed that the waiting lasted forever. At last Mr. Foster said, "Well, then, I'm beat," and he sat down. The crowd applauded him anyway, for what he had done. He had won respect that night.

"Xanthophyll," said Pa. It seemed impossible now that anyone could spell that dreadful word, but Laura thought, Pa can, he *must*, he's *GOT* to!

"X-a-n, zan," said Pa; "t-h-o, tho, zantho; p-h-y—" He seemed slower, perhaps, than he was. "Double-l," he said.

Mr. Clewett clapped the speller shut. There had never been such thundering applause as that applause for Pa. He had spelled down the whole town.

Then, still warm and all stirred up, everyone was getting into wraps.

"I don't know when I've had such a good time!" Mrs. Bradley said to Ma.

"The best of it is, to think we'll have another meeting next Friday," said Mrs. Garland.

Still talking, the crowd was streaming out and lanterns went jogging toward Main Street.

"Well, do you feel some better, Laura?" Pa asked, and she answered, "Oh, yes! Oh, didn't we have a good time!"

CHAPTER 19

The Whirl of Gaiety

Now there was always Friday evening to look forward to, and after the second Literary, there was such rivalry between the entertainers that there was news almost every day.

The second Literary was entirely charades, and Pa carried off the honors of the whole evening. Nobody could guess his charade.

He played it alone, in his everyday clothes. Walking up the central aisle, he carried two small potatoes before him on the blade of his ax. That was all.

Then he stood twinkling, teasing the crowd, and giving hints. "It has to do with the Bible," he said. "Why, every one of you knows it." He said, "It's something you often consult." He even said, "It's helpful in understanding Saint Paul." He teased, "Don't tell me you all give up!"

Every last one of them had to give up, and Laura was almost bursting with pride and delight when at last Pa told them, "It's Commentators on the Ac's."

As this sunk in, up rose a roar of laughter and applause.

On the way home, Laura heard Mr. Bradley say, "We'll have to go some, to beat that stunt of Ingalls!" Gerald Fuller, in his English way, called, "I say, there's talent enough for a musical program, what?"

For the next Literary, there was music. Pa with his fiddle and Gerald Fuller with his accordion made such music that the schoolhouse and the crowd seemed to dissolve in an enchantment. Whenever they stopped, applause roared for more.

It seemed impossible ever to have a more marvelous evening. But now the whole town was aroused, and families were driving in from the homestead claims to attend the Literaries. The men in town were on their mettle; they planned a superb musical evening. They practiced for it, and they borrowed Mrs. Bradley's organ.

On that Friday they wrapped the organ carefully in quilts and horse blankets, they loaded it into Mr. Foster's ox wagon and took it carefully to the schoolhouse. It was a beautiful organ, all shining wood, with carpeted pedals and a top climbing up in tapering wooden pinnacles, tiny shelves, and diamond-shaped mirrors. Its music rack was a lace pattern in wood, with red cloth behind it that showed through the holes, and on either side was a round place on which to set a lamp.

The teacher's desk was moved away, and that organ set in its place. On the blackboard Mr. Clewett wrote out the program. There was organ music by itself, organ music with Pa's fiddle, and organ music with the singing of quartets and duets and solos. Mrs. Bradley sang,

> Backward, turn backward,
> Oh Time in thy flight.
> Make me a child again,
> Just for tonight.

Laura could hardly bear the sadness of it. Her throat swelled and ached. A tear glittered on Ma's cheek before she could catch it with her handkerchief. All the women were wiping their eyes, and the men were clearing their throats and blowing their noses.

Everyone said that surely nothing could be better than that musical program. But Pa said mysteriously, "You wait and see."

As if this were not enough, the church building was roofed at last, and now every Sunday there were two church services and Sunday school.

It was a nice church, though so new that it still looked raw. As yet there was no bell in the belfry, nor any finish on the board walls. Outside, they were not yet weathered gray, and inside they were bare boards and the studding. The pulpit and the long benches with boxed-in ends were raw lumber, too, but it was all fresh and clean-smelling.

In the small entry built out from the door there was room enough to stamp snow off boots and shoes, and to settle clothing blown awry by the wind, before going into the church. The coal heater and the people warmed the church, and Mrs. Bradley had lent her organ, so there was organ music with the singing.

Laura even enjoyed Rev. Brown's preaching. What he said did not make sense to her, but he looked like the picture of

John Brown in her history book, come alive. His eyes glared, his white mustache and his whiskers bobbed, and his big hands waved and clawed and clenched into fists pounding the pulpit and shaking in air. Laura amused herself, too, by changing his sentences in her mind, to improve their grammar. She need not remember the sermon, for at home Pa required her and Carrie only to repeat the text correctly. Then, when the sermon was over, there was more singing.

Best of all was Hymn Eighteen, when the organ notes rolled out and everybody vigorously sang;

We are going forth with our staff in hand
Through a desert wild in a stranger land,
But our faith is bright and our hope is strong,
And the Good Old Way is our pilgrim song.

Then, all together letting out their voices in chorus louder than the swelling organ song,

'Tis the Good Old Way by our fathers trod,
'Tis the Way of Life and it leadeth unto God,
'Tis the only path to the realms of Day,
We are going home in the GOOD OLD WAY!

With Sunday school and morning church, Sunday dinner and dishes, and going to church again in the evening, every Sunday fairly flew past. There was school again on Monday, and the rising excitement of waiting for the Friday Literary; Saturday was not long enough for talking it all over, then Sunday came again.

As if all this were not more than enough, the Ladies' Aid planned a great celebration of Thanksgiving, to help pay for the church. It was to be a New England Supper.

Laura rushed home from school to help Ma peel and slice and stew down the biggest pumpkin that Pa had raised last summer. She carefully picked over and washed a whole quart of small white navy beans, too. Ma was going to make a mammoth pumpkin pie and the largest milkpan full of baked beans, to take to the New England Supper.

There was no school on Thanksgiving Day. There was no Thanksgiving dinner, either. It was a queer, blank day, full of anxious watching of the pie and the beans and of waiting for the evening. In the afternoon they all took turns, bathing in the washtub in the kitchen, by daylight. It was so strange to bathe by daylight, and on Thursday.

Then Laura carefully brushed her school dress, and brushed and combed and braided her hair and curled her bangs afresh. Ma dressed in her second-best, and Pa trimmed his whiskers and put on his Sunday clothes.

At lamp-lighting time, when they were all hungry for supper, Ma wrapped the great pan of beans in brown wrapping paper and a shawl, to keep the beans hot, while Laura bundled Grace into her wraps and hurried into her own coat and hood. Pa carried the beans, Ma bore in both hands the great pumpkin pie, baked in her large, square bread-baking tin. Laura and Carrie carried between them a basket full of Ma's dishes, and Grace held on to Laura's other hand.

As soon as they passed the side of Fuller's store they could see, across the vacant lots behind it, the church blazing with light. Wagons and teams and saddle ponies were already gathering around it, and people were going into its dimly lighted entry.

All the bracket lamps on the inside walls of the church were lighted. Their glass bowls were full of kerosene and their light shone dazzling bright from the tin reflectors behind their clear glass chimneys. All the benches had been set back against the walls, and two long, white-covered tables stretched glittering down the middle of the room.

"Oo, look!" Carrie cried out.

Laura stood stock-still for an instant. Even Pa and Ma almost halted, though they were too grown-up to show surprise. A grown-up person must never let feelings be shown by voice or manner. So Laura only looked, and gently hushed Grace, though she was as excited and overwhelmed as Carrie was.

In the very center of one table a pig was standing, roasted brown, and holding in its mouth a beautiful red apple.

Above all the delicious scents that came from those tables rose the delicious smell of roast pork.

In all their lives, Laura and Carrie had never seen so much food. Those tables were loaded. There were heaped dishes of mashed potatoes and of mashed turnips, and of mashed yellow squash, all dribbling melted butter down their sides from little hollows in their peaks. There were large bowls of dried corn, soaked soft again and cooked with cream. There were plates piled high with golden squares of corn bread and slices of white bread and of brown, nutty-tasting graham bread. There were cucumber pickles and beet pickles and green tomato pickles, and glass bowls on tall glass stems were full of red tomato preserves and wild-chokecherry jelly. On each table was a long, wide, deep pan of chicken pie, with steam rising through the slits in its flaky crust.

Most marvelous of all was the pig. It stood so lifelike, propped up by short sticks, above a great pan filled with baked apples. It smelled so good. Better than any smell of any other food was that rich, oily, brown smell of roasted pork, that Laura had not smelled for so long.

Already people were sitting at the tables, filling and refilling their plates, passing dishes to each other, eating and talking. Already the rich, pale meat, steaming hot inside its rim of crackling brown fat, was being sliced away from one side of the pig.

"How much pork have you got there?" Laura heard a man ask as he passed back his plate for more, and the man who was carving answered, while he cut a thick slice, "Can't say exactly, but it weighed a good forty pounds, dressed."

There was not a vacant place at the table. Up and down behind the chairs Mrs. Tinkham and Mrs. Bradley were hurrying, reaching between shoulders to refill cups with tea or coffee. Other ladies were clearing away used plates and replacing them with clean ones. As soon as anyone finished eating and left his place, it was taken, though the supper cost fifty cents. The church was almost full of people, and more were coming in.

This was all new to Laura. She felt lost and did not know what to do, until she saw Ida busily washing dishes at a table in a corner. Ma had begun to help wait on table, so Laura went to help Ida.

"Didn't you bring an apron?" Ida asked. "Then pin this towel on, so I can't splash your dress." Being a minister's daughter, Ida was used to church work. Her sleeves were rolled up, her dress was covered by a big apron, and she laughed and chattered while she washed dishes at a great rate and Laura as swiftly wiped them.

"Oh, this supper's a great success!" Ida rejoiced. "Did you ever think we'd get such a crowd!"

"No," Laura answered. She whispered, "Will anything be left for us to eat?"

"Oh, yes!" Ida answered confidently, and she went on, low, "Mother Brown always sees to that. She's keeping back a couple of the best pies and a layer cake."

Laura did not care so much for the fruit pies and the cake, but she did hope that some of the pork might be left when her turn came to go to the table.

Some was left when Pa got places for Carrie and Grace and himself. Laura glimpsed them, eating happily, while she went on wiping dishes. As fast as she wiped plates and cups, they were whisked away to the tables, while even faster, it seemed, more dirty ones were piled around the dishpan.

"We really need help here," Ida said cheerfully. No one had expected such a crowd. Ma was fairly flying about, and so were most of the other ladies. Faithfully Laura kept on wiping dishes. She would not leave Ida to cope with them alone, though she grew hungrier and hungrier, and had less and less hope of getting anything to eat.

It was a long time before the tables began to be deserted. At last only the members of the Ladies' Aid, and Ida and Laura, were still hungry. Then plates and cups, knives and forks and spoons, were washed and wiped again, one table was set again, and they could sit down. A pile of bones lay where the pig had been, but Laura was happy to see that plenty of meat remained on them, and some chicken pie was left in the pan. Quietly Mrs. Brown brought out the kept-back layer cake and the pies.

For a little while Laura and Ida rested and ate, while the women complimented each other's cooking and said what a success the supper had been. There was a clamor of talking all along the crowded benches by the walls, and in the corners and around the stove the men stood talking.

Then the tables were finally cleared. Laura and Ida washed and wiped dishes again, and the women sorted them out and packed them into baskets with whatever food was left. It was a compliment to Ma's cooking that not a bite of the pumpkin pie nor a spoonful of the beans remained. Ida washed the baking pan and the milkpan, Laura wiped them, and Ma crowded them into her basket.

Mrs. Bradley was playing the organ, and Pa and some others were singing, but Grace was asleep and it was time to go home.

"I know you are tired, Caroline," said Pa as he carried Grace homeward, while Ma carried the lantern to light the way and Laura and Carrie followed, lugging the basket of dishes. "But your Aid Society sociable was a great success."

"I *am* tired," Ma replied. A little edge to her gentle voice startled Laura. "And it wasn't a sociable. It was a New England Supper."

Pa said no more. The clock was striking eleven when he unlocked the door, and next day was another school day, and tomorrow night was the Friday Literary.

It was to be a debate, "Resolved: That Lincoln was a greater man than Washington." Laura was eager to hear it, for Lawyer Barnes was leading the affirmative and his arguments would be good.

"They will be educational," she said to Ma while they were hurriedly getting ready to go. She was really carrying on an argument with herself, for she knew that she should be studying. She had missed two whole evenings of study in that one week. Still, there would be a few days at Christmas, between the school terms, when she could make up for lost time.

The Christmas box had gone to Mary. In it Ma carefully placed the nubia that Laura had crocheted of soft, fleecy wool, as white as the big snowflakes falling gently outside the windows. She put in the lace collar that she had knitted of finest white sewing thread. Then she put in six handkerchiefs that Carrie had made of thin lawn. Three were edged with narrow, machine-made lace, and three were plainly hemmed. Grace could not yet make a Christmas present, but she had saved her pennies to buy half a yard of blue ribbon, and Ma had made this into a bow for Mary to pin at her throat, on the white lace collar. Then they had all written a long Christmas letter, and into the envelope Pa put a five-dollar bill.

"That will buy the little things she needs," he said. Mary's teacher had written, praising Mary highly. The letter said, too, that Mary could send home an example of her bead work if she could buy the beads, and that she needed a special slate to write on, and that perhaps later on they would wish her to own another kind of special slate on which to write Braille, a kind of writing that the blind could read with their fingers.

"Mary will know that we are all thinking of her at Christmas time," said Ma, and they were all happier in knowing that the Christmas box was on its way.

Still, without Mary it was not like Christmas. Only Grace was wholly joyous when at breakfast they opened the Christmas presents. For Grace there was a real doll, with a china head and hands, and little black slippers sewed on her cloth feet. Pa had put rockers on a cigar box to make a cradle for the doll, and Laura and Carrie and Ma had made little sheets and a pillow and a wee patchwork quilt, and had dressed the doll in a nightgown and a nightcap. Grace was perfectly happy.

Together Laura and Carrie had bought a German-silver thimble for Ma, and a blue silk necktie for Pa. And at Laura's plate was the blue-and-gilt book, Tennyson's *Poems.* Pa and Ma did not guess that she was not surprised. They had brought from Iowa a book for Carrie, too, and kept it hidden. It was, *Stories of the Moorland.*

That was all there was to Christmas. After the morning's work was done, Laura at last sat down to read "The Lotus Eaters." Even that poem was a disappointment, for in the land that seemed always afternoon the sailors turned out to be no good. They seemed to think they were entitled to live in that magic land and lie around complaining. When they thought about bestirring themselves, they only whined, "Why should we ever labor up the laboring wave?" Why, indeed! Laura thought indignantly. Wasn't that a sailor's job, to ever labor up the laboring wave? But no, they wanted dreamful ease. Laura slammed the book shut.

She knew there must be beautiful poems in such a book, but she missed Mary so much that she had no heart to read them.

Then Pa came hurrying from the post office with a letter. The handwriting was strange, but the letter was signed, Mary! She wrote that she placed the paper on a grooved, metal slate, and by feeling the grooves she could form the letters with a lead pencil. This letter was her Christmas present to them all.

She wrote that she liked college and that the teachers said she was doing well in her studies. She was learning to read and to write Braille. She wished that she might be with them on Christmas, and they must think of her on Christmas day as she would be thinking of them all.

Quietly the day went by after the letter was read. Once Laura said, "If only Mary were here, how she would enjoy the Literaries!"

Then suddenly she thought how swiftly everything was changing. It would be six more years before Mary came home, and nothing could ever be again the same as it had been.

Laura did no studying at all between those school terms, and January went by so quickly that she had hardly time to catch her breath. That winter was so mild that school was not closed for even one day. Every Friday night there was a Literary, each more exciting than the last.

There was Mrs. Jarley's Wax Works. From miles around, everyone came that night. Horses and wagons and saddle ponies were tied to all the hitching posts. The brown Morgans stood covered with neatly buckled blankets, and Almanzo Wilder stood with Cap Garland in the crowded schoolhouse.

A curtain of white sheets hid the teacher's platform. When this curtain was drawn aside, a great gasp went up, for all along the wall and across each end of the platform was a row of wax figures, life-size.

At least, they looked as if they were made of wax.

Their faces were white as wax, except for painted-on black eyebrows and red lips. Draped in folds of white cloth, each figure stood as motionless as a graven image.

After some moments of gazing on those waxen figures, Mrs. Jarley stepped from behind the drawn-back curtain. No one knew who she was. She wore a sweeping black gown and a scoop bonnet, and in her hand she held the teacher's long pointer.

In a deep voice she said, "George Washington, I command thee! Live and move!" and with the pointer she touched one of the figures.

The figure moved! In short, stiff jerks, one arm lifted and raised from the folds of white cloth a wax-like hand gripping a hatchet. The arm made chopping motions with the hatchet.

Mrs. Jarley called each figure by its name, touched it with the pointer, and each one moved jerkily. Daniel Boone raised and lowered a gun. Queen Elizabeth put on and took off a tall gilt crown. Sir Walter Raleigh's stiff hand moved a pipe to and from his motionless lips.

One by one all those figures were set in motion. They kept on moving, in such a lifeless, waxen way that one could hardly believe that they were really alive.

When finally the curtain was drawn to, there was one long, deep breath, and then wild applause. All the wax figures, naturally alive now, had to come out before the curtain while louder and louder grew the applause. Mrs. Jarley took off her bonnet and was Gerald Fuller. Queen Elizabeth's crown and wig fell off, and she was Mr. Bradley. There seemed no end to the hilarious uproar.

"This is the climax, surely," Ma said on the way home.

"You can't tell," Pa said teasingly, as if he knew more than he would say. "This whole town has its ginger up now."

Mary Power came next day to visit with Laura, and all the afternoon they talked about the waxworks. That evening when Laura settled down to study she could only yawn.

"I might as well go to bed," she said, "I'm too slee—" and she yawned enormously.

"This will make two evenings you've lost this week," said Ma. "And tomorrow night there's church. We are living in such a whirl of gaiety lately that I declare— Was that a knock at the door?"

The knock was repeated, and Ma went to the door. Charley was there, but he would not come in. Ma took an envelope that he handed her, and shut the door.

"This is for you, Laura," she said.

Carrie and Grace looked on wide-eyed, and Pa and Ma waited while Laura read the address on the envelope. "Miss Laura Ingalls, De Smet, Dakota Territory."

"Why, what in the world," she said. She slit the envelope carefully with a hairpin and drew out a folded sheet of gilt-edged notepaper. She unfolded it and read aloud;

Ben M. Woodworth
requests the pleasure of
your company at his home
Saturday Evening
January 28th
Supper at Eight o'clock

Just as Ma sometimes did, Laura sat limply down. Ma took the invitation from her hand and read it again.

"It's a party," Ma said. "A supper party."

"Oh, Laura! You're asked to a party!" Carrie exclaimed. Then she asked, "What is a party like?"

"I don't know," Laura said. "Oh, Ma, what will I do? I never went to a party. How must I behave at a party?"

"You have been taught how to behave wherever you are, Laura," Ma replied. "You need only behave properly, as you know how to do."

No doubt this was true, but it was no comfort to Laura.

CHAPTER 20

The Birthday Party

All the next week Laura thought of the party. She wanted to go and she did not want to. Once, long ago when she was a little girl, she had gone to Nellie Oleson's party, but that was a little girl's party. This would be different.

At school Ida and Mary Power and Minnie were excited about it. Arthur had told Minnie that it would be a birthday party, for Ben's birthday. From politeness they could hardly say a word about it, because Nellie was with them at recess, and Nellie had not been invited. She could not have come, because she lived in the country.

On the night of the party, Laura was dressed and ready at seven o'clock. Mary Power was coming to go with her to the depot, but she would not come for half an hour yet.

Laura tried to read again her favorite of Tennyson's poems,

> Come into the garden, Maud,
> For the black bat, night, has flown,
> Come into the garden, Maud,
> I am here at the gate alone;
> And the woodbine spices are wafted abroad
> And the musk of the rose is blown.

She could not sit still. She took one more look into the looking glass that hung on the wall. She wished so much to be tall and slim that she almost hoped to see a slender, tall girl. But in the glass she saw a small, round girl in a Sunday-best dress of blue cashmere.

At least it was a young lady's dress, so long that it hid the high tops of her buttoned shoes. The full-gathered skirt was gathered as full in the back as it could possibly be. Over it fitted the tight basque that came down in points in front and in back, and buttoned snugly with little green buttons straight up the front. A band of blue-and-gold-and-green plaid went all around the skirt just above the hem, and narrow strips of plaid edged the pointed bottom of the basque and went around the wrists of the tight, long sleeves. The upstanding collar was of the plaid, with a frill of white lace inside it, and Ma had lent Laura her pearl-shell pin to fasten the collar together under her chin.

Laura could not find one fault with the dress. But, oh! how she wished she were tall and willowy, like Nellie Oleson. Her waist was as round as a young tree, her arms were slender but round, too, and her very small hands were rather plump and capable-looking. They were not thin and languid like Nellie's hands.

Even the face in the glass was all curves. The chin was a soft curve and the red mouth had a short, curving upper lip. The nose was almost right, but the least bit of a saucy tilt kept it from being Grecian. The eyes, Laura thought, were too far apart, and they were a softer blue than Pa's. They were wide-open and anxious. They did not sparkle at all.

Straight across the forehead was the line of curled bangs. At least, her hair was thick and very long, though it was not golden. It was drawn back smooth from the bangs to the heavy mat of the coiled braid that covered the whole back of her head. Its weight made her feel really grown-up. She turned her head slowly to see the lamplight run glistening on its brown smoothness. Then suddenly she realized that she was behaving as if she were vain of her hair.

She went to the window. Mary Power was not yet in sight. Laura so dreaded the party that she felt she simply could not go.

"Sit down and wait quietly, Laura," Ma gently admonished her. Just then Laura caught sight of Mary Power, and feverishly she got into her coat and put on her hood.

She and Mary Power said hardly anything as they walked together up Main Street to its end, then followed the railroad track to the depot, where the Woodworths lived. The upstairs windows were brightly lighted, and a lamp burned in the telegraph office downstairs, where Ben's older brother Jim was still working. He was the telegraph operator. The electric telegraph's chattering sounded sharp in the frosty night.

"I guess we go into the waiting room," Mary Power said. "Do we knock, or just go right in?"

"I don't know," Laura confessed. Oddly, she felt a little better because Mary Power was uncertain, too. Still her throat was thick and her wrists were fluttering. The waiting room was a public place, but its door was shut and this was a party.

Mary Power hesitated, then knocked. She did not knock loudly, but the sound made them both start.

No one came. Boldly Laura said, "Let's go right in!"

As she spoke, she took hold of the door handle, and suddenly Ben Woodworth opened the door.

Laura was so upset that she could not answer his, "Good evening." He was wearing his Sunday suit and stiff white collar. His hair was damp and carefully combed. He added, "Mother's upstairs."

They followed him across the waiting room and up the stairs to where his mother was waiting in a little hall at their head. She was as small as Laura, and plumper, and she was daintiness itself, in a soft, thin gray dress with snowy white ruffles at throat and wrists. But she was so friendly that Laura felt comfortable at once.

In her bedroom they took off their wraps. The room was as dainty as Mrs. Woodworth. They hesitated to lay their coats on the dainty bed, with its knitted white coverlet and ruffled pillow shams. Thin, ruffled white muslin curtains were draped back at the windows, and on a little stand-table a knitted lace doily lay under the lamp. White knitted lace to match was spread on the bureau top, and white lace was draped across the top of the mirror frame.

Mary Power and Laura looked into the mirror, and with their fingers they fluffed up their bangs, slightly flattened by their hoods. Then in the friendliest way Mrs. Woodworth said, "If you've finished your primping, come into the sitting room."

Ida and Minnie, Arthur and Cap and Ben were already there. Mrs. Woodworth said, smiling, "Now when Jim comes up from work, our party will be complete." She sat down and began to talk pleasantly.

The sitting room was pleasant with shaded lamplight and cozy with warmth from the heater. Dark red cloth curtains were draped at the windows, and the chairs were not set against the wall but gathered about the stove, where the coals glowed through the isinglass of the stove's door. Besides the plush photograph album on the center-table's marble top, there were several other books standing on its lower shelf. Laura longed to look into them, but it would not be polite to be so inattentive to Mrs. Woodworth.

After a few moments Mrs. Woodworth excused herself and went into the kitchen. Then a stillness settled on everyone. Laura felt that she should say something, but she could think of nothing to say. Her feet seemed too big and she did not know what to do with her hands.

Through a doorway she saw a long table covered with a white cloth. China and silver sparkled on it, in the light of a lamp that hung suspended on long gilt chains from the ceiling. Glittering glass pendants hung down all around the edge of the lamp's milk-white shade.

It was all so pretty, but Laura could not forget her feet. She tried to draw them farther back beneath her skirts. She looked at the other girls, and knew that she must say something, for no one else could. Yet it was more than she could do, to break that silence. Her heart sank as she thought that, after all, a party was as uncomfortable as a sociable.

Then footsteps came springing up the stairs, and Jim came breezing in. He looked around at them all, and gravely asked, "Are you playing Quaker meeting?"

They all laughed. After that they were able to talk, though all the time they heard small clinks of china from the other room where Mrs. Woodworth was moving about the table. Jim was so much at ease that he called out, "Supper ready, mother?"

"Yes, it is," Mrs. Woodworth said from the doorway. "Won't you all come into the dining room?"

It seemed that the Woodworths used that room only for eating in.

Eight places were set at the table, and on each of the plates was a soup plate full of steaming oyster soup. Ben's place was at the head of the table, Jim's at the foot. Mrs. Woodworth told each of the others where to sit, and said that she would wait on them all.

Now Laura's feet were under the table, her hands had something to do, and it was all so bright and gay that she was no longer bashful.

In the very center of the table was a silver castor holding cut-glass bottles of vinegar, mustard and pepper sauce, and tall salt- and pepper-shakers. The plate at each place was of white china with a wreath of tiny, many-colored flowers around the edge. Beside each plate a white napkin stood up, folded in such a way that it partly opened out like a large flower.

Most marvelous of all, in front of each plate was an orange. Not only that; for these oranges, too, had been made into flowers. The orange's peel had been cut down from the top in little pointed sections, and each section was curled inward and down, like a flower's red-gold petals. Held within these petals, the flesh of the orange curved up, covered with its thin, white skin.

The oyster soup alone was treat enough to make a party, and to go with it Mrs. Woodworth passed a bowl of tiny, round oyster crackers. When the last drop of that delicious soup had been spooned up and swallowed, she took away the soup plates, and she set on the table a platter heaped with potato patties. The small, flat cakes of mashed potatoes were fried a golden brown. She brought then a platter full of hot, creamy, brown codfish balls, and then a plate of tiny, hot biscuits. She passed butter in a round glass butter dish.

Mrs. Woodworth urged generous helpings, not once, but twice. Then she brought cups of coffee, and passed the cream and sugar.

After all this, she cleared the table again, and brought in a white-frosted birthday cake. She set it before Ben and placed a stack of small plates beside it. Ben stood up to cut the cake. He put a slice on each small plate, and Mrs. Woodworth set one at each place. They waited then until Ben had cut his own slice of cake.

Laura was wondering about the orange before her. If those oranges were meant to be eaten, she did not know when nor how. They were so pretty, it was a pity to spoil them. Still, she had once eaten part of an orange, so she knew how good an orange tastes.

Everyone took a bite of cake, but no one touched an orange. Laura thought that perhaps the oranges were to be taken home. Perhaps she could take home an orange, to divide with Pa and Ma and Carrie and Grace.

Then everyone saw Ben take his orange. He held it carefully over his plate, stripped off the petaled peeling, and broke the orange into its sections. He took a bite from one section, then he took a bite of cake.

Laura took up her orange, and so did everyone else. Carefully they peeled them, divided them into sections, and ate them with the slices of cake.

All the peelings were neat on the plates when supper was finished. Laura remembered to wipe her lips daintily with her napkin and to fold it, and so did the other girls.

"Now we'll go downstairs and play games," Ben said.

As they all got up from the table, Laura said low to Mary Power, "Oughtn't we to help with the dishes?" and Ida asked right out, "Sha'n't we help wash the dishes first, Mrs. Woodworth?" Mrs. Woodworth thanked them, but said, "Run along and enjoy yourselves, girls! Never mind the dishes!"

The big waiting room downstairs was bright with light from the bracket lamps, and warm from the red-hot heating stove. There was plenty of room to play the liveliest games. First they played drop-the-handkerchief, then they played blind-man's-buff. When at last they all dropped panting onto the benches to rest, Jim said, "I know a game you've never played!"

Eagerly they all wanted to know what it was.

"Well, I don't believe it's got a name, it's so new," Jim answered. "But you all come into my office and I'll show you how it's played."

In the small office there was barely room for them all to stand in a half-circle, as Jim told them to do, with Jim at one end and Ben at the other end, crowded against Jim's worktable. Jim told them all to join hands.

"Now stand still," he told them. They all stood still, wondering what next.

Suddenly a burning tingle flashed through Laura; all the clasped hands jerked, the girls screamed, the boys yelled. Laura was frightfully startled. She made no sound and did not move.

All the others began excitedly to ask, "What was that? What was it? What did you do, Jim? Jim, how did you do that?" Cap said, "I know it was your electricity, Jim, but how did you do it?"

Jim only laughed and asked, "Didn't you feel anything, Laura?"

"Oh, yes! I felt it," Laura answered.

"Then why didn't you yell?" Jim wanted to know.

"What was the use?" Laura asked him, and Jim could not tell her that.

"But what was it?" she demanded, with all the others, and Jim would answer only, "Nobody knows."

Pa, too, had said that nobody knows what electricity is. Benjamin Franklin had discovered that it is lightning, but nobody knows what lightning is. Now it worked the electric telegraph, and still nobody knew what it was.

They all felt queer, looking at the little brass machine on the table, that could send its clicking messages so far and fast. Jim made one click on it. "That's heard in St. Paul," he said.

"Right now?" Minnie asked, and Jim said, "Right now."

They were standing silent when Pa opened the door and walked in.

"Is the party over?" he asked. "I came to see my girl home." The big clock was striking ten. No one had noticed how late it was.

While the boys put on their coats and caps that had been hanging in the waiting room, the girls went upstairs to thank Mrs. Woodworth and tell her good night. In the dainty bedroom they buttoned their coats and tied on their hoods and said Oh! what a good time they had had! Now that the dreaded party was over, Laura only wished that it could last longer.

Downstairs Rev. Brown had come for Ida, and Laura and Mary Power walked home with Pa.

Ma was waiting up when Laura and Pa came in.

"I can see what a good time you've had, by the way your eyes are shining," Ma smiled at Laura. "Now slip quietly up to bed, for Carrie and Grace are asleep. Tomorrow you can tell all of us about the party."

"Oh, Ma, each one of us had a whole orange!" Laura couldn't help saying then, but she saved the rest to tell them all together.

CHAPTER 21

The Madcap Days

AFTER the party, Laura hardly cared about studying. The party had made such a jolly friendliness among the big girls and boys that now at recess and noon on stormy days they gathered around the stove, talking and joking.

The pleasant days between snowstorms were even livelier. Then they all played at snowballing each other outdoors. This was not ladylike, but it was such fun! They came in panting and laughing, stamping snow from their shoes and shaking it from coats and hoods in the entry, and they went to their seats warm and glowing and full of fresh air.

Laura was having such a good time that she almost forgot about improving her opportunity in school. She stayed at the head of all her classes, but her grades were no longer 100. She made mistakes in arithmetic, sometimes even in history. Once her arithmetic grade went down to 93. Still, she thought she could make up lost time by studying hard next summer, though she knew by heart the true words:

> Lost, between sunrise and sunset,
> One golden hour, set with sixty diamond minutes.
> No reward is offered, for it is gone forever.

The little boys brought their Christmas-present sleds to school. Sometimes the big boys borrowed them, and took the girls sled-riding. The boys pulled the sleds, for there were no hills to slide down, and this winter no blizzards made big, hard snowdrifts.

Then Cap and Ben made a hand-bobsled, big enough for all four girls to crowd into. The four boys pulled it. At recess they raced at great speed, far out on the prairie road and back. At noon they had time to go even farther.

At last Nellie Oleson could not bear standing alone at the window and watching this. She had always disdained to play outdoors in the cold that might roughen her delicate complexion and chap her hands, but one day at noon she declared that she would go for a sled ride.

The sled was not large enough for five, but the boys would not agree to let any one of the other girls stay behind. They coaxed all five girls into the sled. The girls' feet stuck out from the sides, their skirts had to be gathered in till their woolen stockings showed above their high shoetops. Away they went, out on the snowy road.

They were windblown, disheveled, red-faced from cold and wind and laughter and excitement as the boys swung in a circle over the prairie and ran toward town, drawing the sled behind them. They whisked past the schoolhouse and Cap shouted, "Let's go up and down Main Street!"

With laughter and shouts the other boys agreed, running even faster.

Nellie shrieked, "Stop this minute! Stop! Stop, I tell you!"

Ida called, "Oh boys, you mustn't!" but she could not stop laughing. Laura was laughing, too, for they were such a funny sight, heels kicking helplessly, skirts blowing, fascinators and mufflers and hair whipping in the wind. Nellie's screaming only added to the boys' merriment as they ran the faster. Surely, Laura thought, they wouldn't go onto Main Street. Surely they would turn back any minute.

"No! No! *Arthur*, no!" Minnie was screaming, and Mary Power was begging, "Don't! Oh, please don't!"

Laura saw the brown Morgan horses standing blanketed at the hitching posts. Almanzo Wilder, in a big fur coat, was untying them. He turned to see what caused the girls' screaming, and at the same instant Laura knew that the boys meant to take them all past him, past all the eyes on Main Street. This was not funny at all.

The other girls were making such a commotion that Laura had to speak low, to be heard.

"Cap!" she said. "Please make them stop. Mary doesn't want to go on Main Street."

Cap began to turn at once. The other boys pulled against him, but Cap said, "Aw, come on," and swung the sled.

They were on their way back to the schoolhouse and the bell was ringing. At the schoolhouse door they scrambled out of the sled good-naturedly, all but Nellie. Nellie was furious.

"You boys think you're smart!" she raged. "You—you—you *ignorant Westerners!*"

The boys looked at her, sober and silent. They could not say what they wanted to, because she was a girl. Then Cap glanced anxiously at Mary Power, and she smiled at him.

"Thank you, boys, for the ride," Laura said.

"Yes, thank you all, it was such fun!" Ida chimed in.

"Thank you," Mary Power said, smiling at Cap, and his flashing smile lighted up his whole face.

"We'll go again at recess," he promised, as they all trooped into the schoolhouse.

In March the snow was melting, and final examinations were near. Still Laura did not study as she should. All the talk now was about the last Literary of that winter. What it would be was a secret that everyone was trying to guess. Even Nellie's family was coming to it, and Nellie was going to wear a new dress.

At home, instead of studying, Laura sponged and pressed her blue cashmere and freshened its lace frill. She so wanted a hat to wear instead of her hood that Ma bought for her half a yard of beautiful brown velvet.

"I know you'll take the very best care of the hat," Ma made excuse to herself, "and it will be perfectly good to wear for some winters to come."

So on Saturdays Mary Power and Laura made their hats. Mary's was of dark blue cloth, trimmed with a twist of black velvet and blue, all from her father's scrap bag. Laura's was of that lovely brown velvet, so soft to touch, and with a tawny-golden sheen to its silkiness. She wore it for the first time to the Literary.

In the schoolhouse no preparation was to be seen, except that the teacher's desk had been moved from the platform. People crowded three in a seat, and every inch of standing room was jammed. Even on the teacher's desk, boys stood tightly crowded. Mr. Bradley and Lawyer Barnes pressed back the mass of people, to keep the center aisle clear. No one knew why, and no one knew what was happening when a great shout went up from the people outside who were trying to get in.

Then up the center aisle came marching five black-faced men in raggedy-taggedy uniforms. White circles were around their eyes and their mouths were wide and red. Up onto the platform they marched, then facing forward in a row suddenly they all advanced, singing,

> Oh, talk about your Mulligan Guards!
> These darkies can't be beat!

Backward, forward and backward and forward they marched, back and forth, back and forth.

> Oh TALK aBOUT your MULLigan GUARDS!
> These DARKies CAN't be BEAT!
> We MARCH in TIME and CUT a SHINE!
> Just WATCH these DARKies' FEET!

The man in the middle was clog dancing. Back against the wall stood the four raggedy black-faced men. One played a jew's-harp, one played a mouth organ, one kept the time with rattling bones, and one man clapped with hands and feet.

The cheering started; it couldn't be stopped. Feet could not be kept still. The whole crowd was carried away by the pounding music, the grinning white-eyed faces, the wild dancing.

There was no time to think. When the dancing stopped, the jokes began. The white-circled eyes rolled, the big red mouths blabbed questions and answers that were the funniest ever heard. Then there was music again, and even wilder dancing.

When the five darkies suddenly raced down the aisle and were gone, everyone was weak from excitement and laughing. It did not seem possible that the whole evening had gone. The famous minstrel shows in New York surely could not be better than that minstrel show had been. Then a question ran through the whole jostling crowd, "Who were they?"

In their rag-tag clothing and with their blackened faces, it had been hard to know who they were. Laura was sure that the clog dancer was Gerald Fuller, for she had once seen him dance a jig on the sidewalk in front of his hardware store. And as she remembered the black hands that had held the long, flat, white bones between their fingers and kept them rattling out the tunes, she would have been certain that that darky was Pa, if the darky had had whiskers.

"Pa couldn't have cut off his whiskers, could he?" she asked

Ma, and in horror Ma answered, "Mercy, no!" Then she added, "I hope not."

"Pa must have been one of the darkies," Carrie said, "because he did not come with us."

"Yes, I know he was practicing to be in the minstrel show," said Ma, walking faster.

"Well, but none of the darkies had whiskers, Ma," Carrie reminded her.

"My goodness," Ma said. "Oh my goodness." She had been so carried away that she had not thought of that. "He couldn't have," she said, and she asked Laura, "Do you suppose he would?"

"I don't know," Laura answered. She really thought that, for such an evening, Pa would have sacrificed even his whiskers, but she did not know what he had done.

They hurried home. Pa was not there. It seemed a much longer time than it was, before he came in, cheerfully asking, "Well, how was the minstrel show?"

His long brown whiskers were as they had always been.

"*What did you do with your whiskers?*" Laura cried.

Pa pretended to be surprised and puzzled, asking, "Why, what is wrong with my whiskers?"

"Charles, you'll be the death of me," Ma said, helplessly laughing. But looking closely, Laura saw the smallest white smudge in the laughing-wrinkles at the corner of his eye, and she found a very little black grease in his whiskers.

"I know! You blacked them and smoothed them down behind that high coat-collar!" she accused him, and he could not deny it. He had been the darky who rattled the bones.

Such an evening came once in a lifetime, Ma said, and they all sat up late, talking about it. There would be no more Literaries that winter, for spring was coming soon.

"We'll move back to the claim as soon as school lets out," Pa said. "How will all of you like that?"

"I must be looking over my garden seeds," Ma said thoughtfully.

"I'll be glad to go. Grace and I'll pick violets again," said Carrie. "Won't you be glad, Grace?" But Grace was almost asleep on Ma's lap in the rocking chair. She only opened one eye and murmured, "Vi'lets."

"How about you, Laura?" Pa asked. "I've been thinking that by now you might want to stay in town."

"I might," Laura admitted. "I do like living in town better than I ever thought I would. But everyone will be moving out to hold down claims all summer, and we'll come back to town next winter, won't we?"

"Yes, I really think we will," said Pa. "We might as well, as long as I can't rent this building, and it is safer for you girls, going to school. Though we might as well have stayed on the claim this winter. Well, that's the way it goes. Get all ready for a hard winter, and there's not so much as one blizzard."

He said it so comically that they all burst out laughing at the joke on them.

After that, there was moving to think about, and in the warming air scented with damp earth, Laura felt less than ever like studying. She knew she could pass the examinations, even if her grades were not as high as they should be.

When her conscience pricked her, she thought rebelliously that she wouldn't see Ida and Mary Power and Minnie and the boys again, all summer long. She promised herself that she would study really hard, next summer.

In the examinations she did not make one perfect grade. Her history grade was only 99, and in arithmetic she earned only 92 plus. That was her record, and she could never change it now.

Then suddenly she knew that there must be no more self-indulgence. There were only ten months left, before she would be sixteen years old. Summer was before her, with blue skies and great blowing white clouds, the violets blooming in the buffalo wallow and the wild roses spangling the prairie grasses, but she must stay in the house and study. She must. If she did not, perhaps next spring she could not get a teacher's certificate, and Mary might have to leave college.

CHAPTER 22

Unexpected in April

EVERYTHING was settled in the little house on the homestead. Outdoors the snow was all gone, a green mist of new grass lay over the prairie, and plowed land spread black and sweet-smelling under the warm sun.

For two hours that morning Laura had studied. Now as she cleared away the dinner dishes she saw her slate and schoolbooks waiting and she felt the soft breeze beguiling her to go walking with Carrie and Grace in the spring weather. She knew she had to study.

"I think I'll go to town this afternoon," said Pa as he put on his hat. "Is there anything you want me to get, Caroline?"

Suddenly the breeze was icy cold, and Laura looked quickly from the window. She exclaimed, "Pa! There's a blizzard cloud!"

"Why, it can't be! This late in April?" Pa turned to see for himself.

The sunlight went out, the sound of the wind changed as it rose. The storm struck the little house. A whirling whiteness pressed against the window and the cold came in.

"On second thought," said Pa, "I believe I'd rather stay home this afternoon."

He drew a chair close to the stove and sat down. "I'm glad all the stock is in the stable. I was going to get picket ropes in town," he added.

Kitty was frantic. This was the first blizzard she had known. She did not know what to make of it, when all her fur stood up and crackled. Trying to soothe her, Grace discovered that a spark would snap from her wherever she was touched. Nothing could be done about that, except not to touch her.

Three days and nights the blizzard raged. Pa put the hens in the stable lest they freeze. It was so cold that the dismal days were spent close to the stove, and though the light was dim, Laura doggedly studied arithmetic. "At least," she thought, "I don't want to go walking."

On the third day, the blizzard left the prairie covered with fine, hard snow. It was still frozen when Pa walked to town next day. He brought back news that two men had been lost in that blizzard.

They had come from the East on the train, in the warm spring morning. They had driven out to see friends on a claim south of town, and just before noon they had set out to walk to another claim two miles away.

After the blizzard, the whole neighborhood turned out to search for them, and they were found beside a haystack, frozen to death.

"Being from the East, they didn't know what to do," said Pa. If they had dug into the haystack and plugged the hole behind them with hay, they would have kept each other warm and they might have lived through the blizzard.

"But whoever could have expected such a blizzard, so late," said Ma.

"Nobody knows what will happen," Pa said. "Prepare for the worst and then you've some grounds to hope for the best, that's all you can do."

Laura objected. "You were all prepared for the worst last winter, Pa, and all that work was wasted. There wasn't one blizzard till we were back here and not prepared for it."

"It does seem that these blizzards are bound to catch us, coming or going," Pa almost agreed.

"I don't see how anybody can be prepared for anything," said Laura. "When you expect something, and then something else always happens."

"Laura," said Ma.

"Well, it does, Ma," Laura protested.

"No," Ma said. "Even the weather has more sense in it than you seem to give it credit for. Blizzards come only in a blizzard country. You may be well prepared to teach school and still not be a schoolteacher, but if you are not prepared, it's certain that you won't be."

That was so. Later Laura remembered that Ma had once been a schoolteacher. That evening when she had put away her books to help Ma get supper, she asked, "How many terms of school did you teach, Ma?"

"Two," said Ma.

"What happened then?" Laura asked.

"I met your Pa," Ma answered.

"Oh," Laura said. Hopefully she thought that she might meet somebody. Maybe, after all, she would not have to be a schoolteacher always.

CHAPTER 23

Schooltime Begins Again

AFTERWARD it seemed to Laura that she did nothing but study that whole summer long. Of course this was not true. She brought water from the well in the mornings, she milked and moved the picket pins and taught the new calf to drink. She worked in the garden and in the house, and in haying time she trod down the great loads of hay that Pa drove away to town. But the long, hot, sticky hours with schoolbooks and slate seemed to overshadow all else. She did not go to town even on Fourth of July. Carrie went with Pa and Ma but Laura stayed at home to take care of Grace and study the Constitution.

Letters came often from Mary, and every week a long letter went to her in return. Even Grace was able to write little letters, as Ma taught her, and these were always sent to Mary with the others.

The hens were laying now. Ma saved the best eggs for setting, and twenty-four chicks hatched. The smaller pullet eggs Ma used in cooking, and for one Sunday dinner, with the first green peas and new potatoes, they ate fried chicken. The other cockerels Ma let grow up. They would be larger to eat, later on.

The gophers came again, and Kitty grew fat in the cornfield. She caught more gophers than she could eat, and at all hours of the day she could be heard mrreowling proudly as she brought a fresh-killed one to lay at Ma's feet or Laura's or Carrie's or Grace's. She wanted to share her good food, and her puzzled look showed plainly that she could not understand why the whole family did not eat gophers.

The blackbirds came again. Though they were not so many this year, and Kitty caught some of them, still they did damage enough. Again the mellow fall weather came, and Laura and Carrie walked to school.

There were more people in town now, and in all the country around. The school was so crowded that all the seats were filled, and in some of the front seats three of the smaller pupils sat.

There was a new teacher, Mr. Owen, a son of the Mr. Owen whose bay horses had almost won the Fourth of July race. Laura liked and respected him very much. He was not very old, but he was serious and industrious and enterprising.

From the first day, he ruled with a firm hand. Every pupil was obedient and respectful, every lesson was thoroughly learned. On the third day of school, Mr. Owen whipped Willie Oleson.

For some time, Laura did not quite know what she thought about that whipping. Willie was bright enough, but he had never learned his lessons. When he was called upon to recite, he let his mouth fall open and all the sense went out of his eyes. He looked less than halfwitted, he hardly looked human. It made anyone turn sick to see him.

He had begun doing this, to tease Miss Wilder. He seemed unable to collect his scattered mind enough to understand anything she said to him. At recess he would do this again, to amuse the other boys. When Mr. Clewett taught, he thought that Willie was a halfwit, and required nothing of him. The habit had grown on Willie, until now at any time he could be seen mooning about with his mouth dropped open and his eyes empty. Laura really thought that Willie's mind completely left him at these times.

The first time that Willie goggled at Mr. Owen was when his name was asked for the school record. Mr. Owen was startled, and Nellie spoke up. "He's my brother, Willie Oleson, and he can't answer questions, they confuse him."

Several times that day and the next, Laura saw Mr. Owen glance sharply at Willie. Willie was always drooling and staring blankly. When he was called upon to recite, Laura could not bear to see his idiot face. On the third day, Mr. Owen quietly said, "Come with me, Willie."

He had his pointer in his hand. With the other hand firm on Willie's shoulder, he took Willie into the entry and shut the door. He did not say anything. From their seat nearest the door, Ida and Laura heard the swish and thud of the pointer. Everyone heard Willie's howls.

Mr. Owen came quietly in with Willie. "Stop blubbering," he said. "Go to your seat and study. I expect you to know and recite your lessons."

Willie stopped blubbering and went to his seat. After that, one look from Mr. Owen cleared some of the idiot look from Willie's face. He seemed to be trying to think, and to act like other boys. Laura often wondered whether he could pull his mind together after he had let it go to pieces so, but at least Willie was trying. He was afraid not to try.

Laura and Ida, Mary Power and Minnie, and Nellie Oleson had kept their old seats. They were all tanned brown from the summer sun, except Nellie, who was paler and more ladylike than ever. Her clothes were so beautiful, though her mother did make them over from castoffs, that Laura grew dissatisfied with her brown school dress and her blue cashmere for best. She did not complain, of course, but she wanted to.

Hoops had finally come in, and Ma bought a set for Laura. She let down the hem of the brown dress, and made it over so cleverly that it could be worn over hoops perfectly well, and the full blue cashmere needed no changing. Still, Laura felt that all the other girls were better dressed.

Mary Power had a new school dress. Minnie Johnson had a new coat and new shoes. Ida's clothes came out of a missionary barrel, but Ida was so sweet and merry that she looked perfectly dear in anything. When Laura dressed for school, it seemed to her that the more she fussed with her appearance the more dissatisfying it was.

"Your corset is too loose," Ma tried to help her one morning. "Pull the strings tighter and your figure will be neater. And I can't think that a lunatic fringe is the most becoming way to do your hair. It makes any girl's ears appear larger to comb the hair up back of them and to have that mat of bangs above the forehead."

Ma was anxiously helpful, but some sudden thought made her laugh softly to herself.

"What is it, Ma? Tell us!" Laura and Carrie begged.

"I was only thinking of the time your Aunt Eliza and I combed our hair up off our ears and went to school that way. The teacher called us up front and shamed us before the whole school, for being so unladylike and bold as to let our ears be seen." Ma laughed softly again.

"Is that the reason you always wear those soft wings of hair down over your ears?" Laura cried.

Ma looked a little surprised. "Yes, I suppose it is," she answered, still smiling.

On the way to school Laura said, "Carrie, do you know I've never once seen Ma's ears?"

"They're probably pretty ears, too," said Carrie. "You look like her, and your ears are little and pretty."

"Well," Laura began; then she stopped and spun round and round, for the strong wind blowing against her always made the wires of her hoop skirt creep slowly upward under her skirts until they bunched around her knees. Then she must whirl around and around until the wires shook loose and spiraled down to the bottom of her skirts where they should be.

As she and Carrie hurried on she began again. "I think it was silly, the way they dressed when Ma was a girl, don't you? Drat this wind!" she exclaimed as the hoops began creeping upward again.

Quietly Carrie stood by while Laura whirled. "I'm glad I'm not old enough to have to wear hoops," she said. "They'd make me dizzy."

"They are rather a nuisance," Laura admitted. "But they are stylish, and when you're my age you'll want to be in style."

Living in town was so exciting that fall that Pa said there was no need of Literaries. There was church every Sunday, prayer meeting every Wednesday night. The Ladies' Aid planned two sociables, and there was talk of a Christmas tree. Laura hoped there would be one, for Grace had never seen a Christmas tree. In November there was to be a week of revival meetings at the church, and Mr. Owen, with the school board's approval, was planning a School Exhibition.

School would go on without interruption until the School Exhibition just before Christmas. So the big boys did not wait until winter, but came to school in November. More smaller pupils had to be crowded three in a seat to make room for them.

"This school needs a larger building," Mr. Owen said to Laura and Ida one day at recess. "I am hoping that the town can afford to build one next summer. There really is a need for a graded school, even. I am counting a great deal upon the showing we make at the School Exhibition, to acquaint the people with the school and its needs."

After that, he told Laura and Ida that their part in the Exhibition would be to recite the whole of American history, from memory.

"Oh, do you think we can do it, Laura?" Ida gasped when he had left them.

"Oh, yes!" Laura answered. "You know we like history."

"I'm glad you've got the longer part, anyway," said Ida. "I've only got to remember from John Quincy Adams to Rutherford B. Hayes, but you've got all that about the discoveries and the map and the battles, and the Western Reserve and the Constitution. My! I don't know how you ever can!"

"It's longer, but we've studied it more and reviewed it oftener," said Laura. She was glad to have that part; she thought it more interesting.

The other girls were talking eagerly about the revival meetings. Everyone in town and from all the near-by country would go to them. Laura did not know why, for she had never been to a revival meeting, but when she said that she should stay at home and study, Nellie exclaimed in horror, "Why, people who don't go to revival meetings are *atheists!*"

The others did not say a word in Laura's defense, and Ida's brown eyes pleaded anxiously when she said, "You are coming, aren't you, Laura?"

The revival meetings would last a whole week, and besides the daily lessons, there was the School Exhibition to prepare for. Monday night Laura hurried home from school to study till supper time; she thought about history while she washed the dishes, and then snatched a little time with her books while Pa and Ma were dressing.

"Hurry, Laura, or we'll be late! It's church time now," said Ma.

Standing before the glass, Laura hurriedly set her darling brown velvet hat evenly on her bangs, and fluffed them out. Ma waited by the door with Carrie and Grace. Pa shut the stove's draft and turned down the lamp wick.

"Are you all ready?" he asked; then he blew out the lamp. By his lantern light they all went out, and he locked the door. Not a window on Main Street was lighted. Behind Fuller's Hardware the last lanterns were bobbing across the vacant lots toward the brightly lighted church, and wagons, buggies, and blanketed horses stood thick in the shadows around it.

The church was crowded, and hot from the dazzling lamps and the coal heater. Graybeards sat close around the pulpit, families were in the middle seats, and young men and boys filled the back seats. Laura saw everyone she knew and many strangers, as Pa led the way up the aisle, looking for a vacant place. He stopped at next to the front seat, and Ma with Grace, then Carrie and Laura, edged past knees and sat down.

Reverend Brown rose from his chair behind the pulpit and gave out a hymn, Number 154. Mrs. Brown played the organ, and everyone stood up and sang.

> There were ninety and nine that safely lay
> In the shelter of the fold,
> But one was out on the hills away,
> Far off from the gates of gold,
> Away on the mountains wild and bare,
> Away from the tender shepherd's care.

If a revival meeting could be nothing but singing, Laura would have loved it, though she felt that she should be studying, not wasting time in enjoyment. Her voice rose clear and true as Pa's, as they sang,

> Rejoice, for the Lord brings back His own!

Then the long prayer began. Laura bent her head and closed her eyes, while Reverend Brown's harsh voice singsonged on and on. It was a great relief to stand up at last, and sing again. This was a hymn with a dancing swing and a throbbing beat.

> Sowing the seed by the daylight fair,
> Sowing the seed by the noonday glare,
> Sowing the seed by the fading light,
> Sowing the seed in the solemn night,
> Oh, what shall the harvest be-e-e,
> Oh, what shall the harvest be?

Reverend Brown's preaching went on with the throbbing and swinging. His voice rose and fell, thundered and quivered. His bushy white eyebrows raised and lowered, his fist thumped the pulpit. "Repent ye, repent ye while yet there is time, time to be saved from damnation!" he roared.

Chills ran up Laura's spine and over her scalp. She seemed to feel something rising from all those people, something dark and frightening that grew and grew under that thrashing voice. The words no longer made sense, they were not sentences, they were only dreadful words. For one horrible instant Laura imagined that Reverend Brown was the Devil. His eyes had fires in them.

"Come forward, come forward and be saved! Come to salvation! Repent, ye sinners! Stand up, stand up and sing! Oh, lost lambs! Flee from the wrath! Pull, pull for the shore!" His hands lifted them all to their feet, his loud voice sang,

Pull for the shore, sailor!
Pull for the shore!

"Come! Come!" his voice roared through the storm of singing, and someone, a young man, came stumbling up the aisle.

Heed not the stormy winds,
Though loudly they roar.

"Bless you, bless you, my sinning brother, down on your knees and God bless you; are there any more? Any more?" Reverend Brown was shouting, and his voice roared again into the song, "Pull for the Shore!"

The first words of that hymn had made Laura want to laugh. She remembered the tall thin man and the pudgy little one, so solemnly singing it, and all the storekeepers popping from the torn screen doors. Now she felt that all the noise and excitement was not touching her.

She looked at Pa and Ma. They were quietly standing and quietly singing, while the dark, wild thing that she had felt was roaring all around them like a blizzard.

Another young man, and then an older woman, went forward and knelt. Then church was over, yet somehow not over. People were pressing forward to crowd around those three and wrestle for their souls. In a low voice Pa said to Ma, "Come, let's go."

He carried Grace down the aisle toward the door. Ma followed with Carrie, and behind her Laura followed close. In the back seats all the young men and boys stood watching the people passing by. Laura's dread of strangers came over her and the open door ahead seemed a refuge from their eyes.

She did not notice a touch on her coat sleeve until she heard a voice saying, "May I see you home?"

It was Almanzo Wilder.

Laura was so surprised that she could not say a word. She could not even nod or shake her head. She could not think. His hand stayed on her arm and he walked beside her through the door. He protected her from being jostled in the crowded entry.

Pa had just lighted his lantern. He lowered the chimney and looked up, just as Ma turned back and asked, "Where's Laura?" They both saw Laura with Almanzo Wilder beside her, and Ma stood petrified.

"Come on, Caroline," said Pa. Ma followed him, and after one wide-eyed stare, Carrie did, too.

The ground was white with snow and it was cold, but there was no wind, and stars shone brightly in the sky.

Laura could not think of a word to say. She wished that Mr. Wilder would say something. A faint scent of cigar smoke came from his thick cloth overcoat. It was pleasant, but not as home-like as the scent of Pa's pipe. It was a more dashing scent, it made her think of Cap and this young man daring that dangerous trip to bring back the wheat. All this time she was trying to think of something to say.

To her complete surprise, she heard her own voice, "Anyway, there's no blizzard."

"No. This is a nice winter, not much like the Hard Winter," said he.

Again there was silence, except for the crunch of their feet on the snow-covered path.

On Main Street, dark groups hurried homeward, with lanterns that cast big shadows. Pa's lantern went straight across the street. Pa and Ma and Carrie and Grace went in and were at home.

Laura and Almanzo stood outside the closed door.

"Well, good night," he said, as he made a backward step and raised his cap. "I'll see you tomorrow night."

"Good night," Laura answered, as she quickly opened the

door. Pa was holding the lantern up while Ma lighted the lamp, and he was saying, "—trust him anywhere, and it's only walking home from Church."

"But she's only fifteen!" said Ma.

Then the door was shut. Laura was inside the warm room. The lamp was lighted, and everything was right.

"Well, what did you think of the revival meeting?" Pa asked, and Laura answered, "It isn't much like Reverend Alden's quiet sermons. I like his better."

"So do I," said Pa. Then Ma said it was past bedtime.

Several times next day, Laura wondered what young Mr. Wilder had meant by saying that he would see her that night. She did not know why he had walked home with her. It was an odd thing for him to do, for he was grown-up. He had been a homesteader for a few years, so he must be at least twenty-three years old, and he was Pa's friend more than hers.

That night in church she did not mind the sermon at all. She only wished she need not be there, when so many people, all together, grew so excited. She was glad when Pa said again, "Let's go."

Almanzo Wilder stood in the line of young men near the door, and Laura was embarrassed. She saw now that several young men were taking young ladies home. She felt her cheeks flushing and she did not know where to look. Again he asked, "May I see you home?" and this time she answered politely, "Yes."

She had thought what she would have said last night, so now she spoke about Minnesota. She had come from Plum Creek and he had come from Spring Valley, but before that he had lived in New York State, near Malone. Laura thought she kept the conversation going quite well, until they reached the door where she could say, "Good night."

Every night that week he saw her home from the revival meeting. She still could not understand why. But the week soon ended, so that again she could spend the evenings in study, and she forgot to wonder about Almanzo in her dread of the School Exhibition.

CHAPTER 24

The School Exhibition

THE room was warm and the lamp burned clear and bright, but Laura's chilly fingers could hardly button her blue cashmere basque and it seemed to her that the looking glass was dim. She was dressing to go to the School Exhibition.

She had dreaded it for so long that now it did not seem real, but it was. Somehow she had to get through it.

Carrie was frightened, too. Her eyes were very large in her thin face, and she whispered to herself, " 'Chisel in hand stood the sculptor boy,' " while Laura tied on her hair ribbon. Ma had made a new dress of bright plaid woolen for Carrie to wear when she spoke her piece. "Ma, please hear me say my piece again," she begged.

"There isn't time, Carrie," Ma replied. "We're almost late as it is. I'm sure you know it perfectly well. I'll hear you say it on the way. Are you ready, Laura?"

"Yes, Ma," Laura said faintly.

Ma blew out the lamp. Outdoors a cold wind was blowing and snow blew white along the ground. Laura's skirts whipped in the wind, her hoops crawled up maddeningly, and she feared that the curl was coming out of her bangs.

Desperately she tried to remember all that she must say, but she could not get beyond, "America was discovered by Christopher Columbus in 1492. Columbus, a native of Genoa in Italy—" Carrie was breathlessly chanting, " 'Waiting the hour when at God's command——' "

Pa said, "Hullo, they've got the church lighted up."

Both the schoolhouse and the church were lighted. A thick, dark line of people with splotches of yellow lanternlight was moving toward the church.

"What's up?" Pa asked, and Mr. Bradley answered, "So many have come, they can't all get into the schoolhouse. Owen's moving us into the church."

Mrs. Bradley said, "I hear you're going to give us a real treat tonight, Laura."

Laura hardly knew what she answered. She was thinking, "Christopher Columbus, a native of Genoa in Italy—America was discovered by Christopher Columbus in 1492. Christopher Columbus, a—" She had to get past Columbus.

In the entry the crowd was so jammed that she feared her wire hoops were pressed out of shape. There was no more room for wraps on the hooks there. The aisles were packed with people trying to find seats. Mr. Owen was heard repeating, "These front seats are reserved for the scholars. Pupils please come forward to these seats."

Ma said she would take care of the wraps. She helped Carrie out of her coat and hood while Laura took off her coat and hat and nervously felt her bangs.

"Now, Carrie, you have only to do as well as you have been doing," Ma said as she straightened Carrie's full plaid skirt. "You know your piece perfectly."

"Yes, Ma," Carrie whispered. Laura could not speak. Dumbly she guided Carrie up the aisle. On the way Carrie pressed back against her and looked up pleadingly. "Do I look all right?" she whispered.

Laura looked at Carrie's round, scared eyes. One wisp of fair hair straggled above them. Laura smoothed it back. Then Carrie's hair was perfectly sleek from the middle parting to the two stiff braids hanging down her back.

"There, now you look just right!" Laura said. "Your new plaid dress is beautiful." Her voice did not seem to be hers, it was so serene.

Carrie's face lighted up, and she went wriggling past Mr. Owen to her classmates in the front seat.

Mr. Owen said to Laura, "The pictures of the Presidents are being put up on the wall here, just as they were in the schoolhouse. My pointer is on the pulpit. When you come to George Washington, take up the pointer, and point to each President as you begin to speak about him. That will help you remember the proper order."

"Yes, sir," Laura said, but now she knew that Mr. Owen was worrying, too. She, of all persons, must not fail, because hers was the principal part in the Exhibition.

"Did he tell you about the pointer?" Ida whispered, as Laura sat down beside her. Ida looked like a dim copy of her usual happy self. Laura nodded, and they watched Cap and Ben, who were tacking up the pictures of the Presidents on the board wall, between the studding. The pulpit had been moved back against the wall to leave the platform clear. They could see the long school pointer lying on it.

"I know you can do your part, but I'm scared," Ida quavered.

"You won't be when the time comes," Laura encouraged her. "Why, we are always good in history. It's easier than the mental arithmetic we've got to do."

"I'm glad you have the beginning part, anyway," Ida said. "I couldn't do that, I just *couldn't*."

Laura had been glad to have that part because it was more interesting. Now there was only a jumble in her head. She kept trying to remember all that history, though she knew it was too late now. But she must remember it. She dared not fail.

"Please come to order," Mr. Owen said. The School Exhibition began.

Nellie Oleson, Mary Power and Minnie, Laura and Ida and Cap and Ben and Arthur filed up onto the platform. Arthur was wearing new shoes, and one of them squeaked. In a row, they all faced the church full of watching eyes. It was all a blur to Laura. Rapidly Mr. Owen began to ask questions.

Laura was not frightened. It did not seem real that she was standing in the dazzle of light, wearing her blue cashmere and reciting geography. It would be shameful to fail to answer, or to make a mistake, before all those people and Pa and Ma, but she was not frightened. It was all like a dream of being half-asleep, and all the time she was thinking, "America was discovered by Christopher Columbus—" She did not make one mistake in geography.

There was applause when that was over. Then came grammar. This was harder because there was no blackboard. It is easy enough to parse every word in a long, complex-compound sentence full of adverbial phrases, when you see the sentence written on slate or blackboard. It is not so easy to keep the whole sentence in mind and not omit a word nor so much as a comma. Still, only Nellie and Arthur made mistakes.

Mental arithmetic was even harder. Laura disliked arithmetic. Her heart beat desperately when her turn came and she was sure she would fail. She stood amazed, hearing her voice going glibly through problems in short division. "Divide 347,264 by 16. Sixteen into 34 goes twice, put down 2 and carry 2; sixteen into 27 goes once, put down 1 and carry 11; sixteen into 112 goes seven times, put down 7 and carry naught; sixteen into 6 does not go, put down naught; sixteen into 64 goes 4 times, put down 4. Three hundred and forty-seven thousand, two hundred and sixty-four divided by sixteen equals—twenty-one thousand, seven hundred and four."

She need not multiply back to make sure the answer was right. She knew it was right because Mr. Owen set another problem.

At last he said, "Class dismissed."

Through a great noise of applause, they all turned and filed back to their seat. Now the younger pupils would speak their pieces. Then Laura's turn would come.

While one after another the girls and boys were called to the platform and recited, Laura and Ida sat still and stiff with dread. All the history that Laura knew raced madly through her mind. "America was discovered . . . The Congress of the Confederated Colonies in Philadelphia assembled . . . 'There is only one word in this petition which I disapprove, and that is the word Congress . . .' Mr. Benjamin Harrison rose and said, 'There is but one word in this paper, Mr. President, which I approve, and that is the word, Congress.' . . . 'And George the Third . . . may profit by their example. If this be treason, gentlemen, make the most of it!' . . . Give me liberty or give me death. . . . We hold these truths to be self-evident. . . . Their feet left bloody tracks upon the snow. . . ."

Suddenly Laura heard Mr. Owen say, "Carrie Ingalls."

Carrie's thin face was strained and pale as she made her way to the aisle. All the buttons up the back of her plaid dress were buttoned outside-in. Laura should have thought to button her up; but no, she had left poor little Carrie to do the best she could, alone.

Carrie stood very straight, her hands behind her back and her eyes fixed above the crowd. Her voice was clear and sweet as she recited,

> Chisel in hand stood a sculptor boy
> With his marble block before him,
> And his face lit up with a smile of joy

As an angel dream passed o'er him.
He carved that dream on the yielding stone
With many a sharp incision;
In Heaven's own light the sculptor shone—
He had caught that angel vision.

Sculptors of life are we as we stand,
With our lives uncarved before us,
Waiting the hour when at God's command
Our life-dream passes o'er us.
Let us carve it then on the yielding stone
With many a sharp incision.
Its Heavenly beauty shall be our own—
Our lives, that angel vision.

She had not once faltered, nor missed a single word. Laura was proud, and Carrie flushed rosily as she marched smiling down to her place amid a loud clapping of hands.

Then Mr. Owen said, "Now we will listen to a review of the history of our country from its discovery to the present time, given by Laura Ingalls and Ida Wright. You may begin, Laura."

The time had come. Laura stood up. She did not know how she got to the platform. Somehow she was there, and her voice began. "America was discovered by Christopher Columbus in 1492. Christopher Columbus, a native of Genoa in Italy, had long sought permission to make a voyage toward the west in order to discover a new route to India. At that time Spain was ruled by the united crowns of——"

Her voice was shaking a little. She steadied it and went carefully on. It did not seem real that she was standing there, in her blue cashmere held grandly out by the hoops, with Ma's pearl pin fastening the lace cascade under her chin, and her bangs damp and hot across her forehead.

She told of the Spanish and the French explorers and their settlements, of Raleigh's lost colony, of the English trading companies in Virginia and in Massachusetts, of the Dutch who bought Manhattan Island and settled the Hudson Valley.

At first she spoke into a blur, then she began to see faces. Pa's stood out from all the others. His eyes met hers and they were shining as slowly he nodded his head.

Then she was really launched upon the great history of

America. She told of the new vision of freedom and equality in the New World, she told of the old oppressions of Europe and of the war against tyranny and despotism, of the war for the independence of the thirteen new States, and of how the Constitution was written and these thirteen States united. Then, taking up the pointer, she pointed to George Washington.

There was not a sound except her voice as she told about his poor boyhood, his work as a surveyor, his defeat by the French at Fort Duquesne, and then of his long, disheartening years of war. She told of his unanimous election as the First President, the Father of his Country, and of the laws passed by the First Congress and the Second, and the opening of the Northwest Territory. Then, after John Adams, came Jefferson, who wrote the Declaration of Independence, established religious freedom and private property in Virginia, and founded the University of Virginia, and bought for the new country all the land between the Mississippi and California.

Next came Madison, the War of 1812, the invasion, the defeat, the burning of the Capitol and the White House in Washington, the brave sea-battles fought by American sailors on America's few ships, and at last the victory that finally won independence.

Then came Monroe, who dared to tell all the older, stronger nations and their tyrants never again to invade the New World. Andrew Jackson went down from Tennessee and fought the Spanish and took Florida, then the honest United States paid Spain for it. In 1820 came hard times; all the banks failed, all business stopped, all the people were out of work and starving.

Then Laura moved the pointer to the picture of John Quincy Adams. She told of his election. She told of the Mexicans who had fought a war of independence, too, and won it, so that now they could trade where they pleased. So down from the Missouri went the Santa Fe traders, across a thousand miles of desert, to trade with Mexico. Then the first wagon wheels rolled into Kansas.

Laura had finished. The rest was Ida's part.

She laid down the pointer and bowed in the stillness. A loud crash of applause almost made her jump out of her skin. The noise grew louder and louder until she felt as if she must push against it to reach her seat. It did not stop even when at last she reached her place beside Ida and weakly sat down. It went on until Mr. Owen stopped it.

Laura was trembling all over. She wanted to say an encouraging word to Ida, but she could not. She could only sit and rest, and be thankful that the ordeal was past.

Ida did very well. She did not make one mistake. Laura was glad to hear the loud applause for Ida, too.

After Mr. Owen had dismissed the audience, getting out of the church was slow work. Everyone stood between the seats and in the aisles, talking about the Exhibition. Laura could see that Mr. Owen was pleased.

"Well, little Half-Pint, you did a fine job," Pa said when Laura and Carrie had pushed through the crowd to him and Ma. "You did, too, Carrie."

"Yes," said Ma. "I am proud of you both."

"I did remember every word," Carrie agreed happily. "But, oh, I am glad it's over," she sighed.

"*So—am—I*," said Laura, struggling into her coat. Just then she felt a hand on the coat collar, helping her, and she heard a voice say, "Good evening, Mr. Ingalls."

She looked up into the face of Almanzo Wilder.

He did not say anything and neither did she, until they were out of the church and following Pa's lantern along the snowy path. The wind had died down. The air was very cold and still, and there was moonlight on the snow.

Then Almanzo said, "I guess I ought to have asked you if I may see you home."

"Yes," Laura said. "But anyway, you are."

"It was such a tussle, getting out of that crowd," he explained. He was silent a minute and then asked, "May I see you home?"

Laura could not help laughing, and he joined in.

"Yes," Laura said. She wondered again why he was doing this, when he was so much older than she. Mr. Boast, or any friend of Pa's, might see her safely home if Pa was not there to do it, but now Pa was there. She thought he had a pleasant laugh. He seemed to enjoy everything. Probably his brown horses were tied on Main Street, so he was going that way, anyway.

"Are your horses tied on Main Street?" she asked him.

"No," he answered. "I left them blanketed on the south side

of the church, out of the wind." Then he said, "I am making a cutter."

Something in the way he said it gave Laura a wild hope. She thought how wonderful it would be to go sleighriding behind those swift horses. Of course he could not mean to ask her, still she felt almost dizzy.

"If this snow holds, there ought to be some good sleighing," he said. "It looks like we're going to get another mild winter."

"Yes, it does, doesn't it?" Laura answered. She was sure now that he would not ask her to go sleighing.

"It takes some little time to build just right," he said, "and then I'm going to paint it, two coats. It won't be ready to take out till some time after Christmas. Do you like to go sleighing?"

Laura felt as if she were smothering.

"I don't know," she replied. "I never went." Then boldly she burst out, "But I'm sure I would like to."

"Well," he said, "I'll come around some time in January and maybe you'd like to go for a little spin and see how you like it. Some Saturday, say? Would that suit you?"

"Yes. Oh, *yes!*" Laura exclaimed. "Thank you."

"All right, then I'll be around, in a couple of weeks if this weather holds," he said. They had come to the door, and he took off his cap and said good night.

Laura fairly danced into the house.

"Oh, Pa! Ma! what do you think! Mr. Wilder's making a cutter, and he's going to take me sleighriding!"

Pa and Ma glanced at each other, and it was a sober glance. Laura quickly said, "If I may go. May I? Please?"

"We will see when the time comes," Ma answered. But Pa's eyes were kind as he looked at Laura and she was sure that when the time came, she could go sleighriding. She thought what fun it must be, to go speeding swiftly and smoothly through the cold, sunny air, behind those horses. And she could not help thinking in delight, "Oh, won't Nellie Oleson be *mad!*"

CHAPTER 25

Unexpected in December

NEXT day was blank and limp. They would not try again to have Christmas without Mary. The only presents hidden away were for Carrie and Grace, and though Christmas was not until tomorrow, they had opened that morning the small Christmas box from Mary.

There would be a whole week without school. Laura knew that she should improve the time in study, but she could not settle down to her books.

"It's no fun studying at home when Mary isn't here to study with," she said.

Dinner was over and the house all in order, but it seemed empty without Mary in her rocking chair. Laura stood looking around the room as though searching for something she had lost.

Ma laid down her church paper. "I declare I can't get used to her being gone, either," she said. "This piece by a missionary is interesting, but I have read aloud to Mary for so long that I can't properly read to myself."

"I wish she hadn't gone!" Laura burst out, but Ma said she must not feel so.

"She is doing so well in her studies, and it is wonderful that she is learning so many things—running a sewing machine, and playing the organ, and doing such pretty beadwork."

They both looked toward the small vase made of tiny beads, blue and white, strung on fine wire, that Mary had made and sent home to them all for Christmas. It stood on the desk near Laura. She went to it and stood fingering the bead fringe around it as Ma talked on.

"I am a little worried about how we are going to find the money for the new summer clothes she needs, and we must manage to send her a little spending money. She should have a Braille slate of her own, too. They are expensive."

"I'll be sixteen, two months from now," Laura said hopefully. "Maybe I can get a certificate next summer."

"If you can teach a term next year, we may be able to have Mary come home for a summer vacation," said Ma. "She has been away so long, she ought to come home for a little while, and it would cost only the railroad fare. But we must not count our chickens before they are hatched."

"I'd better be studying, anyway," Laura sighed. She was ashamed of her moping idleness, when Mary had the patience to do such perfect work with tiny beads that she could not see.

Ma took up her paper again and Laura bent over her books, but she could not rouse herself from her listlessness.

From the window, Carrie announced, "Mr. Boast is coming! And there's another man with him. That's him now, at the door!"

" 'That is he,' " said Ma.

Laura opened the door and Mr. Boast came in, saying, "How do you do, everyone? This is Mr. Brewster."

Mr. Brewster's boots, his thick jacket and his hands showed that he was a homesteader. He did not have much to say.

"How do you do?" said Ma as she placed chairs for them both. "Mr. Ingalls is over town somewhere. How is Mrs. Boast? I am disappointed that she did not come with you."

"I didn't plan to come," said Mr. Boast. "We just stepped in to speak to this young lady," and his black eyes flashed a look at Laura.

She was very much startled. She sat very straight, as Ma had taught her, with her hands folded in her lap and her shoes drawn back beneath her skirts, but her breath caught. She could not think what Mr. Boast meant.

He went on. "Lew Brewster, here, is looking for a teacher for the new school they are starting in their district. He came in to the School Exhibition last night. He figures that Laura's the teacher they want, and I tell him he can't do better."

Laura's heart seemed to leap and fall back, and go on falling.

"I am not old enough yet," she said.

"Now, Laura," Mr. Boast said to her earnestly, "there is no need to tell your age unless someone asks you. The question is, Will you teach this school if the county superintendent gives you a certificate?"

Laura was speechless. She looked at Ma and Ma asked, "Where is the school, Mr. Brewster?"

"Twelve miles south of here," Mr. Brewster replied.

Laura's heart sank even further. So far from home, among strangers, she would have to depend entirely upon herself, with no help at all. She could not come home until the school term was over. Twelve miles and back was too far to travel.

Mr. Brewster went on, "It's a small neighborhood. The country around there isn't settled up yet. We can't afford more than a two-months' school, and all we can pay is twenty dollars a month and board."

"I'm sure that seems a reasonable sum," said Ma.

It would be forty dollars, Laura thought. Forty dollars! She had not realized that she could earn so much money.

"Mr. Ingalls would rely on your advice, I know, Mr. Boast," Ma added.

"Lew Brewster and I knew each other back East," said Mr. Boast. "It's a good chance for Laura if she'll take it."

Laura was so excited that she could hardly speak. "Why, yes," she managed to stammer. "I would be glad to teach the school if I could."

"Then we must hurry along," said Mr. Boast as he and Mr. Brewster stood up. "Williams is in town, and if we can catch him before he starts home, he'll come over and give you the examination right now."

They said good day to Ma and hurried away.

"Oh, Ma!" Laura gasped. "Do you think I can pass?"

"I believe you can, Laura," Ma said. "Do not be excited nor frightened. There is no occasion to be. Just pretend that it is a school examination and you will be all right."

It was only a moment before Carrie exclaimed, "That's him now——"

" 'This is he,' " Ma said almost sharply.

"That's he coming—— It don't sound right, Ma——"

" 'Doesn't sound right,' " said Ma.

"Right straight across from Fuller's Hardware!" cried Carrie.

The knock came at the door. Ma opened it. A large man, with a pleasant face and friendly manner, told her that he was Williams, the county superintendent.

"So you're the young lady that wants a certificate!" he said to Laura. "There's not much need to give you an examination. I heard you last night. You answered all the questions. But I see your slate and pencil on the table, so we might as well go over some of it."

They sat together at the table. Laura worked examples in arithmetic, she spelled, she answered questions in geography. She read Marc Antony's oration on the death of Caesar. She felt quite at home with Mr. Williams while she diagrammed sentences on her slate and rapidly parsed them.

Scaling yonder peak, I saw an eagle
wheeling near its brow.

" 'I' is the personal pronoun, first person singular, here used as the subject of the verb 'saw,' past tense of the transitive verb 'to see.' 'Saw' takes as its object the common generic noun, 'eagle,' modified by the singular article, 'an.'

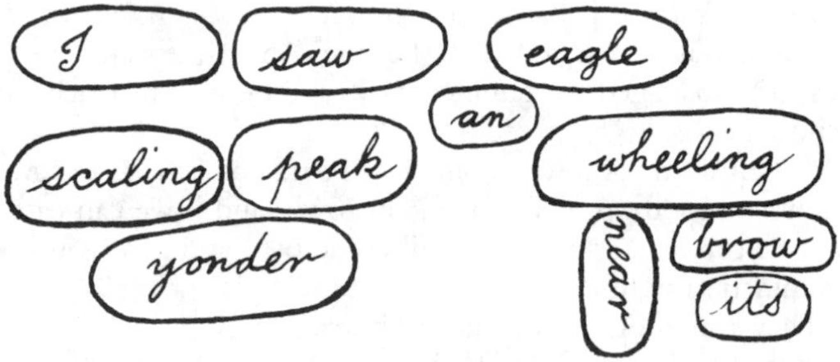

" 'Scaling yonder peak' is a participial phrase, adjunct of the pronoun, 'I,' hence adjectival. 'Wheeling' is the present participle of the intransitive verb, 'to wheel,' here used as adjunct to the noun, 'eagle,' hence adjectival. 'Near its brow' is a prepositional phrase, adjunct of the present participle of the verb 'to wheel,' hence adverbial."

After only a few such sentences, Mr. Williams was satisfied. "There is no need to examine you in history," he said. "I heard your review of history last night. I will cut your grades a little for I must not give you more than a third grade certificate until next year. May I have the use of pen and ink?" he asked Ma.

"They are here at the desk," Ma showed him.

He sat at Pa's desk and spread a blank certificate on it. For moments there was no sound but the faint scratch of his sleeve

DEPARTMENT OF EDUCATION

DAKOTA COUNTY OF KINGSBURY

Teacher's Certificate

This is to certify that *Miss Laura Ingalls*
Has been examined by me and found competent to give instruction in *Reading, Orthography, Writing, Arithmetic, Geography, English Grammar, and History*
and having exhibited satisfactory testimonials of Good Moral Character, is authorized by this

Third Grade Certificate

to teach those branches in any common school in the county for the term of twelve months.

Dated this *24th* day of
December, 1882 *Geo. A. Williams,*
Supt. of Schools,
Kingsbury county, D.T.

Result of examination:

Reading, 62, Writing, 75, History, 98, English Grammar, 81, Arithmetic, 80, Geography, 85 on the paper as he wrote. He wiped the pen-point on the wiper, corked the ink bottle again, and stood up.

"There you are, Miss Ingalls," he said. "Brewster asked me to tell you that the school opens next Monday. He will come for you Saturday or Sunday, depending on the looks of the weather. You know it is twelve miles south of town?"

"Yes, sir. Mr. Brewster said so," Laura replied.

"Well, I wish you good luck," he said cordially.

"Thank you, sir," Laura answered.

When he had said good day to Ma and gone, they read the certificate.

Laura still stood in the middle of the room, holding that certificate, when Pa came in.

"What is it, Laura?" he asked. "You look as if you expect that paper to bite you."

"Pa," Laura said, "I am a schoolteacher."

"What!" said Pa. "Caroline, what is this?"

"Read it." Laura gave him the certificate and sat down. "And he didn't ask me how old I am."

When Pa had read the certificate and Ma had told him about the school, he said, "I'll be jiggered." He sat down and slowly read the certificate again.

"That's fine," he said. "That's pretty fine for a fifteen-year-old." He meant to speak heartily but his voice had a hollow sound, for now Laura was going away.

She could not think what it would be to teach school twelve miles away from home, alone among strangers. She did not want to think of it. She did not want to go. The less she thought of it the better, for she must go, and she must meet whatever happened as it came.

"Now Mary can have everything she needs, and she can come home this next summer," she said. "Oh, Pa, do you think I—I *can* teach school?"

"I do, Laura," said Pa. "I am sure of it."

THESE HAPPY GOLDEN YEARS

CONTENTS

CHAPTER I

Laura Leaves Home

SUNDAY afternoon was clear, and the snow-covered prairie sparkled in the sunshine. A little wind blew gently from the south, but it was so cold that the sled runners squeaked as they slid on the hard-packed snow. The horses' hoofs made a dull sound, clop, clop, clop. Pa did not say anything.

Sitting beside him on the board laid across the bobsled, Laura did not say anything, either. There was nothing to say. She was on her way to teach school.

Only yesterday she was a schoolgirl; now she was a schoolteacher. This had happened so suddenly. Laura could hardly stop expecting that tomorrow she would be going to school with little sister Carrie, and sitting in her seat with Ida Brown. But tomorrow she would be teaching school.

She did not really know how to do it. She never had taught school, and she was not sixteen years old yet. Even for fifteen, she was small; and now she felt very small.

The slightly rolling, snowy land lay empty all around. The high, thin sky was empty overhead. Laura did not look back, but she knew that the town was miles behind her now; it was only a small dark blot on the empty prairie's whiteness. In the warm sitting room there, Ma and Carrie and Grace were far away.

Brewster settlement was still miles ahead. It was twelve miles from town. Laura did not know what it was like. She did not know anyone there. She had seen Mr. Brewster only once, when he came to hire her to teach the school. He was thin and brown, like any homesteader; he did not have much to say for himself.

Pa sat looking ahead into the distance while he held the reins in his mittened hands and now and then chirruped to the horses. But he knew how Laura felt. At last he turned his face toward her and spoke, as if he were answering her dread of tomorrow.

"Well, Laura! You are a schoolteacher now! We knew you would be, didn't we? Though we didn't expect it so soon."

"Do you think I can, Pa?" Laura answered. "Suppose . . . just suppose . . . the children won't mind me when they see how little I am."

"Of course you can," Pa assured her. "You've never failed yet at anything you tried to do, have you?"

"Well, no," Laura admitted. "But I . . . I never tried to teach school."

"You've tackled every job that ever came your way," Pa said. "You never shirked, and you always stuck to it till you did what you set out to do. Success gets to be a habit, like anything else a fellow keeps on doing."

Again there was a silence except for the squeaking of the sled runners and the clop-clop-clop of the horses' feet on the hard snow. Laura felt a little better. It was true; she always had kept on trying; she had always had to. Well, now she had to teach school.

"Remember that time on Plum Creek, Half-Pint?" Pa said. "Your Ma and I went to town, and a blizzard came up? And you got the whole woodpile into the house."

Laura laughed out loud, and Pa's laugh rang like great bells in the cold stillness. How little and scared and funny she had been, that day so long ago!

"That's the way to tackle things!" Pa said. "Have confidence in yourself, and you can lick anything. You have confidence in yourself, that's the only way to make other folks have confidence in you." He paused, and then said, "One thing you must guard against."

"What, Pa?" Laura asked.

"You are so quick, flutterbudget. You are apt to act or speak first, and think afterward. Now you must do your thinking first and speak afterward. If you will remember to do that, you will not have any trouble."

"I will, Pa," Laura said earnestly.

It was really too cold to talk. Snug enough under the heavy blankets and quilts, they went on silently toward the south. The cold wind blew against their faces. A faint trace of sled runners stretched onward before them. There was nothing else to see but the endless, low white land and the huge pale sky, and the horses' blue shadows blotting the sparkle from the snow.

The wind kept Laura's thick black woolen veil rippling

before her eyes. Her breath was frozen in a patch of frost in the veil, that kept slapping cold and damp against her mouth and nose.

At last she saw a house ahead. Very small at first, it grew larger as they came nearer to it. Half a mile away there was another, smaller one, and far beyond it, another. Then still another appeared. Four houses; that was all. They were far apart and small on the white prairie.

Pa pulled up the horses. Mr. Brewster's house looked like two claim shanties put together to make a peaked roof. Its tar-paper roof was bare, and melted snow had run into big icicles that hung from the eaves in blobby columns larger around than Laura's arms. They looked like huge, jagged teeth. Some bit into the snow, and some were broken off. The broken chunks of ice lay frozen into the dirty snow around the door, where dishwater had been thrown. There was no curtain at the window, but smoke blew from the stovepipe that was anchored to the roof with wires.

Mr. Brewster opened the door. A child was squalling in the house, and he spoke loudly to be heard. "Come in, Ingalls! Come in and warm yourself."

"Thank you," Pa replied. "But it's a long twelve miles home and I better be going."

Laura slid out from under the blankets quickly, not to let the cold in. Pa handed her Ma's satchel, that held her change of underclothes, her other dress, and her schoolbooks.

"Good-by, Pa," she said.

"Good-by, Laura." His blue eyes smiled encouragement to her. But twelve miles was too far to drive often; she would not see him again for two months.

She went quickly into the house. Coming from the bright sunshine, she could not see anything for a moment. Mr. Brewster said, "This is Mrs. Brewster; and Lib, here's the teacher."

A sullen-looking woman stood by the stove, stirring something in a frying pan. A little boy was hanging onto her skirts and crying. His face was dirty and his nose needed a handkerchief.

"Good afternoon, Mrs. Brewster," Laura said as cheerfully as she possibly could.

"Just go in the other room and take off your wraps," Mrs.

Brewster said. "Hang them behind the curtain where the sofa is." She turned her back on Laura and went on stirring the gravy in the pan.

Laura did not know what to think. She could not have done anything to offend Mrs. Brewster. She went into the other room.

The partition stood under the peak of the roof, and divided the houses into two equal parts. On either side of the partition, the rafters and the tar-paper roof sloped down to low walls. The board walls were well battened down every crack. They were not finished inside; the bare studding stood against them. This was like Pa's house on the claim, but it was smaller and had no ceiling overhead.

The other room was very cold, of course. It had one window looking out at empty prairie covered with snow. Against the wall under the window was the sofa, a boughten sofa with a curved wooden back and one end curved up. A bed was made up, on the sofa. Brown calico curtains hung against the wall at each end of it, on a string that ran across above the window, so they could be pulled together and hide the sofa. Opposite it, a bed stood against the wall, and at the foot of the bed there was just space enough for a bureau and a trunk.

Laura hung her coat and muffler and veil and hood on nails behind the calico curtain, and set Ma's satchel on the floor under them. She stood shivering in the cold, not wanting to go into the warm room where Mrs. Brewster was. But she had to, so she did.

Mr. Brewster sat by the stove, holding the little boy on his knee. Mrs. Brewster was scraping the gravy into a bowl. The table was set, with plates and knives carelessly askew on a smudged white cloth; the cloth was crooked on the table.

"May I help you, Mrs. Brewster?" Laura said bravely. Mrs. Brewster did not answer. She dumped potatoes angrily into a dish and thumped it on the table. The clock on the wall whirred, getting ready to strike, and Laura saw that the time was five minutes to four.

"Nowadays breakfast is so late, we eat only two meals a day," Mr. Brewster explained.

"Whose fault is it, I'd like to know!" Mrs. Brewster blazed

out. "As if I didn't do enough, slaving from morning to night in this . . ."

Mr. Brewster raised his voice. "I only meant the days are so short . . ."

"Then say what you mean!" Mrs. Brewster slammed the high chair to the table, snatched the little boy and sat him in it, hard.

"Dinner's ready," Mr. Brewster said to Laura. She sat down in the vacant place. Mr. Brewster passed her the potatoes and salt pork and gravy. The food was good but Mrs. Brewster's silence was so unpleasant that Laura could hardly swallow.

"Is the schoolhouse far from here?" she tried to ask cheerfully.

Mr. Brewster said, "Half a mile, cross-lots. It's a claim shanty. The fellow that homesteaded that quarter section couldn't stick it out; he gave up and went back East."

Then he, too, was silent. The little boy fretted, trying to reach everything on the table. Suddenly he flung his tin plate of food on the floor. Mrs. Brewster slapped his hands, and he screamed. He went on screaming and kicking the table leg.

At last the meal was over. Mr. Brewster took the milk pail from its nail on the wall and went to the stable. Mrs. Brewster sat the little boy on the floor and gradually he stopped crying, while Laura helped to clear the table. Then she got an apron from Ma's satchel, tied it over her brown princess dress, and took a towel, to dry the dishes while Mrs. Brewster washed them.

"What's your little boy's name, Mrs. Brewster?" she asked. She hoped that Mrs. Brewster would be more pleasant now.

"John," said Mrs. Brewster.

"That's such a nice name," Laura said. "People can call him Johnny while he's little, and then when he grows up, John is a good name for a man. Do you call him Johnny now?"

Mrs. Brewster did not answer. The silence grew more and more dreadful. Laura felt her face grow burning hot. She went on wiping the dishes blindly. When they were done, Mrs. Brewster threw out the dishwater and hung the pan on its nail. She sat in the rocking chair and rocked idly, while Johnny crawled under the stove and dragged the cat out by its tail. The cat scratched him and he bawled. Mrs. Brewster went on rocking.

Laura did not dare to interfere. Johnny screamed, Mrs. Brewster sullenly rocked, and Laura sat in the straight chair by the table and looked out at the prairie. The road went straight across the snow and far away, out of sight. Twelve miles away was home. Ma was getting supper now; Carrie was home from school; they were laughing and talking with Grace. Pa would come in, and swing Grace up in his arms as he used to lift Laura when she was little. They would all go on talking at the supper table. Later they would sit in the lamplight, cosily reading while Carrie studied; then Pa would play the fiddle.

The room grew dark, and darker. Laura could not see the road any more. At last Mr. Brewster came in with the milk. Then Mrs. Brewster lighted the lamp. She strained the milk and set the pan away, while Mr. Brewster sat down and opened a newspaper. Neither of them spoke. The unpleasant silence settled heavily down.

Laura did not know what to do; it was too early to go to bed. There was no other paper, and not a book in the room. Then she thought of her schoolbooks. Going into the cold, dark bedroom she groped in Ma's satchel and found her history book by the sense of touch. Taking it into the kitchen she sat down by the table again and began to study.

"At least, nothing hinders my studying," she thought grimly. She felt hurt and sore as if she had been beaten, but gradually she forgot where she was, by keeping her mind fixed on history. At last she heard the clock strike eight. Then she stood up and said good night politely. Mrs. Brewster did not answer, but Mr. Brewster said, "Good night."

In the bedroom Laura shivered out of her dress and petticoats, and into her flannel nightgown. She got under the covers on the sofa and pulled the calico curtains around it. The pillow was of feathers, and there were sheets, and plenty of quilts, but the sofa was very narrow.

She heard Mrs. Brewster talking angrily and very fast. The quilts were over Laura's head, so that only the tip of her nose was out in the cold, but she could not help hearing Mrs. Brewster's quarreling. ". . . suits you, but I keep a boarder!" she heard, and ". . . this horrible country out here! Schoolteacher, indeed! . . . been a teacher myself, if I hadn't married a . . ."

Laura thought: "She doesn't want to board the teacher, that is all. She'd be as cross to anybody else." She did her best not to hear any more, and to go to sleep. But all night, in her sleep, she was careful not to fall off the narrow sofa, and she was dreading tomorrow when she must begin to teach school.

CHAPTER 2

First Day of School

LAURA heard a stove lid rattle. For one instant she was in bed with Mary, and Pa was building the morning fire. Then she saw the calico curtain and she knew where she was, and that today she must begin to teach school.

She heard Mr. Brewster take down the milk pail, and the door slammed behind him. On the other side of the curtain Mrs. Brewster got out of bed. Johnny whimpered, and was still. Laura did not move; she felt that if she lay still enough, she might keep the day from coming.

Mr. Brewster came in with the milk, and she heard him say, "I'm going to start a fire in the schoolhouse. I'll be back by the time breakfast's ready." The door slammed behind him again.

All at once, Laura threw back the covers. The air was biting cold. Her teeth chattered and her fingers were so stiff that she could not button her shoes.

The kitchen was not so cold. Mrs. Brewster had broken the ice in the water pail and was filling the teakettle, and she replied pleasantly to Laura's "Good morning." Laura filled the wash basin and washed her hands and face at the bench by the door. The icy water made her cheeks tingle, and her whole face was rosy and glowing in the looking glass above the bench while she combed her hair before it.

Slices of salt pork were frying, and Mrs. Brewster was slicing cold boiled potatoes into another frying pan on the stove. Johnny fussed in the bedroom, and Laura quickly pinned her braids, tied on her apron, and said, "Let me fix the potatoes while you dress him."

So while Mrs. Brewster brought Johnny to the stove and made him ready for breakfast, Laura finished slicing the potatoes, and salted and peppered and covered them. Then she turned the slices of meat and set the table neatly.

"I'm glad Ma told me to bring this big apron," she said. "I like a real big apron that covers your whole dress, don't you?"

Mrs. Brewster did not answer. The stove was red now and

the whole room was warm, but it seemed bleak. Nothing but short, necessary words were said at the breakfast table.

It was a relief to Laura to put on her wraps, take her books and her tin dinner pail, and leave that house. She set out on the half-mile walk through the snow to the schoolhouse. The way was unbroken, except for Mr. Brewster's footsteps, which were so far apart that Laura could not walk in them.

As she floundered on, plunging into the deep snow, she suddenly laughed aloud. "Well!" she thought. "Here I am. I dread to go on, and I would not go back. Teaching school can not possibly be as bad as staying in that house with Mrs. Brewster. Anyway, it cannot be worse."

Then she was so frightened that she said aloud, "I've *got* to go on." Black soft-coal smoke rose against the morning sky from the old claim-shanty's stovepipe. Two more lines of footprints came to its door, and Laura heard voices inside it. For a moment she gathered her courage, then she opened the door and went in.

The board walls were not battened. Streaks of sunshine streamed through the cracks upon a row of six homemade seats and desks that marched down the middle of the room. Beyond them on the studding of the opposite wall, a square of boards had been nailed and painted black, to make a blackboard.

In front of the seats stood a big heating stove. Its round sides and top were cherry-red from the heat of the fire, and standing around it were the scholars that Laura must teach. They all looked at Laura. There were five of them, and two boys and one girl were taller than she was.

"Good morning," she managed to say.

They all answered, still looking at her. A small window by the door let in a block of sunshine. Beyond it, in the corner by the stove, stood a small table and a chair. "That is the teacher's table," Laura thought, and then, "Oh my; I am the teacher."

Her steps sounded loud. All the eyes followed her. She put her books and dinner pail on the table, and took off her coat and hood. She hung them on a nail in the wall by the chair. On the table was a small clock; its hands stood at five minutes to nine.

Somehow she had to get through five minutes, before the time to begin school.

Slowly she took off her mittens and put them in the pocket of her coat. Then she faced all the eyes, and stepped to the stove. She held her hands to it as if to warm them. All the pupils made way for her, still looking at her. She must say something. She must.

"It is cold this morning, isn't it?" she heard herself say; then without waiting for an answer, "Do you think you can keep warm in the seats away from the stove?"

One of the tall boys said quickly, "I'll sit in the back seat; it's the coldest."

The tall girl said, "Charles and I have to sit together, we have to study from the same books."

"That's good; then you can all sit nearer the stove," Laura said. To her joyful surprise, the five minutes were gone! She said, "You may take your seats. School will begin."

The little girl took the front seat; behind her sat the little boy, then the tall girl and Charles, and behind them the other tall boy. Laura rapped her pencil on the table. "School will come to order. I will now take your names and ages."

The little girl was Ruby Brewster; she was nine years old. She had brown hair and sparkling brown eyes, and she was as soft and still as a mouse. Laura knew she would be sweet and good. She had finished the First Reader, and in arithmetic she was learning subtraction.

The little boy was her brother Tommy Brewster. He was eleven, and had finished the Second Reader, and reached short division.

The two sitting together were Charles and Martha Harrison. Charles was seventeen; he was thin and pale and slow of speech. Martha was sixteen; she was quicker, and spoke for them both.

The last boy was Clarence Brewster. He, too, was older than Laura. His brown eyes were even brighter and livelier than his little sister Ruby's, his dark hair was thick and unruly, and he was quick in speaking and moving. He had a way of speaking that was almost saucy.

Clarence, Charles and Martha were all in the Fourth Reader. They had passed the middle of the spelling book, and in arithmetic they were working fractions. In geography they had studied the New England states, and they answered questions so well that Laura set them to learn the Middle Atlantic states. None of them had studied grammar or history, but Martha had brought her mother's grammar and Clarence had a history book.

"Very well," Laura said. "You may all begin at the beginning in grammar and history, and exchange the books, to learn your lessons."

When Laura had learned all this, and assigned their lessons, it was time for recess. They all put on their wraps and went out to play in the snow, and Laura breathed a sigh of relief. The first quarter of the first day was over.

Then she began to plan; she would have reading, arithmetic, and grammar recitations in the forenoon, and, in the afternoon, reading again, history, writing, and spelling. There were three classes in spelling, for Ruby and Tommy were far apart in the spelling book.

After fifteen minutes, she rapped on the window to call the pupils in. Then until noon she heard and patiently corrected their reading aloud.

The noon hour dragged slowly. Alone at her table, Laura ate her bread and butter, while the others gathered around the stove, talking and joking while they ate from their dinner pails. Then the boys ran races in the snow outdoors, while Martha and Ruby watched them from the window and Laura still sat at her table. She was a teacher now, and must act like one.

At last the hour was gone, and again she rapped on the window. The boys came briskly in, breathing out clouds of frosty breath and shaking cold air from their coats and mufflers as they hung them up. They were glowing from cold and exercise.

Laura said, "The fire is low. Would you put more coal on, please, Charles?"

Willing, but slowly, Charles lifted the heavy hod of coal and dumped most of it into the stove.

"I'll do that next time!" Clarence said. Perhaps he did not mean to be impertinent. If he did mean to be, what could Laura do? He was a chunky, husky boy, bigger than she was, and older. His brown eyes twinkled at her. She stood as tall as possible and rapped her pencil on the table.

"School will come to order," she said.

Though the school was small, she thought best to follow the routine of the town school, and have each class come forward to recite. Ruby was alone in her class, so she must know every answer perfectly, for there was no one to help her by answering some of the questions. Laura let her spell slowly, and if she made a mistake, she might try again. She spelled every word in her lesson. Tommy was slower, but Laura gave him time to think and try, and he did as well.

Then Martha and Charles and Clarence recited their spelling. Martha made no mistakes, but Charles missed five words and Clarence missed three. For the first time, Laura must punish them.

"You may take your seat, Martha," she said. "Charles and Clarence, go to the blackboard, and write the words you missed, three times each."

Charles slowly went, and began to write his words. Clarence glanced back at Laura with a saucy look. Rapidly he wrote large and sprawling letters that covered his half of the blackboard with only six words. Then turning toward Laura, and not even raising his hand for permission to speak, he said, "Teacher! The board's too small."

He was making a joke of punishment for failing in his lesson. He was defying Laura.

For a long, dreadful moment he stood laughing at her, and she looked straight at him.

Then she said, "Yes, the board is small, Clarence. I am sorry, but you should erase what you have written and write the words again more carefully. Make them smaller, and there will be room enough."

He had to obey her, for she did not know what she could do if he did not.

Still grinning, good-naturedly he turned to the blackboard and wiped out the scrawls. He wrote the three words three times each, and below them he signed his name with a flourish.

With relief, Laura saw that it was four o'clock.

"You may put away your books," she said. When every book was neat on the shelves beneath the desk tops, she said, "School is dismissed."

Clarence grabbed his coat and cap and muffler from their nail and with a shout he was first through the doorway. Tommy was at his heels, but they waited outside while Laura helped Ruby into her coat and tied her hood. More soberly, Charles and

Martha wrapped themselves well against the cold before they set out. They had a mile to walk.

Laura stood by the window and watched them go. She could see Mr. Brewster's brother's claim shanty, only half a mile away. Smoke blew from its stovepipe and its west window glinted back the light from the sinking sun. Clarence and Tommy scuffled in the snow, and Ruby's red hood bobbed along behind them. So far as Laura could see from the eastern window, the sky was clear.

The school shanty had no window from which she could see the northwest. If a blizzard came up, she could not know that it was coming until it struck.

She cleaned the blackboard, and with the broom she swept the floor. A dustpan was not needed, the cracks between the floorboards were so wide. She shut the stove's drafts, put on her wraps, took her books and dinner pail, and shutting the door carefully behind her, she set out on her morning path toward Mrs. Brewster's house.

Her first day as a teacher was over. She was thankful for that.

CHAPTER 3

One Week

As she went trudging through the snow, Laura made herself feel cheerful. Mrs. Brewster was hard to get acquainted with, Laura thought, but she could not always be cross. Perhaps this evening would not be unpleasant.

So Laura went in, snowy and glowing from the cold, and spoke cheerfully to Mrs. Brewster. But to all her efforts, Mrs. Brewster answered shortly or not at all. At supper, no one said a word. The stillness was so sullen and hateful that Laura could not speak.

After supper she helped with the work again, and sat again in the darkening room while Mrs. Brewster silently rocked. She felt sick from wanting to be at home.

As soon as Mrs. Brewster lighted the lamp, Laura brought her schoolbooks to the table. She set herself lessons, and determined to learn them before bedtime. She wanted to keep up with her class in town, and she hoped she could study hard enough to forget where she was.

She sat small in her chair, for the silence seemed to press against her from all sides. Mrs. Brewster sat idle. Mr. Brewster held Johnny asleep on his lap, and stared into the fire through the stove's open draft. The clock struck seven. It struck eight. It struck nine. Then Laura made an effort, and spoke.

"It is getting late, and I'll say good night."

Mrs. Brewster paid no attention. Mr. Brewster started, and said, "Good night."

Before Laura could hurry into bed in the cold dark, Mrs. Brewster began to quarrel at him. Laura tried not to hear. She pulled the quilts over her head and pressed her ear tight against the pillow, but she could not help hearing. She knew then that Mrs. Brewster wanted her to hear.

For Mrs. Brewster said she'd not slave for a hoity-toity snip that had nothing to do but dress up and sit in a schoolhouse all day; she said that if Mr. Brewster did not put Laura out of the house, she'd go back East without him. She went on and on, and the sound of her voice made Laura feel sick; it was a sound that enjoyed hurting people.

Laura did not know what to do. She wanted to go home, but she must not even think of home or she might cry. She must think what to do. There was nowhere else to stay; the other two houses in the settlement were only claim shanties. At the Harrisons', there were four in the one room, and at Mr. Brewster's brother's house there were five. They could not possibly make room for Laura.

She did not really make Mrs. Brewster any work, she thought. She made her bed and helped with the kitchen work. Mrs. Brewster was quarreling now about the flat country and the wind and the cold; she wanted to go back East. Suddenly Laura understood; "She isn't mad at *me*, she's only quarreling about me because she wants to quarrel. She's a selfish, mean woman."

Mr. Brewster did not say a word, Laura thought: "I've just got to bear it, too. There isn't anywhere else I can stay."

When she woke in the morning she thought: "I have only to get through one day at a time."

It was hard to stay where she was not wanted. She took care to make no work for Mrs. Brewster, and to help her all she could. Politely she said, "Good morning," and smiled, but she could not keep on smiling. She had not known before that it takes two to make a smile.

She dreaded the second school day, but it passed smoothly. Clarence idled instead of studying, and Laura dreaded that she must punish him again, but he knew his lessons. Perhaps she would have no trouble with him.

It was strange that she was so tired at four o'clock. The second day was over, and the first week would be half gone at noon tomorrow.

Suddenly Laura caught her breath, and stood stock-still on the snowy path. She had thought of Saturday and Sunday; two whole days in that house with Mrs. Brewster. She heard herself say aloud, "Oh, Pa. I can't."

It was whimpering; she was ashamed when she heard it. No one else had heard. All around her the prairie was empty, white and far and still. She would rather stay there in the clean cold than go into the mean house or go back tomorrow to the anxious school day. But the sun was setting, and tomorrow it would rise; everything must go on.

That night Laura dreamed again that she was lost in a blizzard. She knew the dream; she had dreamed it sometimes, ever since she really had been lost with Carrie in a blizzard. But this blizzard was worse than before; now the stinging snow and the wind's hard blows tried to drive her and Carrie off the narrow sofa. Laura held onto Carrie with all her might for a long time, but suddenly Carrie was not there; the blizzard had got her. Laura's heart stopped in horror. She could not go on, she had no more strength; she sank down, down, into the dark. Then Pa came driving from town on the bobsled; he called to Laura, "How about going home for Saturday, Half-Pint?" Ma and Mary and Carrie and Grace were so surprised! Mary said happily, "Oh, Laura!" Ma's whole face lighted with her smiling. Carrie hurried to help Laura take off her wraps, and Grace jumped up and down, clapping her hands. "Charles, why didn't you tell us!" Ma said, and Pa answered, "Why, Caroline, I said I'd do a little hauling. Laura's little." And Laura remembered how, at the dinner table, Pa had drunk his tea and pushed back his cup and said, "Guess I'll do a little hauling this afternoon." Ma said, "Oh, Charles!" Laura had not gone away from home at all; she was there.

Then she woke up. She was at the Brewsters', and it was Wednesday morning. But the dream had been so real that she still almost believed it. Pa might come to take her home over Saturday. It was like him, to plan such a surprise.

There had been a snowstorm in the night. She had to break her path to the schoolhouse again. The early sunshine was faintly pink on miles of pure snow and every little shadow was thin blue. As Laura plunged and plowed through the soft drifts, she saw Clarence breaking a path for Tommy and Ruby behind him. They floundered to the school-shanty's door at the same time.

Little Ruby was covered from head to foot with snow, even her hood and her braids were snowy. Laura brushed her and told her to keep her wraps on until the room was warmer. Clarence put more coal on the fire while Laura shook her own wraps and swept the snow through the cracks between the floor boards. The sunshine streaming through the window made the shanty look warm, but it was colder than outdoors. But soon the good stove's warmth made their breaths invisible; it was nine o'clock, and Laura said, "School will come to order."

Martha and Charles came in panting, three minutes late. Laura did not want to mark them tardy; they had to break their path, the whole mile. A few steps in deep snow are easy, and fun, but breaking a path is work that grows harder with every step. For a moment Laura thought of excusing Martha and Charles, this one time. But that would not be honest. No excuse could change the fact; they *were* tardy.

"I am sorry I must mark you tardy," she said. "But you may come to the stove and get warm before you take your seat."

"We're sorry, Miss Ingalls," Martha said. "We didn't know it would take so long."

"Breaking a path is hard work, I know," said Laura, and suddenly she and Martha were smiling to each other, a friendly smile that made Laura feel as if teaching school were easy. She said, "Second Reader class, rise. Pass to the front." And Ruby, the Second Reader class, rose and came to stand before her.

The whole morning went smoothly. At noon, Ruby came to Laura's desk and shyly offered her a cookie. After dinners were eaten from the dinner pails, Clarence asked her to come out and snowball, and Martha said, "Please do. Then we will have three on a side."

Laura was so pleased to be asked, and so eager to be out in the sunshine and clean snow, that she went. It was great fun. She and Martha and Ruby fought against Charles, Clarence, and Tommy. The air was full of snowballs. Clarence and Laura were quickest of all, dodging and scooping and molding the snow with their mittened hands and throwing and dodging again. Laura was glowing warm, and laughing, when a great burst of snow exploded in her eyes and her open mouth and plastered her whole face.

"Oh gee, I didn't mean to," she heard Clarence saying.

"Yes, you did! It was a fair hit," Laura answered, blindly rubbing her eyes.

"Here, let me; stand still," he said. He took hold of her shoulder as if she were Ruby, and wiped her face with the end of her muffler.

"Thank you," Laura said. But she knew that she must not

play any more. She was too small and too young; she would not be able to keep her pupils in order if she played games with them.

That very afternoon Clarence pulled Martha's hair. Her brown braid whisked across his desk as she turned her head, and he caught it and gave it a tug.

"Clarence," Laura said. "Do not disturb Martha. Give your attention to your lessons."

He gave her a friendly grin that said as plainly as words, "All right, if you say so; I don't have to."

To her horror, Laura almost smiled. Barely in time, she kept her look stern. Now she was sure that she would have trouble with Clarence.

Wednesday was gone. There were only Thursday and Friday. Laura tried not to expect that Pa would come for her, but she could not stop hoping. It would be so like Pa to come and save her from a miserable two days in Mrs. Brewster's house. But of course he did not know how miserable it was. She must not expect him. But surely he might come, if the weather were good. If he came, there were only two more evenings to endure, and then—Friday night at home! Still she did not expect him; she must not, or she would be so disappointed if he did not come. They were missing her at home, she knew; if the weather were pleasant, surely he would come.

But Friday morning the sky was stormy and the wind was colder.

All day at school Laura listened to the wind, afraid that its sound would change to a blizzard's howl and the shanty suddenly shake and the window go blank.

The wind blew colder through the cracks. Its sound rose, and from every drift the snow scudded across the prairie. Laura knew now that Pa would not come. Twenty-four miles in such weather was too much for the horses.

"How am I going to get through the time till Monday?" Laura thought.

Wretchedly she turned her eyes from the window, and saw Charles sitting half-asleep. Suddenly he jumped, wide awake. Clarence had jabbed his arm with a pin. Laura almost laughed, but Clarence caught her glance and his eyes laughed. She could not let this pass.

"Clarence," she said. "Why aren't you studying?"

"I know all my lessons," he replied.

She did not doubt it. Clarence learned quickly; he could keep up with Martha and Charles and have plenty of idle time.

"We will see how well you know your spelling," she said. She tapped upon her table. "Third spelling class, rise. Come forward."

The shanty trembled in the wind that every moment howled louder around it. Heat from the red-cheeked stove melted the snow that was blown through the cracks and made wet streaks on the floor. Clarence correctly spelled every word that Laura gave him, while she wondered whether she should dismiss school early. If she waited and the storm grew worse, Charles and Martha might never reach their home.

It seemed to her that the wind had a strangely silvery sound. She listened; they all listened. She did not know what to make of it. The sky was not changed; gray, low clouds were moving fast above the prairie covered with blowing snow. The strange sound grew clearer, almost like music. Suddenly the whole air filled with a chiming of little bells. Sleigh bells!

Everyone breathed again, and smiled. Two brown horses swiftly passed the window. Laura knew them; they were Prince and Lady, young Mr. Wilder's horses! The sleigh bells rang louder, and stopped; then a few bells shook out small tinkles. The brown horses were standing close outside the south wall, in the shelter of the shanty.

Laura was so excited that she had to steady her voice. "The class may be seated." She waited a moment; then, "You may all put away your books. It is a little early, but the storm is growing worse. School is dismissed."

CHAPTER 4

Sleigh Bells

CLARENCE dashed outdoors, and back again, shouting, "It's someone for you, Teacher!"

Laura was helping Ruby into her coat. "Tell him I will be there in a minute."

"Come on, Charles! You ought to see his horses!" Clarence slammed the door so that the shanty shook. Laura quickly put on her coat and tied her hood and muffler. She shut the stove's drafts, thrust her hands into her mittens and took her books and dinner pail. She made sure the door was fastened behind her. All the time she was so excited that she could hardly breathe. Pa had not come, but she was going home, after all!

Almanzo Wilder was sitting in a cutter so low and small that it was hardly more than a heap of furs on the snow behind Prince and Lady. He was muffled in a buffalo coat and a fur cap with flaps that was as snug as a hood.

He did not step out into the storm. Instead, he lifted the fur robes and gave Laura his hand to help her step into the cutter. Then he tucked the robes around her. They were furry, warm buffalo skins, lined with flannel.

"You want to stop at Brewster's?" he asked.

"I must, to leave the dinner pail and get my satchel," Laura said.

In the Brewster house Johnny was screaming angrily, and when Laura came out of the house she saw Almanzo looking at it with disgust. But it was all behind her now; she was going home. Almanzo tucked the robes snugly around her, the sleigh bells began merrily ringing, and swiftly behind the brown horses she was going home.

She said through her thick black woolen veil, "It's nice of you to come for me. I was hoping Pa would come."

Almanzo hesitated. "We . . . ell. He was figuring he would, but I told him it's a drive that would be pretty hard on his team."

"They'll have to bring me back," Laura said doubtfully. "I must be at school Monday morning."

"Maybe Prince and Lady could make the drive again," Almanzo said.

Laura was embarrassed; she had not meant to hint. She had not even thought of his bringing her back. Again, she had spoken before she thought. How right Pa's advice had been; she should always, always, think before she spoke. She thought: "After this, I shall always think before I speak," and she said, without thinking how rude it would sound, "Oh, you needn't bother. Pa will bring me back."

"It would be no bother," Almanzo said. "I told you I'd take you for a sleigh ride when I got my cutter made. This is the cutter. How do you like it?"

"I think it's fun to ride in; it's so little," Laura answered.

"I made it smaller than the boughten ones. It's only five feet long, and twenty-six inches wide at the bottom. Makes it snugger to ride in, and lighter for the horses to pull," Almanzo explained. "They hardly know they're pulling anything."

"It's like flying!" Laura said. She had never imagined such wonderful speed.

The low clouds raced backward overhead, the blown snow smoked backward on either side, and swiftly onward went the glossy brown horses, streaming music from their strings of bells. There was not a jolt nor a jar; the little cutter skimmed the snow as smoothly as a bird in air.

Almost too soon, though not soon enough, they were flashing past the windows of Main Street, and here was Pa's front door again, opening, and Pa standing in it. Laura was out of the cutter and up the steps before she thought; then, "Oh, thank you, Mr. Wilder; good night!" she called back all in a breath, and she was at home.

Ma's smile lighted her whole face. Carrie came running to unwind Laura's muffler and veil, while Grace clapped her hands and shouted, "Laura's come home!" Then Pa came in and said, "Let's look at you. Well, well, the same little flutterbudget!"

There was so much to say and to tell. The big sitting room had never looked so beautiful. The walls were dark brown now; every year the pine boards grew darker. The table was covered with the red-checked cloth, and the braided rag rugs were gay on the floor. The rocking chairs stood by the white-curtained windows; Mary's boughten chair, and the willow chair that Pa had made for Ma so long ago in the Indian Territory. The patchwork cushions were in them, and there was Ma's work-basket and her knitting with the needles thrust into the ball of yarn. Kitty lazily stretched and yawned, and came to curve purring against Laura's ankles. There on Pa's desk was the blue-bead basket that Mary had made.

The talking went on at the supper table; Laura was more hungry for talk than food. She told about each one of her pupils at school, and Ma told of Mary's latest letter; Mary was doing so well in the college for the blind, in Iowa. Carrie told all the news of the school in town. Grace told of the words she had learned to read, and of Kitty's last fight with a dog.

After supper, when Laura and Carrie had done the dishes, Pa said as Laura had been hoping he would, "If you'll bring me the fiddle, Laura, we'll have a little music."

He played the brave marching songs of Scotland and of the United States; he played the sweet old love songs and the gay dance tunes, and Laura was so happy that her throat ached.

When it was bedtime and she went upstairs with Carrie and Grace, she looked from the attic window at the lights of the town twinkling here and there, through the wind and the blowing snow. As she snuggled under the quilts she heard Pa and Ma coming up to their room at the head of the stairs. She heard Ma's pleasant low voice and Pa's deeper one answering it, and she was so glad to be at home for two nights and nearly two days that she could hardly go to sleep.

Even her sleep was deep and good, without fear of falling off a narrow sofa. Almost at once, it seemed her eyes opened; she heard the stove lid rattle downstairs, and knew that she was at home.

"Good morning!" Carrie said from her bed, and Grace bounced up and cried, "Good morning, Laura!" "Good morning." Ma smiled when Laura entered the kitchen, and Pa came in with the milk and said, "Good morning, flutterbudget!" Laura had never noticed before that saying, "Good morning," made the morning good. Anyway, she was learning something from that Mrs. Brewster, she thought.

Breakfast was so pleasant. Then briskly, and still talking, Laura and Carrie did the dishes, and went upstairs to make the beds. While they were tucking in a sheet, Laura said, "Carrie, do you ever think how lucky we are to have a home like this?"

Carrie looked around her, surprised. There was nothing to be seen but the two beds, the three boxes under the eaves where they kept their things, and the underside of the shingles overhead. There was also the stovepipe that came up through the floor and went out through the roof.

"It *is* snug," Carrie said, while they spread the first quilt and folded and tucked in its corners. "I guess I never did think, exactly."

"You wait till you go away," Laura said. "Then you'll think."

"Do you dreadfully hate to teach school?" Carrie asked her, low.

"Yes, I do," Laura almost whispered. "But Pa and Ma mustn't know."

They plumped up the pillows and set them in their places, and went to Laura's bed. "Maybe you won't have to, long," Carrie consoled her. They unbuttoned the straw tick and thrust their arms deep into it, stirring up the straw. "Maybe you'll get married. Ma did."

"I don't want to," Laura said. She patted the tick smooth and buttoned it. "There. Now the bottom quilt. I'd rather stay home than anything."

"Always?" Carrie asked.

"Yes, always," Laura said, and she meant it with all her heart. She spread the sheet. "But I can't, not all the time. I have to go on teaching school."

They tucked in the quilts and plumped up Laura's pillow. The beds were done. Carrie said she would do the sweeping. "I always do, now," she said, "and if you're going to Mary Power's, the sooner you go the sooner you'll be back."

"I only have to find out if I'm keeping up with my class," Laura said. Downstairs, she set the wash-boiler on the stove and filled it with pails of water from the well. Then while it was heating, she went to see Mary Power.

She had quite forgotten that she had ever disliked the town. It was bright and brisk this morning. Sunlight glinted on the icy ruts of snow in the street and sparkled on the frosty edges of the board sidewalk. In the two blocks there were only two vacant lots on the west side of the street now, and some of the stores were painted, white or gray. Harthorn's grocery was painted red. Everywhere there was the stir and bustle of morning. The storekeepers in thick coats and caps were scraping trodden bits of snow from the sidewalk before their stores, and talking and joking as they worked. Doors slammed; hens cackled, and horses whinnied in the stables.

Mr. Fuller, and then Mr. Bradley, lifted their caps and said good morning to Laura as she passed. Mr. Bradley said, "I hear you're teaching Brewster school, Miss Ingalls."

Laura felt very grown-up. "Yes," she said, "I am in town only over Saturday."

"Well, I wish you all success," said Mr. Bradley.

"Thank you, Mr. Bradley," said Laura.

In Mr. Power's tailor shop, Mary's father sat cross-legged on his table, sewing busily. Mary was helping her mother with the morning's work in the back room.

"Well, look who's here!" Mrs. Power exclaimed. "How's the schoolteacher?"

"Very well, thank you," Laura replied.

"Do you like teaching school?" Mary wanted to know.

"I'm getting along all right, I guess," Laura said. "But I'd rather be home. I'll be glad when the two months are over."

"So will all of us," Mary told her. "My, we do miss you at school."

Laura was pleased. "Do you?" she said. "I miss you, too."

"Nellie Oleson tried to get your seat," Mary went on. "But Ida wouldn't let her. Ida said she's keeping that seat for you till you come back, and Mr. Owen said she can."

"Whatever did Nellie Oleson want my seat for?" Laura exclaimed. "Hers is just as good, or almost."

"That's Nellie for you," said Mary. "She just wants anything that anybody else has, that's all. Oh Laura, she'll be fit to be tied when I tell her that Almanzo Wilder brought you home in his new cutter!"

They both laughed. Laura felt a little ashamed, but she could not help laughing. They remembered Nellie's bragging that she was going to ride behind those brown horses. And she never had done it yet.

"I can hardly wait," Mary said.

Mrs. Power said, "I don't think that's very nice, Mary."

"I know it isn't," Mary admitted. "But if you only knew how that Nellie Oleson's always bragging and showing off, and picking on Laura. And now to think that Laura's teaching school, and Almanzo Wilder's beauing her home."

"Oh, no! He isn't!" Laura cried out. "It isn't like that at all. He came for me as a favor to Pa."

Mary laughed. "He must think a lot of your Pa!" she began to tease; then she looked at Laura and said, "I'm sorry. I won't talk about it if you don't want to."

"I don't mean that," Laura said. Everything is simple when you are alone, or at home, but as soon as you meet other people you are in difficulties. "I just don't want you to think Mr. Wilder's my beau, because he isn't."

"All right," Mary said.

"And I only ran in for a minute," Laura explained. "I put wash-water on, and it must be hot now. Tell me where you are in your lessons, Mary."

When Mary told her, Laura saw that she was keeping up with the class by her studying at night. Then she went home.

All that day was such a happy time. Laura did her washing and sprinkled and ironed the clean, fresh clothes. Then in the cozy sitting room she ripped her beautiful brown velvet hat, talking all the time with Ma and Carrie and Grace. She brushed and steamed the velvet and draped it again over the buckram frame, and tried it on. It looked like a new hat, even more becoming than before. There was just time enough to brush and sponge and press her brown dress, and then to help Ma get an early supper. Afterward, they all bathed one by one in the warm kitchen, and went to bed.

"If I could only live like this always, I'd never want anything more," Laura thought as she went to sleep. "But maybe I appreciate it more because I have only tonight and tomorrow morning . . ."

The morning sunshine and the sky had their quiet, Sunday look, and the town was quiet with a Sunday stillness when Laura and Carrie and Grace and Ma sedately went out on Sunday morning. The morning work was done, the beans for Sunday dinner were baking slowly in the oven. Pa carefully closed the heating-stove's drafts, and came out and locked the door.

Laura and Carrie went ahead; Pa and Ma came behind them, holding Grace's hands. All fresh and clean and dressed in Sunday best, they walked slowly in the cold Sunday morning, taking care not to slip on the icy paths. Carefully along the street and single file across lots behind Fuller's store, everyone else was going toward the church, too.

As she went in, Laura looked eagerly over the partly filled seats, and there was Ida! Ida's brown eyes danced when she saw Laura, and she slid along the seat to make room, and gave Laura's arm a squeeze. "My, I'm glad to see you!" she whispered. "When did you come?"

"Friday after school. I've got to go back this afternoon," Laura answered. There was a little time to talk before Sunday School.

"Do you like teaching?" Ida asked.

"No, I do not! But don't tell anybody else. I'm getting along all right so far."

"I won't," Ida promised. "I knew you would. But your place at school is awfully empty."

"I'll be back. It's only seven weeks more," Laura said.

"Laura," Ida said. "You don't care if Nellie Oleson sits with me while you're gone, do you?"

"Why, Ida Brow . . ." Laura began. Then she saw that Ida was only teasing. "Of course not," she said. "You ask her and see if she will."

Because they were in church and could not laugh, they sat silently shaking and almost choking in their effort to keep their faces sober. Lawyer Barnes was rapping the pulpit to bring the Sunday School to order, and they could not talk any more. They must rise and join in the singing.

Sweet Sabbath School! more dear to me
Than fairest palace dome,
My heart e'er turns with joy to thee,
My own dear Sabbath home.

Singing together was even better than talking. Ida was such a dear, Laura thought, as they stood side by side holding the hymn book open before them.

Here first my willful, wandering heart
The way of life was shown;
Here first I sought the better part
And gained a Sabbath home.

Clear and sure, Laura's voice held the note while Ida's soft alto chimed, "Sabbath home." Then their voices blended again,

My heart e'er turns with joy to thee,
My own dear Sabbath home.

Sunday School was the pleasant part of church. Though they could talk only to the teacher about the lesson, Ida and Laura could smile at each other and sing together. When Sunday School ended, there was only time to say, "Good-by. Good-by." Then Ida must sit with Mrs. Brown in the front seat while Reverend Brown preached one of his long, stupid sermons.

Laura and Carrie went to sit with Pa and Ma and Grace. Laura made sure that she remembered the text, to repeat at home when Pa asked her; then she need not listen any more. She always missed Mary in church. Mary had always sat so properly beside her, watchful that Laura behaved. It was strange to think that they had been little girls, and now Mary was in college and Laura was a schoolteacher. She tried not to think of Mrs. Brewster's, and of school. After all, Mary had gone to college, and now Laura was earning forty dollars; with forty dollars, Mary could surely stay in college next year. Maybe everything comes out all right, if you keep on trying. Anyway, you have to keep on trying; nothing will come out right if you don't. "If I can only manage Clarence for seven weeks more," Laura thought.

Carrie pinched her arm. Everyone was standing up, to sing the Doxology. Church was over.

Dinner was so good. Ma's baked beans were delicious, and the bread and butter and little cucumber pickles, and everyone was so comfortable, so cheerful and talking. Laura said, "Oh, I do like it here!"

"It's too bad that Brewster's isn't a better place to stay," said Pa.

"Why, Pa, I haven't complained," Laura said in surprise.

"I know you haven't," said Pa. "Well, keep a stiff upper lip; seven weeks will soon be gone, and you'll be home again."

How pleasant it was, after the dishes were done, when they were all settled in the front room for Sunday afternoon. Sunshine streamed through the clean windows into the warm room, where Ma sat gently rocking, and Carrie and Grace pored over the pictures in Pa's big green book, *The Wonders of the Animal World.* Pa read items from the *Pioneer Press* to Ma, and at his desk Laura sat writing a letter to Mary. Carefully with Ma's little pearl-handled pen that was shaped like a feather, she wrote of her school and her pupils. Of course she wrote of nothing unpleasant. The clock ticked, and now and then Kitty lazily stretched and purred a short purr.

When the letter was finished, Laura went upstairs and packed her clean clothes in Ma's satchel. She brought it downstairs and into the front room. It must be time to go, but Pa sat reading his paper and took no notice.

Ma looked at the clock and said gently, "Charles, surely you must hitch up, or you'll be late starting. It's a long way to go and come, and dark comes early nowadays."

Pa only turned a page of the paper and said, "Oh, there's no hurry."

Laura and Ma looked at each other in amazement. They looked at the clock, and again at Pa. He did not stir, but his brown beard had a smiling look. Laura sat down.

The clock ticked, and Pa silently read the paper. Twice Ma almost spoke, and changed her mind. At last, not looking up, Pa said, "Some folks worry about my team."

"Why, Charles! There isn't anything wrong with the horses?" Ma exclaimed.

"Well," said Pa. "They're not as young as they used to be, for a fact. They can still hold out pretty well, though, for twelve miles and back."

"Charles," Ma said helplessly.

Pa looked up at Laura and his eyes were twinkling. "Maybe I don't have to drive 'em so far," he said. Sleigh bells were coming down the street. Clearer and louder they came; then rang all at once and stopped by the door. Pa went to the door and opened it.

"Good afternoon, Mr. Ingalls," Laura heard Almanzo Wilder

say. "I stopped by to see if Laura would let me drive her out to her school."

"Why, I'm sure she'd like a ride in that cutter," Pa replied.

"It's getting late, and too cold to tie 'em without blanketing," Almanzo said. "I'll drive down the street and stop on my way back."

"I'll tell her," Pa answered, and shut the door while the bells jingled away. "How about it, Laura?"

"It is fun to ride in a cutter," Laura said. Quickly she tied on her hood and got into her coat. The bells were coming; she had hardly time to say good-by before they stopped at the door.

"Don't forget the satchel," Ma said, and Laura turned back to snatch it up.

"Thank you, Ma. Good-by," she said and went out to the cutter. Almanzo helped her in and tucked the robes around her. Prince and Lady started quickly; all the bells rang out their music, and she was on her way back to her school.

CHAPTER 5

A Stiff Upper Lip

ALL that week, everything went wrong; everything. Nothing gave Laura the least encouragement.

The weather was sullen. Dull clouds lay low and flat above the gray-white prairie, and the wind blew monotonously. The cold was damp and clammy. The stoves smoked.

Mrs. Brewster let the housework go. She did not sweep out the snow that Mr. Brewster tracked in; it melted and made puddles with the ashes around the stove. She did not make their bed nor even spread it up. Twice a day she cooked potatoes and salt pork and put them on the table. The rest of the time she sat brooding. She did not even comb her hair, and it seemed to Laura that Johnny squalled with temper that whole week.

Once Laura tried to play with him, but he only struck at her and Mrs. Brewster said angrily, "Leave him alone!"

After supper he went to sleep on his father's knee, and Mr. Brewster just sat. The air seemed to smoulder with Mrs. Brewster's silence, and he sat, Laura thought, like a bump on a log. She had heard that said, but she had not realized what it meant. A bump on a log does not fight anyone, but it cannot be budged.

The silence was so loud that Laura could hardly study. When she went to bed, Mrs. Brewster quarreled at Mr. Brewster. She wanted to go back East.

Laura could hardly have studied well, anyway; she was so worried about her school. In spite of all she could do, everything went from bad to worse.

It began on Monday, when Tommy did not know one word of his spelling lesson. Ruby would not let him have the speller, he said.

"Why, Ruby!" Laura said in surprise. Then sweet little Ruby turned into a very spitfire. Laura was so startled that before she could stop them, Ruby and Tommy were quarreling.

Sternly Laura stopped that. She went to Tommy's seat and

gave him the speller. "Now learn that lesson," said she. "You may stay in at recess and recite it to me."

Next day, Ruby did not know her lesson. She stood before Laura with her hands behind her, innocent as a kitten, and said, "I could not learn it, Teacher. You gave Tommy the speller."

Laura remembered to count ten. Then she said, "So I did. Well, you and Tommy may sit together to learn your spelling."

They were not studying the same lessons in the book, but they could hold it open in two places. Leaning to one side, Tommy could study his lesson while Ruby, leaning to the other side, could study hers. In that way, Laura and Mary used to learn their different lessons in Ma's speller.

But Tommy and Ruby did not. They sat silently struggling, each to open the book wider at his place. Again and again Laura said sharply, "Tommy! Ruby!" But neither of them learned their spelling well.

Martha could not work her arithmetic problems. Charles sat idly staring at the window, where nothing was to be seen but the gray weather. When Laura told him to keep his eyes on his lessons, he stared day-dreaming at a page. Laura knew he was not seeing it.

She was too little. When Martha and Charles and Clarence stood before her to recite, they were too much for her. Though she did her best, she could not interest them in learning even geography and history.

On Monday, Clarence knew part of his history lesson, but when Laura asked him when the first settlement was made in Virginia, he answered carelessly, "Oh, I didn't study that part."

"Why didn't you?" Laura asked.

"The lesson was too long," Clarence replied, with a look from narrow, laughing eyes that said, "What are you going to do about that?"

Laura was furiously angry, but as her eyes met his she knew that he expected her to be angry. What could she do? She could not punish him; he was too big. She must not show any anger.

So she kept quiet, while she turned the pages of the history consideringly. Her heart was faint, but she must not let him know that. Finally she said, "It is too bad that you did not learn this. It will make your next lesson so much longer, for we must not keep Charles and Martha back."

She went on hearing Charles and Martha recite the lesson. Then she gave them all another lesson of the usual length.

The next day Clarence did not know his history at all. "It's no use trying to learn such long lessons," he said.

"If you do not want to learn, Clarence, you are the loser," Laura told him. She kept on asking him questions in his turn, hoping that he would grow ashamed of answering, "I don't know." But he did not.

Every day she felt more miserably that she was failing. She could not teach school. Her first school would be a failure; she would not be able to get another certificate. She would earn no more money. Mary would have to leave college, and that would be Laura's fault. She could hardly learn her own lessons, though she studied them not only at night, but at noon and recess. When she went back to town, she would be behind her class.

All the trouble came from Clarence. He could make Ruby and Tommy behave, if he would; he was their older brother. He could learn his lessons; he was much smarter than Martha and Charles. How she wished that she were big enough to give Clarence the whipping he deserved.

Slowly the week dragged by, the longest and most miserable week that Laura had ever known.

On Thursday, when Laura said, "Third arithmetic class, rise," Clarence stood up quickly and Charles began to move languidly, but Martha half rose and yelled, "Ow!" and sat down as if she were jerked.

Clarence had driven his knife through her braid and pinned it to his desk. He had done it so quietly that Martha knew nothing of it until she tried to stand up.

"Clarence!" Laura said. He did not stop laughing. Tommy was laughing, Ruby was giggling, even Charles was grinning. Martha sat red-faced, with tears in her eyes.

Laura was in despair. They were all against her; she could not discipline them. Oh, how could they be so mean! For an instant she remembered Miss Wilder, who had failed to teach the school in town. "This is the way she felt," Laura thought.

Then suddenly she was very angry. She yanked the knife up,

and clicked it shut in her fist. She did not feel small as she faced Clarence. "Shame on you!" she said, and he stopped laughing. They were all still.

Laura marched back to her table, and rapped on it. "Third class in arithmetic, rise! Come forward."

They did not know the lesson; they could not solve the problems, but at least they went through the motions of trying. Laura felt tall and terrible, and they obeyed her meekly. At last she said, "You may all repeat this lesson tomorrow. Class is dismissed."

Her head ached as she went toward Mrs. Brewster's hateful house. She could not be angry all the time, and discipline was no good if the pupils would not learn their lessons. Ruby and Tommy were far behind in spelling, Martha could not parse a simple compound sentence nor add fractions, and Clarence was learning no history. Laura tried to hope that she could do better tomorrow.

Friday was quiet. Everyone was dull and listless. They were only waiting for the week to end, and so was she. The hands of the clock had never moved so slowly.

In the afternoon the clouds began to break and the light grew brighter. Just before four o'clock, pale sunshine streamed eastward across the snowy land. Then Laura heard sleigh bells faintly ringing.

"You may put away your books," she said. That miserable week was ended, at last. Nothing more could happen now. "School is dismissed."

The music of the bells came ringing louder and clearer. Laura's coat was buttoned and her hood tied when Prince and Lady passed the window with the dancing bells. She snatched up her books and dinner pail, and then the worst thing of all happened.

Clarence opened the door, thrust his head in, and shouted, "Teacher's beau's here!"

Almanzo Wilder must have heard. He could not help hearing. Laura did not know how she could face him. What could she say? How could she tell him that she had given Clarence no reason to say such a thing?

He was waiting in the cold wind, and the horses were not blanketed; she must go out. It seemed to her that he was smiling, but she could hardly look at him. He tucked her in and said, "All snug?"

"Yes, thank you," she answered. The horses went swiftly, their strings of bells merrily ringing. It would be better to say nothing of Clarence, Laura decided; as Ma would say, "Least said, soonest mended."

CHAPTER 6

Managing

WHILE Pa played the fiddle that evening at home, Laura felt much better. Two weeks were gone, she thought; there were but six more. She could only keep on trying. The music stopped, and Pa asked, "What's the trouble, Laura? Don't you want to make a clean breast of it?"

She had not meant to worry them; she intended to say nothing that was not cheerful. But suddenly she said, "Oh, Pa, I don't know what to do!"

She told them all about that miserable week at school. "What can I do?" she asked, "I must do something; I *can't* fail. But I am failing. If only I were big enough to whip Clarence. That's what he needs, but I can't."

"You might ask Mr. Brewster to," Carrie suggested. "He could make Clarence behave himself."

"Oh, but Carrie!" Laura protested. "How can I tell the school board that I can't manage the school? No, I can't do that."

"There you have it, Laura!" Pa said. "It's all in that word, 'manage.' You might not get far with Clarence, even if you were big enough to punish him as he deserves. Brute force can't do much. Everybody's born free, you know, like it says in the Declaration of Independence. You can lead a horse to water, but you can't make him drink, and good or bad, nobody but Clarence can ever boss Clarence. You better just manage."

"Yes, I know, Pa," Laura said. "But how?"

"Well, first of all, be patient. Try to see things his way, so far as you can. Better not try to make him do anything, because you can't. He doesn't sound to me like a really vicious boy."

"No, he isn't," Laura agreed. "But I guess I just don't know how to manage him."

"If I were you," Ma gently began, and Laura remembered that Ma had been a schoolteacher, "I'd give way to Clarence, and not pay any attention to him. It's attention he wants; that's why he cuts up. Be pleasant and nice to him, but put all your attention on the others and straighten them out. Clarence'll come around."

"That's right, Laura, listen to your Ma," said Pa. " 'Wise as a serpent and gentle as a dove.' "

"Charles!" said Ma. Pa took up his fiddle and began saucily playing to her, "Can she make a cherry pie, Billy boy, Billy boy; can she make a cherry pie, charming Billy?"

Sunday afternoon, when Laura was flying over the sunny snow in the cutter, Almanzo Wilder said, "It chirks you up to go home over Sunday. I've got an idea it's pretty tough, staying at Brewster's."

"It's my first school, and I never was away from home before," Laura answered. "I get homesick. I do appreciate your driving so far to take me home."

"It's a pleasure," he said.

It was polite of him to say so, but Laura saw no pleasure for him in that long, cold drive. They hardly said a word the whole way, because of the cold, and she knew very well that she would not be entertaining, anyway. She could hardly ever think of anything to say to strangers.

The horses were so warm from trotting that they must not stand one moment in the cold wind, so at the Brewsters' door he stopped them only long enough for Laura to jump quickly out. As they went on, he touched his fur cap with his gloved hand and called through the sleigh bells' music, "Good-by till Friday!"

Laura felt guilty. She had not expected him to make that long drive every week. She hoped he did not think that she was expecting him to do it. Surely, he was not thinking of . . . well, of maybe being her beau?

She was almost used to Mrs. Brewster's miserable house. She had only to forget it, as well as she could; to study until bedtime, and in the mornings to make her bed neatly, swallow her breakfast and wipe the dishes, and get away to school. There were only six weeks more, now.

On Monday morning, school began as glumly as it had ended on Friday. But Laura was determined to make a change, and she began at once.

When Tommy had stumbled through his reading lesson she smiled at him and said, "Your reading is improving, Tommy.

You deserve a reward. Would you like to copy your spelling lesson on the blackboard?"

Tommy smiled, so she gave him the spelling book and a new piece of chalk. When he had copied his lesson, she praised his writing and told him that now he could study his spelling from the board. She gave the spelling book to Ruby.

"Your reading lesson was very good, too," she said to Ruby. "So tomorrow, would you like to copy your spelling lesson on the blackboard?"

"Oh, yes, ma'am!" Ruby answered eagerly, and Laura thought, "There! that's one thing managed."

Clarence fidgeted, dropped his books, and pulled Martha's hair, but Laura remembered Ma's advice and did not see him. Poor Martha did not know her grammar lesson at all; she was so hopelessly confused about complex and compound sentences that she had stopped trying to understand them. She answered only, "I don't know. I don't know."

"I think you must take this lesson over, Martha," Laura had to say, and then she had an inspiration and went on, "I would like to go over it again myself. I am trying to keep up with my class in town, and grammar is hard. If you would like to, we can go through this lesson together at the noon hour. Would you like to?"

"Yes, I would," Martha answered.

So at noon, when they had eaten their dinners, Laura took up her grammar and said, "Ready, Martha?" Martha smiled back at her.

Then Clarence asked, "Is that why you study all the time, to keep up with your class in town?"

"Yes, I study at night but I have to study here, too," Laura answered, passing by him toward the blackboard. Clarence whistled, "Whew!" under his breath, but Laura paid no attention.

At the blackboard she worked with Martha until Martha could diagram a complex compound sentence all by herself. Martha said, "I understand it now! After this, I won't dread the grammar recitation so much."

So that was the trouble, Laura thought. Martha had dreaded grammar so much that she could not learn it.

"Don't dread a lesson," Laura said. "I'll always be glad to

study any of them with you, if you want me to." Martha's brown eyes smiled almost like Ida's as she said, "I would like to, sometimes. Thank you." Laura wished that she need not be the teacher; she and Martha were the same age, and might have been friends.

She had decided what to do about Clarence's history lessons. He was far behind Charles and Martha, but Laura asked him no questions that he could not answer, and when she set the lesson for next day she said, "This doesn't mean you, Clarence; it would make your lesson far too long. Let me see. How many pages are you behind?"

He showed her, and she said, "How many do you think you can learn? Would three be too much?"

"No," he said. There was nothing else he could say, no contention he could make.

"Then the class is dismissed," Laura said. She wondered what Clarence would do. Pa's advice and Ma's was working well so far, but would it work with Clarence?

She did not ask him many questions next day, but he seemed to know the three pages perfectly. Charles and Martha were now nine pages ahead of him. Laura set them seven pages more, and said to Clarence, "Would another three pages be too much? You may take that much if you like."

"I'll learn it," Clarence said, and this time he looked at Laura with a friendly smile.

She was so surprised that she almost smiled back. But she said quickly, "Make it shorter if it is too much."

"I'll learn it," Clarence repeated.

"Very well," Laura said. "Class dismissed."

She was becoming adjusted to the pattern of the days. A silent breakfast in the chill of early morning, a shivering walk to the cold school shanty; then the usual round of recitations, with recess and noon breaking it into four equal parts. Then the cold walk back to the Brewsters' house for a cheerless supper, an evening of study, and sleep on the narrow sofa. Mrs. Brewster was always sullen and silent. She seldom even quarreled at Mr. Brewster any more.

The week passed and Friday came again. When the history class came forward to recite, Clarence said, "You may hear me recite as far as Martha and Charles. I've caught up with them."

Laura was amazed. She exclaimed, "But how could you, Clarence?"

"If you can study at night, I can," Clarence said. Laura almost smiled at him again. She could have liked him so much, if she had not been the teacher. The brown sparkles in his eyes were like the blue sparkles in Pa's. But she was the teacher.

"That is good," she said. "Now you can all three go on together."

With four o'clock came the music of sleigh bells, and Clarence loudly whispered, "Teacher's beau!"

Laura's cheeks grew hot, but she said quietly, "You may put away your books. School is dismissed."

She dreaded that Clarence might shout again, but he did not. He was well on his way toward home with Tommy and Ruby when Laura shut the shanty door behind her and Almanzo tucked her again into the cutter.

CHAPTER 7

A Knife in the Dark

THE third week went by, and the fourth. Now there were only four weeks more. Though every morning Laura was anxious about the school day ahead, still it was not as bad as the Brewsters' house, and every afternoon at four o'clock she drew a breath of relief; one more day had gone well.

There were no blizzards yet, but February was very cold. The wind was like knives. Every Friday and Sunday, Almanzo Wilder had made the long, cold drive, to take her home. Laura did not know how she could get through the week, without looking forward to Saturday at home. But she felt sorry for Almanzo, who was making those cold drives for nothing.

Much as she wanted to go home every week, she did not want to be under such an obligation to anyone. She was going with him only to get home, but he did not know that. Perhaps he was expecting her to go driving with him after she went home to stay. She did not want to feel obliged to go with him, neither could she be unfair, or deceitful. She felt that she must explain this to him, but she did not know how.

At home, Ma worried because she was thinner. "Are you sure you get enough to eat at Brewster's?" Ma asked, and Laura answered, "Oh, yes, a great plenty! But it doesn't taste like home cooking."

Pa said, "You know, Laura, you don't *have* to finish the term. If anything worries you too much, you can always come home."

"Why, Pa!" Laura said, "I couldn't *quit.* I wouldn't get another certificate. Besides, it's only three weeks more."

"I'm afraid you're studying too hard," Ma said. "You don't look like you get enough sleep."

"I go to bed every night at eight o'clock," Laura assured her.

"Well, as you say, it's only three weeks more," said Ma.

No one knew how she dreaded to go back to Mrs. Brewster's. It would do no good to tell them. Being at home every Saturday raised her spirits and gave her courage for another week. Still, it was not fair to take so much from Almanzo Wilder.

He was driving her out to the Brewsters' that Sunday afternoon. They hardly ever spoke during those long drives; it was too cold to talk. The jingling sleigh bells sounded frosty in the sparkling cold, and the light cutter sped so fast that the north wind following it was not very sharp on their backs. But he must face that wind all the way back to town.

The Brewsters' shanty was not far ahead when Laura said to herself: "Stop shilly-shallying!" Then she spoke out. She said, "I am going with you only because I want to get home. When I am home to stay, I will not go with you any more. So now you know, and if you want to save yourself these long, cold drives, you can."

The words sounded horrid to her as she said them. They were abrupt and rude and hateful. At the same time, a dreadful realization swept over her, of what it would mean if Almanzo did not come for her again. She would have to spend Saturdays and Sundays with Mrs. Brewster.

After a startled moment, Almanzo said slowly, "I see."

There was no time to say more. They were at Mrs. Brewster's door, and the horses must not stand and get chilled. Quickly Laura got out, saying, "Thank you." He touched his hand to his fur cap and the cutter went swiftly away.

"It is only three weeks more," Laura said to herself, but she could not keep her spirits from sinking.

All that week the weather grew colder. On Thursday morning Laura found that the quilt had frozen stiff around her nose while she slept. Her fingers were so numb that she could hardly dress. In the other room the stove lids were red hot, but the heat seemed unable to penetrate the cold around it.

Laura was holding her numbed hands above the stove when Mr. Brewster burst in, tore off his boots and began violently rubbing his feet. Mrs. Brewster went quickly to him.

"Oh, Lewis, what's the matter?" she asked so anxiously that Laura was surprised.

"My feet," Mr. Brewster said. "I ran all the way from the schoolhouse but there's no feeling in them."

"Let me help," his wife said. She took his feet into her lap and helped him rub them. She was so concerned and so kind that she seemed like another woman. "Oh, Lewis, this dreadful country!" she said. "Oh, am I hurting you?"

"Go on," Mr. Brewster grunted. "It shows the blood's coming back into them."

When they had saved his half-frozen feet, Mr. Brewster told Laura not to go to school that day. "You would freeze," he said.

She protested, "But the children will come, and I must be there."

"I don't think they'll come," he said. "I built a fire, and if they do come, they can get warm and go home again. There will be no school today," he said flatly.

That settled it, for a teacher must obey the head of the school board.

It was a long, wretched day. Mrs. Brewster sat huddled in a quilt, close to the stove, and sullenly brooding. Mr. Brewster's feet were painful, and Johnny fretted with a feverish cold. Laura did the dishes, made her bed in the freezing cold, and studied her schoolbooks. When she tried to talk, there was something menacing in Mrs. Brewster's silence.

At last it was bedtime. Laura hoped desperately that tomorrow she could go to school; meantime, she could escape by going to sleep. The cold in the bedroom took her breath away and stiffened her hands so she could hardly undress. For a long time she lay too cold to sleep, but slowly she began to be warmer.

A scream woke her. Mrs. Brewster screamed, "You kicked me!"

"I did not," Mr. Brewster said. "But I will, if you don't go put up that butcher knife."

Laura sat straight up. Moonlight was streaming over her bed from the window. Mrs. Brewster screamed again, a wild sound without words that made Laura's scalp crinkle.

"Take that knife back to the kitchen," Mr. Brewster said.

Laura peeped through the crack between the curtains. The moonlight shone through the calico, and thinned the darkness so that Laura saw Mrs. Brewster standing there. Her long white flannel nightgown trailed on the floor and her black hair fell loose over her shoulders. In her upraised hand she held the butcher knife. Laura had never been so terribly frightened.

"If I can't go home one way, I can another," said Mrs. Brewster.

"Go put that knife back," said Mr. Brewster. He lay still, but tensed to spring.

"Will you or won't you?" she demanded.

"You'll catch your death of cold," he said. "I won't go over that again, this time of night. I've got you and Johnny to support, and nothing in the world but this claim. Go put up that knife and come to bed before you freeze."

The knife stopped shaking, as Mrs. Brewster's fist clenched on the handle.

"Go put it back in the kitchen," Mr. Brewster ordered.

After a moment, Mrs. Brewster turned and went to the kitchen. Not until she came back and got into bed did Laura let the curtains fall together again. Softly she drew the bedcovers over her and lay staring at the curtain. She was terribly frightened. She dared not sleep. Suppose she woke to see Mrs. Brewster standing over her with that knife? Mrs. Brewster did not like her.

What could she do? The nearest house was a mile away; she would freeze if she tried to reach it in this cold. Wide awake, she stared at the curtains and listened. There was no sound but the wind. The moon went down, and she stared at the dark until the gray winter daylight came. When she heard Mr. Brewster build the fire and Mrs. Brewster beginning to cook breakfast, she got up and dressed.

Nothing was different; breakfast was the usual silent meal. Laura went to school as soon as she could get away. She felt safe there, for the day. It was Friday.

The wind was blowing fiercely. Fortunately it was not a blizzard wind, but it scoured hard particles of snow from the frozen drifts and drove them through every crack in the shanty's north and west walls. From all sides the cold came in. The big coal heater seemed to make no impression on that cold.

Laura called the school to order. Though she was near the stove, her feet were numb and her fingers could not grip a pencil. She knew that it was colder in the seats.

"Better put your coats on again," she said, "and all of you come to the fire. You may take turns sitting in the front seat or standing by the stove to get warm. Study as best you can."

All day the snow was blown low across the prairie, and through the schoolroom's walls. Ice froze thick on the water pail, and at noon they set their dinner pails on the stove to thaw the frozen food before they ate it. The wind was steadily growing colder.

It cheered Laura to see how well every pupil behaved. Not one took advantage of the disorder to be idle or unruly. No one whispered. They all stood by the stove, studying, and quietly turning about to warm their backs, and all their recitations were good. Charles and Clarence took turns, going out into the wind to get coal from the bin and keep up the fire.

Laura dreaded the day's end. She was afraid to go back to the house. She was sleepy; she knew that she must sleep, and she feared to sleep in Mrs. Brewster's house. All day tomorrow and Sunday she must be in that house with Mrs. Brewster, and much of the time Mr. Brewster would be at the stable.

She knew that she must not be afraid. Pa had always said that she must never be afraid. Very likely, nothing would happen. She was not exactly afraid of Mrs. Brewster, for she knew that she was quick, and strong as a little French horse. That is, when she was awake. But she had never wanted so much to go home.

It had been right to tell Almanzo Wilder the truth, but she wished that she had not done it so soon. Still, he would not have come so far in such bitter cold, anyway. Every moment the wind blew stronger, and colder.

At half past three they were all so cold that she thought of dismissing school early. The mile that Martha and Charles must walk, worried her. On the other hand, she should not cut short the pupils' opportunity for learning, and this was not a blizzard.

Suddenly she heard sleigh bells. They were coming! In a moment they were at the door. Prince and Lady passed the window, and Clarence exclaimed, "That Wilder's a bigger fool than I thought he was to come out in this weather!"

"You may all put away your books," Laura said. It was much too cold for the horses to stand outdoors. "It is growing colder, and the sooner everyone reaches home, the better," she said. "School is dismissed."

CHAPTER 8

A Cold Ride

"CAREFUL of the lantern," was all that Almanzo said as he helped her into the cutter. Several horse blankets were spread over the seat, and on their ends, under the fur buffalo robes, a lantern stood burning to warm the nest for Laura's feet.

When she ran into the house, Mr. Brewster said, "You aren't thinking of such a thing as driving in this cold?"

"Yes," she answered. She lost no time. In the bedroom, she buttoned on her other flannel petticoat, and pulled over her shoes her other pair of woolen stockings. She doubled her thick black woolen veil and wrapped it twice around her face and hood, and wound its long ends around her throat. Over that she put her muffler, crossed its ends on her chest, and buttoned her coat over all. She ran out to the cutter.

Mr. Brewster was there, protesting. "You folks are fools to try it," he said. "It is not safe. I want him to put up here for the night," he said to Laura.

"Think you'd better not risk it?" Almanzo asked her.

"Are you going back?" she asked him.

"Yes, I've got stock to take care of," he said.

"Then I'm going," she said.

Prince and Lady started swiftly into the wind. It struck through all the woolen folds and took Laura's breath away. She bent her head into it, but she felt it flowing like icy water on her cheeks and chest. Her teeth clenched to keep from chattering.

The horses were eager to go. Their trotting feet drummed on the hard snow and every sleigh bell cheerily rang. Laura was thankful for the speed that would soon reach shelter from the cold. She was sorry when they trotted more slowly. They dropped into a walk, and she supposed that Almanzo was slowing them for a rest. Probably horses must not be driven too hard against such a bitter wind.

She was surprised when he stopped them, and got out of the cutter. Dimly through the black veil she saw him going to their drooping heads, and she heard him say, "Just a minute, Lady," as he laid his mittened hands on Prince's nose. After a moment he took his hands away with a scraping motion, and Prince tossed his head high and shook music from his bells. Quickly Almanzo did the same thing to Lady's nose, and she too, tossed up her head. Almanzo tucked himself into the cutter and they sped on.

Laura's veil was a slab of frost against her mouth that made speaking uncomfortable, so she said nothing, but she wondered. Almanzo's fur cap came down to his eyebrows, and his muffler covered his face to his eyes. His breath froze white on the fur and along the muffler's edge. He drove with one hand, keeping the other under the robes, and often changing so that neither hand would freeze.

The horses trotted more slowly again, and again he got out and went to hold his hands on their noses. When he came back Laura asked him, "What's the matter?"

He answered, "Their breath freezes over their noses till they can't breathe. Have to thaw it off."

They said no more. Laura remembered the cattle drifting in the October blizzard that began the Hard Winter; their breath had smothered them, till they would have died if Pa had not broken the ice from their noses.

The cold was piercing through the buffalo robes. It crept through Laura's wool coat and woolen dress, through all her flannel petticoats and the two pairs of woolen stockings drawn over the folded legs of her warm flannel union suit. In spite of the heat from the lantern, her feet and her legs grew cold. Her clenched jaws ached, and two sharp little aches began at her temples.

Almanzo reached across and pulled the robes higher, tucking them behind her elbows.

"Cold?" he asked.

"No," Laura answered clearly. It was all she could say without letting her teeth chatter. It was not true, but he knew that she meant she was not so cold that she could not bear it. There was nothing to do but go on, and she knew that he was cold, too.

Again he stopped the horses and got out into the wind, to thaw the ice from their noses. Again the bells rang out merrily.

The sound seemed as cruel, now, as the merciless wind. Though her veil made a darkness, she could see that the sun was shining bright on the white prairie.

Almanzo came back into the cutter.

"All right?" he asked.

"Yes," she said.

"I've got to stop every couple of miles. They can't make more," he explained.

Laura's heart sank. Then they had come only six miles. There were still six miles to go. They went on swiftly against the cutting wind. In spite of all she could do, Laura shook all over. Pressing her knees tight together did not stop their shaking. The lantern beside her feet under the fur robes seemed to give no warmth. The pains bored into her temples, and a knot of pain tightened in her middle.

It seemed a long time before the horses slowed again, and again Almanzo stopped them. The bells rang out, first Prince's, then Lady's. Almanzo was clumsy, getting into the cutter again.

"You all right?" he asked.

"Yes," she said.

She was growing more used to the cold. It did not hurt so much. Only the pain in her middle kept tightening, but it was duller. The sound of the wind and the bells and the cutter's runners on the snow all blended into one monotonous sound, rather pleasant. She knew when Almanzo left the cutter to thaw the ice from the horses' noses again but everything seemed like a dream.

"All right?" he asked. She nodded. It was too much trouble to speak.

"Laura!" he said, taking hold of her shoulder and shaking her a little. The shaking hurt; it made her feel the cold again. "You sleepy?"

"A little," she answered.

"Don't go to sleep. You hear me?"

"I won't," she said. She knew what he meant. If you go to sleep in such cold, you freeze to death.

The horses stopped again. Almanzo asked, "Making it all right?"

"Yes," she said. He went to take the ice from the horses' noses. When he came back he said, "It's not far now."

She knew he wanted her to answer. She said, "That's good."

Sleepiness kept coming over her in long, warm waves, though she was holding her eyes wide open. She shook her head and took burning gulps of air, and struggled awake, but another wave of sleepiness came, and another. Often when she was too tired to struggle any longer, Almanzo's voice helped her. She heard him ask, "All right?"

"Yes," she said, and for a moment she would be awake; she heard the sleigh bells clearly and felt the wind blowing. Then another wave came.

"Here we are!" she heard him say.

"Yes," she answered. Then suddenly she knew that they were at the back door of home. The wind was not so strong here; its force was broken by the building on the other side of Second Street. Almanzo lifted the robes and she tried to get out of the cutter, but she was too stiff; she could not stand up.

The door flashed open, and Ma took hold of her, exclaiming, "My goodness! are you frozen?"

"I'm afraid she's pretty cold," Almanzo said.

"Get those horses into shelter before they freeze," Pa said. "We'll take care of her."

The sleigh bells dashed away, while with Pa and Ma holding her arms, Laura stumbled into the kitchen.

"Take off her shoes, Carrie," Ma said as she peeled off Laura's veil and knitted woolen hood. The frost of her breath had frozen the veil to the hood and they came away together. "Your face is red," Ma said in relief. "I'm thankful it isn't white and frozen."

"I'm only numb," Laura said. Her feet were not frozen, either, though she could hardly feel Pa's hands rubbing them. Now in the warm room she began to shake from head to foot and her teeth chattered. She sat close by the stove while she drank the hot ginger tea that Ma made for her. But she could not get warm.

She had been cold so long, ever since she got out of bed that morning. In the Brewsters' cold kitchen her place at the table was farthest from the stove and near the window. Then came the long walk through the snow to school, with the wind blowing against her and whirling up under her skirts; the long, cold day in the schoolhouse, and then the long ride home. But there was nothing to complain of, for now she was at home.

"You took a long chance, Laura," Pa said soberly. "I did not know that Wilder was starting until he had gone, and then I was sure he'd stay at Brewster's. It was forty below zero when that crazy fellow started, and the thermometer froze soon afterward. It has been steadily growing colder ever since; there's no telling how cold it is now."

"All's well that ends well, Pa," Laura answered him with a shaky laugh.

It seemed to her that she never would get warm. But it was wonderful to eat supper in the happy kitchen, and then to sleep safely in her own bed. She woke to find the weather moderating; at breakfast Pa said that the temperature was near twenty below zero. The cold snap was over.

In church that Sunday morning Laura thought how foolish she had been to let herself be so miserable and frightened. There were only two weeks more, and then she could come home to stay.

While Almanzo was driving her out to the Brewsters' that afternoon she thanked him for taking her home that week.

"No need for thanks," he said. "You knew I would."

"Why, no, I didn't," she answered honestly.

"What do you take me for?" he asked. "Do you think I'm the kind of a fellow that'd leave you out there at Brewster's when you're so homesick, just because there's nothing in it for me?"

"Why, I . . ." Laura stopped. The truth was that she had never thought much about what kind of a person he was. He was so much older; he was a homesteader.

"To tell you the whole truth," he said, "I was in two minds about risking that trip. I figured all week I'd drive out for you, but when I looked at the thermometer I came pretty near deciding against it."

"Why didn't you?" Laura asked.

"Well, I was starting out in the cutter, and I pulled up in front of Fuller's to look at the thermometer. The mercury was all down in the bulb, below forty, and the wind blowing colder every minute. Just then Cap Garland came by. He saw me there, ready to go out to Brewster's for you, and looking at the thermometer. So he looked at it, and you know how he grins? Well, as he was going on into Fuller's, he just said to me over his shoulder, 'God hates a coward.' "

"So you came because you wouldn't take a dare?" Laura asked.

"No, it wasn't a dare," Almanzo said. "I just figured he was right."

CHAPTER 9

The Superintendent's Visit

"I HAVE only to get through one day at a time," Laura thought, when she went into the house. Everything was still all wrong there. Mrs. Brewster did not speak; Johnny was always miserable, and Mr. Brewster stayed at the stable as much as he could. That evening while she studied, Laura made four marks on her notebook, for Monday, Tuesday, Wednesday, Thursday. She would mark off one of them every night; when they were gone, there would be only one week more.

Day after day the weather grew colder again, but still there was no blizzard. The nights passed quietly, though Laura lay half-asleep and woke often. Each evening she crossed out a mark. It seemed to make time pass more quickly, to look forward to crossing out one more day.

All Wednesday night she heard the wind howling and snow beating on the window. She dreaded that there might be no school next day. But in the morning the sun was shining, though there was no warmth in it. A bitter wind rolled the snow low across the prairie. Laura gladly faced it as she fought her way to the school shanty, breaking her path again.

Snow was blowing through the cracks, and once more she let her pupils stand by the stove to study. But slowly the red-hot stove warmed the room, until at recess Laura could hardly see her breath when she blew it above Clarence's back seat. So when she called the school to order she said, "The room is warmer now. You may take your seats."

They were hardly in their places, when a sudden knock sounded on the door. Who could it be? she wondered. As she hurried to the door, she glanced through the window, but nothing was to be seen. At the door stood Mr. Williams, the county superintendent of schools.

His blanketed team stood tied to a corner of the school shanty. The soft snow had muffled the sounds of their coming, and they had no bells.

This was the test of Laura's teaching, and how thankful she

was that the pupils were in their seats. Mr. Williams smiled pleasantly, as she gave him her chair by the red-hot stove. Every pupil bent studiously to work, but Laura could feel how alert and tense they were. She was so nervous that it was hard to keep her voice low and steady.

It heartened her, that each one tried hard to do his best for her. Even Charles made an effort, and surpassed himself. Mr. Williams sat listening to recitation after recitation, while the wind blew low and loud and the snow drifted through the cracks in the walls.

Charles raised his hand and asked, "Please may I come to the stove to warm?" Laura said that he might, and without thinking to ask permission, Martha came too. They were studying from the same book. When their hands were warm, they went back to their seat, quietly, but without asking permission. It did not speak well for Laura's discipline.

Just before noon, Mr. Williams said that he must go. Then Laura must ask him if he wished to speak to the school.

"Yes, I do," he answered grimly, and as he rose to his full height of six feet, Laura's heart stood still. Desperately she wondered what she had done that was wrong.

With his head nearly touching the ceiling he stood silent a moment, to emphasize what he intended to say. Then he spoke.

"Whatever else you do, *keep your feet warm.*"

He smiled at them all, and again at Laura, and after shaking her hand warmly, he was gone.

At noon Clarence emptied the coal hod into the stove, and went out into the cold to fill it again at the bin. As he came back he said, "We'll need more coal on the fire before night. It's getting colder, fast."

They all gathered close to the stove to eat their cold lunches. When Laura called the school to order she told them to bring their books to the fire. "You may stand by the stove or move about as you please. So long as you are quiet and learn your lessons, we will let that be the rule as long as this cold weather lasts."

The plan worked well. Recitations were better than ever before, and the room was quiet while they all studied and kept their feet warm.

CHAPTER 10

Almanzo Says Good-by

THAT Saturday at home, Ma was worried about Laura. "Are you coming down with something?" she asked. "It isn't like you to sit half-asleep."

"I feel a little tired. It isn't anything, Ma," Laura said.

Pa looked up from his paper. "That Clarence making trouble again?"

"Oh, no, Pa! He's doing splendidly, and they are all as good as can be." She was not exactly lying, but she could not tell them about Mrs. Brewster and the knife. If they knew, they would not let her go back, and she must finish her school. A teacher could not walk away and leave a term of school unfinished. If she did, she would not deserve another certificate, and no school board would hire her.

So she made a greater effort to hide from them her sleepiness and her dread of going back to Mrs. Brewster's house. There was only one more week.

By Sunday afternoon the weather had moderated. The temperature was only fifteen degrees below zero when Laura and Almanzo set out. There was hardly any wind and the sun shone brightly.

Out of a silence Laura said, "Only one more week, and I'll be so glad when it's over."

"Maybe you will miss the sleigh rides?" Almanzo suggested.

"This one is nice," Laura said. "But mostly it is so cold. I should think you'd be glad not to drive so far any more. I don't know why you ever started making these long drives; you didn't need to take them to get home, the way I do."

"Oh, sometimes a fellow gets tired of sitting around," Almanzo replied. "Two old bachelors get pretty dull by themselves."

"Why, there are lots of people in town! You and your brother needn't stay by yourselves," Laura said.

"There hasn't been anything going on in town since the school exhibition," Almanzo objected. "All a fellow can do is hang around the saloon playing pool, or in one of the stores watching the checker players. Sometimes he'd rather be out with better company, even if it does get cold, driving."

Laura had not thought of herself as good company. If that was what he wanted, she thought, she should make an effort to be more entertaining. But she could not think of anything entertaining to say. She tried to think of something, while she watched the sleek brown horses, trotting so swiftly.

Their dainty feet spurned the snow in perfect rhythm, and their blue shadows flew along the snow beside them. They were so gay, tossing their heads to make a chiming of the bells, pricking their ears forward and back, lifting their noses to the breeze of their speed that rippled their black manes. Laura drew a deep breath and exclaimed, "How beautiful!"

"What is beautiful?" Almanzo asked.

"The horses. Look at them!" Laura answered. At that moment, Prince and Lady touched noses as though they whispered to each other, then together they tried to break into a run.

When Almanzo had gently but firmly pulled them into a trot again, he asked, "How would you like to drive them?"

"Oh!" Laura cried. But she had to add, honestly, "Pa won't let me drive his horses. He says I am too little and would get hurt."

"Prince and Lady wouldn't hurt anybody," Almanzo said. "I raised them myself. But if you think they're beautiful, I wish you could've seen the first horse I ever raised, Starlight. I named him for the white star on his forehead."

His father had given him Starlight as a colt, back in New York State when he was nine years old. He told Laura all about gentling Starlight, and breaking him, and what a beautiful horse he was. Starlight had come west to Minnesota, and when first Almanzo came out to the western prairies, he had come riding Starlight. Starlight was nine years old then, when Almanzo rode him back to Marshall, Minnesota, one hundred and five miles in one day, and Starlight came in so fresh that he tried to race another horse at the journey's end.

"Where is he now?" Laura asked.

"At pasture on Father's farm back in Minnesota," Almanzo told her. "He is not as young as he used to be, and I need a double team for driving out here, so I gave him back to Father."

The time had passed so quickly that Laura was surprised to see the Brewsters' ahead. She tried to keep up her courage, but her heart sank.

"What makes you so quiet, so sudden?" Almanzo asked.

"I was wishing we were going in the other direction," Laura said.

"We'll be doing that next Friday." He slowed the horses. "We can delay it a little," he said, and she knew that somehow he understood how she dreaded going into that house.

"Till next Friday, then," he smiled encouragingly, as he drove away.

Day by day and night by night that week went by, until there was only one more night to get through. Tomorrow was Friday, the last day of school. When that one night and one day were over, she would go home to stay.

She so dreaded that something might happen, this last night. Often she woke with a start, but all was quiet and her heart slowly ceased thumping.

Friday's lessons were unusually well-learned, and every pupil was carefully well-behaved.

When afternoon recess was over, Laura called the school to order, and said there would be no more lessons. School would be dismissed early, because this was the last day.

She knew that she must make some closing speech to the school, so she praised them all for the work they had done. "You have made good use of the opportunity you had to come to school," she told them.

"I hope that each of you can get more schooling, but if you cannot, you can study at home as Lincoln did. An education is worth striving for, and if you can not have much help in getting one, you can each help yourself to an education if you try."

Then she gave Ruby one of her name-cards, of thin, pale pink cardboard with a spray of roses and cornflowers curving above her printed name. On the back she had written, "Presented to Ruby Brewster, by her teacher, with kind regards. Brewster School, February, 1883."

Tommy was next, then Martha and Charles, and Clarence. They were all so pleased. Laura let them have a moment to enjoy looking at the pretty cards, and carefully place them in their books. Then she told them to make ready their books, slates, and pencils, to carry home. For the last time she said, "School is dismissed."

She had never been more surprised than she was then. For instead of putting on their wraps as she expected, they all came up to her desk. Martha gave her a beautiful, red apple. Ruby shyly gave her a little cake that her mother had baked for her gift. And Tommy and Charles and Clarence each gave her a new pencil that he had carefully sharpened for her.

She hardly knew how to thank them, but Martha said, "It's us, I mean we, that thank you, Miss Ingalls. Thank you for helping me with grammar." "Thank you, Miss Ingalls," Ruby said. "I wish it had frosting on it." The boys did not say anything, but after they had all said good-by and gone, Clarence came back.

Standing by Laura's table and leaning against it he looked down at his cap in his hands and muttered, "I'm sorry I was so mean."

"Why, Clarence! That's all right!" Laura exclaimed. "And you have done wonderfully well in your studies. I am proud of you."

He looked at her with his old saucy grin, and shot out of the room, slamming the door so that the shanty shook.

Laura cleaned the blackboard and swept the floor. She stacked her books and papers and shut the drafts of the stove. Then she put on her hood and coat and stood at the window waiting until the sleigh bells came jingling and Prince and Lady stopped at the door.

School was out. She was going home to stay! Her heart was so light that she felt like singing with the sleigh bells, and fast as the horses trotted, they seemed slow.

"You won't get there any faster, pushing," Almanzo said once, and she laughed aloud to find that she was pushing her feet hard against the cutter's dashboard. But he did not talk much, and neither did she. It was enough to be going home.

Not until she had thanked him nicely and said good night and was in the sitting room taking off her wraps, did she remember that he had not said, "Good night." He had not said, "I'll see you Sunday afternoon," as he had always said before. He had said, "Good-by."

Of course, she thought. It was good-by. This had been the last sleigh ride.

CHAPTER II

Jingle Bells

WAKING next morning was happier than Christmas. "Oh, I'm at home!" Laura thought. She called, "Carrie! Good morning! Wake up, sleepyhead!"

She almost laughed with joy as she shivered into her dress and skipped downstairs to button her shoes and comb her hair in the warming kitchen where Ma was getting breakfast.

"Good morning, Ma!" she sang.

"Good morning," Ma smiled. "I declare you look better already."

"It's nice to be home," Laura said. "Now what shall I do first?"

She was busy all that morning, helping with Saturday's work. Though usually she disliked the dryness of flour on her hands, today she enjoyed kneading the bread, thinking happily that she would be at home to eat the fresh, brown-crusted loaves. Her heart sang with the song on her lips; she was not going back to the Brewsters' ever again.

It was a beautifully sunny day, and that afternoon when the work was all done, Laura hoped that Mary Power would come to visit with her while they crocheted. Ma was gently rocking while she knitted by the sunny window, Carrie was piecing her quilt block, but somehow Laura could not settle down. Mary did not come, and Laura had just decided that she would put on her wraps and go to see Mary, when she heard sleigh bells.

For some reason, her heart jumped. But the bells rang thinly as they sped by. There were only a few bells; they were not the rich strings of bells that Prince and Lady wore. Their music had not died away, when again sleigh bells went tinkling past. Then all up and down the street, the stillness sparkled with the ringing of the little bells.

Laura went to the window. She saw Minnie Johnson and Fred Gilbert flash by, then Arthur Johnson with a girl that Laura did not know. The full music of double strings of bells came swiftly, and Mary Power and Cap Garland dashed by in a cutter. So that was what Mary was doing. Cap Garland had a cutter and full strings of sleigh bells, too. More and more laughing couples drove up and down the street, in sleighs and cutters, passing and repassing the window where Laura stood.

At last she sat soberly down to her crocheting. The sitting room was neat and quiet. Nobody came to see Laura. She had been gone so long that probably no one thought of her. All that afternoon the sleigh bells were going by. Up and down the street her schoolmates went laughing in the sunny cold, having such a good time. Again and again Mary and Cap sped past, in a cutter made for two.

Well, Laura thought, tomorrow she would see Ida at Sunday School. But Ida did not come to church that Sunday; Mrs. Brown said that she had a bad cold.

That Sunday afternoon the weather was even more beautiful. Again the sleigh bells were ringing, and laughter floating on the wind. Again Mary Power and Cap went by, and Minnie and Fred, and Frank Harthorn and May Bird, and all the newcomers whom Laura barely knew. Two by two they went gaily by, laughing and singing with the chiming bells. No one remembered Laura. She had been away so long that everyone had forgotten her.

Soberly she tried to read Tennyson's poems. She tried not to mind being forgotten and left out. She tried not to hear the sleigh bells and the laughter, but more and more she felt that she could not bear it.

Suddenly, a ringing of bells stopped at the door! Before Pa could look up from his paper, Laura had the door open, and there stood Prince and Lady with the little cutter, and Almanzo stood beside it smiling.

"Would you like to go sleigh riding?" he asked.

"Oh, yes!" Laura answered. "Just a minute, I'll put on my wraps."

Quickly she got into her coat and put on her white hood and mittens. Almanzo tucked her into the cutter and they sped away.

"I didn't know your eyes were so blue," Almanzo said.

"It's my white hood," Laura told him, "I always wore my dark one to Brewster's." She gave a gasp, and laughed aloud.

"What's so funny?" Almanzo asked, smiling.

"It's a joke on me," Laura said. "I didn't intend to go with you any more but I forgot. Why did you come?"

"I thought maybe you'd change your mind after you watched the crowd go by," Almanzo answered. Then they laughed together.

Theirs was one of the line of sleighs and cutters, swiftly going the length of Main Street, swinging in a circle on the prairie to the south, then speeding up Main Street and around in a circle to the north, and back again, and again. Far and wide the sunshine sparkled on the snowy land; the wind blew cold against their faces. The sleigh bells were ringing, the sleigh runners squeaking on the hard-packed snow, and Laura was so happy that she had to sing.

Jingle bells, jingle bells,
Jingle all the way!
Oh what fun it is to ride
In a one-horse open sleigh.

All along the speeding line, other voices took up the tune. Swinging out on the open prairie and back, fast up the street and out on the prairie and back again, the bells went ringing and the voices singing in the frosty air.

Jingle bells, jingle bells,
Jingle all the way!

They were quite safe from blizzards because they did not go far from town. The wind was blowing, but not too hard, and everyone was so happy and gay for it was only twenty degrees below zero and the sun shone.

CHAPTER 12

East or West, Home Is Best

GLADLY Laura set out to school with Carrie on Monday morning. As they picked their way across the icy ruts of the street, Carrie said with a happy sigh, "It's good to be walking to school together again. It never seemed right without you."

"I feel the same way," Laura answered.

When they went into the schoolhouse, Ida exclaimed joyfully, "Hello, Teacher!" and everyone turned from the stove to gather around Laura. "How does it seem to be coming to school yourself?" Ida asked; her nose was swollen and red from the cold, but her brown eyes were gay as ever.

"It seems *good*," Laura answered, squeezing Ida's hand while all the others welcomed her back. Even Nellie Oleson seemed friendly.

"Quite a few sleigh rides you've been having," Nellie said. "Now you're home again, maybe you'll take some of us with you."

Laura only answered, "Maybe." She wondered what Nellie was scheming now. Then Mr. Owen left his desk and came to greet Laura.

"We are glad to have you with us again," he said. "I hear you did well with your school."

"Thank you, sir," she answered. "I am glad to be back." She wanted to ask who had spoken to him about her teaching, but of course she did not.

The morning began a little anxiously, for she feared that she might be behind her class, but she found that she had more than kept up with it. The recitations were all reviews of lessons that she had learned during the wretched evenings at the Brewsters'. She knew them perfectly; she was still sailing at the head of the class with flying colors, and she was feeling happily confident until the morning recess.

Then the girls began to talk about their compositions, and

Laura discovered that Mr. Owen had told the grammar class to write, for that day's lesson, a composition on "Ambition."

The grammar class would be called to recite immediately after recess. Laura was in a panic. She had never written a composition, and now she must do in a few minutes what the others had been working at since yesterday. They had all written their compositions at home, and Mrs. Brown had helped Ida write hers. Mrs. Brown wrote for the church papers, so Ida's composition would be good.

Laura had no idea how to begin. She knew nothing about ambition. The only thought in her head was that she was going to fail in a class that she had always led. She must not fail, she couldn't. She would not. But how did one write a composition? Only five minutes were left.

She found herself staring at the yellow leather cover of the dictionary on its stand by Mr. Owen's desk. Perhaps, she thought, she might get an idea from reading the definition of ambition. Her fingers were chilly as she hurriedly turned the A pages, but the definition was interesting. Back at her desk, she wrote as fast as she could, and kept on writing desperately while the school was called to order. Miserably she felt that her composition was not good, but there was no time to write it over nor to add anything more. Mr. Owen was calling the grammar class to recite.

One by one, as he called upon them, the others read their compositions, while Laura's heart sank. Each one seemed better than her own. At last Mr. Owen said, "Laura Ingalls," and all the class rustled as everyone looked at her expectantly.

Laura stood up, and made herself read aloud what she had written. It was the best that she had been able to do.

AMBITION.

Ambition is necessary to accomplishment. Without an ambition to gain an end, nothing would be done. Without an ambition to excel others and to surpass one's self there would be no superior merit. To win anything, we must have the ambition to do so.

Ambition is a good servant but a bad master. So long as we control our ambition, it is good, but if there is danger of our being ruled by it, then I would say in the words of Shakespeare, "Cromwell, I charge thee, fling away ambition. By that sin fell the angels."

That was all. Laura stood miserably waiting for Mr. Owen's comment. He looked at her sharply and said, "You have written compositions before?"

"No, sir," Laura said. "This is my first."

"Well, you should write more of them, I would not have believed that anyone could do so well the first time," Mr. Owen told her.

Laura stammered in astonishment. "It is s . . . so short . . . It is mostly from the dictionary . . ."

"It is not much like the dictionary," Mr. Owen said. "There are no corrections. It grades one hundred. Class is dismissed."

It couldn't be marked higher. Laura still was at the head of her class. She felt confident now that with steady work she would keep her place at the head of her classes, and she looked forward happily to writing more compositions.

Time no longer dragged. That week went by in a flash, and on Friday when Laura and Carrie went home to dinner Pa said, "I have something for you, Laura."

His eyes were twinkling as he drew his pocketbook from his pocket. Then one by one he laid in her hand four ten-dollar bills.

"I saw Brewster this morning," Pa explained. "He gave me this for you, and said you taught a good school. They would like to have you back next winter. But I told him you wouldn't go so far from home again in the wintertime. I know it wasn't pleasant at Brewster's even if you didn't complain, and I'm proud that you stuck it out, Laura."

"Oh, Pa! It was worth it," Laura said breathlessly. "Forty dollars!"

She had known that she was earning forty dollars, but the bills in her hand made the fact seem real for the first time. She looked at them, hardly able to believe it even now. Four ten-dollar bills; forty dollars.

Then she held it out to Pa. "Here, Pa. Take it and keep it for Mary. It's enough so that she can come home on her vacation this summer, isn't it?"

"Plenty for that, and then some," said Pa, as he folded the bills again into his pocketbook.

"Oh, Laura, aren't you going to have anything at all for teaching your school?" Carrie exclaimed.

"We'll all see Mary this summer," Laura answered happily. "I was only teaching school for Mary." It was a wonderful feeling, to know that she had helped so much. Forty dollars. As she sat down to the good dinner in the pleasant kitchen of home, she said, "I wish I could earn some more."

"You can if you want to," Ma said unexpectedly. "Mrs. McKee said this morning she would like to have you help her on Saturdays. She has more dressmaking than she can do alone, and she will pay you fifty cents and dinner."

"Oh!" Laura cried out. "Did you tell her I will, Ma?"

"I said you might if you'd like to," Ma smiled.

"When? Tomorrow?" Laura eagerly asked.

"Tomorrow morning at eight o'clock," said Ma. "Mrs. McKee said she wouldn't be ready for you till that late. Only from eight to six, she said, unless there's a rush, and she'll give you your supper if you stay to finish up something in the evening."

Mrs. McKee was the town's dressmaker. The McKees were newcomers who lived in a new house, between Clancy's dry-goods store and the new office building at the corner of Main and Second Street. Laura had met Mrs. McKee at church, and liked her. She was tall and slender with kind blue eyes and a pleasant smile. Her light brown hair was worn in a knot at the back of her head.

So now Laura's time was full, and all of it was pleasant. The crowded days at school went swiftly by, and all the week Laura looked forward to the day of sewing busily in Mrs. McKee's living room—that was always in such spotless order that Laura hardly noticed the cook-stove at one end.

On Sunday morning there was Sunday School and church, and every pleasant Sunday afternoon there was the sleigh-ride party. Prince and Lady came down the street with their full strings of sweet-toned bells gaily ringing, and stopped at the door for Laura, and she went with Almanzo in the little cutter behind the prettiest and fastest-stepping horses in the Sunday parade.

But best of all were the mornings and the evenings at home. Laura realized that she had never appreciated them until now. There were no sullen silences, no smoldering quarrels, no ugly outbreaks of anger.

Instead there was work with pleasant talk, there were happy little jokes and evenings of cozy studying and reading, and the music of Pa's fiddle. How good it was to hear the old familiar tunes as the fiddle sang them in the warm, lamplighted room of home. Often Laura thought how happy and how fortunate she was. Nothing anywhere could be better than being at home with the home folks, she was sure.

CHAPTER 13

Springtime

ON A Friday afternoon in April Laura and Ida and Mary Power walked slowly home from school. The air was soft and moist, the eaves were dripping, and the snow was slushy underfoot.

"Spring is almost here again," Ida said. "Only three more weeks of school."

"Yes, and then we'll be moving out to the claim again," said Mary. "You will, too, Laura, won't you?"

"I suppose so," Laura answered. "I declare, it seems the winter's hardly begun, and now it's gone."

"Yes, if this warm spell lasts the snow will be almost gone tomorrow," Mary said. That meant that there would be no more sleigh rides.

"It's nice on the claim," Laura said. She thought of the new calves and the baby chicks, and the garden growing, of lettuce and radishes and spring onions, and violets and the wild roses in June, and of Mary's coming home from college.

With Carrie she crossed the slushy street and went into the house. Both Pa and Ma were in the sitting room, and there in Mary's rocking chair sat a stranger. As Laura and Carrie stood hesitating near the door, he rose from his seat and smiled at them.

"Don't you know me, Laura?" he asked.

Then Laura did know him. She remembered his smile, so like Ma's.

"Oh, Uncle Tom! It's Uncle Tom!" she cried.

Pa laughed. "I told you she'd know you, Tom." And Ma smiled, so like his smile while he shook hands with Laura and Carrie.

Carrie did not remember him; she had been only a baby in the Big Woods of Wisconsin. But Laura had been five years old when they went to the sugaring-off dance at Grandma's, and Uncle Tom had been there. He had been so quiet that she had hardly thought of him since then, but now she remembered the news that Aunt Docia had told of him when she stopped at the house by Plum Creek in Minnesota.

He was a small, quiet man with a gentle smile. Looking at him across the supper table, Laura could hardly believe that for years he had been a foreman of logging crews, taking the log drives out of the Big Woods and down the rivers. Although he was so small and soft-spoken, he had bossed the rough men and handled the dangerous log drives fearlessly. Laura remembered Aunt Docia's telling how he plunged in among the floating logs of a drive and, clinging to them, had dragged an injured man from the river to safety; this, though he could not swim.

Now he had much to tell Pa and Ma and Laura. He told of his wife Aunt Lily and their baby Helen. He told of Uncle Henry's family, Aunt Polly, Charley and Albert.

After they left Silver Lake they had not gone to Montana, after all. They had stopped in the Black Hills. They were all there yet, except Cousin Louisa. She had married and gone on to Montana. As for Aunt Eliza and Uncle Peter, they were still living in eastern Minnesota, but Alice and Ella and Cousin Peter were somewhere in Dakota Territory.

Carrie and Grace listened wide-eyed. Carrie remembered nothing of all these people, and Grace had never seen the Big Woods, nor a sugaring-off dance, nor known the Christmases when Uncle Peter and Aunt Eliza came visiting with the cousins Alice and Ella and Peter. Laura felt sorry for her little sister who had missed so much.

Suppertime passed quickly, and when the evening lamp was lighted and the family gathered around Uncle Tom in the sitting room, Pa still kept him speaking of the lumber camps and log drives, of roaring rivers and the wild, burly men of the logging camps. He told of them mildly, speaking in a voice as soft as Ma's, and smiling her gentle smile.

Pa said to him, "So this is your first trip West," and Uncle Tom answered quietly, "Oh, no. I was with the first white men that ever laid eyes on the Black Hills."

Pa and Ma were struck dumb for a moment. Then Ma asked, "Whatever were you doing there, Tom?"

"Looking for gold," said Uncle Tom.

"Too bad you didn't find a few gold mines," Pa joked.

"Oh, we did," Uncle Tom said. "Only it didn't do us any good."

"Mercy on us!" Ma softly exclaimed. "Do tell us all about it."

"Well, let's see. We started out from Sioux City, eight years ago," Uncle Tom began. "In October of '74. Twenty-six of us men, and one man brought along his wife and their nine-year-old boy."

They traveled in covered wagons, with ox teams, and some saddle horses. Each man had a Winchester and small arms, and ammunition enough to last for eight months. They loaded supplies of flour, bacon, beans, and coffee into the wagons, and depended on hunting for most of their meat. Hunting was good; they got plenty of elk, antelope, and deer. The greatest trouble was lack of water on the open prairie. Luckily it was in early winter; there was plenty of snow, and they melted it at night to fill the water barrels.

The storms halted them some; during the blizzards they stayed in camp. Between storms the snow made hard going, and to lighten the loads they walked; even the woman walked a great part of the way. A good day's journey was fifteen miles.

So they pushed on into the unknown country, seeing nothing but the frozen prairie and the storms, and now and then a few Indians at a distance, till they came to a strange depression in the land. It barred their way, and stretched as far as they could see ahead and on both sides. It looked like an impossibility to get the wagons down into it, but there was nothing to do but cross it, so with considerable trouble they got the wagons down onto this sunken plain.

From the floor of it, strange formations of bare earth towered up all around them, hundreds of feet high. Their sides were steep, sometimes overhanging, cut and whittled by the winds that blew forever. No vegetation grew on them, not a tree nor a bush nor a blade of grass. Their surface looked like dry caked mud, except in places where it was stained with different and brilliant colors. The floor of this sunken land was scattered thick with petrified shells and skulls and bones.

It was a heathenish place to be in, Uncle Tom said. The wagon wheels crunched over the bones, and those tall things seemed to turn as you went by, and some of them looked like faces, and outlandish idols. The wagons had to go between them, following the gulches or valleys. Winding around among those queer things, they got lost. It was three days before they could find their way out of that place, and it took a day's hard work to get the wagons up on its rim.

Looking back over it, an old prospector told Uncle Tom that it must be the Bad Lands of which he had heard tales from the Indians. And he added, "I think that when God made the world He threw all the leftover waste into that hole."

After that, they went on across the prairie until they came to the Black Hills. There they found shelter from the fierce prairie winds, but the going was hard because the valleys were full of snow and the hills were steep.

They had been traveling seventy-eight days when they made their last camp on French Creek. Here they cut pine logs from the hills, and built a stockade eighty feet square. They chopped the logs thirteen feet long, and set them upright, tightly together, sinking the bottom ends three feet into the ground. It was hard digging, the ground being frozen. On the inside of this wall, they battened it with smaller logs, pegged over every crack between the larger logs, with heavy wooden pegs.

At each corner of the square stockade they made stout log bastions, standing out, to give them a crossfire along the outside of the walls. In these bastions, and also along the walls, they cut portholes. The only entrance to this stockade was a double gate, twelve feet wide, made of large logs solidly pegged together with wooden pins. It was a good stockade, when they got it finished.

Inside it they built seven little log cabins, and there they lived through the winter. They hunted for their meat, and trapped for furs. The winter was bitter cold, but they pulled through, and toward spring they found gold, nuggets of it, and rich gold dust in the frozen gravel and under the ice in the creek beds. About the same time, the Indians attacked them. They could hold off the Indians all right, in that stockade. The trouble was that they would starve to death in it, if they could not get out of it to hunt. The Indians hung around, not fighting much but driving back any party that started out, and waiting for them to starve. So they cut down rations and tightened their belts, to hang on as long as they could before they had to kill their ox teams.

Then one morning they heard, far off, a bugle!

When Uncle Tom said that, Laura remembered the sound, long ago, echoing back from the Big Woods when Uncle George blew his army bugle. She cried out, "Soldiers?"

"Yes," Uncle Tom said. They knew they were all right now; the soldiers were coming. The lookouts yelled, and everybody crowded up into the bastions to watch. They heard the bugle again. Soon they heard the fife and drum, and then they saw the flag flying, and the troops coming behind it.

They threw open the gate and rushed out, all of them, fast as they could to meet the soldiers. The soldiers took them all prisoner, there where they were, and kept them there, while some of the troops went on and burned the stockade, with everything in it. They burned the cabins and the wagons, and the furs, and killed the oxen.

"Oh, Tom!" Ma said as if she could not bear it.

"It was Indian country," Uncle Tom said mildly. "Strictly speaking, we had no right there."

"Had you nothing at all to show for all that work and danger?" Ma mourned.

"Lost everything I started out with, but my rifle," said Uncle Tom. "The soldiers let us keep our guns. They marched us out on foot, prisoners."

Pa was walking back and forth across the room. "I'll be durned if I could have taken it!" he exclaimed. "Not without some kind of scrap."

"We couldn't fight the whole United States Army," Uncle Tom said sensibly. "But I did hate to see that stockade go up in smoke."

"I know," Ma said. "To this day I think of the house we had to leave in Indian Territory. Just when Charles had got glass windows into it."

Laura thought: "All this happened to Uncle Tom while we were living on Plum Creek." For some time no one spoke, then the old clock gave its warning wheeze and slowly and solemnly it struck, only once.

"My goodness! look at the time!" Ma exclaimed. "I declare,

Tom, you've held us spellbound. No wonder Grace is asleep. You girls hurry up to bed and take her with you, and Laura, you throw down the featherbed from my bed, and quilts, and I'll make a bed down here for Tom."

"Don't rob your bed, Caroline," Uncle Tom protested. "I can sleep on the floor with a blanket, I've done so, often enough."

"I guess Charles and I can sleep on a straw-tick for once," said Ma. "When I think how you slept cold and uncomfortable, so many nights on that trip."

The cold winter of Uncle Tom's story was still in Laura's mind, so strongly that next morning it was strange to hear the Chinook softly blowing and the eaves dripping, and know that it was springtime and she was in the pleasant town. All day while she was sewing with Mrs. McKee, Pa and Ma were visiting with Uncle Tom, and next day only Laura and Carrie and Grace went to Sunday School and church. Pa and Ma stayed at home in order not to waste a moment of Uncle Tom's short visit. He was leaving early Monday morning for his home in Wisconsin.

Only scattered patches of snow were left on the muddy ground. There would be no more sleighing parties, Laura knew, and she was sorry.

Pa and Ma and Uncle Tom were talking of people she did not know, while they all sat around the table after a late Sunday dinner, when a shadow passed the window. Laura knew the knock at the door, and she hastened to open it, wondering why Almanzo had come.

"Would you like to go for the first buggy ride of spring?" he asked. "With Cap and Mary Power and me?"

"Oh, yes!" she answered. "Won't you come in, while I put on my hat and coat?"

"No, thank you," he said, "I'll wait outside."

When she went out she saw that Mary and Cap were sitting in the back seat of Cap's two-seated buggy. Almanzo helped her up to the front seat and took the reins from Cap as he sat down beside her. Then Prince and Lady trotted away up the street and out on the prairie road toward the east.

No one else was out driving, so this was not a party, but Laura and Mary and Cap were laughing and merry. The road was slushy. Water and bits of snow spattered the horses and buggy and the linen lap robes across their knees. But the spring wind was soft on their faces and the sun was warmly shining.

Almanzo did not join in the merry talk. He drove steadily, without a smile or a word, until Laura asked him what was the matter.

"Nothing," he said, then he asked quickly, "Who is that young man?"

No one was in sight anywhere. Laura exclaimed, "What young man?"

"That you were talking with, when I came," he said.

Laura was astonished. Mary burst out laughing. "Now don't be jealous of Laura's uncle!" she said.

"Oh, did you mean him? That was Uncle Tom, Ma's brother," Laura explained. Mary Power was still laughing so hard that Laura turned, just in time to see Cap snatch a hairpin from Mary's knot of hair.

"Suppose you pay some attention to me," Cap said to Mary.

"Oh, stop it, Cap! Let me have it," Mary cried, trying to seize the hairpin that Cap held out of her reach, while he snatched another one.

"Don't, Cap! Don't!" Mary begged, putting both hands over the knot of hair at the back of her neck. "Laura, help me!"

Laura saw how desperate the situation was, for she alone knew that Mary wore a switch. Cap must be stopped, for if Mary lost any more hairpins, her beautiful large knot of hair would come off.

Just at that instant, a bit of snow flung from Prince's foot fell into Laura's lap. Cap's shoulder was turned to her as he struggled with Mary. Laura nipped up the bit of snow and neatly dropped it inside his collar at the back of his neck.

"Ow!" he yelled. "Looks like you'd help a fellow, Wilder. Two girls against me is too many."

"I'm busy driving," Almanzo answered, and they all shouted with laughter. It was so easy to laugh in the springtime.

CHAPTER 14

Holding Down a Claim

UNCLE TOM went East on the train next morning. When Laura came home from school at noon, he was gone.

"No sooner had he gone," said Ma, "than Mrs. McKee came. She is in distress, Laura, and she asked me if you would help her out."

"Why, of course I will, if I can," Laura said. "What is it?"

Ma said that, hard as Mrs. McKee had worked at dress-making all that winter, the McKees could not afford to move to their claim yet. Mr. McKee must keep his job at the lumber-yard until they saved money enough to buy tools and seed and stock. He wanted Mrs. McKee to take their little girl, Mattie, and live on the claim that summer, to hold it. Mrs. McKee said she would not live out there on the prairie, all alone, with no one but Mattie; she said they could lose the claim, first.

"I don't know why she is so nervous about it," said Ma. "But it seems she is. It seems that being all alone, miles from any-body, scares her. So, as she told me, Mr. McKee said he would let the claim go. After he went to work, she was thinking it over, and she came to tell me that if you would go with her, she would go hold down the claim. She said she would give you a dollar a week, just to stay with her as one of the family."

"Where is the claim?" Pa inquired.

"It is some little distance north of Manchester," said Ma. Manchester was a new little town, west of De Smet. "Well, do you want to go, Laura?" Pa asked her.

"I guess so," Laura said. "I'll have to miss the rest of school, but I can make that up, and I'd like to go on earning some-thing."

"The McKees are nice folks, and it would be a real accom-modation to them, so you may go if you want to," Pa decided.

"It would be a pity, though, for you to miss Mary's visit home," Ma worried.

"Maybe if I just get Mrs. McKee settled on the claim and

used to it, I could come home long enough to see Mary," Laura pondered.

"Well, if you want to go, best go," Ma said. "We needn't cross a bridge till we come to it. Likely it will work out all right, somehow."

So the next morning Laura rode with Mrs. McKee and Mattie on the train to Manchester. She had been on the cars once before, when she came west from Plum Creek, so she felt like a seasoned traveler as she followed the brakeman with her satchel, down the aisle to a seat. It was not as though she knew nothing about trains.

It was a seven mile journey to Manchester. There the trainmen unloaded Mrs. McKee's furniture from the boxcar in front of the passenger coach, and a teamster loaded it onto his wagon. Before he had finished, the hotelkeeper was banging his iron triangle with a spike, to call any strangers to dinner. So Mrs. McKee and Laura and Mattie ate dinner in the hotel.

Soon afterward the teamster drove the loaded wagon to the door, and helped them climb up to sit on the top of the load, among the rolls of bedding, the kitchen stove, the table and chairs and trunk and boxes of provisions. Mrs. McKee rode in the seat with the teamster.

Sitting with their feet hanging down at the side of the wagon, Laura and Mattie clung to each other and to the ropes that bound the load to the wagon, as the team drew it bumping over the prairie. There was no road. The wagon wheels sank into the sod in places where it was soft from the melting snow, and the wagon and its load lurched from side to side. But it went very well until they came to a slough. Here where the ground was lower, water stood in pools among the coarse slough grass.

"I don't know about this," the teamster said, looking ahead. "It looks pretty bad. But there's no way around; we'll just have to try it. Maybe we can go across so quick the wagon won't have time to sink down."

As they came nearer to the slough, he said, "Hang on, everybody!"

He picked up his whip and shouted to the horses. They went fast, and faster, till urged on by his shouts and the whip they broke into a run. Water rose up like wings from the jouncing wagon wheels, while Laura hung onto the ropes and to Mattie with all her might.

Then all was quiet. Safe on the other side of the slough, the teamster stopped the horses to rest.

"Well, we made it!" he said. "The wheels just didn't stay in one place long enough to settle through the sod. If a fellow got stuck in there, he'd be stuck for keeps."

It was no wonder that he seemed relieved, for as Laura looked back across the slough she could see no wagon tracks. They were covered with water.

Driving on across the prairie, they came finally to a little new claim shanty, standing alone. About a mile away to the west was another, and far away to the east they could barely see a third.

"This is the place, ma'am," the teamster said. "I'll unload, and then haul you a jag of hay to burn, from that place a mile west. Fellow that had it last summer, quit and went back East, but I see he left some haystacks there."

He unloaded the wagon into the shanty, and set up the cook-stove. Then he drove away to get the hay.

A partition cut the shanty into two tiny rooms. Mrs. McKee and Laura set up a bedstead in the room with the cook-stove, and another in the other room. With the table, four small wooden chairs, and the trunk, they filled the little house.

"I'm glad I didn't bring anything more," said Mrs. McKee.

"Yes, as Ma would say, enough is as good as a feast," Laura agreed.

The teamster came with a load of hay, then drove away toward Manchester. Now there were the two straw-ticks to fill with hay, the beds to make, and dishes to be unpacked. Then Laura twisted hay into sticks, from the little stack behind the shanty, and Mattie carried it in to keep the fire going while Mrs. McKee cooked supper. Mrs. McKee did not know how to twist hay, but Laura had learned during the Hard Winter.

As twilight came over the prairie, coyotes began to howl and Mrs. McKee locked the door and saw that the windows were fastened.

"I don't know why the law makes us do this," she said. "What earthly good it does, to make a woman stay on a claim all summer."

"It's a bet, Pa says," Laura answered. "The government bets a man a quarter-section of land, that he can't stay on it five years without starving to death."

"Nobody could," said Mrs. McKee. "Whoever makes these laws ought to know that a man that's got enough money to farm, has got enough to buy a farm. If he hasn't got money, he's got to earn it, so why do they make a law that he's got to stay on a claim, when he can't? All it means is, his wife and family have got to sit idle on it, seven months of the year. I could be earning something, dressmaking, to help buy tools and seeds, if somebody didn't have to sit on this claim. I declare to goodness, I don't know but sometimes I believe in woman's rights. If women were voting and making laws, I believe they'd have better sense. Is that wolves?"

"No," Laura said, "It's only coyotes, they won't hurt anybody."

They were all so tired that they did not light the lamp, but went to bed, Laura and Mattie in the kitchen and Mrs. McKee in the front room. When everyone was quiet, the loneliness seemed to come into the shanty. Laura was not afraid, but never before had she been in such a lonely place without Pa and Ma and her sisters. The coyotes were far away, and farther. Then they were gone. The slough was so far away that the frogs could not be heard. There was no sound but the whispering of the prairie wind to break the silence.

The sun shining in Laura's face woke her to an empty day. The little work was soon done. There was nothing more to do, no books to study, no one to see. It was pleasant for awhile. All that week Laura and Mrs. McKee and Mattie did nothing but eat and sleep, and sit and talk or be silent. The sun rose and sank and the wind blew, and the prairie was empty of all but birds and cloud shadows.

Saturday afternoon they dressed for town and walked the two miles to Manchester to meet Mr. McKee and walk home with him. He stayed until Sunday afternoon when they all walked to town again and Mr. McKee took the train back to De Smet and his work. Then Mrs. McKee and Laura and Mattie walked back to the claim for another week.

They were glad when Saturday came, but in a way it was a relief when Mr. McKee was gone, for he was such a strict

Presbyterian that on Sunday no one was allowed to laugh or even smile. They could only read the Bible and the catechism and talk gravely of religious subjects. Still, Laura liked him, for he was truly good and kind and never said a cross word.

This was the pattern of the weeks that passed, one after another, all alike, until April and May were gone.

The weather had grown warmer, and on the walks to town they heard the meadow larks singing beside the road where spring flowers bloomed. One warm Sunday afternoon the walk back from Manchester seemed longer than usual and tiring, and as they lagged a little along the way Mrs. McKee said, "It would be pleasanter for you to be riding in Wilder's buggy."

"I likely won't do that any more," Laura remarked. "Someone else will be in my place before I go back." She thought of Nellie Oleson. The Olesons' claim, she knew, was not far from Almanzo's.

"Don't worry," Mrs. McKee told her. "An old bachelor doesn't pay so much attention to a girl unless he's serious. You will marry him yet."

"Oh, no!" Laura said. "No, indeed I won't! I wouldn't leave home to marry anybody."

Then suddenly she realized that she was homesick. She wanted to be at home again, so badly that she could hardly bear it. All that week she fought against her longing, hiding it from Mrs. McKee, and on Saturday when they walked again to Manchester there was a letter waiting for her.

Ma had written that Mary was coming home, and Laura must come if Mrs. McKee could find anyone else to stay with her. Ma hoped she could do so, for Laura must be at home when Mary was there.

She dreaded to speak of it to Mrs. McKee, so she said nothing until at the supper table Mrs. McKee asked what was troubling her. Then Laura told what Ma had written.

"Why, of course you must go home," Mr. McKee said at once. "I will find someone to stay here."

Mrs. McKee was quiet for a time before she said, "I don't want anyone but Laura to live with us. I would rather stay by ourselves. We are used to the place now, and nothing ever happens. Laura shall go home and Mattie and I will be all right alone."

So Mr. McKee carried Laura's satchel on the Sunday afternoon walk to Manchester, and she said good-by to Mrs. McKee and Mattie and got on the train with him, going home.

All the way she thought of them, standing lonely at the station, and walking the two miles back to the lonely shanty where they must stay, doing nothing but eating and sleeping and listening to the wind, for five months more. It was a hard way to earn a homestead, but there was no other way, for that was the law.

CHAPTER 15

Mary Comes Home

LAURA was so glad to be at home again, out on Pa's claim. It was good to milk the cow, and to drink all she wanted of milk, and to spread butter on her bread, and eat again of Ma's good cottage cheese. There were lettuce leaves to be picked in the garden, too, and little red radishes. She had not realized that she was so hungry for these good things to eat. Mrs. McKee and Mattie could not get them, of course, while they were holding down their claim.

At home now there were eggs, too, for Ma's flock was doing well. Laura helped Carrie hunt for nests that the hens hid in the hay at the stable and in the tall grass nearby.

Grace found a nest of kittens hidden in the manger. They were grandchildren of the little kitten that Pa had bought for fifty cents, and Kitty felt her responsibility. She thought that she should hunt for them as well as for her own kittens. She brought in more gophers than all of them could eat, and every day she piled the extra ones by the house door for Ma.

"I declare," Ma said, "I never was so embarrassed by a cat's generosity."

The day came when Mary was coming home. Pa and Ma drove to town to fetch her, and even the train seemed special that afternoon as it came at last, unrolling its black smoke into a melting line low on the sky. From the rise of ground behind the stable and the garden, they saw the white steam puff up from its engine and heard its whistle; its far rumbling was still, and they knew that it had stopped in town and that Mary must be there now.

What excitement there was when at last the wagon came up from the slough, with Mary sitting on the seat between Pa and Ma. Laura and Carrie both talked at once and Mary tried to talk to both at the same time. Grace was in everyone's way, her hair flying and her blue eyes wide. Kitty went out through the doorway like a streak, with her tail swelled to a big brush. Kitty did not like strangers, and she had forgotten Mary.

"Weren't you afraid to come all by yourself on the cars?" Carrie asked.

"Oh, no," Mary smiled. "I had no trouble. We learn to do things by ourselves, at college. It is part of our education."

She did seem much more sure of herself, and she moved easily around the house, instead of sitting quiet in her chair. Pa brought in her trunk, and she went to it, knelt down and unlocked and opened it quite as if she saw it. Then she took from it, one after another, the presents she had brought.

For Ma there was a lamp mat of woven braid, with a fringe all around it of many-colored beads strung on stout thread.

"It is beautiful," Ma said in delight.

Laura's gift was a bracelet of blue and white beads strung on thread and woven together, and Carrie's was a ring of pink and white beads interwoven.

"Oh, how pretty! how pretty!" Carrie exclaimed. "And it fits, too; it fits perfectly!"

For Grace there was a little doll's chair, of red and green beads strung on wire. Grace was so overcome as she took it carefully into her hands that she could hardly say thank you to Mary.

"This is for you, Pa," Mary said, as she gave him a blue silk handkerchief. "I didn't make this, but I chose it myself. Blanche and I . . . Blanche is my roommate. We went downtown to find something for you. She can see colors if they are bright, but the clerk didn't know it. We thought it would be fun to mystify him, so Blanche signaled the colors to me, and he thought we could tell them by touch. I knew by the feeling that it was good silk. My, we did fool that clerk!" and, remembering, Mary laughed.

Mary had often smiled, but it was a long time since they had heard her laugh out, as she used to when she was a little girl. All that it had cost to send Mary to college was more than repaid by seeing her so gay and confident.

"I'll bet this was the prettiest handkerchief in Vinton, Iowa!" Pa said.

"I don't see how you put the right colors into your beadwork," Laura said, turning the bracelet on her wrist. "Every little bead in this lovely bracelet is right. You can't do that by fooling a clerk."

"Some seeing person puts the different colors in separate

boxes," Mary explained. "Then we only have to remember where they are."

"You can do that easily," Laura agreed. "You always could remember things. You know I never could say as many Bible verses as you."

"It surprises my Sunday School teacher now, how many of them I know," said Mary. "Knowing them was a great help to me, Ma. I could read them so easily with my fingers in raised print and in Braille, that I learned how to read everything sooner than anyone else in my class."

"I am glad to know that, Mary," was all that Ma said, and her smile trembled, but she looked happier than when Mary had given her the beautiful lamp mat.

"Here is my Braille slate," said Mary, lifting it from her trunk. It was an oblong of thin steel in a steel frame, as large as a school slate, with a narrow steel band across it. The band was cut into several rows of open squares, and it would slide up and down, or could be fastened in place at any point. Tied to the frame by a string was a pencil-shaped piece of steel that Mary said was a stylus.

"How do you use it?" Pa wanted to know.

"Watch and I'll show you," said Mary.

They all watched while she laid a sheet of thick, cream-colored paper on the slate, under the slide. She moved the slide to the top of the frame and secured it there. Then with the point of the stylus she pressed, rapidly, here and there in the corners of the open squares.

"There," she said, slipping the paper out and turning it over. Wherever the stylus had pressed, there was a tiny bump, that could easily be felt with the fingers. The bumps made different patterns, the size of the squares, and these were the Braille letters.

"I am writing to Blanche to tell her that I am safely home," said Mary. "I must write to my teacher, too." She turned the paper over, put it in the frame again, and slipped the slide down, ready to go on writing on the blank space. "I will finish them later."

"It is wonderful that you can write to your friends and they can read your letters," said Ma. "I can hardly believe that you are really getting the college education that we always wanted you to have."

Laura was so happy that she felt like crying, too.

"Well, well," Pa broke in. "Here we stand talking, when Mary must be hungry and it's chore time. Let's do our work now, and we will have longer to talk afterward."

"You are right, Charles," Ma quickly agreed. "Supper will be ready by the time you are ready for it."

While Pa took care of the horses, Laura hurried to do the milking and Carrie made a quick fire to bake the biscuit that Ma was mixing.

Supper was ready when Pa came from the stable and Laura had strained the milk.

It was a happy family, all together again, as they ate of the browned hashed potatoes, poached fresh eggs and delicious biscuit with Ma's good butter. Pa and Ma drank their fragrant tea, but Mary drank milk with the other girls. "It is a treat," she said. "We don't have such good milk at college."

There was so much to ask and tell that almost nothing was fully said, but tomorrow would be another long day with Mary. And it was like old times again, when Laura and Mary went to sleep as they used to, in their bed where Laura for so long had been sleeping alone.

"It's warm weather," Mary said, "so I won't be putting my cold feet on you as I used to do."

"I'm so glad you're here that I wouldn't complain," Laura answered. "It would be a pleasure."

CHAPTER 16

Summer Days

IT WAS such a joy to have Mary at home that the summer days were not long enough for all their pleasures. Listening to Mary's stories of her life in college, reading aloud to her, planning and sewing to put her clothes in order, and once more going with her for long walks in the late afternoon, made the time go by too swiftly.

One Saturday morning Laura went to town to match Mary's last winter's best dress in silk, to make a new collar and cuffs. She found just what she wanted in a new milliner's and dressmaker's shop, and while Miss Bell was wrapping the little package she said to Laura, "I hear you're a good sewer. I wish you would come and help me. I'll pay you fifty cents a day, from seven o'clock to five, if you'll bring your dinner."

Laura looked around the pleasant, new place, with the pretty hats in two windows, bolts of ribbon in a glass showcase, and silks and velvets on the shelves behind it. There was a sewing machine, with an unfinished dress lying across it, and another lay on a chair nearby.

"You can see there is more work here than I can do," Miss Bell said in her quiet voice. Miss Bell was a young woman and Laura thought her handsome with her tall figure and dark hair and eyes.

Laura decided that it would be pleasant to work with her.

"I will come if Ma is willing I should," she promised.

"Come Monday morning if you can," said Miss Bell.

Laura left the shop and went up the street to the post office to mail a letter for Mary. There she met Mary Power, who was on her way to do an errand at the lumberyard. They had not seen each other since the buggy ride in early spring, and there was so much to talk about that Mary begged Laura to come with her.

"All right, I will," said Laura. "I'd like to ask Mr. McKee how Mrs. McKee and Mattie are getting along, anyway."

They walked slowly, talking all the way up the street, across the cindery railroad tracks and the dusty street to the corner of the lumberyard, and there they stood talking.

A yoke of oxen was coming slowly into town on the country road from the north, hauling a lumber wagon. A man walked beside the farther ox, and Laura idly watched him as he swung a long whip. The oxen trudged along until nearly to the corner, then started ahead quickly.

Laura and Mary stepped back. The man commanded, "Whoa! Haw!" But the oxen did not turn left. They swung to the right, around the corner.

"Gee, then! Go where you're a mind to!" the driver ordered them, impatiently, but joking. Then he looked at the girls, and they exclaimed together, "Almanzo Wilder!"

He raised his hat with a cheerful flourish to them, and hurried along the street with the oxen.

"I didn't know him without his horses!" Laura laughed.

"And the way he was dressed," Mary disparaged him. "In those rough clothes and ugly heavy shoes."

"He is likely breaking sod, and that is why he had oxen. He wouldn't work Prince and Lady so hard," Laura explained, more to herself than to Mary Power.

"Everybody is working," Mary remarked. "Nobody can have any fun in the summertime. But Nellie Oleson is going to ride behind those horses yet, if she possibly can. You know the Olesons' claim is a little way east of the Wilder boys' claims."

"Have you seen her lately?" Laura asked.

"I never see anybody," Mary answered. "All the girls are out on their fathers' claims, and Cap is teaming every day. Ben Woodworth is working at the depot, and nobody can get a word with Frank Harthorn nowadays, he works all the time in the store since his father has made him a partner. Minnie and Arthur are out with their folks on their homestead, and here I haven't seen you since early April."

"Never mind, we'll see each other all next winter. Besides, I am coming to town to work if Ma says I may," and Laura told Mary that she expected to sew for Miss Bell.

Suddenly she saw that the sun was almost overhead. She stopped only a moment in the lumberyard office, to hear from Mr. McKee that Mrs. McKee and Mattie were getting along all right, though they still missed her. Then quickly she said good-by to Mary and hurried away on her walk home. She had stayed in town too long. Though she walked so fast that she was almost running, dinner was ready when she reached home.

"I am sorry I stayed so long, but so many things happened," she made excuse.

"Yes?" Ma inquired, and Carrie asked, "What happened?"

Laura told of meeting Mary Power and of seeing Mr. McKee. "I visited too long with Mary Power," she confessed. "The time went so quickly that I did not know it was so late." Then she told the rest. "Miss Bell wants me to work for her in her shop. May I, Ma?"

"Why, Laura, I declare I don't know," Ma exclaimed. "You have only just got home."

"She will pay me fifty cents a day, from seven o'clock to five, if I bring my own dinner," Laura told them.

"That is fair enough," said Pa. "You take your own dinner, but you get off an hour early."

"But you came home to be with Mary," Ma objected.

"I know, Ma, but I will see her every night and morning and all day Sunday," Laura argued. "I don't know why, but I feel I ought to be earning something."

"That is the way it is, once you begin to earn," Pa said.

"I will be earning three dollars a week," said Laura. "And seeing Mary, too. We will have lots of time to do things together, won't we, Mary?"

"Yes, and I will do all your housework while you're gone," Mary offered. "Then on Sundays we'll have our walks."

"That reminds me, the new church is done," said Pa. "We must all go to church tomorrow morning."

"I'll be so glad to see the new church! I can hardly believe there is one!" Mary said.

"It's there sure enough," Pa assured her. "We'll see for ourselves tomorrow."

"And the next day?" Laura asked.

"Yes, you may go to work for Miss Bell. You can try it for awhile anyway," Ma said.

Sunday morning Pa hitched the horses to the wagon, and they all rode to church. It was large and new, with long seats that were comfortable to sit in. Mary liked it very much, after the small chapel at college, but she knew hardly anyone there. On the way home she said, "There were so many strangers."

"They come and they go," Pa told her. "No sooner do I get acquainted with a newcomer than he sells the relinquishment of his claim and goes on West, or else his family can't stand it here and he sells out and moves back East. The few that stick are so busy that we don't have time to know each other."

"It doesn't matter," Mary said. "I will soon be going back to college, and I know everyone there."

After the Sunday dinner, when the work was done, Carrie sat down to read the *Youth's Companion*, Grace went to play with the kittens in the clean grass near the door, Ma rested in her rocking chair by the open window, and Pa lay down for his Sunday nap. Then Laura said, "Come, Mary, let's go for our walk."

They walked across the prairie to the south, and all along their way the wild June roses were blooming. Laura gathered them until she filled Mary's arm with all she could hold.

"Oh, how sweet!" Mary kept saying. "I have missed the spring violets, but nothing is sweeter than prairie roses. It is so good to be home again, Laura. Even if I can't stay long."

"We have until the middle of August," said Laura. "But the roses won't last that long."

"'Gather ye roses while ye may,'" Mary began, and she quoted the poem for Laura. Then as they walked on together in the rose-scented warm wind, she talked of her studies in literature. "I am planning to write a book some day," she confided. Then she laughed. "But I planned to teach school, and you are doing that for me, so maybe you will write the book."

"I, write a book?" Laura hooted. She said blithely, "I'm going to be an old maid schoolteacher, like Miss Wilder. Write your own book! What are you going to write about?"

But Mary was diverted from the subject of books. She inquired, "Where is that Wilder boy, that Ma wrote me about? It seems like he'd be around sometime."

"I think he is too busy on his claim. Everybody is busy," Laura answered. She did not mention seeing him in town. For some reason that she could not explain, she felt shy of talking about it. She and Mary turned and went rather quietly back to the house, bringing into it the fragrance of the roses they carried.

Swiftly that summer went by. Every weekday Laura walked to town in the early morning, carrying her lunch pail. Often Pa walked with her, for he was doing carpenter work on new buildings that newcomers were building. Laura could hear the hammers and saws while she sewed steadily all day long, pausing only to eat her cold lunch at noon. Then, often with Pa, she walked home again. Sometimes there was a pain between her shoulders from bending over her work, but that always disappeared during the walk, and then came the happy evening at home.

At supper she told of all she had seen and heard in Miss Bell's shop, Pa told any news he had gathered, and they all talked of the happenings on the claim and in the house: how the crops were growing, how Ma was getting along with Mary's sewing, how many eggs Grace had found, and that the old speckled hen had stolen her nest and just came off with twenty chicks.

It was at the supper table that Ma reminded them that tomorrow was Fourth of July. "What are we going to do about it?"

"I don't see that we can do anything, Caroline. No way that I know of, to prevent tomorrow's being the Fourth," Pa teased.

"Now, Charles," Ma reproached him, smiling. "Are we going to the celebration?"

There was silence around the table.

"I cannot hear you when you all talk at once," Ma teased in her turn. "If we are going, we must think about it tonight. I've been so enjoying having Mary here that I forgot about the Fourth, and nothing is prepared for a celebration."

"My whole vacation is a celebration, and it seems to me enough," Mary said quietly.

"I have been in town every day. It would be a treat to me to miss a day." Then Laura added, "But there are Carrie and Grace."

Pa laid down his knife and fork. "I'll tell you what. Caroline, you and the girls cook a good dinner, I will go to town in the morning and get some candy and firecrackers. We will have our own Fourth of July celebration right here at home. What do you say to that?"

"Get lots of candy, Pa!" Grace begged, while Carrie urged, "And lots of firecrackers!"

Everyone had such a good time next day that they all agreed it was much more fun than going to town. Once or twice Laura wondered if Almanzo Wilder were in town with the brown horses, and the thought of Nellie Oleson just crossed her mind. But if Almanzo wanted to see her again, he knew where she was. It was not her place to do anything about it, and she didn't intend to.

All too soon the summer was gone. In the last week of August Mary went back to college, leaving an emptiness in the house. Now Pa cut the oats and wheat with his old hand cradle, because the fields were still so small that they would not pay for having a harvester. When the corn was ripe he cut it and shocked it in the field. He was thin and tired from all the hard work he had done, in town and in the fields, and he was restless because people were settling the country so thickly.

"I would like to go West," he told Ma one day. "A fellow doesn't have room to breathe here any more."

"Oh, Charles! No room, with all this great prairie around you?" Ma said. "I was so tired of being dragged from pillar to post, and I thought we were settled here."

"Well, I guess we are, Caroline. Don't fret. It's just that my wandering foot gets to itching, I guess. Anyway I haven't won that bet with Uncle Sam yet, and we stay right here till we win it! till I can prove up on this homestead claim."

Laura knew how he felt for she saw the look in his blue eyes as he gazed over the rolling prairie westward from the open door where he stood. He must stay in a settled country for the sake of them all, just as she must teach school again, though she did so hate to be shut into a schoolroom.

CHAPTER 17

Breaking the Colts

OCTOBER days had come, and the wild geese were flying south, when once more Pa loaded the furniture on the wagon and they all moved back to town. Other people were moving in from the country, and the seats in the schoolhouse were filling up.

Most of the big boys were not coming to school any more. Some had moved to the claims to stay. Ben Woodworth was working in the depot, Frank Harthorn was busy in the store, and Cap Garland was working with his team, hauling hay and coal or anything he was hired to move in town or country. Still there were not seats enough in the schoolhouse, for the country was full of newcomers whose children came to school. The smaller pupils were crowded three in a seat, and it was certain now that a larger schoolhouse must be built before next winter.

One day when Laura and Carrie came from school, they found company sitting with Ma in the front room. The man was a stranger, but Laura felt that she should know the young woman who looked at her soberly. Ma was smiling; she said nothing for a moment, while Laura and the woman looked at each other.

Then the woman smiled, and Laura knew her. She was Cousin Alice! Alice, who with Ella and Peter had come to spend Christmas in the log house in the Big Woods. Alice and Mary had been the big girls then; Ella had been Laura's playmate. Now while Laura greeted Alice with a kiss, she asked, "Did Ella come, too?"

"No, she and her husband couldn't come," Alice said. "But here is a cousin you haven't met yet, my husband, Arthur Whiting."

Arthur was tall, with dark hair and eyes; he was pleasant and Laura liked him, but though he and Alice stayed a week, he always seemed to be a stranger. Alice was so much like Mary that she belonged in the family, and Laura and Carrie hurried home from school because Alice would be sitting in the sunny front room with Ma.

In the evenings they all popped corn and made taffy, listened to Pa's fiddle, and endlessly talked of old times and of plans for the future.

Arthur's brother, Lee, was Ella's husband, and they had taken adjoining claims only forty miles away. Peter was coming out in the spring.

"It has been such a long time since we were together in the Big Woods, and now we are gathering out here on the prairie," Alice said one evening.

"If only your mother and father would come," Ma said wistfully.

"I think they will stay in eastern Minnesota," Alice told her. "They only came that far, and there they seem contented."

"It's a queer thing," said Pa. "People always moving west. Out here it is like the edge of a wave, when a river's rising. They come and they go, back and forth, but all the time the bulk of them keep moving on west."

Alice and Arthur stayed only a week. Early Saturday morning, well wrapped up, with heated flatirons at their feet and hot baked potatoes in their pockets, they set out on their forty-mile sleigh ride home. "Give my love to Ella," Laura said, as she kissed Alice again for good-by.

It was wonderful sleighing weather, clear and colder than zero, with deep snow and no sign of a blizzard cloud. But this winter there were no more sleighing parties. Perhaps the boys were working their horses too hard all the week. Now and then Laura saw Almanzo and Cap at a distance; they were breaking a pair of colts to drive and seemed to be having a busy time.

On Sunday afternoon Laura saw them passing several times. Sometimes Almanzo, and sometimes Cap, was braced in the cutter, holding with all his might to the reins, while the wild colts tried to break away and run. Pa looked up from his paper once and said, "One of those young fellows will break his neck yet. There's not a man in town would tackle handling that team."

Laura was writing a letter to Mary. She paused and thought how fortunate it was that during the Hard Winter, Almanzo and Cap had taken chances no one else would take, when they had gone after wheat for the starving people.

She had finished her letter and folded it, when someone

knocked at the door. Laura opened it, and Cap Garland stood there. With his flashing grin that lighted his whole face, he asked, "Would you like a sleigh ride behind the colts?"

Laura's heart sank. She liked Cap, but she did not want him to ask her to go sleigh riding, and all in an instant she thought of Mary Power and of Almanzo and she did not know what to say.

But Cap went on speaking. "Wilder asked me to ask you, because the colts won't stand. He'll be by here in a minute and pick you up, if you'd like to go."

"Yes, I would!" Laura exclaimed. "I'll be ready. Come in?"

"No thanks, I'll tell him," Cap replied.

Laura hurried, but the colts were pawing and prancing impatiently when she came. Almanzo was holding them with both hands, and said to her, "Sorry I can't help you," as she got herself into the cutter. As soon as she was seated, they dashed away down the street.

No one else was out driving, so the street was clear as the colts fought to break away from Almanzo's grip on the lines. Far out on the road south of town they went racing.

Laura sat quietly watching their flying feet and laid-back ears. This was fun. It reminded her of a time long ago when she and Cousin Lena let the black ponies run away across the prairie. The wind blew hard and cold on her face, and bits of snow pelted back onto the robes. Then the colts tossed their heads, pricked up their ears, and let Almanzo turn their frisky steps back toward town.

He looked at her curiously. "Do you know there isn't a man in town except Cap Garland who will ride behind these colts?" he asked.

"Pa said so," Laura replied.

"Then why did you come?" Almanzo wanted to know.

"Why, I thought you could drive them," Laura said in surprise, and asked in her turn, "But why don't you drive Prince and Lady?"

"I want to sell these colts, and they've got to be broken to drive first," Almanzo explained.

Laura said no more as the colts tried again to run. They were headed toward home and wanted to get there quickly. It took all Almanzo's attention and muscle to hold them to a fast and fighting trot. Main Street flashed by in a blur, and far out on the prairie to the north Almanzo quieted the colts and turned them again. Then Laura laughed, "If this is breaking them, I'm glad to help!"

They said little more until an hour had gone by and the winter sun was sinking. Then as Almanzo held the colts and Laura quickly slipped out of the cutter at Pa's door, he said, "I'll come for you Sunday." The colts jumped and dashed away before Laura could reply.

"I am afraid to have you ride behind those horses," Ma said as Laura came in.

Pa looked up from his paper. "Does seem like Wilder is trying to get you killed. But I'd say you are enjoying it from the way your eyes are shining," he added.

After this, Almanzo came on Sunday afternoons to take Laura for a sleigh ride. But he and Cap always drove the colts first, more than half the afternoon, to quiet them, and nothing that Laura could say would persuade Almanzo to let her ride before the colts were somewhat tired.

There was a Christmas tree that year at the new church. Laura and Carrie remembered a Christmas tree long ago in Minnesota, but Grace had never seen one. Laura thought the best part of that Christmas was seeing Grace's delighted face when she looked at the Christmas tree with its lighted candles shining, the bright-colored mosquito-bar bags of candy and the presents hanging from its branches.

But while she was waiting for Grace's Christmas doll to be brought to her from the tree, Laura was given a package which surprised her so much that she was sure there was some mistake. It was a small black leather case lined with blue silk. Against the lovely blue shone, all white, an ivory-backed hairbrush and comb. Laura looked again at the wrapping paper; her name was plainly written on it, in a handwriting she did not know.

"Whoever could have given me such a present, Ma?" she asked.

Then Pa leaned to admire it, too, and his eyes twinkled. "I could not swear who gave it to you, Laura," he said. "But I can tell you one thing. I saw Almanzo Wilder buying that very case in Bradley's drugstore," and he smiled at Laura's astonishment.

CHAPTER 18

The Perry School

THE first March winds were blowing hard the next Thursday when Laura came home from school. She was breathless, not only from struggling with the wind, but from the news she brought. Before she could tell it, Pa spoke.

"Could you be ready to move to the claim this week, Caroline?"

"This week?" said Ma in surprise.

"The school district's going to put up a schoolhouse on Perry's claim, just south of our south line," Pa said.

"All the neighbors will help build it, but they want to hire me to boss the job. We ought to be moved out before I begin, and if we go this week, there'll be plenty of time to finish the schoolhouse before the first of April."

"We can go any day you say, Charles," Ma answered.

"Day after tomorrow, then," said Pa. "And there is something else. Perry says their school board would like to have Laura teach the school. How about it, Laura? You will have to get a new certificate."

"Oh, I would *like* to have a school so near home," said Laura. Then she told her news. "Teachers' examinations are tomorrow. Mr. Owen announced them today. They will be at the schoolhouse, so there's no school tomorrow. I do hope I can get a second-grade certificate."

"I am sure you can," Carrie encouraged her stoutly. "You always know your lessons."

Laura was a little doubtful. "I have no time to review and study. If I pass, I have to do it on what I know now."

"That is the best way, Laura," Ma told her. "If you tried to study in a hurry you would only be confused. If you get a second grade we will all be glad, and if it is only third grade we will be glad of that."

"I will try my best," was all that Laura could promise. Next morning she set out alone, and nervously, to the teachers' examinations at the schoolhouse. The room seemed strange, with only a few strangers sitting here and there among empty seats, and Mr. Williams at the desk instead of Mr. Owen.

The lists of questions were already written on the blackboard. All morning there was silence, except for the scratching of pens and small rustles of paper. Mr. Williams gathered the papers at the end of every hour, whether they were finished or not, and graded them at his desk.

Laura finished each of her papers in good time, and that afternoon, with a smile, Mr. Williams handed her a certificate. His smile told her, even before she quickly saw the words he had written on it, "Second Grade."

She walked home, but really she was dancing, running, laughing and shouting with jubilation. Quietly she handed the certificate to Ma, and saw Ma's smile light her whole face.

"I told you so! I told you you would get it," Carrie gloated.

"I was sure you would pass," Ma praised her, "if you didn't get bothered by your first public examination among strangers."

"Now I will tell you the rest of the good news," Pa smiled. "I thought I'd save it as a reward, for after the examination. Perry says the school board will pay you twenty-five dollars a month for a three months' school, April, May, and June."

Laura was nearly speechless. "Oh!" she exclaimed. Then, "I didn't expect . . . Why! Why, Pa . . . that will be a little more than a dollar a day."

Grace's blue eyes were perfectly round. In solemn awe she said, "Laura will be rich."

They all burst out laughing so merrily that Grace had to join in, without knowing why. When they were sober again, Pa said, "Now we'll move out to the claim and build that schoolhouse."

So during the last weeks of March, Laura and Carrie walked to school again from the claim. The weather was spring-like in spite of March winds, and every evening when they came home they saw that more work had been done on the little schoolhouse that was rising from the prairie a little way to the south.

In the last days of March, the Perry boys painted it white. There never had been a prettier, small schoolhouse.

It stood snowy white on the green land, and its rows of windows shone brightly in the morning sunshine as Laura walked toward it across the short, new grass.

Little Clyde Perry, seven years old, was playing by the doorstep where his First Reader had been carefully laid. He put the key of the new door into Laura's hand and said solemnly, "My father sent you this."

Inside, too, the schoolhouse was bright and shining. The walls of new lumber were clean and smelled fresh. Sunshine streamed in from the eastern windows. Across the whole end of the room was a clean, new blackboard. Before it stood the teacher's desk, a boughten desk, smoothly varnished. It gleamed honey-colored in the sunlight, and on its flat top lay a large Webster's Unabridged Dictionary.

Before this desk stood three rows of new, boughten seats. Their smooth honey-colored finish matched the teacher's desk. The ends of the outside rows were tight against the walls; between them there was space for the third row and the two aisles. There were four seats in each row.

Laura stood a moment in the doorway, looking at that fresh, bright expensive room. Then going to her desk, she set her dinner pail on the floor beneath it and hung her sunbonnet on a nail in the wall.

A small clock stood ticking beside the big dictionary; its hands stood at nine o'clock. It must have been wound last night, Laura thought. Nothing could be more complete and perfect than this beautiful little schoolhouse.

She heard children's voices at the door, and she went to call her pupils in.

Besides Clyde, there were two others, a little boy and a girl who said their name was Johnson. They were both in the Second Reader. That was the size of the school. In all the term, no more children came.

Laura felt that she was not earning twenty-five dollars a month, teaching only three children. But when she said this at home, Pa replied that these three were as much entitled to schooling as if there were a dozen, and that she was entitled to pay for the time that she spent teaching them.

"But, Pa," she protested. "Twenty-five dollars a month!"

"Don't let that worry you," he answered. "They are glad to have you at that price. Large schools are paying thirty dollars."

It must be right, since Pa said so. Laura contented herself by giving each little pupil the very best of schooling. They were all quick to learn. Besides reading and spelling, she taught them to write words and figures, and how to add and subtract. She was proud of their progress.

Never had she been so happy as she was that spring. In the fresh, sweet mornings she walked to her school, past the little hollow blue with violets that scented all the air. Her pupils were happy, too, every one as good as gold, and eager and quick to learn. They were as careful as she, not to mar or dim the freshness of their shining new schoolhouse.

Laura took her own books to school, and while her little pupils studied at their desks, between recitations, she studied at hers, with help from the big dictionary. At recess and during the long noon hour, she knitted lace while the children played. And always she was aware of the cloud shadows chasing each other outside the windows, where meadow larks sang and the little striped gophers ran swiftly about their affairs.

After each happy day, there was the walk home past the little hollow where the violets grew, spreading their fragrance on the air.

Sometimes on Saturday Laura walked westward across the prairie to Reverend Brown's house—on his claim. It was a long mile and a half walk, and she and Ida always made it longer by going to the highest point of the rise of ground beyond the house. From there they could see the Wessington Hills, sixty miles away, looking like a blue cloud on the horizon.

"They are so beautiful that they make me want to go to them," Laura said once.

"Oh, I don't know," Ida replied. "When you got there, they would be just hills, covered with ordinary buffalo grass like this," and she kicked at a tuft of the grass where the green of spring was showing through last year's dead blades.

In a way, that was true; and in another way, it wasn't. Laura could not say what she meant, but to her the Wessington Hills were more than grassy hills. Their shadowy outlines drew her with the lure of far places. They were the essence of a dream.

Walking home in the late afternoon, Laura still thought of the Wessington Hills, how mysterious their vague shadow was against the blue sky, far away across miles after miles of green, rolling prairie. She wanted to travel on and on, over those miles, and see what lay beyond the hills.

That was the way Pa felt about the West, Laura knew. She knew, too, that like him she must be content to stay where she was, to help with the work at home and teach school.

That night Pa asked her what she planned to do with all her school money when she got it.

"Why," Laura said, "I'll give it to you and Ma."

"I'll tell you what I have been thinking," said Pa. "We should have an organ when Mary comes home, so she can keep up the music she's learning in college, and it would be nice for you girls, too. Some folks in town are selling out and going back East, and they have an organ. I can get it for one hundred dollars. It is a good organ, I tried it to see. If you will pay your school money for it, I can make up the other twenty-five dollars, and besides I can build another room on this house so we will have a place to put it."

"I would be glad to help buy the organ," Laura said. "But you know I won't have the seventy-five dollars till after my school is out."

"Laura," Ma put in, "You should think about getting yourself some clothes. Your calicoes are all right for school, but you need a new summer dress for best; your year before last's lawn is really past letting down any more."

"I know, Ma, but think of having an organ," said Laura. "And I think I can work for Miss Bell again, and earn some clothes. The trouble is that I haven't got my school money yet."

"You are certain to get it," Pa said. "Are you sure you want to buy an organ with it?"

"Oh, yes!" Laura told him. "There's nothing I'd like more than to have an organ, that Mary can play when she comes home."

"Then that's settled!" Pa said happily. "I'll pay down the twenty-five, and those folks'll trust me for the balance till you get it. By jinks! I feel like celebrating. Bring me my fiddle, Half-Pint, and we'll have a little music without the organ."

While they all sat in the soft spring twilight, Pa played and sang merrily:

> Here's to the maiden of bashful sixteen,
> Here's to the woman of fifty,
> Here's to the flaunting extravagant queen,

And here's to the housewife that's thrifty!
Here's to the charmer whose dimples we prize,
Now to the maid who has none, sir!
Here's to the girl with a pair of blue eyes,
And here's to the nymph with but one, sir!

His mood changed, and so did the fiddle's. They sang,

Oh, I went down south for to see my Sal,
Sing polly-wolly-doodle all the day!
My Sally was a spunky gal,
Sing polly-wolly-doodle all the day.
Farewell, farewell, farewell my fairy fay,
I'm off to Louisiana
For to see my Susy Anna,
Singing polly-wolly-doodle all the day!

The dusk was deepening. The land flattened to blackness and in the clear air above it the large stars hung low, while the fiddle sang a wandering song of its own.

Then Pa said, "Here is one for you girls." And softly he sang with the fiddle,

Golden years are passing by,
Happy, happy golden years,
Passing on the wings of time,
These happy golden years.
Call them back as they go by,
Sweet their memories are,
Oh, improve them as they fly,
These happy golden years.

Laura's heart ached as the music floated away and was gone in the spring night under the stars.

CHAPTER 19

The Brown Poplin

Now that Ma had spoken of her clothes, Laura saw that she should do something about them. So early Saturday morning she walked to town to see Miss Bell.

"Indeed I shall be glad to have your help," said Miss Bell. "I've been at my wit's end to keep up with all the work, there are so many new people in town. But I thought you were teaching school."

"Not on Saturdays," Laura laughed. "Beginning in July, I can work all week if you like."

So every Saturday she sewed all day long for Miss Bell. Before her school ended, she was able to buy ten yards of a beautiful brown poplin which Miss Bell had ordered from Chicago. And every evening when she went home there was something new to see, for Ma was making up the brown poplin for her, and Pa was building the new room for the organ.

He built it across the east end of the house, with a door in the north looking toward town, and windows in both the east and the south walls. Under the southern window he built a low seat, wide enough for one person to sleep on, so that it could be used as an extra bed.

One evening when Laura came home, the new room was complete. Pa had brought the organ; it stood against the north wall by the door. It was a beautiful organ, of polished walnut, with a tall back. Its overhanging canopy of shining wood almost touched the ceiling. Beneath that, three perfect little mirrors of thick glass were set into the rich walnut, and on either side of the music rack was a solid shelf for a lamp. The slanting music rack was of open woodwork cut in scrolls and backed with red cloth. It lifted on hinges, and revealed behind it a storage space for songbooks. Beneath this, the long, smooth lid folded back into the organ, or unfolded and dropped down to cover the row of black and white keys. Above the keys was a row of stops, marked tremolo and forte and other names, that changed the tone of the organ when they were pulled out. Underneath the keys were two levers, that folded back against the organ, or opened out so that a player's knees could work them. Pressed outward, they made the music louder. Just above the floor were two slanting pedals, covered with carpet, that a player's feet must press down and let up, to pump the organ.

With this beautiful organ, there was a walnut stool. It had a round top, standing on four curved legs. Grace was so excited about this stool that Laura could hardly look at the organ.

"Look, Laura, looky," Grace said, and she sat on the stool and whirled. The top of the stool worked on a screw, and it rose or sank under Grace as she whirled.

"We must not call this a claim shanty any more," said Ma. "It is a real house now, with four rooms."

She had hung white muslin curtains at the windows; they were edged with white knitted lace. The black whatnot stood in the corner by the south window; the carved wooden bracket with the china shepherdess on it was hung on the eastern wall. The two rocking chairs sat comfortably by the east window and bright patchwork cushions lay on the wooden seat under the south window.

"What a pleasant place to sew in," Ma said, looking at this new sitting room with a happy smile. "I shall hurry your dress now, Laura. Perhaps I can have it finished by Sunday."

"There is no hurry," Laura told her. "I don't want to wear it until I have my new hat. Miss Bell is making the very hat I want, but it will take two more Saturdays' work to pay for it."

"Well, how do you like your organ, Laura?" Pa said, coming in from the stable. In the other room, which was only a kitchen now, Carrie was straining the milk.

"My goodness, Grace!" Ma exclaimed, just as Grace and the organ stool crashed on the floor. Grace sat up, too frightened to make a sound, and even Laura was horrified, for the stool lay in two pieces. Then Pa laughed.

"Never mind, Grace," he said. "You only unscrewed it all the way. But," he said sternly, "you stay off this stool, after this."

"I will, Pa," she said, trying to stand up. She was too dizzy. Laura set her on her feet and held her steady, and tried to say to Pa how much the organ pleased her. She could hardly wait until Mary came to play it while Pa played the fiddle.

At supper Ma said again that this was not a claim shanty any more. The kitchen was so spacious now, with only the stove, the cupboard, the table and chairs in it.

"This won't be a claim, either, by year after next," Pa reminded her. "Another eighteen months, and I'll be able to prove up; it will be our land."

"I hadn't forgotten, Charles," said Ma. "I'll be proud when we have our patent from the government. All the more reason to call this place a house, from now on."

"And next year, if all goes well, I'm going to get it sided and painted," Pa promised himself.

When Laura came home next Saturday she brought her new hat, after all. She carried it carefully, well wrapped in paper to protect it from dust.

"Miss Bell said I'd better take it, before someone else saw it and wanted it," she explained. "She says I can do the work for it afterward, just as well."

"You can wear it to church tomorrow," Ma told her. "For I have your dress finished." The brown poplin was laid out on Laura's bed, all pressed and shimmering, for her to see.

"Oh, let's see your hat, too," Carrie asked, when they had all admired the dress, but Laura would not unwrap it.

"Not now," she refused. "I don't want you to see it, until I put it on with the dress."

Next morning they were all up bright and early, to have time to get ready for church. It was a fresh, clear morning; the meadow larks were singing and the sunshine drinking the dew from the grass. All ready in her starched Sunday lawn and Sunday hair ribbons, Carrie sat carefully on her bed, to watch Laura dress.

"You do have beautiful hair, Laura," she said.

"It isn't golden, like Mary's," Laura answered. But in the sunshine as she brushed it, her hair was beautiful. It was fine, but very thick, and so long that the shimmering brown length of it, unbraided, fell below her knees. She brushed it back satin-smooth, and coiled and pinned the mass of braids. Then she took the curlers out of her bangs and carefully arranged the curly mass. She put on her knitted white-lace stockings, and buttoned her high, well-polished black shoes.

Then carefully over her under-petticoats she put on her hoops. She liked these new hoops. They were the very latest style in the East, and these were the first of the kind that Miss Bell had got. Instead of wires, there were wide tapes across the front, almost to her knees, holding the petticoats so that her dress would lie flat. These tapes held the wire bustle in place at the back, and it was an adjustable bustle. Short lengths of tape were fastened to either end of it; these could be buckled together underneath the bustle, to puff it out, either large or small. Or they could be buckled together in front, drawing the bustle down close in back, so that a dress rounded smoothly over it. Laura did not like a large bustle, so she buckled the tapes in front.

Then carefully over all she buttoned her best petticoat, and over all the starched petticoats she put on the underskirt of her new dress. It was of brown cambric, fitting smoothly around the top over the bustle, and gored to flare smoothly down over the hoops. At the bottom, just missing the floor, was a twelve-inch-wide flounce of the brown poplin, bound with an inch-wide band of plain brown silk. The poplin was not plain poplin, but striped with an openwork silk stripe.

Then over this underskirt and her starched white corset-cover, Laura put on the polonaise. Its smooth, long sleeves fitted her arms perfectly to the wrists, where a band of the plain silk ended them. The neck was high, with a smooth band of the plain silk around the throat. The polonaise fitted tightly and buttoned all down the front with small round buttons covered with the plain brown silk. Below the smooth hips it flared and rippled down and covered the top of the flounce on the underskirt. A band of the plain silk finished the polonaise at the bottom.

Around the brown silk neckband Laura placed a blue ribbon two inches wide. She pinned it together at her throat with the pearl bar pin that Ma had given her. The ends of the ribbon fell in streamers to her waist.

Then, Laura unwrapped her hat. Carrie sighed with delight when she saw it.

It was a sage-green, rough straw, in poke-bonnet shape. It completely covered Laura's head and framed her face with its flaring brim. It was lined with shirred silk, blue. Wide blue ribbons tied under her left ear and held the bonnet securely in place.

The blue of the lining, the blue ribbon bow, and the blue neck ribbon, exactly matched the blue of Laura's eyes.

Pa and Ma and Grace were ready for church when she came out of the bedroom, with Carrie following her. Pa looked from the top of Laura's head to the bottom of the brown poplin flounce, where the soft black toes of her shoes peeped out. Then he said, "They say that fine feathers make fine birds, but I say it took a fine bird to grow such feathers."

Laura was so pleased that she could not speak.

"You look very nice," Ma praised, "but remember that pretty is as pretty does."

"Yes, Ma," Laura said.

"That's a funny hat," said Grace.

"It isn't a hat. It's a poke bonnet," Laura explained to her.

Then Carrie said, "When I'm a young lady, I'm going to earn me a dress just exactly like that."

"Likely you'll have a prettier one," Laura answered quickly, but she was startled. She had not thought that she was a young lady. Of course she was, with her hair done up and her skirts almost touching the ground. She was not sure she liked being a young lady.

"Come," Pa said. "The team is waiting, and we'll be late to church if we don't hurry."

The day was so pleasant and sunny that Laura hated to sit in the church, and Reverend Brown's long sermon seemed even duller than usual. The wild prairie grass was green outside the open windows and the light wind enticed her as it softly brushed her cheek. It seemed that there should be more, in such a day, than going to church and going home again.

Ma and Carrie and Grace changed at once into their every-day dresses, but Laura did not want to. She asked, "May I keep my Sunday dress on, Ma? if I wear my big apron and am very careful?"

"You may if you want to," Ma gave permission. "No reason that anything should happen to your dress if you take care."

After dinner, and after the dishes were washed, Laura wandered restlessly out of the house. The sky was so blue, the floating piles of cloud were so shimmering and pearly, and far and wide the land was green. In a row around the house the young cottonwoods were growing; the little saplings that Pa had planted were twice as tall as Laura now, spreading their slender branches and rustling leaves. They made a flickering shade in which Laura stood, looking east and south and west at the lovely, empty day.

She looked toward town, and while she looked a buggy came dashing around the corner by Pearson's livery barn and out along the road toward the Big Slough.

The buggy was new, for the sun flashed and sparkled from its wheels and top. The horses were brown and trotted evenly. Were they the colts that she had helped break? Surely, they were, and as they turned toward her and crossed the slough, she saw that Almanzo was driving them. They came trotting up, and the buggy stopped beside her.

"Would you like to go for a buggy ride?" Almanzo asked, and as Pa came out of the house Laura replied in the words she had always used.

"Oh yes! I'll be ready in a minute."

She tied on her poke bonnet, and told Ma that she was going for a buggy ride. Carrie's eyes were shining, and she stopped Laura and stood tiptoe to whisper, "Aren't you glad you didn't change your dress?"

"I am," Laura whispered back, and she was. She was glad that her dress and her bonnet were so nice. Carefully Almanzo spread the linen lap robe, and she tucked it well under her flounce to cover the brown poplin from dust. Then they were driving away in the afternoon sunshine, southward toward the distant lakes, Henry and Thompson.

"How do you like the new buggy?" Almanzo asked.

It was a beautiful buggy, so black and shining, with glossy red spokes in the wheels. The seat was wide; at either end of it gleaming black supports slanted backward to the folded-down top behind, and the seat had a lazy-back, cushioned. Laura had never before been in a buggy so luxurious.

"It is nice," Laura said, as she leaned comfortably back against the leather cushion. "I never rode in a lazy-back buggy before. The back isn't quite as high as the plain wooden ones, is it?"

"Maybe this will make it better," Almanzo said, laying his arm along the top of the back. He was not exactly hugging Laura, but his arm was against her shoulders. She shrugged, but his arm did not move away. So she leaned forward, and shook the buggy whip where it stood in the whipsocket on the dashboard. The colts jumped forward and broke into a run.

"You little devil!" Almanzo exclaimed, as he closed both hands on the lines and braced his feet. He needed both hands to control those colts.

After a time the colts were calmer and quieter, and trotting again.

"Suppose they had run away?" Almanzo then asked her indignantly.

"They could run a long way before they came to the end of the prairie," Laura laughed. "And there's nothing to run against between here and there."

"Just the same!" Almanzo began, and then he said, "You're independent, aren't you?"

"Yes," said Laura.

They drove a long way that afternoon, all the way to Lake Henry and around it. Only a narrow tongue of land separated it from Lake Thompson. Between the sheets of blue water there was width enough only for a wagon track. Young cottonwoods and choke-cherry trees stood slim on either side, above a tangle of wild grapevines. It was cool there. The wind blew across the water, and between the trees they could see the little waves breaking against the shore on either side.

Almanzo drove slowly, as he told Laura of the eighty-acre field of wheat he had sown, and the thirty acres of oats.

"You know I have my homestead and my tree claim both to work on," he said. "Besides that, Cap and I have been hauling lumber for a long ways, out around town to build houses and schoolhouses all over the country. I had to team, to earn money for this new buggy."

"Why not drive the one you had?" Laura sensibly wanted to know.

"I traded that on these colts last fall," he explained. "I knew I could break them on the cutter in the winter, but when spring came, I needed a buggy. If I'd had one, I'd have been around to see you before this."

As they talked, he drove out from between the lakes and around the end of Lake Henry, then away across the prairie to the north. Now and then they saw a little new claim shanty. Some had a stable, and a field of broken sod nearby.

"This country is settling up fast," Almanzo said as they turned west along the shore of Silver Lake and so toward Pa's claim. "We have driven only forty miles and we must have seen as many as six houses."

The sun was low in the west when he helped her out of the buggy at her door.

"If you like buggy rides as well as sleigh rides, I will be back next Sunday," he said.

"I like buggy rides," Laura answered. Then suddenly she felt shy, and hurried into the house.

CHAPTER 20

Nellie Oleson

"I DECLARE," Ma said. "It never rains but it pours." For strangely enough, Tuesday evening a young man who lived on a neighboring claim came by, and asked Laura to go buggy riding with him next Sunday. On Thursday evening, another young neighbor asked her to go buggy riding with him next Sunday. And as she was walking home Saturday evening, a third young man overtook her and brought her home in his lumber wagon, and he asked her to go riding with him next day.

That Sunday Almanzo and Laura drove north past Almanzo's two claims, to Spirit Lake. There was a small claim shanty on Almanzo's homestead. On his tree claim there were no buildings at all, but the young trees were growing well. He had set them out carefully, and must cultivate and care for them for five years; then he could prove up on the claim and own the land. The trees were thriving much better than he had expected at first, for he said that if trees would grow on those prairies, he thought they would have grown there naturally before now.

"These government experts have got it all planned," he explained to Laura. "They are going to cover these prairies with trees, all the way from Canada to Indian Territory. It's all mapped out in the land offices, where the trees ought to be, and you can't get that land except on tree claims. They're certainly right about one thing; if half these trees live, they'll seed the whole land and turn it into forest land, like the woods back East."

"Do you think so?" Laura asked him in amazement. Somehow she could not imagine those prairies turned into woods, like Wisconsin.

"Well, time will show," he answered. "Anyway, I'm doing my part. I'll keep those trees alive if it can be done."

Spirit Lake was beautiful and wild. There Almanzo drove along a rocky shore, where the water was deep and the waves ran foaming before the wind and dashed high on the rocks.

There was an Indian mound by Spirit Lake, too. It was said to be a burial place, though no one knew what was in it. Tall cottonwoods grew there, and choke-cherries smothered in wild grapevines.

On the way back, they came into town past the Olesons' claim. It was on the section line a mile east of Almanzo's homestead. Laura had not seen Nellie Oleson's home before, and she felt a little sorry for her; the shanty was so small, standing among the wild grass in the wind. Mr. Oleson had no horses, only a yoke of oxen, and the place was not improved as Pa's was. But Laura barely glanced at it, for she did not want to spoil the beautiful day by even thinking of Nellie Oleson.

"Good-by, then, till next Sunday," Almanzo said, as he left her at her door. The whole country seemed different to her, now that she had seen Lakes Henry and Thompson, and Spirit Lake with its strange Indian mound. She wondered what next Sunday would show.

Sunday afternoon as she watched the buggy coming across Big Slough she saw, to her surprise, that someone was with Almanzo. She wondered who it could be, and if perhaps he did not intend to go for a drive that day.

When the horses stopped at the door, she saw that Nellie Oleson was with him. Without waiting for him to speak, Nellie cried, "Come on, Laura! Come with us for a buggy ride!"

"Want some help, Wilder?" Pa asked, going toward the colts' heads, and Almanzo said that he would be obliged. So Pa held the bridles, while Almanzo waited to help Laura into the buggy, and in stupefied surprise Laura let him. Nellie moved over to make room for her, and helped her tuck the lap robe around the brown poplin.

As they drove away, Nellie began to talk. She admired the buggy; she exclaimed over the colts; she praised Almanzo's driving; she gushed about Laura's clothes. "Oh," she said, "Laura, your poke bonnet is just utterly too-too!" She never stopped for an answer. She did so want to see Lakes Henry and Thompson; she had heard so much about them; she thought the weather was just utterly too-too, and the country was nice, of course not anything like New York State, but that couldn't really be expected out West, could it?

"Why are you so quiet, Laura?" she asked without stopping and went on, with a giggle, "My tongue wasn't made to lie still. My tongue's made to go flippity-flop!"

Laura's head ached; her ears rang with the continuous babble, and she was furious. Almanzo seemed to be enjoying the drive. At least, he looked as though he were being amused.

They drove to Lakes Henry and Thompson. They drove along the narrow tongue of land between them. Nellie thought the lakes were just utterly too-too; she liked lakes, she liked water, she liked trees and vines and she just adored driving on Sunday afternoons; she thought it was just too utterly too-too.

The sun was rather low as they came back, and since Laura's house was nearest, they stopped there first.

"I'll be along next Sunday," Almanzo said as he helped Laura out of the buggy, and before Laura could speak, Nellie chimed in, "Oh, yes! we will come by for you. Didn't you have a good time! Wasn't it fun! Till Sunday, then, don't forget, we'll be by, good-by, Laura, good-by!" Almanzo and Nellie drove away toward town.

All that week Laura debated with herself, to go or not to go. It was no pleasure to her to go driving with Nellie. On the other hand, if she refused to go, Nellie would be pleased; that was what Nellie wanted. Trust Nellie to find some way to go driving with Almanzo every Sunday.

Laura made up her mind to go with them.

Next Sunday's drive began much like the one before. Nellie's tongue went flippity-flop. She was in gay spirits, chattering and laughing to Almanzo and almost ignoring Laura. She was sure of triumph, for she knew that Laura would not long endure this situation.

"Oh, Mannie, you have those wild colts so well broken, you handle them so wonderfully," she cooed, leaning against Almanzo's arm.

Laura bent to tuck the dust robe more closely in at her feet, and as she straightened up again, she carelessly let the end of the robe flutter out on the strong prairie wind. The colts left the ground in one leap and ran.

Nellie screamed and screamed, clutching at Almanzo's arm, which he very much needed to use just then. Laura quietly tucked down the end of the lap robe and sat on it.

When it was no longer flapping behind them, the colts soon quieted and went on in their well-trained trot.

"Oh, I never was so frightened, I never was so frightened in my life," Nellie chattered and gasped. "Horses are such wild things. Oh, Mannie, why did they do it? Don't let them do it again."

Almanzo looked sidewise at Laura and said nothing.

"Horses are all right if you understand them," Laura remarked. "But I suppose these are not like the horses in New York."

"Oh, I would never understand these western horses. New York horses are quiet," Nellie said, and then she started talking of New York. She talked as though she knew it well. Laura knew nothing of New York State, but she knew that Nellie did not, either, and that Almanzo did.

They were nearing the turn toward home when Laura said, "We are so near the Boasts'. Don't you think it would be nice to go see them?"

"If you like," said Almanzo. Instead of turning west, he drove straight on north across the railroad tracks and farther out across the prairie to Mr. Boast's homestead claim. Mr. and Mrs. Boast came out to the buggy.

"Well, well, so the buggy carries three," Mr. Boast teased, his black eyes sparkling. "It's a wider seat than the cutter seat. The cutter was built for two."

"Buggies are different," Laura told him.

"They seem . . ." Mr. Boast began, but Mrs. Boast interrupted. "Now, Rob!" she exclaimed. "You'd better be asking the folks to get out and stay awhile."

"We can't stay," Laura said. "We only stopped for a minute."

"We are just out for a drive," Almanzo explained.

"Then we will turn around here," Nellie said with authority.

Laura spoke quickly, "Let's go a little further. I've never been over this road. Is there time to go a little further, Almanzo?"

"It's a good road straight north," Mr. Boast said. His eyes laughed at Laura. She was sure he guessed what was in her mind, and her eyes laughed back at him as Almanzo started the colts and they went on north. Beyond Mr. Boast's claim they crossed an end of the Slough that ran northeast from Silver Lake. Here a road turned toward town, but it was wet and boggy as Laura had known it would be, so they kept on driving north.

"This is stupid, this isn't any fun; call this a good road?" Nellie fretted.

"It is good so far," Laura said quietly.

"Well! we won't come this way again!" Nellie snapped. Then quickly she recovered her happy vivacity, telling Almanzo how much she enjoyed driving just anywhere with such a good driver and fine team.

Another road branched to the west and Almanzo turned the team into it. Nellie's home was only a little way ahead. As Almanzo helped her from the buggy at her door, she clung to his hand a moment, saying how much she had enjoyed the drive and, "We'll go another way next Sunday, won't we, Mannie?"

"Oh, it's too bad I suggested going that way, Nellie, if you minded it so much," said Laura, and Almanzo said only, "Good-by," and took his place beside Laura.

There was quietness between them for a little while as they drove toward town. Then Laura said, "I am afraid I have made you late for your chores by wanting to take that road."

"It doesn't matter," he reassured her. "The days and nights are as long as they ever were, and I don't have a cow."

Again they were silent. Laura felt that she was dull company after Nellie's lively chatter, but she was determined that Almanzo would decide that. She would never try to hold him, but no other girl was going to edge her out little by little without his realizing it.

At home again, as Almanzo and Laura stood beside the buggy, he said, "I suppose we'll go again next Sunday?"

"We'll not all go," Laura answered. "If you want to take Nellie for a drive, do so, but do not come by for me. Good night."

She went quietly into the house and shut the door.

Sometimes when she was walking to her school, past the hollow that was growing greener with violets' leaves then blue with their blossoms, Laura wondered if Almanzo would come next Sunday. Sometimes when her three little pupils were diligently studying, she looked up from her own studies and saw the cloud shadows moving over the sunny grass beyond the windows, and wondered. If he didn't, he didn't; that was all. And she could only wait until next Sunday.

On Saturday she walked to town and sewed all day for Miss Bell. Pa was breaking sod at home, to make a larger wheat field, so Laura stopped at the post office to see if there were any mail, and there was a letter from Mary! She could hardly wait to get home, to hear Ma read it, for it would tell when Mary was coming home.

No one had written Mary about the new sitting room and the organ that was waiting for her there. Never had anyone in the family had such a surprise as that organ would be for Mary.

"Oh, Ma! a letter from Mary!" she cried, bursting in.

"I'll finish the supper, Ma, you go read it," said Carrie. So Ma took a hairpin from her hair, and as she carefully slit the envelope she sat down to read the letter. She unfolded the sheet and began to read, and it was as if all the light went out of the house.

Carrie gave Laura a frightened look, and after a moment Laura asked quietly, "What is it, Ma?"

"Mary does not want to come home," Ma said. Then, quickly, "I do not mean that. She asks if she may spend her vacation with Blanche, at Blanche's home. Stir the potatoes, Carrie; they'll be too brown."

All through supper they talked about it. Ma read the letter aloud. Mary wrote that Blanche's home was not far from Vinton, and she very much wanted that Mary should visit it. Her mother was writing to Ma, to invite Mary. Mary would like to go, if Pa and Ma said she might.

"I think she should," Ma said. "It will be a change for her, and do her good."

Pa said, "Well," and so it was settled. Mary was not coming home that year.

Later, Ma said to Laura that Mary would be at home to stay when she finished college, and it might be that she would never have another opportunity to travel. It was nice that she could have this pleasant time and make so many new friends while she was young. "She will have it to remember," Ma said.

But that Saturday night, Laura felt that nothing would ever be right again. Next morning, though the sun was shining and the meadow larks singing, they did not mean anything, and as she rode to church in the wagon she said to herself that she would ride in a wagon all the rest of her life. She was quite sure now that Almanzo would take Nellie Oleson driving that day.

Still, at home again she did not take off her brown poplin, but put her big apron on as she had done before. Time went very slowly, but at last it was two o'clock, and looking from the window Laura saw the colts come dashing over the road from town. They trotted up and stopped at the door.

"Would you like to go for a buggy ride?" Almanzo asked, as Laura stood in the doorway.

"Oh, yes!" Laura answered. "I'll be ready in a minute."

Her face looked at her from the mirror, all rosy and smiling, as she tied the blue ribbon bow under her left ear.

In the buggy she asked, "Wouldn't Nellie go?"

"I don't know," Almanzo replied. After a pause he said in disgust, "She is afraid of horses." Laura said nothing, and in a moment he continued, "I wouldn't have brought her the first time, but I overtook her walking in the road. She was walking all the way to town to see someone, but she said she'd rather go along with us. Sundays at her house are so long and lonely that I felt sorry for her, and she seemed to enjoy the drive so much. I didn't know you girls disliked each other."

Laura was amazed, that a man who knew so much about farming and horses could know so little about a girl like Nellie. But she said only, "No, you wouldn't know, because you did not go to school with us. I will tell you what I'd like to do, I'd like to take Ida driving."

"We will, sometime," Almanzo agreed. "But today is pretty fine, just by ourselves."

It was a beautiful afternoon. The sun was almost too warm, and Almanzo said that the colts were so well broken now that they could raise the buggy top. So together, each with a hand, they raised it and pressed the hinge of the braces straight to hold it up. Then they rode in its shade with the gentle wind blowing through the open sides.

After that day, nothing was ever said about the next Sunday, but always at two o'clock Almanzo drove around the corner of Pearson's livery barn, and Laura was ready when he stopped at the door. Pa would look up from his paper and nod good-by to her, then go on reading, and Ma would say, "Don't be out too late, Laura."

June came and the wild prairie roses bloomed. Laura and Almanzo gathered them beside the road and filled the buggy with the fragrant blossoms.

Then one Sunday at two o'clock the corner of Pearson's barn remained empty. Laura could not imagine what might have happened, till suddenly the colts were at the door, and Ida was in the buggy, laughing merrily.

Almanzo had gone by the Reverend Brown's, and persuaded Ida to come. Then for a surprise, he had crossed the Big Slough west of the town road; this brought them to Pa's land a little south of the house, and while Laura watched toward the north, they had come up from the opposite direction.

They drove that day to Lake Henry, and it was the merriest of drives. The colts behaved beautifully. They stood quietly while Ida and Laura filled their arms with the wild roses and climbed back into the buggy. They nibbled at the bushes by the road while Almanzo and the girls watched the little waves ripple along the shores of the lakes on either hand.

The road was so narrow and so low that Laura said, "I should think the water might be over the road sometimes."

"Not since I have known it," Almanzo answered, "but perhaps, many years or ages ago, the two lakes were one."

Then for awhile, they sat in silence and Laura thought how wild and beautiful it must have been when the twin lakes were one, when buffalo and antelope roamed the prairie around the great lake and came there to drink, when wolves and coyotes and foxes lived on the banks and wild geese, swans, herons, cranes, ducks, and gulls nested and fished and flew there in countless numbers.

"Why did you sigh?" Almanzo asked.

"Did I?" said Laura. "I was thinking that wild things leave when people come. I wish they wouldn't."

"Most people kill them," he said.

"I know," Laura said. "I can't understand why."

"It is beautiful here," said Ida, "but we are a long way from home and I promised Elmer I'd go to church with him tonight."

Almanzo tightened the reins and spoke to the colts while Laura asked, "Who's Elmer?"

"He is a young man who has a claim near Father Brown's and he boards at our place," Ida told her. "He wanted me to go walking with him this afternoon, but I thought I'd rather go with you, this once. You've never seen Elmer . . . McConnell," she remembered to add.

"There are so many new people, and I can't keep track even of the ones I know," Laura said.

"Mary Power is going with the new clerk in Ruth's bank," Ida told her.

"But Cap!" Laura exclaimed. "What about Cap Garland?"

"Cap's smitten with a new girl who lives west of town," Almanzo told them.

"Oh, I think it's a pity we don't all go in a crowd any more," Laura lamented. "What fun the sleighing parties were, and now everyone's paired off."

"Oh, well," Ida said. "'In the spring a young man's fancy lightly turns to thoughts of love.'"

"Yes, or it's this," and Laura sang,

Oh whistle and I'll come to you, my lad,
Oh whistle and I'll come to you, my lad,
Though father and mither and a' should gae mad,
Oh whistle and I'll come to you, my lad.

"Would you?" Almanzo asked.

"Of course not!" Laura answered. "That's only a song."

"Better whistle for Nellie, she'd come," Ida teased, and then she said soberly, "But she is afraid of these horses. She says they aren't safe."

Laura laughed delightedly. "They were a little wild, the time she was with us," she said.

"But I can't understand it. They are perfectly gentle," Ida insisted.

Laura only smiled and tucked the dust robe in more securely. Then she saw Almanzo looking sidewise at her behind Ida's head, and she let her eyes twinkle at him. She didn't care if he did know that she had frightened the colts to scare Nellie, on purpose.

All the miles home they rode talking and singing, until they came to Laura's home, and as she left them she asked, "Won't you come with us next Sunday, Ida?"

Blushing, Ida answered, "I would like to, but I . . . I think I'm going walking with Elmer."

CHAPTER 21

Barnum and Skip

JUNE was gone, and Laura's school was out. The organ was paid for. Laura learned to play a few chords with Pa's fiddle, but she would rather listen to the fiddle alone, and after all, the organ was for Mary's enjoyment when Mary came home.

One evening Pa said, "Tomorrow's Fourth of July. Do you girls want to go to the celebration in town?"

"Oh no, let's have it as it was last year," Carrie said. "I don't want to be in a crowd where they shoot off firecrackers. I'd rather have our own firecrackers at home."

"I want lots of candy at home," Grace put in her vote.

"I suppose Wilder will be around with that team and buggy, Laura?" Pa asked.

"He didn't say anything about it," Laura answered. "But I don't want to go to the celebration, anyway."

"Is this unanimous, Caroline?" Pa wanted to know.

"Why, yes, if you agree with the girls," Ma smiled at them all. "I will plan a celebration dinner, and the girls will help me cook it."

All the next morning they were very busy. They baked fresh bread, a pieplant pie, and a two-egg cake. Laura went to the garden, and with her fingers dug carefully into the hills of potatoes to find new potatoes. She gathered enough potatoes for dinner, without injuring one plant by disturbing its roots. Then she picked the first of the green peas, carefully choosing only the plump pods.

Ma finished frying a spring chicken while the new potatoes and the peas were cooked and given a cream dressing. The Fourth of July dinner was just ready, all but steeping the tea, when Pa came home from town. He brought lemons for afternoon lemonade, firecrackers for the evening, and candy for all the time after dinner.

As he gave the packages to Ma, he said to Laura, "I saw Almanzo Wilder in town. He and Cap Garland were hitching up a new team he's got. That young fellow missed his vocation; he ought to be a lion tamer. Those horses are wilder than hawks. It was all he and Cap could do to handle them. He said to tell you if you want to go for a buggy ride this afternoon, be ready to climb in when he drives up, for he won't be able to get out to help you. Said to tell you, there's another team to break."

"I do believe he wants to break your neck!" said Ma. "And I hope he breaks his own, first."

This was so unlike Ma's gentle self that they all stared at her.

"Wilder will manage the horses, Caroline. Don't worry," Pa said confidently. "If ever I saw a born horseman, he's one."

"Do you really not want me to go, Ma?" Laura asked.

"You must use your own judgment, Laura," Ma replied. "Your Pa says it is safe, so it must be."

After they had slowly enjoyed that delicious dinner, Ma told Laura to leave the dishes and go put on her poplin if she intended to go driving. "I'll do up the work," Ma said.

"But you have worked all morning," Laura objected. "I can do it and still have time to dress."

"Neither of you need bother about the dishes," Carrie spoke up. "I'll wash, and Grace will wipe. Come on, Grace. You and I are older than Mary and Laura were when they did the work."

So Laura was ready and waiting at the door when Almanzo came. She had never seen the horses before. One was a tall bay, with black mane and tail. The other was a large brown horse, spotted with white. On one side of his brown neck a white spot resembled a rooster. A streak of white in the brown mane looked like the rooster's tail.

Almanzo stopped this strange team and Laura went toward the buggy, but the brown horse reared straight up on his hind legs, with front feet pawing the air, while the bay horse jumped ahead. Almanzo loosened the reins and as the horses sprang away he called, "I'll be back."

Laura waited while he drove around the house. When he stopped the horses again, she went quickly to the buggy, but stepped back as again the spotted horse reared and the bay jumped.

Pa and Ma were beside Laura; Carrie stood in the doorway clutching a dish towel, and Grace looked out beside her. They all waited while Almanzo drove around the house again.

Ma said, "You'd better not try to go, Laura," but Pa told her, "Caroline, she will be all right. Wilder will handle them."

This time as Almanzo stopped the horses he turned them a little, cramping the buggy to give Laura a better chance to get between the wheels. "Quick," he said.

Hoops and all, Laura moved quickly. Her right hand grasped the folded-down braces of the buggy top, her right foot touched the buggy step, and as the spotted horse reared and the bay horse leaped, her left foot stepped into the buggy and she dropped into the seat. "Drat these hoops!" she muttered, while she settled them inside the speeding buggy, and covered her brown poplin with the dust robe.

"Don't touch the buggy top!" Almanzo said, and then they were silent. He was fully occupied in keeping control of the horses, and Laura made herself small on her side of the seat to keep out of the way of his straining arms as he tried to pull the horses down out of their run.

They went north because they were headed that way. As they streaked through town Laura caught a glimpse of a thickly scrambling crowd getting out of the way, and Cap Garland's grin as he waved his hand to her.

Later she thought with satisfaction that she had sewed the ribbon ties to her poke bonnet herself; she was sure the stitches would not give way.

The horses settled to a fast trot, and Almanzo remarked, "They said you wouldn't go, and Cap said you would."

"Did he bet I would?" Laura asked.

"I didn't, if that's what you want to know," Almanzo answered. "I wouldn't bet about a lady. Anyway, I wasn't sure how you'd like this circus I'm driving."

"What became of the colts?" Laura inquired.

"I sold them."

"But Prince and Lady . . ." Laura hesitated. "I am not criticizing these horses, I just wondered if anything is wrong with Prince and Lady."

"Nothing is wrong. Lady has a colt and Prince doesn't drive so well without Lady. I had an offer of three hundred dollars for the colts, they're a well-matched, well-broken team and worth it, but you can't be sure of a fair price every day. This team cost me only two hundred. That's a clear gain of a hundred dollars, and I figure I can sell these for more than they cost me, if I want to, when they're broken. I think it will be fun to break them, don't you?"

"Oh, yes!" Laura answered. "We will teach them to be gentle."

"That's what I figured. By the way, the spotted one's named Barnum, and the bay is Skip. We won't go by the picnic grounds; the firecrackers would make them wild again," Almanzo said.

The horses went on mile after mile at a swift trot on the road across the open prairie. Rain had fallen the night before and water stood in pools wherever the road dipped, but Barnum and Skip refused to get their feet wet. They jumped across every puddle, taking the buggy flying over it with them and not a spatter fell on Laura's poke bonnet.

The Fourth of July sun was hot, and Laura wondered why Almanzo did not suggest raising the buggy top until he said, "I'm sorry, but if we raised the top these horses would be frantic. I don't know if I could hold them. Cap and I together couldn't hitch them to the buggy till we put the top down."

So they rode in the sunshine with the prairie wind blowing and white clouds sailing the blue sky overhead. They drove to Spirit Lake, around the end of it and beyond; then by different roads they went home again.

"We have driven sixty miles," Almanzo said as they neared the house. "I think the horses will stand to let you out. I daren't get out to help you, for fear they would leave me."

"I can get out myself," Laura said. "Don't let the horses get away. But won't you stay to supper?"

"I'd like to, but I must get the horses back to town before I stop them, so Cap can help me unhitch. Here we are. Don't jiggle the buggy top as you step down between the wheels."

Laura tried not to, but she did jar it a little; Barnum reared, Skip leaped and they dashed away.

When Almanzo came next Sunday, Laura knew what to expect. She was quick to spring into the buggy the first time the horses stopped.

They were headed east, and they ran that way. After a while they went more quietly, and Almanzo drove them by a roundabout way to the twin lakes. Rapidly, but without rearing or plunging, they passed over the narrow road between the lakes, and on the homeward road they trotted.

"I have been driving them some this week, and I guess they are beginning to get the idea that they might as well behave," Almanzo remarked.

"But they are not as much fun when they behave," Laura complained.

"You think not? Well, then let's teach them what a buggy top is for. Catch hold!"

Barely in time to do her part, Laura caught the front brace at her side of the buggy top and lifted it as Almanzo lifted his side. Quickly she pressed back on the hinge in its middle, straightening and clamping it as Almanzo did. The top was up and held firmly in place, just in the nick of time.

Skip sprang, and Laura caught her breath as Barnum reared. Up and up he went, forefeet pawing the air higher still, and his huge back rising in front of the dashboard. Nearer it came and nearer, in one more instant it would topple backward upon the buggy. Then with a great leap Barnum came down, far ahead, running with Skip. The buggy top swayed with the swiftness of its going and fear of it increased their speed.

Almanzo's arms were rigid as he held the reins that were taut and straight as wires. Laura shrank back in her corner of the seat, held her breath and hoped they would not break.

At last the horses tired, and slowed to a trot. Almanzo drew a deep breath and relaxed a little. "Was that better?" he smiled at Laura.

Laura laughed shakily. "Much better, so long as the harness holds together," she said.

"The harness will hold. I had it made to order at Schaub's harness shop. Every strap is sound leather and it's double-riveted and wax-sewed. In time these horses will learn the difference between running and running away," he said confidently. "They were runaways, you know."

"Were they?" said Laura, and her laugh was still a little shaky.

"Yes, that's why I got them so cheap. They can run, but they can't run away from us. After awhile they'll learn that they can't, and they'll stop trying and be a good team."

"The buggy top is still up, and still scaring them. How will we ever get it down?" Laura wanted to know.

"We don't need to put it down. Just be careful not to shake it when you're getting out, and I'll leave it up."

The dangerous instant, in getting in or out of the buggy, was the instant that she was between the wheels. She had to be quicker than the horses, and go between the wheels without being caught.

When Almanzo stopped the horses at her door, very carefully Laura stooped under the buggy top's braces without touching them, and quickly she got to the ground. Her skirts swooshed as she went, and the horses jumped and were gone.

She was surprised that her knees felt weak as she went into the house. Pa turned to look at her.

"Safely home again," he said.

"There isn't a bit of danger," Laura told him.

"No, of course not, but just the same I shall feel better when those horses are quieter. I suppose you're going again next Sunday?"

"I think so," Laura answered.

Next Sunday the horses were much quieter. They stood while Laura got into the buggy. Then quickly they started and trotted swiftly away. Almanzo drove them through town and northward. As the miles slipped behind them, their shining coats became dark with sweat.

Almanzo gently tried to pull them back to a walk. "Better slow down, boys, you'll be cooler if you do," he told them, but they refused to slacken their speed. "Oh, well, if you want to go, it won't hurt you," he added.

"It is terribly warm," Laura said, raising the bangs from her forehead to let the wind blow underneath them. The heat of the sun was intense and strangely smothering.

"We can raise the top," Almanzo said, but doubtfully.

"Oh, no, let's don't!" Laura objected. "The poor things are warm enough, without running away . . . without running," she corrected herself.

"It is pretty warm to excite them so much," Almanzo agreed. "It might not hurt them, but I'd rather not risk it, if you don't mind the sun."

As time passed the horses trotted more slowly. Still they would not walk, but trotted onward steadily until Laura suggested turning homeward earlier than usual because of the weather signs.

The wind came in short, hot puffs from every direction, and thunderclouds were in the west. Almanzo agreed, "It does look like rain."

Turned toward home, the horses trotted more swiftly, but it was a long way to go. Ghostly whirlwinds sped invisible over the prairie, twisting the grass in small circles as they went, as if unseen fingers were stirring it.

"Dust devils," Almanzo remarked, "Only there is no dust, nothing but grass. They say they're a sure sign of cyclone weather."

The thunderheads piled up in the west; the whole sky looked stormy. The sun was shooting angry red beams of light across the dark clouds when Laura came home. Almanzo hurried away to reach his claim and make things snug there before the rain fell.

But the storm held off. Night came, black and oppressive, with still no rain, and Laura slept uneasily. Suddenly she woke in a glare of light; Ma stood by the bedside, holding a lamp. She shook Laura's shoulder.

"Quick, Laura!" she said. "Get up and help Carrie get her clothes, and come! Pa says there's a bad storm coming."

Laura and Carrie snatched up their clothes and followed Ma, who had snatched up Grace and her clothes and a blanket and was hurrying to the open trapdoor of the cellar.

"Go down, girls, quickly. Hurry," she told them. They tumbled hastily down into the small cellar under the kitchen.

"Where is Pa?" Laura asked.

Ma blew out the lamp. "He is outdoors, watching the cloud. He can get here quickly, now that we are all down out of his way."

"Why did you blow out the lamp, Ma?" Grace almost whimpered.

"Get into your clothes as well as you can, girls," Ma said. "We don't want the lamp, Grace; we don't want any risk of fire."

They could hear the roaring of wind, and a strange wild note was in it. Flashes of lightning glared into the darkness. The kitchen overhead was brighter than fire for an instant, then the dark was blacker and seemed to press on the eyeballs.

Ma dressed Grace, while Laura and Carrie somehow got into their clothes. Then they all sat on the earth floor, with their backs against the earth wall, and waited.

Laura knew they were safer in the cellar, but she could hardly bear the closed-in, underground feeling of it. She wanted to be out in the wind with Pa, watching the storm. The wind roared. The lightning slapped her open eyes with glare and darkness. Overhead in the kitchen the clock, pathetically ignorant of the storm, struck one.

It seemed a long time before Pa's voice came down through the darkness. "You may come up now, Caroline. The storm passed west of us, between here and the Wessington Hills."

"Oh, Pa, it wasn't near enough to get the Reverend Brown's, was it?" Laura asked.

"No. I doubt if this house would have stood if it had come that near," Pa answered.

Cramped and chilled from sitting so long uncomfortably in the cold cellar, they all crawled wearily into their beds.

All through August the weather was hot, and there were many thunderstorms. Several times Ma roused Laura and Carrie in the night, to go down cellar with her and Grace while Pa watched the storm clouds. The wind blew with terrific force, but it was always a straight wind; and the worst of it passed to the west.

Frightened as she was in these terrifying nights, Laura felt a strange delight in the wild strength of the wind, the terrible beauty of the lightning and the crashes of thunder.

But in the morning they were all tired and heavy-eyed. Pa said, "It seems we have to have about so many electric storms. If we don't get them in blizzards in the wintertime, we get them in cyclones and thunderstorms in the summer."

"We can't do anything about it, so we must take them as they come," said Ma.

Pa rose from the table, and stretched as he yawned. "Well, I can make up my sleep when the cyclone season is over. Right now I have to cut the oats," and he went out to his work.

He was cutting the oats and wheat again with the old cradle. A harvester cost more money than he had, and he would not go in debt for one.

"This giving a mortgage on everything he owns, to buy a two-hundred-dollar machine, and paying ten per cent interest on the debt, will ruin a man," he said. "Let these brash young fellows go in debt for machinery and break up all their land. I'm going to let the grass keep on growing, and raise cattle."

Since he had sold Ellen's big calf to send Mary to college, he had bought another cow. Ellen's little calf had grown up, other calves had grown up, until now he had six cows and heifers, besides this year's calves, so he needed a great deal of grass and hay.

On the last Sunday in August, Almanzo came driving Barnum single. Barnum reared, but Laura was quick, and when his feet touched the ground again she was safely in the buggy seat.

When Barnum had almost reached town and had settled to a trot, Almanzo explained. "I want to break him to drive single. He is so large and strong and such a good-looker that he will be worth more as a single driver than in a team. He must get over this way of starting, though."

"He is a beauty," Laura agreed, "and I believe he is really gentle. Let me drive him; I would like to see if I could."

Almanzo seemed doubtful, but he gave her the lines. "Keep a tight rein on him," he said. "Don't let him get the start of you."

Laura had not realized before how very small her hands were. They looked and felt tiny, holding those leather lines, but she was strong. She drove around the corner by the livery barn and all the way up Main Street, Barnum trotting as fast as he could.

"Did you see them turn and stare?" said Almanzo. "They never expected to see a woman driving that horse."

Laura saw nothing but Barnum. Across the railroad tracks and on through Poverty Flat, the new part of town, she drove. But her arms were growing tired, and a little way out of town she gave the lines back to Almanzo.

"When my arms are rested, I want to drive again," she told him.

"You may," he promised. "You may drive all you want to. It gives my arms a rest, too."

The next time she took the lines they felt alive. Through

them she got the feel of Barnum's mouth. A kind of thrill came up the lines to her hands. "I do believe Barnum knows I'm driving," she said in surprise.

"Of course he does. He doesn't pull so hard, either. Watch him!" Almanzo took the lines. At once they grew tauter and seemed almost to stretch.

"He leans on the bit, with me," Almanzo said. Abruptly he changed the subject. "Do you know your old schoolteacher, Clewett, is going to start a singing school?"

Laura had not heard this. Almanzo said, "I'd like to have you go with me, if you will."

"I would like to, very much," she answered.

"All right, next Friday night. I'll come for you at seven." Almanzo went on, "He's got to learn to walk. He's never been known to walk yet when he was hitched up. Seems to think that if he can keep on going fast enough he can get away from the buggy."

"Let me take him again," Laura said. She loved the feel of Barnum's mouth coming to her hands through the lines. It was true that he did not pull so hard when she was driving him. "He is really gentle," she said again, though she knew that he had always been a runaway.

All that afternoon she took turns with Almanzo, driving, and before he stopped to let her get out at home, he reminded her, "Friday night, at seven. I'll be driving Barnum single, and he may act up, so be ready."

CHAPTER 22

Singing School

SCHOOL began next day in the new brick schoolhouse on Third Street in town. This was a two-story schoolhouse, with two teachers. The small children were in the downstairs room, and the older ones upstairs.

Laura and Carrie were in the upstairs room. It seemed strangely large and empty, without the small children. Yet almost all the seats were filled with boys and girls whom they did not know. Only a few back seats were empty, and these would be filled when the weather grew too cold for farm work and the big boys came to school.

At recess Ida and Laura stood at an upstairs window, looking down at the children playing outdoors, and talking with Mary Power and Minnie Johnson. Ida and Elmer were coming to the singing school Friday night, and so were Minnie and her brother, Arthur, and Mary Power with her new beau, Ed.

"I wonder why Nellie Oleson isn't coming to school," Laura wondered, and Ida said, "Oh, hadn't you heard? She's gone back to New York."

"Not really!"

"Yes, she's gone back there to stay with some relatives. You know what I bet, I bet she talks all the time about how wonderful it is in the West!" Ida laughed. They all laughed.

All alone among the empty seats one of the new girls was sitting by herself. She was very blonde, and tall and slender, and she looked unhappy. Suddenly Laura knew how she felt. They were all having such a good time, and there she sat, left out and lonely and shy, as Laura used to feel.

"That new girl looks nice, and she looks lonesome," Laura said in a low voice. "I'm going to go talk to her."

The new girl's name was Florence Wilkins. Her father had a claim northwest of town, and she intended to be a schoolteacher. Laura had been sitting with her and talking only a little while, when the others came from the window and gathered around them. Florence was not coming to the singing school. She lived too far away.

On Friday evening, Laura was ready promptly at seven, in her brown poplin and her brown velvet hat, and promptly at seven Almanzo came. Barnum stopped, and Laura jumped into the buggy so quickly that Almanzo started him again before he had time to rear.

"That's the first time," Almanzo said. "He's getting slower about rearing. Maybe sometime he'll forget it."

"Maybe," Laura doubted it. She quoted, "'May bees don't fly in September.'"

Singing school was to be in the church, and as they came into town Almanzo said that they would better leave a little early, before the others came out, because a crowd around Barnum would excite him. Laura replied, "When you think it is time, just leave, and I will come."

Almanzo tied Barnum to one of the hitching posts, and they went into the lighted church. He had paid tuition for two, and bought a singing book. The class was already there, and Mr. Clewett was seating them. He placed the bass singers in a group, the tenors in another, and sopranos and altos in groups.

Then he taught them the names and values of the notes, the holds, the slurs, and the rests, and the bass, tenor, and treble clefs. After this, he allowed a short recess, and basses, altos, tenors, and sopranos all mixed together, talking and laughing, until Mr. Clewett called them to order again.

They practiced singing scales. Mr. Clewett gave the pitch with his tuning fork again and again. When almost all of them managed to sound very nearly the same note, they were off, up and down the scale, singing "do, re, mi, fa, sol, la, si, do." Exhausted from climbing so high, the voices all gladly came down again, "Do, si, la, sol, fa, mi, re, do!"

Up and down and up and down they sang, sometimes striking the notes and sometimes not, but always with a good will. Laura had taken a place at the end of a seat, and she watched for a sign from Almanzo. When quietly he went to the door, she slipped away and followed.

While they hurried to the buggy he said, "I'll help you in before I untie him. Likely he'll rear as soon as he is untied, but not before if you don't tighten the lines. Take a good hold on them, but don't move them until he starts. I'll try to get in before he comes down, but if I can't make it, you must hold him. Let him run, but don't let him run away. Drive him around the church and pass me again. Don't be afraid, you can drive him. You have, you know."

She had never driven him when he was starting, Laura thought, though she said nothing. Climbing quickly into the buggy, she took hold of the lines where they lay across the dashboard. She gripped them tightly but did not move them.

At the hitching post, Almanzo untied Barnum. The instant his head was free, Barnum reared. Up and up he went until he stood straight on his hind legs; he was down again and running before Laura could catch her breath. The buggy wheels left the ground and struck it with a jolt.

Laura held firmly to the lines. Barnum was racing away on the open prairie beyond the church. She pulled steadily harder with her right arm than with the left, and to her joy Barnum turned that way. He came swiftly around in a very neat circle. The church whirled in its center, and as its side turned toward her, Laura pulled with all her strength on both lines evenly. But Barnum did not stop. They flashed past Almanzo, still standing at the hitching post.

With Barnum's first leap, Laura's heart had leaped too, up into her throat where it nearly choked her. Now they were out on the prairie again. She pulled steadily on the right-hand line, and again Barnum turned. Very quickly the other side of the church was coming toward her, and Laura pulled on both lines. Barnum almost paused, then with a rearing plunge he was running again.

This time Laura's heart stayed in its place. She pulled with her right arm, and Barnum circled neatly. They passed around the church, and Laura rose a little from the seat. With all her weight she pulled. And Barnum stopped. He reared at once, and leaped and ran.

"All right, run," Laura thought. She held him firmly; she guided him around the circle on the prairie, and again she braced her feet and pulled with all her might. This time, Almanzo got into the buggy. As he did so, the church door opened. All the singing school pupils came pouring out, and someone shouted, "Need help?"

Barnum rose straight up in the air, and came down running.

Almanzo's hands closed on the lines ahead of Laura's, and slid back as she let go. She was glad to let him have the lines.

"Just in time," he said. "We never would have got away if that crowd had swarmed around us. Was it too much for you?"

Laura was shaking. Her hands were numb, and it was hard to keep her teeth from chattering, so she only said, "Oh, no."

For a moment or two Almanzo spoke to Barnum, who soon began to trot. Then Laura said, "Barnum wasn't bad. He was just tired of standing still so long."

"He was plain mad about it," Almanzo said. "Next time we'll leave at recess." He added, "Let's go home the long way, it is such a nice night for a drive."

He turned Barnum to the road that crossed the western end of Big Slough. The wind blew softly in the prairie grass, and above the dark land hung myriads of large stars quivering with light.

On and on Barnum trotted, gently now as if he, too, were enjoying the quietness of the night and the brilliant stars.

Almanzo spoke quietly. "I don't know when I ever saw the stars so bright."

Then Laura began to sing softly.

In the starlight, in the starlight,
Let us wander gay and free,
For there's nothing in the daylight
Half so dear to you and me.
Like the fairies in the shadow
Of the woods we'll steal along,
And our sweetest lays we'll warble,
For the night was made for song.
When none are by to listen,
Or to chide us in our glee,
In the starlight, in the starlight,
Let us wander, gay and free.

Barnum stopped at the door and stood quietly while Laura got out. Almanzo said, "I'll be along Sunday afternoon."

"I will be ready," Laura answered. Then she went in.

Pa and Ma were waiting up for her. Ma gave a little sigh of

relief, and Pa asked, "Does that devil horse of Wilder's drive all right at night?"

"He is really a gentle horse," said Laura. "And he stood so quietly when I got out. I like him."

Ma was satisfied, but Pa looked at her sharply. It was not a lie; she had spoken the truth, and she could not tell them how she had driven Barnum. That would worry them, and perhaps they would forbid her to do it again. She intended to drive Barnum. When she and Barnum were used to each other, perhaps, just perhaps, she could make him act gently.

CHAPTER 23

Barnum Walks

NEXT Sunday Barnum was as bad as he had ever been. He refused to stand, and Laura had to wait for a third stop before she could leap into the buggy. Then he reared and tried to run, pulling so hard that after a time Almanzo complained, "He is pulling this buggy by the bit and my arms."

"Let me try," Laura offered. "It will rest your arms."

"All right," Almanzo agreed. "For a minute, but you'll have to hold hard."

He let go of the lines when she had a firm grip on them, just behind his. Laura's arms took the force of Barnum's pull; his strength flowed up the lines with the thrill she had felt before. Oh, Barnum! she begged silently; please don't pull so hard, I want so much to drive you.

Barnum sensed the change of drivers and stretched his neck a little farther, feeling the bit; then his trot became slower. He turned the corner by the livery barn, and dropped into a walk.

Barnum was walking. Almanzo was silent and Laura hardly breathed. A little by a tiny little she eased on the lines. Barnum went on walking. The wild horse, the runaway, who never before had been seen to walk when hitched to a buggy, walked the whole length of Main Street. He reached out twice, feeling the bit with his mouth and, finding it to his liking, arched his neck and walked proudly on.

Almanzo said, low, "Better tighten the lines a little so he won't get the jump on you."

"No," Laura answered. "I am going to let him carry the bit easily. I think he likes it."

All along the street, everyone stopped to stare. Laura did not like to be so conspicuous, but she knew that she must not be nervous now; she must be calm, and keep Barnum walking. "I wish they wouldn't stare," she almost whispered, looking straight ahead at Barnum's placid ears.

In a low tone, too, Almanzo replied, "They have been expecting he would run away with us. Better not let him walk until he starts trotting himself. Tighten the lines and tell him to go. Then he will understand that he trots because you want him to."

"You take him," Laura offered. She felt a little dizzy, from the excitement.

Almanzo took the lines and at his command, Barnum trotted.

"Well, I'll be darned! how did you do it?" he asked then. "I've been trying ever since I've had him, to get him to walk. What did you do?"

"I didn't do anything," Laura said. "He is really a gentle horse."

All the rest of that afternoon, Barnum walked or trotted when told to do so, and Almanzo bragged, "He'll be gentle as a lamb after this."

He was mistaken. On Friday night Barnum again refused to stand, and when finally Laura landed in the buggy, Almanzo reminded her that they would leave singing school at recess. But, though Barnum had not been tied so long as before, he was in such a temper that Laura drove him around and around the church until they barely got away as singing school was over.

Laura loved singing school. It began with singing scales to limber up the voices. Then Mr. Clewett taught them a simple exercise, the first in the book. He gave them the pitch with his tuning fork again and again, until all their voices chimed with it. Then they sang.

> Gaily now our boat is sailing,
> O'er the blue and sparkling wave.

When they could sing this very well, they learned another. This was the song of the grass.

> All around the open door,
> —Smiling on the rich and poor,
> Here I come! Here I come!
> Creeping everywhere.

Then they sang rounds.

> Three blind mice, see how they run,
> they all ran after the farmer's wife
> she cut off their tails with a carving

knife three blind mice see how they
run they all ran after

The basses chased the tenors that chased the altos that chased the sopranos around and around until they were all lost and exhausted from laughing. It was such fun! Laura could last longer than anyone because Pa had taught her and Carrie and Grace to sing "Three Blind Mice" long ago.

Barnum grew so gentle that Laura and Almanzo could stay till the evening's end, and at recess he and the other young men took striped paper bags of candy from their coat pockets and passed them around to the girls. There were pink-and-white striped peppermint balls, and sticks of lemon candy and peppermint candy and horehound candy. And on the way home Laura sang.

Oh childhood's joys are very great,
A-swingin' on his mother's gate,
A-eatin' candy till his mouth
Is all stuck up from north to south,
But though I have to mind the rule,
I'd rather go to singing school!

"That's why I thought you'd like to go," Almanzo said. "You're always singing."

Each singing school night the class sang farther and farther over in the book. On the last night they sang the anthem at the very end, page one hundred forty-four. "The Heavens Declare the Glory."

Then singing school was ended. There would be no more such gay evenings.

Barnum no longer reared and plunged. He started quickly, with a little jump, into a smooth trot. The air was chilled with the breath of coming winter. The stars were brilliant and hung low in the frosty air. Looking at them, Laura sang the anthem again.

The heavens declare the glory of God and
The Firmament showeth His handiwork.
Day unto day uttereth speech, and
Night unto night showeth knowledge.
There is no speech nor language
Where their voice is not heard.

There was no sound but the soft clip-clop of Barnum's feet as he walked along the grassy prairie road.

"Sing the starlight song," Almanzo asked, and Laura sang again, softly,

In the starlight, in the starlight,
At the daylight's dewy close,
When the nightingale is singing
His last love song to the rose;
In the calm clear night of summer
When the breezes softly play,
From the glitter of our dwelling
We will softly steal away.
Where the silv'ry waters murmur
By the margin of the sea,
In the starlight, in the starlight,
We will wander gay and free.

Again silence came and was unbroken while Barnum of his own accord turned north toward the house. Then Laura said, "I've sung for you, now I'll give you a penny for your thoughts."

"I was wondering . . ." Almanzo paused. Then he picked up Laura's hand that shone white in the starlight, and his sun-browned hand closed gently over it. He had never done that before. "Your hand is so small," he said. Another pause. Then quickly, "I was wondering if you would like an engagement ring."

"That would depend on who offered it to me," Laura told him.

"If I should?" Almanzo asked.

"Then it would depend on the ring," Laura answered, and drew her hand away.

It was later than usual when Almanzo came next Sunday.

"Sorry to be so late," he said, when Laura was settled in the buggy and they were driving away.

"We can take a shorter drive," Laura answered.

"But we want to go to Lake Henry. This is about our last chance for wild grapes, now they are frosted," Almanzo told her.

It was a sunny afternoon, warm for the time of year. On either side of the narrow road between the twin lakes, ripened wild grapes were hanging from their vines in the trees. Almanzo drove slowly, and reaching from the buggy he and Laura picked the clusters of grapes. They ate of their tangy sweetness as they watched the water rippling in the sunshine and heard the little waves lapping on the shore.

As they drove home the sun went down in a flaming western sky. Twilight settled over the prairie, and the evening wind blew softly through the buggy.

Then driving with one hand, with the other Almanzo lifted Laura's, and she felt something cool slip over her first finger while he reminded her, "You said it would depend on the ring. How do you like this one?"

Laura held her hand up to the first light of the new moon. The gold of the ring and its flat oval set shone in the faint moon radiance. Three small stones set in the golden oval glimmered.

"The set is a garnet, with a pearl on each side," Almanzo told her.

"It is a beautiful ring," Laura said. "I think . . . I would like to have it."

"Then leave it on. It is yours and next summer I will build a little house in the grove on the tree claim. It will have to be a little house. Do you mind?"

"I have always lived in little houses. I like them," Laura answered.

They had almost reached home. Lamplight shone from its windows and Pa was playing the fiddle. Laura knew the song, it was one that he often sang to Ma. His voice rose with its music and he sang,

A beautiful castle I've built for thee
In dreamland far away,
And there, gentle darling, come dwell with me,
Where love alone has sway.
Oh, sweet will be our blisses,
Oh, rare will be our blisses!
We'll tell our time by the lovers' chime
That strikes the hour with kisses.

Barnum was quiet while Laura and Almanzo stood beside the buggy when Pa's song was finished. Then Laura held up her face in the faint moonlight. "You may kiss me good night," she said, and after their first kiss she went into the house while Almanzo drove away.

Pa laid down his fiddle when Laura came in. He looked at her hand where the ring sparkled in the lamplight.

"I see it is settled," he said. "Almanzo was talking to me yesterday and I guess it's all right."

"If only you are sure, Laura," Ma said gently. "Sometimes I think it is the horses you care for, more than their master."

"I couldn't have one without the other," Laura answered shakily.

Then Ma smiled at her, Pa cleared his throat gruffly, and Laura knew they understood what she was too shy to say.

CHAPTER 24

Almanzo Goes Away

EVEN at home Laura felt that her ring was conspicuous. Its smooth clasp was strange on her first finger, and the garnet and pearls were constantly catching the light. Several times on the way to school next morning she almost took it off and tied it into her handkerchief for safekeeping. But, after all, she was engaged; that could not always be a secret.

She did not mind being almost late to school that morning. There was barely time to slide into her seat with Ida before Mr. Owen called the room to order, and quickly she opened a book so that it hid her left hand. But just as she was beginning to study, a glitter caught her eye.

Ida's left hand was resting on the desk where Laura would be sure to see the broad circlet of gold shining on the first finger.

Laura looked from the ring to Ida's laughing, blushing face and shy eyes, and then she broke a school rule. She whispered, "Elmer?" Ida blushed even rosier, and nodded. Then under the edge of the desk, Laura showed Ida her own left hand.

Mary Power and Florence and Minnie could hardly wait until recess to pounce upon them and admire their rings. "But I'm sorry you have them," Mary Power said, "for I suppose both of you will be quitting school now."

"Not me," Ida denied. "I am going to school this winter, anyway."

"So am I," said Laura. "I want to get a certificate again in the spring."

"Will you teach school next summer?" Florence asked.

"If I can get a school," Laura replied.

"I can get the school in our district if I can get a certificate," Florence told them, "but I'm afraid of teachers' examinations."

"Oh, you will pass," Laura encouraged her. "There's nothing much to it, if only you don't get confused and forget what you know."

"Well, I'm not engaged, nor do I want to teach," said Mary

Power. "How about you, Ida? Are you going to teach for awhile?"

Ida laughed, "No, indeed! I never did want to teach. I'd rather keep house. Why do you suppose I got this ring?"

They all laughed with her, and Minnie asked, "Well, why did you get yours, Laura? Don't you want to keep house?"

"Oh, yes," Laura answered. "But Almanzo has to build it first." Then the big new bell clanged in the cupola, and recess was over.

There was no singing school now, so Laura did not expect to see Almanzo until the next Sunday. She was surprised when Pa asked her, Wednesday night, whether she had seen Almanzo.

"I saw him at the blacksmith shop," Pa told her. "He said he'd see you after school if he could, and if not, to tell you he didn't have time. It seems he and Royal are leaving next Sunday for Minnesota. Something's come up, and Royal's got to go sooner than he expected."

Laura was shocked. She had known that Almanzo and his brother planned to spend the winter with their folks in Minnesota, but he had not intended to go so soon. It was shocking that the whole pattern of the days could be broken so suddenly. There would be no more Sunday drives.

"It may be best," she said. "They will be sure to reach Minnesota before snow falls."

"Yes, they'll likely have good weather for the trip," Pa agreed. "I told him I'd keep Lady while they're gone. He's going to leave the buggy here, and he said you are to drive Lady as much as you please, Laura."

"Oh, Laura! will you take me driving?" Carrie asked, and Grace cried, "Me, too, Laura! Me, too?"

Laura promised that she would, but the rest of that week seemed oddly empty. She had not realized before how often, during a week, she had looked forward to the Sunday drives.

Early next Sunday morning, Almanzo and his brother Royal came. Royal was driving his own team, hitched to his peddler's cart. Almanzo drove Lady, hitched single to his shining, lazy-back buggy. Pa came out of the stable to meet them, and Almanzo drove the buggy under the hay-covered shed. There he unhitched Lady, then led her into the stable.

Afterward, leaving Pa and Royal talking, he came to the kitchen door. He hadn't time to stop, he told Ma, but he would like to see Laura for a moment.

Ma sent him into the sitting room, and as Laura turned from plumping up the cushions on the window seat, the ring on her hand sparkled in the morning light.

Almanzo smiled. "Your new ring is becoming to your hand," he said.

Laura turned her hand in the sunshine. The gold of the ring gleamed, the garnet glowed richly in the center of the flat, oval set, and on either side of it the pearls shimmered lustrously.

"It is beautiful, this ring," she said.

"I would say the hand," Almanzo replied. Then, "I suppose your father told you that Royal and I are going home sooner than we expected. Royal decided to drive through Iowa, so we are starting now. I brought Lady and the buggy over, for you to use whenever you please."

"Where is Prince?" Laura asked.

"One of my neighbors is keeping Prince, and Lady's colt, and Cap is keeping Barnum and Skip. I'll need all four of them in the spring." A shrill whistle sounded from outside. "Royal is calling, so kiss me good-by and I'll go," Almanzo finished.

They kissed quickly, then Laura went with him to the door and watched while he and Royal drove away. She felt left behind and unhappy. Then at her elbow Carrie asked, "Are you going to be lonesome?" so soberly that Laura smiled.

"No, I'm not going to be lonesome," she answered stoutly. "After dinner we will hitch up Lady and go for a drive."

Pa came in and went to the stove. "It's getting so a fire feels good," he said. "Caroline, what would you think of staying here all winter, instead of going to town? I've been figuring. I believe I can rent the building in town this winter, and if I can, I can tar paper and side this house. Maybe even paint it."

"That would be a gain, Charles," Ma said at once.

"Another thing," Pa continued. "We have so much stock now, it would be a big job to move all the hay and fodder. With this house sided outside, and good thick building paper inside, we'd be snug here. We can put up the coal heater in the sitting room and get our winter's supply of coal. There's a cellarful of vegetables from the garden, pumpkins and squashes from the field. Even if the winter's so bad I can't get to town often, we won't need to worry about being hungry or cold."

"That is true," said Ma. "But, Charles, the girls must go to school, and it's too far for them to walk in the wintertime. A blizzard might come up."

"I will drive them there and back," Pa promised. "It's only a mile, and it will be a quick trip with the bobsled and no load."

"Very well," Ma consented. "If you rent the building in town, and want to stay here, I am satisfied to do so. I will be glad not to move."

So before snow fell, all was snug on the homestead claim. In its new siding the little house was really a house, no longer a claim shanty. Inside, thick gray building paper covered all the pine-board walls. They had grown so brown with time, that the lighter paper brightened the rooms, and the freshly starched white muslin curtains gave them a crisp look.

When the first heavy snows came, Pa put the wagon box on the bobsled runners, and half-filled it with hay. Then on school days, Laura and Carrie, with Grace snuggled between them, sat on the blanket-covered hay, with other blankets tucked over and around them, while Pa drove them to the schoolhouse in the morning and brought them home at night to the warmly welcoming house.

Every afternoon on his way to the school, he stopped at the post office, and once or twice a week there was a letter for Laura, from Almanzo. He had reached his father's home in Minnesota; he would come back in the spring.

CHAPTER 25

The Night Before Christmas

On Christmas Eve again, there was a Christmas tree at the church in town. In good time, the Christmas box had gone to Mary, and the house was full of Christmas secrets as the girls hid from each other to wrap the presents for the Christmas tree. But at ten o'clock that morning, snow began to fall.

Still it seemed that it might be possible to go to the Christmas tree. All the afternoon Grace watched from the window, and once or twice the wind moderated. By suppertime, however, it was howling at the eaves, and the air was thick with flying snow.

"It's too dangerous to risk it," Pa said. It was a straight wind, blowing steadily, but you never could tell; it might turn into a blizzard while the people were in the church.

No plans had been made for Christmas Eve at home, so everyone had much to do. In the kitchen Laura was popping corn in the iron kettle set into a hole of the stove top from which she had removed the stove lid. She put a handful of salt into the kettle; when it was hot she put in a handful of popcorn. With a long-handled spoon she stirred it, while with the other hand she held the kettle's cover to keep the corn from flying out as it popped. When it stopped popping she dropped in another handful of corn and kept on stirring, but now she need not hold the cover, for the popped white kernels stayed on top and kept the popping kernels from jumping out of the kettle.

Ma was boiling molasses in a pan. When Laura's kettle was full of popped corn, Ma dipped some into a large pan, poured a thin trickle of the boiling molasses over it, and then buttering her hands, she deftly squeezed handfuls of it into popcorn balls. Laura kept popping corn and Ma made it into balls until the large dishpan was heaped with their sweet crispness.

In the sitting room Carrie and Grace made little bags of pink mosquito netting, left over last summer from the screen door.

They filled the bags with Christmas candy that Pa had brought from town that week.

"It's lucky I thought we'd want more candy than we'd likely get at the Christmas tree," Pa took credit to himself.

"Oh!" Carrie discovered. "We've made one bag too many. Grace miscounted."

"I did not!" Grace cried.

"Grace," Ma said.

"I am not contradicting!" cried Grace.

"Grace," said Pa.

Grace gulped. "Pa," she said. "I didn't count wrong. I guess I can count five! There was candy enough for another one, and it looks pretty in the pink bag."

"So it does, and it is nice to have an extra one. We haven't always been so lucky," Pa told her.

Laura remembered the Christmas on the Verdigris River in Indian Territory, when Mr. Edwards had walked eighty miles to bring her and Mary each one stick of candy. Wherever he was tonight, she wished him as much happiness as he had brought them. She remembered the Christmas Eve on Plum Creek in Minnesota, when Pa had been lost in the blizzard and they feared he would never come back. He had eaten the Christmas candy while he lay sheltered three days under the creek bank. Now here they were, in the snug warm house, with plenty of candy and other good things.

Yet now she wished that Mary were there, and she was trying not to think of Almanzo. When he first went away, letters had come from him often; then they had come regularly. Now for three weeks there had been no letter. He was at home, Laura thought, meeting his old friends and the girls he used to know. Springtime was four months away. He might forget her, or wish that he had not given her the ring that sparkled on her finger.

Pa broke into her thoughts. "Bring me the fiddle, Laura. Let's have a little music before we begin on these good things."

She brought him the fiddle box and he tuned the fiddle and resined the bow. "What shall I play?"

"Play Mary's song first," Laura answered. "Perhaps she is thinking of us."

Pa drew the bow across the strings and he and the fiddle sang:

Ye banks and braes and streams around
The castle of Montgomery,
Green be your woods and fair your flowers,
Your waters never drumlie;
There summer first unfolds her robes
And there the langest tarry,
For there I took the last fareweel
Of my sweet Highland Mary.

One Scots song reminded Pa of another, and with the fiddle he sang:

My heart is sair, I dare na tell,
My heart is sair for somebody.
Oh! I could make a winter night,
A' for the sake o' somebody.

Ma sat in her rocking chair beside the heater, and Carrie and Grace were snug in the window seat, but Laura moved restlessly around the room.

The fiddle sang a wandering tune of its own that made her remember June's wild roses. Then it caught up another tune to blend with Pa's voice.

When marshalled on the mighty plane,
The glittering hosts bestud the sky
One star alone of all the train
Can catch the sinner's wandering eye.
It was my light, my guide, my all,
It bade my dark forebodings cease,
And through the storm and dangers thrall
It led me to the port of peace.
Now safely moored, my perils o'er,
I'll sing, first in night's diadem
Forever and forever more,
The Star—the Star of Bethlehem.

Grace said softly, "The Christmas star."

The fiddle sang to itself again while Pa cocked his head, listening. "The wind is rising," he said. "Good thing we stayed home."

Then the fiddle began to laugh and Pa's voice laughed as he sang,

> Oh, do not stand so long outside,
> Why need you be so shy?
> The people's ears are open, John,
> As they are passing by!
> You can not tell what they may think,
> They've said strange things before
> And if you wish to talk awhile,
> Come in and shut the door!
> Come in! Come in! Come in!

Laura looked at Pa in amazement as he sang so loudly, looking at the door. "Come in! Come in! Come . . ."

Someone knocked at the door. Pa nodded to Laura to go to the door, while he ended the song. "Come in and shut the door!"

A gust of wind swirled snow into the room when Laura opened the door; it blinded her for a moment and when she could see she could not believe her eyes. The wind whirled snow around Almanzo as, speechless, she stood holding the door open.

"Come in!" Pa called. "Come in and shut the door!" Shivering, he laid the fiddle in its box and put more coal on the fire. "That wind blows the cold into a fellow's bones," he said. "What about your team?"

"I drove Prince, and I put him in the stable beside Lady," Almanzo answered, as he shook the snow from his overcoat and hung it with his cap on the polished buffalo horns fastened to the wall near the door, while Ma rose from her chair to greet him.

Laura had retreated to the other end of the room, beside Carrie and Grace. When Almanzo looked toward them, Grace said, "I made an extra bag of candy."

"And I brought some oranges," Almanzo answered, taking a paper bag from his overcoat pocket. "I have a package with Laura's name on it, too, but isn't she going to speak to me?"

"I can't believe it is you," Laura murmured. "You said you would be gone all winter."

"I decided I didn't want to stay away so long, and as you will speak to me, here is your Christmas gift."

"Come, Charles, put the fiddle away," said Ma. "Carrie and Grace, help me bring in the popcorn balls."

Laura opened the small package that Almanzo gave her. The white paper unfolded; there was a white box inside. She lifted its lid. There in a nest of soft white cotton lay a gold bar pin. On its flat surface was etched a little house, and before it along the bar lay a tiny lake, and a spray of grasses and leaves.

"Oh, it is beautiful," she breathed. "Thank you!"

"Can't you thank a fellow better than that?" he asked, and then he put his arms around her while Laura kissed him and whispered, "I am glad you came back."

Pa came from the kitchen bringing a hodful of coal and Ma followed. Carrie brought in the pan of popcorn balls and Grace gave everyone a bag of candy.

While they ate the sweets, Almanzo told of driving all day in the cold winds and camping on the open prairie with no house nor shelter near, as he and Royal drove south into Nebraska. He told of seeing the beautiful capitol building at Omaha; of muddy roads when they turned east into Iowa, where the farmers were burning their corn for fuel because they could not sell it for as much as twenty-five cents a bushel. He told of seeing the Iowa state capitol at Des Moines; of rivers in flood that they crossed in Iowa and Missouri, until when faced with the Missouri River they turned north again.

So with interesting talk the evening sped by until the old clock struck twelve.

"Merry Christmas!" Ma said, rising from her chair, and "Merry Christmas!" everyone answered.

Almanzo put on his overcoat, his cap and mittens, said good night, and went out into the storm. Faintly the sleigh bells rang as he passed the house on his way home.

"Did you hear them before?" Laura asked Pa.

"Yes, and nobody was ever asked to come in oftener than he was," said Pa. "I suppose he couldn't hear me in the storm."

"Come, come, girls," Ma said. "If you don't get to sleep soon, Santa Claus will have no chance to fill the stockings."

In the morning, there would be all the surprises from the stockings, and at noon there would be the special Christmas feast, with a big fat hen stuffed and roasted, brown and juicy, and Almanzo would be there, for Ma had asked him to Christmas dinner. The wind was blowing hard, but it had not the shriek and howl of a blizzard wind, so probably he would be able to come tomorrow.

"Oh, Laura!" Carrie said, as Laura blew out the lamp in the bedroom. "Isn't this the nicest Christmas! Do Christmases get better all the time?"

"Yes," Laura said. "They do."

CHAPTER 26

Teachers' Examinations

THROUGH a March snowstorm Laura rode to town with Pa in the bobsled, to take the teachers' examinations. There was no school that day, so Carrie and Grace stayed at home.

Winter had been pleasant on the claim, but Laura was glad that spring was coming soon. Vaguely as she rode in the nest of blankets on the hay, she thought of the pleasant winter Sundays with the family and Almanzo in the cosy sitting room, and she looked forward to long drives again through the summer sunshine and wind; she wondered if Barnum would still be gentle after the long winter in a stable.

As they neared the schoolhouse, Pa asked if she were nervous about the examinations.

"Oh, no," she answered through the frosty veil. "I am sure I can pass. I wish I were as sure of getting a school I will like."

"You could have the Perry school again," said Pa.

"I would rather have a larger one with more pay," Laura explained.

"Well," Pa said cheerfully as they stopped at the schoolhouse, "the first bridge is the examinations, and here we are! Time enough to cross the next bridge when we come to it."

Laura was impatient with herself because she felt timid when she went into the room full of strangers. Nearly every desk was occupied, and the only person she knew was Florence Wilkins. When she touched Florence's hand, she was startled; it was cold as ice, and Florence's lips were pale from nervousness. Laura felt so sorry for her that she forgot her own timidity.

"I'm scared," Florence said in a low, shaking voice. "All the others are old teachers, and the examination is going to be hard. I know I'll never pass."

"Pooh! I bet they're scared, too!" Laura said. "Don't worry; you'll pass all right. Just don't be frightened. You know you've always passed examinations."

Then the bell rang, and Laura faced the lists of questions. Florence was right; they were hard. Working her way through them, Laura was tired when intermission came. By noon she felt her own heart failing; she began to fear she would not get a certificate, but she worked doggedly on until at last she was through. Her last paper was collected with the others, and Pa came to take her home.

"I don't know, Pa," she said in answer to his question. "It was harder than I expected, but I did the best I could."

"No one can do better than that," Pa assured her.

At home, Ma said that no doubt it would be all right. "Now don't fret! Forget about it until you hear the results of the examinations."

Ma's advice was always good, but Laura repeated it to herself every day and almost every hour. She went to sleep telling herself: "Don't worry," and woke up thinking with dread: The letter may come today.

At school, Florence had no hope for either of them. "It was too hard," she said. "I'm sure only a few of the oldest teachers passed it."

A week went by, with no word. Laura hardly expected Almanzo to come that Sunday, for Royal was sick with the grippe. Almanzo did not come. There was no letter on Monday. There was no letter on Tuesday.

A warm wind had melted the snow to slush and the sun was shining, so on Wednesday Pa did not come for Laura. She and Carrie and Grace walked home. The letter was there; Pa had got it that morning.

"What does it say, Ma?" Laura cried as she dropped her coat and crossed the room to pick up the letter.

"Why, Laura!" Ma said in astonishment. "You know I'd no more look at another person's letter than I'd steal."

With shaking fingers Laura tore the envelope and took out a teacher's certificate. It was a second-grade one.

"It's better than I expected," she told Ma. "The most I hoped for was third grade. Now if I can only have the good luck to get the right school!"

"A body makes his own luck, be it good or bad," Ma placidly said. "I have no doubt you will get as good as you deserve."

Laura had no doubt that she would get as good a school as she could get, but she wondered how to make herself the good luck to get the one she wanted. She thought about little else that night, and she was still thinking about it next morning when Florence came into the schoolroom and came directly to her.

"Did you pass, Laura?" she asked.

"Yes, I got a second-grade certificate," Laura answered.

"I didn't get any, so I can't teach our school," Florence said soberly, "but this is what I want to tell you: You tried to help me, and I would rather you taught our school than anyone else. If you want it, my father says you may have it. It is a three months' school, beginning the first of April, and it pays thirty dollars a month."

Laura could hardly get the breath to answer, "Oh, yes! I do want it."

"Father said, if you did, to come and see him and the board will sign the contract."

"I will be there tomorrow afternoon," Laura said. "Thank you, Florence, *so* much."

"Well, you have always been so nice to me, I am glad of a chance to pay some of it back," Florence told her.

Laura remembered what Ma had said about luck, and she thought to herself: "I believe we make most of our luck without intending to."

CHAPTER 27

School Days End

AT THE end of the last day of school in March, Laura gathered her books, and stacked them neatly on her slate. She looked around the schoolroom for the last time. She would never come back. Monday she would begin teaching the Wilkins school, and sometime next fall she and Almanzo would be married.

Carrie and Grace were waiting downstairs, but Laura lingered at her desk, feeling a strange sinking of heart. Ida and Mary Power and Florence would be here next week. Carrie and Grace would walk to school without her, always after this.

Except for Mr. Owen at his desk, the room was empty now. Laura must go. She picked up her books and went toward the door. At Mr. Owen's desk she stopped and said, "I must tell you good-by, for I shall not be coming back."

"I heard you were going to teach again," Mr. Owen said. "We will miss you, but we will look for you back next fall."

"That is what I want to tell you. This is good-by," Laura repeated. "I am going to be married, so I won't be coming back at all."

Mr. Owen sprang up and walked nervously across the platform and back. "I'm sorry," he said. "Not sorry you are going to be married, but sorry I didn't graduate you this spring. I held you back because I . . . because I had a foolish pride; I wanted to graduate the whole class together, and some weren't ready. It was not fair to you. I'm sorry."

"It doesn't matter," Laura said. "I am glad to know I could have graduated."

Then they shook hands, and Mr. Owen said good-by and wished her good fortune in all her undertakings.

As Laura went down the stairs she thought: "The last time always seems sad, but it isn't really. The end of one thing is only the beginning of another."

After Sunday night supper at home, Almanzo and Laura drove through town and northwest toward the Wilkins' claim. It was three and a half miles from town, and Barnum walked. The twilight deepened into night. Stars came out in the vastness of the sky and the prairie stretched dim and mysterious far away. The buggy wheels turned softly on the grassy road.

In the stillness Laura began to sing:

The stars are rolling in the sky,
The earth rolls on below,
And we can feel the rattling wheel
Revolving as we go;
Then tread away my gallant boys,
And make the axle fly!
Why should not wheels go round-about,
Like planets in the sky?

Almanzo laughed aloud. "Your songs are like your father's! They always fit."

"That is from the 'Old Song of the Treadmill,'" Laura told him. "But it did seem to fit the stars and buggy wheels."

"There's only one word wrong in it," Almanzo agreed. "No buggy wheels of mine will ever rattle. I keep 'em tight and greased. But never mind. When the wheels roll around in this direction for three months more, you will be through teaching school, for good!"

"I suppose you mean, for better or worse," Laura said demurely. "But it better be for good."

"It will be," Almanzo said.

CHAPTER 28

The Cream-Colored Hat

THE new schoolhouse stood on a corner of Mr. Wilkins' claim, only a little way from his house. When Laura opened its door on Monday morning, she saw that it was an exact replica of the Perry schoolhouse, even to the dictionary on the desk, and the nail in the wall for her sunbonnet.

This was a happy omen, she thought; and it was. All her days in that school were pleasant. She felt herself a capable teacher now, and she dealt so well with every little difficulty that none ever lasted until the next day. Her pupils were friendly and obedient, and the little ones were often funny, though she kept her smiles unseen.

She boarded at the Wilkins', and they were all friendly to Laura and pleasant to each other. Florence still went to school and at night told Laura all the day's happenings. Laura shared Florence's room, and they spent the evenings cosily there with their books.

On the last Friday in April, Mr. Wilkins paid Laura twenty-two dollars, her first month's salary, less two dollars a week for her board. Almanzo drove her home that evening, and next day she went with Ma to town to buy materials. They bought bleached muslin for underwear, chemises and drawers, petticoats and nightgowns; two of each. "These, with what you have, should be plenty," said Ma. They bought stronger, bleached muslin, for two pairs of sheets and two pairs of pillow cases.

For Laura's summer dress they bought ten yards of delicate pink lawn with small flowers and pale green leaves scattered over it. Then they went to Miss Bell's to find a hat to go with the dress.

There were several beautiful hats, but Laura knew at once which one she wanted. It was a fine, cream-colored straw with a narrow brim, rolled narrower at the sides. The brim in front came down over the middle of Laura's forehead. Around the crown was a band of satin ribbon a little darker than the straw, and three ostrich tips stood straight up at the crown's left side.

They were shaded in color, from the light cream of the straw to slightly darker than the satin ribbon. The hat was held on the head by a fine, white silk elastic cord that scarcely showed because it fitted under the mass of Laura's braided hair.

As they walked up the street after they had bought that hat, Laura begged Ma to take five dollars and spend it for herself.

"No, Laura," Ma refused. "You are a good girl to think of it, but there is nothing that I need."

So they came to the wagon, waiting for them in front of Fuller's hardware store. Something bulky stood in the wagon box, covered with a horse blanket. Laura wondered what it was, but she had no time to look, for Pa untied the horses quickly and they all started home.

"What have you got in back, Charles?" Ma asked.

"I can't show you now, Caroline. Wait until we get home," Pa answered.

At home he stopped the wagon close to the house door. "Now, girls," he said, "take your own packages in, but leave mine alone until I get back from putting up the horses. Don't you peek under the blanket either!"

He unhitched the horses and hurried them away.

"Now whatever can that be?" Ma said to Laura. They waited. As soon as possible, Pa came hurrying back. He lifted the blanket away, and there stood a shining new sewing machine.

"Oh, Charles!" Ma gasped.

"Yes, Caroline, it is yours," Pa said proudly. "There'll be a lot of extra sewing, with Mary coming home and Laura going away, and I thought you'd need some help."

"But how could you?" Ma asked, touching the shiny black iron of the machine's legs.

"I had to sell a cow anyway, Caroline; there wouldn't be room in the stable next winter unless I did," Pa explained. "Now if you will help me unload this thing, we will take its cover off and see how it looks."

A long time ago, Laura remembered, a tone in Ma's voice when she spoke of a sewing machine had made Laura think that she wanted one. Pa had remembered that.

He took the endgate out of the wagon, and he and Ma and Laura lifted the sewing machine carefully down and carried it into the sitting room, while Carrie and Grace hovered around excitedly. Then Pa lifted the box-cover of the machine and they stood in silent admiration.

"It is beautiful," Ma said at last, "and what a help it will be. I can hardly wait to use it." But this was late on Saturday afternoon. The sewing machine must stand still over Sunday.

Next week Ma studied the instruction book and learned to run the machine, and the next Saturday she and Laura began to work on the lawn dress. The lawn was so crisp and fresh, the colors so dainty, that Laura was afraid to cut it lest she make a mistake, but Ma had made so many dresses that she did not hesitate. She took Laura's measurements; then, with her dressmaker chart, she made the pattern for the waist, and fearlessly cut the lawn.

They made the waist tight-fitting, with two clusters of tucks down the back, and two in front. Down the center of the front, between the tucks, tiny, white pearl buttons buttoned the waist. The collar was a straight, upstanding fold of the lawn; the sleeves were long, gathered at the shoulders and close-fitting to the waist, finished with a hem the width of the tucks.

The skirt was gathered very full all round into a narrow waistband, which buttoned over the bottom of the waist to secure them from slipping apart. All down the full skirt, tucks went around and around it, spaced evenly a little way apart, and beneath the bottom tuck was a full-gathered ruffle four inches wide that just touched Laura's shoe tips.

This dress was finished when Almanzo brought Laura home on the last Friday in May.

"Oh! it is pretty, Ma!" Laura said when she saw it. "All those tucks are so even, and stitched so beautifully."

"I declare," said Ma, "I don't know how we ever got along without that sewing machine. It does the work so easily; tucking is no trouble at all. And such beautiful stitching. The best of seamstresses could not possibly equal it by hand."

Laura was silent a moment, looking at her new, machine-stitched dress. Then she said, "Mr. Wilkins paid me another month's salary today, and I really don't need it. I have fifteen dollars left of my April pay. I will need a new dress for next fall . . ."

"Yes, and you will need a nice wedding dress," Ma interrupted.

"Fifteen dollars ought to buy the two," Laura considered. "They, with the clothes I have, will be enough for a long time. Besides, I will have another twenty-two dollars next month. I wish you and Pa would take this fifteen dollars. Please, Ma. Use it to pay for Mary's visit home, or to buy the clothes she needs."

"We can manage without taking the money for your last term of school," Ma said quietly.

"I know you can, but there are so many things for you and Pa to manage. I would like to help again just this once. Then I would feel all right about going away and not helping any more, and having all these nice clothes for myself," Laura urged.

Ma yielded. "If it will please you to do so, give the money to your Pa. Since he spent the cow money for the sewing machine, he will be glad to have it, I know."

Pa was surprised and objected that Laura would need the money herself. But when she explained and urged again, he took it gladly. "It will help me out of a pinch," he admitted. "But this is the last one. From now on I think we will have clear sailing. The town is growing so fast that I am going to have plenty of carpenter work. The cattle are growing fast, too. Beats all how they multiply, and they live off the homestead, and next year I win my bet with Uncle Sam and this homestead will be ours. So you need never worry about helping any more, Half-Pint. You have done your share and then some."

When she drove away with Almanzo that Sunday evening, Laura's heart was brimming with contentment. But it seemed that always there must be some wish unsatisfied. Now she regretted that she would miss Mary's coming home. Mary was coming that week, and Laura would be teaching a class in fractions in Wilkins' school when Mary came.

On Friday afternoon, Almanzo drove Prince and Lady, and they trotted fast all the way home. As they came near the door of home, Laura heard the music of the organ. Before Almanzo stopped the horses she was out of the buggy and running into the house.

"See you Sunday," he called after her, and she fluttered her ringed hand in answer. Then she was giving Mary a big hug before she could get up from the organ stool, and the first thing Mary said was, "Oh, Laura! I was so surprised to find the organ waiting here for me."

"We had to keep the secret a long time," Laura answered, "But it didn't spoil by keeping, did it? Oh, Mary, let me look at you. How well you're looking!"

Mary was even more beautiful than ever. Laura would never grow tired of looking at her. And now there was so much to tell each other that they talked every moment. Sunday afternoon they walked once more to the top of the low hill beyond the stable, and Laura picked wild roses to fill Mary's arms.

"Laura," Mary asked soberly, "do you really want to leave home to marry that Wilder boy?"

Laura was serious, too. "He isn't that Wilder boy any more, Mary. He is Almanzo. You don't know anything about him, do you? or not much since the Hard Winter."

"I remember his going after the wheat, of course. But why do you want to leave home and go with him?" Mary persisted.

"I guess it's because we just seem to belong together," Laura said. "Besides, I have practically left home anyway; I am away so much. I won't be any further away than I am at Wilkins'."

"Oh, well, I guess it has to be that way. I went away to college, and now you're going away. That's growing up, I suppose."

"It's strange to think," Laura said. "Carrie and Grace are older now than we used to be. They are growing up, too. Yet it would be even stranger if we stayed as we were for always, wouldn't it?"

"There he is coming now," said Mary. She had heard the buggy and Prince's and Lady's hoofs, and no one could have guessed that she was blind, to see her beautiful blue eyes turned toward them as if she saw them. "I've hardly seen you," she said. "And now you have to go."

"Not till after supper. I'll be back next Friday, and besides, we'll have all July and most of August together," Laura reminded her.

At four o'clock on the last Friday in June, Almanzo drove Barnum and Skip up to the Wilkins' door to take Laura home. As they drove along the familiar road, he said, "And so another school is finished, the last one."

"Are you sure?" Laura replied demurely.

"Aren't we?" he asked. "You will be frying my breakfast pancakes sometime along the last of September."

"Or maybe a little later," Laura promised. He had already begun to build the house on the tree claim.

"In the meantime, how about the Fourth of July? Do you want to go to the celebration?"

"I'd much rather go for a drive," Laura answered.

"Suits me!" he agreed. "This team's getting too frisky again. I've been working on the house and they've had a few days' rest. It's time we took the ginger out of them on some more of those long drives."

"Any time! I'm free now." Laura was gay. She felt like a bird out of a cage.

"We'll have the first long drive on the Fourth, then," said Almanzo.

So on the Fourth, soon after dinner, Laura put on her new lawn dress for the first time, and for the first time she wore the cream-colored hat with the shaded ostrich tips. She was ready when Almanzo came.

Barnum and Skip stood for her to get into the buggy, but they were nervous and in a hurry to go. "The crowd excited them, coming through town," Almanzo said. "We will only go to the end of Main Street, where you can see the flags, then we will go south, away from the noise."

The road south toward Brewster's was so changed that it hardly seemed to be the same road that they had traveled so many times to Laura's first school. New claim shanties and some houses were scattered over the prairie, and there were many fields of growing grain. Cattle and horses were feeding along the way.

Instead of being white with blowing snow, the prairie was many shades of soft green, but the wind still blew. It came from the south and was warm; it blew the wild grass and the grain in the fields; it blew the horses' manes and tails streaming behind them; it blew the fringes of the lap robe that was tucked in tightly to protect Laura's delicate lawn dress. And it blew the lovely, cream-colored ostrich feathers off Laura's hat.

She caught them with the very tips of her fingers as they were being whirled away. "Oh! Oh!" she exclaimed in vexation. "It must be they were not sewed on well."

"Miss Bell hasn't been in the West long enough yet," Almanzo said. "She is not used to prairie winds. Better let me put those feathers in my pocket before you lose them."

It was suppertime when they came home, and Almanzo stayed to help eat the cold remains of the Fourth of July dinner. There was plenty of cold chicken and pie; there was a cake and a pitcher of lemonade made with fresh, cold water from the well.

At supper Almanzo proposed that Carrie go with him and Laura to see the fireworks in town. "The horses have had such a long drive that I think they will behave," he said, but Ma replied, "Of course Laura will go if she wishes; she is used to circus horses. But Carrie better not." So Laura and Almanzo went.

They kept the horses well outside the crowd, so that no one would be trampled or run over. In an open space at a safe distance they sat in the buggy and waited until a streak of fire rose in the darkness above the crowd and exploded a star.

At the first flash Barnum reared and Skip leaped. They came down running, and the buggy came down and ran after them. Almanzo swung them in a wide circle, bringing them to face the fireworks again just as another star exploded.

"Don't bother about the horses," he told Laura. "I'll manage them. You watch the fireworks."

So Laura did. After each explosion of beauty against the darkness, Almanzo drove the circle, always bringing Barnum and Skip around in time to face the next rush and blossom of fire. Not until the last shower of sparks had faded did Almanzo and Laura drive away.

Then Laura said, "It is really a good thing that you have my feathers in your pocket. If they had been on my hat while I was watching the fireworks, they would have been twisted off, we whirled so fast."

"Are they in my pocket yet?" Almanzo exclaimed in surprise.

"I hope so," said Laura. "If they are, I can sew them on my hat again."

The feathers were still in his pocket, and as he handed them to her at home he said, "I will be by for you Sunday. These horses do need exercise."

CHAPTER 29

Summer Storm

THE heat was intense that week, and in church on Sunday morning Laura gasped for air. Shimmering heat waves quivered upward outside the windows, and the fitful little breezes were hot.

When church was over, Almanzo was waiting outside to take Laura home. As he helped her into the buggy he said, "Your mother asked me to dinner, and afterward we will exercise these horses again. It will be hot this afternoon," he said in the buggy, "but driving will be pleasanter than sitting in the house, if it doesn't storm."

"My feathers are sewed on tight," Laura laughed. "So let the wind blow."

Soon after Ma's good Sunday dinner, they set out, driving southward over the gently rolling, endless prairie. The sun shone fiercely, and even in the shade of the swiftly moving buggy top, the heat was oppressive. Instead of flowing smoothly and cool, the breeze came in warm puffs.

The shimmering heat-waves made a silvery appearance that retreated before them on the road ahead, like water, and phantom winds played in the grasses, twisting them in frantic writhings and passing on, up and away.

After a time, dark clouds began to gather in the northwest, and the heat grew still more intense.

"This is a queer afternoon. I think we'd better go home," Almanzo said.

"Yes, let's do, and hurry," Laura urged. "I don't like the way the weather feels."

The black mass of clouds was rising quickly as Almanzo turned the horses toward home. He stopped them and gave the reins to Laura. "Hold them while I put on the buggy curtains. It's going to rain," he said.

Quickly, behind the buggy, he unbuttoned the straps that held the top's back curtain rolled up. He let it unroll, and buttoned it at the sides and bottom, tightly closing in the back of the buggy. Then from under the seat he brought out the two side curtains, and buttoned them along their tops and sides to the sides of the buggy top, closing them in.

Then, back in his seat, he unrolled the rubber storm apron, and set the pleat in its bottom edge over the top of the dashboard, where it fitted snugly.

Laura admired the cleverness of this storm apron. There was a slot in it that fitted over the whipsocket, so the whip stood up in its place. There was a slit, through which Almanzo passed the lines; he could hold them in his hands under the storm apron, and a flap fell over the slit, to keep rain from coming in. The apron was so wide that it came down to the buggy box on either side, and it buttoned up to the side frames of the buggy top.

All this was done quickly. In a moment or two, Laura and Almanzo were snugly sheltered in a box of rubber curtains. No rain could come through the apron, the curtains, nor the buggy top overhead. Above the edge of the storm apron, that was as high as their chins, they could look out.

As Almanzo took the lines from Laura and started the horses, he said, "Now let it rain!"

"Yes," Laura said, "if it must, but maybe we can beat the storm home."

Almanzo was already urging the team. They went swiftly, but even more swiftly the black cloud rose, rolling and rumbling in the sky. Laura and Almanzo watched it in silence. The whole earth seemed silent and motionless in terror. The sound of the horses' fast-trotting feet and the tiny creaks of the speeding buggy seemed small in the stillness.

The swelling great mass of clouds writhed and wrestled, twisting together as if in fury and agony. Flickers of red lightning stabbed through them. Still the air was motionless and there was no sound. The heat increased. Laura's bangs were damp with perspiration, and uncurled on her forehead, while trickles ran down her cheeks and her neck. Almanzo urged on the horses.

Almost overhead now, the tumbling, swirling clouds changed from black to a terrifying greenish-purple. They seemed to draw themselves together, then a groping finger slowly came out of them and stretched down, trying to reach the earth. It reached, and pulled itself up, and reached again.

"How far away is that?" Laura asked.

"Ten miles, I'd say," Almanzo replied.

It was coming toward them, from the northwest, as they sped toward the northeast. No horses, however fast they ran, could outrun the speed of those clouds. Green-purple, they rolled in the sky above the helpless prairie, and reached toward it playfully as a cat's paw torments a mouse.

A second point came groping down, behind the first. Then another. All three reached and withdrew and reached again, down from the writhing clouds.

Then they all turned a little toward the south. One after another, quickly, all three points touched the earth, under the cloud-mass and traveling swiftly with it. They passed behind the buggy, to the west, and went on southward. A terrific wind blew suddenly, so strong that the buggy swayed, but that storm had passed. Laura drew a long, shaking breath.

"If we had been home, Pa would have sent us down cellar," she said. "And I would have been glad to go," she added.

"We'd have needed a cellar, if that storm had come our way. I never did run to a cyclone cellar, but if I ever meet a cloud like that, I will," Almanzo admitted.

The wind abruptly changed. It blew from the southwest and brought a sudden cold with it.

"Hail," Almanzo said.

"Yes," said Laura. Somewhere, hail had fallen from that cloud.

Everyone at home was glad to see them. Laura had never seen Ma so pale, nor so thankful. Pa said that they had shown good judgment in turning back when they did. "That storm is doing bad damage," he said.

"It's a good idea, out here in this country, to have a cellar," said Almanzo. He asked what Pa thought of their driving out across country, where the storm had passed, to see if anyone needed help. So Laura was left at home, while Pa and Almanzo drove away.

Though the storm was gone and the sky now clear, still they were nervous.

The afternoon passed, and Laura had changed into her weekday clothes and with Carrie's help had done the chores, before Pa and Almanzo came back. Ma set a cold supper on the table, and while they ate they told what they had seen in the path of the storm.

One settler not far south of town had just finished threshing his wheat crop from a hundred acres. It had been a splendid crop, that would have paid all his debts and left money in the bank. He and the threshers had been working that day to finish the job, and he was on a strawstack when they saw the storm coming.

He had just sent his two young boys to return a wagon he had borrowed from a neighbor to help in the threshing. He got into his cyclone cellar just in time. The storm carried away his grain, strawstacks and machinery, wagons, stables and house; everything. Nothing was left but his bare claim.

The two boys on the mules had disappeared completely. But just before Pa and Almanzo reached the place, the older boy had come back, stark naked. He was nine years old. He said that he and his brother were riding the mules home, running, when the storm struck them. It lifted them all together and carried them around in a circle, in the air, still harnessed together side by side. They were whirled around, faster and faster and higher, until he began to get dizzy and he shouted to his little brother to hold on tight to his mule. Just then the air filled thickly with whirling straw and darkened so that he could see nothing. He felt a jerk of the harness breaking apart, and then he must have fainted. For the next thing he knew, he was alone in clear air.

He could see the ground beneath him. He was being carried around in a circle, all the time sinking a little, until finally he was not far above the earth. He tried to spring up, to get his feet under him, then struck the ground running, ran a little way, and fell. After lying there a few moments to rest, he got up and made his way home.

He had come to the ground a little more than a mile from his father's claim. There was not a shred of clothing left on him; even his high, laced boots had disappeared, but he was not hurt at all. It was a mystery how his boots had been taken from his feet without so much as bruising them.

Neighbors were searching far and wide for the other boy and the mules, but not a trace could be found of them. There could be hardly a hope that they were alive.

"Still, if that door came through," Almanzo said.

"What door?" Carrie wanted to know.

That was the strangest thing that Pa and Almanzo had seen that day. It happened at another settler's claim, farther south. Everything had been stripped clean off his place, too. When this man and his family came up from their cyclone cellar, two bare spots were all that were left of stable and house. Oxen, wagon, tools, chickens, everything was gone. They had nothing but the clothes they wore, and one quilt that his wife had snatched to wrap around the baby in the cellar.

This man said to Pa, "I'm a lucky man; I didn't have a crop to lose." They had moved onto their claim only that spring, and he had been able to put in only a few sod potatoes.

That afternoon about sunset, as Pa and Almanzo were coming back from searching for the lost boy, they came by this place and stopped for a moment. The homesteader and his family had been gathering boards and bits of lumber that the storm had dropped, and he was figuring how much more he would have to get to build them some kind of shelter.

While they stood considering this, one of the children noticed a small dark object high in the clear sky overhead. It did not look like a bird, but it appeared to be growing larger. They all watched it. For some time it fell slowly toward them, and they saw that it was a door. It came gently down before them. It was the front door of this man's vanished claim shanty.

It was in perfect condition, not injured at all, not even scratched. The wonder was, where it had been all those hours, and that it had come slowly down from a clear sky, directly over the place where the claim shanty had been.

"I never saw a man more chirked up than he was," said Pa. "Now he doesn't have to buy a door for his new shanty. It even came back with the hinges on it."

They were all amazed. In all their lives, none of them had ever heard of a stranger thing than the return of that door. It was awesome to think how far or how high it must have gone in air during all those hours.

"It's a queer country out here," Pa said. "Strange things happen."

"Yes," said Ma. "I'm thankful that so far they don't happen to us."

That next week Pa heard in town that the bodies of the lost boy and the mules had been found the next day. Every bone in them was broken. The clothing had been stripped from the boy and the harness from the mules. No scrap of clothing or harness was ever found.

CHAPTER 30

Sunset on the Hill

ONE Sunday Laura did not go driving, for it was Mary's last day at home. She was going back to college next day.

The weather was so very warm that at breakfast Ma said she believed she would not go to church. Carrie and Grace would stay at home with her, while Laura and Mary went with Pa in the wagon.

Pa was waiting for them when they came from the bedroom, ready to go.

Laura wore again her sprigged, pale pink lawn dress and her new hat with the ostrich tips now sewed on tightly.

Mary's dress was a blue lawn with small white flowers scattered over it. Her hat was a white straw sailor with a blue ribbon band. Beneath its brim in back of her hair was a great mass of twisted gold, and golden bangs curled richly on her forehead, above her eyes as blue as her ribbons.

Pa looked at them for a moment. His eyes shone and his voice was proud as he exclaimed in mock dismay, "Jerusalem Crickets, Caroline! I'm not spruce enough to beau two such fine-looking young ladies to church!"

He looked nice, too, in his black suit with the black velvet collar on the coat, his white shirt and dark blue tie.

The wagon was waiting. Before he dressed Pa had combed and brushed the two farm horses and spread a clean horse blanket on the wagon seat. The team drowsed while Pa carefully helped Mary up over the wheel, then gave his hand to Laura. Over their laps they spread the light dust robe and carefully Laura tucked its edge well around her full-gathered tucked lawn skirt. Then in the sunshine and the hot wind, slowly they rode to church.

It was so crowded that morning that they could not find three empty places together. So Pa went forward to sit with the graybeards in the amen corner, while Laura and Mary sat side by side near the middle of the church.

Reverend Brown was preaching earnestly and Laura was

wishing that with so much sincerity he could say something interesting, when she saw a small plump kitten straying up the aisle. Idly she watched it pounce and play, until it wandered onto the platform and stood arching its back and rubbing against the side of the pulpit. As its round, kitten eyes looked at the congregation, Laura believed she could hear its purring.

Then, at her side in the aisle, a small dog passed, trotting briskly. It was a little black-and-tan, with slender legs and a perky short tail, and its quick, business-like trot was natural to it. It was not seeking anyone nor going anywhere, but merely sight-seeing in the church, until it spied the kitten. For an instant the little dog stiffened, then with a firecracker explosion of shrill yaps, it leaped.

The kitten's back rose in an arch, its tail swelled, and in a flash it vanished from Laura's view.

The strange thing was that it seemed to vanish utterly. There was no chase, and the little dog was silent. Reverend Brown went on preaching. Laura barely had time to wonder, when she felt a slight swaying of her hoops, and looking down she saw the tip of the kitten's tail slide out of sight beneath the pink lawn ruffle.

The kitten had taken refuge under her hoops, and now it began climbing up inside of them, clutching and clawing its way from wire to wire. Laura felt an impulse to laugh, but she controlled it and sat solemn as a judge. Then the little dog passed anxiously, peering and sniffing in search of the kitten, and a sudden vision of what would happen if he found it made Laura shake from head to foot with suppressed laughter.

She could feel her ribs swelling against her corsets and her cheeks puffing out and her throat choking. Mary did not know what amused Laura, but felt that she was laughing and pushed her elbow against Laura's side, whispering, "Behave yourself."

Laura shook all the harder and felt her face growing purple. Her hoops kept swaying under her skirts as the kitten cautiously crept down them again. Its little whiskered nose and eyes peeped from beneath the pink ruffle, then, seeing nothing of the dog, it popped out suddenly and scampered down the aisle toward the door. Laura listened, but she heard no yapping so she knew that the kitten had escaped.

On the way home Mary said, "Laura, I am surprised at you. Will you never learn to behave yourself properly in church?"

Laura laughed until she cried, while Mary still sat disapproving and Pa wanted to know what had happened.

"No, Mary, I never will," Laura said at last, wiping her eyes. "You might as well give me up as a hopeless case." Then she told them, and even Mary had to smile.

Sunday dinner and the afternoon passed quietly in family talk, and when the sun was sinking Mary and Laura took their last walk together to the top of the low hill to see the sunset.

"I never see things so well with anyone else," Mary said. "And when I come again you will not be here."

"No, but you will come to see me where I am," Laura answered. "There will be two homes for you to visit."

"But these sunsets . . ." Mary began, and Laura interrupted.

"The sun will set on Almanzo's farm, too, I hope," she teased. "There is no little hill there, but there are ten whole acres of little trees. We shall walk among them and you shall see them. There are cottonwoods, of course, but besides, there are box elders and maples and willows. If they live, they will be a beautiful grove. Not just a windbreak around the house, like Pa's, but a real little woods."

"It will be strange, to see these prairies wooded," Mary said.

"Everything changes," said Laura.

"Yes." They were silent a little while, then Mary said, "I wish I could be at your wedding. Don't you want to put it off till next June?"

Slowly Laura answered, "No, Mary. I'm eighteen now and I've taught three terms of school, that's one more than Ma taught. I don't want to teach any more. I want to be settled this winter in our own home.

"It will be just the ceremony, anyway," she added. "Pa could not afford a wedding and I would not want the folks to go to any expense. When you come back next summer my house will be all ready for you to visit me in."

"Laura," Mary said. "I'm sorry about the organ. If I'd known . . . but I did want to see Blanche's home, too, and it was near, and saved Pa the cost of my railroad journey, and I didn't realize that anything would ever change, here at home. I felt it was always here, to come back to."

"It really is, Mary," Laura told her. "And don't feel bad at all about the organ. Just remember what a nice time you had at Blanche's. I am glad you went, truly I am, and so is Ma. She said so at the time."

"Did she?" Mary's face lighted. Then Laura told her what Ma had said of being glad that she was having good times while she was young, to remember. The sun was sinking now, and she told how its glory of crimson and gold flamed upon the sky and faded to rose and gray.

"Let's go back to the house now," Mary said. "I can feel the change in the air."

They stood a moment longer with hands clasped, facing the west, then slowly they walked down the slope past the stable.

"Time passes so quickly now," said Mary. "Do you remember when the winter was so long, it seemed that summer would never come. And then in summertime, winter was so long ago we almost forgot what it was like?"

"Yes, and what good times we had when we were little," Laura answered. "But maybe the times that are coming will be even better. You never know."

CHAPTER 31

Wedding Plans

AS ALWAYS, Mary's going away made an emptiness in the house. The next morning Ma said briskly, "We will get at your sewing now, Laura. Busy hands are a great help to being cheerful."

So Laura brought the muslins, Ma cut them out, and the airy sitting room filled with the sewing machine's hum and the busy cheerfulness of Ma's and Laura's sewing together.

"I have an idea for making the sheets," said Laura. "I'm not going to sew those long seams down the middle with over-and-over stitch by hand. If I lap the edges flat and sew with the machine down the center, I do believe they'll be smooth enough and even more serviceable."

"It may well be," said Ma. "Our grandmothers would turn in their graves, but after all, these are modern times."

All the white sewing was quickly done on the machine. Laura brought out the dozens of yards of white thread lace that she had knitted and crocheted, and like magic the machine's flashing needle stitched the lace edgings to the open ends of the pillow cases, the throats and wrists of the high-necked, long-sleeved nightgowns, the necks and armholes of the chemises, and the leg-bands of the drawers.

Busily working with the white goods, Ma and Laura discussed Laura's dresses.

"My brown poplin openwork dress is good as new," Laura said. "And my pink sprigged lawn *is* new. What more do I need?"

"You need a black dress," Ma answered decisively. "I think every woman should have one nice black dress. We'd better go to town Saturday and get the goods. A cashmere, I think. Cashmere wears well, and it is always dressy for all but the very hottest days of summer. Then when that dress is out of the way, you must get something pretty for your wedding."

"There will be plenty of time," Laura said. In the rush of summer work, Almanzo had little time to work on the house.

He had taken Ma and Laura one Sunday to see its skeleton of studding standing by the piles of lumber, back from the road behind the grove of little sapling trees.

There were to be three rooms, the large room, a bedroom, and a pantry, with a lean-to over the back door besides. But after Laura had seen how these were planned, Almanzo did not take her to look at the house again. "Leave it to me," he said. "I'll get a roof over it before snow flies."

So they made their long Sunday drives to the twin lakes or to Spirit Lake and beyond.

On Monday morning Ma unfolded the soft lengths of sooty black cashmere and carefully fitting the newspaper pattern pieces to the goods so that none would be wasted, she cut confidently with her large shears. She cut out and pinned together all the skirt gores, the bodice pieces, and the sleeves. After dinner the sewing machine was threaded with black, and started.

It was humming steadily, late that afternoon, and Laura was basting the pieces of cambric lining to the cashmere pieces, when she looked up from her work and saw Almanzo driving up to the house. Something had happened, she was sure, or he would not come on Tuesday. She hurried to the door, and he said, "Come for a little drive. I want to talk to you."

Putting on her sunbonnet, Laura went with him.

"What is it?" she asked as Barnum and Skip trotted away.

"It is just this," Almanzo said earnestly. "Do you want a big wedding?"

She looked at him in amazement, that he should have come to ask her that, when they would see each other next Sunday. "Why do you ask?" she inquired.

"If you don't, would you be willing and could you be ready to be married the last of this week, or the first of next?" he asked even more anxiously. "Don't answer till I tell you why. When I was back in Minnesota last winter, my sister Eliza started planning a big church wedding for us. I told her we didn't want it, and to give up the idea. This morning I got a letter; she has not changed her mind. She is coming out here with my mother, to take charge of our wedding."

"Oh, *no!*" Laura said.

"You know Eliza," said Almanzo. "She's headstrong, and she always was bossy, but I could handle this, if it was only Eliza.

My mother's different, she's more like your mother; you'll like her. But Eliza's got Mother's heart set on our having a big church wedding, and if they are here before we're married, I don't see how I can tell Mother, 'No.' I don't want that kind of a wedding, and I can't afford what it would cost me. What do you think about it?"

There was a little silence while Laura thought. Then she said quietly, "Pa can't afford to give me that kind of a wedding, either. I would like a little longer to get my things made. If we are married so soon I won't have a wedding dress."

"Wear the one you have on. It is pretty," Almanzo urged.

Laura could not help laughing. "This is a calico work dress. I couldn't possibly!" Then she sobered, "But Ma and I are making one that I could wear."

"Then will you, say the last of this week?"

Laura was silent again. Then she summoned all her courage and said, "Almanzo, I must ask you something. Do you want me to promise to obey you?"

Soberly he answered, "Of course not. I know it is in the wedding ceremony, but it is only something that women say. I never knew one that did it, nor any decent man that wanted her to."

"Well, I am not going to say I will obey you," said Laura.

"Are you for woman's rights, like Eliza?" Almanzo asked in surprise.

"No," Laura replied. "I do not want to vote. But I can not make a promise that I will not keep, and, Almanzo, even if I tried, I do not think I could obey anybody against my better judgment."

"I'd never expect you to," he told her. "And there will be no difficulty about the ceremony, because Reverend Brown does not believe in using the word 'obey.' "

"He doesn't! Are you sure?" Laura had never been so surprised and so relieved, all at once.

"He feels very strongly about it," Almanzo said. "I have heard him arguing for hours and quoting Bible texts against St. Paul, on that subject. You know he is a cousin of John Brown of Kansas, and a good deal like him. Will it be all right, then? The last of this week, or early next?"

"Yes, if it is the only way to escape a big wedding," said

Laura, "I will be ready the last of this week or the first of next, whichever you say."

"If I can get the house finished, we'll say the last of this week," Almanzo considered. "If not, it will have to be next week. Let's say when the house is finished we will just drive to Reverend Brown's and be married quietly without any fuss. I'll take you home now and I may have time to get in a few more licks on the house yet tonight."

At home again, Laura hesitated to tell of the plan. She felt that Ma would think the haste unseemly. Ma might say, "Marry in haste, repent at leisure." Yet they were not really marrying in haste. They had been going together for three years.

It was not until suppertime that Laura found courage to say that she and Almanzo had planned to be married so soon.

"We can't possibly get you a wedding dress made," Ma objected.

"We can finish the black cashmere and I will wear that," Laura answered.

"I do not like to think of your being married in black," said Ma. "You know they say, 'Married in black, you'll wish yourself back.' "

"It will be new. I will wear my old sage-green poke bonnet with the blue silk lining, and borrow your little square gold pin with the strawberry in it, so I'll be wearing something old and something new, something borrowed and something blue," Laura said cheerfully.

"I don't suppose there's any truth in these old sayings," Ma consented.

Pa said, "I think it is a sensible thing to do. You and Almanzo show good judgment."

But Ma was not wholly satisfied yet. "Let Reverend Brown come here. You can be married at home, Laura. We can have a nice little wedding here."

"No, Ma, we couldn't have any kind of a wedding and not wait to have Almanzo's mother here," Laura objected.

"Laura is right, and you think so yourself, Caroline," said Pa.

"Of course I do," Ma admitted.

CHAPTER 32

"Haste to the Wedding"

CARRIE and Grace eagerly offered to do all the housework, so that Ma and Laura could finish the cashmere, and every day that week they sewed as fast as they could.

They made a tight-fitting basque, pointed at the bottom back and front, lined with black cambric lining and boned with whalebones on every seam. It had a high collar of the cashmere. The sleeves were lined, too. They were long and plain and beautifully fitted, with a little fullness at the top but tight at the wrists. A shirring around each armhole, in front, made a graceful fullness over the breast, that was taken up by darts below. Small round black buttons buttoned the basque straight down the front.

The skirt just touched the floor all around. It fitted smoothly at the top, but was gored to fullness at the bottom. It was lined throughout with the cambric dress lining, and interlined with crinoline from the bottom to as high as Laura's shoes. The bottom of the skirt and the linings were turned under and the raw edges covered with dress braid, which Laura hemmed down by hand on both edges, so that no stitches showed on the right side.

There was no drive that Sunday. Almanzo came by for only a moment in his work clothes, to say that he was breaking the Sabbath by working on the house. It would be finished, he said, by Wednesday; so they could be married Thursday. He would come for Laura at ten o'clock Thursday morning, for the Reverend Brown was leaving town on the eleven o'clock train.

"Then better come over with your wagon, Wednesday, if you can make it, for Laura's things," Pa told him. Almanzo said he would, and so it was settled, and with a smile to Laura he drove quickly away.

Tuesday morning Pa drove to town, and at noon he came back bringing Laura a present of a new trunk. "Better put your things into it today," he said.

With Ma's help, Laura packed her trunk that afternoon. Her old rag doll, Charlotte, with all her clothes carefully packed in a cardboard box, she put in the very bottom. Laura's winter clothes were laid in next, then her sheets and pillow cases and towels, her new white clothes and calico dresses and her brown poplin. The pink lawn was carefully laid on top so that it would not be crushed. In the hatbox of the trunk's till, Laura put her new hat with the ostrich tips, and in the shallow till itself she had her knitting and crochet needles and worsted yarns.

Carrie brought Laura's glass box from the whatnot saying, "I know you want this."

Laura held the box in her hand, undecided. "I hate to take this box away from Mary's. They shouldn't be separated," she mused.

"See, I've moved my box closer to Mary's," Carrie showed her. "It doesn't look lonesome." So Laura put her box carefully in the trunk till, among the soft yarns, where it could not be broken.

The trunk was packed, and Laura shut down the lid. Then Ma spread a clean, old sheet across the bed. "You will want your quilt," she said.

Laura brought her Dove-in-the-Window quilt that she had pieced as a little girl while Mary pieced a nine-patch. It had been kept carefully all the years since then. Ma laid it, folded, on the sheet, and upon it she placed two large, plump pillows.

"I want you to have these, Laura," she said. "You helped me save the feathers from geese that Pa shot on Silver Lake. They are good as new; I have been saving them for you. This red-and-white-checked tablecloth is like those I have always had; I thought it might make the new home more homelike if you saw it on your table," and Ma laid the tablecloth, still in its paper wrapping, on the pillow. She drew the corners of the old sheet together over all, and tied them firmly. "There, that will keep the dust out," she said.

Almanzo came next morning with Barnum and Skip hitched to his wagon. He and Pa loaded the trunk and the pillow bundle into it. Then Pa said, "Wait a minute, don't hurry away, I'll be back," and he went into the house. For a moment or two all the others stood by the wagon, talking, and waiting for Pa to come from the door.

Then he came around the corner of the house, leading Laura's favorite young cow. She was fawn-colored all over, and gentle. Quietly Pa tied her behind the wagon, then threw her picket rope into the wagon as he said, "Her picket rope goes with her."

"Oh, Pa!" Laura cried. "Do you really mean I may take Fawn with me?"

"That is exactly what I do mean!" Pa said. "Be a pity if you couldn't have one calf out of all you have helped to raise."

Laura could not speak, but she gave Pa a look that thanked him.

"You think it is safe to tie her behind those horses?" Ma asked, and Almanzo assured her that it was safe, and said to Pa that he appreciated the gift of a cow.

Then turning to Laura he said, "I'll be over in the morning at ten o'clock."

"I will be ready," Laura promised, but as she stood watching Almanzo drive away, she was unable to realize that tomorrow she would leave home. Try as she would, she could not think of going away tomorrow as meaning that she would not come back, as she had always come back from drives with Almanzo.

That afternoon the finished black cashmere was carefully pressed, and then Ma made a big, white cake. Laura helped her by beating the egg whites on a platter with a fork, until Ma said they were stiff enough.

"My arm is stiffer," Laura ruefully laughed, rubbing her aching right arm.

"This cake must be just right," Ma insisted. "If you can't have a wedding party, at least you shall have a wedding dinner at home, and a wedding cake."

After supper that night, Laura brought Pa's fiddle to him, and asked, "Please, Pa, make some music."

Pa took the fiddle from the box. He was a long time tuning it; then he must resin the bow carefully. At last he poised the bow above the fiddle strings and cleared his throat. "What will you have, Laura?"

"Play for Mary first," Laura answered, "And then play all the old tunes, one after another, as long as you can."

She sat on the doorstep and just inside the door Pa and Ma sat looking out over the prairie while Pa played "Highland

Mary." Then while the sun was going down he played all the old tunes that Laura had known ever since she could remember.

The sun sank from sight, trailing bright banners after it. The colors faded, the land grew shadowy, the first star twinkled. Softly Carrie and Grace came to lean against Ma. The fiddle sang on in the twilight.

It sang the songs that Laura knew in the Big Woods of Wisconsin, and the tunes that Pa had played by the campfires all across the plains of Kansas. It repeated the nightingale's song in the moonlight on the banks of the Verdigris River, then it remembered the days in the dugout on the banks of Plum Creek, and the winter evenings in the new house that Pa had built there. It sang of the Christmas on Silver Lake, and of springtime after the long, Hard Winter.

Then the fiddle sounded a sweeter note and Pa's deep voice joined its singing.

Once in the dear dead days beyond recall
When on the world the mists began to fall,
Out of the dreams that rose in happy throng,
Low to our hearts love sang an old sweet song.
And in the dusk where fell the firelight gleam
Softly it wove itself into our dream.

Just a song at twilight, when the lights are low
And the flickering shadows softly come and go,
Though the heart be weary, sad the day and long,
Still to us at twilight comes love's old song,
Comes love's old sweet song.

Even today we hear of love's song of yore,
Deep in our hearts it swells forever more.
Footsteps may falter and weary grow the way,
Still we can hear it at the close of day,
So to the end when life's dim shadows fall,
Love will be found the sweetest song of all.

CHAPTER 33

Little Gray Home in the West

LAURA was ready when Almanzo came. She was wearing her new black cashmere dress and her sage-green poke bonnet with the blue lining and the blue ribbon bow tied under her left ear. The soft black tips of her shoes barely peeped from beneath her flaring skirt as she walked.

Ma herself had pinned her square gold brooch with the imbedded strawberry at Laura's throat, against the bit of white lace that finished the collar of her dress.

"There!" Ma said. "Even if your dress is black, you look perfect."

Gruffly Pa said, "You'll do, Half-Pint."

Carrie brought a fine white handkerchief, edged with lace matching the lace on Laura's collar. "I made it for you," she said. "It looks nice in your hand, against your black dress."

Grace just stood near and admired. Then Almanzo came, and they all watched at the door while Laura and Almanzo drove away.

Once Laura spoke. "Does Reverend Brown know we are coming?"

Almanzo said, "I saw him on my way over. He will not use the word, 'obey.' "

Mrs. Brown opened the sitting room door. Nervously she said that she would call Mr. Brown, and asked them to sit down. She went into the bedroom and closed the door.

Laura and Almanzo sat waiting. In the center of the sitting room a marble-topped table stood on a crocheted rag rug. On the wall was a large colored picture of a woman clinging to a white cross planted on a rock, with lightning streaking the sky above her and huge waves dashing high around her.

The door of the other bedroom opened and Ida slipped in and sat down in a chair near the door. She gave Laura a frightened smile and then twisted her handkerchief in her lap and looked at it.

The kitchen door opened and a tall, thin young man quietly

slipped into a chair. Laura supposed he was Elmer but she did not see him, for Reverend Brown came from the bedroom, thrusting his arms into his coat sleeves. He settled the coat collar to his neck and asked Laura and Almanzo to rise and stand before him.

So they were married.

Reverend Brown and Mrs. Brown and Elmer shook their hands, and Almanzo quietly handed Reverend Brown a folded bill. Reverend Brown unfolded it, and at first did not understand that Almanzo meant to give him all of ten dollars. Ida squeezed Laura's hand and tried to speak, but choked; quickly she kissed Laura, slipped a soft little package into her hand, and ran out of the room.

Laura and Almanzo came out into the sun and wind. He helped her into the buggy and untied the horses. They drove back through town. Dinner was ready when they came back. Ma and the girls had moved the table into the sitting room, between the open door and the open windows. They had covered it with the best white tablecloth and set it with the prettiest dishes. The silver spoons in the spoon holder shone in the center of the table and the steel knives and forks were polished until they were as bright.

As Laura hesitated shyly at the door, Carrie asked, "What's that in your hand?"

Laura looked down. She was holding in her hand with Carrie's handkerchief, the soft little package that Ida had given her. She said, "Why, I don't know. Ida gave it to me."

She opened the small tissue-paper package and unfolded the most beautiful piece of lace she had ever seen. It was a triangular fichu, of white silk lace, a pattern of lovely flowers and leaves.

"That will last you a lifetime, Laura," Ma said, and Laura knew that she would always keep and treasure this lovely thing that Ida had given her.

Then Almanzo came from stabling the horses, and they all sat down to dinner.

It was one of Ma's delicious dinners, but all the food tasted alike to Laura. Even the wedding cake was dry as sawdust in her mouth, for at last she realized that she was going away from home, that never would she come back to this home to stay. They all lingered at the table, for they knew that after dinner came the parting, but finally Almanzo said that it was time to go.

Laura put her bonnet on again, and went out to the buggy as Almanzo drove to the door. There were good-by kisses and good wishes, while he stood ready to help her into the buggy. But Pa took her hand.

"You'll help her from now on, young man," he said to Almanzo. "But this time, I will." Pa helped her into the buggy.

Ma brought a basket covered with a white cloth. "Something to help make your supper," she said and her lips trembled. "Come back soon, Laura."

When Almanzo was lifting the reins, Grace came running with Laura's old slat sunbonnet. "You forgot this!" she called, holding it up. Almanzo checked the horses while Laura took the sunbonnet. As the horses started again, Grace called anxiously after them, "Remember, Laura, Ma says if you don't keep your sunbonnet on, you'll be brown as an Indian!"

So everyone was laughing when Laura and Almanzo drove away.

They drove over the road they had traveled so many times, across the neck of Big Slough, around the corner by Pearson's livery barn, up Main Street and across the railroad tracks, then out on the road toward the new house on Almanzo's tree claim.

It was a silent drive until almost the end, when for the first time that day Laura saw the horses. She exclaimed, "Why, you are driving Prince and Lady!"

"Prince and Lady started this," Almanzo said. "So I thought they'd like to bring us home. And here we are."

The tracks of his wagon and buggy wheels had made a perfect half-circle drive curving into the grove of little sapling trees before the house. There the house sat, and it was neatly finished with siding and smoothly painted a soft gray. Its front door was comfortably in the middle, and two windows gave the whole house a smiling look. On the doorstep lay a large, brown shepherd dog, that rose and politely wagged to Laura as the buggy stopped.

"Hello, Shep!" Almanzo said. He helped Laura down and unlocked the door. "Go in while I put up the horses," he told her.

Just inside the door she stood and looked. This was the large room. Its walls were neatly plastered a soft white. At its far end stood a drop-leaf table, covered with Ma's red-checked tablecloth. A chair sat primly at either end of it. Beside it was a closed door.

In the center of the long wall at Laura's left, a large window let in the southern sunshine. Companionably placed at either side of it, two rocking chairs faced each other. Beside the one nearest Laura, stood a small round table, and above it a hanging lamp was suspended from the ceiling. Someone could sit there in the evening and read a paper, while in the other chair someone could knit.

The window beside the front door let still more sunny light into that pleasant room.

Two closed doors were in the other long wall. Laura opened the one nearest her, and saw the bedroom. Her Dove-in-the-Window quilt was spread upon the wide bed, and her two feather pillows stood plumply at the head of it. At its foot, across the whole length of the partition was a wide shelf higher than Laura's head, and from its edge a prettily flowered calico curtain hung to the floor. It made a perfect clothes closet. Against the wall under the front window stood Laura's trunk.

She had seen all this quickly. Now she took off her poke bonnet and laid it on the shelf. She opened her trunk and took out a calico dress and apron. Taking off her black cashmere, she hung it carefully in the curtain closet, then slipped into the blue calico dress and tied on the crisply ruffled, pink apron. She went into the front room as Almanzo came into it through the door by the drop-leaf table.

"All ready for work, I see!" he said gaily, as he set Ma's basket on the chair near him. "Guess I'd better get ready for my work, too." He turned at the bedroom door to say, "Your Ma told me to open your bundle and spread things around."

"I'm glad you did," Laura told him.

She looked through the door by the table. There was the lean-to. Almanzo's bachelor cook-stove was set up there, and pots and frying pan hung on the walls. There was a window, and a back door that looked out at the stable beyond some little trees.

Laura returned to the front room. She took up Ma's basket, and opened the last door. She knew it must be the pantry door, but she stood in surprise and then in delight, looking at that pantry. All one wall was covered with shelves and drawers, and a broad shelf was under a large window at the pantry's far end.

She took Ma's basket to that shelf, and opened it. There was a loaf of Ma's good bread, a ball of butter, and what had been left of the wedding cake. She left it all on the shelf while she investigated the pantry.

One whole long wall was shelved from the ceiling halfway down. The upper shelves were empty, but on the lowest was a glass lamp, Almanzo's bachelor dishes, and two pans of milk, with empty pans near. At the end, where this shelf was above the window shelf in the corner, stood a row of cans of spices.

Beneath this shelf were many drawers of different sizes. Directly below the spices, and above the window shelf, were two rather narrow drawers. Laura found that one was almost full of white sugar, the other of brown sugar. How handy!

Next, a deep drawer was full of flour, and smaller ones held graham flour and corn meal. You could stand at the window shelf and mix up anything, without stirring a step. Outside the window was the great, blue sky, and the leafy little trees.

Another deep drawer was filled with towels and tea towels. Another held two tablecloths and some napkins. A shallow one held knives and forks and spoons.

Beneath all these drawers there was space for a tall, stoneware churn and dasher, and empty space for other things as they should come.

In a wide drawer of the bottom row was only a crust of bread and half a pie. Here Laura put Ma's loaf of bread and the wedding cake. She cut a piece from the ball of butter, put it on a small plate, and placed it beside the bread. Then she pushed the drawer shut.

By the iron ring fastened in the pantry floor, she knew there was a trap door. She straightened the ring up, and pulled. The trap door rose, and rested against the pantry wall opposite the shelves. There, beneath where it had been, the cellar stairs went down.

Carefully covering the ball of butter, Laura carried it down the stairs into the cool, dark cellar, and set it on a hanging shelf that swung from the ceiling. She heard steps overhead, and as she came up the cellar stairs she heard Almanzo calling her name.

"I thought you were lost in this big house!" he said.

"I was putting the butter down cellar so it would keep cool," said Laura.

"Like your pantry?" he asked her, and she thought how many hours he must have worked, to put up all those shelves and to make and fit those many drawers.

"Yes," she said.

"Then let's go look at Lady's big little colt. I want you to see the horses in their stalls, and the place I have fixed for your cow. She's picketed out to grass now, just out of reach of the young trees." Almanzo led the way through the lean-to and outdoors.

They explored the long stable and the yard beyond it. Almanzo showed her the new haystacks on the north, to shelter the yard and stable when the winter winds came. Laura petted the horses and the colt, and Shep as he followed close at their heels. They looked at the little maples and box elders and willows and cottonwoods.

Quickly, the afternoon was gone. It was time for chores and supper.

"Don't build a fire," Almanzo told her. "Set out that bread and butter your mother gave us; I'll milk Fawn, and we'll have bread and new milk for supper."

"And cake," Laura reminded him.

When they had eaten supper and washed the few dishes, they sat on the front doorstep as evening came. They heard Prince blow out his breath, whoof! as he lay down on his bed of clean hay in the stable. They saw the dim bulk of Fawn on the grass, where she lay chewing her cud and resting. Shep lay at their feet; already he was half Laura's dog.

Laura's heart was full of happiness. She knew she need never be homesick for the old home. It was so near that she could go to it whenever she wished, while she and Almanzo made the new home in their own little house.

All this was theirs; their own horses, their own cow, their own claim. The many leaves of their little trees rustled softly in the gentle breeze.

Twilight faded as the little stars went out and the moon rose and floated upward. Its silvery light flooded the sky and the prairie. The winds that had blown whispering over the grasses all the summer day now lay sleeping, and quietness brooded over the moon-drenched land.

"It is a wonderful night," Almanzo said.

"It is a beautiful world," Laura answered, and in memory she heard the voice of Pa's fiddle and the echo of a song,

Golden years are passing by,
These happy, golden years.

THE FIRST FOUR YEARS

CONTENTS

Prologue

THE stars hung luminous and low over the prairie. Their light showed plainly the crests of the rises in the gently rolling land, but left the lower draws and hollows in deeper shadows.

A light buggy drawn by a team of quick-stepping dark horses passed swiftly over the road which was only a dim trace across the grasslands. The buggy top was down, and the stars shone softly on the dark blur of the driver and the white-clothed form in the seat beside him, and were reflected in the waters of Silver Lake that lay within its low, grass-grown banks.

The night was sweet with the strong, dewy fragrance of the wild prairie roses that grew in masses beside the way.

A sweet contralto voice rose softly on the air above the lighter patter of the horses' feet, as horses and buggy and dim figures passed along the way. And it seemed as if the stars and water and roses were listening to the voice, so quiet were they, for it was of them it sang.

In the starlight, in the starlight,
At the daylight's dewy close,
When the nightingale is singing
His last love song to the rose;
In the calm clear night of summer
When the breezes gently play,
From the glitter of our dwelling
We will softly steal away.
Where the silv'ry waters murmur
By the margin of the sea,
In the starlight, in the starlight,
We will wander gay and free.

For it was June, the roses were in bloom over the prairie lands, and lovers were abroad in the still, sweet evenings which were so quiet after the winds had hushed at sunset.

CHAPTER I

The First Year

IT WAS a hot afternoon with a strong wind from the south, but out on the Dakota prairie in 1885 no one minded the hot sunshine or the hard winds. They were to be expected: a natural part of life. And so the swiftly trotting horses drawing the shining black-top buggy swung around the corner of Pearson's livery barn, making the turn from the end of Main Street to the country road Monday afternoon at four o'clock.

Looking from a window of the low, three-room claim shanty a half mile away, Laura saw them coming. She was basting cambric lining to the bodice pieces of her new black cashmere dress and had just time to put on her hat and pick up her gloves when the brown horses and the buggy stopped at the door.

It was a pretty picture Laura made standing at the door of the rough claim shanty, the brown August grass under her feet and the young cottonwoods standing in their square around the yard.

Her dress of pink lawn with its small sprigs of blue flowers just cleared her toes. The skirt was full, and tucked to the waist. The little tight waist with long sleeves and high neck had a bit of lace at the throat. The sage-green, rough-straw poke bonnet lined with blue silk softly framed her pink cheeks and her large blue eyes with the bangs of her brown hair above them.

Manly said nothing of all this, but he helped her into the buggy and tucked the linen lap robe carefully about her to keep off the dust. Then he tightened the reins and they dashed away for an unexpected weekday afternoon drive. South twelve miles across bare prairie to lakes Henry and Thompson, along the narrow neck of land between them where chokecherries and wild grapes grew. Then over the prairie again east and north to Spirit Lake fifteen miles away. Forty or fifty miles in all, but always "around the square" to come home.

The buggy top was up to make a shade from the heat of the sun; the horses' manes and tails flew out on the wind; jack rabbits ran and prairie chickens scuttled out of sight in the grass.

Striped gophers ducked into their holes and wild ducks flew overhead from one lake to another. Breaking a somewhat lengthy silence, Manly said, "Can't we be married soon? If you don't want a big wedding, and you would be willing, we could be married right away. When I was back in Minnesota last winter, my sister started planning a big church wedding for us. I told her we didn't want it, and to give up the idea, but she hasn't changed her mind. She is coming out here with my mother, to take charge of our wedding. But harvest is right on hand. It will be an awfully busy time and I'd like us to be settled first."

Laura twisted the bright gold ring with its pearl-and-garnet setting around and around on the forefinger of her left hand. It was a pretty ring and she liked having it, but . . . "I've been thinking," she said. "I don't want to marry a farmer. I have always said I never would. I do wish you would do something else. There are chances in town now while it is so new and growing."

Again there was a little silence; then Manly asked, "Why don't you want to marry a farmer?" And Laura replied, "Because a farm is such a hard place for a woman. There are so many chores for her to do, and harvest help and threshers to cook for. Besides a farmer never has any money. He can never make any because the people in towns tell him what they will pay for what he has to sell and then they charge him what they please for what he has to buy. It is not fair."

Manly laughed. "Well, as the Irishman said, 'Everything is evened up in this world. The rich have their ice in the summer but the poor get theirs in the winter.' "

Laura refused to make a joke of it. She said, "I don't always want to be poor and work hard while the people in town take it easy and make money off us."

"But you've got it all wrong," Manly told her seriously. "Farmers are the only ones who are independent. How long would a merchant last if farmers didn't trade with him? There is a strife between them to please the farmer. They have to take trade away from each other in order to make more money, while all a farmer has to do is to sow another field if he wants to make a little extra.

"I have fifty acres of wheat this year. It is enough for me, but if you will come live on the farm, I will break the ground this fall and sow another fifty acres next spring.

"I can raise more oats too and so raise more horses, and it pays to raise horses.

"You see, on a farm it all depends on what a man is willing to do. If he is willing to work and give his attention to his farm, he can make more money than the men in town and all the time be his own boss."

Again there was a silence, a rather skeptical silence on Laura's part, broken at last by Manly, who said, "If you'll try it for three years and I haven't made a success in farming by that time, I'll quit and do anything you want me to do. I promise that at the end of three years we will quit farming if I have not made such a success that you are willing to keep on."

And Laura consented to try it for three years. She liked the horses and enjoyed the freedom and spaciousness of the wide prairie land, with the wind forever waving the tall wild grass in the sloughs and rustling through the short curly buffalo grass, so green on the upland swells in spring and so silvery-gray and brown in summer. It was all so sweet and fresh. In early spring the wild violets carpeted and made fragrant the little hollows of the grassland, and in June the wild prairie roses blossomed everywhere. Two quarter sections of this land, each with 160 acres of rich black soil, would be theirs, for Manly had already proven up on a homestead and he also had a tree claim on which he was growing the ten acres of trees required by law to get title. The 3405 trees were planted about eight feet apart each way. Between the two claims lay a school section where anyone could cut the hay, first come first served.

It would be much more fun living on the land than on the town street with neighbors so close on each side, and if only Manly were right— Well, she had promised to try the farm anyway.

"The house on the tree claim will be finished in a couple of weeks," Manly was saying. "Let's be married the next week. It will be the last week in August and before the rush of harvest begins. Let's just drive over to Reverend Brown's and then go home to our new house."

But Laura objected to this because she would not be paid for the last month of her school teaching until October and needed the money for clothes.

"What's the matter with the clothes you have?" Manly asked. "You always look nice and if we are married suddenly, that way we won't need fine clothes.

"If we give Mother time enough, she and the girls will come out from the east and we will have to have a big wedding in the church. I can't afford the expense and your one month's salary would not be enough for you."

This was a surprise, for Laura had not thought of such a thing. In the wild new country, the folks back east never seemed to be real and certainly were not considered in the making of plans, but she remembered with something of a shock that Manly's folks back in eastern Minnesota were well off and that one sister had a homestead claim near by. They would be sure to come if they knew the wedding date, and his mother had asked for that in her latest letter.

She could not ask her Pa to go to any expense for the wedding. It was all he could do to keep up with the family expenses until there would be some return from their 160 acres of wild land. Nothing much could be expected from the raw sod the first year it was turned over, and his farmland was newly broke.

There seemed no other way than to be married suddenly because of the help it would be to have a home and housekeeper in the rush of fall work coming on. Manly's mother would understand and not be offended. It would be thought the right and sensible way to do it by the neighbors and friends, for they were all engaged in the same struggle to establish themselves in their homes on the new prairie land.

And so on Thursday, the twenty-fifth of August, at ten o'clock in the morning, the quick-stepping brown horses and the buggy with the shining top flashed around the corner at Pearson's livery barn, came swiftly over the half mile, and drew up at the door of the little claim house in its hollow square of young cottonwoods.

Laura stood at the door, her Ma and Pa on either hand, her two sisters grouped behind her.

They all gaily tried to help her into the buggy. Her wedding dress was the new black cashmere she had thought would be so serviceable, for a married woman should have a black dress.

All her other clothing and her few girlhood treasures had been packed in a trunk and were waiting in Manly's newly finished house.

As Laura looked back, Ma, Pa, and Carrie and Grace were grouped among the young trees. They threw kisses and waved their hands. Bright green leaves of the cottonwoods waved too in the stronger wind of afternoon and there was a little choke in Laura's throat for they seemed to be saying good-by, and she saw her Ma brush her hand quickly across her eyes.

Manly understood, for he covered Laura's hand with one of his and pressed it strongly.

The preacher lived on his homestead two miles away and it seemed to Laura the longest drive she had ever taken, and yet it was over all too soon. Once in the front room, the ceremony was quickly performed. Mr. Brown came hurriedly in, slipping on his coat. His wife and his daughter, Ida, Laura's dearest friend, with her betrothed, were the witnesses and those present.

Laura and Manly were married for better or worse, for richer or poorer.

Then back to the old home for a noon dinner, and in the midst of good wishes and cheerful good-bys, once more into the buggy and away for the new home on the other side of town. The first year was begun.

The summer wind blew softly, and the sunshine was bright where it shone through the east windows that first morning. It was an early sun, but breakfast was even earlier, for Manly must not be late at the Webbs' for the threshing. All the neighbors would be there. Since they would expect Mr. Webb to give them a good day's work in exchange, as their turns with the threshers came, no one could afford to be late and hold up the gang at Webb's place. So the first breakfast in the new home was a hurried affair. Then Manly drove away with the brown horses hitched to the lumber wagon, and Laura was alone for the day.

It would be a busy day, there was so much to do putting the little new house in order.

Before beginning, Laura looked the place over with all the pride of possession.

There was the kitchen-dining-living room, all in one but so nicely proportioned and so cannily furnished that it answered all purposes delightfully.

The front door in the northeast corner of the room opened onto the horseshoe-shaped drive before the house. Just south of it was the east window where the morning sun shone in. In the center of the south wall was another bright window.

The drop-leaf table stood against the west wall with one leaf raised and a chair at either end. It was covered with Ma's bright red-and-white checked tablecloth on which stood the remains of the early breakfast. A door at the end of the table led into the storm shed, and there was Almanzo's cook-stove with pots and frying pans on the walls. Then there was a window and a back door that opened toward the south.

Just across the corner from the door into the shed was the pantry door. And such a pantry! Laura was so delighted with the pantry that she stood in the doorway for several minutes, admiring it. It was narrow, of course, but long. Opposite her at the far end was a full-sized window, and just outside the window stood a young cottonwood tree, its small green leaves fluttering in the morning wind.

Inside before the window was a broad work shelf just the right height at which to stand. On the wall at the right a strip of board ran the whole length and in it were driven nails on which to hang dishpans, dish towels, colanders, and other kitchen utensils.

But the wall to the left was all a beautiful cabinet. Manly had found a carpenter of the old days who though old and slow did beautiful work, and the pantry had been his pride and a labor of love to Manly.

The wall was shelved the whole length. The top shelf was only a short space from the ceiling, and from it down, spaces between the shelves were wider until there was room for tall pitchers and other dishes to stand on the lower shelf. Beneath the lowest shelf was a row of drawers as well made and fitted as boughten furniture. There was a large wide drawer to hold a baking of bread. There was one drawer that already held a whole sack of white flour, a smaller one with graham flour, another with corn meal, a large shallow one for packages, and two others: one already filled with white sugar and the other one with brown. And one for Manly's wedding present of silver knives and forks and spoons. Laura was so proud of them. Underneath the drawers was an open space to the floor and here stood the stone cookie-jar, the doughnut jar, and the jar of lard. Here also stood the tall stone churn and the dasher. The churn looked rather large when the only cow giving milk was the small fawn-colored heifer Pa had given them for a wedding present, but there would be more cream later when Manly's cow should be fresh.

In the center of the pantry floor, a trap door opened into the cellar.

The door into the bedroom was just across the corner from the front door. On the wall at the foot of the bed was a high shelf for hats. A curtain hung from the edge of the shelf to the floor, and on the wall behind it were hooks for hanging clothes. And there was a carpet on the floor!

The pine floors of the front room and pantry were painted a bright clean yellow. The walls of all the house were white plaster, and the pine woodwork was satin-smooth and oiled and varnished in its natural color.

It was a bright and shining little house and it was really all theirs, Laura thought. It belonged to just Manly and her.

The house had been built on the tree claim, looking forward to the time when the small switches of trees should be grown. Already Manly and Laura seemed to see it sitting in a beautiful grove of cottonwoods and elms and maples which were already planted along beside the road. The hopeful little trees stood in the half-circle of the drive before the house. They were hovering close on each side and at the back. Oh, surely, if they were tended well, it would not be long before they sheltered and protected the little house from the summer's heat and the winter's cold and the winds that were always blowing! But Laura could not stand idly in the pantry dreaming and watching the cottonwood leaves blowing. There was work to be done. She cleared the breakfast table quickly. It was only a step from it to the pantry where everything was arranged on the shelves as it belonged; the dirty dishes she piled in the dishpan on the work shelf before the window. The tea kettle of hot water on the stove was handy too, and soon everything was clean and the door closed upon a pantry in perfect order.

Next Laura polished the stove with a flannel cloth, swept the floor, dropped the table leaf and spread a clean, bright red tablecloth over it. The cloth had a beautiful border and made the table an ornament fit for anyone's front room.

In the corner between the window to the east and the window to the south was a small stand-table with an easy armchair at one side and a small rocker at the other. Above it suspended from the ceiling was a glass lamp with glittering pendants. That was the parlor part of the room, and when the copies of Scott's and Tennyson's poems were on the stand it would be complete. She would have some geraniums growing in cans on the windows soon and then it would be simply beautiful.

But the windows must be washed. They were spattered with plaster and paint from the house-building. And how Laura did hate to wash windows!

Just then there was a rap at the screen door, and Hattie, the hired girl from the farm adjoining, was there. Manly had stopped as he drove to the threshing and asked that she come and wash the windows when she could be spared!

So Hattie washed the windows while Laura tidied the little bedroom and unpacked her trunk. Her hat was already on the shelf and the wedding dress hanging on its hook behind the curtain.

There were only a few dresses to hang up, the fawn-colored silk with the black stripes, and the brown poplin she had made. They had been worn many times but were still nice. There was the pink lawn with the blue flowers. It would not be warm enough to wear that more than once or twice again this summer. Then there was the gray calico work dress to change with the blue she was wearing.

And her last-winter's coat looked very good hanging on the hook beside Manly's overcoat. It would do for the winter that was coming. She didn't want to be an expense to Manly right at the beginning. She wanted to help him prove that farming was as good as any other business. This was such a lovely little home, so much better than living on a town street.

Oh, she did hope Manly was right, and she smiled as she repeated to herself, "Everything is evened up in this world."

Manly was late home, for threshers worked as long as there was daylight to see by. Supper was on the table when he came in from doing the chores, and as they ate, he told Laura the threshers would come next day, would be there at noon for dinner.

It would be the first dinner in the new home and she must cook it for the threshers! To encourage her, Manly said, "You'll get along all right. And you can never learn younger."

Now Laura had always been a pioneer girl rather than a farmer's daughter, always moving on to new places before the fields grew large, so a gang of men as large as a threshing crew to feed by herself was rather dismaying. But if she was going to be a farmer's wife that was all in the day's work.

So early next morning she began to plan and prepare the dinner. She had brought a baking of bread from home, and with some hot corn bread there would be plenty. Pork and potatoes were on hand and she had put some navy beans to soak the night before. There was a pieplant in the garden; she must make a couple of pies. The morning flew too quickly, but when the men came in at noon from the thresher, dinner was on the table.

The table was in the center of the room with both leaves raised to make room, but even then some of the men must wait for the second table. They were all very hungry but there was plenty of food, though something seemed to be wrong with the beans. Lacking her Ma's watchful eye, Laura had not cooked them enough and they were hard. And when it came to the pie—Mr. Perry, a neighbor of Laura's parents, tasted his first. Then he lifted the top crust, and reaching for the sugar bowl, spread sugar thickly over his piece of pie. "That is the way I like it," he said. "If there is no sugar in the pie, then every fellow can sweeten his own as much as he likes without hurting the cook's feelings."

Mr. Perry had made the meal a jolly one. He told tales of when he was a boy in Pennsylvania. His mother, he said, used to take five beans and a kettle of water to make bean soup. The kettle was so large that after they had eaten all the bean broth and bread they could, they had to take off their coats and dive for a bean if they wanted one. Everyone laughed and talked and was very friendly, but Laura felt mortified about her beans and her pie without any sugar in. She had been so hurried when she made the pies but how could she have been so careless? Pieplant was so sour, that first taste must have been simply terrible.

The wheat had turned out only ten bushels to the acre, and wheat was selling at fifty cents a bushel. Not much of a crop. It had been too dry and the price was low. But the field of oats had yielded enough to furnish grain for the horses with some to spare. There was hay in great stacks, plenty for the horses and cows and some to sell.

Manly was very cheerful and already planning for next year. He was in a great hurry to begin the fall plowing and the breaking of new sod land, for he was determined to double his acreage next year—or more, if possible. The wheat for seed was stored in the claim shanty on the homestead, for there was no granary on the tree claim. The rest of the wheat was sold.

Now was a busy, happy time. Manly was early in the field, plowing, and Laura was busy all day with cooking, baking, churning, sweeping, washing, ironing and mending. The washing and ironing were hard for her to do. She was small and slender but her little hands and wrists were strong and she got it done. Afternoons, she always put on a clean dress and sat in the parlor corner of the front room sewing, or knitting on Manly's socks.

Sundays they always went for a buggy ride and as the horses trotted along the prairie roads Laura and Manly would sing the old singing-school songs. Their favorite was "Don't Leave the Farm, Boys."

> You talk of the mines of Australia,
> They've wealth in red gold, without doubt;
> But, ah! there is gold on the farm, boys—
> If only you'll shovel it out.

Chorus:

> Don't be in a hurry to go!
> Don't be in a hurry to go!
> Better risk the old farm awhile longer,
> Don't be in a hurry to go!

And Laura thought of the golden wheat stored in the homestead claim shanty and she was glad.

The drives were short these days for the plowing was hard work for pretty, quick-stepping Skip and Barnum, the driving team.

Manly said they were not large enough to do all the breaking of the new sod land. One day he came home from town leading two large horses hitched behind the wagon, and they were drawing a new sulky breaking plow. Now Manly said he could hitch all four horses to the big plow. Then there would be no trouble in getting the land broke for his crops next year. The horses had been a bargain because their owner was in a hurry to sell and get away. He had sold the relinquishment of his homestead to a man from the east and was going farther west and take up another claim where government land could still be found.

The sulky plow had cost fifty-five dollars, but Manly had only paid half down and given a note for the rest to be paid next year. The plow turned a furrow sixteen inches wide in the tough grass sod and would pay for itself in the extra acres Manly could get ready for crops since he could ride instead of walking and holding a narrow walking plow.

After that Laura would go out in the morning and help hitch the four horses to the plow. She learned to drive them and handle the plow too and sometimes would plow several times around the field. She thought it great fun.

Shortly after this Manly came from town again and behind the wagon was a small iron-gray pony. "Here," he said to Laura, "is something for you to play with. And don't let me hear any more about your father not letting you learn to ride his horses. This one is gentle and won't hurt you."

Laura looked at the pony and loved it. "I'll call her Trixy," she said. The pony's feet were small and her legs fine and flat. Her head was small with a fine mealy nose and ears pointed and alert. Her eyes were large and quick and gentle, and her mane and tail were long and thick. That night after supper, Laura chose her saddle from the descriptions and pictures in Montgomery Ward's catalogue and made the order for it ready to mail the first trip to town. She could hardly wait for the saddle to come but she shortened the two weeks' time by making friends with Trixy. It was a beautiful all-leather saddle, tan-colored and fancy-stitched with nickel trimmings.

"And now," said Manly, "I'll put the saddle on Trixy and you and she can learn together. I'm sure she'll be gentle even if she never has been ridden, but better head her onto the plowed ground. It will be harder going for her—so she won't be so frisky—and a soft place for you to light if you fall off." So when Laura was safely in the saddle, her left foot in the leather slipper stirrup, her right knee over the saddle horn with the leaf-horn fitting snuggly about it, Manly let go the bridle and Laura and Trixy went out on the plowed ground. Trixy was good and did her best to please even though she was afraid of Laura's skirt blowing in the wind. Laura didn't fall off, and day after day they learned horseback riding together.

It was growing late in the fall. The nights were frosty and soon the ground would freeze. The breaking of the new fifty-acre field was nearly finished. There were no Sunday afternoon drives now. Skip and Barnum were working too hard at the plowing to be driven. They must have their day of rest. Instead, there were long horseback rides, for Manly had a saddle pony of his own, and Fly and Trixy, having nothing else to do, were always ready to go. Laura and Trixy had learned to foxtrot and to lope together. The little short lope would land them from the side of the road across the wheel track onto the grass-covered middle. Another jump would cross the other wheel track. Trixy would light so springily on her dainty feet that there was never a jar.

One day as they were loping down a road Manly said, "Oh, yes! Trixy can jump short and quick, but Fly can run away from her"—and Fly started. Laura bent low over Trixy's neck, touched her with her whip, and imitated, as near as she could manage, a cowboy yell. Trixy shot ahead like a streak, leaving Fly behind. Laura stopped her and sat a little breathless until Manly came up. But when Manly protested at the sudden start she said airily, "Oh, Trixy told me she was going in plenty of time."

After that it was proven many times that Trixy was faster—often on a twenty-mile ride over the open prairie before breakfast.

It was a carefree, happy time, for two people thoroughly in sympathy can do pretty much as they like.

To be sure, now and then Laura thought about the short crop and wondered. Once she even saved the cream carefully and sent a jar of fresh butter to town for sale, thinking it would help pay for the groceries Manly was getting. With the butter, she sent five dozen eggs, for the little flock of hens, picking their living around the barn and the straw stacks and in the fields, were laying wonderfully well.

But Manly brought the butter back. Not a store in town wanted it at any price and he had been able to get only five cents a dozen for the eggs. Laura couldn't help any in that way. But why worry? Manly didn't.

When the breaking was finished, the hay barn back of the house was made more snug for winter. It was a warm place for the stock, with hay stacked tightly on each side against the skeleton frame. Hay was stacked even over the roof, about four feet thick at the eaves and a little thicker at the peak of the roof to give plenty of slant to shed water.

With a long hay knife, Manly had cut two holes through the haystack on the south side of the barn. Then he had put windows over the holes inside the barn for, he said, the stock must have light even with the door shut.

When the barn was made snug, it was butchering time.

But Ole Larsen, the neighbor across the road, butchered first. Mr. Larsen was always borrowing. It was the cause of disagreement between Manly and Laura, for Laura objected to tools and machinery being used and broken and not returned. When she saw Manly going afoot to the back end of Ole Larsen's field to get some machine that should have been at his own barn, she was angry, but Manly said one must be neighborly.

So when Mr. Larsen came over to borrow the large barrel in which to scald his hog in the butchering, she told him to take it. Manly was in town but she knew he would lend it.

In a few minutes Mr. Larsen came back to borrow her wash boiler to heat water to scald the hog. Soon he was back again to borrow her butcher knives for the work, and again a little later to get her knife whetstone to sharpen the knives. Grimly Laura said to herself if he came next to borrow their fat hog to kill she would let him have it. But he had a hog of his own.

And after all that, he did not bring over a bit of the fresh meat as good neighbors always did.

A few days later Manly butchered his fat hog and Laura had her first experience making sausage, head cheese, and lard all by herself. Hams and shoulders and spareribs were frozen in the storm shed and fat meat was salted down in a small barrel.

Laura found doing work alone very different from helping Ma. But it was part of her job and she must do it, though she did hate the smell of hot lard, and the sight of so much fresh meat ruined her appetite for any of it.

It was at this time that the directors of the school were able to pay Laura the salary for the last month she had taught. The money made Laura feel quite rich and she began planning how she should spend it. Manly told her if she bought a colt with it she could double the money in a short time by selling it when it was grown. So that was what they decided to do, and Manly bought a bay two-year-old that promised to grow out well.

Laura didn't bother to name the colt. It was just to be sold again, so what was the use? But the animal was fed well, brushed and cared for, to make it grow well.

One blustery day Manly started early for town, leaving Laura very much alone. She was used to being the only person on the place and thought nothing of it, but the wind was so cold and raw that she had not opened the front door. It was still locked from the night. In the middle of the morning, busy with her work, Laura looked out the window and saw a little bunch of horsemen coming across the prairie from the southeast. She wondered why they were not traveling on the road. As they came nearer she saw there were five of them, and they were Indians.

Laura had seen Indians often, without fear, but she felt a quick jump of her heart as they came up to the house and without knocking tried to open the front door. She was glad the door was locked, and she slipped quickly into the back room and locked the outside door there.

The Indians came around the house to the back door and tried to open that. Then seeing Laura through the window they made signs for her to open the door, indicating that they would not hurt her. But Laura shook her head and told them to go away. Likely they only wanted something to eat, but still one never could tell. It was only three years ago that the Indians nearly went on the warpath a little way west, and even now they often threatened the railroad camps.

She wouldn't open the door but watched them as they jabbered together. She couldn't catch a word that she could understand, and she was afraid. They weren't acting right. Why didn't they go away!

Instead they were going to the barn—and her new saddle was hanging in the barn and Trixy was there . . . Trixy! Her pet and comrade!

Laura was afraid; in the house there was comparative safety, for they'd hardly break in. But now Laura was angry too, and as always, she acted quickly. Flinging the door open, she ran to the barn, and standing in the door, ordered the Indians out. One of them was feeling the leather of her beautiful saddle and one was in the stall with Trixy. Trixy was afraid too. She never liked strangers and she was pulling at her halter and trembling.

The other Indians were examining Manly's saddle and the buggy harness with its bright nickel trimmings. But they all came and gathered around Laura just outside the door. She stormed at them and stamped her foot. Her head was bare and her long brown braids of hair blew out on the wind while her purple eyes flashed fire as always when she was angry or very much excited.

The Indians only stared for a moment; then one of them grunted an unintelligible word and laid his hand on Laura's arm. Quick as a flash she slapped his face with all her might.

It made him angry and he started toward her, but the other Indians laughed, and one who seemed to be the leader stopped him. Then with signs pointing to himself, his pony, and then with a sweep of his arm toward the west, he said, "You go—me—be my squaw?"

Laura shook her head, and stamping her foot again, motioned them all to their ponies and away, telling them to go.

And they went, riding their running ponies without saddles or bridles.

But as they went their leader turned and looked back at Laura where she stood, with the wind blowing her skirts around her and her braids flying, watching them go away across the prairie into the west.

Wild geese were flying south. By day the sky was full of them flying in their V-formations, the leaders calling and their followers answering until the world seemed full of their calls. Even at night they could be heard as their seemingly endless numbers sailed ahead of the cold coming down out of the north.

Laura loved to watch them high against the blue of the sky, large V's and smaller V's with the leader at the point, his followers streaming behind, always in perfect V-formation. She loved to hear their loud, clear honk, honk. There was something so wild and free about it, especially at night when the lonely, wild cry sounded through the darkness, calling, calling. It was almost irresistible. It made Laura long for wings so that she might follow.

Manly said, "The old saying is that 'everything is lovely when the geese honk high,' but I believe we will have a hard winter, the geese are flying so high and in such a hurry. They are not stopping to rest on the lakes nor to feed. They are hurrying ahead of a storm." For several days, the wild geese hurried southward; and then one still, sunny afternoon a dark cloud line lay low on the northwest horizon. It climbed swiftly, higher and higher, until the sun was suddenly overcast, and with a howl the wind came and the world was blotted out in a blur of whirling snow.

Laura was in the house alone when the wind struck the northwest corner with such force the whole house jarred. Quickly she ran to the window but she could see only a wall of whiteness beyond the glass. Manly was in the barn, and at the sudden shriek of the storm he, too, looked out a window. Then, although it was only mid-afternoon, he fed the horses and cows for the night, milked the heifer in the little pail in which he had taken out some salt, and shutting the barn door carefully and tightly behind him, started for the house. As soon as he was away from the shelter of the hay at the barn door, the full force of the storm struck him. It seemed to come from every direction at once. Whichever way he turned his head he faced the wind. He knew the direction in which the house lay but he could see nothing of it. He could see nothing but a blur of white. It had grown intensely cold and the snow was a powdered dust of ice that filled his eyes and ears, and since he must breathe he felt smothered. After taking a few steps he could not see the barn. He was alone in a whirling white world.

Keeping his face in the right direction, Manly went ahead;

but soon he knew he had gone far enough to be at the house, yet he could not see it. A few steps more and he stumbled against an old wagon that had been left some little distance south of the house. In spite of his guarding against it, the wind had blown him south of his way, but now he knew where he was. So again setting his face in the right direction he went on. Again, he knew he should have reached the house but he had not. If he should become hopelessly confused he might not find it at all but wander out on the open prairie to perish, or he might even freeze within a few feet of the house before the storm was over. No shout of his could be heard above the wind. Well, he might as well go on a little farther, no use standing still. Another step, and his shoulder just lightly brushed something. He put up his hand and touched the corner of a building. The house! He had almost missed it and headed out into the storm.

Keeping his hand on the wall he followed it and came to the back door.

Blown in with the storm, as he opened the door, he stood and blinked the snow from his eyes in the warmth and shelter of the house he had so nearly missed. He still clutched the milk pail. In the struggle with the storm he had not spilled the milk—because it was frozen.

For three days and nights the blizzard raged. Before Manly went to the barn again, he followed the house wall to where the long rope clothesline was tied at the corner. With his hand on the rope, he followed it to the back of the house. Unfastening it at the corner, he followed the house around to the door and fastened the rope there, and to the loose end he tied a shorter rope, the drying line he had put up in the storm shed. Now unreeling the rope as he went he could go to the haystack at the barn door, make the rope fast, and follow it back to the house safely. After that he went to the barn and cared for the stock once a day.

While the blizzard shrieked and howled and raged outside, Laura and Manly both stayed indoors. Laura kept the fire going from the store of coal in the storm shed. She cooked from the stores in her pantry and cellar and she sang at her knitting in the afternoon. Old Shep and the cat lay companionably on the rug before the cook-stove and there was warmth and comfort in the little house standing so sturdily in the midst of the raging elements.

Late in the afternoon of the fourth day the wind went down. It lost its whirling force and blew the loose snow scudding close to the ground, packing it into hard drifts that lay over the prairie with bare ground showing between. The sun shone again with a frosty light and huge sundogs stood guard on each side of it. And it was *cold*! Laura and Manly went outdoors and looked over the desolate landscape. Their ears still throbbed to the tumult of the storm, and the silence following it was somehow confusing.

"This has been very bad," Manly said. "We will hear of plenty of damage from this." Laura looked at the smoke rising from the stovepipe in their neighbor's house across the road. She had not been able to see it for three days. "Larsens are all right anyway," she said.

Next day Manly drove to town to get a few supplies and to learn the news.

The house was bright and cheerful when he came home. The last rays of the afternoon sun were shining in at the south window, and Laura was ready to help him off with his coat as he came in from the barn after putting up his team and doing the night feeding.

But Manly was very sober. After they ate supper he told Laura the news.

A man south of town, caught at his barn by the storm as Manly had been, had missed the house going back. He had wandered out on the prairie and had been found frozen to death when the wind went down.

Three children going home from school had become lost, but found a haystack and dug into it. They had huddled together for warmth and had been drifted in. When the storm stopped, the oldest, a boy, had dug out through the snow, and searchers had found them. They were weak from hunger but not frozen.

Range cattle had drifted before the storm for a hundred miles. Blinded and confused they had gone over a high bank of the Cottonwood River, the later ones falling on top of the first, breaking through the ice of the river and floundering in the water and loose snow until they had smothered and frozen to death. Men were dragging them out of the river now, hundreds of them, and skinning them to save the hides. Anyone who had lost cattle could go look at the brands and claim his own.

The storm so early in the season was unexpected, and many people had been caught out in the snow and had frozen their hands and feet. Another storm came soon, but people were prepared now and no damage was done.

It was too cold for horseback riding, and snow covered the ground, so Manly hitched the driving team to the cutter (the little one-seated sleigh) on Sunday afternoons. Then he and Laura drove here and there, over to Pa's farm to see the home folks or to the Boasts, old friends who lived several miles to the east. But the drives were always short ones; no twenty or forty miles now. It was too dangerous, for a storm might come up suddenly and catch them away from home.

Barnum and Skip were not working now. They were fat and frisky and enjoyed the sleigh rides as much as Laura and Manly. They pranced and danced purposely to make their sleigh bells ring more merrily while their ears twitched alertly and their eyes shone.

Trixy and Fly, the saddle ponies, Kate and Bill, the working team, were growing fat in the barn and took their exercise in the haystack-sheltered barnyard at the back.

The holidays were near and something must be done about them. The Boast and the Ingalls families had spent them together whenever they could. Thanksgiving dinner at Boasts', Christmas dinner at the Ingalls' home. Now with Laura and Manly, there was a new family, and it was agreed to add another gathering to those two holidays. New Year's should be celebrated at the Wilders'.

Christmas presents were hardly to be thought of, the way the crops had turned out, but Manly made handsleds for Laura's little sisters, and they would buy Christmas candy for all.

For themselves, they decided to buy a present together, something they could both use and enjoy. After much studying of Montgomery Ward's catalogue, they chose to get a set of glassware. They needed it for the table and there was such a pretty set advertised, a sugar bowl, spoon-holder, butter dish, six sauce dishes, and a large oval-shaped bread plate. On the bread plate raised in the glass were heads of wheat and some lettering which read "Give us this day our daily bread."

When the box came from Chicago a few days before Christmas and was unpacked, they were both delighted with their present.

The holidays were soon over and in February Laura's nineteenth birthday came. Manly's twenty-ninth birthday was just a week later so they made one celebration for both on the Sunday between.

It wasn't much of a celebration, just a large birthday cake for the two of them, and a little extra pains were taken in the cooking and arranging of the simple meal of bread, meat, and vegetables.

Laura had become quite a good cook and an expert in the making of light bread.

With work and play, in sunshine and storm, the winter passed. There was very little visiting or having company, for neighbors were rather far away (except for the Larsens across the road) and the days were short. Still, Laura was never lonely. She loved her little house and the housework. There were always Shep and the cat, and a visit to the horses and cows at the barn was, she thought, as good as visiting people any day.

When Trixy lipped her hand or rested her soft nose on her shoulder, or Skip, the scamp, searched her pocket for a lump of sugar, she felt that they were very satisfactory friends.

The wild geese were coming back from the southland. They flew overhead from one lake to the other, where they rested on the water and fed along the shores.

The ground was bare of snow, and although the nights were cold and the wind often chilly, the sunshine was warm and spring had come. Manly was getting his plows and harrows in order for working the land to be ready for the sowing of wheat and oats. He must get an early start at the work for there were a hundred acres to sow in wheat and a fifty-acre oatfield on the homestead. At the shanty on the homestead Laura held the grain sacks while he shoveled the wheat into them. He was hauling them to the home barn to be handy for the sowing. The shanty was cold. The grain sacks were coarse and rough to the touch and the wheat was dusty.

Watching the plump wheat kernels slide into the open mouth of the sack made Laura dizzy. If she took her eyes from them, they were drawn irresistibly to the newspapers pasted on the shanty walls and she read the words over and over. She was unreasonably annoyed because some of them were bottom side up but she must read them anyway. She couldn't take her eyes from them. Words! Words! The world was full of words and sliding wheat kernels!

And then she heard Manly saying, "Sit down a minute! You're tired."

So she sat down, but she was not tired. She was sick. The next morning she felt much worse and Manly got his own breakfast.

For days she fainted whenever she left her bed. The doctor told her to lie quietly. He assured her she would feel much better before long and that in a few months, nine to be exact, she would be quite all right. Laura was going to have a baby.

So that was it! Well, she mustn't shirk. She must get around and do the work in the house so that Manly could get the crops in. So much depended on this year's crops, and there was no money to hire help.

Soon Laura was creeping around the house, doing what must be done, and whenever possible relieving her dizzy head by lying down for a few minutes. The little house grew to look rather dingy for she couldn't give it the care it had always had. As she went so miserably about her work she would smile wryly now and then as she remembered a saying of her mother's: "They that dance must pay the fiddler." Well, she was paying, but she would do the work. She *would* help that much in spite of everything.

The trees were not growing very well. The dry weather of the summer had been hard on them, and they must be given extra care, for years from now there must be the ten acres with the right numbers of growing trees in order to prove up on the tree claim and get a title to the land.

So Manly plowed around the little trees and then mulched them with manure from the barnyard.

Laura missed the drives over the greening prairie in the freshness of early spring. She missed the wild violets that scented the air with their fragrance, but when wild rose time came in June she was able to ride behind Skip and Barnum along the country roads where the prairie roses on their low bushes made glowing masses of color from pale pink to deepest red and the air was full of their sweetness. On one such drive she asked abruptly out of a silence, "What shall we name the child?"

"We can't name it now," Manly replied, "for we don't know if it will be a boy or a girl."

And after another silence Laura said, "It will be a girl and we will call her Rose."

It rained often that spring. It rained through the summer and the little trees took courage and waved their little green leaves in the wind while they stretched taller every day. The wild blue stem grass grew on the high prairie, and the slough grass grew rank in the sloughs where water stood in the lowest places.

And, oh, how the wheat and oats did grow! For it rained!

The days went by and by and the wheat headed tall and strong and green and beautiful. Then the grain was in the milk and in just a few days more the crop would be safe. Even if it turned dry now there would be a good crop, for the stalks would ripen the wheat.

At last one day Manly came in from the field. He had been looking it over and decided it was ready to cut.

The wheat, he said, was perfect. It would go all of forty bushels to the acre and be Number One hard. The price would start at seventy-five cents a bushel delivered at the elevator in town.

"Didn't I tell you," he said, "that everything evens up? The rich have their ice in the summer, but the poor get theirs in the winter." He laughed and Laura laughed with him. It was wonderful.

In the morning Manly had to go to town and buy a new binder to harvest the wheat. He had waited until he was sure there would be a good crop before buying it, for it was expensive: two hundred dollars. But he would pay half after the grain was threshed and the other half in a second payment after threshing next year. He would only have to pay eight percent interest on the deferred payment, and could give a chattel mortgage on the machine and cows to secure the debt. Manly went early to town; he wanted to be back in time to begin cutting the grain.

Laura was proud when Manly drove into the yard with the new machine. She went out and watched while he hitched on the four horses and started for the oatfield. The oats were ripest and he would cut them first.

As Laura went back into the house she did a little mental arithmetic—one hundred acres at forty bushels to an acre would be four thousand bushels of wheat. Four thousand bushels of wheat at seventy-five cents a bushel would be— Oh, how much would it be? She'd get her pencil. Four thousand bushels at seventy-five cents a bushel would be three thousand dollars. It couldn't be! Yes, that was right! Why, they would be rich! She'd say the poor *did* get their ice!

They could pay for the mowing machine and the hayrake Manly had bought a year ago and could not pay for because the crop had been so poor. The notes of seventy-five dollars and forty dollars and the chattel mortgage on Skip and Barnum would be due after threshing. Laura did not mind the notes so much, but she hated the chattel mortgage on the horses. She'd almost as soon have had a mortgage on Manly. Well, it would soon be paid now, *and* the note for the sulky plow with its chattel mortgage on the cows. She thought there were some store accounts but was not sure. They couldn't be much anyway. Perhaps she could have someone to do the work until the baby came. Then she could rest; she needed rest, for, not being able to retain her food for more than a few minutes, she had not much to live on and was very emaciated. It would be nice to let someone else do the cooking. The smell of cooking always made her feel so nauseated now.

Manly cut the fifty acres of oats with the new McCormick binder that day. He was jubilant at night. It was a wonderful crop of oats and early tomorrow he would begin on the wheat.

But, the next morning, when Manly had cut twice around the wheatfield, he unhitched and came back to the barn with the team. The wheat would be better for standing a couple of days longer. When he came to cut into it, it was not quite so ripe as he had thought, and he would take no chance of shrunken kernels by its being cut a little green, Manly said. But it was even heavier than he had figured, and if it didn't go

above forty bushels to the acre, he was mistaken. Laura felt impatient. She was in a hurry for the wheat to be cut and safely stacked. From the window she could see the shining new binder standing at the edge of the grain and it looked impatient too, she thought.

After noon that day the DeVoes came by. Cora stopped to spend some time while her husband Walter went on to town. The DeVoes were about the same age as Manly and Laura and had been married about as long. Laura and Cora were very good friends and it was a pleasant afternoon except for being rather uncomfortable from the heat.

As the afternoon passed it grew hotter and there was no wind, which was unusual. It left one gasping for breath and feeling smothered.

About three o'clock Manly came in from the barn and said it was going to rain for sure. He was glad he had not been cutting the wheat to have it lie in a rainstorm before he could get it shocked. The sunshine darkened, and the wind sighed and then fell again as it grew darker yet. Then the wind rose a little, and it grew lighter, but the light was a greenish color. Then the storm came. It rained only a little; then hailstones began to fall, at first scattering slowly, then falling thicker and faster while the stones were larger, some of them as large as hens' eggs.

Manly and Cora watched from the windows. They could not see far into the rain and the hail, but they saw Ole Larsen, across the road, come to his door and step out. Then they saw him fall, and someone reached out the door, took hold of his feet, and dragged him in. Then the door shut.

"The fool," Manly said, "he got a hailstone on the head."

In just twenty minutes the storm was over, and when they could see as far as the field, the binder was still there but the wheat was lying flat. "It's got the wheat, I guess," Manly said. But Laura could not speak.

Then Manly went across the road to find out what had happened to Mr. Larsen. When he came back, in a few minutes, he said that Mr. Larsen had stepped out to pick up a hailstone so large that he wished to measure it. Just as he stooped to pick it up, another one hit him on the head. He was unconscious for several minutes after he was dragged in by the heels, but was all right now except for a sore head.

"And now let's make some ice cream," Manly said. "You stir it up, Laura, and I'll gather up hailstones for ice to freeze it."

Laura turned to Cora where she stood speechless, looking out of the window. "Do you feel like celebrating, Cora?" she asked.

And Cora answered, "No! I want to get home and see what has happened there. Ice cream would choke me!"

The storm had lasted only twenty minutes but it left a desolate, rain-drenched and hail-battered world. Unscreened windows were broken. Where there were screens, they were broken and bent. The ground was covered with hailstones so thickly, it looked covered with a sheet of ice, and they even lay in drifts here and there. Leaves and branches were stripped off the young trees and the sun shone with a feeble, watery light over the wreck. The wreck, thought Laura, of a year's work, of hopes and plans of ease and pleasure. Well, there would be no threshers to cook for. Laura had dreaded the threshing. As Ma used to say, "There is no great loss without some small gain." That she should think of so small a gain bothered Laura.

She and Cora sat white and silent until Walter drove up to the door, helped Cora into the wagon, and drove away almost forgetting to say good-by in their anxiety to get home and learn how bad the storm had been there.

Manly went out to look at the wheatfield and came in sober enough. "There is no wheat to cut," he said. "It is all threshed and pounded into the ground. Three thousand dollars' worth of wheat planted, and it's the wrong time of the year."

Laura was muttering to herself, "the poor man gets his—."

"What's that?" Manly asked.

"I was only saying," Laura answered, "that the poor man got his ice in the summer this time."

At two o'clock the next day hailstones were still lying in drifts in low places.

Though plans are wrecked, the pieces must be gathered up and put together again in some shape. Winter was coming. Coal must be bought to last through. That would cost between sixty and one hundred dollars. Seed grain would have to be bought for next spring's sowing. There were notes on the machinery coming due.

There was the binder that had been used to cut only fifty

acres of oats; there was the sulky plow and the mower and rake, the seeder that had sown the grain in the spring and the new wagon. There was too the five hundred dollars still due on the building of the house. "Five hundred dollars debt on the house!" Laura exclaimed. "Oh, I didn't know that!"

"No," Manly said. "I didn't think there was any need to bother you about that."

But something must be done about all this, and he would go to town tomorrow and see what could be done. Perhaps he could raise money with a mortgage on the homestead. That was proved up on, thank goodness. He couldn't give a mortgage on the tree claim. That belonged to Uncle Sam until Manly had raised those trees. And Laura thought she could hear her father singing, "Our Uncle Sam is rich enough to give us all a farm!" Sometimes Laura was afraid her head was a little flighty, but that extra five hundred dollars' debt had been something of a shock. Five hundred and two hundred was seven hundred, and the wagon and the mower . . . She must stop counting it or she would have her head queer.

Manly found he could renew all his machinery notes for a year by paying the interest. He could even make the first payment on the binder after the next harvest, postponing the second payment to the year after. He could sell all the wild hay he had for four dollars a ton delivered at the railroad in town. Buyers wanted it to ship to Chicago.

But he could not raise money with a mortgage on the homestead unless they were living on it. He must have money to pay the interest due, for living expenses and for seed. There was no way to get the money except by moving to the homestead. If they were living on the homestead he could mortgage it for eight hundred dollars.

A newcomer would buy Kate and Bill for more than Manly had paid for them. Manly would not need them, for he had found a renter for the tree claim on shares; Manly would furnish the seed.

Skip and Barnum, with Trixy and Fly to do the driving, could do the work on the one place.

If someone else worked the tree claim, Manly could raise more crops on the homestead and have more profit from the farms than if he tried to work both claims all by himself.

An addition would have to be built on the homestead claim shanty before they moved but they could do with one new room and a cellar underneath through using the original shanty for a storeroom.

So it was decided. Manly hurried to stack the oats, which the hail had threshed to the ground, but the oat straw made good animal feed to take the place of hay and that would leave more hay to sell.

When the oats were hauled to the homestead and stacked, Manly dug the hole in the ground for the cellar, and over it built the one-room addition to the claim shanty. Then he built the frame of a barn, cut slough hay, and when it was dry stacked it around the frame to make a hay barn.

Everything was ready now for the moving. Manly and Laura moved to the homestead the next day after the barn was finished.

It was the twenty-fifth of August. And the winter and the summer were the first year.

CHAPTER 2

The Second Year

IT WAS a beautiful day, that twenty-fifth of August, 1886, when Manly and Laura moved to the homestead.

"A fine day, as fine as our wedding day just a year ago, and it's a new start just as that was. And a new home, if it is some smaller.

"We'll be all right now. You'll see! 'Everything evens up in the end. The rich man—' "

His voice trailed silent but Laura couldn't help finishing the Irishman's saying to herself: "The rich man has his ice in the summer and the poor man gets his in the winter." Well, they had got theirs in that hailstorm and in the summer too.

But she mustn't think about that now. The thing to do was to get things arranged in the new home and make it cheerful for Manly. Poor Manly, he was having a hard time and doing his very best. The house wasn't so bad. The one new room was narrow (twelve feet by sixteen) and not very long, facing the south with a door and a window on a narrow porch, closed at the west end by the old claim shanty.

There was a window in the east end of the room. The looking glass was hung beside it in the south corner and the parlor table stood under it. The head of the bed came close to the window on the other side and extended along the north wall.

The kitchen stove was in the northwest corner of the room and a kitchen cupboard stood beside it. The kitchen-dining table stood against the west wall close to the south end.

The carpet from the old bedroom was across the east end of the room, and the armchair and Laura's little rocking chair stood on it, close to each other between the windows. The sun came in through the east window in the mornings and shone across the room. It was all very snug and pleasant.

The room that had been the claim shanty was convenient as a storage room, and the stock were comfortable in their new barn. Sheltered from the north and west by the low hill and facing the south, it would be warm in winter.

The whole place was new and fresh. The wind waved the tall grass in the slough that stretched from the foot of the hill by the barn to the south and to the east line of the farm. The house was at the top of the low hill and there would always be grassland in front of it. The plowland lay to the north of the hill out of sight from the house. Laura was glad of that. She loved the sweep of unbroken prairie with the wild grasses waving in the winds. To be sure, the whole place was grassland now, except for a small field. Ten acres of cultivated land were required by law before proving up on a homestead. But the grass to the north of the house was upland, blue stem, and not the tall slough grass that grew so rankly in low places. It was haying time, and every day counted in the amount of hay that could be put up before winter.

Because of the hailstorm, hay would be the only crop this year. So as soon as breakfast was over on the day after the moving, Manly hitched Skip and Barnum to the mowing machine and began cutting hay.

Laura left her morning's work undone and went with him to see the work started, and then because the air was so fresh and the new-cut hay so clean and sweet, she wandered over the field, picking the wild sunflowers and Indian paintbrush. Presently she went slowly back to the house and her unfinished tasks.

She didn't want to stay in the house. There would be so much of that after the baby came. And she felt much better out in the fresh air. So after that she did as little as possible in the house, and instead stayed out in the hayfield with Manly.

When he loaded the hay in the big hayrack to haul to the barn, Laura, already in the wagon, stepped up on each forkful as it was pitched in and so gradually rose with the load until she was on the top, ready to ride to the barn. At the barn she slid down the hay into Manly's arms and was safely on the ground.

Manly made the stacks in the field with a bull rake. The bull rake was a long wide plank with long wooden teeth set in it at intervals for the whole length. A horse was hitched at each end, and, walking one on each side of a long windrow of hay, they pulled the plank sideways. The long teeth slipped under the hay and it piled up in front of the plank and was pushed along the ground.

When there was enough of a load and it was where the stack was to be, Manly tipped the plank. It went over the top of the hay which was left in a pile. Several of these piles started the stack. Then as the horses came to it, one went on each side of the stack, the rake went on up, Manly followed it and spilled the hay on top of the stack and then went down the other end after another load.

Barnum was good and always walked along with his end of the plank on his side of the stack. But Skip stopped when he had no driver, so Laura drove Skip the length of the stack and then sat against the sweet hay on the sunny side while Manly would bring up another load with the rake.

When the stack was high enough, Manly raked down the sides with his pitchfork and gathered up all the scattered hay around and against it, making all neat and even. Then he topped the stack with a load of hay from the wagon.

So the nice fall weather passed. Nights grew cooler, frost came. The haying was finished.

Manly had mortgaged the homestead for eight hundred dollars, so now he could buy the coal for winter, and it was stored in the storeroom.

The taxes of sixty dollars (there were no taxes on the tree claim because they had no title yet) were paid. Interest, on the notes given for machinery, was paid. There was money for seed in the spring and to live on, they hoped, until next harvest.

The hay had helped. Manly had sold thirty tons at four dollars a ton, and the $120 was a year's income from crops.

Wild geese were late coming from the north, and when they did, seemed in no hurry to go on south. Instead they fed in the sloughs and flew from one lake to the other, where the water was nearly covered with them as they swam about. The sky was filled with their V-shaped flocks and the air rang to their calls. Manly hurried into the house for his gun one day.

"A flock of geese is coming over so low, I believe I can get one," he told Laura.

Quickly he went out the door, and forgetting that the old gun kicked, he held it up before his face, sighted and pulled the trigger.

Laura followed him just in time to see him whirl around with his hand to his face.

"Oh, did you hit a goose?" she asked.

"Yes, but I didn't quite kill it," he answered, as he wiped the blood from his nose.

The flock of geese went on unharmed to join their kindred at the lake.

It was going to be an open winter; the geese knew there was no hurry to go south.

The small field was soon plowed and the hurry of work was over.

In November, the snow came and covered the ground, making good sleighing. Manly and Laura, well bundled up and covered with robes, went often for sleigh rides on sunny afternoons. Because Laura felt so much better outdoors, Manly made a handsled and a breast-collar-harness for Old Shep.

On pleasant days Laura hitched Shep to the handsled and let him pull her on it down the hill to the road. Then together they would climb the hill, Shep pulling the sled and Laura walking beside him to take another ride down until she was tired from the walking and the fun. Shep never got tired of it, and at times when the sled tipped against a drift and Laura rolled into the snow he seemed actually to laugh.

And so November passed and December came.

The sun was shining on the morning of the fifth of December, but it looked stormy in the north.

"Better play outdoors all you can today, for it may be too stormy tomorrow," Manly said.

So, soon after breakfast Laura hitched Shep to the sled and took the day's first ride down the hill. But she stayed out only a little while.

"I don't feel like playing," she told Manly when he came up from the barn. "I would rather curl up by the stove." And again after the dinner work was done she sat idly by the stove in her little rocking chair, which worried Manly.

Along in the afternoon Manly went to the barn and came back with the horses hitched to the sleigh.

"I'm going for your Ma," he said. "Keep as quiet as you can until we come." It was snowing hard now as from the window Laura watched him drive down the road with the team trotting their best. She thought that the pace would have won them the prize at the Fourth of July races.

Then she walked the floor or sat by the stove until Manly came back with her Ma.

"My goodness," Ma exclaimed, as she warmed herself by the fire. "You should not be up. I'll get you to bed right away."

And Laura answered, "I'll have a long time to stay in bed. I am going to stay up now as long as I can."

But soon she made no objections and only vaguely knew when Manly drove away again to fetch a friend of her Ma's from town.

Mrs. Powers was a friendly, jolly Irish woman. The first Laura knew of her being there was hearing her say, "Sure she'll be all right, for it's young she is. Nineteen you say; the very age of my Mary. But we'd better have the doctor out now, I'm thinking." When Laura could again see and know what went on around her, Ma and Mrs. Powers were standing one on each side of her bed. And was that Manly at the foot? No! Manly had gone for the doctor. Then were there two Ma's and two Mrs. Powerses? They seemed to be all around her.

What was that old hymn Pa used to sing?

. . . angel bank
Come and around me stand,
Oh, bear me away on your snowy wings
To—

She was being borne away on a wave of pain. A gust of cold, fresh air brought her back and she saw a tall man drop his snowy overcoat by the door and come toward her in the lamplight.

She vaguely felt a cloth touch her face and smelled a keen odor. Then she drifted away into a blessed darkness where there was no pain.

When Laura opened her eyes, the lamp was still shining brightly over the room, and Ma was bending over her with the doctor standing beside her. And in the bed by her side was a little warm bundle.

"See your little daughter, Laura! A beautiful baby, and she weighs just eight pounds," Ma said.

"It's a fine girl you are yourself," Mrs. Powers said from where she was sitting by the fire. "A fine, brave girl, and baby'll be good because of it. You'll be all right now."

So Manly took the doctor and Mrs. Powers home, but Ma stayed, and Laura went to sleep at once with her hand resting gently on little Rose.

Rose was such a good baby, so strong and healthy that Ma stayed only a few days. Then Hattie Johnson came. "To wash baby this time, instead of windows," she said.

But soon Hattie went and the three, Manly, Laura and Rose, were left by themselves in the little house atop the low hill with the sweep of the empty prairie all around it.

There was not a house near enough for neighbors, but a mile away across the slough a few buildings on the edge of town were in sight.

A hundred precious dollars had gone for doctor bills and medicine and help through the summer and winter so far; but after all, a Rose in December was much rarer than a rose in June, and must be paid for accordingly.

Christmas was at hand and Rose was a grand present. Then the day before Christmas Manly hauled a load of hay to town and brought back the most beautiful clock. It stood nearly two feet high from its solid walnut base to the carved leaf at its very top. The glass door that covered the face was wreathed with a gilt vine on which four gilt birds fluttered, and the pendulum that swung to and fro behind them was the color of gold too.

The clock had such a pleasant, cheerful voice as it said tick, tock, and when it struck the hour its tone was clear and sweet. Laura loved it at once.

The old round, nickel alarm clock could not be depended on to tell the right time, but still it would have answered the need, and Laura said doubtfully, "But ought you—" Then Manly told her he had traded the load of hay for it, and it would be a Christmas present for all three of them. The hay he had kept for feed was holding out so well that there would be more than enough to take the stock through the rest of the winter, and he couldn't have sold the load of hay for money because they were not shipping anymore.

Christmas was a happy time even though it was a stormy day, and they stayed quietly at home.

After the Christmas storm the weather was clear and sunny but cold—twenty-five and thirty below zero on some days.

But one day seemed unusually warm and Laura had been at home so long, she wanted to go for a sleigh ride to see Ma and Pa. Could they take the baby out safely?

They were sure they could. Some blankets were put to warming by the stove. Manly drove the cutter close to the door and made a little warm nest of them in the shelter of the dashboard. Rose was wrapped in her own warm blankets and little red cloak and hood, with a thin blue silk handkerchief lightly covering her face, and tucked tightly in among the blankets in the cutter.

Then away they went, the horses stepping quickly and the sleigh bells singing merrily.

Several times Laura put her hand in among the blankets and touched Rose's face to be sure that she was warm and that there was air beneath the veil.

It seemed only a few minutes until they drove up to the old homeplace and went quickly into the house, where Ma and Pa both scolded them well.

"You're crazy!" Pa said. "Out with that baby when it is fifteen below." And so it was by the thermometer. "She might have smothered," Ma added.

"But I watched. She couldn't have," Laura answered.

And Rose waggled her fingers and cooed. She was warm and happy and had had a good nap.

Laura had never thought it might be dangerous to take the baby out, and she was anxious on the way home and glad when they were safely there. It seemed there was a good deal to taking care of babies.

There were no more sleigh rides for some time, and then one day that was really warm they drove the four miles to see their good friends, the Boasts.

Mr. and Mrs. Boast lived by themselves on their farm. They had no children and could hardly make fuss enough over Rose.

When at last the visit was over and Mr. Boast was standing by the buggy to see them start, he started to speak, then hesitated and finally said in a queer voice, "If you folks will let me take the baby in to Ellie for her to keep, you may take the best horse out of my stable there and lead it home."

Manly and Laura were still in astonishment, and Mr. Boast

went on. "You folks can have another baby and we can't. We never can."

Manly gathered up the reins, and Laura said with a little gasp, "Oh, no! No! Drive on, Manly!" As they drove away, she hugged Rose tightly; but she was sorry for Mr. Boast as he stood still where they had left him, and for Mrs. Boast waiting in the house, knowing, she was sure, what Mr. Boast was going to propose to them.

The rest of the winter passed quickly. There were no more storms and the weather was warm for the season. April came and on all the farms seeding was begun.

On the twelfth of April, Manly went down to the barn to hitch up for the afternoon's work.

When he went into the barn the sun was shining warmly and he had no thought of storm. But when the horses were combed and brushed and harnessed, just as he was starting to take them out, there was a crash as of something smashing against the whole side of the barn. Then he heard the shriek of the wind and looking out could see nothing but whirling snow. A blizzard in April! Why, it was time for spring's work! Manly could hardly believe his eyes. He rubbed them and looked again. Then he unharnessed the team and went to the house. It was quite a little way to go and nothing whatever could be seen except the whirling snow, but there were things scattered along the path—the cutter, the wagon, the bobsled. Taking his direction from the way each stood as he came to it, he went on to the next and came safely to the porch and the house. Laura was anxiously trying to see from the window to the barn, hoping for a glimpse of Manly coming, but she couldn't see him until the door opened.

It was the worst storm of the winter and lasted two days, with no slacking of the wind which held steadily to its high wild shriek.

But all was snug at the house. The stock were safe and warm in the barn, and following the line of sleds and wagon, Manly managed to get safely to them and back once a day to give them water and fill the mangers.

When on the morning of the third day the sun rose bright and the wind came only in low gusts, it looked a wintry world.

A good many people had been caught in the storm and two travelers nearby had lost their lives.

While Mr. Bowers was working in his field, two miles south of town, two strangers had come walking from town. They stopped and inquired the way to Mr. Mathews, saying they were friends of his from Illinois. Mr. Bowers pointed out Mr. Mathews' house to them, in plain sight across the prairie, and the strangers went on their way. Soon the storm struck and Mr. Bowers went from the field to his buildings and shelter.

The day the storm was over, Mr. Bowers saw Mr. Mathews passing on his way to town and inquired about his friends from Illinois. Mr. Mathews had not seen them, so the two went searching for them.

The two strange men were found in a haystack that stood by itself on the open prairie, considerably off the course they should have followed. They had pulled hay out of the stack and lighted it to make a fire. Then they evidently had given up the idea of keeping warm by an open fire in the wind and snow and had crawled into the hole in the haystack. There they had frozen to death.

If they had kept walking, they could have "walked out" the storm, for it lasted only two days. Or if they had been properly dressed, they would not have frozen inside the haystack. But their clothes were thin, for springtime in Illinois, and not for a western blizzard.

The snow was soon gone again, and spring really came, with the singing of meadow larks and the sweetness of violets and new grass as all the prairie turned a beautiful soft green.

Laura put Rose in a clothesbasket with her tiny sunbonnet on her head and set the basket nearby while she and Manly planted the garden.

The old dog Shep was gone. He never had become reconciled to Rose but always was jealous of her. One day he went away and never came back, and his fate was never known. But a friendly, stray Saint Bernard, a huge, black dog, had come to the house and been adopted in Shep's place.

The Saint Bernard seemed to think his special job was to watch over Rose, and wherever she was, there he would be curled around her or sitting up close against her.

The cook-stove was moved into the storeroom, leaving the other room cooler for the hot weather, and in the summer kitchen Laura worked happily, with Rose and the big, black dog playing or sleeping on the floor.

There could be no horseback riding safely with a baby, but Laura did not miss it so much, because Manly fastened a dry-goods box in the front of the road-cart, leaving just enough room for Laura's feet at the end where the driver sat. When the work was done after dinner, Laura would hitch Barnum to the road-cart and with Rose in her pink sunbonnet sitting in the box would drive away wherever she cared to go. Sometimes just to town, but more often to see her Ma and the girls.

At first Ma was afraid to have Rose travel that way, but soon she became used to it. Although Barnum was a fast driver, he was as gentle as a kitten, and the cart on its two wheels was light and safe. Rose could not fall out of the box, and Laura was a good driver. She never had a moment's uneasiness with Barnum hitched to the road-cart.

And Manly didn't care how often she went, just so she came home in time to get supper.

With housework, garden work, caring for and driving with Rose, the summer soon passed and it was haying time again. Now Rose sat in the shelter of a windrow of hay and watched while Laura drove Skip on the bull rake.

Laura and Manly both liked to stay out in the sunny hayfield, and leaving Rose asleep with the big dog watching over her, Laura sometimes drove Skip and Barnum on the mowing machine while Manly raked hay with Fly and Trixy.

There were no threshers to cook for this fall, for the renters on the tree claim had the threshing done.

The yield of grain was not nearly so much as it should have been. The season had been too dry. And the price of wheat was lower—only fifty cents a bushel.

Still there was money enough to pay all the interest and some of the smaller notes, those for the mowing machine and horse rake and for the sulky plow, and the first payment was made on the harvester. There were still the wagon note and the five hundred dollars due on the house and the eight-hundred-dollar mortgage on the homestead. Seed must be kept for the next sowing, taxes must be paid, the coal must be bought, and they must live until after the next harvest.

There would also be the hay again, and this year there were two steers to sell. They were nice large two-year-olds, and they would sell for twelve dollars each; twenty-four dollars would help buy groceries.

They hadn't done so badly, considering the season.

The twenty-fifth of August had come again, and this winter and summer were the second year.

CHAPTER 3

The Third Year

WITH the coming of cool weather, Laura proposed moving the cook-stove back into the bed-sitting room, and she could not understand why Manly put it off, until one day when he came from town with a hard-coal heater.

It was a beautiful stove, the black iron nicely polished and all the nickel trimmings shining brightly.

Manly explained how buying the stove would be a saving in the end. It would take so little coal to keep it going that even though the price per ton was twelve dollars instead of the soft coal price of six, the cost would be less. Then there would be a steady, even heat night as well as day. It would keep them from taking cold by being first warm and then chilly, as with the cook-stove. The nickel top of the new stove was movable and all the cooking except baking could be done on it. On baking days a fire could be made in the summer kitchen.

Rose was creeping, or rather hitching herself, around on the floor these days, and the floor must be kept warm for her.

Laura felt that they couldn't afford the beautiful new stove, but that was Manly's business. She need not bother about it—and he did suffer with the cold. It seemed as though he could never get clothes warm enough. She was knitting him a whole long-sleeved undershirt of fine, soft, Shetland wool yarn for a Christmas surprise.

It was difficult to keep it hidden from him and get it finished, but after Christmas she could knit its mate easily.

Manly wore the new shirt when they drove in the cutter to eat Christmas dinner with the home folks.

It was dark when they started for home again and it had begun to snow. Luckily it was not a blizzard but only a snowstorm and, of course, a wind. Rose was warmly wrapped and sheltered in Laura's arms, with blankets and robes wrapped around them both and Manly in his fur coat beside them.

The going was slow against the storm in the darkness and

after some time Manly stopped the horses. "I believe they're off the road. They don't like to face the wind," he said.

He unwrapped himself from the robes, climbed out of the cutter, and looked closely at the ground, trying to find the tracks of the road, but the snow had covered every sign of it. But finally by scraping away the snow with his feet, he found the wheel tracks of the road underneath and only a little to one side.

So Manly walked the rest of the way, keeping to the road by the faint signs of it that he could find now and then, while all around in the darkness was falling snow and empty open prairie.

They were thankful when they reached home and the warmth of the hard-coal base-burner. And Manly said his new undershirt had proven its worth.

Though the weather was cold, there were no bad blizzards and the winter was slipping by very pleasantly. Laura's Cousin Peter had come up from the southern part of the state and was working for the Whiteheads, neighbors who lived several miles to the north. He often came to see them on Sunday.

To surprise Manly on his birthday Laura asked Peter and the Whiteheads to dinner, cooking and baking in the summer kitchen. It was a pleasant day and warm for winter and the dinner was a great success.

But in spite of the warm day Laura caught a severe cold and had a touch of fever so that she must stay in bed. Ma came over to see how she was and took Rose home with her for a few days. Instead of getting better, the cold got worse and settled in Laura's throat. The doctor when he came said it was not a cold at all but a bad case of diphtheria.

Well, at least Rose was out of it and safe with Ma, if she had not taken it with her. But there were several anxious days, while Manly cared for Laura, until the doctor reported that Rose had escaped the disease.

But then Manly came down with it, and on his morning visit, the doctor ordered him to bed with strict orders to stay there. He said he would send someone out from town to help them. A short time after the doctor went away, Manly's brother Royal came out to care for them. He was a bachelor, living alone, and thought he was the one could best come.

So both in the same room, with the crudest of care, Manly and Laura spent the miserable, feverish days. Laura's attack had been dangerous, while Manly's was light.

At last they were both up and around again, but the doctor had given his last advice and warning against overexertion. Royal, tired and half sick himself, had gone home, and Laura and Manly, well wrapped, had spent a day in the summer kitchen while the sick room was fumigated.

Then after a few days longer, Rose was brought home. She had learned to walk while she had been away and she seemed to have grown much older. But it was very pleasant to have her taking her little running steps around the room, and most of all, it was good to be well again.

Laura thought the trouble was all over now. But that was not to be for many a day yet.

Manly—disregarding the doctor's warning—had worked too hard, and one cold morning he nearly fell as he got out of bed, because he could not use his legs properly. They were numb to his hips and it was only after much rubbing that he could get about with Laura's help.

But together they did the chores; after breakfast, Laura helped him hitch up the wagon and he went to town to see the doctor.

"A slight stroke of paralysis," the doctor said, "from overexertion too soon after the diphtheria."

From that day on there was a struggle to keep Manly's legs so that he could use them. Some days they were better and again they were worse, but gradually they improved until he could go about his usual business if he was careful.

In the meantime spring had come. Sickness with its doctor bills had been expensive. There was no money to go on until another harvest. The renter on the tree claim was moving away and Manly in his condition could not work both pieces of land. The tree claim was not proved up and the young trees must be cultivated to hold it.

Something must be done. And in this emergency a buyer for the homestead came along. He would assume the eight-hundred-dollar mortgage and give Manly two hundred. And so the homestead was sold and Manly and Laura moved back to the tree claim one early spring day.

The little house was in bad order, but a little paint, a few fly screens, and a good cleaning made it fresh and sweet again. Laura felt that she was back home, and it was easier for Manly to walk on the level ground to the barn than it had been for him to climb up and down the hill on the homestead.

He was gradually overcoming the effect of the stroke but still would fall down if he happened to stub his toe. He could not step over a piece of board in his way but must go around it. His fingers were clumsy so that he could neither hitch up nor unhitch his team, but he could drive them once they were ready to go.

So Laura hitched up the horses and helped him get started and then was on hand ready to help him unhitch when he drove them back.

The renter had taken the tree claim with the fall plowing done so he turned it back to Manly plowed. Manly had only to harrow and seed the fields. It was slow work but he finished in good time.

The rains came as needed and the wheat and oats grew well. If it would only keep on raining often—and not hail.

There were three little calves in the barn lot and two young colts running all over the place, plus the colt they had bought with Laura's school money, now a three-year-old and grown out nicely. The little flock of hens were laying nicely. Oh, things weren't so bad after all.

Rose was toddling about the house, playing with the kitten or clinging to Laura's skirts as she went about the work.

It was a busy summer for Laura, what with the housework, caring for Rose, and helping Manly whenever he needed her. But she didn't mind doing it all, for Manly was recovering the use of his hands and feet.

Slowly the paralysis was wearing off. He was spending a great deal of time working among the young trees. It had been too dry for them to grow well the summer before and they were not starting as they should this spring.

Some of them had died. The dead ones Manly replaced, setting the new ones carefully. He pruned them all, dug around their roots, and then plowed all the ground between.

And the wheat and oats grew rank and green.

"We'll be all right this year," Manly said. "One good crop will straighten us out and there never was a better prospect."

The horses were not working hard now. Skip and Barnum did what was necessary and the ponies, Trixy and Fly, were growing fat on their picket ropes. Manly said they should be ridden, but Laura could not leave Rose alone; neither could she take her during the day with safety and pleasure.

It was quiet and there was nothing to do after supper when Rose was put to bed. She was so tired with her play that she slept soundly for hours. So Laura and Manly came to saddling the ponies and riding them on the road before the house, on the run for a half mile south and back, then around the half-circle drive before the house, a pause to see that Rose was still sleeping, and a half mile run north and back for another look at Rose until ponies and riders were both ready to stop. Trixy and Fly enjoyed the races they ran in the moonlight and the shying at the shadow of a bunch of hay in the road or the quick jump of a jack rabbit across it.

Cousin Peter came one Sunday to tell Manly and Laura that Mr. Whitehead wanted to sell his sheep, a hundred purebred Shropshires.

A presidential election was coming in the fall and it looked as though the Democrats were due to win. If they did, Mr. Whitehead, being a good Republican, was sure the country would be ruined. The tariff would be taken off, and wool and sheep would be worth nothing. Peter was sure they could be bought at a bargain. He would buy them himself if only he had a place to keep them. "How much of a bargain? What would you have to pay?" Manly asked.

Peter was sure he could buy them for two dollars apiece since Mr. Whitehead was feeling particularly uneasy about the election. "And the sale of their wool next spring ought nearly to pay for them," he added. There were one hundred sheep. Peter had one hundred dollars due him in wages. That would be half of the money needed to buy them at two dollars each. Laura was thinking aloud. They had land enough by using the school section that lay just south of them: a whole section of land with good grazing and hay free to whoever got there first and used it. For the first time Laura was glad of the Dakota law that gave two sections in every township to the schools. And especially glad that one of them adjoined their tree claim.

"We'd have pasture and hay enough and we could build good shelter," Manly said.

"But the other one hundred dollars?" Laura asked doubtfully.

Manly reminded her of the colt that they had bought with her school money, and said he believed he could sell it now for one hundred dollars. She could buy half the sheep if she wanted to gamble on them.

And so it was decided. If Peter could get the sheep for two hundred, Laura would pay half. Peter was to care for the sheep, herding them on the school section in summer. Together Peter and Manly would put up the hay, with Manly furnishing teams and machinery. Back of the hay barn they would build on another one for the sheep, opening onto a yard fenced with wire. Peter would live with them and help with the chores in return.

A few days after the colt was sold, Peter came driving the sheep into the yard that had been built for them. There were a hundred good ewes and six old ones that had been thrown in for nothing.

Every morning after that, Peter drove the sheep out onto the school section to graze, carefully herding them away from the grass that would be mowed for hay.

The rains came frequently. It even seemed as though the winds did not blow as hard as usual, and the wheat and oats grew splendidly.

The days hurried along toward harvest. Just a little while longer now and all would be well with the crop.

Fearful of hail, Manly and Laura watched the clouds. If only it would not hail.

As the days passed bringing no hailstorm, Laura found herself thinking, Everything will even up in the end; the rich have their ice in the summer but the poor get theirs in the winter. When she caught herself at it, she would laugh with a nervous catch in her throat. She must not allow herself to be under such a strain. But if only they could harvest and sell this crop, it would mean so much. Just to be free of debt and have the interest money to use for themselves would make everything so much easier through the winter that was coming soon.

At last the wheat was in the milk and again Manly estimated that the yield would be forty bushels to the acre. Then one morning the wind blew strong from the south and it was a warm wind. Before noon the wind was hot and blowing harder. And for three days the hot wind blew.

When it died down at last and the morning of the fourth was still, the wheat was dried and yellow. The grains were cooked in the milk, all dried and shrunken, absolutely shriveled. It was not worth harvesting as wheat but Manly hitched Skip and Barnum to the mowing machine and mowed it and the oats, to be stacked like hay and fed without threshing to the stock as a substitute for both hay and grain.

As soon as this was done, haying was begun, for they must cut the hay on the school section ahead of anyone else. It was theirs if they were the first to claim and cut it. Laura and Rose went to the hayfield again. Laura drove the mower while Manly raked the hay cut the afternoon before. And a neighbor boy was hired to herd the sheep while Peter helped Manly stack the hay. They stacked great ricks of hay all around the sheep barn and on three sides of the sheep yard, leaving the yard open on the south side only.

And the twenty-fifth of August came and passed and the third year of farming was ended.

CHAPTER 4

A Year of Grace

FALL plowing was begun as soon as haying was finished, but the work was too hard for Skip and Barnum to do even with the help of the ponies. Trixy and Fly were small and could not pull with strength. They were intended only for riding. Fly objected strenuously at times, kicking savagely when her tugs were being hitched.

Once when Laura was helping Manly hitch the horses to the plow and keeping watch of Rose at the same time, she lost sight of Rose. Immediately she stopped working with the harness, and looking quickly around the yard, said, "Manly, where is Rose?"

And a little hand pulled Fly's tail away from her body, on the opposite side of the four horses abreast, a little face showed between Fly and her tail, and Rose's little voice said, "Here I am!"

Now Manly's hands were not nearly so stiff and clumsy. Perhaps he could soon hitch the straps and buckle the buckles himself.

The team was tired at night. Laura could hardly bear to see them at the unhitching, Skip with his gay head hanging and Barnum's dancing feet standing so patiently still.

Manly said he would have to get another team, for he wanted to break the sixty acres of sod and have the whole 160 acres ready to seed in the spring.

"But the three years are up. Do you call this farming a success?" Laura objected.

"Well, I don't know," Manly answered. "It is not so bad. Of course, the crops have been mostly failures, but we have four cows now and some calves. We have the four horses and the colts and machinery and there are the sheep . . . If we could only get one crop. Just one good crop, and we'd be all right. Let's try it one more year. Next year may be a good crop year and we are all fixed for farming now, with no money to start anything else."

It sounded reasonable as Manly put it. There didn't seem to be anything else they could do, but as for being all fixed—the five hundred dollars still due on the house worried Laura. Nothing had been paid on it. The binder was not yet paid for and interest payments were hard to make. But still Manly might be right. This might be when their luck turned, and one good year would even things up.

Manly bought two Durham oxen that had been broken to work. They were huge animals. King was red and weighed two thousand pounds. Duke was red-and-white spotted and weighed twenty-five hundred pounds. They were as gentle as cows, and Laura soon helped hitch them up without any fear—but she fastened Rose in the house while she did so. They were cheap: only twenty-five dollars each and very strong. Now Skip and Barnum took the ponies' place and did the light work, while the cattle hitched beside them drew most of the load.

The plowing was finished easily and the breaking of the sod was done before the ground froze. It was late in doing so for it was a warm, pleasant fall.

The winter was unusually free of bad blizzards, though the weather was very cold and there was some snow.

The house was snug and comfortable with storm windows and doors, and the hard-coal heater in the front room between the front door and the east window. Manly had made the storm shed, or summer kitchen, tight by battening closely all the cracks between the board sheeting, and the cook-stove had been left there for the winter. The table had been put in its place in the front room between the pantry and bedroom doors, and Peter's cot-bed stood against the west wall of the room where the table used to stand. Geraniums blossomed in tin cans on the window sills, growing luxuriantly in the winter sunshine and the warmth from the hard-coal heater.

The days passed busily and pleasantly. Laura's time was fully occupied with her housework and Rose, while Rose was an earnest, busy little girl with her picture books and letter blocks and the cat, running around the house, intent on her small affairs.

Manly and Peter spent much of their time at the barn, caring for the stock. The barn was long, from the first stalls where the horses and colts stood, past the oxen, King and Duke, the cows and the young cattle, the snug corner where the chickens roosted, on into the sheep barn where the sheep all ran loose.

It was no small job to clean out the barn and fill all the mangers with hay. Then there was the grain to feed to the horses, and they had to be brushed regularly. And all the animals must be watered once a day.

On pleasant days Manly and Peter hauled hay in from the stacks in the fields and fed the animals from that, leaving some on the wagon in the sheep yard for the sheep to help themselves.

This was usually finished well before chore time, but one afternoon they were delayed in starting. Because the snow drifts were deep, they were hauling hay with King and Duke. The oxen could go through deep snow more easily than horses, but they were slower, and darkness came while Manly and Peter were still a mile from home.

It had begun to snow: not a blizzard, but snow was falling thickly in a slow, straight wind. There was no danger, but it was uncomfortable and annoying to be driving cattle, wallowing through snow in the pitch dark and the storm.

Then they heard a wolf howl and another; then several together. Wolves had not been doing any damage recently and there were not so many left in the country, but still they were seen at times, and now and then they killed a stray yearling or tried to get into a flock of sheep.

"That sounds toward home and as though they were going in that direction," Manly said. "Do you suppose they will go into the sheep yard?"

"Not with Laura there," Peter answered. But Manly was not so sure and they tried to hurry faster on their way.

At home Laura was beginning to be anxious. Supper was nearly ready, but she knew Manly and Peter would do the night chores before they ate. They should have been home before now and she wondered what could have happened.

Rose had been given her supper and was sleeping soundly, but Nero, the big, black dog, was uneasy. Now and then he raised his head and growled.

Then Laura heard it—the howl of a wolf! Again the wolf howled, and then several together, and after that, silence.

Laura's heart stood still. Were the wolves coming to the

sheep yard? She waited, listening, but could hear nothing but the swish of the snow against the windows; or was that a sheep blatting?

Must she go to the sheep yard and see that they were all right? She hesitated and looked at Rose, but Rose was still asleep. She would be all right if left alone. Then Laura put on her coat and hood, lighted the lantern, and taking it and the dog with her, went out into the darkness and the storm.

Quickly she went to the stable door, opened it, and reaching inside secured the five-tined stable fork; then shutting fast the door again, she went the length of the barn, flashing her lantern light as far as she could in every direction.

Nero trotted ahead of her, sniffing the air. Around the sheep yard they went but everything was quiet except for the sheep moving restlessly around inside. There was no sight nor sound of the wolves until, as Laura stood by the yard gate listening for the last time before going back to the house, there came again the lone cry of a wolf. But it was much farther to the north than before. The wolves had gone by on the west and all was well, though Nero growled low in his throat. Laura hadn't known she was frightened until she was safely in the house; then she found her knees trembling and sat down quickly.

Rose was still asleep and it was not long before Manly and Peter were there.

"What would you have done if you had found the wolves?" Manly asked.

"Why, driven them away, of course. That's what I took the pitchfork for," Laura answered.

In December Laura felt again the familiar sickness. The house felt close and hot and she was miserable. But the others must be kept warm and fed. The work must go on, and she was the one who must do it.

On a day when she was particularly blue and unhappy, the neighbor to the west, a bachelor living alone, stopped as he was driving by and brought a partly filled grain sack to the house. When Laura opened the door, Mr. Sheldon stepped inside, and taking the sack by the bottom, poured the contents out on the floor. It was a paper-backed set of Waverley novels.

"Thought they might amuse you," he said. "Don't be in a hurry! Take your time reading them!" And as Laura exclaimed in delight, Mr. Sheldon opened the door, closed it behind him quickly, and was gone. And now the four walls of the close, overheated house opened wide, and Laura wandered with brave knights and ladies fair beside the lakes and streams of Scotland or in castles and towers, in noble halls or lady's bower, all through the enchanting pages of Sir Walter Scott's novels.

She forgot to feel ill at the sight or smell of food, in her hurry to be done with the cooking and follow her thoughts back into the book. When the books were all read and Laura came back to reality, she found herself feeling much better.

It was a long way from the scenes of Scott's glamorous old tales to the little house on the bleak, wintry prairie, but Laura brought back from them some of their magic and music and the rest of the winter passed quite comfortably.

Spring came early and warm. By the first of April a good deal of seeding had been done and men were busy in all the fields. The morning of the second was sunny and warm and still. Peter took the sheep out to graze on the school section as usual, while Manly went to the field. It was still difficult for him to hitch up the team, and Laura helped him get started. Then she went about her morning's work.

Soon a wind started blowing from the northwest, gently at first but increasing in strength until at nine o'clock the dust was blowing in the field so thickly that Manly could not see to follow the seeder marks. So he came from the field and Laura helped him unhitch and get the team in the barn.

Once more in the house they could only listen to the rising wind and wonder why Peter didn't bring the sheep in. "He couldn't have taken them far in such a short time and he surely would bring them back," Manly said. Dust from the fields was blowing in clouds so dense that they could see only a little way from the windows, and in a few minutes Manly went to find Peter and the sheep and help if help were needed.

He met Peter with the sheep about four hundred yards or one-quarter of a mile from the barn. Peter was on foot, leading his pony and carrying three lambs in his arms. He and the dog were working the sheep toward their yard. The sheep could hardly go against the wind but they had to face it to get home. They had not been sheared and their fleeces were long and heavy. The poor sheep with their small bodies and little feet carrying such a load of fluffy wool caught too much wind. If a sheep turned ever so little sideways, the wind would catch under the wool, lift the sheep from its feet and roll it over and over, sometimes five or six times before it could stop. Against the strength of the wind it was impossible for the sheep to get to its feet. Peter would lift it up and stand it on its feet headed right so it could walk into the wind. He was tired and the sheep dog and pony were powerless to help, so it was time for Manly to be there.

It took them both over an hour to get all the sheep the four hundred yards and into the yard.

After that they all sat in the house and let the wind blow. Their ears were filled with the roar of it. Their eyes and throats smarted from the dust that was settling over the room even though the doors and windows were tightly closed.

Just before noon there came a knock at the door, and when Manly opened it, a man stood on the step.

"Just stopped to tell you, your wheels are going round," he said, and with a wave of his hand toward the barn, he ran to his wagon, climbed in, and drove on down the road. His face was black with dust and he was gone before they recognized him as the man who had bought their homestead.

Laura laughed hysterically. "Your wheels are going round," she said. "What did he mean?" She and Manly went into the kitchen and looked from the window toward the barn and then they knew. Between the house and barn, the hay wagon with the big hayrack on it had been left standing. The wind had lifted it, turned it over and dropped it bottom side up. The wagon rested on the rack underneath, leaving the wheels free in the air, and every one of the four wheels was turning in the wind.

There was only a cold bite to eat at noon, for no one felt like eating and it was not safe to light a fire.

About one o'clock Laura insisted that she could smell fire and that there must be a prairie fire near, but no smoke could be seen through the clouds of dust.

The wind always rises with a fire, and on the prairie the wind many times blows strongly enough to carry flame from the fire to light grass ahead of the burning, so that the fire travels faster than the grass burns. Once Manly and Peter had raced toward a fire trying to save a large haystack that stood between it and them. They ran their horses' heads up to the stack and jumped off just as a blown flame lit the opposite end of the haystack. Each had a wet grain sack to fight the fire. They scrambled up the stack and slid down the end, scraping the fire off and putting it out at the ground after it had burned back a little way from the end of the stack. They let it run down each side as a back fire and the main fire raced by and on, leaving the haystack with Manly and Peter and horses untouched. The horses had stood with their heads against the stack where they could breathe.

The wind reached its peak about two o'clock, then slackened gradually, so slowly at first it was hardly noticeable, but it died away as the sun went down and was still.

Rose lay asleep with her tired, dusty little face streaked with perspiration. Laura felt prostrated with exhaustion, and Manly and Peter walked like old men as they went out to the barn to see that the stock was all right for the night.

Later they learned that there had been a prairie fire during the sixty-five mile an hour wind, a terrible raging fire that hardly hesitated at firebreaks, for the wind tore flames loose and carried them far ahead of the burning grass. In places the fire leaped, leaving unburned prairie, the flame going ahead and the wind blowing out the slower fire in the grass as a candle is blown out.

Houses and barns with good firebreaks around them were burned. Stock was caught and burned. At one place a new lumberwagon stood in a plowed field a hundred yards from the grass. It was loaded with seed wheat just as the owner had left it when he had gone from the field because of the wind. When he went back, there was nothing left of the wagon and its load except the wagon irons. Everything else had burned.

There was no stopping such a fire and no fighting it in such a wind.

It went across the country, leaving a blackened prairie behind until it reached the river, and then the wind went down with the sun. There it stopped, somewhere between fifty and one hundred miles from where it began.

There was nothing to do but to re-seed the fields, for the seed was blown away or buried in the drifts of soil around the edges of the plowed land.

So Manly bought more seed wheat and oats at the elevator in town, and at last the seeding was finished.

Then the sheep were sheared and the selling of the wool cheered them all, for wool was worth twenty-five cents a pound and the sheep averaged ten pounds of wool apiece. Each sheep had paid for itself and fifty cents more with its wool alone. By the last of May, the lambs had all arrived, and there were so many twins that the flock was more than doubled. Lambing time was a busy time, both day and night, for the sheep must be watched and the lambs cared for. Among the hundred sheep there were only five ewes who could not or would not care for their lambs. These five lambs were brought into the house and warmed and fed milk from a bottle and raised by hand.

Rose spent her time playing in the yard now, and Laura tried to watch her as the little pink sunbonnet went busily bobbing here and there.

Once Laura was just in time to see Rose struggle upright in the tub of water that stood under the pump spout; and with water running down her face and from her spread fingers at each side, Rose said without a whimper, "I want to go to bed."

One afternoon, just after Rose had been washed and combed and dressed in fresh, clean clothes, Laura heard her shrieking with laughter, and going to the door, saw her running from the barn. "O-o-o," Rose called. "Barnum did just like this." And down she dropped in the dusty path, and with arms and legs waving, rolled over and over on the ground. She was such a comical sight that Laura could only laugh too, in spite of the wreck of the clean dress, the dirt on her face and hands and the dust in her hair.

Another time, Laura missed her from the yard and with fear in her heart ran to the barn door. Barnum was lying down in his stall and Rose sat on his side, kicking her heels against his stomach.

Carefully, so as not to disturb his body, the horse raised his head and looked at Laura and she was positive Barnum winked one eye.

After that Laura tried to watch Rose closer, but she couldn't bear to keep her in the house with the spring so fresh and gay outside. The work must be done between moments of looking at Rose through door and window.

Once again she was just in time to see Rose miss an accident by a narrow margin. She had evidently gone farther afield than usual and was just coming back around the corner of the barn. Then Kelpie, Trixy's latest colt, came running around the same corner with another colt chasing her. Kelpie saw Rose too late to turn, too late to stop, so she put an extra spring in her muscles and sailed over Rose's head, while Susan, the other colt, proving, as she always tried to, that she could do anything Kelpie did, followed behind, going neatly over Rose's head.

Then Laura was there, and snatching Rose up, carried her to the house. Rose had not been frightened, but Laura was, and she felt rather sick. How could she ever keep up the daily work and still go through what was ahead. There was so much to be done and only herself to do it. She hated the farm and the stock and the smelly lambs, the cooking of food and the dirty dishes. Oh, she hated it all, and especially the debts that must be paid whether she could work or not.

But Rose *hadn't* been hurt and now she was wanting a bottle to feed one of the pet lambs. Laura would do the same; she'd be darned if she'd go down and stay down or howl about it. What was it someone had said in that story she read the other day? "The wheel goes round and round and the fly on the top'll be the fly on the bottom after a while." Well, she didn't care what became of the top fly, but she did wish the bottom one could crawl up a little way. She was tired of waiting for the wheel to turn. And the farmers were the ones at the bottom, she didn't care what Manly said. If the weather wasn't right they had nothing, but whether they had anything or not they must find it somehow to pay interest and taxes and a profit to the businessmen in town on everything they bought, and they must buy to live. There was that note at the bank Manly had to give to get the money to buy the grain for the re-seeding after the wind storm. He was paying three percent a month on that note. That was where the wool money would have to go. No one could pay such interest as that. But there was all the summer's living before another harvest. Her head spun when she tried to figure it out.

Would there be enough money to pay it? Their share of the wool money was only $125, and how much was that note? A bushel to the acre of seed wheat and $1 a bushel for the seed: $100. Sixty acres of oats and two bushels to the acre of seed: 120 bushels. At 42¢ a bushel, that would be $50.40. Added to the $100 for wheat the note must be for $150.40.

It seemed to make a great difference in the price whether they were selling wheat or buying it. To be sure, as Manly said, there were freight charges out and back and elevator charges. But it didn't seem fair even so.

Anyway, they should pay the note at the bank as soon as possible. If they had to do so they could buy a book of coupons at the grocery store and give a note for that at only two percent a month. It was rather nice that the merchants had got those books with coupons from 25¢ to $5 in twenty-five- or fifty-dollar books. It was convenient and it was cheaper interest. They had not bought any yet, and she had hoped they would not have to. Somehow the thought of it hurt her pride worse than a note at the bank. But pride must not stand in the way of a saving of one percent. She wouldn't think about it anymore. Manly would do as he thought best about it. It was his business and he wasn't worrying.

As spring turned the corner into summer, the rains stopped and the grain began to suffer for lack of moisture. Every morning Manly looked anxiously for signs of rain, and seeing none, went on about his work.

And then the hot winds came. Every day the wind blew strongly from the south. It felt on Laura's cheek like the hot air from the oven when she opened the oven door on baking day. For a week, the hot winds blew, and when they stopped, the young wheat and oats were dried, brown and dead.

The trees on the ten acres were nearly all killed too. Manly decided there was no hope of replanting to have the trees growing to fulfill the law for the claims.

It was time to prove up and he could not. There was only one way to save the land. He could file on it as a pre-emption. If he did that he must prove up in six months and pay the United States $1.25 an acre. The continuous residence would be no trouble, for they were already there. The two hundred dollars cash at the end of the six months would be hard to find, but there was no other way. If Manly did not file on the land someone else would, for if he failed to prove up, the land would revert to the government and be open to settlement by anyone.

So Manly pre-empted the land. There was one advantage: Manly did not have to work among the trees anymore. Here and there one had survived and those Manly mulched with manure and straw from the barn. The mulching would help to keep the land moist underneath and so help the trees to live. The cottonwood tree before Laura's pantry window, being north of the house, had been protected from the full force of the hot winds and from the sun. It was growing in spite of the drought. Laura loved all its green branches that waved just the other side of the glass as she prepared food on the broad shelf before the window and washed the dishes there.

No rain followed the windstorm, but often after that cyclone clouds would form in the sky and then drift away. It was cyclone weather.

One sultry afternoon, Manly was in town and Peter gone with the sheep. Laura finished her work and she and Rose went out in the yard. Rose was playing with her play dishes under the cottonwood tree on the shady side of the house while Laura idly watched the clouds more from force of habit than a real fear, for she had become used to the danger of storms.

The wind had been from the south strongly in the morning, but had died down, and now Laura noticed clouds piling up in the north. There was a solid bank of blackness and before it clouds rolled. Now the wind rose, blowing hard from the south, and watching, Laura saw the dreaded funnel-shaped cloud drop its point toward the ground from the wall of black. The light turned a greenish color, and seizing Rose, Laura ran with her into the house. She quickly shut all the doors and windows before she ran into the pantry to look again, from its window, toward the storm.

The point of the funnel had touched the ground and she could see the dust rise up. It passed over a field of new breaking and the strips of sod were lifted up out of sight. Then it struck an old haystack. There was a blur and the stack disappeared. The funnel-shaped cloud was moving toward the house. Laura lifted the trap door in the pantry floor and taking Rose with her went quickly through it into the cellar, dropping the door shut behind her. Holding Rose tightly, she cowered close in a corner in the darkness and listened to the wind shriek above them, expecting every second that the house would be lifted and carried away.

But nothing happened, and after what seemed hours but was really only a few minutes she heard Manly's voice calling.

Lifting the cellar door Laura carried Rose up the stairs. She found Manly standing by his team in the yard, watching the storm as it passed eastward less than a quarter of a mile north from where they stood. It went on blowing away buildings and haystacks, but only a sprinkle of rain fell on the parched earth. Manly, in town, had seen the storm cloud and hurried home so that Laura and Rose should not be alone.

There were no more cyclones, but the weather continued hot and dry, and August the fifth was especially warm.

In the afternoon Manly sent Peter to bring Laura's Ma, and at four o'clock he sent Peter again to town, this time on his running pony for the doctor. But their son was born before the doctor could get there.

Laura was proud of the baby, but strangely she wanted Rose more than anything. Rose had been kept away from her mother for the sake of quiet, and a hired girl was taking indifferent care of her. When Laura insisted, the girl brought Rose in, a shy little thing with a round baby face herself, to see the little brother.

After that Laura rested easily and soon could take an interest in the sounds from outside, knowing well, from them, what was going on.

One day Peter came to the bedroom door to bid her good morning. He had stuck a long feather in his hatband and as it nodded above his good-natured face he looked so comical that Laura had to laugh.

Then she heard him talking to his pony and calling his dog and knew he was taking the sheep out. He was singing:

> Oh, my! but ain't she handsome!
> Dear me! she's the sweetest name!
> Ky! yi! to love her is my dooty,
> My pretty, little, posy-pink
> Jenny Jerusha Jane.

And Peter and the sheep were gone until night.

Then she heard Rose playing with the pet lambs. They were so large now that three of them went out with the sheep, but the two smallest still hung around the back door and yard to be fed and played with. Often they pushed Rose over, but it was all in the game. Then she heard the hired girl refuse to give Rose a piece of bread and butter, speaking crossly to her, and that Laura could not bear. Calling from her bed, she settled the question in Rose's favor.

Laura felt she must hurry and get her strength back. Rose shouldn't be meanly treated by any hired girl; and besides, there were the wages of five dollars a week. They must be stopped as soon as possible for the time would come soon enough to pay a note.

Laura was doing her own work again one day three weeks later when the baby was taken with spasms, and he died so quickly that the doctor was too late.

To Laura, the days that followed were mercifully blurred. Her feelings were numbed and she only wanted to rest—to rest and not to think.

But the work must go on. Haying had begun and Manly, Peter, and the herd boy must be fed. Rose must be cared for and all the numberless little chores attended to.

The hay was going to be short of what was needed, for it had been so dry that even the wild prairie grass had not grown well. There were more sheep and cattle and horses to feed, so there must be more hay instead of less.

Manly and Peter were putting up hay on some land two miles away a week later. Laura started the fire for supper in the kitchen stove. The summer fuel was old, tough, long, slough hay, and Manly had brought an armful into the kitchen and put it down near the stove.

After lighting the fire and putting the tea kettle on, Laura went back into the other part of the house, shutting the kitchen door.

When she opened it again, a few minutes later, the whole inside of the kitchen was ablaze: the ceiling, the hay, and the floor underneath and wall behind.

As usual, a strong wind was blowing from the south, and by the time the neighbors arrived to help, the whole house was in flames.

Manly and Peter had seen the fire and come on the run with the team and the load of hay.

Laura had thrown one bucket of water on the fire in the hay, and then, knowing she was not strong enough to work the pump for more water, taking the little deed-box from the bedroom and Rose by the hand, she ran out and dropped on the ground in the little half-circle drive before the house. Burying her face on her knees she screamed and sobbed, saying over and over, "Oh, what will Manly say to me?" And there Manly found her and Rose, just as the house roof was falling in.

The neighbors had done what they could but the fire was so fierce that they were unable to go into the house.

Mr. Sheldon had gone in through the pantry window and thrown all the dishes out through it toward the trunk of the little cottonwood tree, so the silver wedding knives and forks and spoons rolled up in their wrappers had survived. Nothing else had been saved from the fire except the deed-box, a few work clothes, three sauce dishes from the first Christmas dishes, and the oval glass bread plate around the margin of which were the words, "Give us this day our daily bread."

And the young cottonwood stood by the open cellar hole, scorched and blackened and dead.

After the fire Laura and Rose stayed at her Pa's for a few days. The top of Laura's head had been blistered from the fire and something was wrong with her eyes. The doctor said the heat had injured the nerves and so she rested for a little at her old home, but at the end of the week Manly came for her.

Mr. Sheldon needed a housekeeper and gave Laura and Manly houseroom and use of his furniture in return for board for himself and his brother. Now Laura was so busy she had no time for worry, caring for her family of three men, Peter, and Rose, through the rest of the haying and while Manly and Peter built a long shanty, three rooms in a row, near the ruins of their house. It was built of only one thickness of boards and tar-papered on the outside, but it was built tightly, and being new, it was very snug and quite warm.

September nights were growing cool when the new house was ready and moved into. The twenty-fifth of August had passed unnoticed and the year of grace was ended.

*

Was farming a success?

"Well, it all depends on how you look at it," Manly said when Laura asked him the question.

They had had a lot of bad luck, but anyone was liable to have bad luck even if he weren't a farmer. There had been so many dry seasons now that surely next year would be a good crop year.

They had a lot of stock. The two oldest colts would be ready to sell in the spring. Some newcomer to the land would be sure to want them, and there were the younger colts coming on. There were a couple of steers ready to sell now. Oh, they'd likely bring twelve or thirteen dollars apiece.

And there were the sheep, twice as many as last year to keep, and some lambs and the six old sheep to sell.

By building the new house so cheaply, they had money left to help pay for proving up on the land.

Maybe sheep were the answer. "Everything will be all right, for it all evens up in time. You'll see," Manly said, as he started for the barn.

As Laura watched him go, she thought, yes, everything is evened up in time. The rich have their ice in the summer, but the poor get theirs in the winter, and ours is coming soon.

Winter was coming on, and in sight of the ruins of their comfortable little house they were making a fresh start with nothing. Their possessions would no more than balance their debts, if that. If they could find the two hundred dollars to prove up, the land would be theirs, anyway, and Manly thought he could.

It would be a fight to win out in this business of farming, but strangely she felt her spirit rising for the struggle.

The incurable optimism of the farmer who throws his seed on the ground every spring, betting it and his time against the elements, seemed inextricably to blend with the creed of her pioneer forefathers that "it is better farther on"—only instead of farther on in space, it was farther on in time, over the horizon of the years ahead instead of the far horizon of the west.

She was still the pioneer girl and she could understand Manly's love of the land through its appeal to herself.

"Oh, well," Laura sighed, summing up her idea of the situation in a saying of her Ma's, "We'll always be farmers, for what is bred in the bone *will* come out in the flesh."

And then Laura smiled, for Manly was coming from the barn and he was singing:

You talk of the mines of Australia,
They've wealth in red gold, without doubt;
But, ah! there is gold in the farm, boys—
If only you'll shovel it out.

APPENDIX

Autobiographical Sketch for "The Junior Book of Authors"

I WAS born in the Little House in the Big Woods of Wisconsin.

From there, with my parents and sisters, I traveled in a prairie schooner across Minnesota, Iowa, Missouri, and Kansas, and into Indian Territory, where we lived in the Little House on the Prairie. Then traveling back to western Minnesota we lived for several years on the banks of Plum Creek. From there we went West again, to the shores of Silver Lake in Dakota Territory. We lived in De Smet, the Little Town on the Prairie, and I married Almanzo of *Farmer Boy*, just as I told in *These Happy Golden Years.*

After our marriage Almanzo and I lived for a while in the little gray house on the tree claim. Then with our little daughter, Rose (now Rose Wilder Lane, the author), we went to live in the piney woods of Florida, where the trees always murmur, where the butterflies are enormous, where plants that eat insects grow in moist places, and alligators inhabit the slowly moving waters of the rivers. But at that time and in that place, a Yankee woman was more of a curiosity than any of these.

At last, in 1894, we came to the Ozarks. There is no other country like the Ozarks in the world. This land is the very oldest land on this continent. It rose long ago from the sea and was a lonely island while all the rest of North America was still under the ocean. The island then was an almost flat slope of drying mud and of sea sand pressed into flat sandstone, and nothing lived on it but little sea-slugs and snails that died when the mud dried. Almanzo still finds their shapes molded in the rocks, and sometimes their small curled shells.

For millions of years the streams have been cutting deeper into the flat slope of the island, while all the rest of North America came up from the sea, until now the Ozark streams have cut such deep valleys that the land between them is steep, high mountains. But the Ozarks are really not mountains, they are valleys. So the skyline is always level and blue like the sea, and nearly always there is a lovely blue haze over all the hillsides cut so deeply in this old, old land.

On one low hill that in the springtime is covered with a blue carpet of wild violets, there is a white farmhouse; a U.S. Highway curves at the foot of the hill. Behind the house is a gulch where a little stream wanders, and behind the gulch rises a steep, high hill where tall oaks grow, and dogwoods and redbuds that bloom in the spring.

Almanzo and I live in this white farmhouse with our pet bulldog, and in the barns and pastures are our milk goats and our Rocky Mountain burro. All summer we gather fresh vegetables and berries from our garden and in the fall we gather walnuts and pecans from our own trees.

Almanzo used to have horses and drive through town faster than the first automobiles, until the marshal once warned him that he was exceeding the speed limit. Before there were automobiles there were no speed limits. But now that Almanzo is past ninety years old he has given up horses and drives a car instead.

Pa and Ma and my sisters all are gone; of the family I alone am left. But Pa's fiddle is in the museum of the South Dakota Historical Society, where every year someone will play on it the songs he used to play.

It has been many years since I beat eggs with a fork, or cleaned a kerosene lamp. Many things have changed since then, but the truths we learned from our parents and the principles they taught us are always true; they can never change. Great improvements in living have been made because every American has been free to pursue his happiness, and so long as Americans are free they will continue to make our country ever more wonderful.

"Dear Children": A Letter from Laura Ingalls Wilder

HARPER & BROTHERS

PUBLISHERS SINCE 1817

49 East 33rd Street, New York 16, N.Y.

Dear Children:

I was born in the "Little House in the Big Woods" of Wisconsin on February 7 in the year 1867. I lived everything that happened in my books. It is a long story, filled with sunshine and shadow, that we have lived since *These Happy Golden Years.* After our marriage, Almanzo and I lived for a little while in the little gray house on the tree claim. In the year 1894 we and our little daughter, Rose, left Dakota in a covered wagon and moved to a farm in the Ozarks. We cleared the land and built our own farm house. Eventually we had 200 acres of improved land, a herd of cows, good hogs, and the best laying flock of hens in the country. For many years we did all our own work, but now almost all of the land has been rented or sold. For recreation, we used to ride horseback or in our buggy—later on, our Chrysler. We read and played music and attended church socials.

In 1949, Almanzo died at the age of 92. We had been married for 63 years. Our daughter, Rose Wilder Lane, the novelist, now lives in Connecticut.

You may be interested to know what happened to some of the other people you have met in my books. Ma and Pa lived for a while on their homestead and then moved into town where Pa did carpentry. After Mary graduated from the College for the Blind she lived at home. She was always cheerful and busy with her work, her books and music. Carrie worked for the *De Smet News* for a while after finishing high school, and then she married a mine owner and moved to the Black Hills. Grace married a farmer and lived a few miles outside of De Smet. All of them have been dead for some years now.

Mary Power married the young banker and did not live many years. Ida married her Elmer and moved to California. Cap Garland was killed in the explosion of a threshing machine engine. Nellie Oleson went East, married, and moved to Louisiana where she is now buried.

Several years before Almanzo's death, he and I took a trip back to De Smet for a reunion with our old friends. Many of the old buildings had been replaced. Everywhere we went we recognized faces, but we were always surprised to find them old and gray like ourselves, instead of being young as in our memories. There is one thing that will always remain the same to remind people of little Laura's days on the prairie, and that is Pa's fiddle, which is now in Memorial Hall of the State Historical Society at Pierre, South Dakota. Every year at a public concert, someone plays on it the songs Pa used to play.

The "Little House" books are stories of long ago. The way we live and your schools are much different now, so many things have made living and learning easier. But the real things haven't changed. It is still best to be honest and truthful; to make the most of what we have; to be happy with simple pleasures and to be cheerful and have courage when things go wrong. Great improvements in living have been made because every American has always been free to pursue his happiness, and so long as Americans are free they will continue to make our country ever more wonderful.

With love to you all and best wishes for your happiness, I am

Sincerely, your friend,

Laura Ingalls Wilder

CHRONOLOGY

NOTE ON THE TEXTS

NOTES

Chronology

1867 Born Laura Elizabeth Ingalls, February 7, near Pepin, Wisconsin, the second child of Charles Phillip Ingalls and Caroline Quiner Ingalls. Mary Amelia is her older sister, born in 1865. (Parents hail from pioneering families. Charles Ingalls, born in Allegany County, New York, in 1836, is among the ninth generation of his family in North America, his ancestor Edmund Ingalls having journeyed from England to Salem, Massachusetts, in 1628. Charles's father, Lansford Whiting Ingalls, moved with his family from New York to Illinois in 1845, and then, in 1853, to Jefferson County, Wisconsin, near the frontier west of Milwaukee. Farming nearby, across the Oconomowoc River, was Charlotte Quiner—later Mrs. Frederick Holbrook—a widow with six children, one of them Caroline Lake Quiner, born 1839. Eventually, three Ingalls offspring married Quiners: in 1859, Henry Quiner wed Polly Ingalls; in 1860, Charles wed Caroline; and in 1861, Peter Ingalls wed Eliza Quiner; Wilder will call the children of these aunts and uncles "double cousins." Around 1862, their Jefferson County property lost in arrears, the extended Ingalls family, including Charles's parents and Henry and Polly Quiner, embarked for western Wisconsin, near Lake Pepin.) Baby Laura born in log cabin built on partially cleared land seven miles north of Pepin, 160 acres purchased in 1863 by father and Henry Quiner with $35 down, remainder of purchase price, $335, mortgaged. Father farms southern half of property, uncle northern. In November, as post–Civil War economy weakens, the men sell halves to each other, enabling individual sale.

1868 Father and uncle sell Wisconsin properties for a thousand dollars each to a Swedish immigrant, Gustaf Gustafson, on installment. Before leaving the state, both purchase eighty acres in Chariton County, Missouri, perhaps sight unseen, from land agent, for nine hundred dollars, also on time.

1869 In August, her father, perhaps accompanied by family, journeys to Chariton County to sign power of attorney enabling grandfather Lansford Ingalls to collect payments from Gustafson in Wisconsin. Later that fall or in early 1870, the

Ingallses travel to Kansas, by this time known as the "Squatter State." They settle on land designated as the Osage Diminished Reserve (north of Indian Territory), where an 1865 treaty prohibits homesteading. The fifty-mile-wide strip along Kansas's southern border is all that remains to the tribe after it ceded millions of acres of Great Plains territory to the U.S. government earlier in the century. With President Grant failing to act on tribe's request for troops to protect land from incursions and theft, the Osage find themselves in desperate circumstances, near starvation. They pledge to keep peace with whites but are hard-pressed by hostile tribes and settlers bent on sparking confrontation; the previous year, they reluctantly signed the Sturges Treaty, allowing for sale of Reserve for pennies an acre to a railroad and their removal to Indian Territory in what is now Oklahoma. Although the treaty is never enacted, news of its signing sets off a land rush of settlers hoping to force the government to open the Reserve. By mid-1869, six hundred settlers illegally occupy land in Montgomery County, Kansas, almost entirely within the Reserve. The Ingallses are soon among them, building thirteen miles southwest of Independence, in Rutland Township, six miles north of state line and southern boundary of the Reserve. At Christmas, settler from across creek brings candy to Ingalls girls.

1870 Tensions rise higher as more than seven thousand settlers have flooded into Montgomery County. In January, a regional Indian Agent warns superiors in Washington, D.C., that Osage may "massacre the inhabitants . . . in a few hours." Federal troops are sent to keep peace while Osage debate Sturges Treaty and their fate; chiefs demand that settlers leave. In later years, Wilder recalls hearing by night, from an Indian encampment near the creek, "the most frightful shouting and screaming," described by father as "war dances." Erroneous news accounts claiming that tribes plan to seize land and destroy settlements fuel alarm among whites. During summer, Congress approves legislation to remove Osage to Indian Territory, but tribe refuses to depart until settlers are cleared from new allotment to the south. General William T. Sherman sends cavalry to Territory to remove settlers; Kansas newspaper mistakenly reports that removal order covers Reserve. Rumors about cavalry's mission may prompt Ingallses to leave Kansas. On August 3, the Ingalls family Bible records birth of third child, Caroline Celestia (Carrie) Ingalls, in Montgomery

County, Kansas; the 1870 federal census, conducted shortly thereafter, also places them there, noting that "settlers had no title." That fall, Gustafson writes Ingalls to say that he cannot meet payments on Wisconsin property. Family departs, traveling through Missouri (having relinquished Chariton County land for lack of funds), where they wait for weather to improve. Along the way, father trades ponies, Pet and Patty, for larger team; Jack, the family dog, goes with ponies.

1871 In May, the Ingallses arrive in Wisconsin, staying with Henry and Polly Quiner until Gustafson moves out of family's cabin. Over the summer, sister Mary attends school a half mile away at Barry Corner with her "double cousins." Laura joins them in the fall for a few months but then is taken out of school. Peter Ingalls and family visit at Christmas; extended clan gathers soon after for dance at grandfather Lansford Ingalls's house.

1873 Panic of 1873 ushers in extended economic stagnation. Parents sell Pepin land; family winters with relatives.

1874 In February, while ice on Mississippi remains thick enough for wagons to cross, the Ingallses set out with Uncle Peter Ingalls and his family for Minnesota, where railroad lines are being established and property is available. Uncle Peter stops at Zumbro River in southeastern Minnesota while parents head further west, arriving in newly established railroad town, Walnut Station (later Walnut Grove), by spring. In October, Charles Ingalls purchases 172 acres and a dugout two miles north of town on Plum Creek, the low price ($430) reflecting crop failures caused by drought and severe infestation by Rocky Mountain locust. Crop losses lead to near-starvation that winter in Minnesota, Kansas, Nebraska, Iowa, Colorado, and Dakota Territory; federal food aid is distributed. Over next four years, locusts consume half the agricultural output of the country. Father works for Eleck Nelson, Norwegian immigrant and neighbor, while family joins Union Congregational Church as charter members, meeting the Reverend Edwin Alden and attending Christmas party in newly built church. Father contributes $26.15 for church bell.

1875 Father builds house on Plum Creek property and sows wheat, which grows well until the largest locust swarm in history, 18 hundred miles long and 110 miles wide, descends upon Great Plains, covering 198 thousand square miles. Consisting of 3.5 trillion insects, the swarm ravages crops, bankrupting farms across west. (Twenty-eight years later, Rocky Mountain locust is extinct, possible victim of ecological changes wrought by farming; last living individual collected in 1902.) Walking two hundred miles to eastern Minnesota, father works harvest for cash. That fall, with mother expecting, the family moves into Walnut Grove. Mary and Laura return from school November 1 to find baby brother, Charles Frederick Ingalls (Freddie, for mother's stepfather Frederick Holbrook), resting beside her in bed. Proud, they hurry home from school each day to see him.

1876 Back in Plum Creek house by spring, the girls walk to school in town, where Laura is awed and irritated by children of local store owner, Nellie and Willie Owens, who feast on candy and flaunt toys and dolls. She will later recall being "fascinated by so many books" at Nellie's birthday party, reading while others play. (The proud Nellie will serve as one of several models for Wilder's character Nellie Oleson.) Another wheat crop falls to hatching locusts, which again denude countryside. Parents sell and move on, planning to manage hotel in Burr Oak, Iowa, with another Walnut Grove couple. On the way, infant Freddie sickens and dies, August 27, while family stays with Peter Ingalls by the Zumbro River. ("One awful day he straightened out his little body and was dead," Laura will remember.) Family endures "cold, miserable" journey to Burr Oak, which they find dirty and dispiriting. Next to a saloon sits the Masters Hotel, where Mary and Laura wait tables and wash dishes; the door between kitchen and dining room sports a bullet hole, "thrilling to us children." Family attends church Christmas program (with young Hamlin Garland in attendance), but the holiday is disappointing, with parents tired and distracted, and girls catching measles.

1877 In January, the family leaves hotel for rooms over grocery, seeking calmer quarters. Unbeknownst to Mary and Laura, townspeople gather below to hear them reading "The Village Blacksmith" and "Paul Revere's Ride." Alarmed after saloon catches fire and when downstairs neighbor is caught dragging his wife around by her hair, family moves again, to house near edge of town, where Grace Pearl Ingalls is born, May 23. A neighbor approaches mother about adopting ten-year-old Laura but is gently rebuffed. Laura enjoys "delightful summer" shepherding the family cow to pasture but becomes aware that parents are deeply concerned about money, father playing "lonesome, longing" tunes on the fiddle and yearning to go west, distressed by bills tying them to Burr Oak. In autumn, pledging not to pay "rich old skinflint" landlord, father sells cow and quietly loads possessions into wagon, awakening children in the middle of night to flee Iowa. Family returns to Walnut Grove and girls to school.

1878 Girls are taught by Samuel Masters (brother of William Masters, former Burr Oak hotel owner, now running hotel in Walnut Grove) and encounter his haughty daughter, Genevieve, later a model for Wilder's character Nellie Oleson. Father builds house behind hotel, runs butcher shop. In summer, Laura works at hotel for fifty cents a week, cleaning, washing dishes, babysitting. Work finished, she reads serials in weekly *New York Ledger*, "great stories they were," furnished with heroines, villains, jewels, and "secret caverns."

1879 Elected justice of the peace, Charles Ingalls works in family's front room where Laura enjoys eavesdropping, fascinated by outbursts of lawyer with an "ungovernable temper." In spring, Mary grows delirious with fever. Seeing her sister's face "drawn out of shape," Laura recalls Mary's favorite oak in Wisconsin as it looked after being struck by lightning. Head shaved, Mary recovers but her eyesight gradually fails; doctors suggest a stroke has damaged optic nerves. Years later, Wilder will remember the last thing Mary saw "was the bright blue of Grace's eyes" as the toddler looked up at her, standing next to her chair. Father asks Laura to "see" aloud for her sister; Wilder will later say her parents were never the same. That summer, father's sister, Laura Ladocia (Docia) Forbes, stops in Walnut Grove on her way west, urging him to accept position as timekeeper and bookkeeper in Dakota Territory, working for her husband, railroad contractor Hiram Forbes. Charles accepts, sells house, and embarks. Mother and sisters meet him later, taking train to Tracy, Minnesota. "Going in the direction which always brought the happiest changes," as Wilder later puts it, family journeys by covered wagon to Silver Lake, stopping at Brookings railroad camp in Dakota Territory, where Laura rides ponies with her cousin, Lena, one of Docia's children. Ingallses winter in surveyors' house on north shore of Silver Lake with boarder, virtually alone in region until Robert Boast, a fellow railroad worker, and his wife arrive at Christmastime. ("We felt as though we had got back to civilization again," Charles Ingalls would recall, long after the Boasts had become close friends.) The Reverend Alden unexpectedly stops by, reporting that a college for the blind exists in Iowa.

1880 Spring land rush looming, father beats crowd by filing claim in February, in Brookings, for 154 acres south of Silver Lake. West of the lake, De Smet is platted as railroad town; father buys two business lots and erects buildings, the first sold for hardware store, the second becoming temporary home. In spring, after hearing of the murder of a fellow homesteader, family moves to shanty near Silver Lake, struggling financially. Laura follows father's example of eating little, leaving food for the rest, "eating raw turnips between meals." Uncle Forbes leaves Mary with handful of greenbacks as he departs for west, having committed what Wilder will later call a "curiously satisfying" scam on the railroad. The Ingallses move to town after violent blizzard of October 15 to be closer to supplies, but are burdened with feeding and sheltering boarders George Masters, his wife Maggie, and their infant, born in the Ingalls home as winter closes in. George Masters (son of the schoolmaster, disowned after hasty marriage) proves shiftless, crowding stove, refusing to help with chores. Blizzards overwhelm town, leaving residents "numbed and dumb," cowering inside. Father and young feedstore owners, brothers Royal and Almanzo Wilder, are only townsfolk to venture out, hauling hay across prairie. (Born February 13, 1857, in upstate New York, fifth of six children of James and Angeline Wilder, Almanzo Wilder moved with his family to Spring Valley, Minnesota, in 1875, riding out to the Dakota Territory in the summer of 1879 with brother Royal and sister Eliza Jane to file on adjoining claims north of proposed town.)

1881 After last train arrives January 4, De Smet is not resupplied with food and fuel for four months. Residents burn hay. Most families have arrived by rail provisioned for a season; with no supplies, Ingallses are "shorter of food than anyone." Possibly in February, Almanzo Wilder and sixteen-year-old De Smet resident Oscar Edmund "Cap" Garland ride miles across prairie and find grain for the town. May 9, a train stalled further east arrives, full of farm machinery, with single emigrant car of provisions, contents distributed after mob threatens to wreck train. "None of us had realized the strain . . . until it broke," Wilder will remember. George Masters and his family head west later that month. The Ingallses return to claim. Laura sews shirts in town, determined to help sister attend college. Corn crop devoured by blackbirds, father sells milk cow for $15. Walking from school to homestead that fall, Laura and sister Carrie get lost in Big Slough, trying to avoid dangerous bull, and stumble on team hitched to hay wagon. Laura catches sight of Almanzo Wilder atop the hay "on his stomach, kicking up his heels," their first encounter. In November, Mary travels with parents to enroll in Iowa College for the Blind, in Vinton, Iowa.

1882 At school, teacher is Eliza Jane Wilder. Classmates include Mary Power, daughter of town tailor; Ida Brown, adopted child of the Reverend Brown; and Genevieve Masters, described in the memoir Wilder will write in 1930 as "the last unbearable straw." Clashes with teacher and Masters but becomes "leader" in school. Courted by several boys and interested in Cap Garland, Laura is squired home after spring revival meeting by Almanzo Wilder. In early December learns that Louis Bouchie, distant relative of Robert Boast, needs teacher at settlement twelve miles from De Smet. Passes teacher's exam at age fifteen and begins teaching Bouchie school immediately, driven home on weekends by Almanzo Wilder.

1883 Completes term at Bouchie school in February, returns to studies in De Smet. In spring, works for dressmaker Martha McKee, keeping McKee company at her claim in May. The following month, sews for Florence Bell, town milliner, alongside Almanzo's sister Laura, who is living with Eliza Jane at her homestead. Back at school in September, writes first composition, on "Ambition." With Ida Brown, delivers recitation on American history at school exhibition. Teacher Ven Owen tells father that Laura has "a wonderful mind and should be given every opportunity for an education."

1884 In spring, takes teacher's exam and receives second-grade certificate. Teaches Perry school for three months, closer to Ingalls homestead, donating money to family to buy organ for Mary. In May, Almanzo Wilder takes her on country drives with team of Morgan horses. The couple attend singing school held at Congregational church that summer and become engaged. Laura and Carrie attend school in the fall while Wilder brothers visit parents in

Spring Valley. Almanzo returns unexpectedly at Christmastime.

1885 Attends school until April, when she quits to teach Wilkins school for three months, work that precludes her from finishing with rest of class. Having proved up on homestead, Almanzo Wilder is completing house on tree claim north of De Smet. Learning that Angeline and Eliza Jane Wilder are planning a big church wedding, Almanzo and Laura move up date and are married August 25 by the Reverend Brown. Since his sister's name is Laura, Almanzo calls her "Bessie"; she calls him "Manly," not caring for his family nicknames ("Manzo" and "Mannie").

1886 Wheat and oat crops appear promising, but the wheat is lost to violent hailstorm. Needing money that fall, Wilders move to shanty on homestead, hoping to mortgage the property. Attended by her mother, Mrs. Power, and doctor, delivers first child, Rose, on December 6.

1887 According to ten-year-old sister Grace Ingalls's diary, "Rose is a big fat baby" by March. After harvesting hay, the Wilders pay off smaller debts and interest on loans but lose stored grain and hay when their barn burns in July. Proving up on their homestead, Charles and Caroline Ingalls move to town permanently.

1888 In March, Laura and Almanzo Wilder contract diphtheria during epidemic, sending Rose, not affected, to stay with Ingallses in De Smet. Almanzo suffers what doctor calls "a slight stroke of paralysis" after returning to work too soon, leaving him severely weakened and limping. Beset by medical bills and debts, unable to work both properties, Wilders sell homestead, moving back to tree claim where they partner with cousin Peter Ingalls, buying a flock of sheep.

1889 In June, sister Mary graduates from Iowa College for the Blind and returns home, where she helps with housework, plays organ, and crafts items for sale. Wilder gives birth to second and only other child, an unnamed boy, who dies less than two weeks later, on August 7. Later that month, house burns down when flaming hay ignites kitchen. Family stays with neighbors until shanty is built. In November, Wilders decide to visit Almanzo's parents in Minnesota. On the eve of South Dakota statehood, severe drought wastes crops and farmers face ruin.

1890 Wilders sell sheep for profit in spring, using cash to purchase tree claim. In May, with Peter Ingalls, they travel by covered wagon to Spring Valley, Minnesota, staying for over a year with James and Angeline Wilder.

1891 In October, inspired by tales of Florida's salutary climate, Wilders embark by train for Westville, a panhandle town where Peter Ingalls has settled with his bride. Wilder will write little about the experience but later will suggest her discomfort at being "a curiosity . . . the only 'Yankee girl.'" Rose Wilder, in her O. Henry Prize–winning story "Innocence" (1922), will evoke a sultry, sinister backwoods where locals brew moonshine and her mother is terrified by cousin's wife, Molly (her name in life and fiction), a monstrous figure reminiscent of "grandfather's big brown horse that . . . once killed a man."

1892–93 In August 1892, Wilders return to De Smet on seventh wedding anniversary, taking house near the Ingallses that remains largely empty aside from cookstove and mattresses, their furniture mortgaged. While Almanzo drives teams and does odd jobs as his health allows, Wilder works as seamstress, leaving Rose with mother and sister Mary. (Rose will later reveal that tree claim was lost at this time.) Financial panic of 1893 closes banks and bankrupts railroads.

1894 A hundred dollars saved, the family decides to seek land in Missouri, tempted by railroad brochure for "Land of the Big Red Apple" and a firsthand report by Frank Cooley, whose children attend school with Rose. July 16, before leaving, Laura asks father to play his fiddle, and he obliges, long into the night. ("In all my life I never heard anything like it," Rose will remember, "gay and strong and reaching, wanting, trying to get to something beyond.") He tells Laura he wants her to have the violin "when the time comes." In scorching heat, family travels by covered wagon alongside the Cooleys. Wilder keeps diary, containing first extended impressions of landscape. On July 24, she writes of Missouri's dramatic bluffs, "I never see a river or lake but it makes me think how I would like to see a world made & watch it through all its changes." In August, sends travel letter to weekly *De Smet News*. "First I ever had published," she will note. Covering 650 miles, arriving last day of August, the Wilders purchase forty wooded, rocky acres east of Mansfield for four hundred dollars. "Rocky Ridge

Farm," as Wilder names it, includes creek, hundreds of apple saplings, and windowless log cabin. Cutting and selling firewood over the winter to buy food, clearing half the land by the following year, the Wilders continue improving house, building barn, and raising chickens.

1896 Grandfather Lansford Ingalls dies, in Webster, Wisconsin, at age eighty-three.

1898 Hoping to pay off mortgage, family moves to Mansfield near railroad station, where they live for over a decade. Wilder runs boarding table for rail travelers and employees while Almanzo buys and runs draying business and eventually sells oil and kerosene. During visit to Mansfield, James Wilder unexpectedly buys Wilders' rented home, giving his son the deed.

1901 October 16, Grace Ingalls marries Nathan Dow in Ingalls home.

1902 In May, word arrives that her father is gravely ill. Wilder travels alone by train to De Smet, where Charles Ingalls dies June 8, age sixty-six. His favorite hymn, "The Sweet By and By," is sung at the funeral. After his death, Wilder will attribute "whatever religion, romance and patriotism I have . . . to the violin and my Father playing in the twilight." She sees mother and sister Mary for the last time.

1903 On the back of an oil-company stock form dated February 1903, writes out two pages of tale inspired by 1879 winter at Silver Lake, fragment found later in envelope labeled "ideas for work." Carrie Ingalls visits Mansfield. That summer, Almanzo Wilder's widowed sister, Eliza Jane Thayer, arrives from Crowley, Louisiana, with her son, Wilder. Since Mansfield offers only mediocre education, Rose persuades parents to send her to Crowley, where she can study Latin and finish high school.

1904–8 Graduating in Louisiana in 1904, Rose Wilder spends next few years working as a telegrapher in the Midwest, moving to San Francisco in 1908.

1909 March 24, Rose Wilder marries Claire Gillette Lane, traveling salesman and reporter for *San Francisco Call*, in San Francisco; newlyweds visit Mansfield.

1910 Wilders sell Mansfield house, moving back to farm around this time.

1911 A recognized expert on poultry, Wilder is invited to speak to a farmers' group. Unable to attend, she writes out her thoughts. In the audience is John Francis Case, editor of the semimonthly farm newspaper *Missouri Ruralist*, who later contacts Wilder to ask if he can publish the address. Signed Mrs. A. J. Wilder, it appears on February 18 as "Favors the Small Farm Home," making the case that poultry, fruit, and dairy produced by a five-acre farm can support a family and a "freer, healthier, happier life" than that in cities. Writes more for *Ruralist* over next few years, including "The Story of Rocky Ridge Farm," signed "A. J. Wilder," but believed to be by his wife. With five hundred dollars inherited from Almanzo's parents, the Wilders relocate and add to farmhouse, constructing stone foundation and fireplace, beamed ceiling, porches, and picture windows; renovation completed by 1913.

1912 On August 1, Carrie Ingalls marries widower David Swanzey in Rapid City, South Dakota, becoming stepmother to his young son and daughter.

1915 Wilder corresponds with daughter Rose Wilder Lane, now writing for *San Francisco Bulletin*. Teeming with money-making schemes, Lane suggests her mother write regularly for *Kansas City Star*, urging her to pursue " 'the story of my life' thing." In August, Wilder travels to San Francisco to visit Lane and the Panama-Pacific International Exposition. Writes long lyrical letters home, exclaiming over city lit up at night and the "blue Pacific . . . beautiful and wonderful." Her letters capture an emotionally fraught and financially complex relationship developing between the Wilders and their daughter; they have lent Rose and Gillette Lane $250 by increasing their mortgage. Beseeching her parents to move to California, Rose pays mother five dollars a week during visit to defray lost poultry revenue and publishes mother's poems in *Bulletin*, signed "Laura Ingalls Wilder," first appearance of professional name. Wilder meets Lane's literary friends, including illustrator Berta Hoerner (later Hader). Trip prolonged through October after Wilder falls from streetcar, hitting her head. She uses recovery to plan articles about Exposition and future writing, asking Almanzo to save her letters.

1916 Helps found the Athenians, women's club devoted to education and the establishment of libraries, taking part in many club activities over the years. Begins writing regularly for *Ruralist*, appearing in nearly every issue for the next eight years. Aimed at farm women, her articles cover practical issues (economical feeding of hens, rat-proofing buildings) while praising country life, and gradually develop into a column. Increasingly personal essays draw on past, recalling love of wildflowers, family's struggles during hard winter, argument with sister over Thanksgiving stuffing, troublesome neighbors.

1917 Becomes editor of *Ruralist* Home section. Begins serving as secretary-treasurer of the Mansfield branch of National Farm Loan Association, offering low-cost loans to farmers through Federal Land Bank in St. Louis.

1918 Rose Wilder Lane divorces, keeping married name.

1919 Wilder publishes first article in a national magazine, *McCall's*, on marrying a farmer. Heavy editing by daughter prompts distress, to which Lane replies, "Don't be absurd." Continues to develop column for *Ruralist*, now called "The Farm Home" (in 1921 retitled "As a Farm Woman Thinks").

1923 Having solidified her reputation with well-known biographies of Henry Ford and Herbert Hoover, Lane publishes Albanian travelogue *The Peaks of Shala*, dedicated to "my mother, Laura Ingalls Wilder," and arrives in Mansfield at Christmas after a four-year absence. Exhausted by Middle East trip, Lane writes for *Country Gentleman*, trying to interest Wilder in same.

1924 Caroline Ingalls dies April 20, age eighty-four. In June, Wilder writes in the *Ruralist* of receiving the news, "Memories! . . . Sometimes I wonder if they are our treasures in heaven or the consuming fires of torment when we carry them with us." Publishes final *Ruralist* column, December 15. Daughter stays in Mansfield until 1926.

1925 Runs for collector of Pleasant Valley Township but loses. Publishes article about Rocky Ridge kitchen in *Country Gentleman*; daughter again dismisses her concerns over revisions, calling it "an ordinary re-write job." Tensions grow between Wilder and Lane, who continues pressing her parents to move (suggesting St. Louis and England). Lane complains that her mother cannot bring herself to trust her "financial judgment or promises." In June, Wilder writes to her mother's sister, Martha Carpenter, in Minnesota, ostensibly asking for Caroline Ingalls's vanity cake recipe for a *Ladies' Home Journal* article but also urging her aunt to send "pages and pages of things you remember," promising to pay a stenographer if necessary. Wilder reveals that she has been ill with something "near to nervous prostration." Carpenter obliges, sending recipes and letters filled with vivid childhood reminiscences: hearing wolves and panthers in the forest, staying in bed while their only clothes were washed, fearing Indians with "painted faces," and surviving on cornmeal cakes, "all we had for awhile." Carpenter also remembers joy of wandering in forest, hearing "the music of the wilds."

1926 Wilders invest in stock market on advice of Rose who tells them, "Fortunately, we can't lose." In Europe again, Lane publishes article in Hearst's *International-Cosmopolitan* detailing suicide attempt and "nightmare" childhood, parents' crop failures, and father's illness and invalidism, claiming responsibility for setting fire to Dakota house.

1927 At sixty, Wilder retires as Home editor of *Ruralist*.

1928 In March, Lane returns, staying for over seven years. Wilder resigns from position at Mansfield Farm Loan Association, having processed almost a million dollars in loans to area farmers. Mary Ingalls, age sixty-three, dies in Keystone, South Dakota, October 17, at the home of Carrie Ingalls Swanzey. Wilders accept daughter's plan to build English cottage for them on their property, across ridge from farmhouse. Budgeting four thousand dollars, Lane ultimately spends eleven thousand on field-stone walls, French doors, and tilework, at the same time renovating and installing electricity in the farmhouse where she will live with a friend, renting from her parents. Lane presents furnished "Rock House" to Wilders for Christmas.

1930 Spurred by financial concerns after stock market crash of previous October (in which both Lane and her parents lost their investments), Wilder writes childhood reminiscence, "Pioneer Girl," during first part of year, showing it to daughter in May. Lane types and lightly revises, sending it to her agent, Carl Brandt, later that month. Ultimately, the memoir is rejected for serialization by *The Atlantic Monthly*, *Country Home*, *Good Housekeeping*, *The Ladies' Home Journal*, and *The Saturday Evening Post*, although the *Post* editor calls it a "grand piece of work." Without telling her mother, Lane types short version intended as text for children's picture book, titles it "When Grandma Was a Little Girl," and sends it to her friend Berta Hader, children's book author and illustrator.

1931 At New York firm of Alfred A. Knopf, children's book editor Marion Fiery reads "When Grandma Was a Little Girl," sent by Hader, and writes to Wilder in February, asking for expansion and revision for eight- to twelve-year-old readers. In May, Wilder completes longer manuscript, passing it to Lane, who types and revises. The following month, the Wilders drive to De Smet for "Old Settlers' Day." With sister Grace, Wilder sifts through her mother's and Mary Ingalls's belongings. The Wilders then drive west to visit Carrie Ingalls Swanzey and her family in Keystone. On leaving, Wilder says to her husband, "The hot wind is blowing us out of Dakota again"; he replies, "It's the last time it will ever have the chance." (They will return, however, twice more.) Fiery accepts Wilder's manuscript, now titled "Little House in the Woods," in September, sending three-book contract the following month. In November, Wilder learns that Knopf plans to close its children's department due to economic depression; Fiery advises her to reject contract and try other publishers. Lane arranges for her agent, George T. Bye, to handle Wilder's subsequent submissions and contracts. In early December, Virginia Kirkus, children's editor at Harper & Brothers, reads Wilder's manuscript on an afternoon train to Connecticut, missing stop in her absorption. "The real magic was in the telling," Kirkus writes later. She immediately accepts the book, retitling it *Little House in the Big Woods* and hiring Helen Sewell as illustrator. (Sewell will provide illustrations and dust jackets for all of Wilder's first editions, most of the later volumes done in collaboration with artist Mildred Boyle.)

1932 Wilder's first book is published in April; it is a selection of Junior Literary Guild for that month, and praised in *New York Herald Tribune* and *New York Times.* By that time, she has completed a manuscript about her husband's childhood in upstate New York. Harper & Brothers returns "Farmer Boy" in September, asking for major revisions. That fall, Lane visits Burr Oak, Iowa, and travels to the Wilder farmhouse near Malone, New York, sending picture postcards and descriptions. In October, *Saturday Evening Post* publishes Lane's serial, "Let the Hurricane Roar," a fictional treatment of her mother's Plum Creek period.

1933 Wilder brings revised "Farmer Boy" to Lane in January. Becomes visibly upset with her daughter after seeing an advertisement for book publication of *Let the Hurricane Roar.* Objects to Lane's use of her parents' real names, insisting "it's all wrong." Years later, Wilder will tell a reader that her daughter's characters have "no connection with my family," labeling the choice of names (changed in later editions) "unfortunate." Lane, profoundly affected by incident, along with other setbacks; falls into severe depression. (Later that fall, Lane takes in an itinerant boy, John Turner, inviting his brother Al the following year.) In March, publisher accepts *Farmer Boy*, offering Depression-era royalties, half the previous rate. Disappointed by terms, Wilder begins third novel, "Indian Country," writing on backs of letters, including those from Iowa fourth graders asking for more books. Over the summer, she and Lane correspond with historians, inquiring about Osage history. *Farmer Boy* published in the fall. At some time during next few years, Wilder works on adult novel about early years of her marriage, titling it "The First Three Years."

1934 In January, writes to friend and newspaper editor Aubrey Sherwood in De Smet, telling him that Lane has been ill for a year, suffering a "nervous breakdown." Finishes draft of "Indian Country" in February; Lane revises in May, limiting point of view to Laura's character and adding transitional scenes. (Early draft employs Mary's point of view.) In July, Wilder sends manuscript to Ida Louise Raymond, Kirkus's successor at Harper & Brothers, who solicits opinions from a midwestern librarian, concerned there is not "enough variety of detail." Wilder learns in August that "Indian Country" is slated for 1935 publication as *Little House on the Prairie* and that she is free to let next novel "shape itself" in her mind.

1935 *Little House on the Prairie* published in September. Lane moves to hotel in Columbia, Missouri, a break with Mansfield that will become permanent. Wilder begins working on fourth novel, about farming at Plum Creek in Minnesota. Sometime over the winter, delivers speech on "My Work" to Sorosis Club in nearby town of Mountain Grove.

1936 Finishes draft of Plum Creek novel, sending it to Lane in March. For the first time, Wilder and her daughter correspond about revisions, wrangling through summer over cuts, additions, and clarifications as grasshoppers multiply in drought-stricken Missouri. "We are doing what we can to kill them," she writes Lane, "but what's the use fighting a judgment of God," interpreting scourge as divine retribution for New Deal agricultural policies (stabilizing prices by limiting production and even destroying crops). Wilder draws maps of Plum Creek showing location of fish trap, dugout, stable, and tableland, answering questions about slate-pencils, summer dresses, and blizzards, sharply emphasizing differences between her childhood and present time, telling Lane "you *must not* have us treated like children of today." Maintains that, in previous century, "children weren't raised to be helpless cowards." In September, after Lane finishes typing and revising, submits Plum Creek manuscript to publisher. Quarrels with Lane about Turner boys and other farmhouse tenants. Lane relinquishes farmhouse (and will not visit Mansfield again until 1949). Wilders leave "Rock House" and return to original home.

1937 In February, Wilder writes Lane to say she has found her mother's handmade book in which her father had written words to two songs, "The Blue Juniata" and "Mary of the Wild Moor," dated 1860. Finds reminiscing increasingly painful as she delves into Silver Lake material and cannot work in the evening: "My brain goes right on remembering and it's H—." Does not feel "first rate" but writes long letters to Lane, as does Almanzo, about experiences traveling to Dakota Territory, filing on claims, and her father's work for railroad. Denounces Missouri senator Harry Truman to Lane as "a liar" while conceding her own farm is "not self-supporting"; admits her heart is hardening toward poor as she relives family struggles. Lane moves from Missouri to New York in June, working on new *Saturday Evening Post* serial, "Free Land," drawn from parents' Dakota experiences. Later that year, Wilder reflects on father's character, summing up with "Pa was no business man. He was a hunter and trapper, a musician and poet." In October, travels with Almanzo to Detroit to deliver speech at Book Fair held by J. L. Hudson Department Store. *On the Banks of Plum Creek* published that month to positive reviews in *The Horn Book* and elsewhere. Lane begins revising Silver Lake manuscript.

1938 In January, Wilder struggles intensely with daughter over Silver Lake material, arguing against opening with "recital of discouragement and calamities" made up of Mary's illness, Jack's death, and father's financial losses. "I *don't like it!*" she says. Defending her opening chapter, "A Journey by Train," in which Laura leads her blind sister by hand across the platform, Wilder writes, "Readers must know all that but they should not be made to think about it." Chides her daughter for introducing latter-day mores: "This is a true story and supposed to show a different (almost) civilization." While Lane wants to replace protagonist, switching to younger Carrie, Wilder insists that Laura must "step up" to take her sister's place, insisting that she has provided "a true picture" of time, setting, and people. "Please don't blur it," she says. Weeks later, she wearies: "Change the beginning of the story if you want. Do anything you please with the dam. stuff if you will fix it up." Lane's *Free Land* is serialized in March and April, then published as novel, becoming a bestseller. That spring, Wilders travel by car across the West, visiting the Grand Canyon and California, stopping in South Dakota on their return. By late summer, Wilder sketches out ten rough chapters of sixth book, "Hard Winter." *On the Banks of Plum Creek* selected as Newbery Honor Book (as is each remaining novel published during her lifetime). Composes letter, "To American Mothers," supporting a bill that requires popular vote on declaration of war, concluding, "Pray that God may save us from another war."

1939 Receives letter early in the year from Ida Louise Raymond, pressing her for Silver Lake manuscript. She tells Lane she will ignore it, having exhausted all excuses: "She can think I have gone to Timbuctoo or am sick or mad or just [too] lazy to write." She then falls ill with serious bout of flu but submits novel to publisher in late spring. Wilder sends "Hard Winter" to daughter in May, saying "I expect you will find lots of fault in it, but we can argue it out later." Expresses indignation about Roosevelt, in concert with Lane's libertarian views. As she and Almanzo prepare to drive to De Smet for Old Settlers' Day, she tells Lane where to find notes for series' final volume, "Prairie Girl," should anything happen. *By the Shores of Silver Lake* is published in fall, Wilder modeling title on that of previous novel.

1940 Writes to agent George Bye in May, thanking him for complimenting "Hard Winter," admitting it was "rather trying, living it all over again." Publisher suggests changing title to *The Long Winter*, arguing that "hard" may prove daunting to young readers. Lane protests, but Wilder yields, regretfully. In June, lets Bye know that seventh novel may "stretch" into eighth. She suggests that a story about "what next happens is taking shape slowly in my mind" but that it is too soon to know if it may become "a completely adult novel." Published that fall, *The Long Winter* garners high praise from reviewers.

1941 When Ida Louise Raymond leaves Harper & Brothers, Wilder is assigned to Raymond's former assistant, editor Ursula Nordstrom. Sends *Little Town on the Prairie* to Bye in July, asking for better terms than previous novel or new contract for *Farmer Boy*, which continues to rankle. In a postscript to him the following month, recalls her teenage years in De Smet as "great days . . . I have a strong feeling of nostalgia for them." Grace Ingalls Dow, age sixty-four, dies November 10, in Manchester, South Dakota.

1942 Writes to Bye agency in September, saying that manuscript of eighth Little House novel (which has received relatively light editing by Lane) has been sent to typist, apologizing for not having it ready sooner.

1943 *These Happy Golden Years* published in March. Writes to a reader that sister Carrie's response was particularly gratifying: "It seemed she was back in those times and all that had happened since was a dream." Wilder suggests to Bye that she considers this book her last but might undertake another story "if it pesters me enough." Lane meets Roger MacBride, fourteen-year-old son of Burt MacBride, an editor at *Reader's Digest*, during meeting about reprinting *Let the Hurricane Roar.*

1944 Wilder deposits her father's violin at South Dakota State Historical Society, in Pierre, requesting that it be played four times a year. (It is now in the collection of the Laura Ingalls Wilder Historic Home and Museum, in Mansfield, Missouri.) Carrie Swanzey visits Mansfield by train; later sells parents' Third Street house, leaving family belongings stored there.

1946 Carrie Ingalls Swanzey, age seventy-five, dies June 2 in Rapid City, South Dakota. Items in storage in De Smet home disposed of by owners who save two portraits of Charles and Caroline Ingalls, sending them to Wilder.

1947 In September, hosts artist Garth Williams, who had recently done drawings for several Harper projects, including E. B. White's *Stuart Little* (1945) and Margaret Wise Brown's *Little Fur Family* (1946); he has been hired by Ursula Nordstrom to illustrate a new uniform edition of "Little House" books, a commission that will occupy much of his next five years. During his stay, Wilder shares family lore, and suggests places from her past for him to visit and photograph. Her husband cautions against risky drive through Dakota blizzards, but Wilder urges artist on, saying, "Oh, *I* would go!"

1948 Wilders sell farm on life-lease, receiving monthly payments and use of property for remaining years.

1949 Declines to attend May 12 opening of Detroit Public Library branch named in her honor, as husband is "not strong" and cannot be left alone, but donates manuscripts of *The Long Winter* and *These Happy Golden Years*. In July, assigns 10 percent of royalties from "Little House" books to Lane. That month, Almanzo Wilder suffers a heart attack, then rallies. He dies October 23, age ninety-two. Neighbors find Wilder embracing him in his chair. Lane informally "adopts" Roger MacBride.

1950 Friends press Wilder to move to town, but she remains at Rocky Ridge, saying of her late husband, "I am very lonely for him, but that would be so wherever I was." Donates manuscript of *Little Town on the Prairie* to Pomona Public Library in California, which dedicates children's room to Wilder in May. Day held in her honor in Hartville, Missouri, in August.

1951 Receives more than nine hundred birthday messages, including cablegram from General Douglas MacArthur, who has used *The Long Winter* in Japanese democratization program. Attends dedication of Mansfield's "Laura Ingalls Wilder Library" on September 28.

1952 In May, Wilder declines invitation to travel to De Smet for Old Settlers' Day. In her last public appearance, during Children's Book Week in November, autographs books at Brown's Book Store, in Springfield, Missouri, where a line of children stretches out the door and into the street. Writes final letter for Lane, to be opened on her death. Harper & Brothers receives inquiry about "offensive" sentence regarding Indians in *Little House on the Prairie*; editor Ursula Nordstrom reports Wilder's apology and approval of revision.

1953 Uniform edition of "Little House" books is published, designed by Helen Gentry with new dust jackets and interior drawings by Garth Williams. Sends telegram to Harper & Brothers: "MARY LAURA AND THEIR FOLKS LIVE AGAIN IN THESE ILLUSTRATIONS." Special "Laura Ingalls Wilder" number of *The Horn Book* appears in December, containing articles by Williams, Virginia Kirkus, and others; Wilder contributes a letter to her readers, as well as her recipe for gingerbread.

1954 Buys new green Oldsmobile and is driven weekly to town. Enjoys birthday parties held in Mansfield. Honored as first recipient of American Library Association's Laura Ingalls Wilder Award, recognizing "substantial and lasting contribution" to children's literature and devised by committee of children's librarians who are "acutely aware of the debt of gratitude" owed her. (Award medal, cast in bronze and featuring a bas-relief portrait of the child Laura, is designed by Garth Williams.) Wilder cannot attend Minneapolis ceremony: "Being 87 years old with a tired heart I have to avoid excitement even if pleasant." Accompanies Lane to her home in Danbury, Connecticut, after daughter's visit.

1955 Remains self-sufficient, telling *Kansas City Star* that she is not afraid to live alone, keeping pistol by screen door and shotgun in her bedroom. "I know how to use them both," she tells reporter. Says companions include barn cat and turtles "that come up out of the holler to see how I am doing." Insists she kept "trying to stop" writing but readers would not have it. "Now I'm 88 and I'm tired," she says, "and no one is going to get me to write any more."

1956 Hospitalized in Springfield, Missouri, during visit by her daughter at Thanksgiving. Treated for diabetes, she rallies and returns home the day after Christmas. Lane, now seventy, writes her own will, naming Roger MacBride as heir.

1957 Dies at Rocky Ridge on February 10, three days after her ninetieth birthday. She is buried in Mansfield Cemetery, where she shares a plot and headstone with her husband. Leaves estate valued at $77,814 and one-page letter dated July 30, 1952, addressed to "Rose Dearest," distributing a few possessions, telling Lane that, when she reads it, "I will be gone and you will have inherited all I have." She assures her that "My love will be with you always," signing it, "Mama Bess." Beneath, in parentheses, she adds her name, Laura Ingalls Wilder. Years earlier she had written, "I am sure that when I come to die, if Father might only be playing for me I should be wafted straight to heaven on the strains of 'The Sweet By and By,' for the pearly gates would surely open."

Note on the Texts

This volume contains the later four novels in Laura Ingalls Wilder's "Little House" series—*By the Shores of Silver Lake* (1939), *The Long Winter* (1940), *Little Town on the Prairie* (1941), and *These Happy Golden Years* (1943)—together with the posthumously published novella *The First Four Years.* (The earlier four novels, published 1932–37, are collected in a companion Library of America volume, *The Little House Books*, Volume One.) The present volume also contains, in an appendix, a biographical essay that Wilder composed for inclusion in *The Junior Book of Authors*, edited by Stanley J. Kunitz and Howard Haycraft (second edition, revised, 1951), and the text of a letter written by Wilder and sent to her readers by her publisher, Harper & Brothers.

In 1937, when Wilder began *By the Shores of Silver Lake*, she was seventy years old and living with her husband on Rocky Ridge Farm, in Mansfield, Missouri. As was her custom, she wrote the first draft of the novel in pencil in dime-store writing tablets. She then mailed the tablets to her daughter, Rose Wilder Lane, a novelist then living in New York City, for criticism, editing, and revision. On the cover of one such tablet, Lane scribbled a note to herself: "No hurry about delivery. Deliver anytime in January, 1938." That deadline passed, and the two corresponded about revisions throughout the rest of the year. This correspondence is preserved in the Rose Wilder Lane papers at the Herbert Hoover Presidential Library, West Branch, Iowa. The Laura Ingalls Wilder Historic Home and Museum preserves two handwritten manuscripts and a typescript with Wilder's revisions, which, like the letters, reveal the author's struggle to relive and accurately describe the traumas of enduring her sister Mary's illness and her parents' struggle with debt. In one manuscript version, Pa is described as a "good farmer" who "paid all his debts," and Laura is so relieved that her sister has survived her fever that "she couldn't feel so very sorrowful" about her blindness. In letters of 1938, Wilder resisted Lane's desire for more emotionalism and instead embraced "this feeling that you call apathy and I call stoicism." Delving further, she wrote that "it seems to me we were rather inclined to be fatalistic—to just take things as they came. I know we all hated a fuss, as I still do." Even as she acquiesced to her daughter's suggestion to be frank in acknowledging the family's losses, she was still concerned that such candidness would be "too sad" for young readers. The novel was delivered to Wilder's editor, Ida Louise Raymond, in May 1939. *By the Shores of Silver Lake* was published, with drawings by Helen Sewell and Mildred Boyle, by Harper & Brothers in October 1939.

Wilder began a first draft of the novel she called "The Hard Winter" in 1938 and continued to work on it through the spring of the following year. She sent a dime-store tablet manuscript to Lane in May 1939. While working on revisions to Lane's typescript, Wilder drew a detailed map of De Smet circa 1880–81, labeling all the businesses in the town, drawing a handcar and an additional schematic showing sightlines from the railroad tracks. She sent revised pages to Lane, asking her to find "the corrected mss I sent back to you." She instructed her, "Don't cut the hymn I had Ma sing to Grace. . . . 'I will sing you a song of that beautiful land—the far away home of the soul / Where no storms ever beat on that glittering strand / While the years of eternity roll.' . . . A land where storms never beat would have been thought of with longing. It has a wailing tune too. The kind Ma sang when she did sing. We must show the effect the winter was having. It nearly broke Ma down when she sang of the land where there were no storms. And Pa when he shook his fist at the wind. Don't leave that out. We have shown that they both were brave, let's show what the winter nearly did to them." Of snow on the Dakota prairie, she wrote, "The prairie was not bare . . . the snow moved over the surface like sand on the desert, there were ripples of it and low drifts." "The Hard Winter" was sent to Harper & Brothers in the fall of 1939 and, in light of the publisher's concern for the children's audience, it was renamed *The Long Winter*, to Wilder's regret. (According to Wilder's biographer William Anderson, "Her editors . . . objected to presenting anything difficult or hard to young readers.") *The Long Winter* was published, with drawings by Helen Sewell and Mildred Boyle, by Harper & Brothers in June 1940. Wilder donated the manuscript to the Detroit Public Library in 1949, where it is held in the Burton Historical Collection. A typescript bearing Wilder's handwritten revisions is among the Rose Wilder Lane papers at the Herbert Hoover Presidential Library, West Branch, Iowa.

When Wilder began planning a seventh "Little House" novel in 1940, she thought it would be her last. She soon found that she had enough material for two books, and she abandoned her outline for "Prairie Girl" for the more focused "Little Town on the Prairie," a title that had been suggested by Harper & Brothers for *The Long Winter*. By Christmas a handwritten draft was ready for Lane's transcription and revisions, which were relatively light. Wilder sent her daughter the manuscript together with a hand-drawn map of De Smet, showing locations of the livery barn and the road to the Ingalls homestead. ("Please don't lose this," she added in a note. "It is the third map I have drawn.") She included pages of detailed corrections and comments, among which was her rationale for belatedly cutting a passage about the Reverend Brown's "meanness": she was concerned that it might offend his relatives and foster grandchildren, "scattered all over the country." (She then passed on a bit of gossip: "Did I ever tell you that Rev. Alden deserted his wife and children and ran away with a girl just after Mary went to college? Fact.") The final typescript was sent to Harper & Brothers in early 1941 and was edited by Ursula Nordstrom, formerly the assistant to Ida Louise Raymond, who had retired in December 1940. (Nordstrom later described Wilder's books to a colleague as "the ONLY manuscripts I ever published here with no repeat absolutely no editorial suggestions from me or anyone else.") *Little Town on the Prairie* was published, with drawings by Helen Sewell and Mildred Boyle, by Harper & Brothers in November 1941. Wilder's handwritten manuscript was donated to the Pomona Public Library, Pomona, California, in 1950.

Wilder took two years to write *These Happy Golden Years*, her final "Little House" novel. On September 10, 1942, she sent an apology to the George T. Bye agency: "I am sorry I have made everyone so much trouble, but I could not get my new story ready any sooner." Later that month, Lane received the manuscript and again did little editing. After Wilder's review and corrections, the final typescript was sent to Ursula Nordstrom. *These Happy Golden Years* was published, with drawings by Helen Sewell and Mildred Boyle, by Harper & Brothers in March 1943. Wilder donated the manuscript to the Detroit Public Library in 1949, where it is held in the Burton Historical Collection.

The texts of these four "Little House" novels are taken from the revised, uniform edition of the "Little House" series, published in hardcover by Harper & Brothers, New York, in 1953.

The date of composition of *The First Four Years* is not known, but textual evidence suggests it was written between 1933 and 1937, with the exception of two adopted readings from the 1939 edition of *By the Shores of Silver Lake*: at 84.23–24, the sentence "For a minute they all admired the great heap of coal" has been restored, and at 90.11, the line "'Hail Columbia, happy land!' (Pa sang with the fiddle)" has been moved from the end of the extract to its proper place at the beginning. Handwritten in pencil on three dime-store tablets, the manuscript bears the title "First Three Years." The first page consists of a rough outline that begins with the words "If not successful in three years, something else," and continues with a list of seasons and remembered events, including the birth of Wilder's daughter. The outline concludes with the single words, "Fire—Leaving." The rest of the manuscript was organized into five sections: an untitled prologue, an untitled first section, "Second Year," "Third Year," and "Year of Grace."

Wilder used both sides of the tablet pages, perhaps an indication that the work was produced early in her novel-writing career. (In composing later novels, she used one side only.) One page was written on the back of a letter dated January 20, 1933, another on the reverse of a manuscript leaf from *Farmer Boy*, published in 1933. Found at the end of the third tablet was the typescript of a poem Wilder wrote in commemoration of "Old Settlers' Day," published in the *De Smet News* for June 20, 1930. Much of the material covered in initial pages of the manuscript is described in greater detail in the final chapters of *These Happy Golden Years*, suggesting that it was drafted before that volume.

Late in 1937, Wilder referred to the manuscript in an exchange between herself, her daughter, and her Harper & Brothers editor, Ida Louise Raymond. In a December 18 reply to Wilder's comment that she was considering an adult novel about the first years of her marriage, Raymond called it "extremely exciting news that you already have a grown-up book in mind." On the back of Raymond's letter, Wilder wrote to Lane: "I thought it might wangle a little more advertising for the L. H. books if I said I might write the grown up one." Wilder reminds Lane: "I asked you if you ever expected to use the framework of The First Three Years and wondered if it would be worth while to write the one grown-up story of Laura and Almanzo to sort of be the cap-sheaf of the 7 volume children's novel. I could write the rough work. You could polish it and put your name to it if that would be better than mine. I just thought about it and wondered." Lane advised her mother to stick to "juveniles," arguing that there was "more money" in that field.

Wilder was still considering the prospect in 1943, writing to her agent George Bye, "I have thought that 'Golden Years' was my last." She had planned, she said, to "spend what is left of my life living, not writing about it, but a story keeps stirring in my mind and if it pesters me enough I may write it down and send it to you."

The manuscript tablets of *The First Four Years* were found in Wilder's Missouri farmhouse after her death in 1957 by Lewis Lichty, the curator of the Laura Ingalls Wilder Historic Home and Museum, and given to Rose Wilder Lane. Lane's adopted heir, Roger MacBride, found them among her papers and brought them to Ursula Nordstrom, children's book editor at Harper & Row (formerly Harper & Brothers). On April 8, 1969, Nordstrom wrote to a friend: "I can't wait to tell you the following: The young man who inherited all the assets of Laura Ingalls Wilder's daughter, Rose Wilder Lane, came in a few days ago and dropped the casual remark that there is a NINTH WILDER MANUSCRIPT, written after *These Happy Golden Years.* I asked why in mercy's name we had never been given it and he explained that it covers the first year of married life for Laura and Almanzo and that there is a faint air of slight disillusion in it, which Laura's daughter thought not suited to the feeling of the 8 published books. He has promised to send it to me as soon as he can get it typed. It is in Laura's handwriting. Isn't that exciting? A voice from the grave! How thrilling it would be to have a new Wilder book! Mrs. Lane died a few months ago and her heir apparently is willing to have us publish the ms. if it is really a finished one."

Later that year, Nordstrom sent the manuscript to Zena Sutherland, a noted expert in children's literature at the University of Chicago, who replied with a letter recommending that the book be published. On November 18, 1969, in reply to Sutherland, Nordstrom wrote that Roger MacBride "would let us do some judicious editing, but I think we just better not. I think maybe we can get [MacBride] to write an introductory note, or something. And just put it out as is. I would hate like hell to tamper with this." Apologizing for "shilly-shallying" about the matter, Nordstrom insisted that "my impulse is not to make any changes here." *The First Four Years*, with pencil drawings by Garth Williams, was published by Harper & Row in February 1971. The book included an introduction by Roger MacBride, in which he offered a "guess" that it was written in the late 1940s. In William Anderson's analysis of the manuscript of *The First Four Years*, "The Literary Apprenticeship of Laura Ingalls Wilder" (*South Dakota History* 13:4, Winter 1983), Anderson dated the work circa 1933–37. He also reported that MacBride and editors at Harper & Row "mutually agreed" to change the estimated date of its composition in later printings of *The First Four Years*, but this was not done.

In editing the manuscript, MacBride and Nordstrom made some minor changes and a few substantive revisions. Overlapping descriptions in the first pages were made consistent with those in *These Happy Golden Years*. Several significant deletions were made by Roger MacBride, who felt that Wilder's description of the birth of her son was too graphic for young readers; these deletions are acknowledged in the Notes in this volume. The present text is taken from that of the first edition.

The text of the "Autobiographical Sketch" is taken from *The Junior Book of Authors* (second edition, revised), a reference work for children's librarians edited by Stanley J. Kunitz and Howard Haycraft (New York: H. W. Wilson Company, 1951). Excerpts from the sketch first appeared in a biographical article on Wilder published in the *Wilson Library Bulletin* for April 1948, suggesting that Wilder's essay was sent to the H. W. Wilson offices sometime early in that year.

The text of the undated letter to readers, printed on Harper & Brothers letterhead, is taken from the copy in the Rose Wilder Lane Papers at the Herbert Hoover Presidential Library in West Branch, Iowa. This "Dear Children" letter exists in several versions. One, perhaps the first, was written during the summer of 1943 shortly after the publication of *These Happy Golden Years.* It appears as "My Family" in *A Little House Reader: A Collection of Writings by Laura Ingalls Wilder*, edited by William Anderson (New York: HarperCollins, 1998). Another was published as "A Letter from Laura Ingalls Wilder" in the special Wilder issue of *The Horn Book Magazine*, in December 1953. The version printed in this volume, which acknowledges Almanzo Wilder's death in October 1949, is from the early 1950s.

This volume presents the texts of the printings chosen as sources but does not attempt to reproduce illustrations, decorations, or other nontextual features of their typographic design. The texts are presented without change, except for the correction of typographical errors and misspellings of proper names. Punctuation and capitalization are not altered, even when inconsistent or irregular. The following is a list of typographical errors corrected, listed by line and page number: 17.21, together."; 21.38, wheatfield; 27.4, low,; 39.36, glacing back; 41.38–39, cottonwood. the; 46.24, back;; 62.12, end of the; 71.34, neck.; 71.40 neckyokes,; 79.23, Brookins; 88.19, done."; 91.6, Rye"; 92.14, stove-pipe; 97.8, feet,; 101.24, Brookins; 106.30, snow flakes; 113.8, and Christmas Candy!"; 113.27, that horses; 115.14, territory; 119.18 and *passim*, Brookins; 127.23, Aden,; 130.33, Brookins; 130.33, shine.; 131.10, Brookins.; 132.12, Brookins; 134.36, Brookins,; 136.32, Brookins; 138.9, Pa. "The; 138.20, territory.; 138.33, Charles."; 139.5, said.; 140.5, said.; 141.24, Brookins; 142.13, Brookins.; 158.40, Brookins.; 164.3, Carolina; 187.5–6, falling. For; 188.9–10, potatoes. She; 194.5, Slap); 202.14, "*The Wonders of The Animal World.*"; 213.32, straw ticks; 224.29, then. . .; 229.17, batching; 234.23, *CHARiot*; 235.12, ON; 261.37, snow.; 263.38, cried.; 270.13, cut."; 276.30, hair-receiver; 279.28, territory.; 290.19, Almanza; 309.29, Boonie Doon,; 314.38, We; 334.6, snow crust.; 335.20, snow crust; 340.10, letup."; 359.36, meat—Oh,; 362.19, in the the; 377.13–14, see. Everyone; 418.17, Mary; 425.20–21, answer. "The; 432.21, insisted. I'll; 436.5, blues; 438.8, that it; 438.8, embrossed; 449.3, Poems,; 453.2, crop. Minnie; 475.21, outdoor; 475.32, book She; 486.38, printed.; 487.3, Woodsworth; 487.21, Ossawatomie; 517.11, and and; 522.24, that she; 532.21, whisp; 557.13, aloud.; 570.4, territory.; 570.17, would.; 572.3, Harthorne's; 572.32, "Her's; 601.6, Ma."; 605.3–4, sleepyhead!" She; 608.3, Carrie Monday; 614.20, territory.; 614.36, asked.; 618.12–13, chinook; 630.34, Mckee; 631.29, Woodsworth; 665.1, to try; 680.21, said,; 680.25, end;; 684.22, "For; 686.21, outside,; 687.25, postoffice,; 692.18, capital; 692.22, capital; 694.21, "The; 695.14, wake; 714.25, said.; 714.31, home."; 736.7–8, Pierson's; 739.33, Pierson's; 745.17, grainery; 745.24, kniting; 757.29, said "that; 761.18, hunred,; 768.23, from; 784.39, Waverly.

Notes

In the notes below, the reference numbers denote page and line of this volume (the line count includes headings). Quotations from Shakespeare are keyed to *The Riverside Shakespeare*, edited by G. Blakemore Evans (Boston: Houghton Mifflin, 1974). Quotations from the Bible are keyed to the King James Version. Quotations from Laura Ingalls Wilder's "Pioneer Girl," an unpublished childhood memoir written in 1930, are taken from a circulating microfilm copy of the autograph manuscript licensed by its owners, the Laura Ingalls Wilder Historic Home and Museum, Mansfield, Missouri, to the State Historical Society of Missouri, Columbia. Quotations from the manuscript of *The First Four Years* are taken from the autograph draft in the collection of the Herbert Hoover Presidential Library. For further biographical information than is contained in the Chronology, see John E. Miller, *Becoming Laura Ingalls Wilder: The Woman Behind the Legend* (Columbia and London: University of Missouri Press, 1998); also Donald Zochert, *Laura: The Life of Laura Ingalls Wilder* (Chicago: Henry Regnery, 1976); William Anderson, *Laura Ingalls Wilder: A Biography* (New York: HarperCollins, 1992); William Holtz, *The Ghost in the Little House: A Life of Rose Wilder Lane* (Columbia and London: University of Missouri Press, 1993); and Pamela Smith Hill, *Laura Ingalls Wilder: A Writer's Life* (Pierre: South Dakota State Historical Society, 2007). See also Laura Ingalls Wilder, *On the Way Home: The Diary of a Trip from South Dakota to Mansfield, Missouri, in 1894*, edited by Rose Wilder Lane (New York: Harper & Row, 1962); *West From Home: Letters of Laura Ingalls Wilder, San Francisco, 1915*, edited by Roger Lea MacBride (New York: Harper & Row, 1974); Laura Ingalls Wilder and Rose Wilder Lane, *A Little House Sampler*, edited by William Anderson (Lincoln: University of Nebraska Press, 1988); *A Little House Reader: A Collection of Writings by Laura Ingalls Wilder*, edited by William Anderson (New York: HarperCollins, 1998); and *A Little House Traveler: Writings from Laura Ingalls Wilder's Journeys Across America*, edited anonymously (New York: HarperCollins, 2006). Most of Wilder's contributions to *Missouri Ruralist*, 1911–24, are collected in *Laura Ingalls Wilder, Farm Journalist: Writings from the Ozarks*, edited by Stephen W. Hines (Columbia and London: University of Missouri Press, 2007). The historical background of De Smet, South Dakota, is covered in John E. Miller, *Laura Ingalls Wilder's Little Town: Where History and Literature Meet* (Lawrence:

University Press of Kansas, 1994), and *The Best of the* "LORE" (De Smet, S.D.: Laura Ingalls Wilder Memorial Society, 2006), a selection of articles from the Wilder Society newsletter. Family background and genealogical information are available in *The Ingalls Family of De Smet* (De Smet, S.D.: Laura Ingalls Wilder Memorial Society, 1995) and in Dorothy Smith, "The Wilder Family Story" (Malone, N.Y.: The Almanzo and Laura Ingalls Wilder Association, 1972). Dating of *The First Four Years* is discussed in William Anderson, "The Literary Apprenticeship of Laura Ingalls Wilder," *South Dakota History* 13:4 (Winter 1983), 285–331. Ursula Nordstrom's correspondence is collected in *Dear Genius: The Letters of Ursula Nordstrom*, edited by Leonard S. Marcus (New York: HarperCollins, 1998). For background on the Sioux Uprising, the Homestead Act, and other events, see *The New Encyclopedia of the American West* (New Haven: Yale University Press, 1998), edited by Howard R. Lamar. *The Ingalls Wilder Family Songbook* (Middleton, Wis.: A-R Editions, 2011), edited by Dale Cockrell, provides music, lyrics, and extensive discussion of the sources of songs in the first eight novels in the "Little House" series.

The "Little House" books, while fiction, are autobiographical; they concern real people, places, and events. Notes are provided on historical figures but not on fictional characters.

BY THE SHORES OF SILVER LAKE

5.11–12 scarlet fever] Wilder seems never to have known the exact nature of her sister's illness. It is clear from her accounts that Mary Ingalls was the only member of the family to fall ill in the spring of 1879. In her memoir, "Pioneer Girl," she explained that doctors believed Mary's stroke was caused by the measles "from which she had never wholly recovered." In a letter to Rose Wilder Lane dated March 23, 1937, Wilder wrote, "Mary had spinal men[in]gitis"; she then canceled the name of the disease and continued, "some sort of spinal sickness. I am not sure if the Dr. named it. She was sick a long time but the Dr. finally did save her. She was paral[y]zed and as she gradually recovered from the stroke her sight went. We learned later when Pa took her from De Smet to Chicago to a specialist that the nerves of her eyes were paral[y]zed and there was no hope."

6.6 homestead] The Homestead Act of 1862 offered 160 acres of land (or a "quarter section," measuring a quarter of a square mile) free to any head of household over age twenty-one. Title was granted after claimant "proved up," or demonstrated that the property had been settled and improved over five years.

6.21 Aunt Docia] Laura Ladocia Ingalls (1845–1918), sister of Charles Ingalls, married a Swiss immigrant, Augustin Eugene Waldvogel, and had two children with him, Lena and Eugene (known as Gene), settling in Pierce

County, Wisconsin, north of Pepin. After Waldvogel shot and killed a man in 1868 and was convicted of murder, "Docia," as she was known, mother of two-year-old Lena and pregnant with Eugene (later called Gene), divorced him and married railroad teamster Hiram Forbes, with whom she had seven more children.

6.27–28 Dakota Territory] Officially established by Congress in 1861, Dakota Territory originally constituted the northernmost portion of the Louisiana Purchase (present-day Dakotas and much of Montana and Wyoming). It was reduced in 1863 to the Dakotas, which were admitted to statehood in 1889.

7.3–7 a hundred . . . Indian Territory] See note 6.6. Wilder's earlier novel *Little House on the Prairie* (1935) locates the Ingallses' cabin in Indian Territory; it was actually in Kansas. Created in 1834, Indian Territory consisted of present-day Kansas, Oklahoma, and Nebraska and was meant to contain five tribes; by 1854, it was reduced to Oklahoma, where many additional tribes were forced to take up residence.

7.26–31 Aunt Ruby . . . child.] Among Charles Ingalls's eight surviving siblings were Ruby Ingalls, George Ingalls, and Polly Ingalls, who married Henry Quiner (brother of Caroline Quiner Ingalls) and had six children, including Charles, or Charley, who appears in *Little House in the Big Woods* (1932). Charles Ingalls's parents were Lansford Whiting Ingalls (1812–1896) and Laura Louise Colby Ingalls (1810–1883).

7.27 Dolly Varden] Nickname of Alma Card (b. 1879?), the only daughter of Joseph and Ruby Ingalls Card, who died in childhood. Dolly Varden was a fictional flirt in Charles Dickens's novel *Barnaby Rudge* (1841); the nickname was shared by another Ingalls baby, Edith Ingalls (b. 1872), the daughter of Ruby's brother Peter.

8.19–20 trains . . . killed.] As train travel became more common in the second half of the nineteenth century, so did spectacular and often fatal accidents, which were graphically described in luridly illustrated newspapers.

14.29 Tracy] Minnesota town eight miles west of Walnut Grove and railroad center for the Chicago and North Western Railway.

21.11–18 "There is . . . times——"] Sung to the tune of "The Happy Land" (1838), a song that first appeared in Sunday school hymnals in the early 1840s. The Scottish poet Andrew Young (1807–1889) wrote the words to accompany a found melody: a traditional "Hindustani Air" arranged, in the 1830s, by Scottish composer Robert Archibald Smith (1780–1829). The most frequently mentioned song in the "Little House" series, it appears in *Little House on the Prairie*, *On the Banks of Plum Creek*, *By the Shores of Silver Lake*, and *The Long Winter*; in the latter it is said to be "Ma's favorite."

30.28–31, 34–37 "I know . . . beware!"] "Beware!" (1865), song by

Charles Moulton (d. 1871), with words, translated from the anonymous German poem "Hüt du dich!," by Henry Wadsworth Longfellow (1807–1882).

31.3–10 "I wouldn't . . . be!"] "The Railroader," American courting song. Evidence suggests that it was written in the early twentieth century, so its use by Wilder may be anachronistic.

38.19 Silver Lake camp] Then the forward construction camp of the Chicago and North Western Railway's Dakota Central branch.

39.5 buffaloes] Some sixty million American bison (commonly called buffalo) once ranged from Canada to Mexico, a principal food source of plains tribes. Throughout the 1800s, professional and sport hunters, along with U.S. Army soldiers, drove the species to near extinction. By 1889, eleven hundred animals remained in the U.S. and Canada.

39.13–16, 19–26 "Oh, come . . . farm!"] "Uncle Sam's Farm" (1850), words by Jesse Hutchinson Jr. (1813–1853), written for the Hutchinson Family Singers, a touring American singing group of 1840s and 1850s that did much to popularize four-part harmony.

41.37 Silver Lake . . . Henry and Thompson] Formed by a glacial depression, Silver Lake lies near Lake Henry; Lakes Henry and Thompson are several miles southeast of what became the town site of De Smet. On a 1914 picture postcard showing the railroad tracks running past Silver Lake, Caroline Ingalls wrote that the image was taken "500 or 700 feet from where the Ingalls family lived in [18]79–80."

41.40 the Jim] James River.

42.4 Spirit Lake] Lake several miles northwest of De Smet.

48.18 buffalo grass] *Bouteloua dactyloides*, a perennial shortgrass native to the semiarid high plains of North America. In answer to a question posed by his daughter in 1937, Almanzo Wilder wrote, "Buffalo grass grew about 6 inches high, very thick, always looked like it was dead or very near it, but cattle would get fat on it."

56.14–17 "A life . . . their cheeks."] Cf. "A Life on the Ocean Wave" (1838), a musical setting, by English composer Henry Russell (1812–1900), of the poem by Epes Sargent (1813–1880): "A life on an ocean wave, / A home on the rolling deep, / Where the scattered waters rave, / And the winds their revels keep!"

56.19–22 "Oh, I wouldn't . . . shirt."] See note 31.3–10.

56.23–24 Broom song] "Buy a Broom!" or "The Bavarian Girl's Song" (1830), song arranged by English music-hall impresario George Alexander Lee, words by Daniel A. O'Meara.

72.16 Better a live . . . lion."] Cf. Ecclesiastes 9:4.

72.18 discretion is . . . valor.] Cf. *1 Henry IV*, V.iv.119–20.

76.20–27 "Where are you going . . . said."] Traditional English nursery rhyme and folk song.

79.23 Brookings. That's sixty miles.] Brookings, South Dakota, some forty miles east of Silver Lake. Wilder acknowledged in a November 18, 1939, letter to Aubrey Sherwood, editor of *The De Smet News*, that she had misspelled the name of this town as "Brookins" throughout *By the Shores of Silver Lake*; she corrected the spelling in her next novel, *The Long Winter*.

86.5–17 "One night . . . across the——"] "Mary of the Wild Moor," popular ballad (c. eighteenth century?), published in Boston in 1845. In 1860, Charles Ingalls transcribed the lyrics of this song and those for "The Blue Juniata" into a handmade book his wife had made.

86.22–33 "I've traveled . . . canoe!"] "Paddle Your Own Canoe" (c. 1865), song by English music-hall entertainer Harry Clifton (1832–1872).

90.11–16 "Hail, Columbia . . . shall find."] "Hail Columbia" (1798), American patriotic song by violinist Philip Phile (d. 1793) with words by Joseph Hopkinson (1770–1842).

90.20 'Highland Mary,'] Song (1792) based on a traditional Scottish air, with words from the poem by Robert Burns, written upon the death of his fiancée, Mary Campbell, in 1786.

90.32–33 'Coming Through the Rye.'] Song (1828) based on a traditional tune, with words from Robert Burns's "Comin' Thro' the Rye" (1782).

91.8–13 "I'm Captain Jinks . . . Army!"] "Captain Jinks" (1868), popular song by Tom Maclagan (1827–1902) with words by English music-hall performer William Horace Lingard (1839–1927).

91.15–18 "I am Mrs. Jinks . . . Army!"] "Mistress Jinks of Madison Square" (1868), song by William Shakespeare Hays (1837–1907) capitalizing on the American success of "Captain Jinks" (see note 91.8–13).

91.24–28 "First! . . . then-the-toe——"] From a Gaelic folk rhyme intended to teach dance steps. See *Nether Lochaber: The Natural History, Legends, and Folk-lore of the Western Highlands*, by the Reverend Alexander Stewart (Edinburgh: William Paterson, 1883).

100.34 the last buffalo wolves] Wolves were extirpated in the Dakotas by the 1920s or 1930s.

105.26 "Away down the River on the O-hi-o!"] From "De Boatmen's Dance" (1843), minstrel song by Daniel Decatur Emmett (1815–1904).

105.27 "Why Chime the Bells So Merrily."] From "The New Year's Come" (1839), song by Jonas B. Phillips (1805–1869) with words by Joseph Philip Knight (1812–1887).

105.28–31 "Jingle bells . . . sleigh!"] "Jingle Bells" (1859), American song by James Lord Pierpont (1822–1893).

105.36–106.5 "Yes, a brighter morn . . . His paths."] "Mountain of the Lord" (1871), American hymn by Robert Lowry (1826–1899). This, along with "Gentle Words and Loving Smiles" and "Lend a Helping Hand" (all of which appear in the present volume), was published in a popular hymnal, *Pure Gold for the Sunday School: A New Collection of Songs Prepared and Adapted for Sunday School Exercises*, by Robert Lowry and W. Howard Doane (New York: Biglow & Main, 1871).

106.8–23 "The sun . . . earth!"] "Gentle Words and Loving Smiles" (1871), American hymn by Robert Lowry (1826–1899). See note 105.36–106.5.

107.6 Boast!] Robert Boast (1848–1921) worked on the Chicago and North Western Railway line and, in 1879, filed on a homestead east of what became De Smet, prior to the founding of the town. He and his wife, Ella Boast (1852–1918), were married ten years before moving from Iowa to Kingsbury County, South Dakota. The Boasts spent that winter in the Surveyor's office.

109.10–21 "Merry, Merry . . . rest."] "Merry, Merry Christmas!" (1870), American song by Mrs. T. J. Cook.

122.12–13 "The Gypsy's Warning."] Popular song (1864) by Henry A. Coard (1812–?). In 1878, it became the first music transmitted electrically when Alexander Graham Bell's assistant, Thomas Watson, sang it to him during a public demonstration of the recently invented telephone.

123.8–15 "When I was young . . . then!"] "I Wish I Were Single Again" (1871), American song by James Cox Beckel (1811–1880).

123.19–22 "She can make . . . mother."] "Billy Boy," traditional American song, likely a parody of the British ballad "Lord Randal."

123.29–30 "I bet my money . . . the gray!"] "Camptown Races" (1850), minstrel song by Stephen Foster (1826–1864).

123.34 "Three blind mice,"] Traditional English round. See note 679.35–37.

124.13–15 "Nellie . . . Vir-gin-ia bride."] "Nelly Was a Lady" (1849), song by Stephen Foster (1826–1864), written for the Christy Minstrels.

124.17–20 "Oh, do you remember . . . frown?"] "Ben Bolt" (1848), song by Nelson Kneass (1823–1868/69?) with words by Thomas Dunn English (1819–1902).

124.22–25 "Oft . . . around me."] "Oft in the Stilly Night" (1818), traditional Scottish melody with words by Thomas Moore (1779–1852).

124.27–30 "Ye banks . . . care?"] "Bonny Doon" (1803?), song attributed to James Miller, with words adapted from Robert Burns's poem "The Banks o' Doon" (1783).

125.5–9, 12–13 "When . . . pilgrim way."] "Lend a Helping Hand," song by William Howard Doane (1832–1915) with words by Fanny J. Crosby (1820–1915). See note 105.36–106.5.

125.22 Reverend Alden!] The Reverend Edwin H. Alden (1836–1911) appears in Wilder's previous novel, *On the Banks of Plum Creek.* He met the Ingalls family in 1874, when he was sent by the Home Missionary Society to found a Congregational church in Walnut Grove, Minnesota.

126.26 Home Missionary Society] Launched in 1826, the American Home Missionary Society was an interdenominational association funding frontier congregations and supplying traveling ministers.

127.4–5 whom . . . chasteneth] Hebrews 12:6.

127.7 one in Iowa.] The Iowa College for the Blind, founded in 1852 in Keokuk, Iowa, later moved to Vinton.

127.35–36 God . . . look down] Cf. I Chronicles 28:9; Psalms 14:2.

130.1–4 "There . . . our King . . ."] See note 21.11–18.

130.22 De Smet . . . days.] De Smet was founded in 1880, a railroad town created during the extension of the Chicago and North Western Railway's Dakota Central branch line (which eventually ran from Tracy, Minnesota, to Pierre, Dakota Territory). The town was named for a Jesuit priest from Belgium, Father Pierre-Jean De Smet (1801–1873), a missionary who traveled throughout the West, working with Native American tribes.

136.5 Mr. Hinz . . . Mr. Harthorns] Henry Hinz (1854–1938) built one of the first buildings in De Smet, a billiard hall and saloon. Edelbert Harthorn (1839–1925) and his son Frank (1864–1950) established a dry goods store, Harthorn & Son, known as the "Red Front Store" for its brightly painted façade.

139.4 Nothing . . . taxes.] Cf. Benjamin Franklin (1706–1790), letter to Jean-Baptiste Leroy, November 13, 1789.

145.34–37 "Oh . . . treeses!"] "The Big Sunflower" (1867), minstrel song by Bobby Newcomb (1847–1888). In a 1936 letter, Wilder wrote that her father always sang the song "if he was particularly cold and miserable."

150.4 claim jumper] In her memoir, "Pioneer Girl," Wilder described how Jack Hunt, a former neighbor of the Ingalls family, was shot and killed by a claim jumper, recalling her father's remark: "people were getting 'too durned thick' and someone might move into our shanty."

152.35 the Wilder boys] Royal and Almanzo Wilder, along with their sister

Eliza Jane, arrived in Dakota Territory in the summer of 1879, filing on adjacent claims.

154.16–23 "Oh, drive . . . man."] "A Motto for Every Man" (1868), song by English music-hall entertainer Harry Clifton (1832–1872). Charles Ingalls's chorus may be his variation on the original; it also appears in Rose Wilder Lane's 1938 novel, *Free Land*, with some minor changes.

154.31–36 "When . . . me."] "The Beacon-Light of Home" (1879), American song by H. M. Estabrooke (1849–1908) with words by George F. St. Clair.

156.34–35 tree claim] The Timber Culture Act of 1873 offered settlers 160 acres of free land, 40 to be planted in trees raised successfully over eight years. So few trees grew that the requirement was later changed to ten acres.

164.10–21 "We . . . door!"] "Keep the Horseshoe over the Door" (1880), song by Irish-American composer Joseph Paul Skelly (1850–1895).

167.21–28 "In Scarlet . . . Allen."] "Barbara Allen," traditional ballad existing in many versions, mentioned by Samuel Pepys in his 1666 diary.

168.1–3 "Home! . . . home."] "Home! Sweet Home!" (1823), song by English composer Henry Rowley Bishop (1786–1855) with words by American librettist John Howard Payne (1791–1852), from their operetta *Clari: or, The Maid of Milan.*

THE LONG WINTER

186.1 "all's well"] Cf. *All's Well That Ends Well*, IV.iv.35.

187.8–9 equinoctial storm.] According to folk wisdom of the time, the equinox caused violent thunderstorms.

194.2 *October Blizzard*] Occurring early in the season, catching farmers unawares, the blizzard of October 15–18, 1880, killed people and livestock, marking the start of what would be known as the "hard winter."

194.5–9 "Oh . . . SLAP!)"] See note 145.34–37.

197.1–11 "Oh . . . die . . ."] "De Floating Scow of Old Virginia," or "Carry Me Back to Old Virginia" (1847), song by Charles T. White (1821–1891), a blackface minstrel performer.

197.23–28, 32–34 "March . . . glory!"] "All the Blue Bonnets" (1832), song, based on a traditional Scottish dance, with words by Sir Walter Scott, from a poem in his novel *The Monastery* (1820).

202.13 the great auk] A woodcut of the great auk answering this description appears in *The Polar and Tropical Worlds: A Description of Man and Nature in the Polar and Equatorial Regions of the Globe*, by Dr. Georg Hartwig

(Springfield, Mass.: Bill, Nichols & Co., 1871), p. 86. The bird may have been a dovekie, *Alle alle*, also known as the "little auk," a diminutive murre-like species with webbed feet, black back, and white breast.

207.3–4 Harthorn's store] See note 136.5.

210.11 'Oh . . . bird!'] Cf. Psalms 55:6.

211.34 Judge Carroll] John H. Carroll, District Court clerk, who conducted the federal 1880 census in Kingsbury County, became the first mayor of De Smet in 1889 and later served in the South Dakota House of Representatives.

212.15–17 Fuller's Hardware . . . General Merchandise.] Fuller's Hardware was owned by Charleton S. G. Fuller (1847–1905), an Englishman who emigrated to the U.S. at age thirteen, founded a hardware store in Brookings in 1879, and the following year traveled east to De Smet. He was later joined in De Smet by his brother Gerald (1848–1930). Power's Tailor Shop was owned by Irish immigrant Thomas P. Power. Daniel Loftus, born 1853, was the proprietor of a grocery and dry goods store; he became a prominent citizen of the town and died there in 1921.

215.3 "How many people . . . now?"] In a *Missouri Ruralist* column, published February 5, 1917, Wilder wrote that "200 people . . . spent the winter of 1880–81 in De Smet." According to postal records, the town grew from 50 to 300 between February 24 and March 15, 1880. The federal census of June 1880 listed over a hundred, including many named in this volume: druggist George Bradley; grocers George Wilmarth, Charles Barker, and Edelbert Harthorn; feedstore owner Jerome Woodruff; hardware dealers Charleton Fuller and his brother Gerald Fuller; station agent Horace Woodworth; hotel keepers Charles Mead, Jerome Beardsley, and Roscoe Sheldon; banker Thomas Ruth; and farmers Royal and Almanzo Wilder. Margaret Garland and her children, Sarah, Florence (a schoolteacher), and Oscar Edmund (Cap), were also in town that winter.

229.27 When he came West . . . old.] Born in 1857, Almanzo Wilder was twenty-two in 1879, when he came to Dakota Territory to file on a homestead. Wilder sought to minimize the ten-year age span between herself and her husband in the novels, sensitive about the appearance of having had (as she wrote to her daughter) "a horr[i]d child marriage." In the 1953 edition of *Farmer Boy*, Almanzo's age is given accurately, as nine years old in 1866. In later volumes, the character is said to be six years older than Laura Ingalls.

230.1 None of the rules worked] The Homestead Act proved vulnerable to fraud. Enforcement of regulations was weak, and land speculators amassed large properties through bribery or fraudulent claims. Approximately 40 percent of homesteaders succeeded in proving up on claims; only a fifth of the trillion acres made available by the federal government was acquired by small farmers.

233.2 *Volga*] Town in Brookings County, thirty-five miles east of De Smet.

234.14 Let 'er go gallagher!] American catchphrase of the late 1800s, with the same sense as "Let 'er rip!"

234.23–26 "We'll *ROLL* . . . be*HIND!*"] "Roll the Old Chariot Along," traditional nineteenth-century sea shanty and spiritual.

239.27 'The Lord helps them that help themselves'] Cf. Benjamin Franklin (1706–1790), *Poor Richard's Almanack*, June 1736.

241.14 "Little Annie . . . Be,"] "Little Annie Rooney" (1889), song by Irish composer and performer Michael Nolan (1867–1910). Published nine years after the winter of 1880, this song is an anachronism.

241.14–15 The Old Grey Mare] "Down in Alabam" (1858), song by J. Warner, performed by Bryant's Minstrels.

241.16 Highland Fling] Traditional Scottish tune, first published 1883.

243.4–5 "Oh, I am as happy . . . Oh!"] See note 145.34–37.

246.29–30 "There's a land . . . afar. . . ."] "Sweet By and By" (1868), American song by Joseph Philbrick Webster (1819–1875) with words by Sanford Fillmore Bennett (1836–1898).

246.32–35 "Jesus is a rock . . . storm."] "A Shelter in the Time of Storm" (1885), hymn, published several years after the hard winter of 1880, by Ira D. Sankey (1840–1908) with words by Vernon J. Charlesworth (1839–1915).

246.36–37 "There a Happy Land . . . Away."] See note 21.11–18.

247.3–7 "Then let the hurricane . . . shore!"] "The Evergreen Shore" (1861), song by William Batchelder Bradbury (1816–1868) with words by William C. Hunter (1811–1877). "The Hurricane Roared" appears as a chapter title in Wilder's original manuscript; the lyrics were used by Rose Wilder Lane as the title of her 1932 *Saturday Evening Post* serial, later published as a novel.

251.10 Tracy cut] See note 14.29.

254.27 *Chicago Inter-Ocean*] Daily and weekly newspaper, 1865–1914.

263.7 Preston] Lake Preston, town in Kingsbury County, Dakota Territory, ten miles east of De Smet.

263.22–23 cousins . . . Peter] Alice, Ella, and Peter Ingalls, three eldest children of Peter Ingalls, Charles Ingalls's brother, and Eliza Quiner Ingalls, Caroline Ingalls's sister.

264.14 Mr. Gilbert] According to newspaper accounts, David Gilbert made twice-weekly trips to Volga by sled throughout the winter of 1880–81 until May 1, when the train tracks were cleared.

265.26–32 "March! . . . glory!"] See note 197.23–28, 32–34.

268.8 Nothing's . . . taxes] See note 139.4.

269.28–30 *Advances . . . Pioneer Press.*] *The Advance: A Congregational Weekly* (1867–1917), periodical for Christian women; *Youth's Companion* (1827–1929), a weekly magazine for children; *Inter-Ocean*, see note 254.27; *The Pioneer Press* (founded in St. Paul in 1849), Minnesota's first daily newspaper.

270.34 Needs must, when the devil drives.] Cited in *Assembly of Gods* (c. 1480) and in John Heywood, *Proverbs* (1546), Part II, 7. Cf. *All's Well That Ends Well* I.iii.29–30.

279.28 Indian Territory] See note 7.3–7.

286.5–6 antelope] Probably pronghorn, *Antilocapra americana*, known colloquially as an antelope and capable of prodigious speed. No true antelope species is native to the Americas.

288.21 You're a mighty . . . Lord] Cf. Genesis 10:9.

290.22–23 father's pastures . . . colt.] The Wilder family settled in Spring Valley, Minnesota, after leaving their farm near Malone, New York, in 1875.

298.33 Pride goes before a fall] Cf. Proverbs 16:18.

299.24–25 "Oh Canaan . . . bound for the . . ."] "On Jordan's Stormy Banks" (1878), hymn by George Frederick Root (1820–1895) with words (1787) by Samuel Stennett (1727–1795). Here the words are combined with those of "Canaan," a traditional hymn.

303.1 The Speech of Regulus] Mary Ingalls was given a copy of *The Independent Fifth Reader*, by J. Madison Watson (New York: A. S. Barnes & Co., 1876), for her twelfth birthday, January 10, 1877. It contains the "Supposed Speech of Regulus" as a lesson in elocution.

303.13 "Old Tubal Cain,"] "Tubal Cain," poem by Charles Mackay (1814–1889).

304.37–305.2 Listen . . . year. . . .] "Paul Revere's Ride" (1861), poem by Henry Wadsworth Longfellow (1807–1882).

305.3–4 "The Swan's Nest"] "The Romance of the Swan's Nest" (1844), poem by Elizabeth Barrett Browning (1806–1861).

308.20 "Livingston's Africa."] See note 202.13. David Livingstone (1813–1873), Scottish missionary and explorer, was said to be "lost to the civilized world" for five years in an 1874 edition of the book.

309.29–30 "Ye banks . . . fair?"] See note 124.27–30.

310.22–25 "I . . . roll."] "The Home of the Soul," song (1866) by Philip Phillips (1834–1895) with words by Ellen Maria Huntington Gates (1835–1920). Often played at nineteenth-century funerals, the hymn was inspired by John Bunyan's Christian allegory *The Pilgrim's Progress* (1678).

317.27–29 "Old . . . three . . ."] Conflation of two poems, "Tubal Cain" (see note 303.13) and "Old King Cole," an English nursery rhyme.

326.23 both nineteen] See note 229.27. Cap Garland, born in 1864, was seventeen in early 1881; Almanzo Wilder, born 1857, was twenty-four.

338.7–18, 21–24 "When . . . harm!"] "We Are All Here" (1880), spiritual attributed to Louis Murray Browne. This song appears in *The Conqueror*, by Ransom H. Randall and C. E. Leslie (Chicago: The Chicago Music Company, 1880), believed to be the singing-school book used by Laura Ingalls and Almanzo Wilder in *These Happy Golden Years.*

338.27–30, 32–35 "De . . . so!"] " 'Twill Nebber Do to Gib It Up So!" (1843), song by Daniel Decatur Emmett (1815–1904), of the Virginia Minstrels.

339.7–10 "Great . . . holiness."] "Great Is the Lord" (1880), hymn with music by Ransom H. Randall (1847–1923?) set to Psalm 48:1. This song appears in *The Conqueror* (1880), by Ransom H. Randall and C. E. Leslie, believed to be the singing-school book described in *These Happy Golden Years.*

339.12–15 "When . . . eyes."] "When I Can Read My Title Clear" (1878), song by Joseph Perry Holbrook (1822–1888) with words by Isaac Watts (1674–1748).

352.17 'Beauty . . . deep.'] Cf. *A Select Second Husband for Sir Thomas Overburie's Wife, Now a Matchlesse Widow* (1616), by John Davies of Hereford (c. 1565–1618).

354.31–32 hundred miles] The round-trip from De Smet to Brookings is approximately eighty miles.

355.25–26 "If . . . dear."] "The May Queen, Part Second: New Year's Eve" (1845), from a three-part cantata, based on the 1832 poem by Alfred, Lord Tennyson; music by Scottish composer William Richardson Dempster (1808–1871).

365.14–33, 366.1–4 "This . . . today."] "Where There's a Will There's a Way" (c. 1867–68), song by English music-hall entertainer Harry Clifton (1832–1872).

LITTLE TOWN ON THE PRAIRIE

372.3 October Blizzard] See note 194.2.

376.2 Dakota Territory] See note 6.27–28.

376.36–37 "as the sparks fly upwards,"] Cf. Job 5:7.

377.17–20 "The Lord . . . waters."] Cf. Psalms 23:1–2.

381.29–30 striped gophers] Thirteen-lined ground squirrel, *Spermophilus tridecemlineatus.*

383.15 a county was being organized] Meetings held at Amos Whiting's homestead claim in February and March 1880 established De Smet as the Kingsbury county seat.

383.38 *The Advance*] See note 269.28–30.

385.21 college for the blind in Iowa.] See note 127.7.

390.5 Mr. Clancy] Character based on Chauncey Clayson, who owned a dry goods store in De Smet; his mother-in-law was Martha White.

390.19 *Inter-Ocean*] See note 254.27.

391.34 thunder-pumps] The American bittern (*Botaurus lentiginosus*) produces a loud, distinctive call known as "thunder-pumping."

397.22–24 For . . . five years.] See note 6.6.

399.6–8 Pull . . . winds—] "Pull for the Shore" (1875), song by Philip Paul Bliss (1838–1876).

399.34 Tay Pay Pryor] Identified in Wilder's "Pioneer Girl" and in the manuscript version of *Little Town on the Prairie* as T. P. Power, town tailor and father of Mary Power. Wilder changed the name in her revisions.

404.1–2 college and manual training] In addition to Braille and traditional humanities and science subjects, course offerings at the Iowa College for the Blind included training in musical instruments, deportment, and crafts (bead-work, sewing, caning, carpet-weaving, and the making of brooms and mattresses).

405.27–28 Hurray! . . . free!] "Marching Through Georgia" (1865), song by Henry Clay Work (1832–1884).

409.13 Lawyer Barnes] Visscher Vere Barnes (1851–1924) served as city attorney of De Smet, as judge of Kingsbury County, and as a territorial legislator.

412.1–7 My country . . . King!] "America" (1832), words by the Reverend Samuel Francis Smith (1808–1895), set to the traditional English music for "God Save the King/Queen."

412.20 "Our father's God, author of liberty—"] See note 412.1–7.

414.20 Almanzo Wilder's] See note 229.27.

418.34 Spanish needle grass] Perhaps *Hesperostipa comata*, also known as speargrass, devil's grass, or needle-and-thread grass.

420.36 *Godey's Lady's Book*] Innovative monthly magazine, published in

Philadelphia from 1830 to 1898, that introduced or perfected many features of nineteenth-century journalism for women: hand-tinted fashion plates, dress patterns, fiction, poetry, "points of ettiquite," and sheet music of parlor songs.

424.6–7 'Her . . . woman.'] Cf. *King Lear* V.iii.273–74.

428.13 "'Sing . . . sixpence—'"] English nursery rhyme.

439.2 *Miss Wilder*] See note 152.35.

441.25 Ida Wright . . . Mrs. Brown.] Edward Brown (1814–1895), cousin of the famous abolitionist John Brown, served as pastor for the Congregational Church in 1880–84. After Brown married his second wife, Laura, in 1867, the couple adopted Ida Belle Wright, who lost most of her family in the Great Chicago Fire of 1871.

445.1–2 double ruffle . . . wear.] Lines from the children's rhyme "Dicky Dilver," describing Dicky's wife: "Fine stockings, fine shoes, / Fine yellow hair, / Double ruffle round her neck / And not a dress to wear."

445.13–15 Then . . . call—] "Whip-Poor-Will's Song" (1865), song by American composer Harrison Millard (1830–1895).

447.27 THE LOTOS-EATERS.] "The Lotus-Eaters" (1832), poem by Alfred, Lord Tennyson. In her memoir, "Pioneer Girl," Wilder describes the book she found in her mother's drawer as "a beautiful book of Scott's poems."

455.31 "Birds . . . agree,"] From a poem by Isaac Watts (1674–1748), "Love Between Brothers and Sisters," in *Divine Songs for Children* (1715).

464.24–25 Bible . . . platter] Cf. Matthew 23:25–26 and Luke 11:39–40.

470.23 nubia] Knitted head scarf for women.

477.25–32 When . . . yet.] The New York monthly *Literary News* for March 1881 printed this verse and other examples of the autograph-album genre submitted by readers during a competition.

478.18 Jake Hopp] Jacob Hopp (1858–1926) arrived in De Smet on April 1, 1880, with a load of printing equipment and soon began publishing the *Kingsbury County News.*

484.5 Ladies' Aid Society] Volunteers organized the first Ladies' Aid Societies during the Civil War to provide food, clothing, medical supplies, and sanitation to hospitals for sick and wounded soldiers.

484.17–21 Rev. Alden . . . West.] See note 125.22.

485.11–12 'lunatic fringe.'] Phrase coined in the 1870s to describe bangs as a hairstyle.

490.18 *Youth's Companions*] See note 269.28–30.

491.6 Gerald Fuller] See note 212.15–17.

496.12–15 Backward . . . tonight.] "Rock Me to Sleep, Mother" (1860), song by Ernest Leslie, pseudonym of Obadiah Bruen Brown (1829–1901), with words by Elizabeth Akers Allen (1832–1911); originally published as a poem in *The Saturday Evening Post*, June 9, 1860, under Allen's pseudonym "Florence Percy."

497.11–14, 17–20 We . . . WAY!] "The Good Old Way" (1871), American hymn by William Howard Doane (1832–1915) with words by Fanny J. Crosby (1820–1915). (See also note 105.36–106.5.) Educated at the New York Institution for the Blind, Crosby wrote the words to many popular hymns.

499.4 graham bread] High-fiber, whole-wheat bread developed in 1829 by American dietitian Sylvester Graham (1794–1851).

502.20 *Stories of the Moorland*] *Stories from the Moorland; or, Tales of the Covenanters* (1869), by American novelist Lizzie Bates (fl. 1867–84), a chronicle of a Scottish farm boy's childhood.

503.15 Mrs. Jarley's Wax Works] Mrs. Jarley, proprietor of a wax work show, appears in Charles Dickens's *The Old Curiosity Shop* (1840). Instructions for "Mrs. Jarley's" amateur waxwork theatricals were subsequently printed in a series of paperback pamphlets in the late 1800s, as well as in books such as *Dick's One Hundred Amusements for Evening Parties, Picnics, and Social Gatherings*, by William Brisbane Dick (Padell Book Co., 1873). The pamphlets provide narrative remarks for the hostess and suggest costumes for her and for historical figures such as George Washington, Queen Elizabeth, and others. An advertisement in the *De Smet Leader* of March 14, 1885, announces that "Mrs. Jarley with her unique group of wax 'figgers'" will appear at the town skating rink.

504.34–39 Ben . . . o'clock] The handwritten invitation to Ben Woodworth's birthday party, on January 28, 1882, was found among Wilder's papers.

506.17–22 Come . . . blown.] From "Maud" (1855), poem by Alfred, Lord Tennyson.

513.20–22 Lost . . . forever.] Aphorism attributed to Horace Mann (1796–1859).

516.4–5, 8–11 Oh . . . FEET!] "Skidmore Guard" (1874), comic march by William Carter (1838–?) with words by Edward Harrigan (1844–1911). Harrigan wrote and starred in vaudeville sketches featuring the Mulligan Guard, a troop of New York City Irish militiamen, squaring off against their blackface rivals, the Skidmore Guard, from the Lower East Side.

523.1 new teacher, Mr. Owen] V. S. L. Owen. In her memoir, "Pioneer Girl," Wilder calls him "Ven Owen."

527.13–18 There . . . care.] "The Ninety and Nine" (1874), American hymn by Ira D. Sankey (1840–1908) with words by Elizabeth Cecelia Clephane (1830–1869). It appears as Hymn 154 in Sankey's *Gospel Hymns No. 5* (1887), a volume owned by Wilder.

527.28–33 Sowing . . . be?] "What Shall the Harvest Be?" (1875), American hymn by Philip Paul Bliss (1838–1876) with words by Emily Sullivan Oakey (1829–1883).

528.11–12 Repent . . . wrath!] Cf. Acts 3:19, Matthew 3:7, Luke 3:7.

528.14–15, 18–19 Pull . . . shore!] See note 399.6–8.

530.29–30 Spring Valley . . . Malone] See note 290.22–23.

531.10–11 " 'Chisel . . . boy,' "] "Life Sculpture," poem by George Washington Doane (1799–1859).

534.19–23 There is . . . Congress.] Thomas Jefferson (1743–1826) recounted this anecdote about Benjamin Harrison's riposte to John Dickinson of Pennsylvania, who, in 1775, objected to the use of the word "Congress" in the Declaration of the Causes and Necessity of Taking Up Arms. It appears in the posthumously published *Memoir, Correspondence, and Miscellanies, from the Papers of Thomas Jefferson*, edited by Thomas Jefferson Randolph (Charlottesville, Va.: F. Carr, 1829).

534.23–25 'And George . . . most of it!'] Cf. Patrick Henry (1736–1799), Speech on the Stamp Act, House of Burgesses, Williamsburg, Virginia, May 29, 1765.

534.25–26 Give me liberty . . . death. . . .] Patrick Henry, Speech at the Second Virginia Convention, Richmond, March 23, 1775.

542.8–9 Scaling . . . brow.] This sentence is parsed in *The Science of the English Language: A Practical Grammar; in which Words, Phrases, and Sentences Are Classified, According to their Offices, and Their Relation to Each Other*, by Stephen Watkins Clark (New York: A.S. Barnes & Co., 1847).

543.3 Teacher's Certificate] The Kingsbury County teacher's certificate found among Wilder's papers is dated December 10, 1883.

THESE HAPPY GOLDEN YEARS

549.25 Brewster settlement] One of the few fictional names in the series. Wilder changed Bouchie to Brewster to disguise the identity of Louis Bouchie, a relative of Robert Boast.

570.4 Indian Territory] See note 7.3–7.

572.3–4 Harthorn's . . . red.] See note 136.5.

572.9 Mr. Fuller . . . Mr. Bradley] See note 215.3.

572.16 Mr. Power's tailor shop] See note 212.15–17.

572.30 Mr. Owen] See note 523.1.

574.29 Lawyer Barnes] See note 409.13.

574.32–35, 575.1–4, 7–8 Sweet . . . home.] "My Sabbath Home" (1871), Sunday school song by William Howard Doane (1832–1915) with words by Christopher Rubey Blackall (1830–1924).

575.14 Reverend Brown] See note 441.25.

575.30 Doxology] Music first appears in Geneva Psalter of 1551; words written c. 1673 by Thomas Ken (1637–1711).

576.7–8 *The Wonders of the Animal World*] See note 202.13.

576.8 *Pioneer Press*] See note 269.28–30.

584.3–4 'Wise . . . dove.'] Cf. Matthew 10:16.

584.6–7 "Can . . . Billy?"] See notes 123.8–15, 19–22, 29–30.

594.20 October blizzard] See note 194.2.

597.10 All's well that ends well] See note 186.1.

599.31 Mr. Williams] George A. Williams (1836–1913), school superintendent of Kingsbury County.

602.26 Starlight] Starlight appears in Wilder's second book, *Farmer Boy* (1933).

606.23 Tennyson's poems.] See note 447.27.

607.14–17, 22–23 Jingle . . . way!] See note 105.28–31.

610.1–2 "Cromwell . . . angels."] *Henry VIII*, III.ii.440–41. The definition of "ambition" in *Webster's Unabridged 1882 Dictionary*, which sat on Ven Owen's desk, cites Shakespeare's lines.

613.28 Uncle Tom!] Caroline Ingalls's brother, Thomas Quiner (1844–1903), worked for the Laird-Norton Lumber Company for over two decades.

614.13–14 Uncle Henry's family] See note 7.26–31.

614.17–19 Cousin Louisa . . . Dakota Territory.] See notes 6.27–28 and 263.22–23.

615.4–7 We started . . . boy.] According to historical accounts such as Annie D. Tallent's memoir *The Black Hills; or, The Last Hunting Ground of the Dakotahs* (St. Louis: Nixon-Jones Printing Co., 1899), Thomas Quiner accompanied an illegal 1874 gold-mining expedition that entered the Black Hills in violation of treaty rights of the Sioux.

620.25 Manchester] Town eight miles west of De Smet.

623.2 a quarter-section of land] See note 6.6.

627.22 Blanche] Mary Blanche Howard, from Webster City, Iowa, partially blinded by cataracts as an infant.

630.12 Miss Bell] Florence Bell (1848–1906), dressmaker and milliner, arrived in De Smet in 1882.

633.4 relinquishment] By law, homesteaders were allowed to give up a claim by relinquishment of the land to the government. Sales of relinquishments to third parties were illegal but common; enforcement was lax.

633.11 *Youth's Companion*] See note 269.28–30.

633.24 'Gather . . . may,'] Cf. "To the Virgins, To Make Much of Time," poem by Robert Herrick (1591–1674).

636.22–23 Cousin Alice!] See note 263.22–23.

640.25 second-grade certificate] Teaching certificates were granted for time periods that varied by state and were awarded according to examination results, with a third-grade certificate often valid for nine months to a year (based on an average score of 70 percent), second grade for eighteen months (on an average score of 80 percent), and first grade for two to three years (90 percent).

641.2 Mr. Williams] See note 599.31.

643.24 Wessington Hills] West of De Smet, in Hand County.

644.37–645.5 Here's . . . sir!] "Let the Toast Pass," or "Here's to the Maiden of Bashful Fifteen" (1777), song by Thomas Linley Sr. (1732–1795) written for Act III, scene iii, of *The School for Scandal*, by Irish dramatist Richard Brinsley Sheridan (1751–1816).

645.7–14 Oh . . . day!] "Polly-Wolly-Doodle" (published anonymously, 1880), American song, perhaps from the minstrel stage.

645.20–27 Golden . . . years.] "Golden Years Are Passing By" (1879), song by Will Lamartine Thompson (1847–1909).

648.8 our patent] Charles Ingalls proved up on his claim in 1886; the paperwork he completed at the Land Office at Watertown, Dakota Territory, is held at the National Archives.

651.27 Henry and Thompson] See note 41.37.

652.26 my homestead and my tree claim] See note 152.35.

654.12 Spirit Lake] See note 42.4.

654.13 tree claim] See note 156.34–35.

662.2–3 Elmer . . . McConnell] Elmer McConnell arrived in De Smet in 1884 and worked on Reverend Edward Brown's farm.

662.14–15 'In . . . love.'] "Locksley Hall" (1842), poem by Alfred, Lord Tennyson.

662.17–20 Oh . . . lad.] "O Whistle and I'll Come to You, My Lad" (1820), song attributed to Scottish fiddler John Bruce, with words adapted from Robert Burns's "Whistle, and I'll Come to Ye" (1793).

663.22 pieplant pie] Pieplant was a common term for rhubarb in the latter nineteenth century.

676.23–34 In the starlight . . . free.] "In the Starlight" (1860?), song by Stephen Ralph Glover (1813–1870), words by Joseph Edward Carpenter (1813–1885).

679.26–27 Gaily now . . . wave.] This song is one of several "Practical Exercises" in *The Conqueror* (1880), believed to be the singing-school book used by Laura Ingalls and Almanzo Wilder.

679.30–33 All around . . . everywhere.] "The Song of the Grass," song by Ransom H. Randall.

679.35–37 Three . . . after] "Three Blind Mice," traditional English round. It appears in *The Conqueror* (1880), believed to be the singing-school book used by Laura Ingalls and Almanzo Wilder.

680.13–18 Oh . . . school!] "The Singin Skewl" (1869), satirical song by "P. Benson Sr.," pseudonym for Charles C. Miller (1831–1920).

680.23–24 "The Heavens Declare the Glory."] American hymn (1880) by Horatio R. Palmer (1834–1907) with words from Psalm 19:1–3. One of the last songs in *The Conqueror* (1880), believed to be the singing-school book used by Laura Ingalls and Almanzo Wilder.

681.3–14 In . . . free.] See note 676.23–34.

682.28–35 A beautiful castle . . . kisses.] "In Dreamland Far Away" (1887), song by Hart Pease Danks (1834–1903) with words by George W. Birdseye (1844–1919), a friend of Stephen Foster. Possibly an anachronism.

690.3–10 Ye banks . . . Mary.] "Highland Mary." See note 90.20.

690.13–16 My . . . somebody.] "My Heart Is Sair for Somebody" (1824–25), song based on a traditional Scottish tune with words from Robert Burns's "For the Sake o' Somebody" (1794). "Somebody" refers to "Bonnie Prince Charlie" (Prince Charles Edward Stuart), second Jacobite pretender to the English throne. The words of Burns's original are "I could wake a winter . . ."

690.23–34 When . . . Bethlehem.] "The Star of Bethlehem" (1878?), song by Charles Heinrich Christopher Zeuner (1795–1857) with words by Henry Kirke White (1785–1806).

691.3–11 Oh . . . in!] "Come In and Shut the Door" (1862), song by

Frederick Buckley (1833–1864), member of the minstrel troupe Buckley's Serenaders, with words by "J.P.H."

698.6–13 The . . . sky?] "The Tread-Mill" (1892), song (composer unknown) with words from a poem by Oliver Wendell Holmes (1809–1894).

718.17–18 promise to obey you?] The Book of Common Prayer (1549) required a pledge of obedience from the bride.

719.10–11 "Marry in haste, repent at leisure."] Cf. *The Old Bachelor* (1693), play by William Congreve (1670–1729).

720.2 "*Haste to the Wedding*"] Traditional fiddle tune, music first printed in 1767.

722.40–723.1 "Highland Mary."] See note 90.20.

723.17–33 Once in . . . all.] "Love's Old Sweet Song" (1884), song by James Lynam Molloy (1837–1909) with words by Graham Clifton Bingham (1859–1913). In the manuscript of *These Happy Golden Years*, Wilder wrote, "I don't know if all this song should be used. I love it all but perhaps it is too much. It seems to me to fit right here. The last song Laura [hears] Pa sing."

730.9–10 Golden years . . . golden years.] See note 645.20–27. In the original 1943 edition of *These Happy Golden Years*, the last words of the novel were followed, on the next page, by a small drawing of Laura and Almanzo on the steps of their new house, beneath which was printed the motto: "The End of the Little House Books."

THE FIRST FOUR YEARS

735.19–30 In the starlight . . . free.] See note 676.23–34. The words of this song are quoted in their entirety in *These Happy Golden Years*; here Wilder supplies the second verse, but substitutes "gently play" for "softly play."

737.27–29 as the Irishman said . . . winter.] H. L. Mencken, in his *New Dictionary of Quotations* (1942), attributes this remark to William Barclay "Bat" Masterson (1853–1921), lawman, confederate of Wyatt Earp, and later a journalist. The words appear in Masterson's last column for the *New York Morning Telegraph*, which was written on the morning of the day of his death, October 25, 1921, and published two days later: "Just think of an honest, hard-working farmer laboring from daylight to dark for forty years of his life. . . . There are those who argue that everything breaks even in this old dump of a world of ours. I suppose these ginks who argue that way hold that because the rich man gets ice in the summer and the poor man gets it in the winter things are breaking even for both. Maybe so, but I'll swear I can't see it that way."

738.23–28 Two . . . school section] Along with his brother Royal and sister Eliza, Almanzo Wilder had been among the first settlers to file for homesteads in Kingsbury County, on August 21, 1879; Almanzo Wilder's claim was located a mile north of the future town site of De Smet. Each of the Wilders also claimed another quarter section under the Timber Culture Act of 1873, which originally required that forty acres be planted in trees. With poor growing conditions, few met the requirement; in 1878, the act was revised to stipulate that 10 out of 160 acres be planted in trees. Thus, Almanzo Wilder had most of two quarter sections to cultivate. The Land Ordinance of 1785 stipulated that each township set aside a "school section"; many states reserved section 16 for school purposes.

738.33 try the farm anyway.] In her manuscript, Wilder wrote and then deleted the following sentence: "Then a coatsleeved arm reached across the top of the buggy seat behind her shoulders and work and money were forgotten."

739.14 Manly's folks] See note 290.22–23.

743.14 Scott's and Tennyson's poems] See note 447.27.

744.20 pieplant] See note 663.22.

745.28–29 "Don't Leave . . . Boys."] The lyrics quoted here are the second verse (slightly altered) and chorus of "Don't Leave the Farm, Boys" (1871), song by Alfred von Rochow with words by Clara F. Berry, as it appears in *The Conqueror* (1880), believed to be the singing-school book described in *These Happy Golden Years.*

746.13 relinquishment] See note 633.4.

746.38 Montgomery Ward] Department store and mail-order business founded in 1872 in Chicago by Aaron Montgomery Ward.

748.23 Larsen] In "Just Neighbors," a *Missouri Ruralist* article of May 20, 1917, Wilder recalls the same neighbor, "Mr. Skelton," in similar terms, as a "good borrower but a very poor hand to return anything." She adds that the family "were kind neighbors later when we really needed their help."

749.10 salary] In her memoir, "Pioneer Girl," Wilder writes of the thirty dollars owed her for teaching the Wilkins' school: "(This was the $30. that bought the colt, that was sold to buy the sheep that with their increase were sold for the money that bought Rocky Ridge.)"

750.5 to the barn] The editors of the Harper & Row edition based on Wilder's manuscript deleted the sentence "Everybody knew Indians would take whatever they took a fancy to . . ." After the phrase "She never liked strangers," they also deleted "and there was something about an Indian that she very much disliked." Of this anecdote, Wilder wrote in the margin of the manuscript, "This is true but happened to a friend of mine."

753.38 Cottonwood River] Perhaps Cottonwood Creek, east of the Badlands.

755.2 "Give us this day our daily bread."] Matthew 6:11.

755.7 twenty-ninth birthday] See note 229.27. In the manuscript, Wilder described her husband as being twenty-five when she was nineteen, a fiction consistent with the time scheme of her earlier novels. The editors of *The First Four Years* corrected the text to reflect Almanzo Wilder's true age.

757.26 Number One hard.] Variety of wheat popular in the 1870s, when millers developed machinery to grind hard grains with high protein content for fine breads and baked goods.

757.31–32 wonderful.] Deleted in editing was the rest of this sentence: "It was wonderful that Manly was going to prove himself right about farming."

761.4–5 "Five hundred dollars debt] The extent to which this debt preyed on Laura Ingalls Wilder's mind can be seen in a letter of March 23, 1937, to Rose Wilder Lane detailing the finances involved in farming in Dakota Territory in the 1880s. (At that time, Lane was working on a serial based on her parents' experiences, "Free Land," published in *The Saturday Evening Post* in March–April 1938.) Almanzo Wilder opened the letter by noting, "Dear Rose, You don't seem to think there is a lot of over head expence in living." Several pages later, his wife wrote, "There was no money in the bank in 1885. There was a debt of $500. for building the house which I didn't know about until some time later."

761.14–15 "Our Uncle Sam . . . farm!"] See note 39.13–16, 19–26.

766.40 Fourth of July races.] In the manuscript, this paragraph continued with the following sentence: "She wanted to go with them, to drive away and away even from herself if that were possible."

767.10 Mrs. Powers] Likely Mary Power's mother, M. Elizabeth Power, an immigrant from Ireland.

767.20–23 . . . angel band . . . To—] The gospel song "Angel Band" (1862), by William Batchelder Bradbury (1816–1868) with words by Jefferson Hascall (1807–1887), refers to Luke 16:22. The lyrics include: "Oh, come, angel band, / Come and around me stand; / Oh, bear me away on your snowy wings / To my eternal home; / Oh, bear me away on your snowy wings / To my eternal home."

768.3 little Rose] The manuscript reads, "resting gently on the little Rose."

769.31–33 the Boasts . . . children] See note 107.6. The Boasts never had children. After Ella Boast was confined to a wheelchair with rheumatoid arthritis in the 1890s, the couple moved from their homestead to De Smet, where Mrs. Boast became known for entertaining groups of town children at parties.

772.32 too dry.] While precipitation during 1885–89 was normal, on average, for the semiarid Dakota prairie, the summers of 1886, 1888, and 1889 were well below average. In June 1891, Grace Ingalls wrote in her diary, "the crops have failed year after year in this place and are likely to this year."

775.16–17 Cousin Peter] See note 263.22–23.

775.38 Royal] See note 152.35.

778.20 presidential election] Tariffs, or taxes on imports, were the chief subject of debate during the presidential campaign of 1888. A supporter of high tariffs, Republican Benjamin Harrison defeated the incumbent Democratic president, Grover Cleveland, winning the electoral college but not the popular vote.

780.20–21 third year] Wilder's manuscript reads, "the third year of trial by farming was ended."

784.18 lone cry of a wolf.] In her manuscript, Wilder wrote of this anecdote, in parentheses: "Note. All true except that I heard the last howl just before I went out and did not go but why spoil a good story for truth's sake."

784.39 Waverley novels] Series of popular historical novels by Sir Walter Scott, beginning with *Waverley* (1814).

790.36 pre-emption] The Preemption Act of 1841 granted to those living on federal land for at least fourteen months the right to "pre-empt" or buy the property for not less than $1.25 an acre before it was offered for sale to the public.

792.20 get there.] The manuscript includes the following sentences, deleted in editing: "There was no merciful chlo[ro]form and the baby weighed 10 lbs. There were many painful days in bed for stitches had to be taken by the Dr. and it was so terribly hot that scalded spots came on Laura's back."

792.35–39 Oh . . . Jane.] "My Jenny Jerusha Jane" (1868), song by W. M. Phelps with words by A. G. Chase, written for the blackface performer Dave Reed of Hooley's Minstrels.

793.14 pay a note.] The manuscript includes the following: "Always those debts were in the back of her mind waiting to come out and be thought about. The Dr. bill would be heavy this time too because of those extra visits."

793.15–16 three weeks later] In the manuscript, the preceding words were deleted: "one awful day." A De Smet newspaper reported on August 10, 1889, "Mr. and Mrs. A. J. Wilder's little child died Wednesday evening," or August 7, 1889. Accounts vary as to how long the child lived, with some biographers suggesting twelve days or less than two weeks. Grace Ingalls noted in her diary on August 27, 1889, that "Laura's little baby boy only a month old died a little while ago, he looked just like Manly."

794.5 more water,] Deleted in editing were the following words: "something in her seemed to break."

794.26 the nerves] Deleted from the published version: "and she must wear dark glass[es] for a long time if she wanted to save her eyes."

795.28 Manly thought he could.] The following sentence was deleted: "How much could she depend on Manly's judgment, she wondered."

795.34 "it is better farther on"] Traditional gospel song, first published in 1877.

796.6–9 You . . . out.] See note 745.28–29.

796.END On the last manuscript page, after the final lyrics of "Don't Leave the Farm Boys," Wilder wrote these slightly altered or misremembered lines from "The Fool's Prayer," a poem by Edward Rowland Sill (1841–1887): "But for our blunders, Lord in shame / Before the face of Heaven we fall. /—oh Lord be merciful to me / a fool."

APPENDIX

799.7 Indian Territory] The Ingallses' cabin was located on the Osage Diminished Reserve in Kansas. Wilder remembered the cabin as being forty miles from Independence, Kansas, which would have placed it in Indian Territory, or what is now Oklahoma. In fact, it was a little over thirteen miles from the town. Wilder took steps to pinpoint the location in 1933 but was not successful. Local historians later discovered the exact piece of property, finding the hand-dug well and unearthing a small horseshoe that may have been thrown by one of the Ingallses' horses, Pet and Patty.

800.11 Rocky Mountain burro] Descendants of donkeys used by nineteenth-century Rocky Mountain miners to carry equipment and supplies.

800.21 Pa's fiddle] Wilder sent Charles Ingalls's fiddle to the South Dakota State Historical Society in Pierre in 1944. The instrument is currently on display at the Laura Ingalls Wilder Home and Museum in Mansfield, Missouri.

801.9–10 sunshine and shadow] A phrase of particular meaning for Wilder, who used it in several contexts. It also appears in an undated poem written by Mary Ingalls after her father's death, "My Father's Violin."

801.23 63 years] The Wilders were married for sixty-four years, from August 25, 1885, to the day of Almanzo Wilder's death, October 23, 1949. The Harper & Brothers letter was occasionally revised; the incorrect figure may have been a holdover from a previous version.

801.26 Ma and Pa] In 1886, Caroline Ingalls bought property on Third Street in De Smet from Eliza Jane Wilder, where Charles Ingalls built their final home the following year, selling the homestead claim in 1892. In De Smet, Charles Ingalls worked as a carpenter and served as Justice of the Peace and deputy sheriff. Recently discovered court cases written in his hand are dated

1883 and 1884. A biographical sketch of Charles Ingalls appears in a *Compendium of Biography* of regional luminaries, published in the 1890s by George A. Ogle & Company of Chicago, perhaps containing information supplied by Ingalls himself. It lists him as a member of the Eastern Star lodge and the Masonic lodge of De Smet, as well as a Populist, a political party active from 1891–1908, opposed to banking and railroad interests and supportive of wheat farmers. Suffering from heart disease, Charles Ingalls died in 1902. Caroline Ingalls died in 1924.

801.28 Mary] After graduating from the Iowa College for the Blind in 1889, Mary Ingalls lived the rest of her life with her parents. In 1892, Charles Ingalls accompanied her to Chicago, where she underwent facial surgery for neuralgia. Rose Wilder Lane described her aunt cleaning house, making clothes for the family, weaving carpets from rags, and creating hairnets and other items for sale. Lane recalled her "wonderful work-basket, a big one, fitted inside with needles and thread and scissors and shuttles," from which she crafted everything from tiny beaded baskets to hammocks, one of which was given to the Wilders and used at their farm in Missouri. Mary Ingalls lived with her mother after her father's death, saying, "I am feet for Ma, and Ma is eyes for me." She died of a stroke in 1928 while visiting Carrie Ingalls Swanzey in Keystone, South Dakota.

801.30 Carrie] Carrie Ingalls taught school briefly and at nineteen apprenticed at the *De Smet Leader*; she may have later worked for the *Kingsbury County Independent*. Around the turn of the century, she moved to western South Dakota where she managed newspapers and established a homestead near the town of Topbar. There she worked for E. L. Senn, known as the "Final Proof King of South Dakota," owner of dozens of newspapers serving homesteaders who were required to publish "proof" sheets for five consecutive weeks before proving up on their claims. In 1911, she moved to Keystone, South Dakota, a mining town, to manage a local paper; the following year, she married David Swanzey, a widower with two young children and a miner known for traveling with Charles Rushmore, a New York attorney, on the day that a granite mountain was named for him. Carrie Swanzey died in Keystone in 1946, at the age of seventy-five.

801.32 Grace] After completing school in De Smet, Grace Ingalls attended Redfield College, northwest of De Smet, for a time, and subsequently taught school. In 1901, she married Nathan Dow in the Ingalls family parlor. The couple lived on a homestead near Manchester, South Dakota. She died in Manchester in 1941, at sixty-four.

802.1 Mary Power] Daughter of Irish immigrants, Mary Power was born in New York in 1866, moving west with her family and arriving in De Smet in 1880, where her father worked as a tailor. Ten years later, Power married Edwin Sanford, a bookkeeper, cashier, and stockholder in the Kingsbury County Bank (where Thomas Ruth, whose name appears in *The Long Winter*, was the